Anne Hamp

# The Two Worlds of Geratica

# The Women of Geratica

Anne Hampton was born in 1971 and lives in Bristol, England.

She doesn't specifically write for one genre, but encompasses politics, spying, action, thriller, murder, mystery, romance, adult, and fantasy themes.

Anne favours strong female lead characters (though she is not a feminist), and approaches adult themes from a sexually dominant woman's perspective – reversing the traditional male/female roles in the bedroom.

# INTRODUCTION

Before reading this book, readers might want some background information, on the society that they are about to encounter.

In a remote galaxy, in a distant corner of the universe, there is a small planet called Geratica (pronounced "Je-ra-tick-a"). It is the *only* planet in this galaxy, and is situated roughly the same distance from their Sun, as we are from ours, and has two moons. Its atmosphere and length of day closely resemble that of Earth's and it is around 5,000 years old. One year is 280 days. One week is 7 days, which means that there are exactly 40 weeks in a year. Each day and week, are referred to by number (for example, Day 1 of Week 20). After 5 days, Day 6 and Day 7 of each week are also referred to as a weekend. They are also recorded in numbers by Day/Week/Year, e.g. Day 1 of Week 2 of Year 5001 would be referred to as 1/2/5001 (though it might be abbreviated to 1/2/01). The time of day is measured and recorded in exactly the same way, as on Earth. It is about 240,000 miles in size, and has a population of around 40,000,000.

It has four regions, with one small ocean, the Geranda (pronounced as in Geratica), which stretches across the planet. Each region is situated on the Geranda, two in Geratica's northern hemisphere and two in its southern equivalent. Castra (Capital of Geratica and slightly the largest) is in the north and borders Volva. In the south, Dumas borders Utipides (pronounced Utipidees).

The core of the planet is not natural, but a living dominant female sex. It was this being that created the planet, and its inhabitants are descended from her. She created the atmosphere surrounding Geratica and constructed a force-field around it, which cannot be penetrated from outside, to protect it from invaders, and created the first two females and males of the Geratican race, who were linked to her and began to build a society based on her ideals. A part of her has always been present in the minds of all Geraticans. It is not cumbersome and they barely notice it, as they go about their daily lives (in fact they can go for a three or four days, without thinking about her at all), but they are aware that she is there. They call her the Divine Being.

Their main source of energy is in the planet's surface, and stems from the core itself. It is extremely strong and powers the entire planet. Miners have the job of extracting it and then it is distributed to storage depots around the planet. It is then converted into gas, electricity, coal (which is used in some Geratican fireplaces, and to power trains), and petrol for cars. From these there are a complex system of pipelines, which supply the gas and electricity to its inhabitants. Some of these lie upon the Geranda ocean bed. Other fuels and goods are transported to the relevant organisations that need it, by road, rail or boat. Cargo vessels travel across the ocean, between the various regions.

At the end of each year, and the beginning of the next, the Divine Being is celebrated in a fortnight- long festival – The Festival of Divinity. This is not so much a belief, but a genuine feeling of gratitude. Because of what they feel in their minds, Geraticans (and this includes both worlds) are in no doubt where they are from and who created them. There is no real thought of any 'afterlife', just a general acceptance that all life must eventually come to its natural end. They do not have any form of religion as such. No-one can do more than speculate however, about the exact nature of the Divine Being.

The build up to the Festival, generally starts in the last couple of weeks of the old year, when decorations are put up all over the land, cards are exchanged, and special festive music is sung and played. It officially begins on Day 1 of Week 40, when Geraticans attend feasts in local city, town or village halls. There is traditionally an official story, written centuries ago as a tribute to the Divine Being, performed by members of the community and narrated by local dignitaries, accompanied by the singing of choristers. There are also one or two speeches made, and traditional festive songs are sung, led by the choristers. It is known as Tribute Day.

Divinity Eve – similar to our Christmas Eve – takes place on the last day of the year.

Divinity Day – similar to our Christmas Day – takes place on Day 1 of the New Year. Families get together, to exchange gifts (children traditionally receive the most), consume festive food and drink, listen to festive music and generally have a good time. They also have their own forms of traditional pantomime, performed in local theatres.

Day 2 of the New Year is known as Queen's Day, when she makes a traditional afternoon address, and a celebratory dinner is given in her honour, in the evening, at her main Palace residence.

Tribute Day, Divinity Day and Queen's Day are statutory holidays for Geraticans. The Festival officially ends on Day 7 of Week 1.

There are 2 other such days – on Day 1 of Week 21, to mark the official beginning of summer, known as Midyear Day and Day 1 of Week 30, known as Harvest Day, when farmers traditionally bring in the first crop of the past year's harvest.

The world is ruled by a monarchy, below which there are the nobility. Then there are senior members of the monarch's staff, who advise the Head of State and administrate their official business. These come from upper middle class 'commoners', to provide a link between the monarchy and the ordinary people. They are followed by parliamentarians, professionals, such as lawyers, doctors etc. Finally, there are the ordinary rank and file workers.

The head of state must always be a queen. By marriage (normally to a member of the nobility), her consort is a prince. Her children are princesses and princes. The eldest princess always succeeds her mother as queen, taking precedence over any older brother. In the event of there being no daughter, the eldest prince's wife succeeds to the throne. (Should there be no direct heir at all, then the nearest female descendant would need to inherit, though this has rarely occurred). It is believed that if there was no female monarch, then the Divine Being would leave her world and Geratica end. This makes securing the succession, of primary importance. The queen's main palace residence is in Castra (where the crown jewels are kept). She also has other residences in each of the other regions of her queendom, and generally holiday's in the other three, about once a year.

Women are the dominant sex on Geratica. Their personalities tend to be naturally strong and confident – though to varying degrees and occasionally some can be less so – and are often matched with a clear clarity of thought. Geratica is a matriarchal society. All major responsibilities are undertaken by them, and they hold all the prominent positions, politically, socially and in the workplace. Scientists and engineers, doctors, nurses, dentists, lawyers, judges, police officers, fire and ambulance service workers, parliamentarians, courtiers, administrative and clerical officers, teachers and lecturers, hospitality workers, train guards, chefs, technical workers such as electricians, plumbers, mechanics, ship's bosuns, train drivers and even aircraft pilots, are all exclusively female. Only girls are educated. Men's working roles are mainly manual – miners, dockers, labourers, farmers (with a woman to manage their estate – often their wives), gardeners, refuse collectors, train firemen, delivery drivers (if they can read), storemen, security guards, oil rig workers, etc. As this is seen as their primary role in life, it is not considered strictly necessary for them to be formally educated as such, academically, though some women do choose to teach the basics to them, in their private households. Their managers and supervisors (and in more recent times, union representatives) are women. Certain occupations can have a mixture of both sexes, such as factory workers, cleaners and (again in the case of men, if they can read) drivers and postal delivery workers. Shops, department stores, post offices, hair salons, as well as pubs, clubs and bars etc are all run and mainly staffed by women, though there can be roles for men in certain instances. In the event of pregnancy, females take maternity leave and their jobs are covered by others, but as the main breadwinners, they nearly always return as soon as possible, afterwards. Nannies are widely employed, and in some cases, domestic cleaners.

In the Geratican nobility, all women are ladies and all men lords.

Some of Geratica's institutions follow slightly different procedures of administration to those of our own.

Naturally, as some women's jobs are better paid than others, depending on their position (though men's are on average, universally similar), some families are better off than others and this creates the kind of class system common to many cultures.

At home, men's roles are usually gardening, decorating and general handiwork that needs doing around the home. Women take charge of the budget and domestic affairs. They are the dominant partner of a marriage, and the Mistress of the house. Traditionally it is customary for men to accept their opinions and wishes. Men take their wives names after marriage.

Geratican children develop faster than humans and education is slightly more intense than the human kind. Girls go to introductory school at age 3 – starting at the beginning of the week following their birthday (or if that be during a school holiday, the first of the new term), then progress to elementary at 5, middle at 7, and senior at 10. They sit their Certificate of Geratica exams at 14, which covers a broad range of subjects (the certificate is awarded if a girl gains at least a pass in six or more of the ten, which must include Mathematics and Geratican Language) and can then leave, or if they wish to go to University, they can stay on to 16 to study an Advanced Certificate of Geratica, in the broadly same subjects. (Though they are able to drop one, other than mathematics, Geratican Language or science). This certificate is awarded if a girl gains at least a pass in five or more of the nine, (which again must include mathematics and Geratican Language). After this there are several universities in which to study for degrees, the most exclusive ones being Castra or Orpington. Their school year is split into 4 terms of 8 weeks' duration, followed by a fortnight's holiday after each. There are no half-terms. Depending on the date that they began school, their academic year begins at the start of the term that it falls in. Girls can be taken out of school at any time, for family holidays, with the school's consent, or parents can wait until the school holidays. This makes the latter very popular times for Geratican adults to take leave from work, especially the ones after the Spring and Summer terms. The holidays actually overlap between the end of one season and the start of the next, but any change in the weather at those times is gradual and often minimal.

The age of consent is 16 on Geratica.

Both the females and males are similar in form to humans, but the females do not have breasts and the males no penis. Both have a vagina. Both also excrete all natural waste through their bottoms. The male is in general, physically stronger in the upper body, and normally taller than the female, but in the lower part, the female has the stronger limbs, particularly in the legs. Overall the male is slightly stronger physically, than the female, but not as much as Earth males are, compared to Earth females.

In the act of reproduction, the main difference to the human kind is that the female extracts the seed from the male and then collects it, rather than the male inserting the seed into the female. She is the dominant sexual partner. The female has a geratis, a bit like the male penis, only much longer, and far more powerful, coiled inside the back of her vagina. The male has a genus, shaped like a ball, on the floor at the back of his. Both have two holes in their vagina, for entry and exit. The female sexual organ is stronger than the male's. Intercourse occurs with partners lying body to body.

When the female becomes sexually aroused by a male, she feels tingles in the lower part of her body, especially in her thighs, as her skin ripples. At the same time her geratis starts to uncoil inside her vagina and can eventually exit, becoming partially visible and erect. This can either be from her left, or right hole, depending on whether she is left or right-handed. The male's arousal will cause his genus to start ballooning. Until intercourse actually begins to take place, this is as far as the geratis can go. Once intercourse starts, it will enter the male's hole, directly opposite the one that it came out of hers, and travel along the wall of his vagina, draping itself over his genus, and then travel back along the other wall, before exiting through his other hole and re-entering the female's directly opposite to that.

The geratis is totally controlled by the female's arousal. As this becomes more and more intense, so the geratis penetrates the genus, grinding over the top, which is the genus's most sensitive spot and making it expand further and further. The geratis gradually expands in width and presses against the walls of the male's vagina, until it completely fills it. This all happens automatically and is directly controlled by the female's arousal only. She can feel the penetration of her geratis on the male's genus and vagina walls and the male feels it, too, but she does not physically do it herself. The geratis operates independently of the female, but driven by her arousal. The act of doing this eventually causes the genus to explode inside the male vagina, causing him to orgasm, and his semen is collected by pores along the surface of the geratis, causing a pleasurable sensation that further induces the female's orgasm. As she comes, her geratis emits juice, which covers the male's vagina walls. The male can taste the sweetness in his mouth, and feel it pour through his veins. Once all of the male's sperm is collected, the geratis retreats back the way it came, to the female's vagina and recoils itself.

The orgasm that both the male and the female experience, is extremely powerful. The intercourse can in theory occur with the female or male in any position, with the woman on top of, beneath, or side-by side with the man. But the standard, and overwhelmingly most popular way amongst Geraticans, is for the female to lie on top, as it is her sexual arousal only, that enables the procedure to happen and this position allows her to control it, according to her passion and desire. She can wrap her arms and legs around the male, and squeeze him between her thighs, as she thrusts her body against the male's. Despite the intensity of their orgasms, Geraticans sexual organs return to normal very quickly after intercourse, and can both be ready to begin the process again, if they so wish, after only a short passage of time. Due to the way that her mind and body are designed a Geratican female tends to naturally have strong sexual confidence, urges and desires, and it is quite standard for her to make love to a male more than once, during the course of a single session of intercourse. Depending on how long she wants to continue, it is possible for her to do it on numerous occasions over the course of a couple of hours, before exhaustion will finally overcome her. It is also possible for the female to orgasm inside of the male without him having one also, simply by her geratis pressing against his vagina walls, whilst penetrating his genus. This means that a female can orgasm more times than a male, if she so wishes.

Intercourse can only happen between a woman and a man. It is possible for two women or two men to become intimate, but full sexual intercourse can never take place, simply because of the way Geraticans' bodies and sexual organs are designed. The geratis only becomes completely aroused by the genus – and vice-versa.

Since it is not possible for sexual intercourse to take place between Geraticans of the same sexual denomination, it also follows that incest – as we would think of it – is not possible between Geratican mothers and daughters, or fathers and sons. But due to their passionate nature, it is not uncommon, and not considered unacceptable, for two females to share a bed together – though it tends to be kept a private affair between themselves. It will often (though not always) be a mother and daughter who are especially close and intimate. If this happens, the most common explanation is that there is an absent father, and the daughter is, to a certain extent, a substitute for him. What they feel for each other is not connected to sexual attraction but purely a deep bond of love and Geratican females are generally extremely affectionate. Of course, it is perfectly possible for two men to be close enough to want to be together in bed, but this is far rarer. On the whole, they do not have quite such strong passions and desires as their female counterparts and their needs are generally most naturally satisfied by what females provide for them.

Clearly also, due to the unique nature of their sexual organs, Geraticans would be unable to have sexual intercourse with people from any other race - unless they came across another kind created by the same type of being.

Traditionally, when a female takes a mate, it is her role to initiate the relationship, and to then decide the terms, that make both partners as equally happy as possible. Once this is done, it is customary for the male to defer to the female's judgement. Similarly, when the female proposes marriage, or an engagement to be married, the male traditionally accepts. The female draws up a contract, setting the terms of the engagement or marriage. It is signed by both parties, and in the case of the latter, witnessed by a town clerk at their wedding ceremony. Historically speaking, a man could be seen as the property of his wife, and it has been a woman's right to punish her husband for disobedience or infidelity (though this is certainly not a regular occurrence today). It can even be their right to do it, should a man back out of a marriage or engagement contract after signing it. But relationships are taken very seriously in Geratica, and the rituals are solemnly observed by the vast majority.

Life expectancy on Geratica is around 85 years for women and 80 for men. Upon death, funerals are held, attended by mourners. The service is conducted by a town clerk and the body is cremated, with the ashes buried in a plot within a cemetery.

The style of dressing amongst Geraticans tends to be traditional. The women are proud of their feminine sex and like to dress elegantly, but sometimes also glamorously, in skirts and gowns. The skirt is considered the ultimate symbol of female authority. 'White collar' women wear skirt suits, blouses and neck-bows to work, or occasionally smart dresses. Men tend to dress in working clothes, but these again will still be smart, with slightly more casual attire worn in the home.

Geratican technology is more advanced than Earth's and they have developed sophisticated scanning techniques, which can pass through the force-field around the planet and probe other worlds in other galaxies (though for many years scanning was the preserve of the elite). They have incorporated ideas learnt from other worlds, whilst rejecting some that they didn't like or agree with. The main species that they have become aware of is the human, from the planet Earth. Their language has gradually evolved into a mixture of English - from Earth - and their own Geratican, which they now refer to as Geratican Language, though the original is still learnt by some girls - known as Ancient Geratican. These Geraticans, whilst sometimes displaying the kinds of character defects common to all societies, and needing a touch of law and order to maintain control and reform themselves, tend, on the whole, to be hospitable, kind and good natured at heart. Crime is relatively low. They are outward looking.

Unfortunately, at some point during the planet's history, there was a schism in the core, so that a parallel world (with women the dominant sex in the same way) was created and from then on, everyone born in one world, began to become connected with someone else (male or female) being born at the same time, or the next in line, on the other. (Even in the case of twins or triplets, etcetera). They don't know each other, or anything about them - not even if they are male or female - and they follow separate, individual paths, but they are aware of each other's presence in their minds, even though they don't sense their thoughts.

After both worlds became aware of each other, the parallel world decided to call itself Geraticai (pronounced "Je-ra-tick-eye"), to distinguish it from the other (though technically they can still be thought of as Geraticans). Their dateline is slightly behind Geratica, as they began life later. Since it is 1,050 years behind Geratica's presumably it was at that time in the planet's history that the schism occurred. The seasons of Geraticai's year (winter, spring, summer and autumn) follow in the same order as on Geratica, but are one behind, therefore perhaps Geraticai's year 1 began during the spring of Geratica's year 1,051, somehow starting with their first winter. Physically and geographically, it is identical to Geratica, with four regions. Spanda (the Capital), Renus, Nerva and Plumas on Geraticai, directly correspond to Castra, Volva, Dumas and Utipides on Geratica. The Nibulus Ocean on Geraticai, directly corresponds to the Geranda Ocean on Geratica. Their language is the same as on Geratica - though they call it Geraticaian - and it has evolved in a similar way.

However, there are occasionally people who are born without being connected to someone on the other world. This can happen on either one. No one is really sure why this is and even exactly where they come from, as they appear to have no biological parents. They simply arrive as older children and are drawn to an adult of the same kind. They are known as Mongrels.

Through their scanning techniques, each world can, up to a point, monitor events on the other.

Once the Geraticans became aware of the existence of two worlds, several attempts were made over the years by both, at traveling through the void to the other, in 'Transportation Capsules' (amongst the elite). The result of each however, was a violent reaction occurring within the planet's core, putting both worlds' stability at risk, endangering everybody's lives, and killing themselves in the process. The only people who were able to do it safely, were the mongrels (and it was usually certain females with the knowledge and specific skills to construct and navigate the capsules). Gradually the attempts by the rest of the Geraticans and Geraticaians to travel became less frequent, until eventually it was decided that it was not possible for them to do it. Many years have now past since the last attempt, and whilst there used to be quite a few mongrels, their numbers were declining, and now it is believed that they are extinct on Geratica. Therefore, there is apparently nobody left on that world who knows precisely how the capsules were constructed, or navigated either. They assume that a similar situation prevails on Geraticai, but cannot be certain.

The extent to which both worlds might need each other to survive is not known for sure.

The prevailing wisdom of the monarchs on Geraticai has been that the destruction of Geratica would result in Geraticai becoming the sole world (though whether that might also have an impact on Geraticai itself in some way is less certain, which has generally had a cautionary effect on them). They traditionally take a belligerent attitude towards Geratica and some even express a wish that it could be detached from them altogether.. They also tended to make use of mongrels, when they found them, to travel to Geratica and spy in secret and sometimes cause problems through discreet meddling, as ordered by their Queen. It is quite a tyrannical regime and its queens are often dictatorial, ruling through a lady chancellor and a high council. There is no parliament. At a lower level, each region has a lady mayor, though this is mainly a comparatively minor role. People on Geraticai tend to have cunning, devious, not to say sometimes nasty streak in them. There is corruption committed at all levels (even by Her Majesty's court, although if that itself is defrauded then the strongest of penalties follow). Having been created slightly after Geratica, they are perhaps slightly more backward, compared with the original world, but they still have sophisticated technology. In fact, a number of people on Geraticai, actually believe that is they who are the original, and Geratica an inferior copy.

The degree to which the people of both worlds exhibit their typical character traits can vary. A few on Geratica are not quite as 'nice' as others, whilst conversely on Geraticai, a few are not quite so 'unpleasant'.

Geraticans have subsequently become more culturally and educationally advanced in general (though there are certainly some intelligent people on Geraticai and there are interests common to both worlds). They in particular, enjoy music, books, cinema, theatre, art, and museums, as well as plenty of good food (traditional Geratican, as well as Earth dishes) and drink. In fact, they have quite strong constitutions and can consume quite vast quantities, in a relatively short space of time. The women in particular, tend to be able to able to drink a substantial amount, before they begin to suffer any ill effects or drunkenness, though this certainly does happen, also. The health of most Geraticans is reasonably good.

Sport isn't of huge interest to them, though the monarchy and nobility are keen hunters on both worlds and this is sometimes a popular spectacle. They breed horses and hounds, specifically for this purpose, as well as farmland animals for food. However, they do not believe in domesticating them. For Geraticans, the purpose of animals is for work, usage, or consumption only. Some females do also indulge in activities such as Crown Green Bowling and Croquet - and many are naturally competitive.

They also have cars (of a similar design to those of 1950s Earth – though more powerful – and driven on the left-hand side of the road), telephones, cinema, radio, but, not yet at least, television. Card games and other such pursuits, are often found in the women's parlours, for entertainment. Gambling sometimes take place within their society – a mainly female activity.

Swimming in the Geranda Ocean, is also popular, but in more recent years the discovery of oil in the sea bed, has resulted in it becoming more industrialised, with oil platforms dotted across it. Now they also use swimming baths, and some women even have them built in their gardens.

Passenger boats still ferry Geraticans across the ocean, to the opposite side of the queendom, and some take holidays in other regions. Geratica does also have a small merchant navy.

Both Geratican worlds have developed the same units of currency (both in value and, since more relatively recent times, design also) and measurement. The currency is called a gero, and in addition, 100 dorkens make up 1 gero.

Politically, the Geratican state is an absolute monarchy, where laws are made in accordance with the queen's views, though Geratica is less brutal than Geraticai and does have a limited constitution. The queen has a court administrator - similar to the lady chancellor on Geraticai (in fact many centuries ago, the Geratican position was called this too) – to advise her, who also meets with members of the privy council - made up of the nobility. (More recently there has been a senior court administrator, with a court administrator as deputy). Nowadays, the privy council is largely ceremonial and has no legal power. Courtiers ensure that all the queen's business is administered, and her bills passed through a parliament. This scrutinises the details and can vote to try and get parts of it amended, and even reject it altogether if it wishes, though this is not a regular occurrence. These positions are all held by women. Parliament is elected every five years, but there are no political parties, only individual members of parliament, representing their constituencies. They can be unseated, if voters think that they're not dealing with issues relating to them effectively or not representing the interests of their constituency, well enough. Only women have suffrage. Once a week, the queen goes to parliament and addresses it, announcing new bills to be debated, followed by half an hour when the MPs can ask her about whatever issue they want. The queen will give her opinion, and state any action she wants to make, if any, assisted if necessary by a court administrator. Geratica is not a dictatorship, and the law courts are allowed to independently administer that which is laid down by Her Majesty's Court (sometimes known as the Royal Court). Even the queen herself would in theory not be above her own law. Complete freedom of speech is allowed. On a lower level, each region does have a lady mayor, as head of a council office, and there is a system of local government below that, with councils headed by a mayor. This is who the town clerk works for. (Even in modern day cities, there is still a town hall, originating from ancient times). But these are all comparatively minor roles, and none are elected.

Geratican women have traditionally taken a very strict approach towards discipline (which some of us in a more liberal society might feel is excessive). Children are brought up to respect 'the rule of their mother's skirt'. Corporal punishment is routinely practised in the home and in schools. Mistresses carry a cane, and most mothers use one to punish bad behaviour and disobedience, to be followed by specific sanctions. Some mothers also possess a whip for extreme offences and if a child is sent before a juvenile court for a serious transgression, they can be sentenced to a horsewhipping in the front courtyard of the Royal Palace, administered personally by the queen and her most senior courtier. The whip used to be held in Geratican schools for the gravest of offences but was withdrawn after some mistresses abused its use. Geraticaian women use the same methods of discipline.

The planet of Geratica has never been invaded – this should be prevented by the force-field – nor has there ever been a war on the original world. However, the monarchy still protects its palaces with guards (of both sexes, but mainly male - though they always answer to female superiors), in order to be prepared, should such a threat materialise.

Finally, I must point out that I am by no means a scientist, and I am certainly not suggesting that any of this could happen! It is a pure fantasy world, but as with all fantasies, they can be based on some real-life themes, and events. Nor am I necessarily saying if I agree or disagree with the Geratican system. I am simply saying "Imagine if ..." I do rather like them though, and hope that you will enjoy meeting them.

**Anne Hampton**

**2015**

## **Author's Note.**

Throughout the 'Geratica' series, when referring to seasons in relation to dates on Geratica and Geraticai, I shall mostly be taking that of the capital region's side of the hemisphere on both worlds – unless specifically stated otherwise.

# PART 1

# CHAPTER 1

# Geratica – Autumn 5010

'Time may move on, but some institutions never alter – thank goodness!'

So thought Linda Radcliffe, as she drove the car through the entrance of Charterhouse College, her daughter's school in Buckmore, to the east of Greenacres. After finding a convenient place to park, she went inside to the lobby, and strode up to the reception.

"Good evening, my name is Mrs Radcliffe, and I'm here to meet the headmistress, for a progress report, regarding my daughter, Alexandra Radcliffe," she announced, in the clear confident manner of a woman who expected to be taken notice of.

The receptionist knew full well who Mrs Radcliffe was. She was the senior court administrator for Queen Alexandra, and she was the most powerful woman in the queendom, after the queen herself.

"If you'd just like to wait in the lobby for a moment, I'll let her know that you're here," she replied.

"Thank you," said Linda, and gave the receptionist a soft smile, which put her a little more at ease.

Linda went and sat down on one of the comfortable armchairs, and crossed her legs, looking more relaxed than she actually felt. She hadn't been looking forward to this. However, as she looked around the lobby, at the paintings of the past principals of the college and many of the Royal family, through the ages, she felt as if she was back studying here again, even though it was now nearly thirty years, since she'd left. It brought back happy memories. This was the most exclusive public school in Geratica. It was very proud of its traditions and indeed, few things did ever change very much.

Now forty-four (forty-five in the New Year), she was indeed the queen's senior court administrator. It was her job to give counsel to the monarch, and see that all her court's business and financial affairs, her meetings with parliament, her speeches and press releases, and her diary of public and private meetings and engagements, were administered effectively – and Linda had a reputation for being *extremely* efficient, and a hard taskmaster, not suffering fools gladly.

Tall and slim with blonde hair to just above her shoulders, she was still considered a very attractive woman. She had a very strong, confident personality, and was highly assertive, often even domineering, though she liked to think she did it in a caring way, genuinely for people's own benefit. She was very much a traditional Geratican woman, who believed that female authority was essential for the good order of the queendom, and that the male role should be subservient to that.

The receptionist came over to her. "If you please Mrs Radcliffe, the headmistress, Mrs Spencer, will see you now. Would you like to follow me?"

"Yes, thank you," replied Linda, pleased that the standards of politeness had not diminished since she had last been a pupil here.

Linda was led into Mrs Spencer's study. "Mrs Radcliffe is here to see you, Headmistress," said the receptionist, waving her hand. Then she left the room, and closed the door.

"Good evening, Linda," said Mrs Spencer, a blonde-haired woman of average height, aged thirty-six.

"Good evening, Elizabeth," replied Linda.

The two women knew each other quite well, both through Alexandra being at the college and also meeting in occasional professional meetings, though they were not personally close.

After exchanging a couple more pleasantries, the receptionist returned, bringing a tray with tea, coffee and biscuits on it. She placed it on a side table, and then withdrew from the room once more.

Elizabeth got up. "Would you like some refreshment?" she asked.

"Yes please. Black coffee would be nice, thank you. No sugar please."

Elizabeth poured coffee for them both and added milk for herself. She picked up the biscuits and looked enquiringly at Linda. "Oh, yes please. Just one. That's most kind of you."

Putting a biscuit into the saucer of each cup of coffee, Elizabeth carried them back her desk, and then the two women got down to business.

"Well, I'm pleased to say Linda," began Elizabeth, "that Alexandra seems to be doing quite well in all of her subjects. She is very quiet and seems a bit withdrawn sometimes though, so she's not always the easiest child for the others to get along with, and only being a day pupil, means that she doesn't get involved in any extra-curricular activities, and is therefore not as well rounded as many of her peers. But she has a curiously pleasing charm about her, when she does manage to speak, I have to admit."

Linda started to feel the heat of her blood running through her veins. Elizabeth always found a way to rile her with her (sometimes deliberately) tactless comments, and this *already* was no exception. She was fiercely protective of her daughter, and now she felt a need to defend her.

"Alexandra is a very shy girl – that can't be denied," she replied slightly tartly, "but I think she is gifted, and on top of that, she works hard – believe me, I make sure that she does. I think you will agree with me that those two things combined, make for promising results. I hope that she will get a place at Castra University. With her ability, and a bit of guidance, coaxing and help, she'll develop more confidence in herself, I'm sure, and then she'll become the kind of woman to make Geratica proud. As to her being a day pupil, as you know, I boarded here as a child – I'm a former head girl of course - and enjoyed it, but I took the decision that being the kind of girl she was, it would be better to let her come home to me each night, for her own happiness and security and I've never regretted it. I'm not sure if she would be doing so well now, if I hadn't and she'd boarded, as I did."

"I'm sorry, I meant no disrespect, Linda," said Elizabeth.

Linda felt like saying that she didn't believe her, but she resisted the temptation, and continued, "I didn't take it that way," raising her hands in a gesture of conciliation, which she hoped looked genuine. "She is actually quite friendly with the boy who lives at the other house in our hamlet, Tom Ryder. His stepmother works with me at the palace. When they are together, he seems to bring something out of her. I think she confides in him and he tells her what he thinks, and that helps her work things out, when she's worried or she's faced with a problem of some kind. She doesn't seem so 'withdrawn' then."

"All of which strengthens my belief, that we need greater equality between men and women in our society, and that boys should be educated in the kind of special schools that you know I have founded in Volva," said Elizabeth.

The two women were now straying into dangerous territory for them. This had long been a topic that they strongly disagreed on, and Linda had been hoping to avoid the subject entirely this evening. She was aware that the headmistress sometimes even used her assembly address at the college to lecture the girls on it according to her own opinion, which Linda disapproved of and suspected that it probably annoyed some of the mistresses here too. Charterhouse College – or any other school – was no place for politics.

It was the end of what had been a long week, and she had told Alexandra that tomorrow, they were going to have a busy day doing housework. Then she had a surprise treat organised for her in the evening and overnight, which would enable her daughter and herself to have a relaxing and pleasurable time together, before the beginning of the new week, the first day of which was going to be especially busy for her at court.

"You *know* my views on that subject, Elizabeth," she remarked coldly. "Quite simply, it is the way we were made on this world. As women, our natural instinct is to govern and lead, and men's natural instinct is to follow. That's what we all feel in our minds. Once we start tampering with that, the whole structure of society and social order will become eroded, and who knows what then might happen. I'm not saying that men should be treated as second class citizens – we should love and respect them very much. But we aren't *supposed* to do things differently to the way we've always done them."

"Yes, yes, we've been through all this before," replied Elizabeth. "I don't see why any change at all is so unacceptable. I don't think it can be right that one sex is 'meant' to treat the other in that way. If we were to try and reach the planet's core, we might be able to find out if something is wrong and change things to redress the balance."

"Well we're still a way off from being capable of doing that," said Linda. "And in any case, why should we throw away all the customs and traditions that have been natural to our race, since the dawn of time?"

"But anyhow, I don't wish to discuss this subject any further tonight and that's final," she continued. "Changing the subject, what has Alexandra's behaviour been like?"

"Exemplary," said Elizabeth. "But then again, you can never be *completely* sure with the quieter ones. Sometimes, all of a sudden, they can reveal their true colours and turn out to be amongst the worst behaved of students."

Anger welled up inside of Linda. She was struggling to control her temper, which could be explosive at times. It seemed as if Elizabeth was deliberately trying to pick possible faults that might undermine her daughter's ability and character in the future, in order to get at her.

"I can assure you *Mrs Spencer*," she countered icily, "that I run a very strict regime in our house. If Alexandra transgresses from the rule of my skirt, she is punished and I am not afraid to use the cane. I assume that is still practised here also and not become another tradition that you've now abandoned, simply because you don't agree with it? If my daughter is a good girl at school – and I am sure that she is – it is because I have brought her up to respect authority, order and tradition."

Now Elizabeth began to get irritated. "I do agree with the cane and yes it most certainly is practised here – *regularly*. As I'm sure you well know. I'd also use the whip if it was still allowed. Those at least, are subjects which you and I do agree on. Please remember Linda that *I* am in charge at Charterhouse. You may be, in the vast majority of this queendom, but when the girls come here, they are under my jurisdiction – within the rule of *my* skirt! Your daughter has never given me, or any of her mistresses, the slightest cause to beat her. I cannot be any clearer than that."

'Unlike *your* daughter,' Linda thought. Elizabeth's own daughter, Gillian, was also a pupil at the college and Linda had heard that, by all accounts she was a bit of a tearaway. But again, she decided to keep this to herself.

"Neither does she often give me cause to beat her at home either," said Linda. "In fact it's probably three or four years since it last happened. She is really a very nice, good natured girl, at heart."

There was a slight pause as they both sipped what remained of their coffee and tried to cool their tempers.

Putting down her cup and saucer, Elizabeth reached inside a folder on her desk and took out several pieces of A4 paper, bound together. "I think we can end on a more positive note," she said. "As you know, I like to show parents an item of work that their daughters have done, which have either particularly impressed or concerned one of their mistresses. And needless to say, this is one of the former. It's an essay that she did for her history prep, under Miss Sanford. It's a lengthy tome, but maybe you'd like to read some of it before you go. The subject matter may be of particular interest to you"

She handed Linda the essay, then took their cups back over to the tray on the side table.

Linda read the title 'A History of the Geratican Monarchy since 1000'. This was when the queendom's records officially began. She was highly skilled at scanning large documents quickly, through her years of experience working at court. It didn't take her long to agree with this mistress's assessment that it was very good, and it wasn't just because Alexandra was her daughter. She had produced one of the most detailed, clear and concise accounts that Linda had ever read on the subject, and she had even included some of her thoughts on the schism in the planet's core, and speculated about what Geraticai might be like.

"I rest my case with this essay," she remarked as she handed it back to Elizabeth. "And this was all her own work, assuredly. I am immensely proud of her."

"As are we," replied Elizabeth. "And there are other good reports. Her music essays also seem to bring her mistress in that particular field to rapture.

Not a subject that interests me and it is, after all an arts subject. You cannot really place it in the same league of importance as science, any more than a humanities subject such as history, for that matter. I stress though, that as headmistress of Charterhouse, this is purely a private opinion and I believe that if she keeps up the good work, generally, then Alexandra might have a chance of making it to Castra."

"Well, unless there's anything else you'd like to discuss, I think that concludes our meeting. It's getting late and I'm sure you're keen to get home for the weekend."

"Yes I am rather," confessed Linda. "I sometimes have to work on Day 1 of a weekend, but this one is free." She got up and held out her hand. "As ever, it's been a pleasure to meet you, Elizabeth."

Elizabeth got up and shook Linda's hand. "The pleasure is mutual," she replied. Both women knew that the other was lying, but they wanted their meeting to end amicably.

As she ushered Linda to the door of her study, Elizabeth asked, "Have you seen much of James recently?"

Linda glanced at her for a moment. Elizabeth's husband, James, was Queen Alexandra's chauffeur and she knew him well. In fact, she was much more fond of him, than she had ever been of Elizabeth. Their home was in the same town as hers – Greenacres.

"From time to time," she replied, eventually. "Mostly, when her Majesty is on an official engagement."

Elizabeth raised an eyebrow in acknowledgement and opened the door. "Goodnight Linda. Have a pleasant weekend," she said.

"Goodnight, Elizabeth. And you," replied Linda. "I'll see myself out."

Then she walked down the corridor and through the lobby, wishing the receptionist a good weekend as she passed her. She was actually seething with rage at Elizabeth's last comments about the superiority of science – which of course had been her subject as a plain mistress. She knew that her daughter was considered gifted in that subject too, but the headmistress had chosen to omit that. Both the arts and science were equally important in their own way, she felt.

Sitting in a chair close to the entrance, was a pupil. Her uniform was spotlessly turned out, and her long blonde hair reached over the shoulders of her slender body. Her school bag was on the ground at her feet. She smiled warmly at Linda, as she approached and then got up to greet her.

"Hello darling," said Linda, her voice full of softness and affection.

"Hello Mother," replied the girl, her voice equally warm. This was Alexandra Radcliffe, the fifteen-year-old daughter, who meant everything to Linda.

Unlike a lot of the pupils at the college and indeed Linda herself years ago, Alexandra did not attend as a boarder, largely because Linda felt she was the kind of girl who would be happier and more secure, if she could come home at night to her mother's loving, counselling and support, but also in part, because Linda had lost her husband ten years previously, and she needed someone to take care of.

They embraced, and Alexandra melted naturally into her mother's arms, as Linda engulfed her in a huge hug, which made her feel as if every part of her was being squeezed tight. She was slightly the shorter, and she looked up into her mother's eyes, lovingly and invitingly, allowing her to take control. Linda kissed her lips, tightening her embrace so much as she did so, that Alexandra murmured softly with pleasure. She returned the kiss, following her mother's lead.

The joy of being reunited with her daughter, helped quench the fire of anger that had burned inside of her, just moments before. "*It's the weekend!*" she said, in a happy voice, as she walked her daughter out of the college, with her arm wrapped around her shoulders. "Let's go. A special treat for you tonight. It's not often I'm here to take you home."

Alexandra held on to her mother's waist. "I'm pleased that you are Mother," she said.

Linda smiled and kissed her again. It was beginning to rain outside and getting chilly. She hurried them both to her car, put Alexandra's bag in the boot and began the drive home.

Once they were out on the main road, Linda glanced across briefly to her daughter. "Well? Do you want me to tell you what Mrs Spencer had to say?"

"I suppose you'd better, Mother," replied Alexandra. "Let's get it over with then."

"Well you've nothing to worry about, sweetheart," said her mother reassuringly. "You're doing very well and I couldn't be more pleased and proud of you. She showed me an essay you did about the history of the monarchy. I was *very* impressed. In fact, I've decided that I'm going to cook your favourite traditional meal for us both tonight, and we'll have a drop of wine with it." She looked back again, with a slight twinkle in her eye. "Not too much though. We've got things to do tomorrow."

Alexandra felt a surge of relief and pride. She always liked it when her mother was pleased with her.

"Thank you, Mother. That'll be lovely. I can't wait!" she said.

"My pleasure, darling," said Linda.

"There's just one thing I would like to say about dear Elizabeth Spencer though," she continued. "Remind me never to recommend her for a job at court. The woman has all the tact of a hound chasing a fox, in Queen Alexandra's hunting party. And what in the world Charterhouse were thinking of, when they appointed a woman with her revolutionary views, to that particular position, I cannot possibly imagine. She'll corrupt the whole system that we at court work so hard to maintain. The headmistress there in my day, would never have spouted such errant nonsense!"

Alexandra had been brought up to be deferential to her mother, using the title of 'Mother', whenever she addressed her and to say 'Yes', or 'No', in obedience, whenever she received instructions or warnings from her. However, she felt that this might be an occasion when it would be safer and more diplomatic to say nothing, and luckily it appeared that her mother was speaking rhetorically.

# CHAPTER 2

The following day, Linda rose early, washed in her bathroom, dressed and then with her sleeves pulled up in preparation for the busy morning of chores ahead, unlocked her daughter's bedroom door, and went inside. As an extremely strict, disciplinarian mother, she always locked Alexandra in her room at night. It was also partly because the girls who boarded at Charterhouse, would be locked in their dormitories (although by the time they got to their last two years, they actually had their own individual chambers), and she thought that she should experience a little of what it was like for them at night. Once her daughter had reached adulthood next year, though, she was certainly going to end the practice.

She went to the window, and drew back the curtains, letting the early morning Autumn light stream into the room. Alexandra was stirring, and as she came to, she squinted through the brightness.

"Good morning, my darling," said Linda and walking over to the bed, leaned over and kissed her daughter's lips as she lay on her back. Alexandra gazed lovingly up into her eyes and retuned it.

"Good morning, Mother," she replied politely.

This tended to be, with slight variations, their daily morning ritual.

"Right," said Linda. "Up you get, now please. Breakfast in thirty minutes, sharp. Don't be late. Understood?"

"Yes Mother," said Alexandra obediently.

"Good." With that Linda left the room and went downstairs.

As Alexandra pushed back the bedclothes and climbed out of bed, she could hear the sound of her mother unlocking the front door. She took off her pyjamas, crossed to her bathroom and washed, then came back and dressed. Sitting at her dressing table she carefully brushed her long blonde hair. She studied herself in the mirror for a moment, and her thoughts drifted briefly, to wonder whether Tom found her attractive.

The smell of the sausage, bacon and eggs that her mother was cooking in the kitchen, was starting to waft its way through the house, and Alexandra's stomach began to rumble. She turned her attention back to her mother's orders. There wasn't much likelihood that she would be late for breakfast now. She was feeling hungry, and she *loved* her mother's cooking. As far as she was concerned, a cooked breakfast was the perfect start to the day. And after having had spaghetti bolognaise, with red wine last night!

All the same, as she made her bed – something her mother inspected regularly – she checked her watch, just to make sure. Her mother would be in one of her strictest moods today, of that she had no doubt. She always was, when she wanted jobs done. In their relationship, her mother was the dominant force. She was very kind and loving and made Alexandra feel protected by her strength, but she was also a strict disciplinarian, and expected her to obey her rules, and defer to her judgement. Alexandra didn't necessarily mind much of the time as, although very intelligent, she wasn't the most confident girl in Geratica and was quite happy to let her mother be in control, and guide her.

Finally, she was ready, and she made her way down to the kitchen.

Linda had put the week's washing through the machine, and it was beginning to spin.

Helping her mother, she laid the table in the breakfast room. Then together, they first each had a bowl of cereal, after which the fried part of the breakfast was finally ready, and there was a silence as they both ate. Alexandra devoured hers, making soft murmurs of approval, as she tasted the flavours on her tongue and they slipped down her throat, to her stomach. She was the first to finish.

"Someone enjoyed that!" said Linda, with a smile.

"Mmm, it was delicious. Thank you, very much, Mother."

Linda's smile broadened. She got up, took their plates and went back to the kitchen. From the stove, she took another helping of sausages and bacon, that she had secretly left slowly simmering and placed it on Alexandra's plate. Then, returning to the breakfast room, she walked up behind her, very quietly.

"Have some seconds then," she said, placing the plate in front of her daughter, and to her pleasure, she saw Alexandra's eyes widen with delight. "Go on, have it whilst I make us some toast."

She planted a light kiss on her daughter's forehead. Alexandra lifted her head, so that she was looking back up at her mother.

"Thank you Mother. I wasn't expecting that!"

Linda glowed once again, and leaned forward. "No, you weren't were you? My pleasure, as always, my little one."

And mother and daughter kissed again, the mother initiating and giving, and the daughter receiving and returning. They were very close.

Half an hour later, and their breakfast, followed by a cup of black coffee each, was over.

Linda looked at her watch. "Right, to business," she said. "Now, I want you to do exactly as I tell you this morning Alexandra, with no fuss. Is that clear?"

"Yes Mother," replied her daughter.

"Crystal clear?"

"I usually do, don't I, Mother?"

"Yes you do. You're very good. Well hopefully this hearty breakfast has built up our strength. Right, here we go then. Time for us to get busy. Sleeves up and pinafore on, Alexandra."

First they washed up, with Linda washing, and Alexandra drying. Afterwards Alexandra was sent out into the back garden, to hang the washing on the line, and then for the next couple of hours, she was following her mother's orders, cleaning, dusting, polishing, and vacuuming. Generally, they split the house between them, when they did this, to save time, meaning that each worked alone. There were five bedrooms – all ensuite.

Eventually, as Alexandra was in the kitchen, just finishing cleaning the cooker, she saw out of the corner of her eye, her mother standing outside the door, with her hands on her hips, looking on closely.

"Am I doing everything OK, Mother?" she asked, though she was certain that she was. Very experienced in housework by now, having helped her mother for many years, she was certain that as the mistress in charge of her own home, as by tradition, a Geratican woman was, she would at least be able to keep it well.

"Yes," said Linda. More than just 'OK' actually. I've told you before about not underselling yourself. Everything's looking spotless. You've worked very hard and I'm pleased. Thank you."

Alexandra felt pleasure, as her mother praised her. She might be strict, but she was always very fair and generous when she thought it was deserved. Her method was a mixture of love and affection, combined with an iron rod of discipline, and control.

"Actually, there were two reasons why I came to see you," said Linda. "Firstly, to check that you weren't shirking – though admittedly that would have been out of character. Secondly, and most importantly, to ask you to put the kettle on. I think it's high time we stopped for a break."

Alexandra smiled. "Certainly, Mother!" she said.

\*\*\*

Whilst they were having another cup of coffee, the phone rang.

Linda had several phones in the house – all linked to the same extension – in the hallway, study, breakfast room, parlour and mistress' bedroom. Each was connected to the security gate at the end of the hamlet drive. If somebody pressed the intercom button for their house, the extension rang. Each phone pick-up point had a scanner screen, which enabled them to see the person outside the gate, after they'd picked up the receiver. If necessary, there was a button on the phone, which if pressed whilst the receiver was up, enabled the receiver to see the gate and talk through the intercom, if they so wished.

When Linda answered the phone in the breakfast room, the screen came to life. Before she could say any more, a strange voice made a rather vulgar noise, and then something was bundled over the gate. Then whoever it was, ran away.

Linda cursed them and slammed down the phone, shutting off the screen in the process.

"Who was that, Mother?" asked Alexandra.

"I don't know for certain, sweetheart, but if I had to hazard a guess, I'd say it was those darned 'Male Rights Protestors'! They threw something over the gate at the bottom of Elmsbrook. Wait here and I'll go and investigate!"

A few minutes later, Linda returned. She showed her daughter a banner. "It was just as I said," she declared. "Male Rights Protestors. Well, what 'right' have they to throw such a thing over the wall of a private hamlet? If that's their mentality, then we'll ignore them anyhow! And *this* will go straight into the bin!"

\*\*\*

After their coffee break, Linda sent Alexandra out to do some shopping at the local grocery store, outside the hamlet, whilst she continued with some vacuuming.

Alexandra quite enjoyed this. The store owner was a friendly lady, who had got to know her quite well. Her mother was a well-known and respected woman anyhow, due to her court connections, and it seemed that most of the local people made a considerable effort to be cordial with her, because they knew she was her daughter. In fact, she suspected that many were anxious to stay on the right side of her, in case they offended her mother, who she knew had a formidable reputation.

She put her security pass through the swipe pad, to the side of the gate at the end of Elmsbrook, and heard the click as it unlocked, and began to open. Once she was outside the hamlet, it automatically shut again. Then, she crossed the road to the store. Two women coming out wished her good morning. Alexandra politely, but shyly returned the greeting.

Mrs Warwicker, or Judith as Linda and Alexandra knew her, was behind the counter as she walked in, serving another woman. After finishing paying, the lady turned to go and saw her.

"Good day to you Miss Radcliffe," she said almost deferentially, nodding her head as she spoke. "Please give my regards to your mother."

"Thank you. I will," replied Alexandra. It was always a custom on Geratica, to be courteous, but as the woman left, Alexandra felt slightly disconcerted that there were quite so many people who clearly knew who *she* was, yet – as in this case – she hadn't the faintest idea who *they* were.

Alexandra asked the store owner. She knew most people. "Who was that, Judith?"

"Mrs Johnson," Judith told her. "She's a seamstress for Lady Sackville."

"I believe Lady Sackville is on the queen's privy council," said Alexandra. "Does my mother actually know this 'Mrs Johnson'? I'm just wondering whether I need to pass her message on."

"I don't think so." She smiled. "I shouldn't worry about it. There must be a lot of people around here, who know who your mother is, but have never personally met her!"

"Exactly," said Alexandra.

She put her mother's shopping basket on the counter, and took the list that she had been given, from her coat pocket.

"Ah, spending your mother's money again, are you, Alexandra?" Judith asked merrily as she took it. "You wouldn't have slipped something onto the list, on the quiet, like, eh?"

Alexandra burst out laughing. "I assume you're joking? I wouldn't dare! My mother keeps meticulous accounts. She'd be furious, if she found out I'd spent more than she'd budgeted for – and she *would* find out too. I'd have to spend my own money, and even then she'd know, because she checks my accounts too!"

"Yes, I know your mother keeps a tight hold on the purse strings," said

Judith, as she began to find the items on the list, and place them by the till. "I collect her bill every quarter, and she always pores over it, to check that I haven't overcharged her. As if I would! Still she controls the whole queendom's finances, as well, so I suppose it's good that we've got someone like that, rather than a reckless over spender, who'd bankrupt us all in a flash."

"Hmm," said Alexandra. During her upbringing, her mother had taught her about the value of money, and what to do with it, with regards to saving and spending, and she was determined to follow her example, when the time came, as she knew it eventually would, that she had a household budget of her own to manage.

At that moment Stephen, Judith's husband, came in from the back of the store, where he'd been moving stock. Alexandra liked him too.

"Ah, it's young Miss Radcliffe," he said as he saw her.

Alexandra smiled at him. "Hello Stephen," she said.

He started walking towards the counter to join his wife, but then stopped suddenly as he remembered something. "Oh, wait a minute," he said. "Judith, didn't someone come in the other day, enquiring about Alexandra?"

"Oh, yes," said Judith. That was Mrs Clark, the woman down the drive from you in Elmsbrook."

"Oh? What did she want?" asked Alexandra, cautiously.

"I don't think it was anything important. I think she's just quite fond of you, as you're friendly with Tom. To tell you the truth, I think she envies your mother for having a daughter. She often tells me that she wishes she could have had one of her own and of course Tom is her stepson, after marriage. But I think she's left it a bit too long for that kind of thing, now."

"Well, she can't have *me*. I'm very happy with my *own* mother, thank you very much!" said Alexandra.

Judith and Stephen both guffawed with laughter. "Well I hardly think she'd go as far as stealing you away!" exclaimed Judith.

Having found all of Linda's groceries, Judith put them through the till, and gave Alexandra the bill for her mother to be charged, as she put everything in her shopping basket.

"Well goodbye then," said Alexandra. "It's always nice to come in here and see you. It won't be long before I'll be back, I'm sure."

"Goodbye Alexandra," said both Judith and Stephen.

"Tell your mother, I'll be collecting her quarterly bill soon, won't you please?" asked Judith.

"I'm sure she'll be glad to hear *that*!" remarked Alexandra, with a smile and then waving goodbye, she left the store and started back home. Her mother would be waiting.

Before she went back through the gate of the hamlet, she checked their house post box on the wall. There was post for her mother – as well as her mother's newspaper, the Geratican Times, which she had delivered at the weekend - so she picked everything up, and put it into the basket. She also checked the box for the other house in Elmsbrook, but it was empty. She and Tom often collected the post if they were passing, sometimes together or sometimes separately, and delivered it to each house. Alternatively, if her mother wanted something urgently, she might be sent down the drive, specifically to fetch it. They also had the good fortune of having a post collection box, right outside the hamlet.

Her mother was just finishing vacuuming the parlour, when she arrived back home. She switched it off, when she saw Alexandra and placed her hands on her hips.

"Did they have everything I wanted?" she asked.

"Yes Mother. It's all there," Alexandra confirmed. "Here's your bill," she added, handing it and the shopping list to her, "and I picked up your post and newspaper."

"So I see. Good. Thank you for that," said Linda. "Right. Now, whilst I sort that out and tidy up the accounts, I'd like ... well that is I *want* you to take the vacuum cleaner upstairs and put it round your bedroom. Then we'll be finished with it."

"OK, at once, Mother," said Alexandra, taking off her coat and pulling up her sleeves.

"Also, whilst I'm in the study, I'll have a quick look through your account book too. I assume it's on your desk?"

"Of course Mother. It's in my top tray. Oh, talking of accounts, Judith asked me to tell you that she'll be round collecting the quarterly bill soon."

"Yes, yes. Yes," said her mother impatiently. "She doesn't need to remind of that. I know when my creditors are due payment. That's just basic household finance!" And with that, she picked up the shopping basket and bustled into the kitchen.

Alexandra smiled to herself. *I said she'd be glad to hear that*, she thought, as she took the vacuum cleaner upstairs and began what she hoped would be her last job of the morning.

After she had finished, she brought the vacuum cleaner back down, and put it back in the Utility room. Her mother was preparing a quick snack in the kitchen.

"OK, I think that's about it for now darling," she said. "Now we'll have something to eat." She smiled. "Well, we need something to get our strength back after all that exertion, don't we?"

"Before I do anything else though Alexandra, please come here," she continued,

Her daughter looked at her, slightly puzzled, but did as she was asked.

Linda reached out and took her in her arms. She looked into her eyes and said, "Thank you for all your hard work this morning, darling. You are a very good girl that any mother would be proud of, and I'm the luckiest one of all, because you're mine!"

Alexandra beamed, but before she could respond her mother had wrapped her in a strong embrace. and was kissing her lips. She murmured with pleasure once again. Just like her mother's cooking, she also loved her hugs. She was also thrilled by the compliment she'd just been given. She thought it was the nicest thing her mother had ever said to her. With all the affection she could muster, she kissed her back.

# CHAPTER 3

After lunch, Alexandra asked her mother if she could go out and call on Tom.

"Of course you can, sweetheart," said Linda. "I'll be here to supervise Mike, when he gets here, and afterwards, I'll bring the washing in, but you're free to go off, and have a nice afternoon."

Mike was a gardener and general handyman. Linda had employed him, after her husband died, to take care of that side of things for them, as and when required.

"I trust that I don't need to remind you of when I expect you back by?" she asked.

On instinct, Alexandra's hand discreetly began to move towards her bottom, as she thought of six strokes of the cane against it. Once before she'd suffered the punishment for returning home just slightly late.

"No Mother," she replied. "I know the rule about being home before dusk, and I won't break it."

"Good," said Linda. She didn't necessarily believe that her daughter would, but every now and again, she liked to give her a gentle reminder that she was the boss, and what her rules were.

"In fact poppet, today I want you back by 4 pm at the latest," she continued. "We're doing something special tonight and you'll need to prepare. Therefore, I'd also prefer it if you didn't invite Tom in when you return. And when you go up to your room to get ready to see him, you'll find out what it is. I think that you'll like it.

"Go on! The sooner you get up those stairs, the sooner you'll know, and the longer you'll be able to spend with Tom."

Alexandra smiled excitedly and her heart began to beat faster. Whatever it was, sounded like it could be a treat!

"Yes, Mother!" she said, her voice slightly breathless and it was all Linda could do, to keep a straight face.

With that, Alexandra went straight through to the stairs and raced up them.

The first thing she noticed when she entered her room, was her favourite gown, laid out on the bed. They must be going out. And presumably somewhere quite glamorous! She loved being able to dress up, and feel like a real Geratican lady, which she knew she would be soon.

Then she spotted the rest of her mother's present to her, on the dressing table. There were three things placed side by side. She picked each one up in turn.

The first was an open envelope, with two tickets inside for a classical music performance taking place tonight, at the Queen Alexandra theatre. The special guest performer was Alexandra's favourite modern day Geratican composer, Philippa Barrington, whom she was studying at Charterhouse, and whose pieces she regularly practised and performed on the piano downstairs in the parlour!

She felt another wave of excitement, flooding through her. This was too good to be true! But whatever could the other things be? Surely, nothing could top that?

She picked up the second item. It was the dinner menu for the restaurant at the Geratica – the most exclusive five-star hotel in the queendom. They were going there too? She couldn't believe it! Her mother had been there a few times, and told her about it. She had also promised to take her there one day.

And so she came to the final part. This turned out to be the thing that amazed her the most. A booking form for tonight, in a bedroom, of the Geratica Hotel, together with a room key!

Alexandra turned to rush back downstairs to thank her mother, but to her surprise, she was standing in the doorway, with her arms folded, smiling.

"Mother!" she exclaimed. "How long have you been there?"

"Almost the entire time you've been up here actually," said Linda. I'm really sorry. I didn't mean to spy, but you couldn't expect me to miss seeing you discover your treat, could you? "

She placed her hands on her hips, still smiling. "Well? Was I right? Do you like it? Hmm?"

"Oh Mother! It's fantastic! "Thank you!" She rushed across to her. Her mother opened her arms and drew her in. Alexandra kissed her, and this time it was Linda who returned it.

"But surely, this is more than one treat, Mother? I can't believe it! How did you manage to arrange it all?"

"Well I don't mean to boast, but *am* a very good organiser, darling!" replied Linda, with a familiar twinkle in her eye that Alexandra knew well.

"The first thing to say is that, although we are officially booked into that room, the key will in fact not fit the lock, as it's actually a miniature copy of the one for the Queen Alexandra Marital Suite! That's *unofficially* where we are staying, though of course the proper key is safe and sound at the Geratica."

"The Queen Alexandra Marital Suite? We're staying there? I didn't think it was finished yet?"

"It is now and it's about to become available. To get back to how I managed to arrange it all, I will confess that it was pure coincidence and luck, really" she added. "The Marital Suite has just been completed, and it's specially built for Queen Alexandra to take her Prince Consort, on their Wedding night – whoever he may be, and whenever it occurs. But at other times, starting from the beginning of next week, it will be available to anyone else prepared to pay for it, whether they are newly-weds or not. And I've managed to pull a few strings, to allow us to check that it's all in tip-top condition, in a secret visit this weekend, before the first official guests start to arrive next week!

"Then I found out that, by pure chance, on the same night that we could stay there, the concert was going to take place, and I knew you'd love that too, so I arranged for us to go to both! It probably won't happen again, so it's now or never. I take it that you wish for 'it' to be 'now', and not 'never'?"

"Definitely, Mother!" exclaimed her daughter.

Linda made the gesture of a fairy godmother waving her magic wand above Alexandra's head. "Then my darling daughter, you shall go to the ball!"

Alexandra giggled. Her mother, despite being extremely strict, had a very kind and loving heart, and she could be funny at the same time.

"Now there's just one more thing to say about this Alexandra. This is an unofficial visit to the Suite, so very few people are going to be aware that we're in there, even amongst the hotel staff. Queen Alexandra knows, as well as Fiona – I had to tell her, as the whole project has been under her control, since its inception – but that's about it. So please keep this under wraps. Understood? I don't want a scandal developing, due to the mistaken belief that I'm doing this purely for a 'freebie'. There is a valid reason for us going, as we want everything to be in good order and spotless before next week, but doubtless there would be some who would see otherwise, and make an issue about it, which would almost certainly become public.

"There really shouldn't be any teething problems, but if we do find anything, I will report it, and it will have to be fixed before the 'opening night', as it were."

"I understand, Mother. I won't say anything," said Alexandra. "But didn't Fiona want to do this herself?"

"Well frankly I think she might have done, yes," replied Linda. "But I'm afraid I rather pulled rank with her! I thought that seeing as I've more or less had nothing to do with this enterprise, Fiona could at least let me make the final inspection. I am the senior of the two of us, don't forget, so if I really put my foot down and insist, then she has little choice but to yield in the end. And that indeed was what happened."

Alexandra thought that she could detect a hint of bitterness in her mother's voice. Perhaps Linda's lack of involvement in the construction of the suite, had been a bone of contention between the two women. Alexandra could imagine her mother finding it very frustrating. She liked to be in control of everything. Of course, when she came home at night, she encountered little or no resistance in achieving that ambition. This sounded like another issue that Alexandra felt it might be diplomatic – and safer – to stay out of.

"What about Tom? I wonder if Fiona's told him? Am I permitted to talk to him about it, Mother?" asked Alexandra.

There was a short pause as Linda thought about it. "Really I should forbid it, because the greater the number of people who know a secret, the bigger the risk that someone could make a mistake and let it slip, or that someone should turn out to be untrustworthy. That's a useful thing for your keen mind to absorb and learn, Alexandra!" she said.

"However, Tom is your best friend, and I've no doubt you're bursting to tell him. I suppose the only person who he is likely to talk about it to, is his stepmother, and she obviously already knows. Very well, you have my permission, *but*, only with the proviso that you swear him to secrecy."

She wagged her finger at her daughter, as she continued, "I mean it Alexandra. This is *very* important! You *must* compel him to talk to nobody about this apart from Queen Alexandra, Fiona, you and myself. Do you hear me?"

"Yes, Mother. Loud and clear. I give you my word that he won't betray us. If he did it would be by accident or force, I'm sure."

"Alexandra, once a secret is betrayed, then whether it was by a genuine accident, by forceful extraction, or by treachery, is irrelevant, because the result is that the damage has already been done in equal measure, by whatever the method was that betrayed it. That's something else for you to remember."

"I do however, accept your word, Alexandra. I hope I won't regret my decision, but I am in a kind mood today."

"Thank you, Mother," said Alexandra. "I won't let you down. I promise. "And thank you again for all of this. I'm really excited, and looking forward to it so much!"

"Don't mention it," replied Linda. "It's my pleasure, really it is. I like making you happy. "

"And I like to make you pleased with me," began Alexandra.

But she was interrupted by the phone.

"Oh, that will be Mike, down at the security gate!" exclaimed Linda. "I didn't realise we'd been up here for so long. Right, I'd better go down and let him in to Elmsbrook, and you get yourself ready and go to Tom. *But remember what I said, and also* make sure you're not late back, because now you know we're going away tonight. I'll explain the exact programme of events then. I made sure that you got your weekend prep done last night, so that's out of the way. Now, I've arranged everything, and as it's your treat, you just relax, and let me take care of you, in every way. If you want my arm around you the whole time, you'll find it's available, and *very* willing and able."

The phone went again. "I must go," said Linda. "I'll be taking Mike out to the back garden, so you just let yourself out when you're ready. See you later."

"Yes Mother," said Alexandra. As far as she was concerned, her mother always liked to take the lead anyhow, and she liked to follow her. That was what made her feel taken care of, as she trusted her implicitly.

They exchanged a brief kiss, and then Linda hurried downstairs.

When she answered the phone in the hall, Alexandra heard her mother say to Mike. "Sorry I took so long. Alexandra and I were having a little game together, upstairs. I'm taking her out tonight, and she's just been finding out about it!"

# CHAPTER 4

Soon afterwards, Alexandra arrived at The Lodge. It had a nameplate on the wall. There was a similar one at The Grange. The Lodge was a smaller house, with four bedrooms (not ensuite).

Fiona, Tom's stepmother, answered the door. About three years younger than her own mother, she was around the same height and build. She had long dark hair and green eyes.

"Hello Alexandra!" she said. "Tom's just upstairs. I think he thought you might be calling, so he's been getting ready."

"Good afternoon, Mrs Clark," replied Alexandra. "Oh right. Well as long as he's decent, I'll go on up to him then."

"No, let him finish" countered Fiona. "He'll be down shortly, when he's ready. Come on into the kitchen and have a chat."

Not wishing to be rude, Alexandra reluctantly followed her. This kind of thing happened quite a lot here. She hoped that Tom wouldn't take too long to come down and rescue her.

"Drink?" asked Fiona.

"No thanks, Mrs Clark," said Alexandra.

"I suppose you've had a busy morning doing housework chores with your mother?"

"Indeed, Mrs Clark."

"I've said it before, although it's not my business. I don't why your mother doesn't get a cleaner in with a pass for the gate, when she's out at work, like I do twice a week with Mrs Turner. Then she wouldn't have it all to do at the weekend."

"We only do a big clean every few weeks, Mrs Clark. Although there are usually still some things to be done, each weekend."

Alexandra thought the main reason was that she didn't want to pay for such a service, when it could be done by herself. She was quite careful with her money.

"What have you been up to then, over the last few days?"

"Not much, Mrs Clark. Just a week at Charterhouse, really."

"Oh yes. Your mother told me that she was going to see your

headmistress. So how are you doing?"

"Quite well, by the sound of it, Mrs Clark."

"And did Mrs Spencer expound her theories of male equality and altering the planet's core?"

"I believe she and my mother had their usual lively debate, Mrs Clark," said Alexandra dryly.

Fiona smirked.

"So what are your plans for this afternoon?" she asked.

"I don't know, but I expect we'll be in the wood at some point, Mrs Clark."

"What will you be doing there?"

Alexandra's eyes glanced, ever so slightly, at the kitchen door. *Come on Tom!'* she thought.

"Well you know, it's a nice, quiet place to walk in, and sit on the seat by the river and talk, Mrs Clark," she replied to Fiona.

She didn't mention the fact, that it was around that spot that her father had fallen in the river and drowned, and that Fiona had been the last person to see him alive. Somehow, it always seemed an awkward topic of conversation between them.

"And what about tonight? Has your mother any special plans?"

"Yes, she did tell me before I left, Mrs Clark. We're going to a concert tonight and then staying at the Geratica overnight, which I'm told you're aware of."

"I knew that your mother was planning it as a surprise, but not whether she'd told you yet. I hope you have a nice time. Of course I am aware of your *unofficial* location in the hotel tonight. I've supervised its construction, for what feels like decades now!"

"Actually, Mrs Clark" said Alexandra, "I was wondering if you'd told Tom about it?"

"Tom? No. I don't tend to tell Colin and Tom all that much about the goings on of the monarch or the affairs of court. I try and keep them separate from my home life. I know your mother tends to involve you more and you've even met Queen Alexandra on occasions. You are female and were named after Her Majesty, after all! But why do you ask?"

"Oh well, only because my mother says that it's a closely guarded secret, Mrs Clark, therefore the fewer people who know about it the better."

Then at last Tom appeared, a tall blue-eyed boy, with fair hair. Their eyes met, and they both smiled. Alexandra certainly found him attractive.

"Hi Tom!" she said. "Are you ready to go out?" She shot him a look to try and convey to him the urgency of her request.

"Ready when you are," he replied.

"Well let's go then. Goodbye Mrs Clark. It's been nice to talk to you." This was the biggest fib that Alexandra had told for a long time, but courtesy committed her to be civil, and she had been brought up to always be polite, as far as it was possible.

"Goodbye Alexandra. As always I shall look forward to our next meeting."

Alexandra nodded in acknowledgement, and after Tom had said goodbye to his stepmother, they left the room. Tom got his coat, and they went out of the house and into the Autumn air.

"Let's walk around the wood first," said Alexandra. It'll be really pretty, and there'll be all the leaves on the ground for us to kick our way through,"

As they walked into the wood via the entrance next door to The Lodge, she added "And I want to talk."

"OK," said Tom. "Whatever you like."

# CHAPTER 5

Alexandra was right, and many of the leaves had fallen from the trees, in some places covering the ground in a sea of gold and brown.

"Come on!" she said happily to Tom. "Let's kick our way through Autumn's golden gown!"

And together they began to kick through the leaves, giggling and laughing, just as they had done for many years previously. 'Autumn's golden gown', was a reference to 'Forever Autumn' by Justin Hayward, a song that Alexandra had picked up from listening to and studying Earth's 20$^{th}$ century pop history, and it was one of her favourites. She 'always loved this time of year', too.

Geratican technology allowed people to pick up music being broadcast on Earth, which was the main other planet with life-forms that they knew of. They could even make copies as they listened. Alexandra had a part of her music collection, exclusively devoted to Earth's music, of many different genres. When it came to pop, she particularly searched for stations that played music from a wide time span. Geratica did have a developing pop culture, but there was nowhere near as much of it. Their world traditionally focused more on the more 'serious' or classical end of the scale. But Alexandra enjoyed Earth's pop, and she felt that if more of their world listened to it, they would, too. (She also liked Geratica's). When searching for the 'classics' of Earth's music, she liked stations which played works from a good variety of composers. Tom had lost count of the amount of tunes and songs that she had bombarded him with in her bedroom. Luckily, they had found that their musical tastes were similar. Alexandra seemed to have a natural taste, and a good ear, for what was good quality in both Geratican and Earth culture, he had decided some time ago. He was happy to let her broaden his somewhat more limited knowledge of music.

Alexandra's thirst for knowledge also never ceased to amaze him either. She was always reading a book and devouring the contents. Tom had never been formally educated – that wasn't the traditional path that boys took on Geratica, though his stepmother had given him a basic grounding herself, in common with a number of other women – but when he was with Alexandra, it was obvious to him that she absorbed everything. She was shy and needed her confidence boosted, but she was highly knowledgeable on many subjects, such as science, Geratican history and geography, maths and Geratican language and literature. On top of that, she seemed to know almost as much about the same subjects on Earth, as well as their politics and cultures. He knew that Earth fascinated her, and that she would like to go there one day, if it was ever possible to do it. And it genuinely wouldn't surprise him, if she did turn out to be the pioneer from their planet, who did achieve that possibility. Alexandra and her mother had a telescope set up in the loft of The Grange, from where they could observe the night sky.

Alexandra and Tom had known each other from an early age. They had both been five, when he and his father, Colin, had moved into The Lodge with Fiona, after they had married, soon after meeting and she had become his stepmother. His biological mother had died when he was very young, and he had no memory of her. That was why, although Colin's surname was now Clark, having taken his wife's name, as was customary on Geratica, Tom's surname was still Ryder, his mother having been Jane Ryder. He was four weeks younger than Alexandra.

Being the only two children in the only two houses of this quiet and secluded hamlet of Elmsbrook, away from the outside world, and in an idyllic setting - with a wood which encircled the back of the hamlet and separated their houses, that they could explore and have completely to themselves to play and talk in - they had naturally become very close. They were also fortunate that their personalities seem to gel, and their tastes and interests often converged. Both considered the other to be their best friend and they confided in each other quite a lot. Although boys weren't formally educated, his stepmother had given him some basic literacy skills at home – which wasn't uncommon. Alexandra felt that he was actually quite intelligent.

At least when they were in Elmsbrook wood, on their own and with no one else there to see them, their relationship had recently developed to the point where Alexandra would take Tom's hand as they walked. They had never discussed it, but it was again something that had started to happen naturally, and both of them liked it. When Alexandra squeezed her fingers around Tom's in a gesture of affection, they both looked into each other's eyes and smiled, but that was as far as they had gone so far, even though both sensed what might be beginning between them. Alexandra particularly, was beginning to find that her dreams at night were starting to have more and more of her romantic and erotic fantasies in them, in which Tom was always the object of her desire, and for the first time, her young female Geratican body was experiencing sexual arousal, which she found highly pleasurable. Her geratis had made its first tentative move outside of her vagina, a few weeks ago, and now this was becoming a more regular occurrence.

Their walk had taken them to their regular spot, by the river, where they could sit on the bench, and take in their surroundings.

As they sat down, Tom asked, "So, you want to talk then?"

"Yes," said Alexandra. "Well, I'll tell you my latest news first. I found out after lunch, just before I came to call on you, that Mother's treating me tonight. And it's got to be the best one she's ever given me! You'll never guess all the things she's managed to arrange!"

"You're obviously excited and bursting to tell me," said Tom. "So go on then. I'm listening."

"Mother told me to be home by 4 pm at the latest, as we were doing something tonight and I'd need to get ready," Alexandra began. "She said that if I went to my room, I'd find out what it was. When I arrived, the clues were all there for me to find."

She told him about everything she'd found, and the night that was in store for her.

"Well, you certainly are going to have a fabulous time, of that I'm sure," he said, when she had finished. "The Queen Alexandra Marital Suite! I suppose if anyone could 'pull strings' to get you in there, for an unofficial visit, before anyone else can, it would be your mother!"

"Yes, but Tom, remember what I told you," said Alexandra. "Tell no one, other than the small circle of people I've mentioned. You *must* swear to me that you won't. Please. This is *very* important. I've given my word to my mother that you won't. If you do, then we'll both be for a flogging outside Queen Alexandra's Palace!"

"Alexandra, it's alright. I promise!" said Tom.

"Alright," replied Alexandra, "but it's just that Mother was very clear – as always – that I should 'compel' you to secrecy."

"Anyway, I can't wait to see the suite," she continued. "I only wish you could too." She squeezed his hand that was still inside of hers. "Maybe I'll be able to take you there myself, sometime!"

The possible implications of what she'd just said made them both blush slightly, as they had never discussed such matters before.

"Of course it's my birthday, coming up this week," said Tom.

"Well, I don't think I can arrange it that quickly!" answered Alexandra. Now they both giggled, and Alexandra squeezed his hand again, playfully.

"I hadn't forgotten, and in fact, that brings me to the next thing I need to tell you about. With Mother's permission, I'm inviting you over for dinner with us, a week today. She'll cook us all a special dinner, and we can drink. We'll be able to get all dressed up, and I'll wear a lovely gown, especially for you."

"Tom, do you find me attractive?" she blurted out. Tom looked at her in surprise, at the sudden personal question. Alexandra was amazed at herself for being so forward, but she had wondered about it for so long, and now she simply had to know.

"Um, er, well," Tom struggled to find the first words. "Well actually, now that you come to mention it, yes I do, very much so. In fact, I'd say you were my idea of the perfect beautiful girl."

Alexandra lost her breath for a moment and her toes tingled as a rush of excitement tore through her. She had always hoped ... but Tom's words were more than she had ever dared dream of!

"Do you really mean that?" she asked hoarsely." You're not just saying that to please me, because I've asked you?"

"Alexandra!" cried Tom. "No. Certainly not! I would never do that. You're my best friend. You know that." This time he squeezed her hand.

"Thank you!" she said softly. "You're mine too."

She squeezed his hand inside of hers, tighter than ever before – so tight in fact, that unless she loosened her grip, Tom would never free himself from her – as images came to her mind, of making love to him in her bed, like she had fantasised about so many times. Immediately – quicker than ever before – the strongest wave of sexual arousal she had yet experienced, took over her geratis, and it extended out of her vagina, the furthest yet, making her feel a deep pleasure, and she was suddenly worried that its force and power, might create such a bulge in her skirt, that it would be visible. With her free hand, she quickly and discreetly covered it, hoping that Tom wouldn't notice. She wanted to kiss him very much, and take the initiative, as Geratican women traditionally did in such activities, but she didn't have the confidence to do it at the moment. Therefore, she wasn't quite ready to reveal to Tom, the extent of her desire. When she did, she wanted him to be in no doubt that she wanted him as her lifelong partner, and also that the relationship be traditional, with her leading, and that meant sexually, too. It was her mother's influence. But she had to feel completely capable of taking that role, first.

Getting a grip on her thoughts, she forced them back to the previous conversation, she and Tom had been having.

"So, if you're free, do you want to come over for dinner?" she asked. "You know it would be just as much of a treat for me as for you, if you did come. I'll have to let Mother know soon though. She might even ask me tonight."

"Well that's no problem. I can tell you now, that I'd love to come," replied Tom. "I'd better check with my stepmother, but I'm sure she won't mind."

"Yes, she's actually next on my agenda for discussion, but I'll come to *her* in a minute," said Alexandra. "First, what are your plans for your birthday itself? Can I see you in the evening, after dinner? I'll be at Charterhouse during the day obviously. You'd have to come to me, because you know I'm not allowed to go out on my own by that time. I could ask my mother to take me down, but she might not be there. I know she says she's going to be really busy, in the early part of next week and might not be home until late. In any case I have another reason for wanting you to come over to me."

"Oh?" enquired Tom. "Sounds interesting. What would that be then?"

Alexandra's voice became soft. "Well," she began, "I said I'd wear a lovely gown for you, and I'd be really happy to be wearing something that you've chosen. I want you to be enjoying what you're seeing on your birthday! Come over and see them all in my room. I'll put them on one by one, and then whichever you think you'll find me most attractive in, will be the one I'll wear, next weekend, *just for you!"*

She could tell by Tom's reaction, that she'd hit a spot that aroused him, which thrilled her. She was capable of seducing him!

"I've seen you in a couple of your gowns, and you did look nice," he said. His genus was ballooning. "OK. I've no hope of resisting an offer like that – especially on my birthday! "Yes, I'd love to come over."

Alexandra glowed. "That's settled then! Is 8.00 p.m. OK for you? That'll give us about an hour, before I'll have to start thinking about getting ready for bed. 'Lock up' is at 9.30 p.m."

"That will be fine, Alexandra." said Tom.

"Good!" replied Alexandra. "I'll also make sure to play some of your favourite music, whilst we're together."

"*Our* favourite music." said Tom.

"Yes, you're right. Most of it I'll like very much too," she agreed.

"Alright," she continued, but changing the subject. "Tom, I need to talk about Fiona."

"What's bugging you?" he asked.

He knew instinctively, that Alexandra had been troubled by something that Fiona had said or done. She was quite sensitive and confided in him her worries and concerns about things in general, a lot. He felt that her worrying, combined with her natural shyness, was often what caused her to sometimes be nervous and lack confidence, despite the fact, that she was quite the cleverest girl he knew, and he really didn't think she had any need to doubt herself or her abilities. In that respect, she was lucky that she had an extremely strong mother, who very much told her what to do, and generally managed her affairs. He knew she was very close to her – closer than he was to his own stepmother, in fact – and he liked and got on well with her too. Fiona was his stepmother and so he did naturally feel a certain loyalty towards her (and also love), but he and Alexandra had both often shared their uneasiness about her, with each other. Despite her being his stepmother, when they talked of her, they often referred to her simply as Fiona.

"Well, this morning, Judith-" began Alexandra.

"Who?" interrupted Tom.

"Judith Warwicker the owner of the grocery store."

"Oh, her," he said. "We only know her as Mrs Warwicker, in our house."

"That's probably the case with most people actually, but possibly because of who Mother is, I think she and her husband like to try and be more intimate with us. But they are genuinely quite friendly people, and I like them.

"Anyhow, whilst I was in their store, shopping for Mother, they told me that Fiona had been in, enquiring about me. I did try to press Judith to tell me what, specifically, she wanted to know, but all she said was that she didn't think it was anything important, and also that she thought Fiona was fond of me."

"Perhaps it really *was* just an innocent enquiry," said Tom.

"Anything is possible, but somehow I rather doubt that, Tom," Alexandra declared. "And my doubts increased this afternoon, when I came to call on you. I wanted to go straight upstairs to you, but she insisted that I come into the kitchen with her, where she grilled me on what I'd been doing recently, where we were going to go this afternoon, and she particularly wanted to know what we were going to do in the wood. What did she think we were going to do? Get undressed and swim in the river? Then she was asking about any special plans that Mother had for tonight, obviously trying to find out if she'd told me where we were going. I was desperate for you to come downstairs, so that I had an excuse to get away."

Tom smiled. "Yes, I could tell. You couldn't get out of the house quick enough! Well I suppose I am her stepson, so she wants some idea of what we'll be doing."

"Tom! Even my own mother, who you know is one of the *strictest* and most controlling, in all Geratica, doesn't make me feel like Fiona. It's almost as if she's stalking me!"

"Hey, now!" said Tom calmly and squeezed her hand again. "Don't upset yourself. I've told you before, she often quizzes me about your goings on, too. I'm on your side and I promise to always be loyal to you. But if she's really starting to get to you like this, then you've got to tell your mother."

"I've considered that. But Fiona's your stepmother, and you're my best friend. They work closely together at court, and I don't want to make things awkward for Mother, there. I think she's got her own views on Fiona, though she keeps them to herself. I don't need to remind you of what happened to Father, just over there." Alexandra pointed to the river, which ran through the centre of the wood, and eventually meandered away out of Elmsbrook. "We've talked about it, so many times. Why were they walking along the riverbank on such a stormy, wet day, when it was muddy and slippery, and Father couldn't swim? He'd tried to learn, but the lessons weren't successful. The current is very strong and it all happened so quickly, but could Fiona truly have done nothing to help him before he was swept away?"

"Well, his body was never found and the police investigation concluded that it was accidental death," said Tom.

"Hmm," said Alexandra. "I don't suppose it ever will be found now. But you've got to understand Tom. That makes it so hard for Mother and I to come to terms with. I was only five, but I do remember him. Still. At least the rest of us in the hamlet can swim!"

"I do understand Alexandra," replied Tom. "I'm here for you if you need me – and I think you do."

Alexandra felt a huge surge of pure love, welling up inside of her and massive sexual arousal. Once again, she anticipated what was happening to her geratis, and she did her best to hide the evidence, as it strained inside her pants.

She wanted Tom so badly now. She was almost certain that he was the boy she eventually wanted to marry. And yet still she couldn't ... She wasn't confident enough to ...

After a while, Alexandra looked at her watch.

"Sorry Tom, but I think today we'd better not hang about too much.

Let's start walking back. I need to get ready for tonight. I promise I'm not going to think about Fiona for a while now. I've got so much to look forward to in the next week, what with my overnight treat, then you coming over to me on your birthday and again for dinner next weekend!"

She released his hand as they got up from the bench, and then did something she hadn't before, linking his arm inside of hers, in union. She hoped that this might send a signal to him that she wanted to move their friendship into a new phase. Although they had never discussed such things, in her own mind, Alexandra now regarded Tom, unofficially, as her long-term boyfriend.

She caught his gaze for a moment and then smiling softly, she pressed his arm to her, inside her own.

"What time are you leaving," asked Tom, as they started walking through the wood, towards the entrance adjacent to The Grange, arm in arm.

"I don't know yet." Alexandra gave Tom a look. "Mother is going to inform me of 'the exact programme of events' when I get home!"

They both smirked slightly. "Mother is in her element when she's organising and co-ordinating things." said Alexandra. "Including me!" she added. "It's sometimes like she's still at court! I wouldn't have it any other way though. I love her very much."

"Yes, I think she's got a very kind heart, underneath all that bossiness." said Tom. "As long as you don't get on the wrong side of her, and you do everything exactly as she says, that is!"

With her free hand, Alexandra gave him a playful jab in the ribs. "Don't be rude!" she said. "That's *my mother* you're talking about, don't forget. She wouldn't hesitate to give you the cane, as well as me, you know!"

"I'm only teasing. You know that," said Tom. "I like her a lot too."

He genuinely respected Mrs Radcliffe (and in any case, Geratican children were traditionally brought up to regard their elders - and especially women – in such a way). But Fiona certainly believed that she dominated her daughter. Then again, he believed that his stepmother probably dominated his father.

"In any case, *I've* experienced the cane too, from my stepmother, as *you* know!" he added.

"Yes, of course I do," replied Alexandra, patting his arm inside of hers.

Tom's upbringing had been slightly more liberal than her own, with not quite so many hard and fast rules and his telling offs and lectures generally milder, with Fiona very rarely seeming to even raise her voice. When she did lose her temper however, which admittedly didn't seem to be very much, she had a nasty, violent, and almost sadistic streak in her. As far as she was aware he had only ever been caned once by his stepmother, when he had gone into her study without permission and read something on her desk. Fiona had gone berserk, and given him a beating on his bare skin of his bottom, that had left him black and blue and in some discomfort, when he walked and went to sit down, for a couple of days. Even her mother had been shocked by his condition, when she had seen him walking down the drive of Elmsbrook to The Lodge and had kindly driven him the rest of the short distance home. It had always seemed a gross over-reaction for such a trivial offence to Alexandra, and had further deepened her mistrust of Fiona.

They could now see the edge of the wood, where it met the drive.

"One other thing," said Tom. "You said just now, that your mother was in her element when she was co-ordinating. Do you mind if I make an observation?"

"Hmm?" asked Alexandra, an inviting expression on her face.

"You sometimes feel shy, nervous and not very confident, and you're happy to let your mother take the lead and be the strong, dominant force in your life, and I don't blame you for that. She's been the perfect mother for you, as you've grown up, and given you exactly what you've needed – someone to manage your life, tell you what to do, and build you up when you need more confidence.

"But when you're with me, you seem more confident, and certainly not unable to take the lead. Look at this very afternoon. You've been the one doing it. You mentioned Fiona being on your 'agenda.' It was a bit like a meeting with you in the chair!"

"Oh, sorry!" exclaimed Alexandra. "I didn't mean it to seem like that. I wanted us to have a nice time together."

"No! No! Don't worry about that, silly. I didn't mind at all, and I did have a *lovely* time. I always do when I'm with you. All I'm trying to say is, that I think you're a far more capable person than you give yourself credit for. You're very intelligent and knowledgeable about many subjects, far more than most other people I know. You have a very logical, analytical and scientific mind and you use it very well. You've thought about what you want to say, you have an agenda in your mind, and then you go through it, ticking every item off, one by one. If there was a problem for the whole world and you were told to solve it, you'd be very nervous, I'm sure, but I'd have every confidence in you achieving it. If you and I did something together and one of us had to speak, you never know, you might just be the better one to do it. You know that I have quite a traditional Geratican man's life, which I'm happy with, and I don't see anything wrong in the typical Geratican woman."

Near to edge of the wood, Alexandra had stopped, forcing Tom to as well. She wanted to hear all his words and study them carefully. Fortunately, she possessed the ability to take in a lot of information in a short space of time. She could already play back in her mind, almost word for word what he had just said.

"Well," she replied, when he had finished. "That was certainly quite an observation! I don't think I've ever heard you speak for so long!"

Alexandra's heart was beating fast. She wasn't sure quite how, but somehow Tom's words were building up confidence inside of her. She was now certain that they were meant to be together, and now she believed, at last, that – with Tom at least – she could fulfil the role that she that she had been brought up to take, and which they both wanted. She sensed that this was the time for her to finally take the initiative.

At the point where they'd stopped, she could just see through to the back garden of The Grange and their apple orchard just beyond the gate, through a small gap in between two bushes. The problem with having a large garden, was that there were many places where people might be, but as her eyes scanned around, to her relief she saw Mike, with her mother close by him. It looked as if they might be there a while yet. She was in luck.

All the while she was thinking as quickly as she could. Her mother had taught her take her role seriously, as the initiator in any serious relationship that she sought, and she felt that Tom would want her to do it in the traditional Geratican manner, also. This could potentially be a hugely significant moment in both their lives, and it was her job to arrange the terms, so that both of them were happy to proceed, and that the relationship had a reasonable chance of success. Once she had, and she'd made the proposal, it would be customary for Tom to defer to her judgement. So she had to get it right! Apart from anything else, she and Tom had always had an unusually special bond together, and she didn't want to do anything that might damage that, or hurt him or her – most particularly him, because she now loved him so much.

# CHAPTER 6

The late afternoon air was getting chilly, as they stood together. Alexandra started to make decisions. The first thing they needed to do was go into her mother's house, to get warmer. This was slightly disobeying her mother's instructions (and she normally followed them to the letter), but on the other hand, she'd only said that she'd *prefer* her not to bring him in, due to her need to prepare for tonight. It was only 3.25 pm however, therefore Alexandra felt that she should just still have enough time, and she hoped that if her mother knew exactly what she had in mind to do, then she wouldn't be too bothered about it. In any case, Alexandra didn't want to tell her mother exactly what she was doing until afterwards – a matter of such personal potential significance was one for her alone to deal with, she felt. If she was lucky, her mother *might* still be in the back garden with Mike, so she could get him in without having to see her beforehand. If not, she would have to give her a *vaguely* truthful reason for bringing him in with her - which she couldn't think of at the moment - but she hoped that her mother would accept it. It would also give her a bit more time to prepare herself. Then she could take Tom upstairs and they could talk.

"Tom, I've decided that there's something else I need to discuss, *extremely* urgently," she began. "But not standing out here. Let's go into The Grange."

Tom looked at her in surprise. She could see that he'd been taken aback, but she still gave him a hard, serious look back and tightened his arm, still inside of hers, against her body, for extra emphasis, as she continued talking.

"Tom, this is *very* important for both of us, and I need to be the boss here. *Please* accept that, and defer to me. I must *insist* and you must *yield*. That's the way we do things, regarding this issue, on this world. And we must do it quickly, or else we might lose the moment and I might lose my nerve."

"Yes, alright," said Tom. "Take me wherever you want, and tell me whatever it is you want to tell me, but could you please do me a favour and soften up a bit? I don't mind you being the boss, but I'm not used to you being quite so assertive!"

Without referring to Tom's request, Alexandra simply said, "Come on," and walked him around the corner and up the long driveway of The Grange. As they went, she said to him in a slightly softer tone, "I'm really sorry Tom. I don't mean to be doing this in a bullying kind of way. But I don't want to tell you all about this, until we're inside, and at the same time I need to stress its importance to us both. Mother's out in the back garden, so we won't have to see her before we go upstairs. Otherwise I'd have had to make some excuse as to why I've brought you back here. I'm not telling her about this, until we're finished."

When they reached the front porch door, she unlocked it and they went inside. "Don't take your coat off down here," she said. Wait until we're in the left hand spare room. I want us to go in there, so that I can see into the back garden, and keep a check on Mother's whereabouts. I wasn't really supposed to invite you in today, because I need to prepare for tonight. But I think there should still be enough time."

"You're disobeying your mother?" asked Tom, incredulously.

"Well, actually Mother only said that she'd prefer me not to." She ushered him through to the stairs, and led him up.

Once they were finally in the room, Alexandra closed the door and then patted the bed, in indication to Tom of where to sit. Then she moved the dressing table chair out into the room, searching for a position where she could see her mother in the garden below, but was far enough from the window for her mother not to be able to look up and see her. Satisfied, she set it down so that she could see Tom on the bed, to one side, and her mother in the garden on the other. This room had in fact been her playroom, when she was younger.

Tom had taken off his coat, and put it on the bed, beside him. Alexandra put hers on the back of the chair, and sat down.

"Right," she said, rolling up her sleeves, in a manner that she hoped might indicate a certain air of assertiveness. She took a deep breath. "This is it. Here I go," she thought nervously.

"Sorry to drag you into another 'meeting' Tom." she said with a slight smile. "Now, please just listen to me, whilst I talk for a while. I'm hoping you're going to both like and accept what I'm about to offer you, so try not to worry. I'm a lot more nervous than you are, believe me."

She was just about to go on, when she noticed Tom's eyes twinkling and his mouth twitching.

"What? What's so funny?" she demanded.

Tom broke out into a chuckle. "I'm sorry Alexandra," he said, "but I think I've already guessed what you're planning to offer me. If you're nervous, and you don't need to tell me that you are, because I know you well, then I'll try and help you. Would you by any chance be proposing a relationship with me?"

Alexandra looked at Tom and for a brief moment betrayed a smile that

Tom immediately interpreted as an admission. "I'm right aren't I?" he declared triumphantly.

"Yes you are, clever clogs," said Alexandra. "Alright, tell me how you guessed!"

"It was what you said, just before we left the wood. That it was a matter in which you had to be the boss, and that it was the way we did it in Geratica. Well there weren't many other things it could be other than this!"

"Well, Mother would probably say that there were plenty more things, but we'll put that to one side for the moment!" Now they both chuckled. Tom had always enjoyed Alexandra's dry wit.

"Actually I'm glad you did," said Alexandra. "I spent the previous ten minutes trying to find the right words to tell you that I wanted to propose this.

"Right, Tom," she continued. "As I was saying at the beginning, I need you to listen for a while, whilst I tell you my reasons, and then *assuming* you're in agreement, you know that I've then got to set out the terms."

"That's fine. You're the boss," said Tom.

"Yes," replied Alexandra. "OK. We've known each other for ten years now. We've grown up together, played together and talked together, and I think we've got a special bond between us, that few other people in Geratica have got.

"We always liked each other, became best friends, and gradually became more and more fond of each other. But I think we've both begun to notice recently, that other more powerful feelings have been developing between us.

"I do genuinely love you very, very much, Tom, my darling. You're my confidante and best friend, and we like the same things and laugh at the same things. When I'm with you, I never want to leave you.

"I've wanted you for months now, but I didn't feel confident enough in my ability to fulfil the role that I've been brought up to take. What ultimately made me decide to propose this relationship, was your 'observation' of me, whilst we were walking towards the end of the wood. I agree with everything you say.

"You understand my weaknesses and your analysis of my thought process is spot on, which pleases me. I'm quite proud of the way I approach things, and if you appreciate that in me, then that's going to help me a lot.

"I know you value my intelligence, and whilst I don't think there's all that much wrong with yours either, it's true that I've worked hard at school, and I do enjoy finding out about things, for pleasure. Of the two of us, I suppose I might, on occasions, have a greater understanding of the way things are done, so you would be able to rely on me to know what's best sometimes.

"I want us to and very much hope that we'll stay together forever. When it comes to setting up a home on our own, I won't expect you to get involved in any financial matters, partly because I don't think you'll want to. I'll naturally take charge of all household matters and you'll do the traditional male tasks.

"I'll admit, I find you very desirable, sexually and you say I'm your idea of the perfect beautiful girl. Laying my cards on the table, once we're both past the age of consent, next year, I will long to take you to bed and make love to you in the traditional sexual position. I think most Geratican females are quite sexually confident, and have very strong, passionate desire, and I don't seem to be any different. Even though I'm still a virgin, I think that I could perform in bed. At least I hope so. But it must be when you feel ready, too, Tom. I'll be happy to wait for you – although please don't make it too long, as by that time, my passion will be burning!

"All of which leads me to now believe that we are perfect match and I'd like us to form a relationship, which I will lead, as the traditional Geratican woman that I know you like, and that I wish to be."

Alexandra paused for a second. That was the proposal set out, at least. She checked her watch glanced out of the window. Her mother was still outside, but it surely wouldn't be long, before she would be back indoors.

"So, Tom," she said, as she looked back at him. "Now it's time for you to give your answer. Is my proposal, of interest to you?"

"Definitely," declared Tom. "Alexandra, I'm certain that you're the girl I want to spend the rest of my life with. I've wanted it for months, too. I was so thrilled when I realised what you must be going to ask me! You've made my dreams come true. I love you with all of my heart. I love your softness, be it your voice, your touch, or simply the way you go about your life. I love your warmth, your kindness, your intelligence and your beauty – especially your long blonde hair! Without hesitation or reservation of any kind, I accept your proposal. Thank you!"

Pure joy now filled Alexandra's face. "My pleasure, Tom. *My darling!*" She placed particular soft emphasis on the last two words, and was pleased to see a smile of satisfaction creep onto his face. A rush of sexual energy swept through her body again, and her geratis stormed out to its furthest yet, straining in her pants once more. This time, she wasn't so concerned about the possibility of the shape in her skirt becoming visible to Tom. However, although at this stage of her life, she didn't know it, her geratis was of a medium length, and this wasn't going to be a problem for her, unlike some other women with longer ones, who – if they wished their feelings to be kept discreet -sometimes had to take steps to try and hide their arousal, usually by adjusting their state of dress slightly, or wearing a thick skirt or gown.

After another quick glance out of the window, Alexandra said "Right. Now I need to set the terms. We might not have much more time, so let's get this done.

"Right," she said again, "Well, I can't see that there are any obvious major impediments to our happiness, by going into this relationship, so I don't think we need very much, beyond the standard Geratican female and male traditional roles. I just want to introduce two conditions, Tom.

"Firstly, this relationship *will* be led by me, but you of all people understand how my lack of confidence and self doubt, sometimes hinders me. It's because you do and have the ability to help me through, that I know you're the boy for me. I'm never going to be as strong as Mother, therefore our relationship and my needs won't be quite the same as what was between Mother and Father. You must promise me that you'll be supportive of me, as you were in the wood just now. That's what will enable me to lead effectively. Without that, it'll be more difficult.

"Secondly – and this is connected to the first – I want us to take things at a steady pace. Not too slowly, but not all in a rush either. I intend to propose marriage eventually, but that's such an important union, that I won't enter into it, until I'm totally sure that our partnership works, enabling me to fulfil my role as a traditional Geratican wife, as effectively as I want to. I'm already at least ninety-five percent sure, but I won't move to our ultimate union, until I reach one hundred percent and no less.

"Well, I think that's all from my side. Is there anything you want to add Tom? It's my job to make sure we establish the basis of our relationship for the benefit of us both."

"No Alexandra," said Tom. "What I said before, will more or less suffice for me. All I might add is that I think you've just once again proved my point. With a bit of confidence, you can make a natural leader."

"Oh no, not natural," denied Alexandra. "It doesn't, and never will, come naturally to me. I have to really force myself to do it. I'm alright with you – it's a huge advantage that we've known each other for years – and I want to be the lady in charge of my own house and family, with all the responsibilities that go with that. But eventually I'll be going into the 'World of Work', and I'm really not sure at all, whether I would ever want to become a manager."

"Anyhow," she continued. "I think that concludes our business. Thank you very, very much for this! I've got a boyfriend – and he's the only one I've ever *really* wanted. This must have turned out to be the best day of my life, so far!"

She got up and took a final glance outside. Then she walked over to Tom. "All that remains is for us to seal the deal!" she said. Then very softly, "You know what *that* means my darling, don't you? Hmm?"

"No," said Tom.

Alexandra leaned over, slipped her arms tentatively around his shoulders and kissed him on the mouth for the very first time, as he sat on the bed. She sensed him going breathless with excitement, as he held on to her waist. For a couple more seconds, they exchanged kisses and then withdrew, both panting from the power of the arousals inside of them.

"Ooh!" exclaimed Alexandra. "That was nice! I'm doing that again on the second night of next week!"

"Yes!" said Tom. "Thank *you* for making me your boyfriend and allowing me to have *you* as my girlfriend!"

Alexandra beamed. "Don't mention it!"

"Oh. One other thing occurs to me," said Tom. "This makes you my stepmother's potential daughter-in-law! Do you want me to tell Fiona about our relationship now, or leave it for a bit?"

Alexandra pulled a face, as she considered. "That woman!" she said. "I've no doubt she'll be delighted, thinking that she can keep tabs on me even more now! No, perhaps it's best if you don't say anything until after I'm back tomorrow. I need to tell Mother first, and I don't want to risk having her blurting it out in some way, before then. It's possible that Mother might be a bit miffed, if she turns out to be the last of the 'potential parents and in-laws' to find out. I'll give you a call tomorrow, when Mother and I have retuned, whatever time that is."

She smiled. "My first official phone call to my boyfriend!"

"OK Boss," said Tom. He felt a ripple of excitement go through him, stronger than he would have expected, at the thought of Alexandra ringing him. He'd be waiting for it all day! She had demonstrated today, what he had always known she possessed – the ability to lead. And he liked it and wanted her to go on doing it. He never wanted to leave her. He wanted to do all the things that they both enjoyed together, forever. He was a traditional Geratican boy, looking for a traditional relationship with a traditional

Geratican girl. And with the gorgeous Alexandra Radcliffe, the most beautiful girl he knew, whose looks conformed to all his fantasies, and whose clearly obvious sexual desires, complemented his exactly, he was certain he'd found her.

"Right, well you'd best be going and I really must get ready for tonight," said Alexandra. "I'll see you back in here on the second night of week thirty-three, for your birthday treat!"

"Ooh, I can't wait. Honestly, I can't!" replied Tom, putting on his coat. "Hope you have a really nice time tonight and overnight."

"Thanks. I hope so too." said Alexandra.

Then she ushered him back downstairs, and out to the front door, where they kissed again, and said goodbye. Alexandra closed the door, turned, and went back to the stairs, and rushed up them to her room, excitedly, from the thought of both what had just happened, and the evening ahead.

# PART 2

# CHAPTER 1

Alexandra was walking on air.

Tom! She couldn't stop thinking about him and every time she did, her heart jumped for joy, and her geratis moved inside of her.

She hummed softly to herself, as she started her various ablutions. She had just washed and dried her hair, and was at her dressing table, making sure that it looked immaculate, before taking a bath, when there was a knock at the door.

She heard her mother's voice. "Alexandra, can I come in?"

"Yes, Mother," she answered. "I'm in my dressing gown."

"Oh, right," said her mother. She opened the door and came in.

Alexandra could see a warm, happy glow on her mother's face and knew she was in a particularly good humour tonight. She was probably looking forward to this, as much as herself.

"Hello my darling," said Linda. "Did you have a nice time with Tom?"

"Yes, Mother. Very much so," answered Alexandra. This was true. "When I got back, I could see that you were in the back garden with Mike, so I thought I'd leave you to it and came up here to make myself up, so that I'd be ready to go in time." This was only half true, but she planned to tell her mother what had actually happened this afternoon, later tonight.

"Good girl. Sensible thinking," said Linda.

"Well, first of all," she continued, "I've just booked a taxi for 6.00 p.m., to take us to the hotel. Then I'll check us in and we'll slip our bits and pieces up to the suite, whilst the taxi waits, and then it's off to the concert which starts at 8.00 p.m., so that should give us time to get ourselves settled in, beforehand. Then after that it's a five-course meal back at the hotel, which will be in the private Dining room, followed, *of course*, by a night in the Queen Alexandra Marital Suite. Tomorrow will start *unsurprisingly* with breakfast, then maybe a leisurely walk about. We'll aim to be back around late afternoon. I may have one or two other things up my sleeve, during tonight and tomorrow, if you're a good girl."

"Oh, I will be, Mother! said Alexandra, "But how can there be more? You've given me lots of treats before, but never so much all together! It's like having a second birthday, this year!"

Linda drew her daughter into her arms. "Because sweetheart, you're a very special girl and as I always tell you, I'm a very clever mother!" She squeezed and kissed her.

"Have we got a box in the theatre, Mother?"

Her mother looked at her, with an expression of mock amazement. "Darling, have you ever known me to take you to a theatre, and not give you a box?"

"I'll take that as a 'yes' then Mother! Thank you!" She returned the kiss, as she clung to her.

"And now I must go and ready myself, too, said Linda. Once you're fully dressed up to the nines, pop downstairs and when I get down, I'll get us a quick aperitif, to get the proceedings under way, before the taxi comes."

"OK Mother," said Alexandra. "What shall I do about the ironing?" This was normally her job and she generally did it in the early evening, after it had been in the airing cupboard for a while.

"Well, you can't do that *and* travel to Avermore, darling!" laughed Linda. "You can leave it for tonight and do it when we're back tomorrow."

"Very good Mother" said Alexandra obediently, as Linda went off to the mistress bedroom.

And so at around 5.30 p.m., they both sat on the sofa in the parlour, Linda sipping a gin and tonic, and Alexandra a sherry, as they waited for the taxi, their overnight cases at their feet. Each were wearing expensive, glamorous, shoulder-less long black evening gowns – the favourite colour of both.

Linda's had four thigh length splits – two at the front, and two at the back. On her arms she wore matching black gloves that stretched to her elbows. A diamond was studded into the upper wrist of each. She had a locket on a chain hanging from her neck. It contained a picture of her dear late husband, Robert. On the whole she kept it discreetly out of view, beneath a blouse, jumper or dress, but on occasions she allowed it to be visible. Tonight was one such. She wanted her daughter and herself to have a really nice time, and if Robert was here, she would naturally have wished the same for him.

Alexandra's had two smaller splits, one at the front and one at the back. On the chest a silver broach was studded into the fabric. Around her neck was a diamond necklace, given to her by her mother on her fourteenth birthday.

The phone rang. "Ah," said Linda. "I think your carriage awaits, my darling." She crossed the parlour to answer it.

The scanner screen flickered into life, as Linda picked up the receiver.

"Hello James," said Linda, the image on the screen immediately giving her confirmation that it was who she was expecting. "Come on in, and then when you reach The Grange, if you wouldn't mind driving to the door, that would be great, thank you."

"Right you are, Linda!" replied the man.

Linda pressed a button on the scanner. Immediately the gate opened. A moment later a car came through, and made its way up the hamlet drive. The gate automatically closed again, behind.

Alexandra got up as Linda put down the phone and the screen became blank again.

"I didn't know you knew any taxi drivers, Mother?"

Linda smiled mischievously as she picked up her daughter's coat and slipped it over her shoulders. "I've a confession to make darling! When I said I'd booked 'the taxi,' I wasn't talking about a public one. I've arranged something slightly more private. The call that I made was simply to confirm the time that he'd arrive."

"So, who is 'he' then, Mother?"

"You're aware that your headmistress's husband, James, works at the palace?"

"Oh yes, Mother. Her daughter Gillian, never ceases to ensure that everyone knows it. He's Queen Alexandra's chauff ..."

Alexandra stopped in surprise, as her mother's "arrangement" became clear to her. Her eyes widened. "*He's* taking us?"

Linda's eyes twinkled merrily as she smiled, and her eyebrows rose and fell. "Yes my lovely. I know him quite well through my work at court. By another stoke of good fortune, he's free, and at our disposal tonight and tomorrow!"

"You mean you've 'arranged' it with Queen Alexandra, Mother?"

She saw her mother's eyebrows twitch up and down again, in acknowledgement.

Alexandra smiled. "My clever Mother!" she said. Is this another of my 'surprises'?"

Linda could contain herself no longer, and she chuckled as her daughter helped her on with her coat. "Well, considering your reaction, then I think that you already know the answer to that particular question, sweetheart!"

she exclaimed.

They exchanged another brief kiss.

The doorbell rang. "Right then!" said Linda. Pick up your case, and this clever mother will take her wonderful, darling daughter, to the ball!"

# CHAPTER 2

Outside, Linda greeted James, and introduced him to Alexandra. James took their cases, and put them in the boot of the car. He was thirty-five and dark haired.

"Alexandra darling, when you get into the back, if you wouldn't mind sitting on the driver's side, please? If I sit on the passenger side it might be easiest, because then I can see both of you to talk to. I've no doubt that James and I will have a natter, and this side might enable him to see me best through the rear view mirror too."

"OK. No problem, Mother," said Alexandra.

"Watch you don't crease your gown as you sit down, now," warned Linda.

"Yes Mother."

James opened the door, and motioned for Alexandra to get in. Your carriage awaits Ma'am," he said, smiling.

Alexandra smiled back. "Thank you, James," she said and got in.

"I'll just get the house properly secure, and then we'll be off," said Linda.

James got back in the car, and twisted around to face Alexandra, on the back seat, a broad grin on his face. "Nice to meet you at last, Alexandra."

"It's a pleasure to meet you too, James. Should I call you that, or Mr Spencer?"

"James will do just fine!" he said.

"You were very polite and formal with Lin ... er, your mother," he remarked. Was that just for my benefit, or is that the norm?"

"Yes it is. I've been brought up to always address my mother in that fashion." She started to take her coat off and settle herself down for the journey.

"I've heard quite a bit about you," said James. "Both from your mother and my wife. Mostly good, I hasten to add!"

"I'm glad to hear it!" replied Alexandra.

By now Linda was about to return to the car. Alexandra had taken off her coat and James had for the first time seen her in all her finery.

"Alexandra you look fantastic! You're going to knock them dead tonight!"

Alexandra beamed. "Thank you!" she said softly.

"I'm surprised to hear that you haven't got a boyfriend!" exclaimed James.

At that moment though, he got out of the car again, and went around to the other side, to meet Linda, who was now ready to go. He opened the door for her, and she thanked him and stepped in. She smoothed her dress as she sat down, and then James closed the door and returned to the driver's seat.

"Right. The Geratica Hotel please James!" ordered Linda.

"Right you are, Ma'am!" replied James. He drove them to the hamlet gate, and Linda handed him her card. He swiped the console, the gate opened and they were away.

Avermore, their destination, was about 20 miles away, to the north of Greenacres. This was also where the Royal Palace was situated, and where Linda and James worked. They hadn't gone very far when Linda said to James, "It's a bit of a novelty for you tonight isn't it, with a different boss in the back of the car?"

"Yes, but she's still called Alexandra, so there's no real confusion," he replied.

Alexandra could feel a huge laugh coming from inside her belly, and she desperately tried to stifle it.

"You cheeky little man. How dare you!" said Linda. "You know exactly who the boss is in this car, and it isn't my daughter, however much this might be her special night!"

"Linda," countered James, "All little men – and their wives too for that matter – realise by your very presence anywhere, wherever it might be, that you are the boss. Even when Queen Alexandra is in the back of the car with us, I know that it is the woman in the passenger seat beside me, who is really running the show and pulling the strings!"

"Hmm, that was better," replied Linda. "Very well. I shan't sack you tonight then. "Maybe I'll put that first comment down to nerves addling your brain. Or maybe it was the sight in your mirror of two beautiful ladies in the back of this car that did it."

Alexandra was now giggling uncontrollably. Linda smiled softly with a twinkle in her eyes. "Something tickling you, sweetheart?" she asked.

"It's you two together, Mother!" said Alexandra, when they had momentarily subsided. "Is it always like this?"

"Well bear in mind that the queen is usually with us, and we all have to observe a certain amount of decorum and deference when dealing with Her Majesty. Despite James' flattery, even I have to defer to Queen Alexandra's judgement, sometimes, although of course if I am advising her in the right way, her judgement will turn out to be correct! The queen is always the boss. But in general I think we both enjoy our jobs, and we are both staunch supporters of Queen Alexandra, so I suppose we do try to have a bit of fun, every now and again. And I will say that, far from slapping us down and telling us to stop, Her Majesty is far more likely to encourage us."

"Yes, we do get on, very well," agreed James. "And I wasn't entirely joking earlier, either. We all know that if an event is to be staged, a Royal visit or walkabout to be organised, or anything like that needs to be done, then nobody will do it better than your mother, Alexandra."

"Thank you James, it's nice to be appreciated sometimes. It's not what I do the job for – I do it out of duty to the monarch and a desire to make Geratica as good a place to live in as possible, but every now and again it is nice ..."

\*\*\*

Amidst all the banter and conversation, Linda still hadn't taken her coat off, and they still had some way to go, so now she slipped it off, and put it down on the seat with her daughter's. Alexandra glanced over at her mother. With a smile, Linda reached out, and took her hand in her own gloved one.

"Are you alright, my darling?" she asked softly.

"Yes, wonderful, Mother!" replied Alexandra.

"Good!"

Linda stroked her daughter's fingers inside of hers, and Alexandra felt the soft velvety touch of her mother's long black glove. It was nice.

With her other gloved hand, her mother ran her fingers up and down her arm.

The car was quiet for a while. James, whilst maintaining his professionalism in transporting his two passengers safely to their destination, nevertheless could not indeed help but have his attention drawn to the two beautiful blonde ladies in his mirror, and most particularly Linda.

They now knew each other well, and were friendly together. He enjoyed her company, always looking forward to their meetings, and having her in the car with him when he chauffeured Queen Alexandra. He was attracted to her strong personality, and had always found her attractive. She was actually nine years his senior, but he thought that she could easily pass for a woman of his age, or probably younger.

Seeing her tonight though, awakened sexual arousal in him, such that he had not experienced for a long time. He had never seen her looking so beautiful. Her tall, slim body (slightly taller than his), with her blonde hair running down her neck to her bare shoulders, her red lips and in that long black gown and gloves. He also couldn't help but notice the long splits in the front of her gown, which exposed the long black stockinged legs that he had always fantasised about being wrapped tight around his, as she made love to him.

Despite having been married for fifteen years (before he had quite reached twenty, largely due to Elizabeth having just discovered that she pregnant with Gillian; when their parents had discovered that they'd had sex before marriage, they had strongly disapproved, as this was considered unacceptable at the time), the marriage had never been a truly happy one – which Linda was aware of – and this partly explained why there had never been more children. It was also a long time since he had had sex that had been an enjoyable or even comfortable experience for him – though it wasn't that he didn't still find Elizabeth attractive. To make matters worse, he knew that Linda, who he was falling in love with, was a widow, available and possibly looking for love again. He dreamed of her making a move on him, but so far she had never taken the initiative (something he knew that she was more than capable of, and the most likely of the two of them to do). Deep down he knew what the real issue was. He had to tell Elizabeth that he wanted to leave her, but he didn't have the courage. If he ever did manage to do that, he thought he *might* have a chance with her.

***

Alexandra was indeed wonderfully happy tonight, both with her achievements of the afternoon, and the excitement of what lay ahead this evening.

Despite her genuine desire for a traditional Geratican relationship, where she would be leading, she had to admit that, back with her mother now, she was happy to let her be dominant, and take control once again. She found this a bit confusing, and decided that, provided she successfully told her mother about her proposal later, then she would ask her opinion on it.

She was also struck by the apparent chemistry between her mother and James. The conversation had started to pick up again now, and the two of them chatted happily about people they knew at the palace and general goings on, though they avoided specific work related issues, out of respect for Alexandra, whose special night it was, and for whom many of them probably wouldn't have much interest for her anyway. Her mother did not have an easy relationship with the headmistress of Charterhouse, but clearly got on well with her husband, to an extent which she hadn't realised before!

***

Eventually, after about a half hour drive, they reached Avermore. Although she had been there on numerous occasions now, Alexandra still loved to see it. Castra was the capital of Geratica, and Avermore was the real heart of Castra, where many of Geratica's most illustrious and historic institutions were based. The Gonder, Castra's biggest river, came into view.

"Tomorrow, after breakfast, I'll give you a tour around the city," said her mother. "Well, that is of course, James will drive, but I shall be directing!"

"Oh, didn't I tell you? Terribly sorry, but I'm on leave tomorrow." James interjected.

"Oh are you indeed?" retorted Linda. "Well we'll soon change that. It's cancelled. There, I said we'd change that. So, there's an end to it!"

"Right you are, Ma'am," said James, as Alexandra began to giggle again. She didn't think she'd enjoyed a car journey more, for a long time.

"When you finish your education, and go out into the big wide world of work, Alexandra," began James, "do you think that you'd like to have your mother as a boss, based on what you've heard tonight?"

"I already know what it would be like, James," Alexandra replied, "She's the boss at home and would be no different in any other situation."

Linda smiled next to her. "Good answer, Alexandra! You're exactly right. *I am*. You see James, it's like I've always told you. My daughter is a sensible girl, who knows what's best for her, and who to get it from. You should take a leaf out of her book sometimes."

James groaned. "Oh I can't win. I might as well just drive, and say no more!"

"Well that's the most sensible thing *you've* said, for the last five minutes," said Linda. "Commit that to memory, and also add this. 'Do not be cheeky to a woman'!"

"Yes Ma'am," said James.

Shortly, Linda pointed up ahead. "Parliament Square, darling." "Remember when you visited Parliament House, before?"

"Yes, of course, Mother," replied Alexandra. The magnificent building; just over two hundred years old, to their right as they approached the square, backing on to the banks of the Gonder as it wound eastwards; looked just the same as it had previously. Some things rarely changed.

Then, James turned the car ninety degrees right, into a quiet, very low speed limit road. "The Royal Avenue," said Linda. One or two elegant houses dotted the route on the right, beside the Gonder. Then Linda squeezed Alexandra's hand, and pointed to the left. They were approaching the even more ancient Royal Palace.

As Alexandra looked across to see it, her mother reached over and put her arm around her shoulders. The car crawled along, and Alexandra took in the palace's vast courtyard, and gazed at the lights that illuminated the many windows, some of which were rooms she knew from previous visits, and some of which she had no idea what lay behind. There were guards at the main gates, and sentries posted outside the official main front entrance. She felt her mother's fingers softly stroke her hair as she looked, giving her a sensation that always made her tingle when they gently brushed through the ends.

"It's always nice to see the palace and Parliament House lit up in the darkness," remarked Linda.

"Do you still work in the same place, Mother?" Alexandra always asked the same question, whenever she came here. She was very proud of her mother's position, and the work that she did. She loved to see the place where it all happened, and she was also sensible enough to realise that she was very lucky. Her mother's relative affluence, and the comfortable and secluded lifestyle that Alexandra had enjoyed growing up in Elmsbrook, were mainly possible through her years of hard work here.

"Yes. It's still around the back of the palace." There was another, more secluded courtyard there and also another main entrance to the palace, which was actually the one which Queen Alexandra normally used. Linda's department and her personal office was close to there. Behind the courtyard, lay many royal gardens and acres of private countryside surrounded the palace, where the queen often hunted.

As Alexandra continued to look, Linda exchanged a glance with James, through his mirror, and they both smiled. She was due to receive another surprise tomorrow.

The car slowly began to move away from the palace until, upon reaching the other end of the royal Avenue, James turned right again into Divinity Hill. This led them to Avermore Bridge, which they crossed to the other side of the Gonder. Then he drove on through a couple more streets.

"Nearly there now, darling," Linda said softly to her daughter.

Alexandra looked about excitedly. She had always wanted to go to the Geratica!

Eventually she saw the hotel sign, and James pulled into the entrance. Looking out of the window, Alexandra could see that it was obviously another highly impressive looking building.

As soon as they stopped, James came and opened Alexandra's door. She picked up her coat, and with James taking her hand, clambered out of the car.

"Thank you James," she said, smiling again. She liked him.

"Here, I'll help you with that," said James as she began to put her coat on.

"Thank you again James!" she replied, as he finished.

"It's a pleasure Miss Radcliffe," he confirmed. "And may I say what a pleasant and well-mannered girl you are. You're a credit to your mother. Or should I say the boss?! Speaking of whom, I'd better go round and ..."

Before he could say or do anything else, there as a banging on the car window, behind Alexandra. Linda had leant over from her side, and was gesticulating wildly at James to come to her side of the car.

"Oh dear, I'm for it now!" he cried, as he started over to her. Alexandra was starting to giggle again. Normally her mother would have probably been the first out of the car, but she was clearly enjoying playing the role of his boss i.e. Queen Alexandra, and having him wait on her."

"Were you just going to leave me sitting there, whilst you were gossiping?" she scolded him. "We haven't got all night you know!"

"I'm sorry, Ma'am" he said. "Here, I'll help you with your coat, too." Giving it to him, Linda turned around to allow him to slip it over her back, and as she did so, James for the first time saw the back of her gown. *Another two thigh length splits!* His sexual arousal began again. She looked even more stunning than he'd thought. He felt a shiver of excitement sweep through his genus, and he licked his dry lips. His loss of composure was so obvious that Alexandra couldn't fail to notice it.

Linda looked around impatiently. "James, what in the world's the matter with you? Come on! We really haven't got all night you know, quite apart from the fact that it's freezing cold!" This time Alexandra didn't think she was joking.

James regained control of himself. "Sorry Ma'am," he repeated. "I probably should have come to your door first, but I thought that seeing it was Alexandra's special night, I'd attend to her. Whilst I was helping her with her coat, I simply complimented her on her manners and told her what a nice girl she was."

"Oh. Did you? Well. That's ..."

After breaking off, she asked her daughter, "Alexandra is this true?"

"Very," replied Alexandra. "In fact he paid a very nice compliment to us both"

"Well, in that case I forgive you, James," she said returning to him. "That was very nice of you. And unusually perceptive too! But now, can we *please* get on! I've got to get us signed in here, and get our cases up to the room, before we go to the theatre!"

"Certainly Ma'am!" said James, and went to the boot and removed their cases.

"Thank you James," said Linda. "Right, I hope we won't keep you too long. We'll see you again in a minute."

They were about to go, when Linda suddenly thought of something and looked back. "James," she said, "it's cold out here, do you want to stay here, or wait in the lobby for us?"

"Oh, yes maybe I will wait in there. Thank you."

And so, the three of them went into the lobby of the Geratica Hotel.

# CHAPTER 3

"Hello. I have a room booked for my daughter and myself," said Linda, as they reached the front desk, "under the name of Radcliffe."

"Good evening Mrs Radcliffe," replied the receptionist, smiling. "We were expecting you." She checked for the booking details, then ran through the necessary formalities with Linda.

Alexandra looked around the vast lobby. She had either eaten in or stayed in many hotels with her mother, over the years, but this was without doubt the biggest of them all.

A woman came out from a room behind the reception desk. From reading her name badge, Alexandra realised that this was the hotel manageress – a Mrs Pauline Entwistle.

"Good evening Mrs Radcliffe!" she said brightly. "May I say what a pleasure it is, to welcome you and your daughter to the Geratica Hotel. We all sincerely hope that you enjoy your stay with us."

"Thank you. I am sure that we will," replied Linda.

"I see that you have cases," said the receptionist. "Would you like a porter to show you to your room?"

Pauline quickly cut in. "That won't be necessary. If you'll just fetch the room key, then I'll show them up personally."

The receptionist looked at Pauline in surprise, but did as she was asked, and handed it to her boss. Alexandra guessed that the hotel manageress was one of the very few who knew of their 'secret'.

"If you'd like to follow me then," she invited and so, whilst James sat in the lobby and waited, Alexandra and her mother followed Pauline across the lobby to the lift, wheeling their cases behind them.

They eventually arrived on top floor of the hotel. "OK Mrs Radcliffe," the manageress began, leading them to one end of the corridor. "I'll just explain some details. The room that you've officially booked – number 200 – is here." She unlocked the door with the key from reception and they stepped inside. "Now, apart from security, there's just one other person who is aware of your unofficial stay in the Queen Alexandra Marital Suite, and that's the head of room service. You'll notice that the bedclothes from the mistress bed have been removed. She personally did this and they're now on the bed of the Marital Suite, which is just across the corridor. It covers most of the top floor of the hotel, as you can see."

The manageress ushered them out, shut the door and gave the key to Linda. Then she led them the short distance of the corridor to the suite. She reached inside her skirt pocket and took out another key. "This will gain you access to the Marital Suite," she declared, as she unlocked this door. Once again she gave the key to Linda, and ushered Alexandra and her inside. "These are the only two rooms on this whole floor, so you should be completely separated from the other guests, but I am posting Security guards here, anyhow."

"If you require anything, such as breakfast in the suite for example, then simply ring room service, and a maid will bring your requirements up, with instructions to just knock and leave the tray outside room 200. Once she has gone, a Security guard will bring the tray to the Marital Suite and knock, to let you know that it's been delivered.

"We prefer people to check out of the hotel by 11.00 a.m. When you do, just before you leave the suite, if you wouldn't mind ringing me on this number." She removed a business card from her suit jacket inside pocket, and handed it to Linda. "Then I can send the head of room service straight up to rearrange things to how they were before you came, and to attend personally to any cleaning duties,

"Well I think that's all I need to tell you. Have you any questions?"

"No. I think that's clear enough," said Linda. "Thank you."

"It's a pleasure, Mrs Radcliffe," said Pauline, smiling. "The only other thing to say is, please feel free to come and see me in my office before you leave the Geratica, to let me know what you think of the suite and whether we need to do anything before this coming week. Ask for me at reception and I'll be informed, then I'll come and take you through. Have a pleasant stay!"

She withdrew from the suite, and closed the door behind her.

Linda smiled at Alexandra. "We're here!"

They were actually standing in what was effectively a small passage, with a door at the end. Linda took her daughter's hand, and together they went through, into the suite itself.

Alexandra gasped. "Mother. It's huge!" she exclaimed.

"Well, it *is* a Royal Suite darling," replied Linda. "Right, well let's just leave the cases here, and go straight out again. We must get to the theatre in reasonable time, before the concert starts. We can have a good look round later."

She went to the bed, which dominated the centre of the Suite, and put her case down to the left side, as you looked at it from the foot – the side that she slept on at home. Alexandra looked about. "I assume that this is the only bed, Mother?" she asked.

Linda looked at her with the slight hint of a smile. "Darling, this is a suite that has been officially designed for Queen Alexandra to bring her Consort to, on her wedding night. I hardly think, they'll be wanting anyone else in here, as they commence their first official night of passion together, do you?

"Yes, this *is* the only bed Alexandra, and I shall be sleeping on my normal side of it tonight. So, unless you want to sleep on the floor – or in room 200 on your own, which would seem a shame, after you've come all this way to be in the suite, then you'll be sleeping on the other side from me tonight – as you would be on this night of the weekend anyway, if we were at home."

This night of the weekend, was usually when Linda gave her daughter one of her treats, letting her sleep the whole night in her arms, next to her. It wasn't just a treat for Alexandra either. Linda missed having her late husband to love and hold and she liked to pour out all of her affection to her daughter, who was the most special and precious thing that she possessed from that all too brief union – even though the feelings were obviously not heightened and driven by sex now, as they had been before.

"Yes Mother!" said Alexandra, as she put her case down on the floor, on her side of the bed. "I do very much want to sleep in a bed that Queen Alexandra will eventually do the same in. And it'll be even more special, because I'll be in your arms."

She started making her way back out from the side of the bed at the same time as her mother paced towards her. As Linda met her daughter, she gave her the biggest kiss she had given her yet that day.

"Right!" she said. "Now let's find James. We've got a concert to see."

They found James, still sat in the lobby. "The Queen Alexandra Theatre, please James," said Linda.

"Right you are, Ma'am," answered James, and they went back to the car.

# CHAPTER 4

At just after 7.30 p.m., Alexandra and her mother were settling into their box in the theatre. Linda had said that it was high time that they had some refreshment, and was busy looking through the cupboards of the tiny kitchen area that was provided for, in each private box. Alexandra was testing the field glasses, to see if she could spot any tiny signs of movement behind the stage curtain. She always wondered what it was like for the performers, just as they were about to go on stage for a concert or play. The thought of performing on stage, or for that matter doing anything that would mean having to speak in public, filled her with dread, but she admired people who did it, in all walks of life. She was also wondering if she might spot Philippa Barrington.

"Well, I think they've got just about all the usual things," said her mother. "But I've spotted some rather nice looking biscuits. Dark chocolate, too. If I make us a both a cup of coffee, shall we give them a quick taste? It seems mean to make them lonely, by shutting them away in the cupboard, when we could be introducing them to our grateful stomachs!"

Alexandra giggled – something she was doing quite a lot of tonight. The main entertainment of the evening hadn't even started yet, but her mother and James had already provided her with plenty.

"That's an interesting way of putting it, Mother! Mmm, yes please." she replied happily.

"OK I'll put the coffee machine on then, darling," said Linda, beaming. "Have you seen anything interesting?" she added, referring to the field glasses.

"Oh, nothing much, Mother. I was just checking to see if they're working properly, really."

"And they are, I trust?"

"Yes, Mother. Perfectly."

"I should think so too!" exclaimed Linda, as she started preparing the coffee. "If they don't, then I shall complain. I pay good money for these boxes and the perks they provide us with. They're not cheap, and contrary to the belief of some, I do *not* get a discount, in the queen's own theatre, through being her senior court administrator!"

Alexandra suppressed another giggle. She sometimes found her mother's indignant outbursts very amusing. "Quite, Mother," she said.

The thought had occurred to her that her mother must have forked out quite a bit of money for all of this. She had obviously got the Suite for free, but she had still booked a room (and quite a luxurious one, by the look of the other that she'd seen), and she presumed that must have come out of her own pocket. It would have been peak rate too, and on top of that they were having a five course meal tonight and breakfast tomorrow – and all that at the Geratica! And still then there was this box, in this theatre, to see this concert! Once again, she realised how lucky she was, that her mother had such a good, responsible and well paid job, to help give her the chance to experience all of these finer things in life.

Linda finished making the coffee, and set it down on the table in front of their seats. As she took her place next to her daughter, she slipped her arm around her shoulders. "Alright my gorgeous darling," she said lovingly, "Now your treat really begins. I'm going to make sure that you have a truly wonderful evening." She leaned over Alexandra, and kissed her three times, full on the lips, and was delighted to see her daughter's eyes close in pleasure as she savoured the feeling.

There was now quite a hum all around the theatre as it filled up. Alexandra always loved this atmosphere, as people arrived, settled into their seats, and began to chat excitedly to each other. Having said that, she always felt glad to be in a nice quiet box, rather than amongst the general throng below. It looked as if it was quite noisy down there, and she doubted that she'd be able to make herself heard, even if she did try to say something. She preferred a quieter and more intimate atmosphere to talk in, such as where she was right now. Here you could enter the box and close the door behind you, and it felt a bit like being in a very small room. On the whole she preferred to be an observer of things, rather than necessarily participating in them.

The lights in the theatre were still on, but they would be dimming very shortly now, as the overture began. Linda picked up the concert programme that she had brought on their arrival and placed it in between Alexandra and herself.

"According to this, Mother," said Alexandra, "Philippa Barrington's performance, is the whole second half of the concert."

"Yes. A real treat for you then," replied Linda. She smiled to herself, inside. If all went according to plan, her daughter would receive her first 'extra' surprise, after the concert.

Then the lights did indeed dim, as the evening's entertainment finally began. Linda reached over and her black gloved hand squeezed Alexandra's, and gently stroked her fingers, as they settled down to watch the concert.

The first half, contained an anthology of many popular pieces, from both Geratica and Earth's classical music history, combined with one or two lesser known, but, (in Alexandra's opinion) equally good works.

At its conclusion, with the lights in the theatre now coming back to life, there was an interval. The noise in the theatre gradually grew, as people began to enthuse about the music they'd just heard, and the experiences they'd had. Then there was a lot of movement, as people got up to stretch their limbs, and some to make their way down their row of seats, and down the aisles to the balconies, where theatre attendants were dotted about, with sandwich boards, selling ice cream. Again, as she watched, Alexandra felt glad that she was safely up in their box. She didn't like the idea of having to squeeze past people like that, and having to race to grab your refreshments, and get back before the performance started again. The other big perk about being here instead, was that you had someone knock on the door, and personally offer it to you, should you be interested.

"What do you think so far, then, sweetheart?" asked her mother.

"It's wonderful, Mother," she replied, smiling happily. "Thank you!"

She kissed her mother's lips.

"Well I hope you'll save some thanks for the end!" said Linda. "That was just your appetiser. Your main course is coming up after the interval." ('And after that, you should be getting a sweet, too!' she thought to herself).

"Talking of food, darling," she continued. "I know we normally sample the ice cream of most theatres we go to, but we do have rather a large meal to negotiate when we get back to the hotel. So shall I tell the girl, when she comes, that we won't have any tonight?"

Alexandra had to think for a second. She really did enjoy the ice creams sold in theatres and cinemas. If they turned it down, then it surely had to be a first for them. On the other hand, though ...

"Yes Mother. Perhaps that's wise," she replied, which, as was usually their way, thus allowed her mother's suggestion to become their decision. And Alexandra knew in her heart that, as also usually seemed to be the way, her mother was right.

Right on cue, there was a knock on the door, and when Linda opened it, she did indeed tell the girl that for the first time ever they regretted that they would have to decline her establishment's kind offer, as they had a prior engagement elsewhere, after the concert.

"I wouldn't mind a couple more of those biscuits though," she said, as she sat back down. "They won't fill us up so much!" She picked up the packet, and offered one to her daughter. During the first half, they had together managed to get through half of them, and Alexandra suspected that a similar thing would happen during the second. She thanked Linda and took one, this time more than happy to once again be allowing her mother's suggestion to become their decision.

"What did *you* think of the first half, Mother?" asked Alexandra.

"I agree with you. It was very good. Classy in fact, is the word that comes to mind."

Her mother was always very exacting, when it came to the standards she expected from most things, and the most vocal of critics when not satisfied, so Alexandra felt that this was high praise indeed, from her.

"Mother. What's James going to do, whilst we're here? Just wait in the car, until we come out?"

"Well, not quite *all* of the time, darling," replied Linda. "There's a rather nice fish and chip shop, just down the road, which we've recently discovered. You can sit in there and eat it, after you've been served. He'll hang around there and amuse himself, whilst we're here, but he'll be waiting outside, once we come out."

Alexandra noticed that her mother had said, '*we've* recently discovered'. Presumably that meant that they sometimes ate together then.

"So, what's your arrangement with Queen Alexandra, regarding him, then, Mother?"

Linda smiled. "James is indeed on leave this weekend. But only because she relieved him of his duties! He had been due to take her on a couple of minor personal excursions, not related to any of her public duties. This is a non-working weekend for her, and as luck would have it, next weekend is the same, so she postponed what she'd planned until then, which meant that he was free for me."

"That was very obliging of her, Mother!"

"Yes it was. But before you ask – no I did not ask her to grant me the favour! That would not be appropriate, and I wouldn't want you to think that I had that much influence over Her Majesty. It was simply that she became aware that we'd be going to the Marital Suite, and staying overnight, so she offered to let me have him for the weekend instead, which would save me having to drive all the way there tonight, and back again tomorrow. That wouldn't have been a major problem, but it was a nice gesture from her, and I'm grateful to her for it. It meant that I could relax a bit more, and you enjoyed the entertainment, didn't you?"

Alexandra grinned. "Yes I did, Mother!" she confirmed.

"As I said earlier," continued Linda, "this was all made possible by some happy pieces of good fortune, really."

"And also, you're a very clever mother."

"Well, yes, of course. That too."

However, that was where their conversation had to end for now, as at that moment, the orchestra began again, and the lights faded, as the second half of the concert began. Linda wrapped an arm around her daughter's shoulders, and with her other hand squeezed her arm, whilst planting a soft kiss on her cheek.

As the curtain lifted, and there was a round of applause. As it died down, the conductor of the royal symphony orchestra addressed the audience.

"Ladies and Gentlemen, please welcome our special guest soloist, for the second half of our musical extravaganza, the esteemed composer, Mrs Philippa Barrington!"

There was now another round of loud applause, as Philippa Barrington appeared from the side of the stage. Tall and slim, she wore a long royal blue gown and her auburn hair was tied back in a matching blue bow. She acknowledged the audience with a smile and a bow of her head, and walked over to the conductor. The two women shook hands, and then Mrs Barrington went over to her piano in the middle of the stage and sat down.

And then she began to play. A ripple of applause went around the theatre. For the next 45 minutes she and the orchestra gave a rendition of one of her most popular symphonies. They finished to thunderous applause, and the audience rose to its feet. The conductor inclined her hand towards Philippa Barrington in acknowledgement. Mrs Barrington graciously accepted the reception. There were shouts of "More!" from some. So, for an encore, she gave a quick melody of the best known parts of some of her other symphonies, which was followed by more rapturous applause, during which the conductor presented her with a bouquet of flowers, on behalf of the orchestra.

Then the conductor turned to the audience. In their box, Linda took Alexandra's hand and squeezed it inside of hers. She was the only member of the audience who knew what was coming next. She had made it clear to the conductor, that she did not want her daughter's name mentioned specifically in the following announcement, as she didn't want people to be looking around the boxes, trying to see her. She knew that would make Alexandra feel embarrassed, and uncomfortable. All the same, she hoped that once her daughter realised that it was her that was being referred to, she wouldn't be too overcome and lose her composure completely, when facing what should be the greatest moment of her life so far.

The conductor addressed the audience for the final time. "Ladies and Gentlemen," she began, "we thank Mrs Philippa Barrington, for her participation in our extravaganza. We know that she has many fans here tonight."

In the box Linda stroked her daughter's fingers, beginning slowly, then quickening the pace as the conductor spoke. The next part would be the big moment.

The conductor continued, "We are also aware though, that there is one young lady amongst us who is a particular devotee of her life and music, through collecting her works, studying her, and both listening to and playing her music."

Linda's gloved fingers danced all over Alexandra's.

"Mrs Barrington, having heard much about her, has therefore kindly offered to meet the lady concerned backstage, as soon as the concert is over, and very much hopes that she will accept."

Now Linda's fingers reached an urgent crescendo, and then her whole hand tightened around her daughter's, so that Alexandra's was completely enveloped by the soft texture of her mother's black velvet glove.

Some people in the audience began to look at each other, knowing that it wasn't them, and wondering who the lucky young lady was.

"All that remains, is to thank you all for coming, and wish you a safe journey home. We hope to see you all again soon."

She spun back around to face the orchestra again and they immediately launched into their signature tune, which would bring the concert to its conclusion.

In their box, Alexandra looked at Linda. The conductor's description of 'the young lady', combined with what her mother's fingers had done to hers, whilst she was speaking, could surely only mean one thing!

Linda smiled, her eyebrows rose and fell and then she nodded. She drew her daughter to her and above the noise of the music, said into her ear, "Yes my darling. It's you. I said that would be your main course and now you can have your dessert!"

Alexandra's jaw dropped.

"Come on!" said Linda, slipping her daughter's coat over her, and putting on her own. "If we leave now, just before the end, we'll be taken backstage. Make sure you hold on to that programme. I think this is one that you'll be keeping!"

Then she ushered Alexandra to the door of the box.

"Mother! I've never met her. I won't know what to say!" said Alexandra.

"It's alright my sweetheart," Linda soothed her. Squeezing her to her, she went on, "I'll be there with you. Just think that you're meeting Philippa Barrington, as you've always wanted to, who you're very knowledgeable about, and now she wants to know about you, too. Keep that in your head, and it'll help relax you a bit. It'll only be for a short while, and I'm sure she's very nice."

In fact, Linda *knew* that she was very nice. She had met her two days ago, for a coffee during her lunch break, along with Alexandra's music mistress, and they had planned this together.

Outside the box they were met by the theatre manager, who was beaming from ear to ear.

Alexandra!" she said. "Come backstage and meet Mrs Barrington!"

# CHAPTER 5

The theatre manageress, led Linda and Alexandra back down the steps from their box, from whence they had come, and then through a side door, with a sign saying 'Staff Only' on it. After walking through a couple of corridors, they came to a small room. The manageress opened the door, and indicated with her hand, inviting them to come through.

"Mrs Barrington, if you please, this is Alexandra Radcliffe," she said. "Miss Radcliffe please meet Mrs Philippa Barrington."

She looked at Linda. "I believe you two are already acquainted?"

Linda nodded in acknowledgement, and Alexandra looked at her in astonishment.

"Well, I'll give you a moment. I'll be outside to escort you back, when you're finished." The manageress left the room, and closed the door.

Philippa Barrington was seated by a piano. She got up, smiling broadly, and walked over to Alexandra, extending her hand.

"Good evening Alexandra," she said.

"Good evening Mrs Barrington," replied Alexandra politely, with a smile.

Mrs Barrington was seated by a piano. She got up, smiling broadly and walked over to Alexandra, extending her hand.

"Oh please, call me Philippa! We don't need to be too formal. I know that you're probably quite nervous, and it might surprise you to learn that I am a little, too. Most of us feel it, when we meet someone new. Your mother may be one of those super-confident exceptions!" She chuckled and her eyes sparkled as she did so.

"Sorry Linda. I didn't mean to be rude," she said.

"Oh, don't worry about that," replied Linda. "People are often commenting on the strength of my personality, in both a positive and negative way, and I'll take that as one of the former!"

"Just to explain, Alexandra," continued Philippa, "I did meet with your mother, and music mistress from Charterhouse, the day before yesterday, to discuss the possibility of meeting you. I hadn't met your mother before, though we had corresponded, but she seemed to deal with me, as if she'd known me for years."

"Take off your coat, and come and sit down with me for a moment." She pulled up another stool to the piano, and motioned for Alexandra to sit on it. Linda took her coat, and put it together with hers, over the backs of a couple of chairs, in the corner of the room. Alexandra was still feeling a bit overawed, but Philippa Barrington had always been a major influence on her culturally, and she did seem very friendly. Her mother was also in the room with her. As she sat down, she began to feel some of the butterflies in her stomach dissipating.

"I've heard a lot about you, Alexandra. Your music mistress was sufficiently impressed by some of your essays on both my life and my works, and even what my legacy might be, to send copies of them to me. Now, I might be biased, but I cannot help but agree! You're clearly a gifted scholar, and I understand that many of your mistresses in other subjects feel the same."

Alexandra's face radiated a warm glow, as she took in Philippa's words of praise. "Thank you Philippa. I am deeply honoured to hear you say that," she said.

For the next couple of minutes Philippa talked with Alexandra about her music and to Linda's relief, she sensed her daughter beginning to gain more confidence and open up. Anyone listening could not fail to realise, that Alexandra knew her subject matter well.

She was pleased with how this encounter had gone, so far. They had managed it in the right way, she felt, and as usual she had played the dominant role in the planning. There was still a bit more to do, though.

Linda checked the clock on the wall. She had told James, simply to wait in the car until they were ready to leave, and had also been given an assurance by Pauline Entwistle, that as long as they were back at the Geratica Hotel, by 11.00 p.m., then they would still be able to have their meal in the private dining room, as the last shift for the kitchen and serving staff finished at 2.00 a.m., when the hotel closed for the night. They should be in time. It was only a short drive.

"I understand that, as well as having an extensive music collection, you can also play the piano," said Philippa.

Alexandra glanced at her mother. "Well, a little. I'm not an expert though."

Philippa smiled. "Well I wouldn't expect you to be an expert! You would be a precocious child indeed to be hailed as an 'expert' at fifteen! We all have to learn our trade, and it often takes years of practice – though some are quicker to achieve it than others."

"You're better than me, and you do play, to entertain other guests at dinner parties sometimes though, don't you?" Linda gently coaxed her daughter. She knew what was going to be proposed next, and wanted to steer her in the right direction.

Philippa opened the piano lid. "Well let's see now. If I was to play this ..." She played the opening bar of one of her symphonies. She indicated the piano to Alexandra. "What would your response be?"

Alexandra's heart beat fast, as she strove to keep her thoughts clear. Her mother's training for combating her nerves, began to kick in. She knew this piece well, and there was no reason why she should get the next notes wrong. All she needed was to do was relax, and keep her mind strong and determined to succeed, and she wouldn't make a mess of it, in front of Philippa Barrington.

Taking a deep breath, she played the next bar. "That's good," said Philippa. "And then ..." she played the next bar and Alexandra the next. They continued until they had played several more bars, with Alexandra gradually gaining in confidence. She felt ecstatic. She was actually playing with Philippa Barrington!

Philippa glanced over to Linda, and gave a very slight nod of her head, as if to say that she was satisfied. Linda moved discreetly nearer to her daughter.

"Alexandra, I think you play more than 'a little'. You have a natural ear," began Philippa. "How would you feel, if I offered to give you some private tuition, at your home? I don't take very many students and consequently when I do, my fee is relatively high, but you would be learning from the experience of one who might be considered an 'expert' in her field, by some, and I think in your case, it might be well worth it – for both of us."

Alexandra was dumbfounded. She wasn't quite sure what to say. In her heart, she knew she wanted it very much! It was like a dream come true, but she could never have believed that it could ever possibly become a reality. Now here it was being offered to her, out of the blue!

Philippa had mentioned that it would cost quite a bit of money though. So that was obviously her mother's department. She would say 'Yes', or 'No'. It would *probably* be 'Yes', but if it *should* be 'No', then that would be that, regardless of her personal feelings. It wouldn't be something that her mother would be prepared to negotiate with her about, though she would sympathise, and try to make it up to her, in other ways.

Almost as if she could read her mind, her mother took her hand and held it within hers. Alexandra looked at Linda and squeezed within her mother's hand with her fingers, often a secret sign between them that told Linda that her daughter needed her help or guidance, or wanted her to take the initiative in some way. Linda squeezed back from the outside, to acknowledge the gesture and send another secret sign back, telling Alexandra that her mother would help her. Mother and daughter were so close and intimate, that they sometimes needed no words to communicate with each other.

"What do you want to do, darling?" asked Linda, in a calm, soothing voice and looking deep into her daughter's eyes. "I think Philippa's made you a 'once in a lifetime' offer. My advice is to take it. I'll make the arrangements with Philippa, if you agree."

As she studied her, a brief, barely perceptible look of delight flashing through Alexandra's eyes told Linda what she needed to know, and she engulfed her daughter's hand and squeezed it in confirmation.

Without further delay, she turned to Philippa and said, "OK Mrs Barrington, we'll accept your most kind offer. Thank you very much."

Philippa Barrington nearly fell off her piano stool in surprise, at Linda's sudden announcement. "But, but ... Alexandra are you definitely sure?" she asked. "If I give my time to you, I need to know that you're fully committed, and not simply doing this because you feel pressurised by your mother."

"Oh no, please believe me, I don't," Alexandra reassured her quickly. "I want to do this very much. And may I also, like my mother, say 'Thank you.' I'm thrilled and deeply honoured to have received this opportunity from someone who you know I hold in such high esteem. In fact, the main reason for my slight hesitation, was that I didn't know what my mother thought."

"Whose opinion is clearly most important, in this relationship!" said Philippa.

"Alexandra and I are a partnership," said Linda, "though it is obvious that I am the senior partner, and the boss. We are very close, and do a lot of things together, but Alexandra at times lacks some of the confidence that she needs, although it is starting to come. I make no secret of the fact that I am a dominant mother, but I am very clear in what I believe she should do and can achieve, and she needs strong guidance when she is unsure of herself. I won't apologise for being the one who makes the final decision. We *are* mother and daughter, after all."

"Please! Please! How the relationship between yourselves works, is no business of mine. I was just observing and I didn't mean to offend you Linda – nor you Alexandra, for that matter. I think you're both very lucky to have one another, actually. I am very much looking forward to working with you, Alexandra."

"And me with you," replied Alexandra. "Times two."

Philippa *was* looking forward to it. Alexandra was clearly a gifted, diligent and hard working student. That much she was more than aware of. She also appeared to be a very nice, well mannered and courteous girl. The perfect student! What was clear to her, however, was that in tutoring this model pupil, she was going to have to contend with a domineering mother. She hoped above all, that she and Alexandra would be left alone to practice, and that Linda wouldn't be looking over her shoulder all of the time. That really would be intolerable!

Having said that, she did rather like Linda too. She could understand a mother being strongly protective and ambitious for her child. She had children of her own.

"Do you have any plans for your future, Alexandra?" she asked. "I don't suppose you've ever thought of a career in music?"

"Well I'm obviously very interested in it, but beyond that I'm not really sure at the moment," Alexandra replied." I'm hoping to get in to Castra next year and then depending on what I end up reading there, I'll decide on my career plans seriously then."

"That sounds sensible. How about playing music professionally?"

Alexandra looked at Philippa. "What, in public you mean? Oh I don't know. I'm not sure if I'd ever have the nerve."

"Perhaps after we've worked together for a while, you might feel comfortable accompanying me?"

Alexandra looked shocked that such a proposal could be considered conceivable and Linda decided that this might be a good time to try and bring the encounter to a conclusion. They needed to leave soon, anyhow.

"Well let's take one thing at a time, shall we?" she began. "I think that perhaps now, it's time that Alexandra and I left, and found our driver. We have to get back to the Geratica by 11.00 p.m., for what I hope will be a rather nice dinner. If you don't mind Philippa, I'll be in touch early next week to discuss our arrangement and, of course, the fee. Thank you for your time and it's been a pleasure to meet you. I'm sure that Alexandra will say that it's been at least as much for her too."

"Oh, definitely much more than that," said Alexandra. "This must have been one of the greatest days of my life!"

"It's been my pleasure!" said Philippa. "Before you go, one last thing; I'm sure you know, Alexandra, that I have a book just about to be released, in the run-up to the Festival of Divinity, containing the complete scores to all of my published works. I have here *a copy* of the original final draft manuscript, complete with my handwritten notes on it. The original will be kept by myself, but the copy ..." she picked up a brown parchment from the top of the piano and held it out for Alexandra to take, "... is yours to keep, if you'd like it."

Once again, Alexandra looked shocked. She slowly took the parchment from Philippa's hands and carefully removed the manuscript from inside. She stared at it with reverence. It was beautifully bound in gold. Gently she opened it, and turned through the pages. She had indeed known that this book was due out, and she had been hoping to get it on Divinity Day. She had never dreamed that she would see *this* though. This was what a book looked like, before it was printed! It was true what Philippa had said too. Dotted in the margins of various pages, were many notes, that she herself had handwritten, regarding final amendments to the finished text, before it was officially printed.

Alexandra looked at Philippa. "Do you really mind? I can keep this?" she asked almost hoarsely.

Philippa smiled. "Of course. I had it copied especially for you."

Alexandra glanced at her mother, with a discreet enquiring look, for a quick confirmation that it would alright to accept the gift. Linda nodded, equally discreetly.

"You must think very highly of me. I can't believe it!" said Alexandra. Thank you, truly, with all of my heart. I shall treasure this forever." She delicately placed the manuscript back inside the parchment.

"And I shall treasure this meeting forever, too, Alexandra," replied Philippa. "I hope that this will be the start of a long and happy relationship for us – in whatever form it may take."

Linda had fetched their coats. She motioned for Alexandra to get up from the piano. She did so quickly, clutching the parchment, realising that her mother was probably now in haste to be getting back to the hotel.

"Well thank you again and goodbye," said Linda as they put on their coats. "As I said I'll be in touch, early next week, but now we really must be going!"

"Of course. I hope you both enjoy your dinner. I'll look forward to hearing from you as you've indicated, Linda, and to meeting you again very soon, Alexandra for our practice sessions."

Linda knocked on the door of the room, and the threesome said their goodbyes and shook hands.

There was the sound of a woman clearing her throat and hastily retracing her steps outside. The door opened and the theatre manageress stood smiling in the doorway.

"Hello again ladies," she said. "Did you enjoy your meeting?"

"Yes, very much, thank you," confirmed Linda. "We're ready to leave now please."

Linda and Alexandra waved goodbye to Philippa and followed the manageress back the way they had come. After thanking her, and saying goodbye, they finally left the theatre.

As instructed, James was waiting in the car. He got out and greeted them as they approached,

"Did you enjoy the concert ladies?" he asked, as he opened the door for Linda.

They both answered enthusiastically in the affirmative.

"And did you enjoy your meeting with Philippa Barrington, Alexandra?" he continued, as he opened the door for her.

She smiled. "You knew!"

"Well yes, I did. Sorry, but I had to keep it quiet. Boss's orders I'm afraid!"

"James!" barked Linda. "Stop gossiping and take us to the Geratica Hotel please. As fast as you can. We're both hungry, and if we don't get there soon, we'll miss dinner!"

"At the double, Ma'am," he answered, as he closed Alexandra's door, got back in the car, and did as Linda had ordered.

# CHAPTER 6

James arrived back at the Geratica Hotel and dropped off his two passengers.

"Right. Meet us back here tomorrow morning at 11.00 a.m. sharp, James," said Linda. Then, in a softer voice, "Thank you for tonight James. *Good night!*"

Alexandra noticed that her mother slipped her hand inside James' arm and gave it a quick squeeze.

"Good night then, both of you. Enjoy your stay at the Geratica!" said James, as he got back in the car, and then drove away.

"And now, my darling, it's time for the second instalment of your special treat," said Linda, wrapping her arm across her daughter's shoulders. "Hold on to your clever mother and she'll take you for the best meal you've ever had!"

"There's nothing I'd like to do more, Mother!" Alexandra told her, gripping her waist.

Linda's strong embrace tightened still further, on hearing her daughter's words. As she was walked across to the hotel entrance by her mother – an experience she always enjoyed – Alexandra thought that she had never felt so happy as she was tonight, after successfully initiating a relationship with Tom, this afternoon, the concert tonight and incredibly, meeting Philippa Barrington. Now, feeling safely secure and protected, as she snuggled to her mother, with a five course meal awaiting her at the Geratica, and the likely prospect of her mother taking her over, in the bed of the Queen Alexandra Marital Suite, surely life could never get *much* better than this?!

"Taking her over," referred to their private description of what happened when Alexandra went to her mother's bed and was smothered underneath her body and lips and wrapped inside her tight embrace, until she lost control and surrendered to her mother's dominant loving.

Inside the hotel, Linda led Alexandra straight through to the dining room, and announced them to the head waitress. Then they were shown to a small private room, leading off from it. Inside, a table was made up for two guests. The head waitress took their coats, and two others helped them to their seats, and placed napkins over their laps. Alexandra carefully placed her parchment under the table, at her feet.

Then they were each given a menu, and Linda the wine list. She selected two bottles of a Utipidean red. One of the waitresses fetched them from the wine rack, and poured a sample for Linda to taste. Alexandra thought that she looked a little nervous, lest her mother should reject it and ask for another. She had never seen anyone do that before, but if anyone would, it would be her mother, she decided.

"That's fine. Thank you," said Linda.

The waitress filled both of their glasses. "I'll let you decide on your order, ladies," she said and withdrew.

As they glanced through their menus, the first course of canapés was served. Eventually they decided on their courses, and when the waitress returned, Linda treated Alexandra by ordering for them both. Normally, nowadays, Alexandra had the confidence to order for herself, but tonight her mother wanted to take care of her completely.

"Thank you, Mother," said her daughter reaching across the table, and touching her gloved hand. Linda responded by wrapping hers around Alexandra's, and squeezing tight.

"We're going to have a very late night tonight, Mother."

"Well, we don't have to go to work or school tomorrow, sweetheart. Just once in a while, is OK. Much earlier to bed tomorrow night, of course!"

Soon they began their soup course.

"By the way, Mother," began Alexandra. "Did you *know* what Philippa was going to propose to me tonight?"

Linda wiped her mouth with her napkin. "Hmm, yes I did darling. I wanted to surprise you! It's true what she said. We did have a meeting the day before yesterday, at lunch time."

"The more I've thought about it, the more I've guessed that might have been the case, Mother. But I wasn't sure in the theatre, whether you *did* know, and whether you'd be in favour of it. I think she was rather surprised when you told her we'd accept, when I hadn't even said anything."

"Well, I can usually read your thoughts quite well," said Linda, between mouthfuls. I'm sorry if I got a bit defensive then, sweetheart, but I'm very proud of our relationship. I think it works well, and we complement each other."

"I don't think she meant anything personal, Mother. And I wouldn't change it for the world, either. I'm not ashamed to admit that I need your strength to help and guide me sometimes. I don't mind you taking control. In fact, I wouldn't be so happy if you didn't. I love you and I need you so much. And thank you very, very much for everything you've given me tonight. I still can't believe it!"

This time Linda reached over the table and touched her daughter's arm. "That's my pleasure, darling. I love you and I need you too. Maybe I need you for different reasons, but I really do, my lovely."

As they ate their third course, the entrée, Alexandra decided to talk to her mother a bit more about James.

"Mother," she asked, "What's James doing tonight then, whilst we're here?"

"He's going home. He'll be there on his own, I think. I don't believe your headmistress is returning this weekend. She very often stays up at Charterhouse. To tell you the truth, they're not the happiest of married couples, and I think the arrangement quite suits them both."

"If you don't mind my asking, Mother, how exactly would you define your relationship with him? It's just that I detected one or two things tonight, which made me think that the two of you might be rather close."

Linda paused in her eating for a second, and raised an eyebrow at her daughter. "Oh, really? Do tell me more."

"Well. It might be just my imagination, Mother, and I might be wrong – and I know it's not my place, or any of my business ..."

"Don't worry about that!" interrupted Linda, impatiently. "Stop floundering and come to the point!"

"If it makes it any easier for you," she continued, a little more gently, "I'll tell you that, once you'd met James tonight, I had been intending to broach this subject with you anyhow, so you've no need to be nervous."

"Oh!" said Alexandra, genuinely surprised. This did indeed make it a little easier.

"OK then, Mother," she continued, a little more confidently, "You both clearly talk and joke a lot, and seem to get on very well. When we were in the theatre and I asked you what he was doing whilst he waited, you said that there was fish and chip shop that 'we'd' discovered. You squeezed his arm when he left the hotel tonight. Not to mention, that when he let you out of the car outside the theatre, even I couldn't fail to notice that he was salivating at the sight of you! I think he finds you extremely attractive, and you *are* wearing your most stunning gown. I've even been wondering whether you might have *planned* to induce that reaction in him!"

Linda continued eating as she listened to her daughter. Once Alexandra had finished talking and herself eating, she touched Alexandra's arm again. "Right. You've spoken and not eaten for a while. Now you get on with your entrée, and I'll take over for a while, OK?"

"Yes Mother," said Alexandra.

"You are as usual, a very perceptive child. A child who is to become a woman before too long, in fact. That's why, I think tonight may be a good time for me to discuss this with you. James and I are indeed close, as you say. Your father has been dead for ten years now, and whilst I will never forget that he was the first true 'love of my life', and the feelings that I had for him will always remain, I've never ruled out the possibility of there being another who could make me feel the same, should he come along. Over the past few years, James has become more and more special to me. We do have many things in common, including a sense of humour, we share the same views in supporting Queen Alexandra, and he has confided in me quite a lot, about the problems in his marriage. Dear Mrs Spencer, needless to say, has slightly progressive views in her idea of James' role in it – a role that he's not comfortable with at all. He wants and needs a traditional marriage. And I know that I could provide it for him. I do love him, very much."

Both Alexandra and Linda had large appetites and it hadn't taken Alexandra long to polish off her entrée. "Are you saying, Mother ...?" she began, but Linda raised her hand to silence her.

"What I'm saying, darling," she continued, "is that James and I would very much like to get together, and I've made it clear to him that I would like to make a proposal. Unfortunately, there are two main difficulties. The first, which we will most likely have to accept, is that Mrs Spencer has always strongly asserted that she will never, under any circumstances, grant James a divorce. Obviously her views on greater rights for males don't quite extend that far!

"The second difficulty that I'm experiencing is getting James to face up to his wife, and tell her that he wants to leave her and be with me. Even though I know it's what he really wants, so far my gentle coaxing of him in that general direction hasn't been successful. He hasn't yet had the nerve to do it, but I am still working on him, and I do believe that, unlike in the case of the first problem, it might happen eventually. I'm planning to intensify my efforts, from now onwards, to finally achieve our ambition, as soon as possible."

"Therefore, this is what I need to discuss with you Alexandra-" At that point she broke off momentarily, as the waitress re-appeared and took their plates. They thanked her politely, and then Linda continued.

"Darling, I need you to tell me, firstly, having met James tonight, what you think of him, whether you like him, etc., and secondly, how you would feel about somebody moving into The Grange and effectively taking on the role that your father had, when you were small."

Alexandra considered the questions for a moment.

"Well, I've obviously only just met James tonight, Mother," she began, "but I will say that I like him. He seemed really nice, and I thought he was genuinely taken with me. You were really funny together, and I really enjoyed being with you both. You do seem well suited.

"As to whether I'd mind him moving in with us, I don't know. I can't say for certain how I would feel, because I've been used to it just being you and me for so long, and I do like that, I can't deny it. But I've always known that you could fall in love with a man again, and wondered whether you would. Most of all, I'd want you to be happy. I wouldn't object, in principle at least – well, I don't suppose any objections from me will stop you doing what you think is best, in the end! I'll be off to university – hopefully Castra – next year, anyhow, so you'd have the house to yourselves on the whole, then."

"Well, yes, I must make it clear that, as you say, I will make the decision in the end, and that will be the end of it," said Linda. "But you do like him and you'd have no objections in principle, to any proposal I make? I don't want to feel that I'm making you suffer something that you won't be able to bear. It's bound to take some getting used to, for you. James and I would both realise that, have no fear, and we'd do everything we can to make you feel as happy and secure, as you've always been with me on our own."

"I do like him and no, I wouldn't have any objections in principle, Mother," confirmed Alexandra. "You know that when it comes to what you want to happen, and what you think is best, both for me and us, I respect your judgement above all else, and I'm happy for you to decide. If you think James is the man for you, then that's good enough for me, and the way it will be. And you'd obviously still be the boss, even if James did come to join us, so in that respect, things wouldn't change."

Linda smiled. "Of course. That goes without saying! I won't tolerate anything but a traditional Geratican relationship, and James will want that too.

"Well, I think that settles that, then," she concluded. "Thank you, sweetheart!"

"Are you prepared to tell me, what these plans of yours to 'intensify your efforts,' entail, Mother?" asked Alexandra.

"No, not yet, darling. Leave that to me for the moment," replied Linda, looking at her daughter across the table, with a slight gleam in her eyes.

Then the two waitresses appeared with their main courses. Once everything was settled, and they were alone and about to eat again, Alexandra decided that she should now tell her mother about the proposal that she herself had made to Tom, this afternoon ...

# CHAPTER 7

Linda was refilling their wine glasses.

"Mother," said Alexandra, "I actually have some news to tell you of, myself."

"Oh?" asked Linda, "What's that then?" She began pouring wine into her daughter's glass.

With a deep breath, Alexandra said quickly, "This afternoon, I proposed a relationship with Tom, and he accepted it."

The sudden and unexpected announcement, caused Linda's concentration to slip momentarily, and as she stared at her daughter, she spilt some drops of wine on the tablecloth.

"Darn it, Alexandra!" she exclaimed as they both dabbed the cloth with serviettes from the table. "That's the first time I've spilt drink, whilst pouring from a bottle, in years! And in the Geratica Hotel, of all places! So embarrassing! If Queen Alexandra had seen that, goodness knows what she would have thought. Why did you have to choose that particular moment, to come out with this? If I'm charged for the spillage on that cloth, I've a good mind to deduct it from your allowance, next week!"

"Sorry Mother," said Alexandra apologetically, whilst at the same time, she tried desperately not to laugh.

"I'm *joking* obviously!" said Linda. "Don't worry about it. Well, I must admit that was one thing I certainly didn't expect you to tell me tonight. And you've waited until now! Better late, than never, I suppose."

"Right, the floor is yours Alexandra," she continued. "Let's hear about it."

And so, as they began to eat again, Alexandra explained to her mother about the way her feelings for Tom had been developing over the past few months, and how the confidence and inspiration to make the proposal had suddenly come to her, as they had been coming back from the wood.

"Oh, so you disobeyed and lied to me then?" Linda exclaimed, when Alexandra confessed to her that, after seeing her in the garden with Mike, she had taken Tom up to the spare room to propose, rather than immediately starting to get ready for her evening out, as she had previously told her.

"Yes, sorry about that, Mother," she said. "But as it was such an important *personal* matter for me to arrange myself, I didn't feel that I wanted you to know about it until afterwards, and even then, I wanted to wait until we had a chance to sit down alone together, for a long period of time. That's why I left it until now. And I hoped that you wouldn't mind so much about me inviting Tom in, after you'd said you'd *prefer* that I didn't today, if my proposal was successful."

"Hmm, well I'll decide whether to cane you or not, tomorrow, once we're back home," said Linda. "I'm joking *again* of course! I can quite understand how you felt. That was a perfectly reasonable, and sensible way of going about it."

Alexandra felt a surge of relief and pride, at her mother's praise for her actions.

"I assume, Alexandra, that you formulated the proposal in the correct, traditional Geratican woman's way? You decided the terms on which the relationship would be based?"

"Yes Mother. I hope I did it in the way that you've always instructed me, and one that that I hoped would make you proud," replied Alexandra.

"Well, without wanting to pry into anything that might be deeply personal, may I hear in a bit more detail, your basic reasons for the proposal?" asked Linda. "Again, just to give you a bit of confidence, I will tell you that my initial reaction to this is favourable. I have always thought that the two of you are a good match – although I confess the suddenness of it, has taken me aback slightly."

"Yes, of course, Mother," said Alexandra. "As I've said, Tom and I have always been friends – best friends in fact. We share the same kind of interests and we've gradually become closer and closer, to the point where I think we have an exceptional and unique bond between us, and I think we've both come to realise that we have strong feelings for each other and – well – I sort of crave, er, that is, I feel a longing ... a need ..."

"You're floundering again, darling," said her mother. "What I assume you mean, is that you feel sexual attraction towards him?"

"Yes, definitely, Mother, and I know for a fact that he does for me too, because I've asked him."

"There's no need to be embarrassed to admit that, sweetheart. I may be your mother, but I've experienced the same you know. And I still remember exactly how it felt, when I was your age."

"Just one thing though." Linda put down her knife, and pointed her finger sternly at her daughter.

"I hope I don't have to remind you that you are both under the legal age of consent? Don't, even for one moment, think about any kind of sexual activity, until you've both at least reached that age. Or you could get into serious trouble, and I'm not *just* talking about with *me*! You could regret it for the rest of your life, in your future education and career, not to mention domestically. Do I make myself clear, Alexandra?"

"Yes, crystal clear, Mother" said Alexandra obediently. "Honestly Mother, I wouldn't allow that to happen."

"Alright, well just so long as it doesn't," replied Linda. "You *are* still both very young, although I think you're both quite sensible, to be fair. But at your age particularly, it can be very easy to succumb to temptation. Again, I remember how difficult I found it, when I was nearly, but not quite yet a woman. Just let what I've said to you, act as a formal warning, which I want you to make Tom aware of too. If I find out you've disobeyed me – and I will – you will be shown no mercy, be in no doubt about that. This will *not* be tolerated; no matter what reason or excuse is given. As to the punishment, you'll be both sure to face the cane and I shall give you, personally, more than the standard dose, at least double, and maybe even a horse whipping, too. All contact with Tom will be suspended, until I think you've learnt your lesson – however long that might take. Do I make myself clear again, Alexandra?"

Alexandra gulped at the severity of her mother's warning. Even though she was used to them, it was still a long time since she'd received such a strong lecture as this. She'd once been given a small taste of the whip (and with her clothes on) – but never received a 'full' horse whipping.

"Yes, Mother. Crystal clear again. I promise you, we won't do anything like that until we're old enough. It hurts me that you don't trust me, Mother! You know I always do as you tell me and respect the rule of your skirt."

Linda softened her tone and put her hand over her daughter's.

"Oh, my darling, of course I don't mean to hurt you, and I do trust you, honestly I do. I'll never say this to you again, I promise, but I really want to get across to you, how seriously I regard this issue. Is that alright? Do you understand my sweetheart? As a matter of fact, I know that I'm the luckiest mother in all of Geratica, to have such a good, obedient daughter as mine, who respects the authority of her skirt."

Alexandra couldn't help but glow with pleasure at that. "Oh, Mother! Yes, I do understand, and thank you."

Linda leaned forward and Alexandra followed her mother's lead. As their faces came together, Linda cupped her daughter's in her hands, and kissed her lips four times, making Alexandra feel even more pleasure.

"Anyway darling," said Linda, returning to her meal. I'm sorry. I distracted you from your account to me. Please continue."

"Yes, Mother. Right, well it was just when we were coming back from the wood this afternoon, that Tom said some things that made me realise that I truly have it in me to be a traditional Geratican woman, in a traditional Geratican relationship, partly because I have the intelligence, and partly because, as he pointed out to me, I'd led our discussion in the wood, all the way. He said that it had been almost like I was chairing a meeting! I tried to make it the same, when I made the proposal in my room, roughly on the lines that I've explained to you. When the moment came that I knew I wanted to do it, I had to act fast, in case we lost the moment, or I, my nerve. Luckily I didn't. I was more assertive with him than normal, to an extent which shocked him, but I told him it was such an important matter that I wanted to discuss, that he had to let me be the boss. In actual fact, before we got to the spare room, he'd already guessed what was coming. He said that there wasn't much else it could have been."

Linda's eyes widened slightly, as she heard all of her daughter's report. By now, they both finished their main course, and were sipping the rest of their wine.

"Well!" she exclaimed, "I'm impressed. I think you handled the situation extremely well. You have indeed made your mother proud."

Alexandra beamed more than she had all day. On top of everything that had happened that day, her mother was pleased with how she'd conducted herself this afternoon!

"All that remains then," continued Linda, "is the question of the terms. Were there any of any significance?"

"Just a couple of things, Mother. I did stress that, although I would be leading, I would need his support to help me, when I lack confidence or feel nervous, and what happened in the wood this afternoon, was an example of what his words could inspire me to do. Also I said that I didn't want to rush things. I thought I would probably want to marry him and I was ninety-five percent certain, but I wouldn't do anything until I was one hundred percent. Tom didn't have anything to add, really and he's very easy going – we both are really – so we ended it there."

"Hmm," said Linda approvingly. "Well done indeed!"

Alexandra smiled again. "Thank you, Mother. You don't know how good it makes me feel to hear you say that."

The waitress re-appeared to clear their main course plates away, and then took their dessert orders.

"Waitress," said Linda, "I am treating my daughter tonight. She has just informed me of some news, of a personal nature, that I am most pleased to hear. I wish us to celebrate it. Please could you open another bottle of this same vintage of wine?"

"Oh. Yes, certainly Mrs Radcliffe. Of course! Right away!" The waitress was anxious to please this guest, of whom she knew of, simply by reputation. She scurried to the wine rack, and brought back the selected bottle. Opening it, she again poured a sample for Linda to taste, and when approval was granted, re-filled both of their glasses.

"Thank you," said Linda. "And if we don't finish this with our dessert course, then if you don't mind, we'd like to take the bottle up to our room, for a nightcap."

"No, that's absolutely fine Mrs Radcliffe" said the waitress. She turned to Alexandra. "And may I also congratulate you on your good news, Miss Radcliffe – whatever it may be." The waitress thought it might be impertinent of her to enquire of the exact nature, as Mrs Radcliffe had said that it was personal.

"Thank you, waitress. That's very kind of you," said Alexandra politely. Her mother had brought her up to be guarded about their personal life, when talking to people, in case of gossip warmongering. She wasn't going to say any more.

"Mother, you'll be making me tipsy!" said Alexandra, when the waitress had left.

"You'll be fine, darling," said Linda. "I know you've learnt how to drink now, and it isn't every day that a mother takes her daughter to the Geratica Hotel and *then* gets told by her, that she is now in a relationship, with the boy she has always hoped for as a prospective son-in-law!"

"Of course, Mother, now Fiona could be my prospective mother-in-law. By the way, no one else knows about this yet. I told Tom to keep it quiet, until I'd told you and we were back home. I said I'd ring him tomorrow to let him know that he could tell his stepmother. It was just that I didn't want Fiona, or anyone else, finding out, before you did."

"Good girl. That was good thinking again. Thank you for that. Did you ask him about next weekend, also?"

"Oh. Yes I did, Mother. He definitely would like to come over. Particularly when I told him that I'd wear whichever one of my gowns he'd most like to see me in, all evening! I hope you don't mind Mother, but I've also invited him around on his actual birthday, when I'm going to put each one of them on and let him decide, whilst some of his favourite music is playing in the background."

"That's on Day 2 of Week 33, isn't it?" asked Linda.

"Yes, Mother. In three days' time."

"Well yes, of course you must see your boyfriend on his birthday. Remember you've got to get your prep done though, and it's a school night. What time will he be coming?"

"I said 8.00 p.m., Mother. I should be finished by then and had supper, which is normally sandwiches, that night. I don't know what time you'll be home?"

"I expect it will be between 7.30 and 8.00, roughly. So, you're planning a bit of a fashion show for him then, are you?" There was a trace of amusement in Linda's voice.

"I do really want to make him happy, Mother. I want him to be really pleased to see me, next weekend."

Linda smiled. "I'm not knocking it, darling! Even if you are my daughter and I'm slightly biased, you are a very attractive girl, and you should always take advantage of the assets that you have. For you that's both beauty, *and* brains, which makes you a very lucky girl indeed. On top of that, you're prepared to work hard to improve yourself even more. You have every reason to be confident in your future, sweetheart. It's all going to come together for you, trust me. You're going to do great things, I just know it, and I can't wait to see how things develop.

"I'll give you a little tip for your demonstration, darling. If there's one gown that you really want him to choose, make sure that it's the last one you show him, and really sell it to him, in a more subtle, than obvious way. Then, when it comes to the final decision that will be the one freshest in his mind. He might still go for another one, but you'll certainly have a good chance of guiding him to your way of thinking. That's what I would have done with your father, anyhow, and now with James. The gown that I chose tonight is my best, and I wanted to give you all the best things tonight, my angel, but I'll not deny that I had half an eye on James, as you suggested earlier."

"Mother. You are incredible! You really know how to get what you want, don't you? I'm not sure I could be that devious. I genuinely want him to choose his favourite. James salivated over you tonight. I want Tom to do the same over me, next weekend!"

Linda burst out laughing. "Well, I suppose that's fair enough! You can deal with your relationship in your own way. Call me 'devious' as much as you like though. I normally do get what I want – and not just by those methods – but you have to learn to play the game of life tactically, darling, and there are also times when it can be useful to use your femininity and sexuality to your advantage. Believe me, men can be seduced very easily and once they are, you can control them completely. And I like total control. There's nothing wrong with being a natural Geratican woman, and you should be proud of it.

"I try to teach you how to get what you want, too, and I think it's slowly beginning to work. You were certainly highly successful this afternoon – I'd say that was your biggest achievement so far. With me behind you, in your corner, you'll stand every chance of fulfilling your ambitions and desires. I'd eventually like to see you marry Tom – I think he's 'the one' for you, unless somebody else suddenly comes out of the blue. So your 'devious' mother, may subtly try to help things along, when the time comes, although I promise I won't try to interfere in your relationship *too* much! But I hope you will both value my advice and counsel."

"Yes, Mother." said Alexandra. "I promise that we will, and thank you. I always have and always will appreciate your help."

"Would you say that you seduced Father, in order to control him compltely, then, Mother?" she asked. "And now you want to do the same with James?"

Linda smiled and for an answer, simply raised her eyebrows.

"Also, Mother, you know that I've always wanted a gown with gloves, like you've got on tonight. But you've always said, I need to be grown up, before you'll let me wear them. I may not be sixteen until the end of next summer, but I think I have grown up a lot in the past few months. They look really attractive and sexy at the same time. I love the feeling of the texture of yours against my skin, and when you stroke my fingers and my hair with them on, I feel so tingly!"

"Yes, you have grown up and maybe it's time now, to allow you the opportunity," said Linda. "Is this something that you think Tom might like too?"

"Yes, definitely, Mother," replied Alexandra.

"So, until such a time that they come into your possession, you'll take up my suggestion, to put it in his mind and keep it there, so that he becomes desperate to see you to wearing them?"

Her daughter laughed. "You see why I say you can be devious sometimes, Mother! *Maybe I'll consider it!*"

"Good. So, we have a deal then, sweetheart!" confirmed Linda, grinning.

The waitress returned with their desserts and they began eating again.

"Who'd have thought it before tonight, darling," said Linda. "We both have had our eye on our chosen man and yet neither of us knew about each other's – at least in my case, not quite the extent to which the relationship had developed!"

"I must admit that I'm finding it a bit strange, when I think of the relationship I have with you, and compare it to the one that I want with Tom," replied Alexandra.

"What do you mean?" asked her mother.

"Well, in our relationship, you've always been the much more dominant one, and I've followed your lead and done as you've told me. It feels natural for it to be that way, and I like it. I can't imagine it ever being any different. I think that having you at the heart of everything is what makes us a good partnership. It's not purely a case of you giving your orders and me obeying – although that obviously does happen. I learn from you, I work hard for you and I like to please you. I feel protected by your strength. I'll always need you in the same way, Mother; I just know it.

"I was never sure if I really could be a traditional Geratican woman. I'll be absolutely honest, Mother, and tell you that I often wondered whether I would end up as one of those women that you don't have any time for. You know, wanting a man to be more dominant than me in a relationship. I certainly don't think I'm going to be a 'woman's woman' – the kind who are more at ease with other women than with men. Indeed, I think the opposite might be true for me on occasions. And yet, more recently with Tom, I've gradually started to realise that I *do* want the kind of relationship that you've brought me up to seek, and deep down, I knew that he was 'the one.' But I didn't have the confidence to initiate it until today, when Tom said his magic words! It just seems odd, that in the two most important relationships that I have, I would want opposite roles in each."

"I don't think it's so odd, darling," said her mother. They had finished their desserts now and Linda took Alexandra's hand in hers.

"I always believed that would choose to take the traditional Geratican woman's role in a relationship. You just needed more confidence and I've seen it growing over the past few months. I think we can say now that you've matured into that type of woman. It's the natural instinct of Geratican women to be the dominant sex, and indeed it's the natural instinct of Geratican men, to follow our lead. It's how we are, and we can't change that. That's what these Male Rights Protesters, and their stupid 'progressive' female allies don't understand!"

As in the case of the previous night, Alexandra decided that it was safest to say nothing on this particular subject. She did support her mother's conservative views (although sometimes with a more liberal attitude), but at the same time, as someone who was never going to be the most confident of Geratican women, she could see how a slightly stronger male role in a relationship, could sometimes be beneficial to both partners.

Once again the waitress re-appeared to take their empty plates. She asked if they would like tea or coffee and Linda ordered two black coffees and ports.

Whilst the waitress went to fetch that, Linda continued, "When you're with other Geratican women though, it's also only going to be natural for the more dominant ones to take control and lead, and the ones less so, to be more natural followers. It's true that I am a more dominant and confident personality than you, and almost certainly, always will be. Don't forget, also, that I am your mother after all, so I really *should* be the one in charge! I think you're right though. Our relationship won't change very much, whatever happens. Our needs in a relationship with a man, will be slightly different. I've always wanted a man who will need me, and want me to take control of everything, because that's what I like to do, and make him feel looked after. In a way, perhaps *you've* been the personification of what I've needed, ever since your father died. Whereas you need a man who you can rely on to support you, and make you feel more confident and secure. That's perfectly understandable. But that doesn't mean that you can't still be the leader of your relationship, and be the one who makes the final decisions in the end. Just as there is no reason why any Geratican wife or girlfriend, who doesn't naturally lead when she is amongst other women, can't afterwards go home to her husband or boyfriend, and do just that."

The waitress came back with a tray, on which there were two glasses of port, a pot of coffee and two cups and saucers. She placed a port and a cup and saucer in front of each of them, and gave Linda the pot of coffee.

"Also sweetheart," said Linda, as she poured coffee for her daughter, "remember that with a man, there will also be a sexual element to the relationship, whereas with a woman there won't and cannot be one, due to the way Geratican bodies are formed. Do you have sexual fantasies?"

"Yes, Mother," said Alexandra, smiling sheepishly. "Every night!"

"Hmm, me too," remarked Linda.

Alexandra was amazed at her mother's candour, as they had certainly never discussed this topic before.

"If it's not too personal a question, in broad terms, what form do your fantasies take? In other words: do you think of yourself as being dominant, or more submissive in sexual intercourse? Or to put it even more plainly, which position turns you on the most, on top or underneath?"

Again, Alexandra smiled. "The traditional Geratican woman's way, Mother. On top. In fact, that's the other thing I've found confusing. Whenever I sleep in your bed, you know that my favourite place is beneath you. I *love* it when you take me over – and take my breath away with it, too! I'll not deny that I'm hoping for that tonight. I used to think I'd probably want to be underneath if I was with a man, too, but my sexual desires have most definitely and very firmly, been the other way around. There's now no doubt in my mind that I want to take control, sexually."

"As you say, darling," replied Linda, "that's the traditional Geratican woman's way. Again it's natural. There may be some who truly believe that a man on top of them is best and I know for a fact that dear Mrs Spencer is one of them, but I'm certain that a huge majority of women on this world would say that there's no better feeling than making love to a man. And *I'm* one of *them*!"

"I've always suspected that to be so, Mother, since I became aware of such things," said Alexandra.

Linda smiled. "Yes, well given the nature of our relationship, again it's always been most likely and natural for me to dominate when you come to my bed, too. But it's not a sexual relationship, where you would naturally want to be dominant, if you were with a man – or more specifically, Tom."

Linda's voice softened and became it's warmest and most loving and affectionate. She stroked her daughter's fingers as she spoke. "And by the way, *my darling*, let me make one thing clear to you. I would *never* bring you to the Queen Alexandra Marital Suite, in the Geratica Hotel, and not take you over in the bed! You can stop *hoping* it *might* happen, and start *knowing* that it *will*! Your clever Mother is going to make your dreams come true tonight, *the way that only she can do*, of that you can have no doubt, *my angel*!"

Alexandra smiled and her eyes widened with delight. Her heart beat fast with excitement. She couldn't wait! Her mother chuckled at her reaction and squeezed her hand.

"Mother," said Alexandra hoarsely, as she tried to get a grip on herself. "Seeing as you've been so candid about the subject tonight, please could you tell me, woman to woman, what making love to a man really feels like?"

Now it was Linda's turn to smile.

"Well! You're really coming out with some things tonight, aren't you, darling? Perhaps it's the wine that's emboldening you!"

"Alright," she continued. "I'll take it that you're aware of what exactly happens to your geratis when you lie over him, and also what it does inside of him. As to how it feels, you really need to find out for yourself – *when* you're old enough! I will tell you a couple of things, though.

"Firstly, what you'll experience will be like nothing you've ever known before, or ever will again. It'll truly make you squeal, and the sheer power of the orgasm may even shock you the first time, until you're more experienced. I've already told you that, as far as I'm concerned, there's no better feeling than making love to a man, and I'm sure that you're going to agree!

"Secondly, particularly at the moment, up until – at the very least – the time that you're actually able to make love – *to Tom* – you are going to experience some extremely powerful feelings of arousal, desire and pure, simple lust. My advice to you, my darling, is to do whatever you feel you need to do to satisfy your feelings, as long as it's legal and you do it in private, either in your bedroom, or else a very quiet, remote place, where you know you'll be alone for a good while."

"But, Mother," protested Alexandra, "What if the only way I can satisfy my desire, is by having a full blown orgasm? I can't do that without Tom actually being with me, can I? In my bed, I've stroked and rubbed my geratis, when it's been aroused, and laid on my front and felt it grind into the sheet – both of which were highly pleasurable experiences, but I can only go so far on my own."

"Purely on your own, yes, you are obviously correct sweetheart," said Linda, "because the geratis is only fully aroused in the presence of a man. Recently however, certain 'stimulators' have started to become available, which – if you like – can make the geratis believe that you are with a man. Then you can take yourself '*all the way*,' as it were. The experience wouldn't be quite like the real thing – but close to as good. I won't say anything more tonight – and you'll have me to stimulate your senses in a moment, anyhow – but I promise I'll see what I can do, when I have some time."

Alexandra gasped. "Ooh Mother!" she cried breathlessly, as her heart began to race again. "That sounds fantastic! Thank you!"

As they sipped the last of their ports, Linda reached over the table, and stroked her daughter's fingers seductively, with the softest of touches, stimulating all of Alexandra's senses. As they looked into each other's eyes, both mother and daughter could tell what was now firmly on the other's mind. They both desperately wanted to be in bed together – and soon. The conversation had stopped, and neither did they need any, to tell Alexandra what her mother wanted to do to her, and for Linda to know that her daughter longed for her to do it.

Finally, Alexandra could bear her longing no longer. She slipped her hand inside her mother's and squeezed urgently.

As usual, Linda read her daughter's thoughts, and took the initiative.

"Right!" she said finally. "*Bedtime!* And I'm not sure which one of us is the most desperate for what's about to happen."

"Oh, definitely me. Without a shadow of doubt, Mother!" said Alexandra, as she quickly rose from her chair, and picked up her parchment.

"I wouldn't be so sure about that, darling. I'm going to be all over you in a minute. I want to give you a loving, such as you've never had before! You've had quite a day, and you deserve it. It'll round things off perfectly."

She met her daughter on the other side of the table and wrapped her arms around her. Alexandra melted submissively into her embrace, and gazed upwards, invitingly, in the way that her mother could never resist. Linda's hold tightened and as she pushed herself against her daughter and gave her a huge kiss on the lips.

"Mother," said Alexandra softly. "What you said you do to me, just then. I want it so badly. Love me in bed!"

Linda needed no more encouragement. She picked up her daughter's wine glass and handed it to her, then picked up her own and the quarter full wine bottle. "Follow me then, my darling!" she said, smiling, her voice matching Alexandra's for softness.

They went out of the room and back into the main dining room, now deserted at this late hour. They met the head waitress.

"Hello!" she said warmly. "I hope you enjoyed your meal, ladies?"

"Yes, we did, thank you very much," replied Linda for them both. "We'll go on up to our room now, and take the rest of our wine with us."

"That's fine, Mrs Radcliffe. I trust everything was to your satisfaction?"

"Yes, yes, very good service. Now, if you'll excuse us, we really are anxious to get to bed."

It had been evident to the staff, throughout the meal, as they had discreetly checked on their progress, in order to clear their plates away, before the following course, that mother and daughter were exceptionally close, and detecting a slight aura of excitement around the pair, the head waitress thought it entirely possible, that they were about to go to bed together.

"Well. I won't keep you then," she replied, smiling. "I hope you both get a good night's sleep. Goodnight."

"Goodnight," said both Linda and Alexandra, and then they hurried away, Alexandra following just behind her mother.

The head waitress smirked. 'If you can keep your hands off each other!' she thought dryly, to herself.

# CHAPTER 8

Arriving back in the top floor corridor, their personal guards saluted as they saw them. Alexandra had never experienced that before.

"Hope you enjoyed your evening ladies," said one, a woman who was obviously in charge. "We'll be outside, if you need anything."

"Yes, we did and thank you," said Linda. "Goodnight!"

She unlocked the suite door, and they went inside. Back in the main area of the suite, they both immediately went to their side of the queen sized bed.

"Before, I do anything else, darling. I'll ring Room Service and order breakfast for tomorrow. If I say our usual weekend morning meal, to be delivered at 9.30, I trust that will be OK?"

"Yes, fine Mother," said Alexandra.

Linda picked up the phone by her side of the bed. Despite the lateness of the hour, they were still in time to order for tomorrow morning, and it only took a moment for her to place it.

After putting down the phone, Linda immediately started to undress, and her daughter followed her lead. They smiled together, their longing for each other burning ever stronger.

"See you in a moment then, darling," said Linda, her voice soft, as she left for her ensuite bathroom, to prepare for bed.

"Yes Mother!" replied Alexandra, her voice betraying her excitement. Once inside her own, she quickly put on her cream nightgown, then began to brush her teeth.

Suddenly, she could hear music softly playing. One of her favourite Philippa Barrington tunes! She opened the door slightly, and saw that her mother had started a music player, and was sat on the bed, in her white dressing gown, with her black nightgown underneath. Her hands revealed that she still had her long black gloves on.

"I put together some music before we left, darling," she said. "I've loaded it up on to the machine, and I've also re-filled our glasses with the rest of the wine,"

"Thank you, Mother. That was thoughtful of you."

She turned to go back to her bathroom.

"Don't keep me waiting now, darling!" said Linda lovingly. "You know much I want you, don't you?"

Alexandra looked back at her. "Yes Mother!" she breathed hoarsely, as a fresh wave of excitement rippled through her.

Back in her bathroom she finished cleaning her teeth in a few seconds, and then she quickly combed her hair. Putting on her own white dressing gown, she was now ready.

She went back into the main room, and over towards the bed. Linda came over, and immediately undid her daughter's dressing gown. After slipping it off her shoulders, and draping it over a chair by the bed, she opened the covers on Alexandra's side of the bed and with an inviting stroke of the sheet, with the palm of her hand, she indicated to her to get in. Alexandra did as she was encouraged to.

"Finish up your wine, darling," said Linda, picking up her glass and giving it to her. Alexandra sat drinking on her side of the bed, and watched her mother return to her own. Already, the tips of her fingers and toes were tingling in anticipation. With a smile, Linda removed her dressing gown also, and then got into bed. She quickly drained her wine glass, and Alexandra had finished hers, too.

"I thought I'd keep my gloves on, as I know how they make you tingle!" said Linda. Her voice was soft and soothing as it always had been ever since Alexandra had been a young girl in her mother's bed, but in the last couple of years, as she was older and they'd become more intimate, her mother had added a seductive flavour to the mixture, and now it aroused all of her senses, and sent waves of excitement rushing through her whole body.

First, Linda reached down, and gently massaged her daughter's toes with her right hand, whilst in the meantime taking Alexandra's right hand inside her left, and stroking her fingers. Then Alexandra lay back, and spread herself in a submissive position, and letting her long blonde hair run over her left shoulder, to allow her mother easy access to it, with her right hand. Linda unfastened both her own and Alexandra's nightgowns, and began to run her gloved hands over her daughter's body. Alexandra's heart raced once again, as the soft black velvet touch of her mother's fingers, made her skin ripple. She gave her first murmur of pleasure.

The song on the music player had now changed to 'I'll Take Care Of You'. It was from Earth's twentieth century music history, although it had never been very well known. The singer was called 'Susan McCann'. It was another song that Alexandra had picked up from scanning Earth's musical archive, and Linda, who shared her daughter's enjoyment of different types of music, particularly liked the words of the song, as, when it came to the crunch, taking care of someone who needed her strength, was what she really liked to do, whether it was her late husband, or James, or her daughter, and she had more or less adopted it as her personal song to Alexandra.

Her passion increasing as the song played, she now began to softly kiss her daughter's body, starting from her belly, and working her way over her chest and shoulders and up her neck, at which point Alexandra sighed and murmured again. Eventually she reached her face, so that she was looking straight into her daughter's eyes from just above. Alexandra was mesmerised by her mother's gaze and read, the loving and caring thoughts that they sent to her.

Then Linda put her mouth to her daughter's ear. "*I love you, my darling, my sweetheart, my angel, with all my heart!*" she whispered. She stroked Alexandra's hair, as her daughter had anticipated that she would want to. "*I want to take care of you and give you all the love that I have!*" she continued to whisper. She kissed Alexandra's lips, just as her fingers expertly brushed the tips of her hair. Her daughter shuddered as she felt more tingles and let out another small murmur. Without stopping, Linda continued and Alexandra murmured again, this time a little louder.

Then the final song that Linda had loaded on to the music player, began. This was the climax that she had been building up to. It was 'Take My Breath Away', by Berlin, yet another song that they had discovered from Earth, and the one that they considered their bedroom signature tune. To her delight, the start of the song sent Alexandra into a peak of longing for her mother's body over hers.

"*Oh please, Mother!*" said Alexandra, into her mother's ear. "*I know I'm becoming a woman, but at the same time, I'll always be a baby who needs her mother to take control, and look after her. Take me over and dominate me with your strong loving. I need it all! Take my breath away, beneath you! Love me as much as you want, just as long as I'm in your arms, beneath your protective body. That always feels so wonderful!*"

Linda could resist no longer, as she heard the kind of words that she most loved to be said to her, spoken by the person she most wanted to hear them from.

She moved right over to Alexandra's side of the bed, and mounted her. She wrapped her legs around her daughter's, and squeezed them tight inside of her. Then she lay down over her, so that they were chest to chest and her lips were above Alexandra's. They could both feel each other's hearts thundering. Linda's was beating just as fast as her daughter's now, as her excitement began to reach its zenith. She wrapped her arms tight around Alexandra's shoulders, and pressed her body deep down into her daughter's. Then, finally she began to kiss and kiss and kiss Alexandra's lips, with a passion.

Alexandra now felt completely smothered. Linda was exceptionally good at co-ordinating her loving technique, and her daughter was in ecstasy, as she felt her kisses over her mouth, the strong embrace of her arms and legs, and her body crushing hers into the bed. She sighed with pleasure as she lay beneath her mother. Linda was so expert, that she knew exactly when to relent slightly in her kissing, so that Alexandra could take in breath. As she started to recover, Linda slipped her tongue inside her daughter's slightly ajar mouth and licked hers – her tongue on Alexandra's, performing in much the same way as her fingers had done over Alexandra's earlier. Her daughter sighed in ecstasy, once again.

Linda now decided to make the decisive push.

"*And now, my baby, I* **shall** *take you over!*" she whispered into her daughter's ear.

She pressed down deeper than ever into Alexandra, and squeezed stronger with her with her arms and legs. Her kisses had even greater urgency.

Alexandra couldn't believe that her mother could love her any stronger than before, but she was! Her excitement reached fever pitch. The ultimate moment of pleasure that she and her mother shared, once a week, was coming on fast. Both mother and daughter were murmuring and sighing together now. Alexandra could tell that her mother was experiencing ecstasy too. Her breath was short and hot, between her kisses and her heart thumped against her daughter's chest.

With one more thrust, Linda's body, arms, legs and lips engulfed her daughter, all at once, and she took her over. Alexandra felt as if her mother was right inside of her body, inflaming all her senses. So tight was the hold on her, and so deeply was she crushed beneath, that she couldn't move. Her mother's kisses poured down like hot lava from a volcano, as her passion reached the very tip of its peak. Alexandra began to lose her breath, felt tingles all over, and her head spun, as she lost control of herself. She felt as if she was floating on the bed, being carried along by her mother, as she dominated her entire body and all of her senses, and she clung on tight.

Linda murmured in ecstasy at the pleasure she felt in taking over her daughter. Then as Alexandra moaned softly, and clawed at her back, always a telling sign that she was beginning to pass the limit that she could take, she stopped, and rolled off her.

For a moment they both lay together, gasping for breath. Not surprisingly, given what she'd just experienced, Alexandra took the longest to recover.

Her mother wrapped her arms around her in a gentle, loving embrace, beside her, and rocked her slowly, like a baby.

"Are you alright, my darling?" she asked tenderly, after a couple of moments.

"Yes Mother. I think I've got most of my breath back now!" She snuggled up to her mother's chest.

"Did you enjoy it? I certainly enjoyed taking you over!"

"I loved it, Mother! I think in two years of you doing that to me that was the best yet! Thank you, Mother!" She looked up and kissed her.

"My pleasure darling!" Linda kissed her daughter back.

Alexandra snuggled to her mother's chest again, and Linda gently squeezed and rocked her with her left arm, and stroked her hair with her right hand. Within seconds she was asleep, worn out after the momentous events of the day.

# PART 3

# CHAPTER 1

A noise awoke Alexandra, next morning. It took her a moment to remember where she was, but then the events of the previous day began to register in her mind.

She stretched out on her back, luxuriously, in the queen sized bed. It was only then that she noticed that her mother was up and looking around the Suite, in her dressing gown. Alexandra realised that it was probably she who had awakened her. To her puzzlement, she found that she couldn't remember having said "Goodnight," to her yesterday, which was unheard of.

Alexandra got out of bed, put her own dressing gown on, and went over to join her mother.

"Ah! Good morning, my darling," said Linda, as she saw her daughter. She stepped across, and took her in her arms. "I trust you had a good night's sleep? You went out like a light, last night!"

"Good morning, Mother," replied Alexandra. "Yes I did sleep well, thank you. Also, I'm sorry, but I don't think I said 'goodnight,' to you last night."

"Oh! Don't worry about that sweetheart," said her mother. "I obviously knocked you out with the power of my loving!"

"Yes, you really were fantastic last night, Mother. Plus, the fact that it turned out to be quite a day for me yesterday – and a late night, too!"

Linda squeezed her tight and gave her a big kiss, which Alexandra tenderly returned.

"Well thank you for the compliment, darling!" said Linda. "It goes without saying, that it felt fantastic for me too, last night! Today should be a more leisurely day, anyhow."

"It was a wonderful dinner, too, Mother," added Alexandra. "Thank you."

"Is everything in order here, then?" she asked.

"Yes, I think so. I'll be making a favourable report to the manageress and to Queen Alexandra herself, of course. Have an exploration yourself, if you like, darling. But try not to break anything! I certainly *would* get charged for that, and it would be *very* embarrassing!"

"No, Mother. I'll try not to!" replied Alexandra.

The suite certainly did seem to have everything that you could conceivably want, whilst you stayed here. As well as the bed and the ensuite bathrooms, there was a huge wardrobe and even a Jacuzzi. The kitchen area was well stocked with all kinds of alcoholic beverages, coffees, teas and nibbles and it had its own fridge, kettle, coffee making machine and toaster. The living area had a table and chairs, as well as an easy chair and sofa and a clock. There was the music player, which her Linda had used last night and a radio. The walls were decorated with fine pictures from Geratican art history.

As she looked around, Alexandra couldn't help but wonder if she really might bring Tom here, one day. The thought of making love to him in the queen sized bed here, was enough to stir a sexual arousal inside of her. She understood exactly what her mother had meant last night, regarding those particular feelings.

There was a knock at the door. Linda looked at the time. "I think our breakfast has arrived, sweetheart," she told her daughter.

She went down the passage, opened the door, and looked out. Sure enough a tray was left on the floor, as the hotel manageress had promised. She picked it up, and not wanting to risk holding it with just one hand, carefully closed the door, using her body to push it to.

"Here we are then, darling," she said on her return. "Breakfast is served. Now, do you want to eat it in bed, as we normally do at home on the second day of the weekend, or seeing as we're here, shall we try out the living area? I think that maybe we didn't ought to risk getting crumbs and stains in the bed of the Marital Suite, don't you?"

"OK Mother. The living area it is then," answered Alexandra. Once more, Linda had directed her daughter to her way of thinking. Alexandra reflected again, on how easily her mother took control to get things done how she wanted. She didn't think that she would ever be capable of doing that, in quite the same way, even though she had taken on board some of the tips that her mother had given her, last night. In any case, when they were together, it did make life a lot easier for her, when things were done in that way. She was genuinely appreciative of her mother's dominance in their relationship, and she knew that she always would be.

"Right. This way then." She led them across the suite, and they sat down at the table to eat.

"Hmm," said Alexandra, approvingly, as she neared the end of her cooked breakfast. "The food in this hotel is delicious Mother. Almost as good as your cooking at home. You know I think that's the ultimate!"

Linda smiled. "Another compliment! Thank you. You're obviously a happy and satisfied young lady, this morning, darling!"

"Definitely Mother. I've never felt so good. This is, without question, the best weekend of my life! In any case, you shouldn't be surprised to hear me complimenting your cooking."

"No, I'm not sweetheart. You devour everything I cook for you. Now, let me ask your opinion on a third subject. Who runs the best household in the whole of Geratica?"

"Well that's simple, Mother! You, obviously!"

"Correct answer, darling," said Linda. "All of which leads to what may be the greatest tip I will ever give you, as far as your domestic situation is concerned.

"Now listen and learn from your clever mother," she continued. She looked at Alexandra with a familiar twinkle in her eyes, that her daughter knew well. "A Geratican woman, who runs an efficient and prosperous household, and is fantastic in both the kitchen and the bedroom, will be the most likely to have a successful and long lasting marriage!"

There was the faintest hint of a smirk on Linda's face, after she had finished, and her eyebrows twitched up and down.

Alexandra giggled so much, that she had to be careful not to choke on the last of her bacon. "Thank you, Mother," she replied. "You can be sure I won't forget that particular piece of advice!"

Linda's smirk broke into a smile. "Good girl," she said, as she got up and took their plates. "Well, I'll leave you to ponder on it, whilst I go and make us some toast and coffee."

Whilst Linda was over in the kitchen area, Alexandra did ponder on it. She still slightly had the giggles. Her mother had quite a dry sense of humour, which, combined with the indomitable strength of her personality, her highly affectionate nature, and her attractive looks, made her, in her daughter's eyes, at least, a highly likeable woman – although you needed to be on the right side of her. She could understand why James might find her so desirable and have fallen in love with her.

The comment was obviously meant as a joke, but Alexandra knew that her mother's witticisms were sometimes based on faint elements of truth, or at least half truth. She actually understood the simple realities of life and what really made people tick, better than most. Her mother *was* fantastic in all of the three parts of a relationship that she had mentioned. And they were indeed the ones at the heart of it. Alexandra, too, wanted to be good at all three roles, and with each day that went passed, she was becoming more and more confident that she could and would be.

She decided that she might inform Tom of her mother's advice, and that she intended to follow it! Her thoughts returned briefly to yesterday afternoon. Tom had said he liked her 'softness'. Well, she could do 'soft', alright! In her relationship with her mother, she was certainly the one who had the softest centre. Her mother's was much tougher, though not quite as hard as people who didn't know her very well, might think.

Alexandra also couldn't wait to tell Tom about everything else that had happened in Avermore, once she was back home.

Linda returned with the tray with toast and coffee on it, as promised. After they had finished eating, she took her daughter's hand. "Let's go and try out the sofa, darling," she said and squeezed it inside of hers at the same time, to emphasise her wish.

Alexandra looked into her mother's eyes. "I'd like that Mother," she said.

Linda took the coffee on the tray, over to the sofa, and set it down on a small table in front of it. They sat down and she poured it for them.

Then she slipped her arms around her daughter's shoulders and looked at her.

"Just one more question, darling," she said tenderly. "Who's the cleverest mother?"

"That's another easy one, Mother," replied Alexandra, reclining on the back of the sofa, and looking up at her. "Definitely you, again!"

Linda leaned over and gave Alexandra her biggest kiss of the day so far, then shifted her slightly on the sofa, and pushed her backwards on to the cushions, so that she came down on top of her daughter. She kissed her again and for a few seconds, they exchanged affection. Alexandra made the familiar sound of pleasure that her mother knew well and loved to hear.

"I didn't realise you wanted to test the sofa, in quite that way, Mother!" remarked Alexandra, once they were sitting up again, and drinking their coffee.

"Well, I genuinely did think it would be nice, to be able to say that we'd sat on the sofa, in the Queen Alexandra Marital Suite, darling, but I will admit that I also had ulterior motives!"

"Devious again, Mother." said Alexandra.

"Or 'clever,' even, maybe!" retorted Linda.

Once they had finished a leisurely cup of coffee, the time on the clock in the Suite was approaching nearly 10.30.

"Right sweetheart," said Linda. "It's time we made a move, I'm afraid. I'll put the rest of the breakfast things, in the kitchen, and then we'd better get dressed, packed up and ready to go. I need to call the manageress, too, to tell the Head of Room Service, that we're leaving before I check us out, by 11.00. Oh and make sure you remember your manuscript."

Fifteen minutes later they were in Pauline Entwistle's office. Mother and daughter were again dressed in the same colour – this time blue. Linda wore a pale blue casual jacket, over a matching blouse and skirt, whilst Alexandra had a royal blue blouse and skirt on, with a coat of the same colour over the top.

The hotel manageress was clearly relieved, when Linda told her that they had found no problems or faults in the Marital Suite. She hoped that they had enjoyed their overnight stay, and they both assured her that they had.

"We very much enjoyed the cooking, and my daughter particularly remarked upon it," said Linda. "Although she was sensible enough to add that it was only 'almost as good as' mine!"

"Oh!" replied Pauline. "Well perhaps we'd better make you the head chef here then, to get us up to the standards that she is accustomed to!"

Alexandra giggled.

"No, thank you," said Linda. "I'm sure I could do the job, but I have rather a lot on my plate in my own at the moment, I'm afraid! And I do rather enjoy it."

And with that, they said their goodbyes, and after Linda had settled their bill with reception, left the hotel to meet up with James once again.

# CHAPTER 2

James was there waiting for them, in good time.

"Good morning, ladies!" he said cheerfully. "Did you enjoy your night at the Geratica Hotel?"

"Good morning, James," replied Linda. "Yes we did. It was wonderful, thank you."

"Pleased to hear it, Ma'am," said James.

He loaded their cases into the boot of the car, then let them both into the back. Alexandra gave him a friendly smile, as he held her door open for him. She was now seeing him in a different light, compared to when she had first met him last night. There was potential for the three of them to be together at The Grange, one day.

As he got into the car himself, he said, "Where to first then, Ma'am?"

Linda reached across the back seat, took her daughter's hand, and stroked her fingers. "The Geratica Science Museum, please James," she ordered.

"Right you are, Ma'am," said James, and they set off.

"And how was your night, James?" asked Linda.

"Oh, you know. Quiet," said James. "Went back home. Listened to a bit of radio, then went to bed."

"Your wife hasn't come home for the weekend, then?"

James glanced at Linda through his rear view mirror. "No," he said.

Linda's eyes discreetly looked over at her daughter, and her eyebrows raised a fraction. Alexandra gave a very slight nod, to acknowledge that what her mother had told her last night, had been correct.

***

After he had dropped them off, Linda told James that they'd meet him again in a couple of hours. She was going to take Alexandra to the Geratica Art Museum afterwards, which was only next door. James said that was fine, and he'd amuse himself, until then.

Linda and Alexandra then spent an enjoyable time strolling around the museums. Alexandra had been taken there by her mother before and she'd been on a school trip, but she still enjoyed seeing all the exhibits and reading the tourist information – a lot of which she was familiar with, through her own studying, both for school and pleasure. It was nice to match historical artefacts in the flesh with what she had seen of them in books. As scientific research and artistic development were continually evolving, there were always new things to see, anyhow. There was even a scientific demonstration, which she particularly enjoyed.

Om the corner of one of the main streets, a man was handing out leaflets to whoever he could get to take them. As he did so, he shouted, "Greater rights for men! Equal representation in society, formal education, and suffrage!"

Linda ushered her daughter past. "In Geratica's name, can we not all be left in peace on day 2 of a weekend?" she said. "The Divine Being created our race in the nature which she saw fit. Women are meant to be the leaders in society and a man's role is to be subservient. There's no need for boys to be formally educated in the same way that girls are, in order for them to be able to fulfil their traditional roles. And as for suffrage, voting decisions should be the preserve of those who are sufficiently educated to truly understand the issues involved. And they are obviously going to be women!"

"Yes Mother," replied Alexandra. She could see her mother's point about the traditional roles played by the two genders. At the same time though, she thought that there were probably *some* men who were sufficiently educated to be able to play greater roles within Geratican society – perhaps even vote. Tom was quit an intelligent boy.

***

Back in the car with James, Linda instructed him to take them to view the Bank of Geratica and then the Tower of Avermore - Geratica's principal prison. He drove them across several streets to Geratica's official state bank, and then across Avermore Bridge, along Divinity Hill and past the turning for the Royal Avenue. The journey continued for a short distance, until they reached the Tower of Avermore to their right. They stopped and looked at the tall building.

"I sincerely that you'll never end up spending time in there, at Her Majesty's pleasure, Alexandra," said Linda.

"So do I, Mother," replied Alexandra.

She knew that many notorious prisoners had been held there, throughout much of Geratica's history – and continued to be today. Until two centuries previously, horsewhips had been routinely used by Her Majesty's Court to extract confessions, if necessary in certain cases – but that practice was since abolished. Some of the prisoners would have later been hanged there too, until Queen Alexandra abolished that activity as well, soon after she ascended to the throne. Her mother had been responsible for drafting the bill which Geratica's parliament passed, to end it. Alexandra was pleased that it had been.

Then they all had a light lunch in a café opposite.

"And now we'll go to the palace, please James," ordered Linda, once they'd finished, she'd paid the bill, and they were back in the car..

"Right you are, Ma'am," he obeyed.

Alexandra looked at Linda in surprise. "We're going to see the palace again, Mother?" she asked.

"Well, that's just it, darling," said Linda. "You only saw it from outside, last night."

"You're taking me inside, Mother?" Alexandra exclaimed excitedly.

Linda smiled. "Yes, for a bit, at least. We'll pop into my office, and you can have a look around the section of the palace, that is my little empire!"

"And if your mother can bribe the palace security, she might even be able to take you to see some of the private palace rooms!" said James, as he turned the car around and started off.

"James Spencer, how *dare* you suggest that I'd do something like that!" said Linda. "What did I tell you last night, about being cheeky to a woman?"

"I'm sorry, Ma'am. Of course, I should have said, 'bribe Queen Alexandra!'"

Alexandra smiled. They were at it again! Her mother noticed.

"That's even worse! And *you* can take that smirk off your face, my girl! Now, both of you behave yourselves, or I swear I'll have Her Majesty commit the pair of you to the tower!"

"Yes, Mother," said Alexandra.

"Yes Ma'am," said James. They got into the car and he turned right, into the Royal Avenue.

***

Arriving at the palace, the guards at the gate let James drive through, when they saw him. He drove around to the back of the palace, and stopped by the rear entrance. James let them out, and this time was able to accompany them.

Linda led them to the entrance and swiped her palace identification pass through the security lock. There was a click and she pushed the main door open.

As they entered, the woman at the desk stood up. "Hello, Mrs Radcliffe. Hello, James. I see you've brought your daughter for a visit, Mrs Radcliffe? How was the Geratica Hotel?"

"We had a most enjoyable overnight stay, thank you, Charlotte," said Linda to the woman. "We've just been to both the science and art museums, and I thought, seeing as we were passing, that I'd bring Alexandra in here, so that she can have a look around my department, whilst there's nobody about. We'll go into my office for a moment. See you later."

"Nice, to meet you, Alexandra," said Charlotte.

"And you, Charlotte," replied Alexandra, smiling politely.

As Linda took them across to her office, Alexandra reflected that "Charlotte," hadn't seemed terribly surprised by her mother's sudden arrival. Their visit had obviously been planned. Why else would her mother have brought her identification pass with her, and been able to open an office staff door outside of normal hours?

Linda unlocked the door of her office and they went inside.

"Here we are then, darling," she said. "Still the same old place. Do you want to sit at your mother's desk, like you did last time?"

Alexandra smiled. "Yes, Mother! Thank you."

She sat down and looked around. As usual, she imagined all the things that her mother had done in this room, over the years. All the budgets she had co-ordinated, the laws that she had overseen, the speeches and statements that she had drafted, and the official engagements and meetings that she had organised. This department was the very heart of the palace machinery of administration. And her mother controlled everything from here! She felt a rush of pride that she was her daughter.

"Are your staff still in the same place, too, Mother?" she asked.

"Yes. I'll take you through to my little empire in a minute, if you like."

"Goodness me, Linda. You've changed!" said a woman's voice at the door. Alexandra looked, and was shocked to see that it was the queen! As it was a non-working day for her, she was in slightly more casual attire than normal, a simple blue polo neck jumper and white skirt. Her long red hair flowed freely across her shoulders, to her tall slender body.

"Your Majesty!" said Linda, curtseying and James bowing.

Alexandra sprang up from the chair and out from her mother's desk. "Your Majesty!" she exclaimed, curtseying. "I'm terribly sorry, Ma'am, I didn't expect to see you." She looked at her mother, who, like Queen Alexandra and James, was spluttering with laughter. "In fact this is only the latest, in a series of shocks that I've had this weekend!"

"It's alright, Alexandra. I didn't mean to startle you!" said the queen. "Go back and sit down. I'm aware that your mother has given you a treat this weekend, and included one or two surprises. This must be one of them! She's a most efficient organiser and administrator you know. My right-hand woman! And she clearly can't keep away from her work. I am most surprised to see her today!"

"Yes. Well, you know. My work is never done, Ma'am," said Linda. "There's always something that needs my attention. And if I didn't do it, who else could?"

"Fiona?" asked the queen, mischievously.

"No, Alexandra," she continued. "The truth is that I knew your mother was planning to bring you here today, so good old Charlotte, at the back door, was instructed to phone through to my private office, and tell them you'd arrived, as soon as you got here, so that I could come down the corridor and meet you! I believe that a receptionist wouldn't normally be at the back on a weekend, but an exception has been made for today."

"Speaking of Fiona, reminds me. How was my Marriage Suite? You know that was always her project, Linda."

"It was fine, Ma'am. It's a very nice place, with everything you could possibly wish for, at your fingertips. I – or should I say, we? – could find no problems at all. "I would highly recommend it to you, Ma'am."

With the greatest respect though, Ma'am, I don't care if it was Fiona's project. I am her senior in rank and I was completely left out of it, despite all of my experience as an administrator. It was the least she could do, to let me have first go."

Queen Alexandra sighed. This had been a sore subject between Linda and Fiona, and there was sometimes a clash of personalities anyhow, as they were both strong characters, who liked – and were used to getting – their own way. Neither was averse to manipulating circumstances to their advantage at times, and Linda particularly, was a shrewd tactician.

"I'm sorry, Linda," she said. She had known her since she was a young princess, shortly to become queen and was close to her and valued her counsel highly. "At the time of its instigation, Fiona was still quite new, and I felt she needed something to get her teeth into. And she does have responsibility for the domestic and catering affairs of this palace, anyhow. That was what we agreed to, when we took her on. You were and still are, very busy. You can't do everything."

Linda opened her mouth to protest, but the queen held up her hand. "However it is finished now, and let us say no more about the subject! Other than for me to say of course, that I am pleased that it has been finished and there are no problems. I will one day visit it myself, but obviously at the moment I have no idea when it will be and with whom."

"Of course, Ma'am. As you wish."

"And did you meet Philippa Barrington last night, Alexandra?" asked the queen.

"Yes Ma'am. That was an incredible experience and I'm now even going to receive tuition from her! Forgive me, Ma'am, but was there anybody but me, who *didn't* know that I was going to meet her?"

Linda and James looked at each other and their mouths creased up, as they tried to suppress their laughter.

The queen chuckled too. "You have your mother's sense of humour! Truthfully, only a handful of us knew, and I imagine out of all us, you only have your music mistress still to meet, since last night. Have you found this weekend, a bit overwhelming?"

"I've found it incredible, Ma'am! It's been the best one of my life! And I've got my mother to thank for it!" She looked at Linda and smiled. Her mother wrapped her arm around her, and kissed her.

"Yes, you're very lucky to have her," said the queen. "We both share that good fortune. She has stolen my chauffeur for the weekend, too!"

"Yes Ma'am, and I'm very grateful to you for that, too. It's been most entertaining!"

The queen smiled and nodded in acknowledgement. "Yes, they're really quite a pair, aren't they? She glanced at them for a second.

Linda and Alexandra exchanged one of their own discreet glances, that they had perfected together. "Perhaps in more ways than one," thought Alexandra.

"Well, the other thing I wanted to do," said the queen, "was to tell you that I will be taking tea in my reception room at 3.30 p.m., and you're welcome to join me. That might give you time to quickly do anything else you might want to, beforehand."

Linda gave the briefest of glances to James and Alexandra, before announcing for them all, "We'd be honoured to. Thank you, Ma'am!"

# CHAPTER 3

They had an hour or so, before their appointment with the queen, and Linda walked her daughter the short distance, up the Royal Avenue, and into Parliament Square, where Parliament House was situated.

Although it wasn't in session at the weekend, visitors could still look around the parliament building, seven days a week. All of Geratica's major tourist attractions were open every day of the year, except for the very first two, Divinity Day and Queen's Day in week one and the other two Bank Holidays, during the year. The only difference on the second day of a weekend, was that the opening hours were slightly shorter. Soon after Queen Alexandra had ascended to the throne in the year 4999, one of Linda Radcliffe's reforms as Court Administrator, had been to open the Royal Palace to the public as a tourist attraction, too.

"It's not quite so impressive in the chamber, when the members are away, and there's no business being done," said Linda. "That was obviously how it was, when you visited here with the school, and watched from up here in the gallery."

"And you were there sitting just over there, behind Queen Alexandra, Mother, whilst she made an address and took questions!" said Alexandra, pointing to the throne in the centre of the chamber, where there were a couple of tables and chairs behind.

"Yes sweetheart. That happens on the third day of each week, as you know. I have to make sure Her Majesty gets all the relevant paperwork that she needs relating to the members' questions, and also give her any advice. or bring her up to date on anything that she's not so familiar with. That's why you saw me talking into her ear quite a lot! Next to me, at the other table, is usually Veronica, my secretary, to take notes from me, regarding any follow-up work to be done. Then sat at the back of the chamber, is obviously the speaker, with her clerks behind her."

"I've often wondered what would happen, if Queen Alexandra turned to ask you about something she knew nothing about, and you didn't know either, Mother!"

Linda chuckled. "Well, of course even your clever mother doesn't know *everything-*"

"That's unusually modest of you, Mother."

Linda slapped her daughter's bottom. "Don't you be so cheeky! That's James' influence on you. I shall have words with him in a minute, when we get back to the palace. I won't have him leading you astray!"

"Sorry, Mother!" said Alexandra, giggling. She knew that she was only being playful.

A smile began to creep across Linda's face. She wrapped her arm back around her daughter's shoulders, where it had been until just then and pulled her in closer to her body.

"What I was about to go on to say, before I was so rudely interrupted by my insolent daughter, is that it can indeed sometimes be the case that we genuinely can't provide an answer. Generally, we either say that we'll look into the matter, and write to the member privately, at a later date, or, if we think it's likely that our ignorance will cause Queen Alexandra and her court some embarrassment, then we basically try to fudge it!"

Alexandra burst out laughing. "Fudge it, Mother! You actually admit that?"

"Well of course I do, darling, but not officially of course. And don't you dare tell anyone I said it, either, or you'll get another smacked bottom! Just to be serious for a moment, Alexandra, remember what I've always told you about *discretion*. That applies to our private life, and also any snippet of confidential information that you might get to hear about, through your relationship with me. I'm wondering if I should have said that to you, myself now."

Alexandra grabbed her mother's hand and squeezed from within. "Mother, please! You've got to trust me! I won't ever betray your confidence. It just sounded so funny to hear that coming from you, that's all.

Linda squeezed back from the outside. "Yes darling. I know we'd been having a bit of fun, and that's something that gives me a lot of pleasure, when we're together. And of *course* I trust you! But you've got to be very careful. Something can come out by any means, and it might be completely by accident, through something of which you've never considered. Oh and by the way, this reminds me – did you pass on my orders, to Tom yesterday afternoon, regarding our trip to the Marital Suite last night?"

"Yes, Mother. Very firmly! We'll be discreet. I promise."

"Good girl." "Anyway, all that having been said, and getting back to this chamber and the members questions, it's also obvious, even to someone with a lot less intelligence than you sweetheart, that we are sometimes evasive in our answers, either because we don't know, or more likely because we don't want to admit something. That state of affairs has existed in politics everywhere, since the dawn of time. But again, we don't say such things *officially*, and *certainly not* in the *public* domain!"

"You do enjoy all of this though, don't you, Mother?"

"Yes my love, I have to say I do. I like all of my job, and enjoy everything it entails, but I admit, I get a particular thrill when I'm in here. It may be a bit pressurised at times, but I don't mind that. I like being at the centre of things in everything I'm involved with, because then I at least get the chance to influence, guide and control things, in the way that I want. For me, there's no point in being a woman in the background, staying in the shadows. I'll never get anything done, or achieve any goals, from there."

Linda squeezed her daughter's hand again. "But that's just my opinion and I realise it's never going to be quite the same for some other women, and *that* I think, is always going to include you. That's why, whenever you're with me, either now, or in the future, I'm happy to take control and lead for both of us."

"Thank you, Mother," said Alexandra. "You know I'm grateful for that. I think the bottom line, is that it's what we both want. For us, in our relationship, it's the natural arrangement."

"Yes. I'd certainly go along with that," said Linda. "You put that very well, darling!"

They exchanged kisses.

Linda looked at the clock in the chamber. "If we start making our way back now, my sweetheart, you might get a bit of time to walk around my little empire. It won't take long, and again there'll obviously be no-one there, but at least you can see where my work at the palace gets administered." She offered her arm, invitingly, for Alexandra's shoulders.

"Yes please, Mother!" said Alexandra and slipped inside her Linda's arm. With her own wrapped around her mother's waist, they started back.

"Has it changed much, since my last visit, Mother?"

"No. Not a lot. We've possibly become a bit more computerised, but otherwise, I think it'll be about the same as you remember, darling."

"*More* computerised? Goodness me, Mother. What will they think of next?"

"Yes, well it has been me who's been responsible for introducing them to the palace, sweetheart, so I can't complain too much! To an extent 'I' am '*they*'! We do tend to import technology and culture quite heavily from Earth and I'm all for that, as I think many of our tastes are similar, but we do have considerable technology of our own, which might be more advanced and powerful, so whether we'll need to be quite such slaves to the things as they are, I would say is debatable. They are an interesting concept though, and have their uses, up to a point.

"Of course, Queen Alexandra's weekly visit to parliament, isn't my only one. I do go over a couple of days a week, towards the end of the day, to oversee the business being administered. I normally try to do it on the first two days of the week, because that's when most of the bills are scheduled to be passed, before the queen officially announces that they have become law, on Day 3, before her question time. Unfortunately, the debates go on until the early evening, which means I'm late home to be with you, which is the only drawback, but it can't be helped. I do actually get to speak then, so in a way, I suppose that's even better. I really feel I can make my views known then, and argue the case for any bill that is proving difficult. But of course, I don't go there, as a member of parliament. I'm only an administrator of the court's business, and even I can't *command* them to accept a bill, much as I wish that I could do sometimes!"

"Hmm. I imagine you do, Mother! But, if Queen Alexandra's court have decided on a bill, then it normally does become law though doesn't it? I can never understand why there are such long debates, when all that usually happens in the end is that the members pass it into law anyhow."

"The key word there is 'normally'," said Linda. "In theory, you're right, the bills that pass through parliament, *normally* become laws. But they don't *have* to. Although our world is governed by an absolute monarchy, we aren't a totalitarian state. A bill gets a maximum of three readings. If it fails after the first, then it has to go back and be amended. Then the process is repeated with its second reading, and so on. If after three readings, enough members are still determined to vote against a bill, and it's rejected, then it goes back to the drawing board and either has to be completely re-written, in order to be put through the process again, which can take a while, or simply scrapped."

"I do take an interest in this, to find out what's going on though, Mother and I've never heard of such a case, during my living memory. The only one I know of is obviously the '4941 Budget Crisis', when one of your unfortunate predecessors – Lady Monica Dixon-Taylor – failed to get that year's budget accepted. We all learn about that at school. The nobility were thought to be so out of touch with the 'commoners', that there was nearly a revolution. She had to resign, and that was what led to your position and department always being selected from upper middle class families, like ourselves, to preserve the link between the monarchy and the ordinary people. It almost became an abdication crisis too, but luckily Queen Matilda the second, survived."

"As usual your historical knowledge is flawless, darling" said Linda.

"But bear in mind that just because you haven't heard of any other cases, that doesn't mean to say there haven't been any. Luckily, since that dark and shameful event in our history, the bills rejected have been relatively minor and of low significance, therefore they haven't really attracted publicity. You can be sure that if such a crisis, or anything on a similar scale, were to happen today though, people certainly would know about it, and the modern day media would make it a huge story. You can also, surely realise, how I feel about that! Every time I go into the parliament chamber, I am *determined* not to suffer the same fate as poor Lady Dickson-Taylor, and that thought generally inspires me to fight even more vigorously to force the court's business through!"

"So roughly how many bills are rejected per year, then Mother?"

"Oh, generally only a handful actually get thrown out after a third reading. Which, when you consider how many bills we administrate each year, isn't bad. I'm also proud to say that I have an exceptionally good success rate, in getting previously rejected bills re-drafted, and then finally put into law. There've not been any 'abandonments.' I don't take 'No', for an answer!"

"As you said last night, Mother," said Alexandra. "You usually do get your way. Thank you for telling me about this. I've learnt something today."

"I wish I could see you doing that part of your job," she continued. "I'd be thrilled to see you speak in parliament! I know they do put highlights of the day's proceedings on the radio, and I've heard you sometimes, but that's not quite the same."

"Well, unfortunately of course, parliament tends to take its recess around the same time as the schools are on holiday, so it's a bit awkward," said her mother. "If you were to come over, straight from Charterhouse, you'd really have to make your own way, and then by the time I eventually got us back home, you wouldn't have much time to do your prep, before bedtime."

"I might be able to do most of it, whilst I watched you, Mother."

Linda gave her daughter a sceptical look. "Darling, you can't possibly concentrate properly on your prep *and* listen to what's going on in parliament. That's ridiculous! You know that's why I tell you to do your homework in the study, where it's quiet, and forbid you to do it in your room with music on."

They had reached the palace gates and been allowed back in by the guards. As they walked back around to the back entrance, Linda squeezed Alexandra against her body. "Listen sweetheart. *I* think it would be nice for you to see that, too. You take a very keen interest in all of these things and I'm *extremely* proud of you for that. I can tell you're disappointed and *if* and I did say *if* I can find a way, I promise that I'll make it happen for you. There are certain practicalities that will have to be overcome, but I do want make you happy, and I actually would like to know that you were up in the gallery, watching me!"

She wrapped her arms around her daughter and engulfed her. "I love you with all of my heart, darling!" she said, and then kissed her.

"Now come along, you! Come inside and see my little empire, and then we have an appointment for tea with the queen!"

# CHAPTER 4

"Charlotte," said Linda, after she and her daughter had got back inside the palace. "I'm just going to take Alexandra to have a quick walk around my little empire, OK? Then we'll be off to take tea with Her Majesty, in her reception room."

"Very good, Mrs Radcliffe," she replied. "I hope you enjoy your tea."

"Oh I'm sure we will," said Linda. "They usually serve some delicious buns with it!"

"Do you think they will today, Mother?" asked Alexandra.

"Well, it is traditional to have something of that kind, when 'one' is taking tea, you know, darling," It's basically a light refreshment, in between *lunch* and *dinner*."

"Yes, Mother. The girls who board at Charterhouse, take it in each other's rooms at 3.15 p.m. – as I'm sure you remember. I've been invited, and gone once or twice, but as it's the end of the day, as far as the official curriculum is concerned, I usually want to get my train home. Of course after tea, the boarders do 'extra-curricular activities,' before their dinner."

"Just to let you know, sweetheart," said Linda as they walked across to the main office of the court administration department. "What you'll be given here will be rather better than what the girls take at Charterhouse! It'll be waitress service, with a trolley, which will have tea and biscuits on it, as well as several cakes and buns. She'll come to each of us, and we'll tell her what we want, and it'll be given to us on a plate."

"Thank you Mother. How many times have you been invited then?"

"Oh, a few times. It's normally, if we need to discuss something rather confidential, private, or personal. You don't just go in, because she wants to gossip! Today should be slightly less formal – unless something's happened that I'm not aware of! This is basically a special invitation from the queen, for you to see a little more of the palace, as part of your treat. It goes without saying that I want you on your best behaviour, though. Understood?"

"Yes, of course, Mother! You knew about this, too, I assume?"

"I knew that there was a possibility, yes," admitted Linda.

Linda took out her identification pass again, as they went across the office to the main part of the court Administration Department, which was what was written on the door. Then she swiped it through the panel to open it, and led them in through, as it clicked shut again behind them.

"Do you always call this 'Your little Empire' Mother? "And does everybody call *you* 'Mrs Radcliffe'?"

Linda looked at her daughter. "It's considered quite old fashioned now, but yes, people who work under me do call me that, because I like people to show politeness, and above all respect to me. You know all about that, dear."

Yes of course, Mother," said Alexandra.

"The exceptions are Fiona and James. As we are often together in the company of the queen, who refers to me by my first name, it becomes awkward then to expect them to refer to me as 'Mrs Radcliffe', if she is talking to me, or referring to me in conversation. For Fiona, that is the only reason, but for James, admittedly there is the added fact, that I do like to be a bit more familiar with him.

"As to the other thing, well it's just my little joke really, and I'll not pretend that it's funny, but again, yes I do say that, sometimes. This might be a relatively small department, but a lot of good and important work is done in here, extremely efficiently, under *my* management and that in turn gives *me* power, which I freely admit I like having. I do have the running of the palace and the court's business from here, and it does feel a bit like being the head of an empire, sometimes!

"Anyhow, we've not got long," continued Linda. "If you remember from last time, that's your now potential mother-in-law's office, right in front of you. Locked of course, whilst she's not here, although I do have a mistress-key to some rooms – hers included – something she is not aware of! And that is of course *confidential*!

"Then we have the room shared by our two secretaries, Veronica and Carol.

"Next door to that is the biggest room that we occupy, where all the clerks work, under the chief administration officer - so that's really the busiest hub of the whole organisation, during the week. I'm not exaggerating when I refer to my empire as 'little'. We are only a dozen staff, in total. Having said that, of course, although the household staff and receptionists have come under Fiona's responsibility, on a day-to-day basis, since she became a court administrator, technically I am still in charge of them overall, too.

"Then coming back on the other side, first we have the most important room – our kitchen. "Well, saying that, I don't use it much. I have my own tea and coffee making facilities in my office, and I don't use the microwave to heat anything up, but it is for my staff, generally.

"I'm sure you remember the other main room in this area, sweetheart. With this heavy iron door keeping it locked!" She pressed a combination on the keypad next to it, and then turned the large handle of the door to open it. When she stepped inside, automatic tracer lights came on. "Here are all our secrets! This room is chock-a-block with records and files relating to our legal and financial business. I don't personally come in here much either, but there are regularly women going in to find things for me, or working on my behalf."

"I remember, I found this room quite daunting, Mother. And I was terrified someone might lock me in, and I'd be trapped with no one able to hear me!" said Alexandra.

"I would never would have let *that* happen to you, darling," said Linda. "The culprit would have been sacked on the spot!"

They went out and Linda locked up the door again.

"Then next to my office is the conference room where meetings take place, either with visitors, or once a week our own departmental one.

"The only other thing of note to show you, is through the door at the end of the corridor, and up the stairs!" she said, leading her daughter towards it. She swiped this door as well, and they trotted up the stairs, which bent around through 180 degrees.

"I suppose this is the next most important room, after the kitchen. The rest room!"

"You mean you allow your staff to stop work and rest, Mother?"

Linda laughed. "Well, I have to sometimes, dear! I do come in here and mingle, quite regularly, although I don't take tea breaks as such. If I'm in the office at lunchtime, then I usually come in, with my sandwiches, although I go elsewhere for a main meal, on the first two days of the week, when I work late. There is a canteen in the palace for staff to use, if they wish – and there's the odd 'liquid lunch' for me at some other times too!"

She looked at the clock on the rest room wall. "Right. That's our tour over, I think. Now, we must get cracking. We *cannot* keep Her Majesty waiting!"

\*\*\*

Linda led the way down the vast corridor towards the small lobby outside Queen Alexandra's reception room.

"So what's James been doing, whilst he's had to wait around for us again, Mother?"

"I don't really know," said Linda. "He's not officially here on duty, but he may have found something to potter about with."

"Oh well, we can find out now," she added. They were nearing the lobby, and James was standing a few metres from it, waiting for Linda to arrive, to announce their arrival to the desk.

They all exchanged greetings and then Linda said to James, "Alexandra was wondering what you'd been doing with yourself, whilst we were away. I've been thinking the same thing!"

"I just thought I'd take the opportunity to check over the boss's car, before tomorrow," he replied.

Linda raised an eyebrow. "You went to The Grange, fully checked over my car, came all the way back again presented yourself here, in that time? Well I never thought I'd say this, James Spencer, but I'm impressed!"

"I *meant* Queen Alexandra, Linda!" said James. "You're not the boss in this Palace and this time, *you* know it. Unless your trip away this afternoon, was for your own coronation, and you're about to tell her Majesty that you've stolen her throne, and she's now redundant?"

Linda's lip curled and her eyes narrowed.

"*Oooh!*" she fumed. "I'll get you back for that! James Spencer, I will not let you best me! No man has *ever* got the better of me in sarcastic humour and don't even think for one *second* that you've become the first!"

With that she marched over to the desk.

Alexandra was in stitches. James winked and chuckled at her. "That got her, didn't it? She'll be licking her wounds for a while now. We might have a bit of peace."

"I wouldn't be so sure about that, James! My mother *hates* anyone or anything getting the better of her! She wasn't fibbing to you, when she said that. She'll be determined to get you back. You probably know that as well I do. She simply *has* to be the boss and she'll want to make sure that she gets back on top somehow!"

They were still laughing when Linda came back. "Pull yourselves together you two, and that's an order! We're to sit and wait in the lobby, and then we'll be called in a couple of minutes."

She led the way in. Alexandra looked at James with a smile and spread her palms upwards, as if to say, "What did I tell you?"

As they sat down, Linda continued.

"Now I mean this! We're about to take tea with the queen of Geratica, and whilst it should be a very enjoyable experience, it is really quite an honour. You do *not* go into her reception room, giggling like a pair of elementary school kids. Understood? Both of you?"

Alexandra knew her mother was now very firmly taking charge. This wasn't a joke.

"Yes Mother, said Alexandra. "We won't let you down, I promise! And I'm sorry."

"Good, but I hope you won't let yourselves down either!"

Alexandra shot an urgent look at James to encourage him to say something. From years of experience, Alexandra had found that when her mother asserted herself like this, you had to placate her, and let her know that you understood and also if necessary, apologise, and let her know that you realised she was right.

"Linda I'm sorry," he said. "Maybe we got a bit carried away."

"That's alright, both of you. I'm sorry I was sharp, but we *must* show some decorum!

The door opened, and an aide to Queen Alexandra came out. She smiled. "Good afternoon, Mrs Radcliffe! Her Majesty will see you now!"

"Thank you!" said Linda, speaking for the threesome. With a last glance and encouraging smile, she led them into the reception room, behind the aide.

# CHAPTER 5

Queen Alexandra greeted them warmly, as they came into the room.

"Your Majesty," they all chorused, Linda and Alexandra curtseying, and James bowing.

"I trust you had a pleasant afternoon," she asked Linda and Alexandra.

"Yes we did rather, thank you Ma'am," said Linda. "I took Alexandra up to Parliament House. You know that our ways of government are of a great interest to her, and she's extremely knowledgeable on its history. She even talked about Lady Dixon-Taylor, failing to get her budget passed, causing the 4941 Budget Crisis!"

"Oh my goodness! How did that come up?" asked the queen? "There's not something you're not telling me is there Linda? Geratica's economy isn't about to go belly-up, I hope?"

Alexandra suppressed a giggle.

"Certainly not, Ma'am," said Linda. "Geratica's finances have never been so healthy, I can assure you! No, we were simply talking about my role in parliament, ensuring that our bills are successfully passed, and become law. I know she'd like to see that in action, some time. We'll see what happens."

"I believe she is knowledgeable on many other subjects, too!" said the queen.

"You are too kind, Ma'am," said Alexandra.

"Nonsense! I hear reports about you all the time, from your mother. Some might say that coming from so close a source, the reports must be biased, but she is very fair-minded person, and I believe them to be true. Every grade and report that you get is excellent, and you're also growing up to be a most charming, polite, and extremely nice young lady. You are very well liked, and respected by everyone who's met you. You'll be sixteen next year and I know you're hoping to go to Castra, and I sincerely hope that you do, too! Our Universities need bright, gifted, as well as very personable ladies, who want to work hard, and know how to conduct themselves in both their public and private life. Now, I think that description perfectly sums you up, Alexandra. I've seen Castra take ladies with less ability, and a lot less personal attributes, get in there, and if you don't, well then frankly, I can't see that Castra deserves to be considered Geratica's premier university!"

Alexandra felt stunned. She hadn't been expecting the queen to heap quite as much praise on her as that, when she'd walked in here just now.

"Well, thank you, Ma'am!" she said. "I'm not sure what to say. I'm not sure if I've had such praise before and for it to come from you of all people, who I respect very much."

"There have been times when she's had praise like that before, Ma'am," said Linda, "but she's a very modest girl, and as people realise, she suffers from a lack of confidence and self-belief sometimes, although that is really starting to come on a pace now, and I like to think that I've played a part in that."

"Yes you have, Mother," said Alexandra. "If I am even half the person who Her Majesty describes, then it couldn't have become possible, without you."

There was a very short pause, as Linda kissed her daughter.

"I think it's fair to say though, Ma'am," she continued, "that she will probably always want someone to give help and support to her, up to a point, throughout her life. And to that end, last night she gave me some most wonderful news. She's found someone, a boy who she's been friendly with for most of her life, in fact, who I know very well and like very much, who she thinks could fit the bill. And I agree with her!"

"Linda, are you telling me, what I think you are?" said the queen.

"Well Ma'am, I think now that I've cued her part up so nicely, it would probably be most appropriate, if the girl herself now came to the stage, and told you exactly what she did yesterday afternoon, in her own words."

Linda had been holding Alexandra's hand, ever since they had come into the room, and now their familiar private communication began, as Alexandra did as her mother had suggested.

"Yesterday afternoon, Ma'am, I proposed a relationship to Tom Ryder, Fiona Clark's stepson, and he accepted!"

"Tom!" exclaimed the queen, "I've heard a lot about him, too. You've been next door neighbours for most of your life, haven't you?"

"Yes. Ten years, to be precise, Ma'am."

Their tea then arrived on a trolley. On the shelves underneath, were a vast array of cakes, buns, jams and other delicacies.

"What perfect timing!" said the queen. "This news does indeed call for a celebration! "Everyone, I hope that you will enjoy the selection of refreshments provided."

Alexandra's eyes nearly popped out of her head and her mouth watered, as she saw what was on the trolley. Her mother hadn't been wrong!

When the waitress asked her what she wanted, she requested tea with no sugar, but then she was stuck. "There's so much to choose from. I can't decide!"

Her tongue was lightly running over her lips.

Linda chuckled. "One thing no-one could accuse my daughter of, is being fussy over food. I've yet to discover anything that she doesn't like and I'd be surprised if it finally turned out to be something on that trolley!"

"Darling, would you like me to choose for you?" she asked, a couple of moments later. "It's just that, if you take much longer, James will never get his tea!"

"It's alright, Mrs Radcliffe!" laughed the waitress "I can come back when your daughter's decided."

"No, no, that won't be necessary," said Alexandra. "Could I have a buttered scone, with some jam, please?"

"Strawberry, raspberry, or apricot?" asked the waitress.

"Oh, in the name of Geratica!" exclaimed Linda. "Here we go again. James, you might as well forget your tea and go out and start the car, now. By the time Alexandra's finished, it'll be time for you to take us home anyhow!" Everybody laughed.

"Mother!" exclaimed her daughter indignantly, "It's alright waitress. I'll have strawberry please."

The waitress, spread a dollop of jam on the scone, put it on a plate and handed it to Alexandra.

"Thank you," she said.

The waitress finally moved on to James. As he told the waitress what he wanted, Linda gave her daughter's hand a quick squeeze. Alexandra squeezed back, her hand as usual, inside her mother's. Their eyes met discreetly, and they secretly communicated, Linda checking that she was OK after her teasing, and Alexandra sending back a message that she was happy.

"So, tell me more then, Alexandra," said the queen. "I've never met Tom, like I have you, but the impression I'd been given, was that although you were best friends, if anything serious was ever going to happen between the two of you, it wasn't an event thought likely to be in any way imminent. So, what suddenly, brought on the inspiration?"

"I think in some ways my mother's already told you, Ma'am. I had been considering it for a little while, but I wasn't sure if I was capable of leading a relationship, in the way that I would want. As my mother says, I don't always have enough confidence. But when I was out with him yesterday, he told me his opinion of my abilities and my intelligence, and it suddenly made me realise that I could. And what gave me the confidence was Tom himself. Although we both want a traditional relationship, with me at the helm, he understands that I will need his support and counsel, to do that. It all came to me very quickly, and I had to rush us indoors to the warm, and up to the spare room, to make the proposal properly, or else I was afraid I'd lose my nerve. But I didn't, and he accepted. So, there you have it."

"I remarked to you last night, that I was surprised to hear that you didn't have a boyfriend though, Alexandra," said James, speaking Alexandra realised, for the first time. "Why didn't you say anything about this then?"

"Sorry James. But I hadn't told my mother yet, and I wanted her to be the first to know. I was always planning to tell her over dinner at the Geratica, and that is indeed what I did. Mrs Clark actually doesn't know yet, either, because I didn't want her to immediately come around and blurt it out, before I'd had the chance to say anything. So Tom is under instructions to tell no one until I phone him later, when my mother and I are back home!"

"So, would I be correct in assuming that, apart from Tom, we in this room are the only ones who currently know about this?" asked the queen.

"You are, Ma'am. Yes," confirmed Alexandra.

"I will admit, that I was a little startled when Alexandra told me, over dinner last night, Ma'am," said Linda. "But I've always believed that Tom is a suitable match for her, and when she informed me of exactly how she'd put the proposal to him, and the terms she'd decided, I must say I was impressed. I think she's done very well and I'm proud of her."

"In fact, Ma'am," said Alexandra, "My mother was so 'startled,' that she spilt wine over the table cloth of the Geratica Hotel private dining room!"

Both the queen and James began to snigger.

"Well Ma'am, I was pouring it into my daughter's glass and the wretched girl chose that particular moment, to drop the bombshell! In fact, it was only a few drops and we soon cleared it up."

She turned her face to Alexandra. "Well, charming! I pay you a lovely compliment, and you repay me by telling Her Majesty that!

"Two can play at *that* game, my girl! Ma'am, what my daughter omitted to tell you in her account, is that she sneaked Tom up to our spare room, to make the proposal and then sneaked him out again without my knowledge or express permission, whilst I was outside with our gardener! Then, when I eventually came back in after he'd gone and realised that she'd returned from her date with Tom, she lied to me! She told me, she'd seen me in the back garden and decided to leave me to it, and start beautifying herself, so that she'd be ready to leave on time, for our excursion! And she says that *I'm* 'devious'! I've told her that I've yet to decide whether to cane her or not, when we return home."

The queen chuckled. "Yes, I was about to say it looks like we've discovered another character trait that your daughter has inherited from you, Linda!"

Now *Alexandra* and James sniggered.

"Alright, that's enough of that, you two!" snapped Linda.

"*You* led me to believe that we were going to the Geratica in an ordinary taxi, Mother," said Alexandra, "rather than being taken by Her Majesty's chauffeur!"

"Well, I'm sure that this is a weekend that will live long in the memory for you, Alexandra," said the queen.

"Definitely, Ma'am. I'll *never* forget it!" she replied.

After a brief pause, Queen Alexandra rose, and as she did so, said, "Well it's been very nice to see you all today!"

Linda rose, and discreetly signalled for Alexandra and James to follow. Their reception was at an end.

"I'm sure you'll be keen to return home soon, for dinner. I wish you a safe journey home."

"Thank you, Ma'am" said Linda. "And then it will off to bed as soon possible, I think. Back to Charterhouse for Alexandra tomorrow, and a busy day for me, I think! Thank you very much for our tea."

The queen pressed a button on her desk. In what seemed like no time at all, the aide re-appeared.

"Goodbye Your Majesty," the threesome said in unison, Linda and Alexandra curtseying, and James bowing again.

"Goodbye," said Queen Alexandra.

The aide then showed them out, and they walked through the lobby, and back into the corridor.

***

Linda turned to Alexandra and James. "Well done, you two!" she said. "Alexandra, do you want to have a quick peek at the state rooms again, before we go home?"

"Oh, yes please, Mother!" she answered.

"Right. Come on then, darling!" She held out an open arm and Alexandra slipped inside of it.

"James, you too," she said.

She led the way down the corridors to the front part of the palace. The official main entrance, was ahead of them, though it was only ever used by tourists visiting, or for special or state occasions, when there were guests arriving.

First they went into the State Dining Room, where there was what was still the longest dinner table that Alexandra had ever seen, with chairs all around. It could sit up to fifty people, she remembered. The room was lushly decorated, with portraits hanging from the walls. She had been a guest here once before, with her mother, a year earlier. She had enjoyed it, and particularly the honour of being an official guest at a Palace function, but it had been at the same time, been quite daunting, with so many people around. She had been, deliberately, placed right at the end of one side of the table, with her mother beside her, Queen Alexandra at the head, and Fiona directly opposite, so she hadn't had to worry about speaking to someone she didn't know. Once again she had been grateful to her mother for looking after her. If she came here again, she thought that she would be able to cope with it a bit better, now that she was becoming more confident.

Then they entered the State Ball Room. It couldn't be denied that it was a beautiful and grand room. However, Alexandra wasn't fond of dancing. She had 'two left feet', as the old Earth saying went and it made her feel very awkward doing it. And she didn't think that it was just down to lack of confidence either. It really was one of the very few things that she simply had no ability in. She considered her mother to be slightly better, but even she didn't particularly like doing it either. It was one of the very few things that her mother seemed to have no desire to get to the centre of, and dominate. Quite the reverse was true, in fact. They didn't mind watching it sometimes and very occasionally might even go to a ballet, but if they were at a social occasion, and it appeared that dancing might be looming, they tended to make themselves scarce.

When her mother organised dinner parties, she always said that if people wanted to dance, that was fine, but they would have to arrange it themselves – in another room of the house. It would never be part of her agenda for an evening's entertainment – along with "party games," another thing they both hated and stayed well clear of. It didn't seem to make her parties any less popular though. They were generally regarded as amongst the most convivial and hospitable, with plenty of good humour, and low music, mixing with the food and wine, of which they served plenty, and the freedom to smoke, if people so wished. Her agenda for the after dinner entertainment, tended to be more reserved, with things like the piano and card games (the latter of which her mother *was* good at and that she thought was far more entertaining than any 'party game', watching some of the ladies becoming *very* competitive!)

There was no one left in the ballroom besides themselves now and shortly the palace would be closing its doors to the public for the night.

Linda went between Alexandra and James and linked one arm each of theirs, inside of hers.

"Right you two," she said as they both looked at her in surprise. "We'll be making our way back home in a moment. Before we do, I just want to talk seriously for a second."

"Alexandra, darling, this was your treat. Have you enjoyed it?"

"Mother! I've loved it! It's been the best weekend of my life. Thank you!" She raised her head and kissed her mother affectionately on the lips.

Linda smiled. "It's been my pleasure sweetheart!" She squeezed her daughter's arm inside of hers and kissed her back.

"James," she asked, looking at him, "Have you enjoyed chauffeuring us, over the last twenty-four hours?"

"Yes, I have. I always enjoy having you in the car with me, Linda. I think you know that. But it has been even more special to have met your charming daughter at last, and have her with us, too!"

"Oh! Thank you James! That's really nice! I've really enjoyed meeting you too!"

Linda squeezed both of their arms inside of her, as tight as she possibly could. She was delighted.

"Good! That's what I was hoping to hear. Right, now I'll say my peace. "I've really enjoyed this trip too. Possibly even more than I'd anticipated – and that's been because of the two of you. I've, obviously, always enjoyed being with the two of you, separately and I always wondered what it might be like, if all three of us were together. Now that it's happened, you two seemed to have taken to each other in the way that I always hoped, and I've found that I like how it feels, and want more!

"Now, I'm sorry I gave you both a telling off earlier and I didn't have any wish to spoil our time together, but whilst I was telling the desk outside the lobby, that we were here, ready to be received by the queen of Geratica, it was becoming obvious that the two of you were not, so I *had* to say something! And it had to be firm, because we were within a moment of going in, and you were giggling like a pair of children on a school trip. I couldn't have you going in like that, and I had to calm you down. It was partly my own fault I know, because I obviously was what made you both laugh, and it was perhaps the wrong time to do that to you, but that still wouldn't have excused a lack of decorum in Queen Alexandra's reception room! I said what I said for the benefit of all us, and you both know that I won't hesitate to give a tongue-lashing, if I think it's necessary or deserved. We may have been joking around about it during this trip, but in all seriousness, when it comes to the crunch and sometimes even before, I think we all know who the boss is here.

"I do acknowledge though, that we've all got on through some very good humour, and there's nothing wrong with that. I repeat that I like us being together, and from now onwards, I'm going to be trying very hard to find ways of making it happen. And maybe I'll do the driving next time, too, to give James a rest!"

Linda unlinked her arms from Alexandra and James.

"OK. Lecture over. I haven't given you much opportunity to respond, but that's deliberate. Now, I suppose you'd better take us home, please James!"

"Right you are, Ma'am," he replied and they headed back out of the palace, to the car.

# CHAPTER 6

The car sped along the road, bound for Greenacres. The atmosphere was initially quieter than before. James was thinking about what Linda had said.

It had almost seemed like Linda had been talking to *two* children! He knew that it was basically just her way, though. She had a naturally domineering personality, and was a natural leader, who asserted herself and took charge of situations very easily.

James didn't really mind at all. It was part of what attracted him to her. If nothing else, it made things a lot easier for him. At least he knew where he stood with her, and he'd discovered over the long period that he'd known her that she was one of those people who was usually right, and was used to being so. Even if it didn't seem that way at the time, she often turned out to be in the end. She often did know best, and he had a lot of respect for her. Both he and Alexandra, quite obviously *did* know who the boss was in the threesome.

It was clear that she was the dominant force in Alexandra's life, as had come to realise, even before he'd met her tonight, through Linda's accounts of their domestic goings on, during their conversations at work. Alexandra's mother was the rock that she needed to cling to. He thought that she was very lucky. He wished that he could too.

Elizabeth had radically different ideas to Linda's traditional ones, regarding the roles that men could potentially take in a relationship. Unfortunately, she often tried to prove that they were correct, through her marriage to him, and this led to tensions. He had no aspirations to do any of the kinds of things traditionally associated with women, in a Geratican relationship, and much preferred Linda's more conservative approach.

He wanted to see Linda and Alexandra again, very much, and after what Linda had said at the end of her little speech, it sounded as if she now wanted to find ways to make it happen. And if Linda Radcliffe wanted something to happen, then, it very often did! But this was obviously, potentially dangerous, whilst he was still with Elizabeth. He was also becoming more and more convinced that she truly did desire him, and wanted to be with him, as much as he wanted to be with her. And he knew that the day was fast approaching, when he would have to tell Elizabeth that he wanted to leave her.

His musings were interrupted by Linda herself.

"James Spencer, you're very quiet. Are you thinking about something?"

"Oh, you know, this and that," he replied.

"Well of course I don't know, unless you tell me, you silly man!" she said and Alexandra smiled. She sensed that her mother was now returning to the attack, regarding their mock war of words earlier.

"I did tell you earlier, that I would get my vengeance for your sarcasm and that you wouldn't finish today having got the better of me, so you can take that as a starter," Linda continued. "What I also wanted to say was that, even my daughter gave me a cheeky comment, which I smacked her bottom for, whilst we were visiting Parliament House! You're obviously becoming a bad influence on her. So, kindly refrain from making any more remarks of that nature – *any at all* – until you've dropped us off and gone back home. Understood? Good. That settles it then. I've won!"

Alexandra giggled once again.

"Right you are, Ma'am!" said James.

"Good. Make sure you keep your word!" replied Linda, glancing over at Alexandra discreetly, with a faint smile of triumph.

It didn't take much longer for them to be back in Greenacres. Once they reached Elmsbrook, after James had opened the gate, with Linda's card, he stopped to allow Alexandra to retrieve her mother's newspaper from their letterbox. Then he drove them up the hamlet drive, and back to the front door of The Grange.

As he took their cases out of the boot of his car for the last time, Linda said, "Well thank you very, very much for what you've done for Alexandra and I, this weekend James. It's been very useful, having you around."

"Yes, thank you, just as much from me too, James." added Alexandra.

"Don't mention it ladies. It was a pleasure to have been of service," replied James. "I've enjoyed your company immensely!"

"And us yours," said Linda, speaking for both herself and her daughter. "Well, Goodnight then. Have a safe journey and I'll see you tomorrow! Wait down at the gate, and I'll let you out, once we're back in the house."

"Goodnight James. See you again soon, I hope!" said Alexandra.

"I hope so too, Alexandra. See you tomorrow Linda. Goodbye ladies!" and James got back into his car and drove away.

\*\*\*

Once they were back inside and Linda had let James out of the hamlet, they settled back in, getting changed and unpacked, and doing various ablutions, ready for the morning. Alexandra carefully selected a place to store her treasured book, given to her by Philippa.

Then Alexandra did her ironing duty, and helped her mother prepare their dinner. As it went into the oven, Alexandra asked her if she could now ring Tom.

"Yes of course you can, darling," she said. "Take it in the study, if you like. I promise I won't be listening in!"

Alexandra grinned. "Thank you, Mother," she said.

"But you know my rule about no more than 15 minutes being allowed to you for calls, and the punishment should this be broken," added Linda in a sterner tone and holding up a finger. "I trust that it won't be necessary to employ such a measure tonight."

Alexandra did know the rule. The punishment prescribed for breaking it was three strokes of the cane on the palm of her hand. Her mother also always had an itemised bill, so that she could see the full details of all calls being charged to The Grange.

"No Mother," she replied. "It won't."

"Right," said Linda. "That's understood then. Dinner should be ready in about 30 minutes, so bear in mind you'll need to be ready to sit down and eat then, and I want you to help me dish up beforehand too."

"Of course, Mother."

"Oh. One other thing. Keep it quiet about James being with us. I'd rather not risk anyone else knowing about that at the moment, given that he's still in this situation with Elizabeth. Understood?"

"Perfectly, Mother."

Then Linda smiled.

"Go on and get on with it then. I'll come and give you a gentle reminder later if you're still on the phone, just in case you should have gotten carried away and forgotten the time!"

"Yes Mother!" replied Alexandra.

\*\*\*

Going into the study, Alexandra closed the door behind her and then settled down at her desk. She and her mother had one each facing each other and the phone was in the middle of them, to be shared, although it was mainly her mother who used it. She actually wasn't very experienced with telephones, and using them still made her feel a bit nervous, but she was getting better, and it should be fine with Tom.

She picked it up and dialled the number of The Lodge, the number of which, her mother had pinned to the board beside them, in case she should ever need to ring Fiona, urgently.

Fiona! She guessed that it would be her who answered it, so she would try to get her to pass her to Tom as quickly as possible.

A second later, Fiona's voice did indeed come on the line.

"Hello?"

"Hello Mrs Clark. Is Tom there, please?"

"Tom? Who's calling?"

"Alexandra, Mrs Clark."

"Oh hello, Alexandra. You're back then. And how did you find 'it?'"

"I'm assuming you mean the Marriage Suite, Mrs Clark? It was fantastic. Mother didn't report any problems at all."

"Phew! Well I'm relieved to hear that! Good. Well, I'll be able to tell Queen Alexandra tomorrow, although I suppose your mother will have gotten in earlier than me, and already done so!"

"In fact, she did it this afternoon, Mrs Clark," said Alexandra.

"What?" exclaimed Fiona.

"She took me to the palace, and we met the queen, Mrs Clark."

"You met Queen Alexandra this afternoon?" Alexandra could sense Fiona bristling with annoyance, down the phone. "On the seventh day of the week?"

"Yes, Mrs Clark! Apparently the receptionist at the back entrance was instructed to contact Queen Alexandra's personal secretary, as soon as we arrived, so that she could come down to my mother's office and greet us."

"So it was obviously pre-arranged."

"Yes, Mrs Clark, although I knew nothing about it until she suddenly came into the room!"

"Nor did I!" remarked Fiona – rather hotly, Alexandra thought.

"We were also invited to take tea with her, in her reception room, Mrs Clark."

"What?" said Fiona, again. "*Today!* What was the occasion? For your mother to report to the queen about the Marriage Suite?"

"No, Mrs Clark, she'd already done that. I don't think it was mentioned at all. I think it was just an informal invitation, for me to see something more of the palace and its work."

"That would normally be a great honour to grant!"

"Oh yes, Mrs Clark. Believe me my mother made sure that I was aware of that fact, before we went in!

"In fact, for my treat, my mother had arranged a *couple* of extra surprises for me, along the way. I was also introduced to Philippa Barrington backstage, at the theatre last night!"

"Were you indeed?" asked Fiona.

"Yes. Sorry Mrs Clark, I don't mean to be rude, but do you think you could get Tom for me and put him on? Our dinner is in the oven, and I really would like to speak to him beforehand. I'm not to spend too long on the phone."

"Alright. Well it's nice to talk to you again," said Fiona.

"Yes. Goodbye, Mrs Clark," said Alexandra.

She heard the conversation at The Lodge, down the telephone.

"Tom!"

There was the sound of a door opening, and footsteps approaching down the hall.

"Alexandra's on the phone for you."

"Oh. Yes, she told me to expect her ... Are you alright? You look a bit red in the face!"

"Yes. I'm fine. I'm just a bit shocked about something, that's all."

Tom took the phone and his stepmother stalked off into the kitchen.

"Hello Alexandra!" he said.

"Hello Tom, *my darling!*" she answered in the softest voice that she could manage down the phone. They both felt a thrill of sexual arousal, as they heard the sound of each other's voices, and pictured the other at the end of the line.

"Did you have a good time?"

"Oh Tom! It was terrific! We'll be having dinner soon, and you know that I'm not allowed to spend long on the phone. So I'll try and be brief. After the concert, I was actually taken backstage to meet Philippa Barrington! And she's going to give me some private tuition at The Grange!"

"Really? I bet you couldn't believe it! How were you? You didn't go to pieces, did you?"

"No, I was OK, but yes, I was stunned, I'll admit. Then we had an absolutely *scrumptious* meal at the Geratica and the Marital Suite was incredible! It was huge! Then today, Mother took me to the Science Museum *and* the Arts Museum, and then we went to the palace to her workplace, and who do you think I met again, Tom?"

"Not Queen Alexandra?"

"The very same. And she invited us to take tea with her, in her reception room! That's why your stepmother was so shocked. I think she was a bit miffed that she hadn't been told we'd be going to see the queen today and she was even more annoyed that I'd been granted an audience with her, in the reception room! 'That's normally a great honour!' she said. You should have seen the selection of cakes that there was! I had a *delicious* buttered scone, with strawberry jam! Before the reception, Mother even took me to see Parliament House again! It's been the best weekend of my life, Tom!"

"It sounds like it," replied Tom, chuckling at Alexandra's boundless enthusiasm.

"You haven't changed your mind about my proposal, I hope, Tom?"

"What? No of course not? You know I'd never humiliate your honour, like that!"

"Good! Well, I told Mother last night, over dinner – even that I brought you into The Grange to ask you - and she was really pleased. She'd always hoped that I'd choose you! So now you can go and give your stepmother another shock!"

"So, how was your first full day as my official boyfriend?" she asked.

"Great! I haven't done anything special, but I've thought about you, the whole time."

"Ooh have you?" said Alexandra. "Hmm, I've thought much the same about you actually, *my darling!*"

They chatted for a while longer, before the study door opened. The eyes of mother and daughter met and Linda sent a message telling Alexandra that she had two more minutes. Alexandra replied with another, promising to obey. Her mother nodded and returned to the kitchen.

"Well I'd better go, Tom," said Alexandra. "Mother just warned me that I'm only allowed to be on the line for another two minutes, and she'll want me ready to help her dish up dinner, soon. So, I'll see you here, on your birthday at 8.00 p.m. Mother says that's OK."

"Would you like me to send you a kiss down the phone?" she asked.

"Ooh yes please!" said Tom.

"*Press your receiver as close as you can to your ear, then darling!*" she said softly and seductively. "*Are you ready?*"

"*Yes!*" he said softly and she could tell by the slight excitement in his voice, that he was as sexually aroused as she had become.

She sent six kisses through the receiver, making a sound of pleasure, as she neared the end. She could hear his breath shortening as he imagined them on his lips. He returned them to her, as she sent them.

"OK then." said Alexandra. I must go. Have a good couple of days. I'll be thinking of you the whole time!"

"Ditto!" said Tom.

"Bye then," they both said, and hung up.

\*\*\*

At The Lodge, Tom went to the kitchen. Fiona was taking some plates out of a cupboard.

"Mother, I've some news to give you," he said. (Although she was actually his stepmother, he still thought of her as his mother. She was the only one that he'd had known, since his biological mother had died when he was a baby, and he had no memory of *her*.)

"You mean *more* news, Tom," said Fiona. "I assume Alexandra's just told you, what she told me earlier. Well? What is it now?"

"Yesterday afternoon, Alexandra proposed a relationship to me and I accepted it."

Fiona stopped what she was doing, and stared at him for a second. "Oh! Well why in the world have you waited until this evening, to tell me?"

"Alexandra wanted to tell her mother herself, rather than risk her finding out from anyone else, beforehand. So she told me not to say anything, until she let me know that she'd done it and it would appear that happened over dinner at the Geratica Hotel, last night! I'm told that her mother was very pleased, and I hope that you are too, Mother!"

"It would also *appear* that I am to be the last to know about everything at the moment, until Linda Radcliffe's wishes and opinions have been satisfied!" Fiona flushed with annoyance, but then seemed to get a grip on herself.

"However, putting that to one side for the time being, yes I am pleased Tom and I congratulate you!" She stepped forward and gave her stepson a hug.

"It seems to have happened very suddenly, though! I knew that the two of you were very close. But I must admit, I thought that Alexandra might be one of those girls who remained single all her life, because although she wanted someone, she never quite had it in her to take the initiative with him. She is after all, quite dominated by her mother. Well, she's finally done it has she?"

"Tom, you must sit with me in the parlour and tell me all about this ..."

\*\*\*

At The Grange Alexandra, also went to the kitchen, to help with the dinner.

"Mother," she said, "I hope I haven't 'put my foot in it', as the old Earth saying goes, but Fiona was talking to me first on the phone, and she asked me about the Marital Suite. I said that it was fine, with no problems, and she said she was relieved, and that she would tell Queen Alexandra tomorrow. And I told her that you already had, because we'd seen her today and that we'd also been granted an audience with her, taking tea in her reception room. She didn't sound very pleased. Should I have not told her tonight?"

"Oh, don't worry about that sweetheart," said Linda. "She'd have found out tomorrow, soon enough, anyhow. I've no doubt she might be a bit put out, but never mind. It's done now."

"Well Tom will now be telling her about my proposal, so that'll be another thing she'll be the last to know about!"

"Yes, well that couldn't be helped. I wouldn't think she'd be too unhappy to see you start a relationship with Tom anyhow, so she should soon get over any hurt feelings she has over that."

Alexandra wished that she could say the same, about gaining Fiona as a potential mother-in-law.

\*\*\*

At 9.30 p.m. that evening Alexandra had been in bed for fifteen minutes reading. Her mother came into the room.

"OK, Alexandra. Time for 'lights out', and 'lock up.' Another busy week, starting tomorrow."

Alexandra finished her page, and put the book on her bedside table. Linda came and sat on the bed.

"Mother," said Alexandra, reaching for her hand. Linda's fingers slipped around her daughter's. "I hope you and James do manage to get together eventually. I think I might enjoy him being around here."

Linda lowered her face to Alexandra's and kissed her. "Do you really mean that sweetheart? You've only just met him this weekend, remember. I obviously hope for him as my partner too, and I think I can make it happen. I will try and get us together as a threesome again soon, as well, so that we can get another feel for what it would be like. Tell me what you think again, then. OK?"

"OK, Mother, and thank you for the best weekend of my life!" said Alexandra.

Linda smiled. "That's fine. You deserved it, for being such a wonderful daughter!" She gave her another big kiss, and Alexandra returned it.

"Don't forget Tom, as well, Mother. I want to be with him too, and I'd love us to take him to Avermore. I don't think he's ever been there."

"Yes of course you do, and you shall darling," said Linda. "I won't interfere with that. And if as you say, he's never been to Avermore, then perhaps we'd better set about filling that glaring gap in his cultural development, soon. Though, just to be clear, you won't be taking him to the Queen Alexandra Marital Suite, just yet!"

Alexandra's eyes widened with delight. "Ooh, that would be *fantastic* Mother!" she exclaimed excitedly.

"Right. Goodnight darling. Sleep tight!" said Linda and kissed her daughter one last time.

"Goodnight Mother. And you." She kissed her back.

Linda got off the bed, switched off Alexandra's bedside light and went to the door. "See you in the morning, then," she said.

"Yes, Mother," replied Alexandra.

Linda switched off the main light, went out, and closed the door. Alexandra heard the sound of the key turning in the lock, and then her mother's footsteps walking away.

She rolled over, and was soon asleep, her dreams filled with thoughts of Tom.

***

Linda went to the study, and poured herself one last nightcap. Sitting at her desk, she unlocked the bottom drawer and took out a small diary/notebook, containing what she privately referred to as 'random thoughts.' and descriptions of daily events (though there wasn't always a lot of time for the latter nowadays). Whenever she was pondering something over a period of time, or making plans for something to happen, she always found it useful to write down anything which occurred to her.

At the moment she was juggling a number of things in her mind. Firstly, and most importantly, there was her desire for James, and what she knew was his for her. This weekend had added a new ingredient to the mix, in that Alexandra was now aware of their feelings for one another, and seemed to be happy about it, in fact she seemed almost excited at the prospect of her mother finding love again. She felt that she could probably turn this to her advantage, coupled to the plans she had already made, to finally achieve her goal of having James truly 'hers.'

After that there were several things that could happen, or be made to happen, at some point in the future.

She now knew that Alexandra was in love and in a relationship, which she approved of. She would certainly take every opportunity to try and help things along for them, and if it did eventually get to the stage where there was the possibility of marriage, then she would discreetly do all that she could behind the scenes, to ensure that they did the right thing. A trip to Avermore, for the two of them, should be quite easy to arrange.

She had told her daughter that she might be able to find her something to relieve her pangs of sexual desire. That was easy enough too. She would order the same toy that she herself often used, and which was locked in a drawer, under her bed upstairs. She could also easily ensure that her daughter got a new gown, with the elbow length gloves that she desired, and now she decided that that the time had come to grant her request. She would arrange a fitting for her soon. It wouldn't be long after all, before the Festival of Divinity at the beginning of the new year, so that might be an obvious gift. She also needed to contact Philippa Barrington, tomorrow, about Alexandra's piano tuition. She reached for her diary, and made notes to action all three of those things. There was actually one more thing for Alexandra to learn tomorrow, regarding the last one.

She also wanted to make her daughter happy, by finding a way for her to come to Parliament House, and watch from the gallery, whilst she was participating in debates. This was the thing that was possibly the least important, but still something that it might be good for her to see. It was also the one that she had the least idea about how to achieve, and likely to be the one most heavily dependent on circumstance or coincidence.

She scribbled the last of her notes down, then put the notebook back in the drawer, and locked it. She drained her glass and took it, as she left the study, turning the light out as she did so. She put it in the kitchen to be washed up tomorrow, and then having locked up and turned out the lights, she went upstairs to bed.

# PART 4

# CHAPTER 1

Linda and Alexandra were dressed for work and school respectively.

Linda wore a white blouse, with the sleeves rolled up, and a black knee length skirt, with two splits, one at the front, above the left knee, and one at the back above her right black stockinged thigh. This was part of a suit, the jacket of which hung in her wardrobe. At her neck she wore a black matching bow.

Alexandra wore her Charterhouse uniform of a white blouse under a grey jumper and skirt, with the college bow at her neck. There was also a matching blazer, which she would put on when they left.

Linda placed a rack of toast on the table between herself and Alexandra. It was breakfast time, the morning after their trip to Avermore, and a new week was beginning. Unlike at the weekend, there wasn't really time to have a full cooked breakfast before they left each morning for work and school, so the daily meal was generally cereal and a couple of slices of toast, together with a strong cup of black coffee.

"So what have you got today then, darling?" asked Linda, as she buttered a first piece of toast. "Science, history and music, are all on Day 1 aren't they?"

"Yes, Mother. As well as maths and Geratican Language," replied Alexandra.

"Quite a wide range then."

"Yes. Today is my heaviest day of the week really, Mother."

"So you'll be seeing Mrs Wood, your music mistress then. You'll be able to tell her all about your meeting with Philippa. I'll make sure to ring her when I get the chance today, to arrange for her to start your tuition – it's in my diary. I *have* got a very busy day today, with Queen Alexandra's engagement at Castra University, when she'll be making a speech of my drafting, followed by a lunch and a walkabout afterwards, as well as meetings and then I'll be in parliament later. But it will be done. If there's one thing that we'll both get out of today, it's that at least I'll be able to tell you what Castra's food is like these days, so that you'll know what to expect, when you're there next year!"

"*If* I'm there, next year, Mother! Let's not get too presumptuous. I've got to at least pass my exams first."

"Have confidence darling! You're doing very well. Think positively!"

At 7.15 a.m. they were ready to go. With their coats buttoned up, gloves on and scarves wrapped around them, they made their way outside, into the chilly Autumn air. Alexandra went down their driveway, and opened the front gate, whilst her mother got the car out of the garage. Then as Linda drove past, she closed it securely after them, and climbed into the passenger seat, beside her. At the end of the hamlet drive, Linda swiped the gate open with her card and, they were away.

"Isn't it cold darling?" she exclaimed. "I think Autumn has truly arrived a little early this year!"

In ten minutes, they were at Greenacres train station, where Alexandra met the 7.40 train, to take her to Charterhouse.

"Right. Have a good day. Work hard and remember to be a good girl, or you'll be in trouble tonight," said Linda.

"Yes Mother. And you," replied Alexandra. Her mother still regularly gave her this warning, just as she was dropping her off, despite the fact that it was rare for her not to do both.

They embraced and kissed, Alexandra looking up into her mother's eyes. Their hands came together for a final time and Linda's squeezed Alexandra's.

Then Alexandra got out of the car. "Bye. See you tonight, then Mother. Love you."

"See you tonight then darling. Love you even more."

Alexandra shut the door and Linda drove off, waving to her daughter as she passed. She waved back.

\*\*\*

At 8.00, Linda pulled up outside the back entrance of the royal Palace. She heard the town clock strike the hour. Taking her briefcase, she went inside, passing Charlotte once again at the reception.

"Good morning Charlotte. Hope you haven't been there all night?!"

Charlotte stood up. "Good morning Mrs Radcliffe. Definitely not, I assure you!" she replied.

"Good. I expect dedication from all Palace staff, but that *would* be taking it to the extreme!"

Linda unlocked her office and went inside, closing the door behind her. She took off, first her coat and hung it on the hook of the door and then her jacket, which she put on the back of her chair.

"Right. First things first," she said to herself. She made herself a cup of coffee, from her machine.

She opened her desk diary and checked it. She was having her weekly meeting with all the court administration team at 9.00, followed by a meeting with the queen in her study at 9.30. At 10.30, she would be meeting up with James, in final preparation for the queen's journey to Castra University, which they had decided to embark upon at 11.00. They were due there at midday, whereupon Queen Alexandra would make the speech and there would follow a three course meal. Queen Alexandra had never been amongst Geratica's slowest eating monarchs (much like her own Alexandra), therefore Linda estimated that they would be finished there at about 1.30 p.m. After a walkabout outside, they would hopefully be back in the royal Limousine by 2.00 p.m., and then arrive back at the palace at around 3.00 p.m. She had yet another meeting with the privy council at 3.30 p.m., and then later she would go to parliament.

Opening her briefcase, she put a stack of documents into her outbox, all with various comments and instructions for action to her staff. She had been through these on Friday night. Her inbox was empty at the moment, but it would be filling up during the day. She wasn't going to get much time for paperwork today, so she'd be taking most of it home tonight. She put a smaller number of documents into her 'pending' tray, for action later and looking through it, she found one thing which she wanted to chase up on this morning. But before that, she needed to informally write down her findings, concerning the marital suite, and pass them through to Fiona, for her to make an official report based on them.

She took a pen from her jacket pocket and reaching for her memo pad, began her day.

***

Meanwhile, Alexandra caught her train as it puffed into the station and stopped before the platform. She was grateful for the comfort of her coat, as she went out of the waiting room, where she had been to shelter from the elements. The combination of the chill in the air, and the feeling of cold dread that always afflicted her as she travelled to Charterhouse, made her wish that her mother's arm was wrapped around her, keeping her warm. She was also dismayed to think, that in about an hour and a half's time, she would have to spend 15 minutes exercising around the yard at Charterhouse, with all the other girls at the college – the traditional start to each day, after assembly, before the official lessons began, which effectively meant walking at a quick pace and breaking into a jog at regular intervals, when the headmistress told them too. Alexandra hated this, wishing that she could just get straight on with what she really came to the college for – her academic studies. And they weren't even allowed to put their coats on! They had to walk, or jog, strictly in their school uniforms – it also served as an inspection from the headmistress, as to how well they were presented.

The station was part of a small branch line, and her mother had organised for her to have a season ticket. All she had to do, was get on and show it to the guard when she came round, and the same when she came back.

She took the seat that was always reserved for her with the ticket and settled herself down, with a book on her lap and her school bag at her feet. It was a distance of about twenty miles to Buckmore, about the same number of miles from Greenacres to the East, as Avermore was to the north. The train would make two stops, on the way. She was due at the station in Buckmore, at 8.00, and then it was a ten-minute walk to the college. There were quite a few people on board – mostly on their way to work.

Alexandra sucked at the finger of her glove, as she heard the whistle blow, and the train puffed away slowly. She took a last look back at Greenacres, with a pang of regret. She had mixed feelings about Charterhouse. It was a lovely public school, with beautiful grounds and surroundings, and it was a great honour to go there, as it was the most famous and prestigious one in Geratica. Her mother had obviously gone there herself and been a head girl, and she paid top whack fees, to send her daughter there. Unlike some of her contemporaries, Alexandra mostly enjoyed the studying – apart from if she ever had to read, say, or present something in front of the class.

Charterhouse had a great reputation, for taking the brightest girls through an entrance examination at senior level (though their mothers had to be able to afford to pay the entrance fee), who were in turn taught by top quality mistresses. Many (though not all) of the girls went on to university - and often one of the two major ones on Geratica – Castra and Orpington. It took girls from all regions of Geratica, though the vast majority were from the capital, Castra – all of Alexandra's class came from there.

There was also a preparatory (or prep) school – Charterhouse Preparatory School. A lake separated it from Charterhouse College. This was again fee-paying, though there was no entrance examination at that level. Both Alexandra and her mother had attended that too.

What she *didn't* like so much though, was the company of all the other girls. Having been very shy and lacking in confidence, as a girl, she had sometimes suffered taunting, and other girls trying to take advantage of her. Also, even though she was extremely proud of her mother and her job, the fact that she was the daughter of a very prominent person in society, sometimes made her the target of jealousy and resentment. Besides that, there was a lot of competition amongst the girls to be top, and she enjoyed being first in the class, as much as the rest – and quite often was – but she was conscious that this again could cause bad feeling.

She knew also that she was considered by some to be a 'Mummy's Girl', a derogatory term used by the boarders, towards those who went home at night and weekends. There might be some truth in that, but she was certainly grateful that her mother had made the decision to let her come home, once the main part of the day was over. She felt she could cope with it better that way. She knew that she'd be terribly homesick for Elmsbrook, her mother and Tom, if she had to stay here all term and without her mother particularly, she'd be insecure and worried, which would lead to her being unhappy and probably then have an adverse effect on her work. There were one or two girls who she was closer to than the rest, but if she could just be there on her own, she'd feel fine! Tom had always been her best friend and she had always felt comfortable amongst men that she had met. She wondered whether she was going to grow to be a woman, who preferred the company of men to that of her own sex.

As the train puffed steadily along, Alexandra began to feel warmer and as she looked out of the carriage window, to the fields, hills and valleys that they passed, she could see the rich golden colours of Autumn on the ground, as the trees had lost their leaves and migrating birds, flying south to a warmer part of Geratica, for the winter. In a few weeks' time it would be the Festival of Divinity, which nearly everybody looked forward to from one year to the next, and the preparations always slowly began around now. Her spirits lifted a bit. It might be cold, but this was her favourite time of year, from now until the Festival.

She arrived at Charterhouse at her usual time of around 8.15. The official day started at 8.30. She went to her form room, took off her coat, and sat at her desk, pulling up her sleeves. She wasn't the only girl who didn't board, but there weren't many in each year, and there were no others in her form class. As the college was so exclusive, the total number of girls attending each year was quite small anyway. She was one of only six in her form class, and none of her subject classes contained any more pupils than that. She looked at her watch. The rest of the girls would be finishing their breakfast in the dining hall, before the start of the day. They would begin to filter in soon. A couple of minutes later, two girls did indeed come through the door. They acknowledged her and she said "Morning," to them. Her day was beginning at almost exactly the same time as her mother's.

# CHAPTER 2

At 9.25, as Alexandra's daily exercise trauma at Charterhouse neared its end, and she would soon be able to get back into the main building to start her first lesson – a double period of science, before break time, her mother was walking down the corridor of the royal Palace, with Fiona, heading for Queen Alexandra's study. Fiona was wearing a long flowing black dress, with a split at the front. Behind them, following a discreet distance behind, to give her superiors the chance to talk privately, was Veronica, Linda's secretary, who was going to take the minutes of their meeting.

"Well Linda," said Fiona. "Tom told me the news last night! Are you pleased?"

"Yes I am. Very," replied Linda. "I think she's made a good choice."

"Well, as Tom is my stepson, I am naturally biased, but I must say I agree with you on that! And I'm pleased for him, too. So, at some time in the future, we will probably be connected by family ties?"

"Hmm, eventually I certainly hope. But I don't think Alexandra will go rushing into anything, too quickly, before she feels that they're both in a position to marry. She's a sensible girl and she puts a lot of logical thought into these things, you know."

"Yes. Well, I was surprised at the suddenness of this, at the weekend."

"I think it was what you might call a 'flash of inspiration!' She is beginning to become more much more confident, and she finally realised that Tom was the one who could enable her to manage a relationship, in the way that will be right for her. She felt she needed to settle the matter urgently, in case they 'lost the moment!' I can understand that. I know that it can happen that way for some women."

"Oh yes. It can!" exclaimed Fiona, her green eyes gleaming. She had proposed marriage to her husband, Colin, the morning after their first date.

They reached the lobby, and Linda told the receptionist that they had arrived. They went into the lobby and sat down. Unlike the previous day when Linda, Alexandra and James had been guests, invited by the queen, today was a working meeting and they would be in her study, entering from the lobby, through another door.

"I understand that there were no problems with the Marital Suite. I trust you had a pleasant stay?" asked Fiona, fighting not altogether successfully, to keep the bitterness she felt from her voice.

"Yes, it was first class, and we did, thank you," said Linda. "I've written a brief memo, telling you about it this morning, and it should be with you, once one of the clerks has sorted the post."

"It might be there already. I haven't checked my inbox yet. I believe also, that you came here with Alexandra yesterday, and *Her Majesty* came to meet *you* to be informed, and that you were also given the given the *honour* of an invitation for an audience with her, in the reception room?" Once again Fiona's voice faintly betrayed her fury. "That obviously must have been pre-arranged. I didn't know."

"We did, yes," confessed Linda. "I'm sorry about that Fiona, but the trip as a whole was organised as, partly unofficial business, and partly a surprise treat for my daughter, so I kept the exact details under wraps, as much as possible, in order for it to be a secret."

Linda actually *wasn't* so sorry, and Fiona didn't believe she *was* either.

The queen's personal aide, Rebecca Hargreaves came out of Queen Alexandra's study.

"Good morning, Ladies," she greeted them. "If you'll follow me, Her Majesty is ready."

"Thank you," said both Linda and Fiona.

They went into the study and were introduced. "Your Majesty," they both said, curtseying.

The queen was in formal attire today. She wore a dark blue suit with a white blouse and a blue bow at her neck.

She acknowledged them with a nod, and motioned for them to sit down by her desk. They each had an agenda in their hand, sent to them by Rebecca on Day 5 of last week. Veronica sat at a table behind them. A window at the side of the room, gave a view of the surrounding countryside. At the back of the study, was a door leading to other parts of the palace.

"Did you both have a good weekend?" asked the queen.

"Yes Ma'am," said both Linda and Fiona.

"If you'll forgive me Ma'am, could I just say at the outset, that Fiona is now up to date in her knowledge of the night before last, and yesterday," said Linda.

"Ah, good!" replied the queen. "In that case, there's no need for you to explain again, your opinion of the Marital Suite, Linda," she continued. "So, please now write an informal note of your findings to Fiona, who should then make a formal report, based on that."

"I already have, Ma'am. That was the first thing I did, this morning. It should be on her desk now in fact."

"Good. And now that subject is – closed indefinitely to any future discussion." She held up a forefinger as she spoke. She was determined not to get into any more arguments about who should have done what.

"We can now move on to the next item on the agenda. I've asked Dr. Clarissa Atkins, who as you know is Geratica's most eminent research scientist to join us, to give us a brief talk on the current consensus, regarding the schism at the planet's core."

Rebecca looked at a monitor. "According to the front desk, she is in the lobby, Ma'am," she said.

"Excellent," said the queen. "Show her in would you please?"

"Ma'am," Rebecca answered, nodding in acknowledgement, and went out.

A moment later she entered with the usual formalities observed and introductions made.

Once she was sat down, Rebecca produced a pot of both coffee and tea and some biscuits. After asking them all for their preferences, she began to serve them, as they continued the meeting.

The queen began, "Thank you for answering my summons Dr. Atkins. As you know, I've asked you here today, to give us your assessment of the current scientific consensus, regarding the planet core's schism. It isn't the most urgent day-to-day matter, but we are always mindful of what might be causing it and how it might be put right, particularly as we are aware of the existence of the parallel world which has been created by it and that the intentions of their inhabitants might be somewhat hostile towards us. So, if you will, the floor is yours."

"Certainly Ma'am," replied Dr. Atkins, as Rebecca withdrew. Taking a deep breath, she began.

"I'll start right from the beginning, if I may. We know that the planet's core is alive, and that *she* is a part of all of us. We all feel her presence. There is no doubt that she created this planet, we are all descended from the original inhabitants that she created, and that our personality traits are taken from her. We know also, that our ruling monarch must always be a queen, and that by tradition, the only way to ensure our planet's survival is to secure the succession to another, when she dies.

"But over the centuries, as our technology has advanced, we have been able to scan our surroundings, and there can also now be no doubt that a parallel world exists. Of course, it would not be visible to anyone looking at Geratica from space. But it *is* there nonetheless, wrapped around us. We can also all feel in our minds, the presence of another being, and we have concluded that there is a connection between the two. We think that at some point in our history, there was a schism in the core, the cause of which we don't know, which created the two worlds and also caused everyone born on our world, to be linked to the next person or persons in line to be born in the other, no matter who that might be. We cannot detect their thoughts, we will never know who they are, what they do, or anything at all about them, but we sense their presence in our minds. Some people, particularly the elderly, report that one day, they no longer feel it, and we assume that this means that the person we are connected to has died. Therefore, we conclude that it is likely that we can live our own independent timelines.

"However," there have been some people in the past, who appeared to have had no biological parents, and were not linked to the other world. They didn't know where they came from either. They just seemed to arrive, already at a certain age. We called them 'Mongrels'. We simply cannot explain it. There is no logical scientific theory, to suggest a reason for it.

"But in more recent years, their numbers have been declining and indeed in our world at least, we know of none that exist now. Again, we can offer no credible explanation for this.

"Of course, as we all know, since the discovery of the parallel world, many attempts have been made to travel to it, in Transportation Capsules, which were created specifically for this purpose. It was mongrels – and normally females – who knew how to construct them. But the attempts all met without success and caused an eruption in the planet's core, destabilising the world, endangering life, and tragically killing the travellers. The only people who have been able to successfully travel were the mongrels. At the risk of making the scientific community sound incredibly ignorant, there again really is no reason that we can think of, as to why this would be so. But it was gradually decided that after all the failures and deaths, it was impossible for non-mongrels to make the journey, and so all attempts ceased. That was many years ago. Before then, the number of mongrels was declining, and now it is believed that they are extinct. Therefore, there is apparently nobody left who knows precisely how the capsules were constructed, or navigated either.

"It is indeed true, from what the mongrels have reported back to us in the past, and our own scanning of the other world's activities, that they do appear to have malevolent feelings towards us. We can only speculate about this, but it might be that the schism in effect caused the core a split personality, which means that one world's inhabitants are born with more dominant malevolent tendencies than the other.

"As to what we can do about it, the only realistic thing would be – at such a time when we were ready – to go to the core and look for ourselves, but we are only just developing the technology to do it. I believe that it might be possible to do it, but it would be terribly dangerous, and my advice would be to wait until the technology is more advanced, when we might also have been able to scan deeper inside the planet's surface, to try and get a good look at what we'd be dealing with down there. *She* is alive, and we simply don't know the extent of her power. Also, if we try to alter how she is operating, even assuming that we can, we *cannot* be sure just what effect it might have on either world. Would one world simply disappear, or would we merge with the people who we are connected with to become completely new ones, with new identities, and the whole structure of our societies mixed up on an effectively new world? We just don't know."

There was a pause as Clarissa finished, and took a large sip of her coffee.

The queen smiled. "Well, thank you very much for that very thorough explanation, Dr. Atkins. I think that your concluding part goes to the heart of the debate. Sooner or later, we will have to decide if we are to attempt to go down to the core, and if so, just what we would do when we got there – assuming that we could do something."

"Alternatively, do we just simply accept that, although we have some neighbours who don't seem to care too much for us, we *have* lived in the same place for at least most of Geratica's entire existence, without serious incident – and since we don't have anybody who can go to the other world anyhow, could we just leave them be, and let both worlds go on independently, but ignoring each other completely?"

"If I could perhaps make a couple of comments, Ma'am?" asked Linda.

"Please do Linda!" said the queen. She exchanged glances with Fiona. They both were fairly sure what at least one of these "comments" was going to be about.

"Firstly," began Linda, "As you all know, I was married to the last mongrel that our world had. He of course died when our daughter was five, so she is at least a half-mongrel."

"Oh, yes Mrs Radcliffe," said Clarissa, "How foolish of me. I should have mentioned who your husband was. I'm sorry if I was insensitive. And you are of course, correct. That does make your daughter a half-mongrel."

"There has never been a known case of a half-mongrel, being any more successful at travelling through the void to the other world, than an ordinary

Geratican, though," said Fiona. "They might have a slightly better chance of surviving the attempt, but even that couldn't be guaranteed 100%."

"Well I'm not suggesting that my daughter is going to make history, as the first Geratican to do that!" exclaimed Linda, "And I wasn't offended Clarissa. I just wanted to make the point."

"The second point that I was going to make," she continued, "was that I certainly *do* know someone who is *very* keen to go down to the planet's core and make alterations to it – alterations which conform to her ideals and aims, I might add, in order to make the male sex more dominant. I'm talking of course, about my daughter's headmistress at Charterhouse, Mrs Elizabeth Spencer!"

Queen Alexandra and Fiona had been right.

"Yes, Mrs Radcliffe," said Clarissa, "I have regular contact with Elizabeth, and she is a respected scientist, even though she later decided to make teaching her career. She often urges me to start making plans to journey down below to the surface, to eventually reach the core, but I tell her she must be patient and wait until we are truly ready."

She continued, "I think Mrs Spencer would like to see the core restored to how she *should* be, for the same reasons as others, but it is true that the woman has strong views on the subject of men's roles in our society, and of their rights, and she sees this as a perfect opportunity to change the inherent character traits in Geraticans of all sexes, accordingly. But this does raise some ethical dilemmas. If the core intended for our gender traits to be as they are – and the evidence is that she did – then do we have a right to change that? Also, a majority of females *and males* seem happy with how things are, in that respect, so is it fair to force a different way of relating to each other, on them, just because a minority of others want it? It'll mean changing the natural way we've always done things on our world."

"Oh, you don't have to tell me that," said Linda. "I've been through these issues, time after time, but she'll never change! One thing I will say though. I don't think we should ever give up on going down to the core, eventually, once we're ready. We can't afford to ignore the other world completely. If they were to find a way to travel to us, we don't know what they might do. We know of their belligerent attitude towards us. There might even be a war! And if nothing else, if the chance is there to go, then surely it's a once in a lifetime opportunity to see it and not to be missed! I'd certainly like to, if I'm still relatively young and healthy enough for it!"

"I'm sure you'd be going, even if you were one hundred Linda," said the queen.

"Whatever is decided about this, although we cannot travel to Geraticai, we must keep on being vigilant and paying close attention to their affairs through our scanning facilities," continued Linda. "We know that their monarchs take a belligerent stance toward us. Mongrels are apparently extinct on Geratica, but we can't be absolutely certain that's the case on Geraticai."

"Of course, Mrs Radcliffe," replied Dr. Atkins.

"Agreed," said Queen Alexandra.

"What are your views on this Fiona?" she asked.

"I'd say I agree with Linda's views, broadly speaking. I do perhaps *empathise* with Elizabeth Spencer's frustrations, a little more than Linda, but that doesn't mean that I *sympathise* with her views, and I too think she doesn't have the right to do what she wants to do at the core."

"Right. Well, *my* view" said the queen, "is that we should try to reach the core, but only when we are ready and once there, if we *can* and we *do* make any adjustments, then it should be to repair the schism that prevents the Divine Being from acting as she intended, only. Not to change our basic characteristics, which I believe she did intend for us to have."

"If that view is the consensus ladies and I think it is?" The queen looked at the three of them then Linda, "Please could you ensure that a letter is sent to Elizabeth Spencer, to that effect? I want to make it clear to her what my position and that of my court is. I hope that will settle the matter. See that that last sentenced is included too."

"As you wish, Ma'am," said Linda, making a note on her pad, and feeling a rush of excitement flow through her. She would take great pleasure in doing that!

"Well, thank you very much for coming, Doctor Atkins," said the queen, shaking her hand and Linda and Fiona followed suit. "It was a very interesting conversation. Goodbye and have a safe journey."

"Goodbye and thank you, Your Majesty," said Clarissa, curtseying.

She followed Rebecca out, acknowledging Linda and Fiona as she went.

"In fact, we've just touched upon the next item on the agenda," said Queen Alexandra. "Male Rights Protesters."

"We've just discussed this in relation to planet's core," she continued. "But with regards to the practicalities of life, here on the surface as we speak, I think we need to decide how to deal with this issue."

"Yes, well Ma'am," began Linda, "you will have noticed, that regarding the education of males, I have made an indirect reference to it in your speech at lunchtime, which I hope will be seen to be us being as diplomatic as we can be.

"This issue is really quite controversial, and actually nowhere near as popular a cause amongst all classes of Geraticans, as these people and their supporters like to claim. As was said earlier, many are happy with the 'status quo' and it is our natural way of doing things. Regarding the issue generally, I think we should take a similar, diplomatic stand to the speech at lunchtime. Geratica is not a dictatorship, and we respect their views, and would not in any way wish to disrespect or hurt men, and indeed acknowledge that they are certainly not stupid, and express our gratitude to them for their support.

"But a supporting role is as far as they can go, without challenging the whole order, structure and fabric of our traditional society. And traditions should be respected. They are what has made us who and what we are, and it would be unnatural for us, both females and males, to abandon our most fundamental one. Many men themselves do *not* want a more dominant role in relationships, and society generally. They *want* women to lead! And the minority should, in the end, accept the view of the majority!"

There was a pause and it took Fiona a moment to realise that Linda had finished.

"Well, I think Linda has just written another speech for you, Ma'am!" she exclaimed. "Again, I am largely in agreement. We should tread carefully though. Sometimes 'minority' views can start to grow in support, and then it becomes more difficult to argue the case purely on 'traditional' lines, particularly if in the near future, enough of the younger Geratican females decide to take up the baton from the likes of Elizabeth Spencer, and express solidarity with the protesters. Then we really might have a headache!"

"Maybe slightly more than a headache, Fiona!" said the queen. "It might be something of a crisis."

"I say again though, Ma'am," said Linda. "As I have said many times before, and will continue to say, until I'm blue in the face, the direction that those progressive revolutionary idiots would take us down simply won't be natural to us! We need to be quite clear in our opinion over that."

She turned to her secretary. "Veronica, don't minute my last description, please! I'm sorry, I shouldn't have said that, but this makes me so angry. If we don't take a diplomatic, *but firm*, stand on this, we could end up with complete social breakdown!"

"Well one thing that I think we're all agreed on, is that this is a very difficult issue," said Queen Alexandra. I agree that diplomacy is always the safest path, but at the same time, public opinion is largely on the side of the more conservative approach, favoured by us, so for the time being at least, there shouldn't be any major problems. My speech today will indeed touch on one element of the subject, so let us see what the response is to that, before we do anything else, and put this to one side for the time being – though being ever mindful of it, also."

"The next subject is the regular weekly update on palace household affairs. Fiona, as always that's your domain."

"Thank you, Ma'am," said Fiona and gave a quick briefing. It was a fairly routine report and the queen indicated her satisfaction, before moving on.

"Now, the final subject that we have on the agenda has been raised by Linda. So, I'll let her introduce it."

"Ma'am, I realise this is a delicate subject, but obviously the matter of a monarch finding a suitor for a marriage, and then establishing an heir after such an event, is always of high importance in our world, for reasons that I know we are all aware of. I was wondering if you had given any more thought to the subject?"

"I appreciate your concern, Linda," began the queen, "and you know that I take this matter very seriously. I think about securing my succession a lot, but although it is of vital importance, I don't want it to be the *only* reason I marry. Most of all, I want to be happy in my marriage, which will hopefully last the rest of my life, or near to it.

"In our history queens have often taken lovers, but that isn't for me, and anyhow, in this day and age, I don't think a monarch could dare risk doing it. If I was discovered, it would be the biggest scandal of our time.

"I am a natural woman, just like any of my female subjects. I want to fall in love, enjoy being with him as much of my time as I can, and to look forward to making love to my husband plenty, every night, just as any other Geratican wife would.

"So, all of that having been said, did you have anyone in mind?"

"Well," said Linda, "There are two or three possibilities, but I think the most obvious candidate for many, would be Lord George Sackville. I believe that the two of you get along well together, and his mother Lady Caroline Sackville, tells me that he very much hopes that you might be interested in something more serious and that if you were to propose it, he would gladly accept. Naturally, he wouldn't say anything of the kind to Your Majesty, directly. If it's genuine love that you are after, then I believe he is the one for you, though of course I wouldn't dream of trying to influence you. It wouldn't be proper!"

The queen smirked. "No, of course you wouldn't Linda! I will, naturally, make my own final decision, but your advice is welcome, and I am prepared to tell you that I agree. Lord George is my most likely suitor. Very well. I believe that there is a meeting of the privy council this afternoon. If you see Lady Caroline, let it be known that he is in favour, and that I shall make a decision soon, but that it will of course, be at a time of my own choosing."

"As you wish, Ma'am," said Linda.

"As you say though, Ma'am, said Fiona, in a more sceptical tone. "You want to be *absolutely* sure, before you commit to anything. Don't forget that you're still young, with a few more years left to decide. You only turned twenty-nine, just last week."

"Thank you for that advice too, Fiona. Twenty-nine is still young – just! But Linda is right. This is a matter which I must come to a decision upon soon. I have been queen for eleven years now."

Fiona bristled slightly, but did her best to hide it and said no more.

"Now ladies, is there any other business that you would like to discuss? If not, then that concludes our meeting."

Neither Linda or Fiona had anything further to say. Both they and Veronica stood up, and Queen Alexandra bid them farewell.

"Goodbye, Your Majesty!" they chorused as they curtseyed and Rebecca led them away.

Once they were outside of the study, Fiona marched out of the lobby and back down the corridor, without waiting for Linda. Since she was alone, she allowed Veronica to catch up with her, and walked with her the rest of the way back to the court administration department.

"Why is Fiona in such a tearing hurry, Mrs Radcliffe?" asked her secretary.

"I'm not sure," replied Linda. "She wasn't here until just before our meeting at 9.00, so maybe she needs to get back to her desk, to see what work has landed in her inbox this morning."

In fact, she thought it more likely that – judging from her last comment – she was unhappy with Queen Alexandra's heavy hint that she was considering a union with Lord George, though she couldn't for the life of her think why. Twenty-nine might be still young, but it wasn't *so* young for a queen still unmarried and without an heir. (Linda had actually been the same age when giving birth to her own daughter). She had a few more child-bearing years left yet, but she would want to get settled into a marriage first – Linda was certain of that. The queen wasn't the type to rush in to anything. She was quite a deep and logical thinker, much like her own Alexandra and herself.

She had never been close to Fiona, ever since Robert's death, just after she had moved into the hamlet. Fiona appeared to have been the last person to see him alive and had sworn that he had been swept away in the strong currents of the river that day, and that it had happened so quickly, she could do nothing. But she would never understand what had possessed him to go anywhere near the river on that stormy day. He couldn't swim, and hated water.

Despite the fact that they were neighbours, they both made their own way to and from work. Linda preferred to be in early, and worked until the end of the day, whereas Fiona had comparatively more of a lie in, and started later. She usually finished earlier, too, which sometimes annoyed her. There could be a personality clash between them sometimes, as they were both strong characters who didn't like not getting their way, though to be fair, Fiona rarely completely lost her temper – or at least she didn't show it. There were certainly times when they fell out though, the Marital Suite being a prime example. When she acted as she was doing now, Linda always couldn't help but think that she was a funny woman.

For all that though, they did have one or two things in common. Both were wealthy, being highly motivated by money, and knowing what to do with it when they got it, and they each enjoyed the lifestyle that their wealth and position could offer them. They both liked to be glamorous, too, projecting an image, both of power and sex appeal.

Arriving back in her office, she made herself another cup of coffee. The meeting had gone well for her, she felt. Providing the speech which she had written for Queen Alexandra was received well, she would enjoy her lunch at Castra University. She had a bit of time, before she was due to see James to begin their preparations for the journey, so she began drafting the letter that the queen had asked her to write to Elizabeth Spencer – with relish.

# CHAPTER 3

"Good Morning, James!" said Linda, arriving in his garage at the palace, punctually. She had a clipboard and another document in her hand.

"Good Morning, Linda!" he replied cheerfully. He was delighted to see her again, and in more ways than one.

Linda checked that there was no one around to see and then closed the garage door behind her. She walked over to where James stood.

"You got home alright then, last night?"

"Yes, no problem. No hold ups, to speak of."

"Good!" said Linda. "James. Alexandra is now aware of our relationship. I was planning to tell her very soon, anyhow, but she immediately picked up on the signs, when we were travelling to Avermore at the weekend, and that was another main topic of conversation over dinner at the Geratica, as well as her own fledgling relationship, and Philippa Barrington. She has told me that she likes you, and it does sound as if – at least in principle – she would be quite pleased if something of an even closer nature developed between us. Have you given any more thought to telling Elizabeth how you feel?"

"Yes! Plenty. Every day!" said James, "But you'll have to give me time."

Linda felt a stab of exasperation, but she covered it up and touched his arm, her fingers lightly stroking it, in the same way as they did with Alexandra's hand.

"I know it's difficult and I'll wait, because I want you more than any other man," she said softly. "But I'm used to getting what I want, when I want it and as my patience starts to run out, I may have to start giving you some help. That time is becoming imminent. I'm more than happy to do that for you, if it will make this any easier."

James looked at her in surprise, his heart beginning to beat faster. "Well, I suppose it might do, yes," he replied, "But what would you do?"

Linda squeezed his arm. "I'm not going to discuss that now, but rest assured I have something in mind. I know you want me to have you, as much as I want to have you myself, so if you think it will make things easier, then I now formally declare that I'm *going* to help you. I'll give you another fortnight and then we'll talk about this for a final time. If by two weeks today, you're still in this position, then I *will* take the initiative. I still won't be able to tell your dear wife for you, but you'll find out what I have in mind, shortly after that, at my house, over dinner.

"So now is your last chance to tell me for definite, James. Do you want to leave Elizabeth and come and live with me, or not? If the answer is 'no', then we'll officially end this, as of right now, today. But, if as I believe, the answer is 'yes', then you will no longer have a choice, after right now, today and I *will* make you mine. There'll be no turning back for you. You'll either tell Elizabeth what we *both* want, in the next fortnight, by your own steam, or I'll initiate my own plan to make it happen, anyhow. Those will be the only two possible outcomes. There will not, I repeat, *will not* be a third option, allowing you to back out of it, after right now, today. Of all the very tiny number of things in the world that I want and have never quite managed to have, you are what I covet the most, James Spencer! I love you and want to lead, guide and take care of you, for the rest of your life, in the way that you want me to, but which your wife will not.

"If that is all clear to you, then please lay your cards on the table, *right now, today* James. This is the moment of decision. Do you want to leave Elizabeth Spencer and become mine?"

James's heart beat faster still. Linda was effectively coming on at him, which he had always hoped for. He had always imagined that it would be strong, but even so, he was still taken aback by her forcefulness. He felt huge attraction, like never before. He loved Linda's tremendous strength of character, and her desire to take control and dominate. She was a truly traditional woman, not like his wife and he knew that there would be no 'role reversals.' He would be able to be a traditional man. Elizabeth was actually slightly changing the original terms of their marriage contract. He just couldn't bear the thought of being stuck with his wife for the rest of his life. He had to do something about it, and now Linda was proposing to help him do just that, by some as yet unknown method. He took the plunge.

"It is clear to me Linda. I want to leave Elizabeth and be with you. I *want* to be yours, as much as you want to *make* me yours!"

Linda's own heartbeat quickened a little now. This was the exact response that she had wanted.

"You're absolutely sure of that? You understand and accept my terms? You'll have to confront Elizabeth now, with or without my help. You can't continue to stay as you are."

"Yes Linda. I am sure and I accept the terms," confirmed James.

Linda smiled. "Well then James Spencer, that's the deal done, and now you're committed! I'll take that as your word, and I trust you. Don't abuse my trust and you'll be fine.

"That being said, I'm confident that you'll be living with Alexandra and myself, this Festival of Divinity. And I meant what I said yesterday. I want us to start getting together regularly from now on, as a potential, and I now believe probable, family unit."

"I did like Alexandra, Linda. She's a lovely girl. Well mannered, well spoken, clearly very intelligent and with her mother's good looks, too! She's a credit to you Linda!"

Linda broke out into her broadest smile of the morning. "Thank you James! I'm not sure which of us you just gave the biggest compliment to!"

"Both of you, equally!" said James.

Linda gave him a peck on the cheek.

"Right!" she said, "To work matters. Is the car ready?"

"Yes, all systems working perfectly, the bodywork washed and polished, and the inside all hovered out."

"Good. Well here's our copy of the route plan we decided upon, last week." Linda gave James a two-page document, with a map and directions on it.

James opened the front passenger's door and put the route plan on the dashboard. Meanwhile Linda got into the back, and checked the inside of the car, ticking everything off her clipboard, as it met with her satisfaction.

She got back out again. "Yes, that's fine James. Excellent. Right, let's just check Her Majesty's security team haven't got any problems. She pulled out a mobile communicator that she had, attached to her skirt belt.

Switching it on, Linda opened the garage doors again, and stepped outside. As it crackled into life, she pressed a button and a voice came on over the speaker.

"Hello, Linda," said Virginia Stewart, head of the royal Security Team.

"Hello, Virginia," said Linda. "James and I are ready. Are all of your officers set to leave at 11am?

"Yes, the cars are all ready to follow, once you get underway, Linda."

"Excellent. I'll let Her Majesty's personal staff know, that we're ready to leave when she is then. Thank you."

She went back into the garage. "Right, drive us down to the back entrance, James! Everyone's ready for Her Majesty."

"Right you are," said James, as they got in, with Linda in the passenger seat. He carefully drove the car out of the garage, got out and locked the doors, then got back in, and they moved towards the entrance. Linda pressed another button on the communicator. This time the voice of Rebecca Hargreaves, came over the speaker.

"Hello Mrs Radcliffe."

"Hello Rebecca. Could you inform Her Majesty that all is well, and that we're ready to go whenever she is?"

"Certainly Mrs Radcliffe" said Rebecca.

"Thank you," said Linda.

The car arrived outside the entrance. They were in good time. A few minutes later Queen Alexandra appeared with her lady-in-waiting, and flanked by her bodyguards. Linda jumped out, and opened the back door for her.

"Your Majesty," she said, curtseying.

The queen acknowledged her, then stepped into the Royal car. James had turned to face her, and he bowed his head. "Your Majesty," he said.

The queen's two personal bodyguards sat either side of her and the lady-in-waiting, in the back of the car. Linda closed the door and then, got back into the passenger seat.

"Are you ready, Ma'am?" asked Linda.

"Yes. Drive on please, James," said Queen Alexandra.

"Ma'am!" said James and they were off.

***

James followed Linda's instructions, as they went further into their journey. He would normally, easily be able to find his way to Castra University, which was in Thetworth, 30 miles to the west of Avermore, but there was always a specific route which they had to follow, decided upon by Linda and himself beforehand (and often heavily dominated by Linda's opinion), taking into account factors such as time and safety. They also had to take into account the cavalcade travelling behind them, containing Queen Alexandra's security, so that they were always on their tail. Therefore, Linda always navigated, something she revelled in, and as usual, the quiet murmur of banter between the pair, gave the queen and her bodyguards some entertainment, as Alexandra had experienced yesterday.

"Try and avoid the pedestrians please, James."

"I've no intention of driving on the pavement, Linda."

"Never mind the women on the pavement, it's those crossing the road, that your eyes should be paying attention to!"

"Forty miles an hour along here, James. That speedometer is dangerously close to the limit!"

"Everything's under control, Linda. I made sure to get my eyes tested earlier this morning and they're fine."

"Good. I'm glad to hear it, but all the same, the fine will come out of your wages if we're stopped!"

"Turn left here. That means this one, James, not the next. Wake up, man!"

"Yes boss. I was just about to indicate. Give me a chance."

"Perhaps I need to send you on a course, to improve your reflexes, then!"

They reached Thetworth at 11.45 and arrived inside the grounds of Castra University at 11.50. As James brought the car to a halt, Linda jumped out and opened the rear passenger door for the queen, and her bodyguard on that side to exit from. Her other bodyguard exited from the other side and raced around the back of the car to join them. The queen's lady-in-waiting followed close behind.

Queen Alexandra was met by Jemima Huddleston, chancellor of Castra University. There were a small number of Male Rights Protestors outside, but the police kept them well away from her. The Royal delegation was shown inside, and the queen was introduced to various dignitaries and officials. By 12.00 she was sat on the stage of the dining hall, in front of the assembled staff and students.

Jemima welcomed her to the university, and spoke of the great honour that they felt in having her as their guest. She then invited her to the podium, to address them.

The speech which Linda had drafted wasn't particularly long. In it, the queen praised the university for its standards of achievement, and for producing many of Geratica's most distinguished people, throughout history.

She expressed her approval for the university's decision to open its doors to non-public school educated girls, from next year, saying that in the modern world, it was only right and proper that the brightest girls from other schools, should get the chance to be educated at Geratica's premier educational establishment, and spoke of her hope that other universities might follow suit.

Queen Alexandra also took the opportunity to acknowledge that a couple of pioneering schools had been set up for the education of boys, and that there were obviously plenty of males, throughout Geratica, with a reasonable level of intelligence. However, whilst this was a laudable gesture, at the moment there were no plans to formally extend compulsory education to both sexes. There was of course nothing to stop any Geratican woman from educating her son as she saw fit, in the privacy of her own home.

The address seemed to go down well and there was much applause in the hall, as she finished and sat back down.

Then it was time for the special lunch held in her honour. Everyone enjoyed a sumptuous three course meal with wine. Although she would be driving back home tonight, Linda was sure that she could allow herself a glass of red. In fact, on average, over the course of a working week, she usually had two or three lunchtime 'tipples', through working lunches such as today, or lunch dates with various people. She'd had a successful morning. Her thoughts turned to Alexandra for a second. She hoped that she was having a good day too.

***

In fact, as the queen had begun her speech, Alexandra was in her music lesson, the last period before lunch, having had Maths for the previous one, after break time.

Mrs Wood came over to her midway through her lesson. She wore the mistress uniform of a white blouse and black skirt, and a neck bow with the college's colours on it. Her black gown was resting on the back of her chair. Today was a 'theory' lesson, as opposed to the 'history' one on Day 4 and the 'practical' lesson at the end of the working week and the class were quietly studying a piece of musical score.

She put her hand on Alexandra's shoulder and said softly into her ear, "I believe you had a surprise at the weekend?"

Alexandra grinned and nodded. "Just a bit!" she whispered.

"Come and take tea with me, this afternoon and we'll talk. I've arranged with Miss Collins, for you to be allowed to finish your Geratican Language lesson 15 minutes early, so that you'll still have time to catch your train home, this afternoon."

Alexandra looked at her in surprise. "Oh. Yes of course, Mrs Wood. Thank you." she said. Her music mistress nodded to her in acknowledgement, and went back to her desk.

As she finished the exercise, Alexandra considered the invitation. She obviously knew what Mrs Wood was going to talk to her about, but she was surprised to be asked to take tea in her chambers for it. That was normally an honour reserved for head girls or college champions.

She was pleased that her mistress had thought to arrange for her to take it 15 minutes earlier than was usual. Normally, when the girls took tea, it was at 3.15, when the official curriculum finished for the day, which was her 'going home' time. She was always welcome to join other girls in their chambers, before leaving, and she had on a couple of occasions, but because her train left the station at 3.45 and she wanted to be there by 3.40 at the latest, it meant that she couldn't stay long. By the time she was out of her last lesson and into her host's chambers, and then the tea was made, she really only had time to quickly gulp it down, almost burning the roof of her mouth in the process, before she had to excuse herself, and dash out of the college.

She didn't really mind missing out on it though. She didn't have many very close friends, so she felt a bit awkward in that kind of situation, anyhow. The train journey home, listening to it chugging along the line and looking out of the window at the scenery and then being back home, and knowing that her mother would soon be there to hug and kiss her, was all much more appealing.

***

Lunch at Charterhouse was at 12.45. All the girls in the college took their lunch together, in one sitting. The dining hall contained several long tables, each with a long bench on both sides. There were also a small number of single tables taken by older girls. Alexandra was seated at one of these. The mistresses, dressed in the uniform of a white blouse, black skirt, and a neck bow with the college colours on it, had two tables reserved for them. Today Elizabeth Spencer, seated at the head of the first mistresses' table, had a radio set up in the dining hall. After the usual formalities had been observed, she informed them that Queen Alexandra had, just a short time ago, given an address to Castra University. As many of the girls aspired to eventually go there, she wanted them all to listen to it, when extracts were broadcast on the one o'clock news.

A murmur of interest went around the hall, most of it favourable Alexandra felt, which pleased her. Queen Alexandra had always been a popular monarch. She could feel some of the girls giving her some knowing looks. Quite a few were aware of her mother's role at court. She coloured slightly with embarrassment at the brief moment of exposure, before Elizabeth switched on the radio. Then all the girls' attention focused on that, enjoying the novelty of listening to whatever was on there, when they were normally in the college eating their lunch, without any outside entertainment.

The address was the second story of the bulletin. The girls listened, mainly in silence, as the queen's voice came on the air. Alexandra studied the expressions and reactions of the other girls, as they heard the words that she knew her mother had written. The part that appeared to cause the biggest reaction amongst some of them was that Castra was to open its doors to non public schoolgirls, from next year. Perhaps they hadn't realised it, and there were one or two who were clearly horrified at the idea of having to mix with what they would consider 'the riff-raff'. They began to talk disapprovingly to each other.

"Silence!" the headmistress admonished them.

Then came the bit about boys' education, and the queen's assertion that there were no plans at the moment, to extend compulsory education to both sexes. Now Alexandra was watching her headmistress. She wasn't surprised to note that she didn't look at all pleased, and in fact, she got the distinct impression that she was now regretting her decision to let them all listen to the address. As soon as the report finished, she snapped off the radio, and without a word of comment to the girls, on what they had just heard, flounced out of the dining hall, crimson blotching her cheeks.

A hubbub went around the hall, as the girls began to talk about both what they'd heard and had just seen. A couple of minutes later, Alexandra noticed Mrs Spencer's daughter, Gillian, discreetly leave also, no doubt to go and search for her.

# CHAPTER 4

At Castra University, with the lunch over, Queen Alexandra said goodbye to the officials and then went outside, where she began an official walkabout, meeting some of the crowd that had congregated to cheer her and wave flags. Thw queen was discreetly flanked by her bodyguards, and once again followed by her lady-in-waiting, with Linda giving directions to the proceedings. Again a number of Male Rights Activists, started to become vocal, but were gradually drowned out, by the cheers.

Then it was time to return to the palace, after what Linda felt had been a successful engagement.

During the brief period that she had, before her next meeting, Linda rang Philippa Barrington. Philippa said that Day 3 of each week, would be the best for her to visit The Grange, and told Linda her fee. She agreed, and it was arranged that she would start this week, at 5.00, for an hour's tutorial.

"Just one thing though, Mrs Radcliffe," Philippa felt she needed to stress this point from the outset. "Alexandra and I will need some privacy, and peace and quiet, in order for me to tutor her effectively. As I said previously, I don't do this very often, but I always ask with respect, that we are left alone in the room together, with the minimum of interference or interruption. I hope you understand."

"Oh yes, of course Philippa. If you're worrying that I might be trying to sit in on your lessons, let me put your mind at rest immediately. I wouldn't do that! Though naturally, I shall demand a full report from my daughter on her progress, afterwards! In fact, I probably I won't be home from work yet, when you arrive, so when I do, I'll just pop my head around the door to say 'hello' and then I'll be starting to prepare our dinner. I also have a weekly delivery from the supermarket that night, too, for the things that I can't buy from the local grocery store, so I'll have plenty to keep me busy!"

"I'm sure that it will work out perfectly, Mrs Radcliffe," said Philippa. "I look forward to seeing you both, the day after tomorrow."

"Yes. And thank you again Philippa, for granting Alexandra this privilege. I know that she considers it a great honour and she is a highly studious girl."

"It will be my pleasure, Mrs Radcliffe!" said Philippa, and they said goodbye.

*\*\**

Later, at the end of her meeting with the privy council, held every fortnight to discuss court business, she caught Lady Caroline Sackville's eye.

"If you please, My Lady, walk with me, and I may have some news to impart, for your ears only."

Lady Caroline inclined her head enquiringly, and they left the room and made their way down the palace corridors, to the front entrance. Linda knew her quite well, having dined at her estate, on several occasions, which was close to Greenacres. Her husband, Lord Randolph, had died of cancer some twenty-three years before.

After exchanging pleasantries, Linda came to the point. "Lady Caroline, I met with Queen Alexandra this morning, and the question of a possible marriage in the near future, was discussed. She asked if you could pass on a message to Lord George that he is in favour, and that she will make a decision soon, though naturally it will be at a time of her own choosing. I would advise you Lady Caroline, that the queen does appear to view your son as her most likely suitor. She has indeed, said as much."

Lady Caroline looked at Linda for a moment and there was a faint trace of excitement in her eyes.

"Oh! That is news indeed, Linda! Please thank Her Majesty for her message and tell her that I shall pass it to Lord George immediately! Good day to you Linda!"

"Good day, My Lady!" replied Linda.

Lady Caroline hurried away, as fast as she could.

\*\*\*

Meanwhile at Charterhouse, at 3.00, Alexandra was able to slip out of her Geratican Language lesson 15 minutes early, as had been pre-arranged. Leaving the classroom, and about to close the door behind her, she noticed Gillian staring at her, with a puzzled look upon her face. No doubt she was wondering where she was going. She half expected her to get up and follow her, but she didn't.

A blonde, slightly shorter than Alexandra, Gillian Spencer was a clever girl who found her studies quite easy. She liked to be top of the class, and considered Alexandra her main rival. In fact, she had been pipped to the post by her on some occasions and, this sparked hatred inside of her.

The curriculum was very broad and remained more or less the same throughout the girls' school careers, though two subjects could be dropped – apart from mathematics, Geratican language and science – once they reached the advanced stage of their education. Gillian's interest lay in science, and she had immediately dropped artistic studies and music. Alexandra, who was gifted in both science and the arts, had nevertheless (after discussion with her mother) also dropped artistic studies, as well as Ancient Geratican. To receive their Advanced Certificate of Geratica, they had to gain at least a pass in five or more of the eight subjects, which had to include mathematics and Geratican language. The dropping of two subjects, allowed an extra period on the timetable for all of the others.

In addition to this competitiveness, Elizabeth Spencer allowed Gillian to take advantage of her mother's position as headmistress, to more or less have a free reign to do what she wanted, and this she exploited to the full – and even sometimes beyond that. As far as the mistresses were concerned she was "untouchable" as Mrs Spencer turned a blind eye to any of her daughter's more sordid activities, and would not tolerate a single word uttered against her reputation. As a result, she regularly broke rules that the other girls were punished for, if they did likewise, and was without doubt the naughtiest girl in the college. Gambling for money at cards was officially strictly forbidden, yet Gillian managed to get away with secretly organising such activities for small groups of girls in her chambers. Normally once girls reached this stage of their time at Charterhouse, and their thoughts were turning towards university and their future careers, behaviour issues weren't quite so prevalent, but in Gillian's case, she was only becoming more daring, sly and devious. Despite this, she had still managed to become Head Girl of the college.

She was also a bully, and often taunted Alexandra, although it sometimes annoyed her, that despite the fact she could obviously make her feel uncomfortable, Alexandra rarely seemed to get riled. Gillian had various protection rackets and corrupt schemes in place, in order to extract money from the other girls. She ran the college tuck shop herself, at break time each morning and at the end of the main school day, assisted by a couple of other girls. Gillan had initially helped herself to the takings whenever she felt like it, which was often. She was clever enough to be able to falsify the accounts, to cover up her deceit. One week, Gillian had been ill and taken to her bed, therefore the running of it had been temporarily taken over by a couple of other girls, and Alexandra had been drafted in to balance the accounts. It hadn't taken her long to realise that something was seriously wrong, and she had informed her house mistress. Once Gillian had recovered, of course no formal action had been taken against her, but she had been made aware that her scheme was discovered. She had been livid with Alexandra for 'grassing' on her, and had confronted her in a deserted place, her with a couple of her friends, as she was leaving the college grounds for the day.

While her friends had held her, to stop her getting away, Gillian had punched her hard in the stomach, knocking the wind out of her and making her gasp for breath on the ground. From that moment on, Alexandra had been barred from the tuck shop, and the money which she had used to use to buy herself a bag of crisps or a chocolate bar, now had to be given to Gillian directly at the beginning of break time, or she was told, she'd receive another thumping. Her mother still thought that she brought something from the shop each day. Alexandra didn't dare tell her, in case she made a complaint to the college, and she got into even more trouble with Gillian.

Gillian also acted discreetly as her mother's eyes and ears, and if she found out anything which might get other girls into trouble, then the news quickly reached the headmistress. She sometimes engineered situations to incriminate other girls, or cause problems for mistresses, to help her mother gain an excuse to implement her plans for the college politically, which often advantaged Gillian in the process.

Still Alexandra had no time to worry about any of that now. Gillian would surely find out the reason, soon enough.

She crossed to the music block, went up to the top the stairs, to her mistress's chambers, and knocked on the door.

Mrs Wood greeted her, and invited her in. She was offered a seat in a comfortable chair opposite the mistress. In between them, was a table with some freshly made tea. Alexandra's eyes also couldn't fail to spot two jam doughnuts, each on a plate.

"Well, thank you for coming Alexandra," said Mrs Wood as she poured the tea.

"Not at all, Mrs Wood. Thank *you*. This is a great honour," said Alexandra, politely.

"So, how was it then?" Mrs Wood handed Alexandra her cup of tea. "Help yourself to a jam doughnut, by the way."

"Thank you. It was wonderful. The performance was fantastic, and then it was announced that there was someone in the audience, who was a big fan of Philippa Barrington, and that she would be available to meet them afterwards. Then I realised it was me! I felt nervous, but my mother was there with me, and I think I handled it OK in the end. I even played part of a symphony with her, and she's offered to give me some private tuition! My mother is going to sort out the arrangements today, when she gets a moment. I gather you knew about it, last week, and you met them both, a couple of days before?"

"Yes. Well, sorry about that, but I was under orders to keep it as a surprise for you, and also, we thought that the less time you had to think about it, the less nervous you would get beforehand. I was always confident that you'd be fine meeting her and that you'd be able to prove yourself capable on the piano, in front of Mrs Barrington.

"I would now like to put a proposal to you Alexandra. We are, as you know, shortly going to be selecting the college champion, who will go on from here to their university, as the girl who made the single, most significant contribution to the college, in her final year, during the calendar year of 5010. We already have one candidate in Gillian Spencer, but, again, as you know, by tradition we always have two and then make the final selection, at the end of term. How would you feel about being put forward by myself?"

Alexandra jumped slightly and had to be careful not to slop her tea in her saucer.

"I don't know," she said, deciding that it might be wisest to put her tea down for a moment, until she'd regained her composure. "What would I be doing?"

"Well, seeing as you're about to start receiving lessons from Philippa Barrington, then maybe you could organise a piano recital for the whole college. You can have complete access to the college symphony orchestra. You would be playing the piano, out in the front of the stage, but the whole orchestra and performance would be under your direction."

Alexandra gaped at her music mistress, as she ate her doughnut. "But, but ... I've never done anything like that before, and I'd never be able to get people to do what I want them to do. My mother's good at that sort of thing, but I'm not!"

"Your mother is a very significant person in your life, isn't she?" said Mrs Wood.

"She's very dominant, yes. She generally knows what I should do and how I should do it. I follow her direction. She's a strict woman, but also very fair."

"And I know that she thinks you would benefit from this," said the mistress. "You have it in you to perform in front of the college and also, although you've never done it before, you *can* put on a performance. We all have to learn how to do new things sometimes, and doing this would be a huge feather in your cap, and at least give Gillian Spencer a run for her money, which I suspect, if you're honest, you'd like to do! It would also give you so much confidence, to achieve the feat. You've come on a lot, but this would really do things for you, as you go – hopefully – to Castra, next year."

"Are you saying that my mother knows about this also? Is that the real reason why Philippa offered me tuition?"

"No, Alexandra," said Mrs Wood. "We both wanted you to be able to meet her, and be given the opportunity to take lessons from her, as we thought you'd get a lot of pleasure out of it. If it wasn't for that fact, we would never push you, but at the same time, we do think that this would be a terrific opportunity for you. It's still completely your decision, though.

"Look, you don't need to decide today, and you'd better make a move soon, to catch your train. Go home and talk about this, with your mother. Hear her advice and then make your own decision. But I'd like to know tomorrow, if possible, and then I can inform Mrs Spencer. The sooner you were to get started on this, the better!"

Alexandra gulped and cleared her throat. "Yes, Mrs Wood," she said nervously and finished her tea.

Her music mistress got up and offered her hand. "Goodbye then Alexandra. Thank you for coming to tea with me. Have a good evening, and talk with your mother. Tell me your decision tomorrow."

Alexandra got up also and shook her hand. "Thank you for the tea, Mrs Wood. It was very nice. I'll do as you say. Goodbye and see you tomorrow."

***

Alexandra stood on the station platform, as her train arrived at the station. As usual it felt good to know that she was free again, away from the other girls, and would soon be home. But this afternoon, there was a certain feeling of apprehension mixed in with it, due to what Mrs Wood had just suggested to her. She boarded the train and took her seat, settling herself down for the journey home, with her school bag at her feet, and as she did so, she considered the situation, sucking the finger of her glove again. This was a comfort-bringing habit that she had – she had been a prolific finger and thumb sucker as a child growing up, especially when she was worried, nervous, or simply deep in thought – and despite her mother having broken her of the habit, as she'd got older, telling her that grown women didn't do that, she still sometimes found something to suck on. After all, there was still almost a year of her childhood left, she told herself.

She suspected that she would end up doing this. If Mrs Wood and her mother were both keen, she didn't think she'd be able to put her foot down and refuse, despite her music mistress saying that it would be her decision. She was a natural follower when around other Geratican females, and didn't always find it easy to stand her ground, even if she wasn't happy. She had never yet met a man who she didn't like, and generally felt more confident in their company. But she did respect her mother's judgement – her counsel often turned out to be wise and correct – and so generally, she did as she was told, which was what her mother expected of her anyway. She simply wasn't allowed to cause too much fuss, once her mother had told her what was what.

Alexandra honestly couldn't imagine *how* she was going to do it though. She hoped that once her mother was home tonight, she wouldn't be too busy to talk for long over supper, and she felt she would probably get her prep done, by the time she would have to get it ready for. She already had the words of a couple of essays that she had to write, in her head, and there they would stay, until she got them down on paper. She would sit at her desk in the study, with a cup of coffee, and write them as soon as she got home, or rather, probably just after her mother had phoned to check if she was there which was usually just after she got in. Her mother worked late for the first two evenings of the week. On the other three evenings, Linda normally came home earlier and she cooked their dinner.

Thinking of her mother made her look forward to being in her arms again tonight, when she got home – Alexandra's favourite moment of the day, during the week, when their differing needs for each other came together – the mother wanting to give her love to her daughter and the daughter wanting to receive love from her mother.

Then her thoughts turned to Tom, and what he might be doing now. He might be coming home too, from his job working on Lady Sackville's estate, just outside of Greenacres, as a trainee gardener, and general labourer. As he was still yet to come of age, his hours of work were less than the working men's. His father dropped him off in the morning on the way to work, and then he returned on the bus in the afternoon. She began to feel the stirrings of strong sexual arousal inside of her, once more, as erotic thoughts entered her mind. She couldn't wait to see him tomorrow. Looking discreetly around, she picked up her school bag, and placed it around her lap, so that it was hidden from view. Then she put her hand over her crotch and ran her forefinger lightly over her erection. Immediately a bolt of sexual energy tore through her, the strongest she had experienced yet, making her gasp and her legs twitch.

She hoped her mother would find her something that she could use to masturbate with, soon. In common with most Geratican women, her sexual desire was intense, and it was agony not being able to satisfy it, and relieve her geratis. Her mother's warning also registered in her mind though. She would have to remember to pass it on to Tom tomorrow, as she'd been ordered to, but she herself had absolutely no intention of allowing them to commit a sexual act, before they were old enough, so her mother needn't worry.

# CHAPTER 5

Alexandra's train reached the station at Greenacres on time at 4.05 p.m. She walked from the station to home, and arrived at 4.25 p.m. She immediately put the fire on, in both the parlour, and the study, before making herself a cup of coffee, and taking it into the latter room. As she sat at her desk, sure enough the phone rang, and Alexandra recognised her mother's telephone number at the palace, on the display screen.

She picked up the receiver. "Hello, Mother," she said.

"Hello darling!" said Linda. "How was your day?"

"Not too bad, Mother," replied Alexandra. "How was yours?"

"Good. But it's not over yet. I'm off to Parliament House in a few moments. I should be home around 7.45, so you're to make sure that the supper is ready for then. Is that clear?"

"Yes, Mother."

"Also, I want you to phone through our weekly order to the supermarket. Will you be alright? I know you're not comfortable on the phone, darling, but you do need to become more confident with it, which I think is beginning to happen. I only tell you to do it once every few weeks, so that you don't have to suffer it too often, and the ordering is *my* responsibility really, but you know that there will come a time when you'll have a phone in your own house, and as the mistress, you'll need to use it sometimes."

Alexandra groaned inwardly, but said, "Yes, I'll be alright Mother. Although I'll be glad when I've done it, certainly."

"Good girl!" said her mother. "I'm sure you won't have any problems, but ring me if you do. My list is on my desk, in the usual place. Place the order now, before it gets too late, then ring me to tell me, before I go to parliament. I mustn't be too late leaving, so don't keep me waiting for too long. Understood?"

"Yes, of course, Mother!" replied Alexandra.

"Good," said Linda. "Now, I've been in touch with Philippa Barrington," she continued, but changing the subject. "Your tuition will be at 5.00 p.m. for an hour, on Day 3 of each week, starting from this one. OK?"

"Very good, Mother. Thank you."

"Have you got much prep?"

"About an average amount, Mother. I was just about to write a couple of essays, when you rang."

"Excellent," said Linda. "Right, Alexandra. Before you do anything else, ring the order through. You might have to wait a moment or two for one of the customer services staff to be free. I'll stay here and wait for you to confirm with me. You'll speak to Veronica first, and then she'll put you through to me. If I should be already gone to parliament, then you'll just have to leave a message with her to pass on to me, and I'll see it when I get back to my office, before I come home. Is that all clear?"

"Crystal clear, Mother!" Alexandra was used to taking in her mother's instructions quickly, through years of training, and she knew the penalty for not following them properly, through years of experience. The cane was behind her mother's desk.

"Good. Well, I'll hang up and let you ring the order through," said Linda. "I'll be waiting for your confirmation, so do it immediately. Speak to you in a moment then, Alexandra. Bye now."

"Bye, Mother," replied Alexandra and hung up.

Linda reached for a document in her in tray. It was a report from the Geratican Scientific Research Centre, on the latest information gathered from scanning outside of their planet, including other lifeforms and their cultures. Glancing at it, there was nothing particularly significant – she could read it at her leisure tonight.

At The Grange, Alexandra pulled up her sleeves nervously and quickly found her mother's list, on her desk, and the telephone number. Then she picked up the phone receiver again, and steeled herself for the effort. She would always hate ringing people up, almost as much as having to answer an incoming call, when she didn't know who it would be. Luckily, having done it a few times now, she knew what to expect, and so far there had indeed been no serious problem, but there could always be a first time.

Alexandra dialled the number, pressing the buttons carefully. When she had first started using the phone, she remembered sometimes getting a wrong number, in her anxious state, but her mother had helped her to deal with her nerves more effectively now. She didn't have to wait long, before a woman's voice came on to the other end of the line, and asked how she could help. Alexandra explained that she wanted to place an order, and gave her mother's account number when asked. The assistant asked her to confirm who the order was for, and she gave her mother's name. Then she was asked for the order details and she read out the items on the list, ticking them off, as she said them – something her mother had taught her to do.

Luckily everything that they needed for the week was in stock, and the assistant confirmed with Alexandra, that their chosen delivery day was Day 3, in the evening.

Then the job was done, and Alexandra thankfully came off the line, puffing out her cheeks. She quickly found her mother's number at the palace, and dialled it, checking her watch as she did so. It hadn't taken too long. She should just catch her mother, before she went to parliament.

"Is Linda Radcliffe still there?" she asked, as Veronica came on the line.

"Yes. Who's speaking please?"

"It's her daughter."

"Oh, hello Alexandra! Nice to speak to you. I gather you were here yesterday, too."

"Yes, that's right," she replied.

"She's just about to leave for parliament, so you'll just manage to speak to her before she goes," said Veronica. "Goodbye Alexandra. I'm putting you through now."

"Goodbye Veronica," said Alexandra.

"Hello darling. Was everything alright?" said Linda, as she came on the line a moment later.

"Yes Mother. There weren't any problems, just as you said. They've got everything and they'll deliver it on Day 3, in the evening."

"Excellent. Very well done, my darling. How did you find it?"

"A bit better, I suppose, Mother, replied Alexandra. "But I still hated it!"

Linda laughed. "Well, I don't suppose it's ever going to be your favourite piece of technology!"

"Certainly not, Mother!" Alexandra confirmed.

"I must go then, my sweetheart." Linda looked out of the window. "The night is starting to draw in. Stay indoors and get on with your work now. You know the rule. Love you lots, and I'm going to give it all to you, when I get home. That's a promise. See you later. Bye darling."

"I can't wait for you to come home and love me lots, Mother. I love you too, and I need you. Bye now."

At the other end of the line, Linda's passion and affection for her daughter, rose to its highest level of the day so far, and she knew it would be even stronger when she got home. She reached over her desk, and touched the photograph that she had of Alexandra in her office.

"*Well here's something for you to be getting on with then, my darling,*" she said softly, and sent a big kiss down the phone as she stroked her daughter's long blonde hair, in the picture.

"Now, I really must go. See you later. Bye now." She put down the phone and gathering her things together, hurried off to Parliament Square.

***

Alexandra worked busily for an hour, her sleeves at her elbows. By that time, she had finished her essays for science and history. She still had mathematics exercises to do, but she had time for a break before that.

She went upstairs to her bedroom and began to prepare a selection of music that she was going to play tomorrow night, when Tom was there. Part of her collection was already devoted to their common tastes, many of which she had introduced him to. This was something that gave her great pleasure. It delighted her, when he enjoyed something that she did too, and it was their good fortune, that it seemed to happen regularly. Tomorrow's compilation would be the very best of it. She always liked to make Tom happy, and tomorrow, especially so.

She put on the six o'clock news, in the middle of doing this, and took in the events of the day, most of which the girls at Charterhouse hadn't heard, due to Mrs Spencer switching off the radio in a fit of pique at lunch time, after hearing the end of the queen's address. That item was still on the bulletin.

As she listened, she finished her compilation, and then wrapped up Tom's birthday present – a bow tie. She was hoping that they might soon get to go to places together, where they could dress up in a smart, formal and stylish fashion.

Then Alexandra checked her gowns, making sure that they were spotless. She remembered her mother's advice at the Geratica Hotel and she smiled to herself. Could she be 'devious' and try and manipulate Tom to choose the one that she herself wanted to wear? The one she'd worn to the concert was certainly her favourite, which her mother knew, and that was why it had been laid out on her bed, when the treat had been revealed. She thought that Tom would like it best, too, but she wasn't sure. Really, she wanted him to truly decide for himself. Her mother liked to be in complete control, and to get her own way, but she was more easy going.

Once again she was experiencing powerful sensations in her geratis, and it had extended so far that it was straining uncomfortably in her pants. She threw herself onto her bed, stomach first, and thrust her geratis down on the bedspread, imagining that Tom was sandwiched between. She gasped again, and almost lost her breath.

After recovering, she went back down to the study. She thought about phoning Tom, before she carried on with her prep, but she thought that they might be having dinner at The Lodge at the moment, and anyhow, it would be sure to set her aflame again. The combination of using the phone, and probably having to talk to Fiona, was not appealing either.

So, she finished her prep, got her school bag ready for tomorrow, and then with her mother due shortly, she put the fire on in the dining room, and began getting the supper of pâté on toast, in the kitchen.

Just as the toast was becoming ready, she heard the familiar sound of her mother's car pulling up outside the house. Alexandra felt a thrill of excitement. She hadn't seen her mother for a full twelve hours, and she was longing to be in her arms, where she felt the safest of all, and experienced so many pleasurable feelings. She took the pieces of bread out of the toaster, and started to spread the pâté over them.

Then she heard her mother come through the front door. "Mmm, something smells good!" she called out. Just as Alexandra was finishing putting the pâté on the last piece of toast, Linda came into the kitchen.

"Hello my darling," she said coming over to her daughter.

"Hello, Mother," replied Alexandra.

Linda wrapped her arms around her daughter, and putting down the knife, Alexandra melted submissively into her mother's strong embrace, gazing lovingly into her eyes. Linda's passion overcame her, and squeezing Alexandra tighter and tighter, she smothered her lips with kisses, until her daughter murmured with pleasure.

"It looks like I'm just in time!" said Linda.

"Yes, Mother. I was just finishing as you came in. We must have a sixth sense!"

"Or I'm your clever mother, sweetheart!" said Linda with a smile, as they took their plates into the dining room. "But either explanation is a possibility!"

Linda took her place at the head of the table, and Alexandra sat to the side of her. Then, they settled down to eat.

As was usual they were quiet for a moment, as they shared their mutual love of food, and satisfied their healthy appetites.

"Mmm," said Linda once again. "This tastes as good as it smelt when I came in. Congratulations darling! It may only be pâté on toast, but I do believe you're developing into a fine cook."

Alexandra smiled with pleasure. She leaned over and kissed her mother, who immediately returned the gesture. "Thank you Mother."

She continued, "We heard the report of Queen Alexandra's address to Castra, on the one o'clock news, at Charterhouse today."

Linda looked at her in surprise. "Oh? How did that happen then?"

"Mrs Spencer had a radio put in the Dining Hall, so that we could hear it, because some of us have ambitions to go there, Mother." Alexandra smiled mischievously. "Do you want me to tell you what her reaction was?"

"Well, I did hope for the 'education of boys' reference to be seen in as diplomatic a light as possible, and the address generally, seems to have had a largely favourable response. But I assume from your expression, Mrs Spencer wasn't happy?"

"You could say that, Mother. She went purple, snapped the radio off, as soon as the report ended, and stormed out! I suspect that she now bitterly regrets her decision to let us listen to it."

Linda gave a chuckle, which shortly became a laugh. "Darn it! I wish I'd seen that! Well, I can't say that I'm terribly surprised, but it's done now. In actual fact, in a couple of days' time, she'll be getting a letter from me, on behalf of Queen Alexandra, spelling out the court's position on this issue, which will most likely make her hit the roof! It should reach Charterhouse in the post on 3/33/10. Keep your head down on that day, darling!"

"Something else happened today, Mother. Mrs Wood invited me for tea in her chambers this afternoon. She arranged that I could leave my last lesson early, so that I'd still have time to get my train home, which was nice of her. She obviously wanted to hear all about my meeting with Philippa, at the weekend, but she also told me that I'm being thought of as a possible candidate for college champion, and what it's proposed I should do."

"Oh, I see," said Linda. "Then you've been told that I knew about this, also?"

"Yes Mother." Alexandra reached for her hand, and as Linda instinctively let her slip hers inside, her daughter squeezed from within. Are you very busy tonight? I've finished my prep and I'm ready for the morning. Mrs Wood wants an answer from me tomorrow, and I really need to talk."

Linda squeezed Alexandra's hand inside of hers. "Yes, of course we can talk, darling. Right. I assume you're wanting a cup of coffee? I'll make it, and you go and sit yourself down in the parlour. I'm here now, to take control. We'll sit on the sofa together and talk, and then I'll help you make a decision."

"Thank you, Mother," said Alexandra and getting up she kissed her again. Then Linda took their plates to the kitchen, on her way to making the coffee, and Alexandra went through to the parlour to wait for her. She could already feel her mother's strength. She *would* take control and guide her to the right path and somehow, when it really came down to it, Alexandra was always happy to let her do it. She was the person who she loved and respected above all others and the one Geratican woman whose dominance she trusted completely, and felt protected by.

***

In the spacious, well-furnished and richly decorated parlour – the largest room of the house, stretching all the way along the right-hand side of the building - Linda set the tray down on the table, in front of the sofa, and poured the coffee. Then she sat down next to her daughter.

"Right," she began, "Would you like my arm around you?"

Alexandra nodded. "Yes please, Mother." Linda slipped it around her shoulders, and gently stroked her hair.

"OK then, my darling, tell Mother how you're feeling about this."

"Apprehensive, is the first word that comes to mind, Mother. And that's the least of it. Frankly I was stunned that such a thing could be suggested. Mother, I'm terrified at the thought of responsibility. You're a natural at it, but I want my future role in Geratica, whatever it may be, to be more in the background. You know that."

"Yes I do sweetheart," said Linda, "and I'm sure that's the direction that you *will* take. That's what will suit you best, and you'll make just as important contribution to Geratica in that role as someone like me can, at court.

"But there will *very occasionally*, throughout your life, be times when you'll need to step out of the shadows, I'm afraid. Look upon this as the first of those. It would give you valuable experience, regardless of whether you became college champion or not, but if you could achieve that feat, it really would be a marvellous addition to your CV and a major asset to you at Castra, or any other university, for that matter – but let's keep our fingers crossed for Castra!"

Linda leant forward and picked up their cups of coffee, handing Alexandra's to her.

"Thank you, Mother," said her daughter and they both were quiet for a moment, as they drank.

Afterwards, Alexandra slipped her hand inside her mother's again. "So your advice is for me to accept this nomination, then Mother? I expected it to be so, but I wanted to tell you how I felt."

"Well, yes it is darling, and I do hope you'll take it. But I'm certainly not going to *tell* you to do something like this, and nor will Mrs Wood. If you really don't feel that you can do it, then that will be that, and no one will think any less of you. But *I* genuinely believe that you can."

Linda squeezed her daughter's hand, from the outside. "You can be sure of all the help and support that you need, behind the scenes, from all of us in your corner. I'll get you through this, sweetheart, I promise. My strength will guide and carry you.

"But you're also an extremely likeable girl, and you'll find that other people that you become responsible for will want to work for you and help you, too. As I've said to you darling, you must learn to play the game and play to your strengths. And obviously you have Philippa Barrington herself, tutoring you. How can you fail? Remember also, that you've got Tom now too. He can give you his support. You know his words can inspire you, and make you realise that you have more confidence than you realise, sometimes."

"That's true, Mother," said Alexandra.

Linda's fingers stroked her daughter's, encouraging her.

"I don't think I can do this, without both you and Tom, Mother. I do understand that it could be a good thing for me to do, and I want to fulfil my true potential. As long as I have you especially Mother, to help and guide me, then I think it might be possible. I need your dominance inside of me. As long as I know I've got that, then my answer will be 'yes,' tomorrow."

Linda wrapped her arms around Alexandra. "That's guaranteed, and you know it!" She pushed her daughter onto her back and lay over her on the sofa. For over a minute, Linda kissed Alexandra's lips, making her daughter tingle and murmur with pleasure, more than once, as she laid smothered beneath her.

"I'm pleased you've decided to accept the nomination, darling," she said, still on top of Alexandra. "I don't think you'll regret it." She gave her daughter on more kiss. "I think you needed a loving tonight!"

"I do have one piece of information to give to you Alexandra," she continued as they sat back up on the sofa. "I believe that James is going to tell Mrs Spencer that he wants to leave her, quite soon."

"Oh!" said Alexandra. "Does that mean ..."

"Never mind what it *might* mean at the moment, darling. I'm just letting you know, and I'll say no more for the moment. Except that, obviously it goes without saying, I want *total discretion*. The last thing we both want is for Elizabeth Spencer to find out from someone else, before James tells her. Do I make myself clear?"

"Yes, of course, Mother," said Alexandra. "I would never tell anyone that! You have my word."

"Good girl," said Linda. "Oh, one more thing, if you're interested. Fiona is pleased that you and Tom are an item now, too."

"Oh. Right, that's good then," said Alexandra. She wasn't surprised to hear that. She was probably delighted that she might be able to keep tabs on her, even more now.

Linda looked at the grandmother clock. "Right. Let's get washed up and then it'll soon be time for you to start getting ready for bed. It's been a long day for me, and there's another ahead tomorrow."

"Yes, Mother," said Alexandra and they went into the kitchen.

***

After saying goodnight to Alexandra, Linda went down to the study and started working through the paperwork that she'd brought home, a glass of port next to her, writing comments, instructions, and memos. After about an hour, she had finally finished, got things ready for the morning, locked up, and turned out the lights for the night.

In her bedroom, she opened the drawer under her bed, and took out a machine. Placing it on the floor, she operated a pump with her foot, and gradually the form of a naked man's torso came into shape. She lifted it up, and placed it inside the bed, on what had used to be Robert's side. Then she began to undress.

The thought of the possibility of James finally being hers, plus the memories that she always had of Robert – at night, especially carnal ones – mixed with the passionate love she had felt for Alexandra earlier, had all combined to inflame her sexual appetite, and her geratis was heaving and straining.

Inside the man's body was a fully functioning, but fake genus, which could arouse a woman's geratis to a certain level of orgasm, even though the man was not real. It could even produce false sperm. Now Linda fitted the other part of the machine to the man's torso – a head, with an eyepiece connected to it by a cable. Climbing into bed beside it, she put the eyepiece on her forehead, just above her right eye.

The eyepiece was able to transmit a series of images to the woman's brain, of any man she desired. She could load any image she wished into the machine, and once it was activated, it would fill her mind.

She could then have both her mind and body stimulated to achieve the interactive effect making love to the man she most desired.

Linda had been amazed to find such a toy on the market, and extremely impressed by the technology that had produced it. It was a state-of-the-art device, and she had paid quite a lot of money for it. Upon testing it, she had been delighted with the results. It was another of these that she was buying for Alexandra – in fact she had ordered it today.

Finally, Linda lay over the body, and switched on the machine. Until just recently, she had only used pictures of Robert to intensify her passion, but now Robert shared the visions in her mind, with James. She was able to control the speed with which the images came to her, and Linda preferred the intermediate setting, so that she could devote equal attention to both of them, and the body laid before her, which she fantasised more and more about being James.

Linda licked her lips. She was as natural a Geratican woman as there was possible to be, and a man's naked body, free for her personal attention, was her ultimate fantasy. She felt her geratis slip inside the male body's vagina hole, run along one wall and loop itself over the genus, before running back the other side, and re-entering her. That one action in itself made her feel pleasure, but she knew, as an experienced Geratican woman, that this was just the start.

Slowly, she began to kiss the body, starting with its lips, then moving down the neck, and across the shoulders, and then over its chest. All the while the visions kept appearing before her eyes, again and again. She returned the path of her kisses, back up to the lips. With her legs locked around those of the body's, and her arms around its neck, she squeezed it tight. She kissed the lips passionately, and as the visions kept appearing in her mind, it seemed as if she was kissing both Robert and James. She thrust her whole body against the toy, and pressed down deep over its vagina. As she began to kiss the body again, it was now, in her mind, no longer an anonymous object, but her wild passionate fantasy of what James's body would be like to make love to. Linda was most attracted to smaller men (partly because she liked to dominate them). Robert (and Christopher before that) had been too. They had in fact both been dark-haired also. She wanted James so badly! Her geratis reached a peak of desire, in both grinding hard against the genus, which was swelling up inside the male vagina and also expanding outwards, until it filled the entire vagina and pressed against its walls.

Linda was in ecstasy and she knew that she was close to coming. She'd always loved this feeling, almost as much as the climax itself. She was breathing heavily, and her legs and feet were tingling all over. Holding the body to her, inside her legs and arms, in an even stronger embrace, the tingles in her thighs became a hot burning which she simply had to quench. She saw Robert and James again, and smothered their lips with her most passionate kisses. She thrust her body downwards, over and over again, and her geratis responded to her desire, by pounding ever harder against what she wanted to be James' genus.

Then the genus exploded and sent a sticky substance – which felt like male sperm, but wasn't – trickling down her geratis and inside of her, and she sizzled with pleasure. Then Linda came, softly moaning in ecstasy, as the fire in every part of her lower body became an orgasm, and caused her to line the male body's vagina walls with a sweet, sticky fluid. In her mind, the images of Robert and James were engulfed in a golden glow, as if they were feeling the sweetness in their veins.

As the orgasm finished, Linda rolled off the male body, and got her breath back. Because the man's body was artificial, the toy couldn't quite replicate the intensity of orgasm, that only passionate intercourse with a real one could, but it was still a perfectly satisfactory one, as far as Linda was concerned. She glanced at the clock. Geraticans recovered from their orgasms quickly, and Linda was exceptionally strong. This had come in useful in her younger days, particularly when she had first been with Robert, and her lustful feelings and desires had been at their peak. She had once made love to him eight times in one night, which even by Geratican women's standards, was prolific. Although she had never been one to boast about such things, she did consider herself 'extremely good' in the bedroom, and she had been delighted that Robert had thought so too. She hoped that James would agree, and that it wouldn't be too long before she found out. Like when she was eating a box of chocolates, Linda now couldn't resist another one, though she must get to sleep after that. She climbed back on top, switched the machine on, and a few minutes later, came again.

Finishing, she switched off the machine and then pressed another button. It even automatically sent fluid around to absorb her love juice, and clean up the vagina!

She dismantled the machine, and put it all back in the drawer, under her bed. Then she got under the covers, turned out the bedside light, and went to sleep.

# CHAPTER 6

The following day was Tom's birthday. As Linda and Alexandra left Elmsbrook for another day, Alexandra dropped his card into The Lodge's letterbox. She would give him his present, when she saw him this evening. At the same time, she put their own dustbin outside of the hamlet gate, to be emptied today – a weekly job of hers, the second part of which would be done this evening, when she took it back up to The Grange, on her arrival back home.

At Charterhouse, during break time at 11.00, Alexandra went to the staff room, and asked for Mrs Wood. She was delighted to hear that Alexandra had decided to accept the nomination for college champion. There had been little doubt in her mind that, once Alexandra talked with her mother, she would be persuaded, anyhow. She told her that she would tell Mrs Spencer, as soon as possible, and that she would speak to her again during her next lesson, to discuss the plans for the concert. Then it would be over to her to begin organising it!

Alexandra left the staff room, shaking slightly with nerves, but also feeling a steely determination not to let all the people who were supporting her down.

One person who was not so delighted with the news though, was Elizabeth Spencer herself.

"You are aware that Gillian Spencer has already been nominated for the sciences, Annabel?" Elizabeth was asking Mrs Wood, in her study at lunch time.

"Yes of course, Elizabeth, but traditionally there are always two candidates, and ideally they are nominated 50-50, between the sciences and the arts. In fact, I believe that Alexandra was considered a possible candidate for the sciences, as well."

Elizabeth pursed her lips in frustration. It wasn't so much the competition to her daughter that bothered her. It was the *candidate*. Most unusually, she had been forced to fight for Gillian's selection as the sciences candidate, as the Head of that department had stated her preference for Alexandra. Her daughter had been furious to find that she was not automatically selected, as she had been used to taking whatever role she liked, during her time at Charterhouse. Eventually though, Elizabeth had got her way.

Now Alexandra was being nominated for the arts, and this time there was no way she could stop it. She desperately wanted Gillian to go to Castra as college champion, but she knew that Alexandra Radcliffe was a serious rival. Not only was she a very bright girl, like her own daughter, but she also had powerful backers.

Firstly, her mother was the stickler to tradition, Linda Radcliffe, who she despised, and who her husband worked with. She had become aware, through picking up on court gossip, during various liquid lunches with Geratican dignitaries, that the pair got on very well, and she was beginning to suspect that James found Linda desirable, and vice-versa. She simply couldn't bear the thought of Linda Radcliffe's daughter taking the glittering prize away from her own.

Alexandra was also highly popular with her mistresses, and was obviously now being heavily promoted by her music mistress, who also happened to be the head of department there. Not only that, but it now appeared that she was a protégé of Philippa Barrington, who even Elizabeth, who was clueless on the subject, realised was considered a major composer in Geratican history.

There was also the issue of Alexandra only being a day pupil, and therefore being a bit of an outsider. She came to Charterhouse to do her work, but she rarely stayed a moment after the official curriculum finished at 3.15, despite being sometimes invited to tea by some of the boarders, and she never got involved in any extra-curricular activities. Elizabeth thought that the award should go to someone who had got a broader experience of the college life, than Alexandra did.

"Oh very well then!" she said icily. "May the best girl win!"

***

At 3.15, Elizabeth watched from her study window, as Alexandra Radcliffe left Charterhouse as usual, to catch the train home. She noticed that today, she seemed to be particularly anxious to get away.

She stepped out of the study, and looked up the corridor. Her daughter was coming down it. She closed the door and walked up to meet her.

"Gillian!" she said. "Come and take tea at my house."

***

"Sit down," said Elizabeth, once they were inside. "I've got some bad news, I'm afraid."

She started making the tea and continued, "You now have a rival candidate for the title of college champion. It's Alexandra Radcliffe!"

"Radcliffe?" sneered Gillian. "She's no competition!"

"Don't be so quick to dismiss her, Gillian! She may be a mouse, but she's bright and her mother is Linda Radcliffe, who is a force to be reckoned with.

"It appears that Alexandra is now to receive private musical lessons from none other than Philippa Barrington, who I'm sure you're aware of. She went to a concert at the weekend, and I gather she was introduced to her backstage, where the offer was made. Now Mrs Wood, the head of music, has decided to get her to organise a music concert, based on Mrs Barrington's works, in which she'll perform on the piano, a la Philippa Barrington, and direct the college symphony orchestra. She'll be given complete freedom to produce the concert, as she sees fit."

"She'll never manage that!" scoffed Gillian. "I've never heard of such a ridiculous idea! Alexandra Radcliffe, directing? The whole thing will be a disaster. She couldn't organise a raffle!"

"Gillian," said Elizabeth." You're not listening to me. Now think girl! Alexandra Radcliffe may be a shy and nervous person, but her mother is anything but! She's famous throughout the queendom, for her administrative skills and she's the controlling force in Alexandra's life, make no mistake about that. What *Mrs* Radcliffe *says*, *Miss* Radcliffe *does*. She may not be able to have any *direct* influence over this proposed performance, but you can bet your life that she will do *indirectly*, behind the scenes. She'll be advising her what to do each day, before she comes in, of that I'm quite sure.

"Alexandra is also a very well liked person in this college, even if most people don't know her very well. There's something about her that people seem to warm to. Perhaps it's that sweet, innocent, unassuming charm that she displays sometimes. Whatever it is, people *will* pull together to help her with this, because it's that nice Alexandra Radcliffe!

"Add to that, the support of Mrs Wood, even before you get to the fact that she's receiving lessons from the very composer whose work she'll be showcasing, and I'd say that she has at least an even chance of pulling this off."

Gillian had stopped snorting. "Well?" she exclaimed indignantly, "So what if she does? Surely a mere concert recital can't be considered a more worthy contribution to Charterhouse, than my thesis and demonstration of

Geratica's crust and my speculation on its core?"

"I would agree with you Gillian, but when it comes to this award, I'm afraid it's the one thing that I cannot have any control over. It's decided independently. Unfortunately, we scientists sometimes have to accept that what *we* consider most interesting and worthy, isn't always shared by the ordinary person on the street. Art, in whatever form it takes, is usually considered beautiful, nice and interesting and maybe sometimes more easy to understand, than science, which is often considered dull, drab and boring. Of course when something goes wrong and they don't understand why, then they come running to us!"

Gillian was scowling now. "I won't let that Mummy's Girl win!" she seethed. "She's already embarrassed me once."

She beat the arm of the chair with her fist, as she went into a rant. "I simply will *not* let some upstart take over as the top cat around here! Especially not the wimpy mouse daughter of Linda Radcliffe. Those Radcliffes will take over Geratica, if we let them!"

Elizabeth was pleased to see this reaction in her daughter. It would help Gillian to do her bidding, which was what she wanted of her now.

"If you're angry Gillian," she said "then channel it into something that will help us both. And this is what I suggest ..."

***

Alexandra got home in a state of great excitement. She would soon be seeing Tom! She had checked The Lodge's letterbox, when she'd come through the hamlet gate, and his card had been collected. Then she had brought the emptied bin back up to The Grange.

As usual her mother phoned shortly after she arrived. Linda said that she'd be home before Tom arrived tonight, but she reminded her of the warning she'd given at the Geratica, and which she wanted passed on.

After they had said goodbye, Alexandra made the sandwiches that they were going to have for their supper tonight and put them in the fridge, then washed and dried her hair. She wanted to look beautiful for Tom, tonight.

Then she got on with her prep. By the time her mother arrived home, she was finished, and they ate their sandwiches in the dining room.

Tom arrived at 8.00 on the dot, and Alexandra was up from her chair, and out to the front porch, immediately after hearing the doorbell. Linda smiled to herself. They were clearly in love and she remembered how it had been between Robert and herself, when they had first got together. Much the same, if she was honest, even though they had been a little older. She had just reached twenty-one, with Robert coming up to the same age.

He had not been her first love, nor had she been a virgin (though Robert still had been one). She had been in a relationship previously, with Christopher, a miner, which had ended at his insistence. Particularly at that time, this went strictly against the traditional way of doing things. Relationships were taken extremely seriously on Geratica, and very often once a woman had proposed one to a man, the bond between them was so strong, that a further proposal of engagement or marriage, and then the actual union itself, unto death, almost inevitably followed. Most marriages were happy and divorce was rare. The failure of her first relationship, brief as it was, which been an engagement to be married, with a contract drawn up and signed, had caused her great heartache. It had taken all of her strength to endure the ordeal, and she had also felt a stigma. Once a contract was signed, the agreement was regarded as final and neither party – let alone *the man* - was expected to walk out of it. Before he left her, she'd horsewhipped him for it.

Linda had then met Robert, also a miner, who she'd married after almost two years of them being together, though she had waited some time before having Alexandra – at twenty-nine. Linda and Robert had by then, been comfortably off, and Linda had already in 4994, brought The Grange (worth 500,000 geros at the time) in the hamlet of Elmsbrook, on the outskirts of the town of Greenacres. As well as being a quiet and relaxing retreat after a long, hard day's work for both Robert and her, they'd been able to bring their daughter up in a peaceful, secluded environment. Just three years after Alexandra's birth, she had climbed the career ladder to the pinnacle of Court Administrator, in 4998. At her urging, Robert had eventually left the mine and gone to work for one of the new oil platforms, that were starting to operate in the Geranda Ocean. (Since the discovery of oil under the ocean bed in 4995, at Court she had been one of the major proponents of its usage, as a potentially rich source of technological and financial reward for the Queendom and its economy. This had turned out to be prescient).

Then of course, when Alexandra was five, and they had been married for nearly twelve years, and together in total for getting close to fourteen, Robert had died in tragic circumstances, causing her even more grief, and taking her to the well, to find strength. Linda was aware that many people considered her to have been grievously unlucky in her personal relationships, and she didn't disagree, but also, always liked to point out that she still was lucky enough to have her daughter, whose moulding by her, into the character that she was now, she considered her finest achievement.

Alexandra brought Tom into the dining room, and Linda got up and shook his hand as she greeted him warmly, and wished him a happy birthday.

"So, you're my potential son-in-law are you? Well, my daughter could have chosen worse! Seriously though, Tom, I couldn't be happier. Congratulations!"

"Thank you, Mrs Radcliffe," replied Tom, politely. "I think I'll be happy with you as a potential mother-in-law, too!"

"Well, I won't keep you both," said Linda. "I know that Alexandra is desperate to put on a fashion show for you, so off you go. I'm making a cup of coffee for Alexandra and me. Do you want a drink, Tom?"

"Oh. Yes, please, Mrs Radcliffe. A black coffee will be fine for me, thank you."

"Three black coffees it is then," said Linda, and went through to the kitchen.

Alexandra took Tom's hand and led him up to her bedroom, where she kissed him.

First of all, she gave him his card and present.

"I've never worn a bow tie before," he said. "I don't know how to tie it!"

"Well," said Alexandra. "I'm sure we can find out, and Mother is bound to know. We could ask her when you come at the weekend, and we're dressed up. Remember to bring it with you."

"Speaking of Mother, there's something I've been ordered to tell you Tom. It's actually a warning from her, to both of us."

"What about?"

Alexandra took a deep breath. "We're both to remember that we're below the age of consent, until we're sixteen, and we are not allowed to have sex until then. If we do and she finds out – which she will – it won't be tolerated, no matter what reason or excuse we give. We'll both be severely punished, which is bound to involve the cane, and I in particular, will get more than the standard dosage, at least double, and possibly even a horse whipping, too. All contact with you will be suspended, until Mother restores it, after however long it takes for her to think that I've learnt my lesson. She was *extremely* assertive about this, Tom, even for her, and she left me in no doubt about how serious an issue this is, and to regard what she'd said, as a formal warning. As I said just now, I was ordered to pass this on to you, so now I have."

There was a knock on the door. "Alexandra. Room service. Are you decent? Can I come in?"

Alexandra giggled. "Yes, it's alright Mother!" she called. "We're just talking at the moment."

Linda opened the door and entered. "I thought you'd be halfway through your gowns by now," she said, as she crossed the room to set the tray down on her daughter's dressing table. As she was retracing her steps, Alexandra took her hand and made eye contact. A few seconds later, she had communicated to her mother the subject that she had just been discussing. Linda gave a discreet nod of acknowledgement.

Before she left the room, she glanced at them both. "It's alright, Tom," she said. "I promise you won't get a lecture like that, every time you come here! But you need to know how seriously this matter will be regarded, even though I hope it isn't necessary to spell out to two sensible young people like you, what the possible consequences of such a rash and foolish act might be. They could impact on all of us, and you would regret it for the rest of your lives. I really don't expect to be discussing this subject again."

She stood in the doorway. "That's it. Enjoy the rest of your evening together!" Linda closed the door and went back downstairs.

Tom's reaction was much the same as Philippa's had been at the theatre, three nights ago. He gaped at the door, and then back at Alexandra, who couldn't help but smile at his bewilderment.

"How did she know what you were saying?" he demanded. "Was she listening at the door, or something?"

"No, of course not!" laughed Alexandra. "I let her know, just then, after she'd given us the coffee."

"*What?*" Tom exclaimed, even more confused. "How?"

"We can, if we want to, communicate without words. It can come in useful at times, particularly if we're in a situation where we can't talk in the normal way, or we need to be discreet."

"You mean you're *telepathic*?"

"No, it's not like that, exactly," replied Alexandra. "I'm not going to give away our secrets! It's quite intimate and I'm not sure if I could explain quite *how* we do it, anyhow, but we do. Mother is especially good – as she is at most things – she can read me like a book. That's why I can never lie to her. I can't keep anything from her. Maybe that's why she started us doing it! As far as I know, this is a purely private thing between us, which nobody else does, anywhere. Obviously, I think you'd need to be very close to someone, to be able to do it, and there is a very strong bond between Mother and myself."

"Do you think we could do it?" asked Tom.

"Possibly. I'd hope so anyway, given what you are to me. I'll have a think about it and maybe seek Mother's opinion."

"Anyhow," said Tom, "I was going to say that of course we wouldn't do that, until we're older. I can see I'm going to be kept in line. Anyone would think that I was your mother's son!"

"Well, like she said," laughed Alexandra, "it won't always be like that! But you know what she's like. If she wants something made clear, then she makes sure that it is. Now that we're in an official relationship, she's probably thinking that there's every chance of you becoming her son-in-law, so in a way you're becoming family!

"I must say, Tom, that if – as I hope – we do eventually marry and share a home of our own, although I'll be running things then, when Mother is around, she will expect her advice to be listened to. I'm sure that in that situation, when it really comes down to it, she'll let us go in whichever direction we – or I – want, but she will be trying to guide us the way *she* thinks we should go, and she'll be hoping that we follow. And most definitely, when we're in her house, it will be her who is the boss, and not me!"

"You mean, she's going to be a 'back seat driver'!" exclaimed Tom.

"Well, I suppose you could put it like that, but that may just be unavoidable, and I should think knowing her as you do, you more or less expected that, when you agreed to become my boyfriend! And truthfully, I won't mind, to a large extent. Remember that her role with me has often been to tell me what to do – and I've always liked that. She won't want to withdraw from that role, completely."

"Anyhow," she continued, picking up the tray from her dressing table, "take your coffee and relax, and I'll get things started!"

After taking a large sip of her own, she went to her music player and started it up, then opened her wardrobe.

As the music began to play quietly in the background, she said softly, "OK, Tom, *my darling*, these are the gowns. You just listen to the music, and I'll put the first one on for you! Smiling sweetly at him, as he sat on her bed, she went into her bathroom to change.

Tom indicated his approval, as she emerged and walked around the room like a model on a catwalk, enjoying herself as she gave a twirl, and posed for him.

She repeated the process for each gown, and was delighted to note the pleasure on Tom's face, and the look in his eyes, that clearly betrayed his sexual arousal. She was becoming 'turned on' too!

Although Alexandra hadn't consciously followed her mother's advice, the last of the gowns did in fact turn out to be her favourite. After finishing showing herself off in it, she changed back, and then came to the moment of truth.

After wearing each one, she had placed it on Tom's lap, so that he now had four gowns resting there. Alexandra came to the bed and sat next to him. Running her fingers lightly down his arms, she asked softly, "Well, *my darling*, have you made a decision? Do you have a favourite?"

Tom took a final look at them all. "They're all fantastic, and you looked gorgeous in every one!" he began.

Alexandra beamed. "Thank you!" she said.

"But, having to choose one, maybe it would be the last one ..."

Alexandra's heart leapt. "Tom, you *sweetie!*" she cried. "That's mine too! It's uncanny how are tastes are so often the same! That's one of the many reasons why I love you so much!"

She took the gowns off his lap and placed them to his side. Then she pushed him onto his back and went down on him on the bed. For the first time in her life she was lying on top of a boy, and it was Tom, the one she had always wanted it to be! She smothered his lips, and kissed them softly, whilst she pressed herself deep into his body. Her thighs tingled beneath her skirt, and she wrapped her legs and arms around him, and squeezed. Her geratis throbbed in her pants, and Tom felt it between his thighs. Ecstasy filled all of Alexandra's senses as she felt more pleasure than ever before, and Tom softly sighed with his own pleasure beneath her. Her geratis strained over the hole of Tom's vagina, wanting to connect with it, and the ecstasy increased still further. Her breath became heavy, and she sighed deeply. Alexandra felt a dampness in her pants and realised that she'd released a small emission. Instinctively, she could tell that they'd reached the point where they could go no further, without her entering Tom, and making love to him. She stopped, rolled off him, and lay panting by his side, as she got her breathing back under control.

"*I love you, Tom, my darling!*" she whispered.

"*I love you, Alexandra!*" Tom whispered back.

They kissed again.

Then Alexandra retrieved her book that she'd been given by Philippa Barrington and proudly showed it to her boyfriend.

"It's beautiful," he said. "And very special, too. You must be very proud."

"Definitely" Alexandra assured him. "I'll treasure it for always."

Eventually they went back downstairs to re-join Linda, before Tom left.

"Well, has the big decision for the weekend been made?" she asked.

"Yes, Mother," replied Alexandra.

Linda said no more about the subject, until Tom had departed. Then she asked her daughter, "Well, which one did he choose then?"

"The one that I wore last weekend, actually, Mother."

Linda smiled in triumph. "I knew it!" she said. "You followed my advice, to leave your favourite to the end, so that it would be freshest in his mind, when he decided. You did try to influence him, didn't you?"

"Yes, Mother!" said her daughter. It was certainly at least half true. She had worn that gown last. Whether she had indeed been trying to manipulate the situation, she wasn't sure, but Alexandra decided that, for the moment, she would let her mother think so, anyhow.

# CHAPTER 7

At Charterhouse the following morning, once assembly was over, the day began as usual, with daily exercise around the yard. To Alexandra's slight alarm, the headmistress seemed to pick out her name more often than usual for chastisement, concerning her level of effort, which puzzled her. She could sense Gillian smirking at her discomfort, not far away.

The first period of the day was the weekly tutorial. As they waited in the classroom for their form mistress to arrive, Gillian asked one of her usual questions to the other girls, at this time of the week.

"Do any of you girls want to get some 'drama lessons', after tea this afternoon?"

As was also usual, one of the girls, Melanie Patterson, who was friendly with Gillian, said "yes," but the others ignored the offer, feeling slightly embarrassed.

"Are you in with us, Mouse?" demanded Gillian. This was her nickname for Alexandra, due to her quiet and shy nature.

Alexandra was well aware of what these 'drama lessons', actually were. Gillian Spencer had been the first girl in the year to lose her virginity – something she was insufferably pleased with herself about – and she had done it by walking out of the school one day, bunking off a double period of History, and visiting a massage parlour. In one of her most audacious money-making schemes, she had then arranged for two of the boys who worked there, to visit Charterhouse twice a week, in the guise of actors, for any of the girls who wanted to see them. Incredibly, so it seemed to Alexandra, not one of the staff seemed to realise what these men really were. They were Gillian's official guests, and no questions were asked. Once safely ensconced in her chambers, the girls could 'break their duck', as Gillian put it, and if they liked it, could carry on seeing them as many times as they liked, providing they paid the fee demanded by the parlour, which Gillian had negotiated at a reduced rate, to take into account their non-earning status. Many of the Charterhouse girls received handsome allowances from their mothers each week, but the normal rates were still a little out of their league, at present. Gillian received a percentage of the takings, which again she had negotiated for herself.

Despite the reduced rate however, in order to gain sufficient funds for their exploits, the girls taking part (in fact by then just Gillian and Melanie), began visiting local retailers and shoplifted goods, which they then sold on at exorbitant prices, to the other girls at the college, during lunchtime.

Alexandra was amazed that *any* of the girls would get involved in seeing escort boys. Her mother would go *ballistic* if she ever thought her daughter had been a part of it.

"No thank you, Spencer," she replied to Gillian. (The girls generally called each other by their first names, but Gillian insisted on addressing them all by their surnames and for them to use hers also.) "I have to get to the station to get my train home, after we finish the daily curriculum."

"Yeah, well of course we all know you're a Mummy's Girl, Radcliffe," said Gillian sarcastically. "I heard you were leaving in a bit of a hurry yesterday night, too."

"It was actually my boyfriend's birthday yesterday, and I was seeing him last night, so I obviously didn't want to be late."

Gillian was momentarily caught off guard, and the others stared at her. "*You've* got a *boyfriend?*" she said incredulously. "I don't believe it. You're just trying to impress us!"

"I swear to you it's true, Spencer," replied Alexandra.

"Who is it then?" Gillian demanded.

"His name's Tom, and he lives in the house at the other end of our hamlet," Alexandra told her.

"Tom Ryder? I've heard of him. He's the son of the woman your mother works with, isn't he?"

"His stepmother actually, but yes, that's otherwise correct."

Gillian smirked at the others. "Well, well, well! Who would have thought it? Mouse is the first to get a boy! I'm surprised she had it in her to propose a relationship!" She looked back at Alexandra and sneered, "Or did your mother do it for you?"

"No, she certainly did not, Spencer!" said Alexandra indignantly. "It was all my own effort."

Gillian smirked again. "I should have thought you'd want to come to the 'drama lessons' then. You'll need to learn what to do, before you go to bed together, and I'll bet Tom will have to go on top, even then! You haven't got a dominant bone in your body. You could never give a man one, let alone two or three a night, like most normal women!"

A couple of the other girls sniggered, and Alexandra went scarlet, both with embarrassment and indignation at Gillian's contempt for her likely ability in the bedroom – a grave insult to a Geratican woman, particularly from one to another. Gillian knew that several of the girls present would probably have started a fight with her for being so rude to them, but she had a certain amount of confidence that Alexandra wouldn't be one of them.

Just then though, their form mistress, Miss Ford came in. "Alright, quiet now girls!" she ordered, as she took off her black gown, placed it over the back of her chair and sat down. Everyone turned their attention to the first period of the day, much to Alexandra's relief.

The tutorial period was mainly just for any administrative work to be caught up on, and also an opportunity to discuss anything that had come up over the previous week. This morning the subject was Queen Alexandra's address to Castra University, which they had heard on the radio in edited format, at lunchtime on 1/33/10.

Generally, the girls' reaction was favourable, and at least in this class, there was no serious contention with the idea of Castra opening up to a wider demographic. The only one to take any serious issue with a part of the address was Gillian, who naturally enough, Alexandra thought, asserted her mother's line over the education of boys. Alexandra had been observing her carefully, throughout the discussion.

"How about you, Alexandra?" asked Miss Ford. "You've not said anything. What did you think?"

Alexandra hated being put on the spot like this, but she was becoming more confident in her ability to make intelligent, reasoned statements, and on this subject she was quite well informed, so she answered as best that she could.

"It's difficult for me to be objective Miss Ford, as obviously it was my mother who wrote the address, but I genuinely think that it set the right balance and tone, and I know that she felt it generally seemed to have been received quite well."

One of the girls sitting near her, Benita Davis, sounded surprised. "What? You mean that Queen Alexandra doesn't write her own speeches?" she asked.

"Oh, no. Obviously, she has the final say over the finished draft, and she wouldn't say anything that she really didn't believe or mean, but her speeches are prepared for her, and my mother does indeed draft most of them. Sorry if any of you didn't realise that."

"You twat, Davis!" said Gillian. "That's what her officials around her are there for!"

In fact, Benita was probably the girl that Alexandra felt closest to at Charterhouse. She knew that she was by no means a "twat."

"Perhaps Miss Ford, we should have a Tutorial devoted to the workings of the royal court, and Radcliffe could give us all a talk on the subject?" suggested Gillian, slyly.

"Thank you Gillian," said the mistress. "That might be an idea for the future."

Gillian nodded in acknowledgement, and Alexandra felt a stab of dread inside of her. Giving a talk to the rest of the class was one of her ultimate nightmares, and what was more, she knew that Gillian Spencer was well aware of it.

The period eventually finished, and Alexandra went off to her next lesson – geography.

Meanwhile, Gillian also resolved to tell her mother about Mrs Radcliffe's opinion of the reaction to the address that she had written, *and* that Alexandra now appeared to have a boyfriend, at break time.

\*\*\*

Once Gillian had arrived at her mother's study later though, she found her in a deep fury.

"I've had a letter from that blasted Linda Radcliffe, on behalf of the queen, telling me *'the official court position'* on the subject of the planet's core!" she fumed. "In a nutshell, she says that, after considering the scientific evidence, the court has decided that we should try to reach the core, but that it's still too dangerous at the moment. We will only go there when we're totally ready, and once there, *if* we *do* make any adjustments, then it will only be to repair the schism that prevents the Divine Being from acting as she intended and even then, only if it's considered safe to do it. Not to change our race's basic characteristics, which Her Majesty believes she intended for us to have. She finishes by saying that Her Majesty hopes that this settles the matter!"

"How does she know what the Divine Being intended? I don't care if she *is* the queen of Geratica! She doesn't know it, any more than I do! We can't know that for certain, until we go down and find out. That's the whole point! And how much longer are we expected to wait, before we finally feel confident enough to do it? Ten years? Fifty? Five Hundred?"

As Elizabeth thought about the kind of traits that she'd like men to have, as a result of altering the gender balance between the sexes, her geratis became aroused. Quite apart from the politics which she was passionate about, it also turned her on sexually.

When Gillian told her the news that she had learnt, about Linda Radcliffe's apparent opinion of the reaction to the address Queen Alexandra had given two days ago, Elizabeth glared at her. "*Mrs* Radcliffe might be holding sway at court at the moment, but regardless of that subject - I'm darned if she's also going to stop me from getting my daughter to Castra, as champion of Charterhouse! Step up your efforts, as I suggested yesterday, Gillian ..."

# CHAPTER 8

That evening, at The Grange, Alexandra got straight on with her prep. She had actually done some of it in the prep room at Charterhouse, whilst she ate her sandwiches during the lunch break, to save some time tonight. Before her mother was home, Alexandra had a telephone call. As she suspected, the screen flickered into life, and it was Philippa Barrington at the gate of Elmsbrook. She pressed the button to open it, and Philippa drove up to the house.

Alexandra showed her into the parlour, and offered her refreshment. She made them both a coffee, and put some biscuits on a plate, and took it all into the room, on a tray.

She felt quite nervous, as this was her first session, but as they began talking, she began to relax. Philippa liked her, and was already confident that she could mould Alexandra into an exceptionally accomplished piano player.

"I know that you've been asked to give a concert of my work, with the college symphony orchestra, for an evening at Charterhouse," she said.

"Yes. You obviously must have known last weekend! I've agreed to do it, although I'll admit, I'm feeling rather daunted by the prospect – not to mention scared to death!"

"Oh good. I'm glad that you accepted the invitation," said Philippa. "I'm sure you do feel very nervous about it, and I know that you aren't a naturally confident girl, but you'll have a good solid team behind you – and that will include me! There's no reason why you shouldn't succeed."

"I suppose not," said Alexandra, her voice betraying her uncertainty. "But I really hate being an organiser, and telling other girls what I think they should do, let alone perform in public at the end of it. It's as if my worst nightmares are all coming at once!"

"Well, I'm sure I'm not alone Alexandra, in believing that your mother is going to play an important role for, in helping you with the organisation, behind the scenes. It will have to *be* behind the scenes, as it's got to be seen officially, as all your own work, but she'll be giving you plenty of advice. You're very lucky to have her, so take that as a positive."

"Yes, I know. My mother's already promised to help me all she can, and I know that she's my best asset. Mother herself is always teaching me that I should use my assets wisely, to my advantage, to help me succeed. She's always been the strong one who leads for both of us, and I'm going to rely on her a lot, whilst I'm doing this, and she says that I can."

There you are then, you're halfway there," said Philippa. "Now, as far as the performance is concerned, I'm in charge of your preparation, and your mother is paying me good money to do it, so let's get to work!"

\*\*\*

A few minutes later, Linda arrived home. She heard the chords from the piano, being played in the parlour, and popped her head around the door. Philippa and Alexandra were busy in practice, and her daughter was so deep in concentration, sleeves pushed to the elbows, that she almost didn't notice her mother standing there.

However, after she did, she stopped immediately and smiled. "Hello Mother!" she said warmly.

"Hello darling," said Linda, as she came into the room, and over to the piano. She leant over her daughter as she sat on her piano stool, and Alexandra lifted her head and reached upwards, offering herself to her mother. Linda wrapped her arms around her, squeezed her tight, and gave her a big long kiss, which Alexandra returned as she gazed lovingly up into her mother's eyes.

Philippa Barrington could clearly see the affection held between the mother and daughter, and this only confirmed further, her belief that Linda Radcliffe was of crucial importance to Alexandra Radcliffe's confidence in achieving her goal.

"Good evening, Philippa," said Linda, as she looked over to the other side of the piano, where the composer had pulled up a chair.

"Good evening Linda," replied Philippa.

"Well, I see you're busy and have both got drinks, so I'll leave you to it," said Linda. "I'll be in the kitchen getting our dinner ready, if you need me, and there should be a delivery from the supermarket in a minute, too, so I hope that won't disturb you too much." She went out, and Philippa and Alexandra continued from where they had been.

\*\*\*

Just as Linda had said, the supermarket delivery arrived about 15 minutes later. She let the lorry through the gate, and up to The Grange, then went out and supervised the dispatch, checking everything that came off, against her order, and directing where it should be placed inside the house, before finally paying the driver, once she was satisfied that all was in order.

Later on, after Philippa had departed, and Alexandra was finishing her prep, as her mother got the dinner, there was another ring on the telephone. The Grange was quite a large house, but although there was some distance between the study and the kitchen, Alexandra could clearly hear her mother's exasperation at the interruption at this particular moment, to her cooking.

"Who in all of Geratica is that, phoning right on dinner time!" she exclaimed. Then she shouted down to the study, "I hope that's not Tom for you, Alexandra!"

Alexandra crossed her fingers that it wasn't. She readied herself to be told by her mother, to answer the phone instead of her, but to her relief, the extension was picked up in the breakfast room. She saw that it wasn't The Lodge, when she looked at the display on the study phone, anyhow. Then she heard her mother say, "Oh. Hello Judith. I'm actually just cooking the dinner, but come on up anyway."

"Alexandra, could you come here a moment please, darling?" she called.

"Yes, Mother," said Alexandra obediently.

"Darling I want you to look after the dinner for me, for a few minutes," said her mother as she entered the breakfast room. "Judith is coming up to get her quarterly bill paid. She does have a habit of calling at the most inconvenient of times, but I don't like to delay these things. Anyhow, the dinner will be ready soon, so just keep an eye on it, and keep it simmering, until I've finished with her. Is that clear?"

"Crystal clear, Mother," said Alexandra.

The doorbell rang. "Right. See you in a tick. Linda went and let Judith in. They went through to the study and Linda checked the quarterly bill against her weekly accounts. Once again satisfied, she paid Judith the money.

"Judith," she said. "Maybe it would be a good idea for you to put the bill in my letterbox, from now onwards. It gets checked every day, and then I could sort the bill out, and send Alexandra down with the money. It would be fairly prompt, I can assure you. I've never had a reputation for keeping my Creditors waiting!"

Judith's standard practice, was to take payment face-to-face, to try and ensure prompt payment – and also to provide a human contact style of service, as all her customers were local – and this approach usually produced good results, but as this was Linda Radcliffe, her most esteemed customer, she decided that she could make an exception for her.

"Oh yes, Mrs Radcliffe. That will do fine, if that's what you'd prefer."

"OK then, Judith. Right, well I'll look forward to receiving your next bill in the letterbox, in 5011!" replied Linda.

She showed her out, and then went back to the kitchen. Alexandra was then appraised of the new arrangement.

"I should have done this before, but other things have always taken priority," said Linda. "She's always calling at a time that's really awkward for me, so now there'll be no need for her to do so at all! Thank you for looking after the dinner for me, sweetheart." She kissed her daughter's forehead.

"That's OK, Mother," said Alexandra.

Linda watched the monitor, ready to let Judith out of Elmsbrook. Then she and her daughter sat down to have their dinner.

# CHAPTER 9

On Day 4, Gillian once again asked Alexandra if she was interested in the 'drama lessons' and once again Alexandra declined.

Gillian now decided that it was now going to be nigh on impossible to tempt Alexandra to indulge in this activity, particularly as it now also appeared that she had an official boyfriend. So tomorrow, she would strike with the 'heavy' treatment.

In her music history lesson, Mrs Wood talked with Alexandra about her first steps in organising the concert. She advised her to select a board of girls who could deal with the administrative side of things, whilst she concentrated on working with the symphony orchestra, and her own private tuition. Alexandra agreed warily and decided that she'd talk to her mother again tonight.

\*\*\*

After dinner that night, with her prep finished, Alexandra sat down with her mother in the study. First, Linda informed her that James would be coming over for dinner with them tomorrow night. The official reason was that, as Linda was going to be hosting a dinner party on the evening of Day 5, next week, which Queen Alexandra was attending, and James would be chauffeuring her to, Linda needed to discuss some confidential matters with him, which couldn't be done at the palace. But this was just a 'front.'

Then they discussed the matter at hand. Linda made some notes on her pad, in front of her.

"Basically," she said, "You need to think of some people who you feel you can trust to do a good job, and not let you down, and if you get on with them, then that would be even better. You'll need somebody who can deal with the book-keeping side of things, to decide on the financial matters, someone who can handle the retail and distribution, i.e. the ticket sales and the refreshments etc. on the night, and someone who can do the marketing to promote it. I'm sure you'd be good at the first, yourself, but you'd be best served finding someone else to do it on a regular basis, so that you'll have time to concentrate on the concert itself.

"Once you've got them in place, the first thing you should do is to think of some kind of fundraising activity that you could encourage the pupils to participate in, so that you can get as much cash in the kitty as possible to fund the concert. Your marketing and retail people should liaise to think of something suitable.

"The other thing I would say to you, Alexandra, is that although you need to keep an overall eye on the whole operation, you must try and delegate the responsibilities for the organisation, as much as possible, so that you've got maximum time to devote to liaising with the symphony orchestra, and to the concert. You'll be practising with Philippa anyhow, so you could decide together on exactly what you might perform, and establish a 'running order,' and then it'll be a matter of holding rehearsals, and obviously, eventually a dress-rehearsal.

"But, first things first. Do you have an idea of who you could bring in to help you with the various responsibilities?"

Alexandra thought about it. "Well, not Gillian Spencer, ideally, Mother, but I think most of the rest of my form are fairly reliable. But I'm not sure who exactly to choose for what."

"I'll make a suggestion to you," said Linda. "Write a letter, inviting applications for the posts, and copy it to all the people who you think are suitable. Then see who's interested. *Hopefully* you'll get at least three responses, and they'll be the ones you'll go with. You'll have to sort out who's best for what, and if you should get more than three, you'd have to decide between some of them, but cross those bridges when you come to them. See what happens first."

"Are you saying I should interview them, Mother?"

"Well no, I don't imagine that will be necessary, unless you should be swamped with applicants, and bear in mind that you'll need to get on with this fairly quickly, if you're to get it staged before the Festival of Divinity – which is obviously a must. You'll probably just need to go with what turns up, and to a degree, hope for the best. My advice to you and your board members, once you've established who they're going to be, would be to sort out between yourselves, immediately, who does what role."

"OK Mother. I'll distribute a letter."

"Well let's get it written then," said Linda. "Then we'll copy it, and you can get it circulated tomorrow. I'm sure that you're more than capable of doing it yourself, but to save time, would you like me to dictate something to you, and then you could type it? Without wishing to boast, you'll be getting the benefit of an 'expert's' assistance!"

"Oh, yes please, Mother!" said her daughter.

So, after Alexandra had taken her own notepad and pen from her desk,

Linda rattled off a letter in no time, which Alexandra gratefully took down. Her mother was taking control, just as her headmistress had predicted to *her* daughter.

# CHAPTER 10

The following day, as Alexandra arrived at Charterhouse, she placed letters in the mailboxes of three of her form class, and one from her music class. The ones she left out from her form class, were Gillian Spencer and her closest partner in crime, Melanie Patterson, who Alexandra knew would not be on her side. Now it would just be a question of waiting for the responses. She desperately hoped that at least three would agree to help her, and that they would be able to fulfil the individual roles that she'd need from them.

\*\*\*

At break time, Alexandra had just entered the yard to stretch her legs before the next period, Geratican Literature, when she was suddenly shoved to the side, and dragged around a corner, by two large girls. As she was brought to a stop, she stood face-to-face with Gillian Spencer and Melanie Patterson. Gillian's arms were folded, and she smiled coldly.

"Well, well, well, Mouse! We meet once again in these circumstances!" she said, sarcastically. "I'll come straight to the point, and repeat one more time, what I asked you yesterday – though I don't expect the answer to be any different. Are you in for the 'drama lessons', or not?"

"*Not,* Spencer!" replied Alexandra. She didn't care what Gillian did to her, there was no way she was going to get mixed up in that.

"Yeah, as I said, I thought as much. Well, Radcliffe, it's your lucky day! I'm not going to have you winded like last time, but nor am I going to make you do it, either!" She smirked. "But what I am going to *insist* upon, is that you help my friend and I with a spot of shoplifting at lunch time. We need some goods to flog, to get more cash."

Alexandra looked at her in alarm. "No!" she cried.

"I told you, I insist, Mouse! You must do this, to make up for not accepting my offer. Think of it as payment. The boys are coming again this afternoon, so I'll give you one last, simple choice. And you must decide now. It's either meeting one of them this afternoon, once the normal curricular activities are completed, or going out with Melanie and me at lunchtime. Or else you *will* get a thumping. Which will it be?"

Alexandra shuddered and started to panic. She was more than a little scared of Gillian, if the truth was known.

Gillian had insulted her, by deriding her likely sexual abilities, and Alexandra suspected she had done it, largely because she genuinely thought it was true, but also to try and goad her into attempting to prove otherwise. The comment had hurt her, and brought back some of her earlier insecurities. When it really came to it, would she be able to make love to a man? Fantasy was sometimes very different from reality. Alexandra certainly felt passion for things – and Tom was top of the list – but it didn't seem to burn inside of her *quite* as fiercely as it did in a lot of Geratican women. She actually had quite strong willpower to resist temptation, too.

Gillian's boast was always that she had, 'given him one, three times, straight off,' during her hour at the parlour. Alexandra wasn't a very physically strong girl (which didn't really bother her) and she couldn't imagine herself having the stamina to make love to Tom more than once at a time. Perhaps Gillian was right. But again, she was aware that was unusual for a Geratican woman.

Alexandra had no desire to go with an escort boy, and she knew her mother would horsewhip her if she found out that she had. It would mean missing her train (the next wasn't due until forty-five minutes later) and arriving late home. Her mother would find out that she was later at least, when she wasn't there to receive her call (and also be home earlier on this night of the week, in any case). If she was later than permitted home, it would then mean a punishment, and a plausible reason for being late would have to be found. In any case, if she *did* go with an escort boy, and then 'couldn't manage it', which she thought was highly possible, given how nervous she'd be, then Gillian would have a field day if she found out – and Alexandra was sure that she would do, somehow – she might even be watching.

That option simply wasn't on, but neither could she face getting a thumping today, either. She couldn't see any other way out of this. She would have to accept the second choice. With a feeling of dread and guilt, she asked Gillian, "What time are you going out at lunchtime?"

Gillian smiled triumphantly. "Meet us at the front entrance, when the bell goes!" she ordered. "But before then ... you must perform an initiation task first, if you're to take part in one of our activities!" She pulled out a black marker pen from her blazer pocket. "Before the next period starts, after break time, write on the classroom wall, 'Miss Hick is Thick'." She held out the pen. "In fact, do it right now and we'll be right behind, watching you!"

Alexandra gulped and took the pen. Then they went to their next lesson, Geratican literature.

***

Alexandra was shaking as she went into the classroom, closely followed by Gillian, Melanie and her two heavies. There was no one else there at the moment. She took off her blazer and put it over the back of the chair, by her usual desk and pulled up her sleeves. She hated herself for what she was going to have to do, both now, and at lunch time, but hopefully, if she could just manage to make it through, it might get Gillian off her back for a while. Quickly, before the bell rang and the others came in, she selected a spot which she hoped Miss Hick would be least likely to spot during the lesson, and sprawled the offensive statement on the wall, in capital letters, trying to disguise her handwriting as much as possible. She wrote as small as she could, whilst at the same time trying to make it big enough to be acceptable to Gillian. Then she turned and held out the pen for Gillian to retrieve.

Gillian smiled wickedly. She'd wondered whether Alexandra really would do it, and she had to admit that Radcliffe had guts, considering that she had most likely, never done anything like that before. She'd passed the test. Gillian had considered getting her to write something on the music block wall, about Mrs Wood, but she had decided that Alexandra would be highly unlikely to agree to that, given her current obligations.

"I'll take that back – *after* the lesson!" she replied.

Alexandra shuddered again. She hoped desperately that the writing wasn't discovered, until at least after the lesson. If it was, and she still had the pen in her possession, it would increase her chances of being exposed as the guilty party. She'd have to hope that they wouldn't be ordered to open their desks, and turn out their pockets, for inspection.

Then the bell rang and Gillian's two heavies, who were not part of this class, left. The three remaining girls went to their desks, and sat down.

Alexandra spent the next 45 minutes in a cold sweat and they seemed to last forever, but eventually the bell rang again at midday, telling the girls to go to their final period of the morning, which for Alexandra was Music practical. Outside the Geratican literature classroom, Alexandra handed Gillian back the marker pen. "See you at lunch time then, Radcliffe!" said Gillian, and she and Melanie went away.

Normally, Alexandra enjoyed her next lesson, but today, given what she was going to do at lunchtime, she felt a knot in her stomach and, most unusually, found it difficult to concentrate. Mrs Wood did ask her if she had made a start on her preparations for the concert and Alexandra told her that she had put letters of invitation for the various roles on the planned board, in some of the girls' mailboxes, and that she was waiting for their responses.

***

At lunchtime, Alexandra put on her blazer, and went to collect her coat from the cupboard in her form room. Then, with her bag over her shoulder, she made her way to the main gates, as Gillian had told her to, nibbling on a sandwich as she walked.

Gillian was there, already waiting for her, along with Melanie. "Are you ready then, Mouse?" she asked chillingly, another huge smirk on her face. "Even now, it's actually not too late for you to turn back and go with an escort boy instead this afternoon, after all. We'll go and do this without you. Although I'll call you a chicken! And don't you dare grass on us either, or I'll definitely thump you!"

Alexandra had never been friendly with Melanie either. She always struck her as not the brightest spark in the box, and Alexandra suspected that she attached herself to Gillian to try and make herself look big. She was quiet like herself, but when she spoke, Alexandra seldom heard anything of any great significance, emanating from her mouth.

"Let's just get on with it, Spencer," she said. "And by the way, this is a one-off. You said nothing about any future involvement of me, in your seedy operations. We'll be even then."

Gillian was slightly surprised. Radcliffe was standing up for herself, better than she had expected. (In fact Alexandra had surprised herself too). She grinned, led the way out of the gates, and they slipped away down a side road.

***

They went into Rimmingtons, one of the most exclusive of Geratica's high street stores, and Gillian led them to the perfumery department.

"Right Radcliffe!" ordered Gillian. "You do the work, and we'll keep watch. Swipe as much of this stuff as you can into your bag, in thirty seconds!" Gillian looked up at the security camera above the floor and reaching up, stretched out a long arm, and placed a strip of black cloth over the lens. This was her standard trick. By the time the store's security realised that something was wrong, they would have done the job and left, and Gillian adjudged that about sixty seconds was long enough, before the alarm would be raised, and they could be caught getting away.

Alexandra shook with nerves, but began to do as Gillian said. She had slipped three things into her bag, when suddenly there was an almighty commotion.

A woman's voice shouted out, "There she is! Stop her!" and a group of security guards rushed over to Alexandra and grabbed her by the arms. The woman – the store detective – then said, "Officers, this girl has been caught trying to steal goods from this store!" Two policewomen then promptly arrested Alexandra, and there then followed a flash of light, as some photographers' cameras snapped pictures of the occurrence. She looked around, but Gillian and Melanie were nowhere to be seen.

"Come with us to the station please, Miss," said one of the officers and Alexandra felt a terrible dread, as she was dragged away and realised to her horror, that she was now in a lot of trouble.

***

The other two girls raced back to Charterhouse, and Gillian went straight to her mother's study. Elizabeth was on the phone when she got there.

"I've got some news!" said Gillian excitedly, as she hung up.

"I know what you're going to tell me," said her mother. "Alexandra Radcliffe's just been arrested for shoplifting in Rimmingtons! I won't ask for details, but I assume the fact that the police were there so quickly, and the presence of the press, was *your* doing?"

Gillian folded her arms and smirked. "Yes!" she said. "I made a couple of phone calls, just before lunch, telling them that the daughter of someone in a prominent position at court, might be planning to do something rather naughty at Rimmingtons! They couldn't help but be interested! *And* earlier on, after break time, I – *persuaded* – her to write a rude message on the wall, before our Geratican Literature lesson. 'Miss Hick is Thick' to be precise!"

"Excellent work, Gillian!" said Elizabeth. "Now I can suspend her, and she'll surely have to go before a court to answer a charge soon, which will inevitably get a good deal of publicity. She cannot possibly be considered for college champion now, and there'll be no one else who can challenge you, like she could. The way *should* be now clear for you to take the title!"

Her daughter grinned greedily.

"Well, I'd better get to the police station, and sort things out there!" she continued. "Then I'll be bringing her back. I shall be giving her a beating – if you want to be in on it, in the manner which we've agreed, then make sure you're around when I return!"

Then, she hurried out to her car.

*\*\*\**

At the station, many eyebrows had been raised in astonishment, to find Alexandra being brought in as a suspect to a shoplifting offence. She was shaking uncontrollably, both through the horror of what she had just done, and the thought of what was going to be happening to her now. The custody sergeant, a lady in her forties, who had known Linda Radcliffe well, for many years, was particularly surprised. Although she had never met her, knowing *of* Alexandra as she did, she was certain that this was hugely out of character for her, and suspected that there was something – or more likely *someone* behind it. Sergeant Geraldine Perkins gave Alexandra a drink of hot coffee, and gently asked her some questions, in the interview room.

Alexandra realised that she had been caught red-handed, and that the best course of action now, was to fully co-operate and tell the police exactly why she had committed the offence. This gradually confirmed Sergeant Perkins' suspicions.

As Elizabeth Spencer arrived, Alexandra was in a custody cell, and Sergeant Perkins had returned to her desk, where she was typing Alexandra's confession. Elizabeth confirmed that she was her headmistress at Charterhouse, that she had been technically responsible for Alexandra when the offence had taken place, and that the girl should not have been outside the college grounds, at the time.

Soon afterwards, Alexandra was brought out to the front desk and asked to read her statement of confession. After agreeing that it was correct, she was asked to sign it, and then told that she was to appear before a juvenile court on the morning of Day 1 of next week and to report by 8.00 a.m., when she would be told when she would be appearing, and assigned to a solicitor, who would represent her. There would be a written letter, sent to her mother. As she was under age, she could not be detained at the station, therefore bail did not apply.

"Well, I'm sorry about this, Sergeant." said Elizabeth. "But I'll take her back to Charterhouse College now, where she will be punished and suspended, and then I'll ask her mother to come and take her home."

"Before you go, Mrs Spencer, would you and Alexandra please take a seat for a moment?" said Sergeant Perkins.

Elizabeth looked at her in surprise. "Yes, of course, Sergeant!" she replied and shepherded Alexandra over to the waiting area.

Sergeant Perkins took Alexandra's statement over to one of the other officers. After a few moments, she came over to them.

"My name is Sergeant Johnson. Mrs Spencer, if you please, drive yourself back to Charterhouse College and send for your daughter and also another of your pupils, a Miss Melanie Patterson. Another officer and myself, will escort Miss Radcliffe. We wish to speak to Miss Spencer and Miss Patterson also, regarding this case."

"What?" demanded Elizabeth. "You do know that it was my daughter's prompt actions that alerted you to Alexandra's crime, don't you?"

"I don't want to comment any further, until we've spoken to her," replied Sergeant Johnson. "Please do as I ask, and we'll meet you at Charterhouse College."

Elizabeth left, looking puzzled. Meanwhile Alexandra was taken out to a police car with Sergeant Johnson and a Constable Walker, and driven back to the college.

# CHAPTER 11

Gillian was in her mother's study, when Elizabeth got back to Charterhouse.

"Where's Radcliffe?" she demanded, looking about.

"She's following behind, escorted by two police officers," said Elizabeth. "They want to talk to you, about this affair, too."

"Me? Why? I didn't do anything, apart from call the police, and the press!"

"I don't know," said Elizabeth. "Did anything else happen, that you haven't told me about?"

"No. Not that I can think of," replied Gillian.

Elizabeth buzzed her secretary and asked for Melanie Patterson to be found, and sent to her immediately.

There was a knock at the door. "Enter!" called Elizabeth.

Sergeant Johnson and Constable Walker came in with Alexandra, whom Gillian looked quizzically at.

"Please be seated officers," said Elizabeth indicating to her conference table, and they all sat down. "Melanie Patterson should be with us in a moment. I've just sent for her. Would you like any refreshments?"

"No thank you," said both of the officers. "We'll wait for Miss Patterson to arrive, before we start," said Sergeant Johnson.

In fact, it was several moments before 'Miss Patterson' finally arrived, during which the tension in the room was palpable. Melanie jumped in shock, as she saw the two policewomen.

"Sit down please, Melanie," said Elizabeth. "This is Sergeant Johnson and this is Constable Walker. They want to talk to you and Gillian, about an incident involving Alexandra Radcliffe at lunchtime.

Sergeant Johnson began, "Miss Radcliffe has admitted that she attempted to steal three items of perfume from Rimmingtons department store at 1.00 p.m. today. We were able to observe, and apprehend her immediately, at the scene, due to a phone call being made to us by Miss Spencer, alerting us to the possibility of the crime."

Alexandra glanced at Gillian, who couldn't resist smirking, yet again. She had guessed as much, by now. This had been a set-up, to get her into trouble.

"However," the sergeant continued, "In her statement to us, she has made certain allegations. First of all, let me say that recently there has been a spate of shoplifting in various department stores, in Buckmore, usually occurring between 1.00 and 2.00 p.m., during the working week, and occasionally at various other times at the weekend. Each case has followed a similar pattern. A security camera has been found to have been tampered with, but by the time of the discovery, the theft has taken place, and the offenders have left the scene. We have never captured any video footage of the incidents, due to the sabotage, but as the incidents began to occur regularly, at similar times, we suspected that it was probably the work of the same group of people, and we have stepped up our surveillance of all department stores in the area. Miss Spencer's phone call was obviously of great interest to us, though not entirely unexpected.

"Now we come to Miss Radcliffe's first allegation. She claims that this morning, you threatened to commit a violent act upon her, unless she agreed to shoplift for you, Miss Spencer. She says that she has never been part of these activities until today, but that you and Miss Patterson have been involved for some time, and that you, Miss Spencer, are in fact the mistress mind of the operation."

Gillian gave a look of shocked innocence. "That's a lie!" she cried. "She knows she's finally been caught, and now she's trying to wriggle out of it and blame me! She's been the one stealing stuff, and then when I do my civic duty, and report her to the authorities, this is how I'm treated!"

"Yes, well, your comments will be noted Miss Spencer, and as I said these are only *allegations*-"

"Allegations from a self-confessed attempted thief!" interrupted Elizabeth.

"Miss Radcliffe has admitted to the attempted theft this lunch time, and that is not in question," said Sergeant Johnson. "What is in question, though, is the matter of the other department store thefts, which she denies any involvement in. My suspicion is that her allegations that you and Miss Patterson have been regularly shoplifting at lunchtime, might well match the times of the recent department store thefts. We think it highly likely that there was more than one person involved."

"If I could just point out something else, please, Sergeant," said Alexandra. "I'm not a boarder here. I go home at night and for the weekends, and I live in Greenacres, 20 miles away from Buckmore. I am normally with my mother or my boyfriend, all the time. If there have been thefts at the weekend, then it must have been the work of others."

"That comment will be noted, too, Miss Radcliffe," said the sergeant as

Constable Walker wrote furiously in her notebook. "Let's now turn to the reason why the goods were stolen. Miss Radcliffe alleges that they are being sold on to other girls at Charterhouse, during lunch time, and that there was a specific reason for Miss Spencer and Miss Patterson to require the money they obtained from this.

"Mrs Spencer, you are aware of the presence of two young men here at the college, a couple of days a week?"

Elizabeth looked at Sergeant Johnson. "Yes. I believe they're actors, giving some of the girls some drama lessons, during their extra-curricular time. A nice gesture, on behalf of my daughter, I feel."

"And they are cleared with you?" asked Sergeant Johnson. "You take responsibility, as headmistress, for their presence here?

"Y-yes," said Elizabeth slowly. "Well, I must admit, I don't think any of us on the staff, have ever met them, but they're Gillian's guests here and I generally let her get on with things as she wishes, without much interference from us. They seem to be popular amongst a small, regular group of girls."

"Very popular!" said Melanie. "They're gorgeous!"

"Hmm, well this 'small regular group of girls' *might* be the very same ones who are responsible for the recent shoplifting incidents. Maybe you should do some checking up on your daughter's male friends, Mrs Spencer. Miss Radcliffe's final allegation is that these men are not actors, but a pair of *escort boys*, procured from a nearby massage parlour, which Miss Spencer visited, in order to lose her virginity. Any girls who were interested could pay for their services at a specially reduced rate obtained by Miss Spencer, and she then got a cut of the takings. Soon though, this group became just Gillian and Melanie. In order to keep paying the rate required however, the girls have had to get their hands on extra cash, and this thieving of goods and the subsequent flogging of them to your pupils, is how they have obtained it. Miss Patterson's last comment, could be seen as very revealing indeed!"

"What?" exclaimed Elizabeth, genuinely shocked. "I can't believe what I'm hearing! Gillian, tell me. Is this true?"

"What proof do you have, in any of these *allegations*?" demanded Gillian, ignoring her mother's question.

"Only Miss Radcliffe's word, against yours. But I think there is sufficient evidence to make both Miss Patterson and yourself, suspects. As I've said, we believe that more than one person has been responsible for these thefts and from what Miss Radcliffe has said, it is highly unlikely that she was involved in any of the ones occurring at the weekend, since she is only a day-pupil here, and would have been nowhere near the area at the time. Her mother and boyfriend, could doubtless confirm her presence with them.

"You've also brought these men into your chambers, who you claim to be actors, and it appears your mother, the headmistress of Charterhouse, is genuinely under the impression that they are, though she admits she's never met them. Yet Miss Radcliffe alleges that every girl in the school knows that they are escort boys. Miss Patterson certainly seems to be more interested in their appearance, than in any acting capacity! I'm told they're due to visit again this afternoon. How very fortunate! When you go to bring them in, we can ask them to tell us some of the plays or films they've been in, and maybe even to quote us a few lines."

Gillian's face froze. "No!" she said. "They're not coming today."

"But you told me that they *were*, earlier, Spencer," said Alexandra.

"Well, they've changed their minds!" snapped Gillian.

"Oh I see," said the sergeant. "So the officers posted outside, who are under orders to radio me, when they see two men arrive, won't be doing so, then?"

"Gillian!" said Elizabeth. You still haven't answered my question. Are these allegations about having escort boys in your chambers, true? Answer me!"

Gillian flushed. "Alright! I admit that the men are escorts." she said.

"*Gillian!*" screamed her mother.

"But that still doesn't connect me with the shoplifting though."

"Well, you say that," said the sergeant, "But even if you've got them working here for a reduced rate, I believe their services still won't be cheap, and you're still only schoolgirls. Where are you getting the money from then? It can't be all out of your allowances."

Gillian pursed her lips. This sergeant was clever, and clearly, now that Radcliffe had spilled the beans, the police were inclined to believe her. This wasn't working out how she'd planned it!

Elizabeth lost patience. "Sergeant, please could I have a word with my daughter alone?"

"Very well, you may," said Sergeant Johnson. "You can have five minutes. We'll be right outside the door."

She got up and led the others out. As they left Alexandra could see that

"Miss Patterson," was now deeply worried. Despite the trouble that she herself was in now, she still couldn't believe how stupid Melanie was to have got *so* deeply involved with this, and it didn't surprise her in the least, that she had all but admitted the truth about the 'actors' to the police, in her one and only comment, during the meeting in the headmistress's study.

*\*\*

Left alone in her study with her daughter, Elizabeth now finally exploded.

"*You stupid girl!*" she shouted and struck Gillian across the face, sending her reeling. Her daughter looked back at her in shock. She had never received so much as a tap from her mother before.

"Do you realise what you've done?" asked Elizabeth. "I've allowed you freedom to do what you want here, and made sure everyone lets you do it, so that you can help me run this college how I wish and be my eyes and ears. I can get you all the privileges and awards you'll ever need, and I let you behave however you like, so long as you're ultimately doing my bidding. I've turned a blind eye to many a thing. But *this!* If it was only the shoplifting which I'm sure you *are* behind, that would be bad enough, but bringing in *escort boys* right under my nose, and pretending that they're actors? What in the name of Geratica did you think you were playing at? There are serious moral issues, attached to that particular activity, and you are underage, Gillian! You've broken the law! I trust that you at least took precautions?"

"Of course," replied Gillian. "We all did."

"There's no way we can stop this getting out!" continued her mother. "Alexandra Radcliffe has told all to the police, and there'll inevitably be further ramifications. The press will have a field day, and you may just have blown everything that we've got here, to pieces!

"For a start, my job could be on the line, once it's found out that I've been letting escort boys into Charterhouse for the pleasure of my daughter and her friends, without even knowing it. Everyone will be saying that Charterhouse is becoming a seedy place, and that I should be better informed about what's going on under my own roof – and they'll be dead right!

"And you, my girl, can kiss goodbye any hope you might have had of going to Castra as college champion! After what's about to come out, I'm afraid the damage to your reputation will be too great for anybody to seriously consider you now. Alexandra's position may be retrievable, but not yours. There might now be great pressure to have you expelled, or sent away to a reform school and even still as headmistress here, I might not be able to prevent it. Did you really think that, after being set up and caught like that, and knowing how much trouble she was in – and boy is she in for a rollicking and punishment from her mother – she wouldn't tell the police everything she knew? What did she have to lose?

"If she remains a candidate for college champion, and we both survive this, then we have only have a couple of options that we can take, in the hope of stopping her now. But please Gillian, *don't* do *anything* until I say so, and then only what I *say*. I'll decide what we do now. I can't risk letting you do something off your own bat, anymore."

Gillian scowled. "I'm sorry. I underestimated Radcliffe. I never would have thought that she'd have the bottle to grass on me again, after what I did to her the last time. There won't be a third occasion!"

Elizabeth scoffed. "Oh! Well it's a fine time to be sorry about it now, after the damage has been done! You're right, there *won't* be another occasion – I'll make sure of that. And when I hear you start to use words like 'grass', it really starts to worry me. You're not playing some fantasy role in a film, Gillian. This is the real world. And in the real world, when people realise that authority has them cornered, and that the game is up, they mostly cut their losses, and look after their own interests, to save their skins. That's what Alexandra has done, and added to that, once her mother has recovered her temper, she'll have her to help deal with the repercussions."

"I hope you aren't thinking of going after her for revenge Gillian, either," she continued. "You're going to be in enough trouble as it is, very soon. You'll only make it worse for yourself. I don't remember you ever being worried about being a 'grass', when you've been working for me!"

"How many girls in total have been involved with this?" she asked.

"There were five initially, but now it's just Melanie and I," replied Gillian.

"As well as the three of you, I shall have to deal with them," said Elizabeth. "And what time are those boys due?"

"3.15 p.m."

"Well then, you can go out and send them away, and then I don't expect to hear any more of them being in this college. *Alright Gillian?*"

"Yes Mother," said Gillian, rather sulkily.

There was another knock on the door.

"Enter!" called Elizabeth.

It was Sergeant Johnson. "Is everything alright, Mrs Spencer," she asked. "Your voice must have been heard all over the college!"

Elizabeth's already red face, went a shade redder, as she realised she might have been overheard in her rage. Although, on the other hand, if people had heard her berating her daughter, maybe that wasn't such a bad thing at the moment. It might help create the impression she needed to portray. A strong headmistress, in complete control of her school, and not tolerating her daughter's outrageous behaviour. Gillian had deserved all that she'd got. She should have given it to her long ago.

"Yes, everything's fine now, Sergeant," she replied. "Please feel free to come back in, when you're ready."

"In that case we'll come back in now," said Sergeant Johnson.

***

"So, Miss Spencer," said Sergeant Johnson, "do you still deny any involvement in the thefts from the stores?"

Gillian glanced at her mother. "No. I admit it. I was the one who organised both the escort boys and the shoplifting. Melanie and I did the latter, so that we could flog the stuff to the girls at lunch time, and make ourselves more cash, so that we could afford the former. I got a percentage of the parlour's takings from the enterprise."

"And was Miss Radcliffe involved in any way, until this lunch time?"

Gillian scowled again as she admitted, simply, "No."

"My daughter tells me that there were initially five girls involved in this, Sergeant, but now it's only herself and Melanie," said Elizabeth.

"Then the other three girls broke the law also, and we will need to speak with them," replied Sergeant Johnson.

"Of course, and I shall deal with them here as well," declared Elizabeth.

The sergeant pulled out her notebook.

"If you wouldn't mind giving me their names, Miss Spencer?"

Gillian obliged and Sergeant Johnson made a note of them.

My daughter has also promised me that she will send those *escort boys* away when they arrive at 3.15 p.m., and that they won't be coming back," said Elizabeth.

"If you don't mind, we'll hang around until we've seen that happen, Mrs Spencer," said the sergeant. "In the meantime, we'll see those other three girls, if you could send for them, please."

"Certainly, Sergeant Johnson."

"The other thing to do," continued the sergeant, "is to ask you, Mrs Spencer to ensure that Miss Spencer is presented at the juvenile court in Buckmore, by 8.00 a.m. on Day 1 of next week. The actual time of the hearing will be confirmed to you then, and you'll be assigned to a solicitor, who will represent you. You'll receive written confirmation."

"Of course, Sergeant," said Elizabeth.

"Miss Patterson, your parents will be contacted soon also, and you will be attending the hearing, too, along with Miss Radcliffe."

Melanie looked as if she was close to tears.

Elizabeth phoned through to her secretary and asked her to send for the other three girls.

"It might take a little time to summon them all here, Sergeant Johnson," she said. "I wonder if I could now see these three girls in private, so that I might explain to them what action the college is going to take over this?"

"You may, Mrs Spencer," replied the sergeant. "For these girls, as far as we're concerned that's all for today. When the others get here, we'll hold them outside until you're finished. Thank you for your time."

\*\*\*

The policewomen now left the study. Mrs Spencer took two chairs from the corner of the room, and placed them in the centre. Then she rolled up her sleeves and picked up the cane from behind her chair.

"Well I'm sure I don't need to tell you how displeased I am with all three of you. Stealing is an extremely serious offence, and girls of your age, should know better. Each one of you has obviously participated in that activity, at some point and left the premises without authorisation to do it. And for two of you, all in order to be able to pay for *escort* boys! I shan't comment any further on that subject, except to say that I am disgusted by it. You're supposed to be about to become mature women. As for actually bringing those people into the college, well that was Gillian's doing, and I've already admonished her about it.

"Alexandra, it has also come to my attention that an offensive slogan was written on a classroom wall about Miss Hick before a Geratican Literature lesson this morning. I know it was you who did it, as you were seen and I believe the source of the information reported to me. This is also totally unacceptable, and I should have thought you would know better."

The source of the information was of course her own daughter, who had put Alexandra up to the act in the first place.

"So Alexandra and Melanie, you will now be taught a lesson, to ensure that you will know better, the next time such a temptation comes your way! Gillian was punished earlier, when I spoke with her alone. You're both going to receive six, on your bare bottoms for stealing whilst being outside of Charterhouse grounds without permission and you Melanie will receive another six, for dirtying yourself with escort boys. Alexandra you will receive four extra for writing on the classroom wall. In other words, ten for you and twelve for Melanie. Each of you, lower your skirts and pants and bend over a chair."

Alexandra felt a sense of dread. She'd never been caned on her bare bottom before, although she'd heard the stories of Mrs Spencer's harsh method of punishment. Even her mother didn't do that. Indeed, she'd never been caned on her bottom at all during her entire time within Charterhouse – from the prep school to the college.

Both girls undid their skirts, lowered their garments and stepped forward tentatively. Before they knew it, they'd been forcibly pushed down over the chairs by the headmistress.

Mrs Spencer gave Alexandra her first two beatings, making her wince, before doing the same to Melanie. Then to Alexandra's horror, she handed the cane to her daughter. Taking great pleasure in being able to beat her sworn rival, Gillian did so hard, and then sadistically made Alexandra wait for an eternity, whilst she held it up above her bottom. Alexandra thought for a moment that the cane had been passed back to Mrs Spencer, and she glanced across to the other chair, but at that moment it came down again, even harder than before. She groaned softly and bit into her sleeve. Gillian did then give the cane back to her mother, who beat Melanie twice more. The girl gritted her teeth as the discomfort in her buttocks intensified. Next, Mrs Spencer did the same to Alexandra and then to Melanie. Neither girl wanted to suffer the humiliation of breaking down.

Alexandra shut her eyes, gripped the back of the chair with all her might, and prepared herself. If the pattern of receivership continued, then she knew it was likely that the next two beatings would follow on immediately, from

Gillian. Sure enough they did. Gillian gave Alexandra two more whacks, before handing the cane once more to her mother. Mrs Spencer caned Melanie twice more, before turning her attention back to Alexandra.

One of Mrs Spencer's biggest failings as a mistress, had always been that she let her temper get the better of her. If a girl made her angry or frustrated enough, or she simply lost patience, she took it out on her. She'd had a reputation as being particularly hard and vicious with the cane. Now her full fury at the possibility, and now even probability, of Linda Radcliffe's girl taking the prize, that she had for so long coveted for her own, came to the fore. She wanted to make Alexandra squeal, and cry out. Glowering, she raised her hand and brought the cane down with all the force she could muster on to Alexandra's bottom, almost leaping up into the air. Then again. Then ... She stopped herself just in time. She wanted to go on and on, at least giving her the same number as Melanie, but she had clearly stated ten beatings, and that was what would have to be. Alexandra's head was buried in her sleeve, muffling the sound of her soft moan of pain, and her eyes had watered.

Mrs Spencer administered four more beatings to Melanie. To her annoyance, she was the one who squealed. Alexandra had shown a level of resilience which surprised her.

"Alright, get up both of you and put your skirts and pants back on!" ordered Elizabeth. The girls struggled to their feet, still wincing and wiping the water from their eyes.

"Now I'm going to suspend all three of you for a week," she said. "Yes, you included, Gillian! Alexandra and Melanie, I shall now ring your mothers and explain, and then they'll come to take you home. Go to the lobby and wait for them. In the meantime, I'll get official letters to them typed up, and they'll be given to you to take home, before you leave."

She pointed to the door. "Get out of my sight, both of you. You have disgraced the good name of Charterhouse!"

Once they were outside, Elizabeth turned to her daughter. "But not as much as you, Gillian," she said coldly.

Alexandra and Melanie were both only too glad to get out of the headmistress's study. Alexandra looked at her watch. Her mother would probably still be at work, but she'd be preparing to come over to the college soon, anyhow, because she was picking her up this afternoon, and James was coming tonight. Normally she would be counting down the minutes until her mother arrived, but today, after what she'd done at lunchtime, it was different. Alexandra was dreading getting home tonight, and she began to shiver. Her mother would be *furious*. She was fully expecting one of the telling offs of her life, and to be caned again.

*** 

At the Royal Palace, Linda got the call from Elizabeth, passed through to her by Veronica, her secretary. She was incredulous at the news, and nearly spilt her final cup of coffee, for the working week.

"I can't believe it! How in all of Geratica, did that situation occur?" she was saying.

"I'm sorry Linda, but it has." Elizabeth explained the situation briefly, though she avoided mentioning her daughter, or the escorts. Linda Radcliffe was going to find out the whole story soon enough, anyhow. She wasn't going to be the one to tell her.

After Mrs Spencer rang off, Linda immediately called through to Queen Alexandra's personal aide, Rebecca Hargreaves and asked her to give a message to the queen that she had an emergency, and that she needed to leave straight away. Then, she gathered up her things and hurried out. First of all, she told Veronica that she was leaving for Charterhouse, right away and wouldn't be back, then found James, and told him the news.

"I'm really sorry, James, but I think that under the circumstances, we'd better postpone tonight, until maybe one day next week. I'm going to have to get to the bottom of this. I can't believe she would choose this moment, to do something so stupid! I'm absolutely livid with her, and she's going to be in *serious* trouble tonight! She might have ruined her whole future. I'll kill her!"

"Try not to fly off the handle too much though, Linda," said James. "Give her the chance to explain it for herself. I'm stunned too. It seems so out of character, and she appeared to be becoming quite mature. I think there's more to this than meets the eye."

"Yes, I think so, too. That's why I said that I want to get to the bottom of this. Well I must go, but I'll ring you tonight, and update you."

They said their goodbyes and then Linda went to her car, and sped towards Charterhouse.

***

Alexandra had been given her official suspension letter, by the headmistress's secretary, and was waiting nervously in the lobby, sucking on her finger, when her mother arrived. She stood up, but unusually there was no exchange of affection between them this afternoon. Linda regarded her daughter coolly, and as their eyes met, Alexandra didn't need any words from her mother, to tell her that she was furious, and that she was going to be severely reprimanded, and punished tonight. Her eyes filled with tears. She was worried about what was in store for her, and she also felt deeply ashamed. She loved and idolised her mother, and she hated displeasing and disappointing her, and knowing that she had let her down.

Linda led the way out, but before they reached the car, Sergeant Johnson, who had stayed to see that the escorts were sent away, and told not to come back, came over to meet them. She introduced herself to Linda.

"Mrs Radcliffe, I'm sure you're now aware of the situation your daughter now finds herself in," she said. "Whilst she was at the station, she made a statement of confession, but also gave us some other information that we have found very useful, and it has enabled us to establish the facts. I have a copy of it here. You might like to read it yourself."

"Oh. Thank you very much, Sergeant," said Linda. This would indeed be of great interest to her.

Once in the car, with mother and daughter having still not exchanged a single word, Linda drove out of the college, and they began a long silent journey home.

# PART 5

# CHAPTER 1

When they got home, Linda at last spoke.

"Put your coat away and go to the study. Immediately!" she ordered.

Alexandra's throat was dry. She could only just manage to croak, "Yes, Mother!"

"Pardon? Speak up girl!" said her mother impatiently.

Alexandra cleared her throat. "Yes Mother!" she repeated more clearly.

"Well, be quick about it then. I told you what you were to do, ten seconds ago!" said Linda.

Her daughter trembled, and stammering "Y-y-yes Mother!" she raced to the cloakroom to remove her coat, and went into the study and sat at her desk. Any hope that she might have had, that her mother might be sympathetic to the predicament that she had got herself into, was now all but gone.

Despite her dominant personality, Alexandra rarely truly feared her mother, but the exceptions were when she was extremely cross with her – and now she clearly was boiling mad. Alexandra felt cold shivers down her spine, and she sucked on her fingers. Then she heard her mother's footsteps as she came down the passage, and another shiver pulsated through her whole body, as she realised that her telling off was about to begin.

Linda came into the room, reading Alexandra's statement that Sergeant Jenkins had given her a copy of. To her relief, from the look of this, and reading between the lines of what the sergeant had told her – that it had enabled them to establish the facts, which appeared to strongly indicate that Gillian Spencer was behind this – she thought that her daughter's position, though serious, did not seem untenable. Alexandra had clearly done something wrong, which she would punished further for, this evening and over the next week, and she would roast her alive for both her behaviour and her stupidity, but she had obviously been bullied into this, and Linda suspected she might know what the reason for it was. *That* was not her daughter's fault.

She finished reading, put the statement on her desk, opposite Alexandra and stood behind her chair, her hands upon her hips.

"Well, I don't know what to say!" she began, and then gave a false chuckle. "Alexandra, correct me if I am wrong, but you've been doing very well in your studies at Charterhouse, have you not?"

"Yes, Mother," said Alexandra.

"You've got a good chance of going to Castra University, yes?"

"Yes Mother."

"You would agree with me, that going to Castra as college champion, would be a great honour, and that you're lucky to have Philippa Barrington to help you possibly achieve that objective?"

"Yes, Mother."

The answer to all of these questions were so obvious, that Alexandra knew where her mother was going with this.

"You've even started a relationship with, Tom, too. Haven't you?"

"Yes, Mother."

"*Well then, please tell me, what in the name of all Geratica, is the meaning of your behaviour today?*" thundered Linda. Alexandra shook visibly, and a couple of trickles urine escaped from her bladder creating a small damp patch in her pants.

"I didn't have a choice, Mother!"

"Didn't have a *choice*?" Linda shouted. "Don't you *dare* try and give me that! No one *has* to go into Rimmingtons and try to take their perfume, without paying for it! And you've no need to steal, in your position!

"So, I ask you again, Alexandra. What is the meaning of this?"

"It's true, Mother! Gillian bullied me and you don't know what she's like! She would have thumped me, if I hadn't either done this at lunchtime, or gone with an escort boy, this afternoon. Well, I wasn't going to do the latter! She originally just tried to get me to get involved with one of those, but I refused. She tried to goad me, by dismissing my likely ability in the bedroom, in front of all my form class, after she found out that I now have a boyfriend. It was such an insult and I was so embarrassed. She said that I'd need to learn what to do from the escort boys. But I still wouldn't join in.

"Then this morning she came at me with two other girls. I don't know who they were, they're just her heavies and not part of the escort operation - that's only Gillian and Melanie now, although there were originally three others. Gillian told me that if I still wouldn't do it, then I *had* to go and help her and Melanie shoplift at lunch time, or else she would have given me a thumping! I didn't realise that she was setting me up! Gillian and Melanie had scarpered, just before the police arrived."

"Set up, or no set up, that's not the point! You should not have *done* that Alexandra!" shouted her mother, banging her desk hard with her fist, to emphasise the word 'done', and making Alexandra jump. "Stealing is morally wrong, no matter what the circumstances. I've always taught you that, and now of all times, you've chosen to break that moral, which you will be *severely* punished for! You may not have actually done it in the end, but you were still caught trying. How would you like it if someone went upstairs to your bedroom right now, and took one of your things? What will Judith Warwicker think? She might not ever trust you to go into her shop again!

"Has Gillian now admitted her involvement in all of this, including bringing in the escorts?"

"Y-yes Mother," stammered Alexandra. "The sergeant basically f-forced her to confirm that she had organised and taken part in all of it. The three of us who went to Rimmingtons at lunch time, are all due at the j-juvenile court together, on Day 1 of next week."

"Alexandra, have you any idea what you put at risk, by doing this today?" demanded Linda. "Having been arrested, you're now going to have a criminal record! That might seriously damage your chances of being accepted at Castra next year, and whether you can still seriously expect to be considered for going there as college champion, I would think now is also going to be uncertain. And after I had gone to great pains to tell your headmistress how well you respected authority, and the rule of law! In case you aren't aware of it, Alexandra, there is a stigma attached to people who have been involved in illegal activity, and it can go against you when you're trying to get a job. And what makes it worse in your case, is that there is going to be a lot of publicity over this, due to you being my daughter. I've warned you about that, on various issues, time and time again. Quite apart from anything else, did you even stop to consider the embarrassment that you would cause me, if you were caught doing this? I thought you and I were the closest partnership in all of Geratica, and that you were an intelligent girl, but I was obviously mistaken on both counts! To cap it all, Mrs Spencer tells me that you even wrote a rude slogan on a classroom wall, about one of your mistresses! So we can add *vandalism* and *disrespect* to your other misdemeanours of being outside the grounds of Charterhouse without authorisation and *attempted theft!*"

"She forced me to do that too, Mother, to test my courage!" wailed Alexandra.

"To test your courage? Do you really think that anything that you've done today, could possibly be called 'courageous'? I don't! I think you've been incredibly stupid, and I'm hurt that all that I've helped to gain for you, you've now thrown back in my face. Your relationship with me clearly isn't as important to you, as I previously thought!"

Alexandra had been in a state of high anxiety and tension, ever since break time at Charterhouse, this morning, and now the words of her mother's last two sentences, finally broke the dam holding back her emotions. She began to sob uncontrollably. Her mother meant everything to her, and the thought that she had done something which might have damaged their relationship, was too much to bear. Her mother's rage at her, and complete lack of support and understanding, was something she didn't experience very often, and she felt lost, alone and frightened. She shook again and the dampness in her pants got a fraction wetter.

"I'm t-t-truly sorry, Mother!" she stammered, between her sobs. "I didn't think enough about it, and I love you more than anyone else in the world, including Tom! But Gillian panicked me, and she'd taunted me about my relationship with Tom. She *would* have been violent to me, Mother – she does do that to people sometimes. I thought that if I just went along with them once, I could get her off my back for a while. And now I've caused all this!" Alexandra broke off, and began to cry again.

"Yes, well I don't doubt you are feeling sorry now, and I accept your apology," said Linda," But this is not the time for you to be making any excuses for your behaviour, which will count for nothing, nor am I in any mood to accept those today. I suppose the only redeeming factor in your otherwise disgraceful behaviour, is that you chose the shoplifting rather than going with an escort boy for underage sexual intercourse. I would never have expected you to do either, but be *very* assured that if it was the latter offence which had been committed, then I'd now be giving you a thrashing from the whip!"

She reached behind her desk and took down the cane that always hung in a prominent position on the study wall.

"Even so Alexandra, I had hoped that *this* object was a thing of the past between us. But if ever there was an indiscretion that warranted a caning it is surely this. I'm sure I don't have to tell you what you're going to receive. Come here!"

Linda sat down in her chair as her daughter began to walk around the desk towards her. Alexandra now felt a terrible urge in her bladder, brought on by dread of the beating her mother was about to give her.

"M-mother!" she stammered, "B-before that, could I please go to the lavatory? I think I might soak my pants during it, if I don't go until afterwards!"

Linda studied her, and noticed a small patch of wetness becoming visible in her skirt. "Oh, goodness me!" she exclaimed exasperatedly. "Go on then, but I'll give you a maximum of two minutes. If you're not back by then, I'll add an extra stroke and I very much mean that!"

"Yes, Mother!" Alexandra dashed out of the study and into the downstairs lavatory. In almost no time at all, Linda heard a huge gushing sound as her daughter emptied her bladder in a long stream.

She had been only too aware of Alexandra's distress, during the rocketing that she had just given her. For a start she'd been stammering, something she had done in times of great anxiety, when she was younger, but had managed to overcome, with her help, before she'd gone to Charterhouse College.

She had chosen her words regarding their relationship, deliberately, because she'd known they'd hit home. She had certainly meant some of what she'd said – she *was* concerned that her daughter had been so easily pushed into breaking a moral code of conduct between them, and that she hadn't thought more about the possible consequences of her actions. She *did* genuinely feel let down by her, after what she had recently done for her. She had thought that Alexandra was maturing into a Geratican woman that she could be proud of, but this without doubt, was a step backwards.

At the same time though, she did have more sympathy with her daughter than she was allowing her to see at the moment, and she knew that as her anger began to subside, this would increase. Alexandra wasn't good at handling bullying and clearly this had been a major factor in what had happened. She suspected that her daughter had suffered at the hands of Gillian Spencer, more than she had previously realised, and again she was hurt that her daughter hadn't confided more in her about it. She did about most other things. It was the main reason why she had decided to send Alexandra to Charterhouse as a day-pupil. She was actually more furious with Gillian, and if she could get her hands on her, she'd much prefer to give her a huge thrashing, than cane her own daughter. She hated having to do it, but Alexandra had to receive a punishment for this, regardless of the circumstances, and she wasn't going to soften up today. The time for some sympathy, heart-to-heart conversation and to kiss and make up, would come tomorrow, after Alexandra had been locked in her room to stew for a while, and she herself had calmed down, and made some discreet, behind-the-scene telephone calls.

Alexandra's reputation was going to take a slight knock for a short time – that was unavoidable. But Linda was sure that Gillian's scheming had badly backfired on her, and that she had overreached herself. She was the one most likely to come off worse, in the long run. She imagined that Mrs Spencer wasn't too pleased with the way things had worked out too. She would suffer the embarrassment of the public finding out about the antics of her daughter, who was one of the pupils in her charge, as headmistress of

Charterhouse and that – so it appeared – she hadn't known about the visits of escort boys to her daughter's chambers, right under her nose. Linda despised her even more now. She was certain that she had pushed Gillian to find a way to discredit Alexandra, and destroy her chances of becoming college champion, because she wanted Gillian to take the title herself.

Linda felt that if she took full control of Alexandra's situation, over the next few days, and played her daughter's cards right for her, then she probably had a good chance of getting her back on track, by the time she returned to Charterhouse, after her suspension.

The toilet flushed and soon Alexandra was back in the study, just within Linda's time limit. With trepidation, she once more walked towards her mother. Neither mother or daughter could look at each other.

Alexandra leant across her mother's knee, and Linda gripped her trembling body tightly, with her left arm, to secure her in position. Then she raised her right hand and brought the cane down on her daughter's bottom. Alexandra flinched. After two more strokes, she wriggled uncomfortably. By the time she had received five, she was beginning to writhe about on her mother's knee. When Linda administered the sixth, and final stroke, which she always made sure was the hardest, so that the memory of that one stayed in her daughter's mind the longest, Alexandra cried out.

"Right. Get up and face me!" ordered Linda.

For the second time in the space of an hour and a half, Alexandra hoisted herself to her feet. She looked at her mother, as she had been asked.

"Now, you're suspended from Charterhouse, next week, and I'm going to 'gate' you at The Grange for the corresponding time. Apart from of course, if you're accompanied by me. It will finish after Day 5 of next week. Is that clear?"

"Yes, Mother. Crystal clear," said Alexandra in her most obedient fashion.

"I'm also suspending your allowance for the next two weeks, and there will be no special treats, until after that. You're to go to your room now, and you won't come out again until I permit it, sometime, during the day, tomorrow. I shall be busy trying to clear up some of the mess you've made! Until then, I'll put each of your meals on a tray, come into your bedroom and leave it on your dressing table, and collect your dishes later. Apart from those occasions, your door will be locked at all times. There will be no conversation between us. Is that understood?"

"Yes, Mother," said Alexandra, her eyes beginning to fill up with tears.

"Also, in case you're wondering, James will not be coming tonight, after all. Due to the circumstances, it simply isn't appropriate for him to be here at the moment. That's another thing that I'm cross with you about. You have upset *My Arrangements*! You know that this is a critical time in my plans, regarding that subject, and I was intending for us to all enjoy an evening here together. I *hope* that I'll be able to rearrange it for some time, early next week. You'd better hope that I can Alexandra, because I shall be most annoyed if my plans are ruined by your stupidity!"

Alexandra gulped, and crossed her fingers, behind her back. Then she took a deep breath, and stammered, "M-mother? W-what about Tom, tomorrow night?"

"We'll see," said Linda simply. "Right. Go to your room now and close the door behind you. In two minutes, I'll be up to lock it. Since we won't be speaking again until tomorrow, I'll say goodnight, now."

"Goodnight Mother."

Alexandra fled the study, and Linda heard her sobbing, as she went upstairs to her bedroom. As she'd been told to expect, a moment later Alexandra heard the lock turning in the door.

# CHAPTER 2

The first thing Linda did was to ring Sergeant Geraldine Perkins at the police station at Buckmore. They knew each other through having been at the same school, many years ago and their paths still crossed sometimes as she lived in Greenacres, too.

They greeted each other and remarked that it was a little while since they had seen each other. Geraldine guessed the reason for Linda's call and said that it had been nice to see Alexandra this afternoon, but she wished it had been under happier circumstances. They briefly discussed the case, and Geraldine told Linda that she had suspected from the start that someone else was probably involved, having some idea of Alexandra's character, and indeed it had turned out that she'd been bullied into it. Linda agreed, though she said that it was no excuse.

She then got to her main business. She wanted the name of the solicitor who would be representing her daughter at the hearing, at the beginning of next week, and a telephone number. She was a little pushed for time, as she needed to get in touch with her before the weekend. Geraldine found the details, and gave them to her. The solicitor's name was Jessica Beale a woman apparently in her thirties, who had been qualified for over ten years. This reasonably pleased Linda. At least it wouldn't be a complete novice who was on her first case. She took the number, and thanked Geraldine. After saying that she hoped they would meet again soon, and goodbye, Linda cut away and immediately rang the number she'd been given, without replacing the receiver.

To her relief Jessica Beale hadn't yet finished for the weekend. She introduced herself, and directed her to the case at the juvenile court that she was defending on Day 1 of next week. After explaining that she was Alexandra Radcliffe's mother, she announced that she would like to be called as a witness. Jessica said that this was fine, and asked her what she wanted to say. Linda explained briefly, but told her that she'd speak in more detail at the court, before the hearing. She also asked her if she knew who the judge was going to be. Jessica told her that it was Lavinia Mountford. Linda knew her, too. They had in fact been at Charterhouse together. This was good news.

As with a lot of people, Jessica knew who she was dealing with, purely by the name. Linda agreed that she and Alexandra would her at the juvenile court at 8.00 a.m. on Day 1 of next week, and said goodbye.

Linda puffed out her cheeks. That was the most important thing done. After making herself what she felt was going to be a well-deserved cup of coffee, she would next, call Queen Alexandra.

***

After getting through to the palace, Linda asked to be put through to Queen Alexandra urgently.

"Your Majesty," she said, as the queen came on the line.

"Linda!" said Queen Alexandra. "Is everything alright? I know what's happened. It's been on the national news!"

Linda was taken aback. "Already, Ma'am? Well, I suppose some of the press *were* present, when the ghastly incident took place. I've not had a chance to catch the news yet, since I brought my daughter home from Charterhouse. I finished giving her the bollocking of her life about twenty minutes ago, and told her to stay in her room until further notice. She's been in there, crying her eyes out for ..." Linda's voice faltered slightly, before recovering. "I can't believe she could have been so stupid!"

It might have only been brief, but Queen Alexandra had noticed her trusted senior court administrator's anguish. One of the things that had made her a popular monarch, was that she was seen as perceptive, and in touch with her subjects' feelings. She was sure that such a close mother and daughter, were probably suffering a crisis in their relationship at the moment, and also that Linda would have punished Alexandra in the traditional Geratican manner – a caning and sanctions – which would have hurt them both, deeply.

"Do you know what the exact circumstances were?" she asked gently.

"Yes, I do, Ma'am. Alexandra did at least have the good sense to provide the police with a full statement, explaining everything. It's about the only sensible thing that she's done all day!

"It was those blasted Spencer women who orchestrated this. She was – up to a point, at least – set up. I've told her that she can't simply use that as an excuse – she still shouldn't have done it – but there's no doubt that heavy pressure was put on her to go into the store and try to steal something, which unfortunately she wasn't strong enough to withstand. Elizabeth Spencer wants Gillian to go to Castra as college champion and she's furious that Alexandra is now standing in her way, and knows that she might be a strong enough candidate to defeat her daughter. Therefore she's instructed Gillian to find a way of discrediting Alexandra, so that she's forced to withdraw from the race.

"Unfortunately for poor Mrs Spencer though, Gillian may well have bitten off more than she can chew. Have the media got hold of the rest of the story yet, Ma'am?"

"The rest? No, there weren't many other details."

"Well I'll tell you then, Ma'am. Confidentially, of course."

"Of course, Linda," said the queen.

"Well it's quite sensational, Ma'am. It transpires that although this was Alexandra's only time in doing this, Gillian and another girl, a Melanie Patterson, have been regularly going out of the college grounds in their lunch hour, and visiting various department stores, to do the very same. Then they've been selling their ill-gotten gains on to other girls at Charterhouse. And you'll never guess what they've been spending the profits on. Gillian Spencer, daughter of Elizabeth, the headmistress, has been secretly smuggling escort boys into her chambers, posing as actors, giving drama coaching to any girls who wanted it, when in fact they were obviously giving them coaching of a totally different kind! And not one mistress knew the truth, let alone the headmistress! I'm told that there were originally three other girls involved, but now it's just the two of them. I understand that they were paying the escorts a reduced rate, but they soon found that they needed to find more cash, so this was what they resorted to, and Gillian was the mistress mind behind it."

"Goodness me!" exclaimed Queen Alexandra. "Has she admitted that?"

"So, I've been told, Ma'am," said Linda. "Alexandra, Gillian and this other girl, are all due to appear before the juvenile court on Day 1 of next week."

"Well surely then, even if Gillian avoids getting sent to a young offenders' institution, there's a strong possibility of her being expelled?"

"I don't know, Ma'am. Normally I would think so, too, but she's always been a special case there. She more or less does what she likes, and Mrs Spencer just lets her get on with it. No one can touch her. At the end of the day, it's Mrs Spencer who's in charge of the boarding school and the decision to expel a girl, ultimately lies with her. The story I've heard recently through the grapevine on the board of governors, is that Gillian is often used by her, as a sort of 'right hand woman' to help her run the place, and be her eyes and ears. Several of the girls who end up in her study for a ticking off, are there because she's got them into trouble or reported them to her."

"This is going to be the biggest scandal to ever hit Charterhouse though," said the queen. The media will find out the whole truth at the hearing next week, if they don't before – we all know what the press are like, and it only takes one person in the know, to be indiscreet. At the very least, Elizabeth Spencer is going to be publicly accused of incompetence. The question will be, whether she has a firm enough foundation there, to withstand the storm that will blow her way."

"Yes. Well I intend to be a part of that storm, Ma'am!" said Linda. "I've had enough of her. Apart from being an ex-pupil myself, I'm obviously now on the board of governors. I'm going to propose a vote of no confidence in her as headmistress, and ask for her to be removed from her post. I'm writing a letter this weekend, to all of the board members, detailing all of the problems that those two Spencers cause the staff and pupils alike, at Charterhouse, and calling for an emergency meeting. I'll have it in the post for Day 1 of next week.

"The judge is going to be Lavinia Mountford, a woman who was at Charterhouse during my time there. I've also found out who the solicitor representing Alexandra will be at the hearing, and asked her to call me as a witness. Then I can say my piece, regarding today, and make the court fully aware of the role that both Elizabeth and Gillian Spencer have played in bringing this situation about.

"After all of that, we'll see how firm her foundations are, Ma'am! I will say that I genuinely believe that she is not the most popular person, amongst the staff."

"It sounds like someone still loves their daughter to death, despite what she's done," said Queen Alexandra. "I know that nothing motivates you more, than channelling all your resources into helping her. With you behind her, I somehow think she's going to pull through. She's a very lucky girl."

"Thank you, Ma'am. I only hope that she realises it!"

"Linda! You know that she does. That's why she's crying so much. She knows she's let you down, and she's desperately upset about it. Don't be too hard on her. She's allowed others to push her into making a mistake, but that doesn't make her a bad girl. And there are actually far worse mistakes that people can make."

Linda was grateful. Queen Alexandra did have a gift for empathy.

"Yes, Ma'am," she replied. "I really did feel terrible about it, but I was determined to be as hard as possible with her tonight, because there's no escaping the fact that she's done wrong. I've punished her severely, and I know she was in a terrible state, because she was stammering and she hasn't done that, since before she went to Charterhouse. But tomorrow I'll make her know I still love her, of that you can be sure."

"I think you're going to have a busy weekend then Linda," said the queen. "I'd better let you go. I'd stay indoors if I were you, anyhow. Now that the media sense there's a story to be had, you can probably expect them outside your hamlet gate!"

Linda pressed the button on the phone to snap on the monitor, so that she could see outside the gate.

"It looks like they're already there, Ma'am. No, I'm not intending to go anywhere this weekend. And Alexandra certainly won't be! She's been suspended from Charterhouse for a week, and I've gated her at The Grange, for a week, running concurrently with that. The one thing that we had planned, was to have Tom Ryder over for a meal tomorrow night – it was his birthday three days ago. I haven't promised it to her yet, but I think I'll still allow Alexandra that. If ever there's a time when she needs him, it's now. I think he'll be good for her."

"Yes, I think so too, Linda. He might have heard about her predicament on the news now."

"The Lodge is going to be one of my next telephone calls, Ma'am."

"Linda, before I go," began Queen Alexandra, "Obviously, I can't interfere with the case in any direct sense, but I would like to show Alexandra some support. I'm on her side, too. If I was to supply a general reference to the court, painting her in the favourable light which I've always seen her in, would that be of help?"

Linda felt a rush of delight inside of her. It certainly could be!

"Thank you, Ma'am! That really would be most kind of you, and might prove very useful. I'll let Alexandra know, tomorrow."

"Excellent! I'll get something sent immediately, and make sure it's with the court by first thing on Day 1 of next week. Do you want to take leave for that day?"

"Yes. Thank you again, Ma'am. That might be best, as I don't know when exactly, during the day, the hearing will take place."

"Of course! I'll make sure 'your little empire' are informed. "Anyhow, have as good a weekend as you can, and try not to worry about this. I'm sure it will all work out in the end."

"I think Alexandra will be the one doing the lion's share of the worrying, Ma'am. It's more in her nature than mine. But I shall be strong for her."

"As always!" exclaimed the queen. "Goodbye Linda, and we'll hopefully see you back at the palace on Day 2 of next week. Good luck to both you, and Alexandra for Day 1."

"Thank you, your Majesty." said Linda, and they each hung up.

*** 

No sooner had Linda put the phone down, then it rang and the monitor screen came to life, as she picked up the receiver. The media presence was pressing the buzzer at the gate, trying to get through to The Grange. Linda slammed the receiver back down, and ignored it. Instead she reached for her notepad, and thinking quickly, began to scribble down a few words. Five minutes later, when she was satisfied with what she had written, she lifted the receiver on the phone again, and pressed a button to enable her to speak to the people at the gate. Quickly and clearly, she read her prepared statement.

*"Good evening, ladies! We are most touched by your anxiousness to gain our acquaintance, but unfortunately my daughter and I, are a little preoccupied at the moment. I am sorry to disappoint you all.*

*"Alexandra has made an error of judgement, which she sincerely apologises for, and will accept whatever punishment it is seen fit for to take, to atone for her mistake.*

*"We would however, like to draw your attention to the fact that we think Miss Gillian Spencer, daughter of Elizabeth, headmistress of Charterhouse College, has made a bigger error of judgement – maybe even several – and that you should perhaps turn your attentions in that direction.*

*"We will obviously be attending the hearing at the juvenile court, on Day 1 of next week, but until then, we will not be going out, or commenting further. That will be all. Thank you, and Goodnight!"*

Linda cut the line, immediately after finishing her statement. She didn't want to give any of the assembled gathering a chance to ask any questions. What she had said, she hoped would keep them busy for a while, and maybe push them in a different direction, if she was lucky. Picking up her contacts book, she sank back into her chair briefly, then after finding the number she required, phoned Philippa Barrington.

Philippa was shocked to hear the news, and said that it didn't seem like Alexandra at all, even if, as it was, she had only met her twice so far. She had seemed such a nice, well-mannered, well brought up, and studious girl.

Linda explained the circumstances as she saw them, and Philippa's opinion was much in keeping with the consensus that seemed to be developing, regarding Alexandra's actions. She asked Linda to wish pass on her good wishes to her daughter, for the hearing, and also said that she would write a letter to the court, outlining her favourable opinion of Alexandra, since meeting her, and stating her view that, if she had strayed from the correct path in some way, then it was completely out of character.

Linda readily agreed, and thanked her. Philippa promised to ensure that it would arrive at Buckmore Juvenile Court, by first thing on Day 1 of next week.

***

Then Linda rang The Lodge. Fiona answered.

"Linda!" she exclaimed. "I've heard the news. What happened? It seems so strange."

"My daughter's been an idiot, that's what's happened!" snapped Linda. "Plus the Spencer double act have been doing their dirty work! Gillian Spencer bullied her into it, and then set her up, basically. I haven't got time to go into all the precise details at the moment Fiona, but I won't be at work on Day 1 of next week, as that's when Alexandra has to appear before Buckmore Juvenile Court, and the case could be heard at any time of the day. Gillian, and the other girl involved, will be there too."

"Look, as you know, we've invited Tom over for dinner tomorrow night, so that he and Alexandra can celebrate his birthday properly, without having to be up for work and school, the following morning. Alexandra is suspended from Charterhouse for a week now, because of this though. Anyhow, despite it all, I think that it would be good for Alexandra to still see Tom tomorrow. He's good for her, and she needs him at the moment. Do you mind if I have a quick word with him, just to make him aware of a couple of things?"

"No, of course not, Linda. Well the very best of luck at the court, if I don't speak to you before then. See you on Day 2 of next week. Goodbye."

She called for her stepson to come to the phone.

"Tom," said Linda, as he came on the line.

"Hello, Mrs Radcliffe," he replied. "How's Alexandra? And what in the name of the Divine Being happened?"

"I'm afraid that Alexandra has got herself into a bit of trouble, and she's going to have to attend a hearing at Buckmore Juvenile Court, on Day 1 of next week. There is a bit more to this than most people realise at the moment though, and I'm hopeful that things will go as well as can be expected. She's suspended from Charterhouse for all of next week, but once the dust has settled, and she goes back, then all being well, she can get back on track. In the short term, this business obviously won't do her any good, but in the long run, so long as she keeps her nose *immaculately* clean, then it should all blow over. But she's got to play her cards right, and I'm going to play them for her!

"Now, you were coming to dinner with us tomorrow night, and that's still on. Alexandra needs you Tom, and together we'll have to help her face the hearing next week. You can be sure that she's going to be extremely worried, and nervous about it."

"Yes, Mrs Radcliffe. I want to be there, too. I'm going to ask for the day off. It'll be very short notice, but that can't be helped. Can I speak to her, please?"

"Oh. No. Sorry, Tom," said Linda. "You'll have to wait until you see her tomorrow, I'm afraid. I've just given her a severe telling off, and she's now locked in her room, until I tell her she can come out – which won't be until sometime tomorrow – and she'll be speaking to no one, until then. And I mean no one! Even I won't be doing so again tonight. There's no escaping the fact that she's done wrong today, Tom, and at the moment, she's in disgrace.

"Regarding tomorrow night though. Just be aware that there have been some people from the media, outside the hamlet, tonight. I hope they won't try to stick around all weekend, and any photographers shouldn't be able to see anything from outside of the security gate. But just in case, I want you to go through the wood, and come in through our back entrance. One of us will let you in through the kitchen porch. It'll be more discreet. Is that clear?"

"Perfectly, Mrs Radcliffe," said Tom. "Whatever you say."

"Also – and this is most important Tom – if anyone should try to contact you, realising that you're now Alexandra's boyfriend, I don't want you to say anything at all. They probably won't, but just to make sure. Refuse any requests for an interview, or a quote! *Discretion!* Do I have your word, boy?"

"Yes, of course, Mrs Radcliffe. I promise. I would never do that!" Tom felt like she was talking to him like her own son again.

"Good," said Linda. "Well, we'll look forward to seeing you at 6.00 p.m.

tomorrow then. I wish it could be in slightly happier circumstances, but that's Alexandra's own fault. It doesn't mean we can't enjoy ourselves though. I'll confirm to Alexandra, that I'm still allowing her to see you, tomorrow. She isn't sure at the moment. She'll be mightily relieved, I think!

\*\*\*

After saying goodbye to Tom, Linda left the study and went to the kitchen to make the dinner. She was planning just one more call tonight – to James, to let him know what the situation was.

As she had told her, Linda took Alexandra's helping up to her bedroom, and left it on the dressing table, then left without a word, locking the door behind her. After she'd finished eating, she waited a few extra minutes, then went back up and took Alexandra's empty plate away, leaving in the same manner as before. She locked the door again – this time for the night.

After washing up and then pouring herself a drink, Linda rang James.

"How did it go?" asked James.

"I suppose I did a bit of what you asked me to, and a bit of what you said not to do," replied Linda. "I did give her a chance to explain herself, but I also flew off the handle, a bit. In fact, things might not be *quite* as bad for Alexandra, as I feared. After she was arrested, she fully co-operated with the police at the station, and gave a very detailed statement, explaining exactly how it all came about. That led to the police going to Charterhouse themselves, to talk to a couple of other girls."

"James," said Linda delicately, "I'm afraid this is where it's going to get a bit awkward. One of the two girls that the police spoke to was your daughter. If they haven't already, the media may soon be asking some questions there, too. I've had them at the gate of Elmsbrook, this evening and I decided I'd have to give a brief statement, through the intercom. I won't be saying any more this weekend, and if anyone tries to get anything out of you, as Elizabeth's husband, or Gillian's father, you're not to either. Understood?"

"Definitely, Linda," said James. "Anyhow, I don't know much about it *myself*, at the moment."

"Well, I'll tell you then," replied Linda. She took a swig of her coffee, settled back in her chair, and filled James in on the events that she now knew had been going on for some time.

"I don't believe it, I really don't!" exclaimed James, when she'd finished. "Gillian's always been closer to her mother, particularly since she's been at Charterhouse, and I've always known that she was a scamp – Alexandra is an absolute angel, compared to her – but I never guessed that she was up to anything as serious as this."

"No, and it appears that Elizabeth didn't either!" remarked Linda. "I imagine there are going to be some serious questions asked about her competence – having escorts smuggled in to her college, right under her nose and *nobody* realised! I've already spoken to Queen Alexandra, and she was suggesting that Gillian would be expelled, and maybe even sent to a young offender's institution. I'm sorry to say, James, but I agree with her, and I think there's every likelihood that Gillian will end up in one of those. But if she should be lucky enough to escape that particular punishment, and she's handed back to Charterhouse, then I don't know what will happen.

"I think it largely depends on whether your dear wife can survive this crisis, and the damage to Charterhouse's reputation. If she goes – and I'd better tell you James, that I'm writing a letter to every member of the board of governors, calling for an emergency meeting to discuss her removal – then I think that Gillian will be kicked out for sure. But if she manages to hold on, it'll still be her ultimate decision, whether she's expelled or not. I suppose, if the press reaction is hostile enough, and public opinion seems to be against Gillian, then Elizabeth's hand could be forced.

"The solicitor who'll be representing Alexandra, seems to be a woman with some experience, and I know the judge from my Charterhouse days, actually. I'll be taking the day off for it, so I won't be in work until Day 2, next week.

"So, I think that there's a reasonable chance that once everything is sorted out, Alexandra's situation may not be too badly affected. She's done wrong, clearly and there's no excuse for it, but she can certainly claim, with some justification, that she was coerced into doing it. Compared to what Gillian might be served, I don't imagine that her punishment will be too severe, from the juvenile court – unlike the one she's received from me! I caned her, gated her at The Grange for a week, and suspended her allowance for a fortnight, with no special treats awarded during that period, either. Once she's finished her suspension period, she'll *hopefully* be able to slip quietly back into Charterhouse, and pick up from where she left off, and still have a chance of getting into Castra. My only worry is that it might be considered unacceptable for a girl with a criminal record – even though in her case it would be very minor – to be a candidate for college champion, which will be a blow to all of us, considering the lengths we've gone, to set up the chance for her."

"I imagine that she'll be pretty upset about it, too, Linda," remarked James.

"Yes she will, but that will in many ways be her own fault," replied Linda. "However, I *will* have to work to make sure that the disappointment doesn't completely destroy her confidence, and affect her whole performance, for the rest of her school year. But anyhow, I'll cross that bridge, when, and if I come to it. Maybe I'm being too pessimistic."

"Let's hope so," said James. "You're not normally someone to let the possibility of something failing, stop you from making sure that it ultimately succeeds, when you want it to. You're the strongest woman I know Linda – that's why I'm attracted to you – and if anyone can pull Alexandra through this, it's you."

"So, you're sending a letter then?" he asked.

"Yes. I'm going to write it this weekend, and send all the copies off, first thing on Day 1 of next week. I've had enough, and what I've heard today is unacceptable. Something's got to be done. Sorry, James, I know she's your wife but ... well, changing the subject slightly. I don't suppose you've spoken to her yet, about our matter?"

"No. Sorry, Linda."

"OK, well I'm not discussing *that* tonight! But obviously, you were due to come over here for dinner tonight. Assuming all is relatively well, by then, would Day 1 of next week be convenient for you? We'll give the same official reason as today, and of course there might be more credibility then, as I won't have been in work to discuss the arrangements for Day 5 of next week, and the night will be getting close."

"I think so, Linda. Thank you," said James.

"I see what you mean about this being awkward though," he continued. "In theory, I suppose I should be at the court next week, supporting Gillian, as her father, and yet you'll be there also with Alexandra, and I'll really be hoping for the same outcome as you, for her. Do you think I should go?"

"It's up to you, James," said Linda. "I can understand that it does make you feel that your loyalties are compromised, and I wouldn't blame you at all, for making a diplomatic excuse and not coming. I won't tell you that you've got to come, in these circumstances."

"But on the other hand," pondered James, "if Elizabeth has any suspicions at all about us – and I honestly don't know about that – then it might make it a bit obvious if I stay away. Perhaps I will come, but I'll have to be sat with Elizabeth and Gillian."

"Well, as I said, it's your decision," replied Linda. "If you *are* there, then I don't see any reason, why we still can't meet in the evening, as planned, either. It's not as if we'll be in any position to discuss the arrangements for the end of the next working week, whilst we're at the juvenile court."

"Anyhow, I must go, so I'll say goodbye now, and I'll see you on Day 1 of next week, whatever happens."

\*\*\*

Finally, Linda listened to the news, and heard the report of her daughter's arrest, and her statement to the press, earlier. As she had hoped, attention now, was beginning to focus on Charterhouse itself.

Then she went to bed. As she got upstairs, she could hear Alexandra still quietly sobbing. She now desperately wanted to hold her in her arms, and comfort her, but she forced herself to remain resolute in her determination that her daughter would have the whole night, and some of tomorrow, to reflect on things.

\*\*\*

In her room, Alexandra heard her mother go to bed. She was feeling truly desperate. She was terrified at the thought that their relationship might be damaged by this. Her mother was the rock that she clung to, and without her, she feared that she would be swept away by the storm. She knew that she had let her down, and everybody else for that matter, after all they had done for her, and she wondered whether she had indeed blown her chance of becoming college champion, and even of going to Castra, at all. Wiping away her tears, she got ready for bed herself. Once there, it took a long while for sleep to come, and when it did, her dreams were troubled. She awoke several times in the night.

# CHAPTER 3

Linda rose early the next morning, and put the week's washing through the machine. Then she checked the gate of Elmsbrook. She couldn't see anybody camped outside. Anyhow, she wouldn't think about the media now. She was going to write her letter to the Charterhouse board of governors.

She made breakfast – cereal and a fully cooked one, though she wouldn't bother with the toast today – and took Alexandra's to her room, and left her once more. Then again, after she'd eaten, she collected her daughter's dishes from her room, washed everything up, and hung the washing on the line outside. Then she went down to the letterbox and picked up her newspaper. Upon returning, she finally sat down at her desk in the study, and began her letter.

\*\*\*

By lunchtime, Linda was finished. She then listened to the latest news bulletin. There didn't seem to have been much change since last night, as far as what the media were saying. Now, she decided that it was time to put her daughter out of her misery. She went up to her bedroom, unlocked the door, and went in. Alexandra was reading, a book and looked up in surprise.

"Good afternoon darling!" she said in a warm voice, that she hoped would break the ice and raise her daughter's confidence. "Shall we have some lunch then?"

"G-good morning M-mother," replied Alexandra nervously.

Linda went to the bed, where Alexandra sat, and slipped her arm around her shoulders.

Alexandra began to speak again, still stammering slightly.

"A-are you s-still ..." she began.

Linda sat down beside her, looked into her eyes, and gently coaxed her, as she had many times a few years ago, to help her daughter to overcome the disability. "Now just relax, take a deep breath, and think. You know what you want to say, and it's me, Mother, so you've no need to be nervous." She squeezed Alexandra's hand, and stroked her fingers, as she softly soothed her.

Alexandra calmed herself. "You're not still angry with me, Mother? I can come out of my room now?"

"Taking those questions in reverse order, Alexandra, said Linda, "firstly, yes, you may come out now and secondly, no, I'm not still angry with you, so you needn't worry. I'm not going to shout at you, anymore. Your period of disgrace, is now over. Come on downstairs, and have a quick bite to eat with me, then we'll wash up and go into the study, and have a more relaxed talk, than we did last night. And Tom will be coming at 6.00 p.m. tonight. I can't pretend that I'm not still a little cross about all of this, but it isn't just your mistake yesterday, which is annoying me. We'll talk about all of that, later. For now, though, let's just go downstairs. Come on."

She stood up, and held out her arm for Alexandra to go inside of. Her daughter accepted, and Linda walked her out of the room, and down the stairs.

"Snuggle yourself up to me, the way you like to, if you want, darling," she said, squeezing Alexandra tight. "I'm here with you, and I'm going to get you through this. Just let me take over, and you'll be OK."

Linda hoped that she sounded 100% confident, to help ease her daughter's fears, although she actually felt that 90% was a more accurate estimate.

Alexandra herself began to feel some strength returning to her. This was more the way things usually were between them. Her mother seemed to have simmered down, and was now talking about taking control of the situation. Now, she didn't feel quite so lost. In time, her mother might forgive her, after all.

So later that afternoon, Linda made them both a cup of coffee, and they sat down at their desks in the study, to talk.

"Right," said Linda, and reached across to take Alexandra's hand. "Now, first of all, I *was* very angry with you last night, and I'm sorry to have frightened you. Your stammer came back, which showed how bad you must have been feeling. I hope you realise how much that upset me, too."

Linda was squeezing her daughter's hand, and stroking her fingers once again, with the softest of touches. Alexandra couldn't really explain it, but somehow her mother always seemed to have some kind of magic in her fingers, as they glided around hers, because they always had a comforting, and sometimes controlling effect on her.

"Now, you've no need to be at all frightened now, I promise you my darling! Yesterday is gone and this is when we make up together, and start to fight back. You and I are a partnership, with me leading. That's the way we do things, and that's why we're so good together.

"As I said earlier, I am still cross, but it's not just with you. You've been a naughty girl, Alexandra, and you deserved to be punished, but that said, I *can* see that you were heavily pushed into doing what you did. That's not an excuse, but it was clearly the only reason for it. Obviously, I'm quite upset that after all the work and effort that's gone in to getting you into a position, where you can possibly achieve great things – particularly from me – you've put it all at risk by doing this, but we'll just have to get over that, and try our hardest to put things right.

"I'm concerned that you crumbled so easily under the pressure though, darling! If the bullying from Gillian was as bad as it seems to have been, then why, in the name of the Divine Being, didn't you say something to me? You know that I'm always here for you to confide in, and you do on most things. That's the main reason why I sent you to Charterhouse as a day-pupil, and not a boarder, so that you could home and talk to me about your feelings, and be guided, looked after, and loved by me. But you've never given me any reason to suspect that there was anything as bad as this going on!"

Alexandra now squeezed her mother's hand from the inside and Linda looked into her eyes, encouraging her to say what she had on her mind.

"Mother," she began. "I'm truly sorry for what I did yesterday. I know I did wrong, and I accept that I deserved to be punished. The worst thing for me, even more than what I might have done to damage my future prospects, is that I've let you down, and that things might never be the same between us again!"

"The last part of that statement is complete nonsense Alexandra!" said her mother. "You *mustn't* think like that darling. You and I have far too solid a relationship, to let three bottles of perfume and a rude statement written on a wall, damage it beyond repair. I've just told you – we'll get over that. I'm far more angry with Gillian, for setting you up, and her 'mistress', Elizabeth, who I believe she was working for, than I am with you. But once again, sweetheart, why didn't you tell me how she was taunting and bullying you? I'd have helped you, and you wouldn't have got into this mess."

"Mother, there's something else you should know about," said Alexandra.

Linda looked at her in alarm. "Alexandra, I hope you're not telling me that there's more to come out regarding this, which I wasn't aware of last night!" she said sternly.

"No, no, Mother!" Alexandra reassured her. "It's nothing connected to that. It's something that happened between us, earlier in 5010, during my last school year."

"Oh," said Linda. "Go ahead then."

"Gillian runs college tuck shop, Mother," began Alexandra. "For a few days, a while ago, she was ill, and some of the other girls who assisted her, had to take over themselves. I was drafted in to take care of the accounts.

"Anyhow, I noticed that the books weren't right. They didn't balance at all, and I realised that Gillian must be fiddling them, and helping herself to the takings. I reported it to our house mistress, and then of course, word got around the rest of the staff. Once Gillian had recovered, they had to tell her that they'd discovered what she'd been doing, although they didn't take any action, and they let her carry on in the same position. It didn't take her long to find out that I'd been checking the accounts though, and she guessed that I'd told someone. She was furious that I'd 'grassed' on her – and that's when I got my first thumping from her."

Linda sat bolt up in her chair, nearly spilling her coffee in her saucer. "She's hit you?" she cried.

"Yes, Mother. It was much the same situation as yesterday – only the first time, she wasn't in any mood to let me off. She got a couple of girls to hold me up, whilst she punched me so hard in the stomach, that all the breath got knocked out of me. As a result, I was blackballed from the tuck shop from then on, and the money that I would have spent on crisps, or a chocolate bar, I had to give directly to her, instead. And that's how it's been ever since."

"What?" exclaimed Linda angrily. "You mean to say that all the money I've given you for that has been going straight into Gillian's pocket?"

"Um ... Yes, Mother, I'm afraid so," said Alexandra sheepishly. "Does that mean that I'll be punished again, for wasting your money?"

"No, it doesn't, Alexandra. I think we've established who really needs to be punished. But yet again, why, for goodness sake, didn't you tell me this, back then?"

"Because I thought that you'd probably report it to the college formally, and that would have got me into even more trouble with Gillian," said Alexandra.

"Well, you've got yourself into even more trouble with the police now, Alexandra – and this time I *will* be taking formal action. I'm even more angry with her now, and determined that she's going to get her just desserts next week!"

"Anyhow, Mother, that's why I knew that Gillian was serious about giving me a thumping yesterday, if I didn't do what she wanted. And if I'd chosen the 'escort boys' option – which I certainly didn't want to – then you would have certainly horsewhipped me if you'd found out, and I just know that you *would* have found out somehow. In any case she'd insulted me by rubbishing my likely sexual ability, in front of my form class, which really embarrassed me. If I had taken that last option, and then not been able to do it, I'd have been a laughing stock, because Gillian would be sure to know, and tell all of Charterhouse! I felt I had to do the shoplifting. That's why I did what I did."

Linda looked at her quizzically. "When you say she'd insulted you, what exactly did she say?" she asked.

"She said that I ought to go to the 'drama lessons' to 'learn how to do it' and that even then, Tom would 'have to be on top'. I'd never be able to ... well, 'give a man one', as she put it, let alone two or three times at a time, like most Geratican women. She's always boasted that she did it three times, during the hour she spent in a massage parlour, when she lost her virginity. Believe me we've been told that on many occasions!

"Anyhow, some of the other girls sniggered when Gillian made those remarks to me, and it started me thinking that maybe she was right. I don't feel as confident as I did before. Perhaps I'm just fantasising and when it really comes to it, I won't be able to manage it."

"Oh, for Geratica's sake, Alexandra!" exclaimed her mother, crossly. "You don't want to listen to all that tosh! That's just girl talk. Young Geratican females have been boasting to each other about their sexual performance, since time began. It's just immaturity. You're *all* still young and inexperienced. If Gillian thinks she's clever, having done it three times in an hour, I can tell her that I beat that, on several occasions with your father, and sometimes the total for a night, might have been considerably more! But it's not a subject that mature, not to mention polite, and well-mannered Geratican ladies, brag about. Yes, we may talk, or sometimes even joke about it, but bragging – if it needs to be done at all – should be reserved for your partner's ears only, in private!

"Gillian's just trying to intimidate you, darling – and she seems to be succeeding. She was probably hoping to goad you into taking part in those 'drama lessons'! I do acknowledge though, that Gillian grossly insulted you. That's not an acceptable thing for one Geratican female to insinuate about another."

Linda felt a deep fury welling up inside of her. Just wait until she got her hands on her – and she was going to, she was determined about that!

"I think she genuinely thought what she said was true, Mother, but you might be partially right," said Alexandra. "There's no doubt though, that I'm not as passionate as some Geratican women, and I'm never going to be the one with the most stamina. The truth is, I'm not even sure myself, whether I've got it in me."

"Darling, there's *no* reason at all, why you won't be able to make love to a man," said Linda firmly. "I won't hear of such nonsense! It's not exactly the most difficult thing in the world to do, after all. Unlike the other main female species that we know of in the universe, we only have to position ourselves in the right place, so to speak, and then our internal sexual organs do the rest for us. All we have to do is build up our passions, and satisfy our desires. From what I've seen of you, when you're with Tom, you have enough passion inside of you to make it happen, sweetheart, I promise.

"In any case, it isn't *all* about 'stamina'! I know that you're also highly sensitive, Alexandra, and your senses become very acute. That's another big factor in making love, and it's bound to contribute extremely heavily towards inducing you to orgasm, darling, and Tom too. Take it from someone older, and more experienced than you. Mother knows what she's talking about, more than an upstart like Gillian Spencer! And no-one knows and understands you better than me. I want the best for you, and if you take my advice and follow my instructions, like a Geratican mother's ultimate good girl that you *nearly* always are for me, then you'll stand a much better chance of getting it, than listening to all that stupid girls talk at Charterhouse. It's a good job you *are* a day pupil there, so that you can come home and hear something sensible in the evening!

"We discussed some of this last weekend. It's true that you're on the less dominant, less confident, and yes, perhaps less passionate side of the Geratican personality, but that certainly doesn't mean you can't be a traditional woman in the bedroom, which I think is what you really want. Your natural urges and desires, will be that way inclined. Maybe your passion won't be quite as strong as some – myself included perhaps – but you are how you are, and you can't do a lot to change something as fundamental as that. It doesn't matter sweetheart. Stamina isn't necessarily important, though it's undeniably nice to have. Quality, not quantity, as they say! What you achieve in making love to Tom once or twice, it might take Gillian three or four times that amount, to achieve the same, with whoever her man might be. You don't know, and it's personal. What goes on in your bedroom, with your partner, is your business and no one else's.

"I will tell you, that for many women, the first orgasm is usually the strongest and most intense, but they quickly recover, and then I always compare it to eating a box of chocolates! You just can't resist having another one, and before you know it, you've had five or six. The orgasms do become slightly less intense, the more you have them, but they're still pleasurable. How many you might have, can also depend on whether your partner can continue for as long as you can. One of you is bound to tire eventually, and it's often the man – but not always.

"Your approach to a box of chocolates, tends to be different to mine. I devour most of it in a very short space of time, and find it extremely difficult to resist, whereas you're often satisfied with just a few at a time. That analogy might apply to your sexual hunger, too. Whereas – just between you and me – I've been known to be prolific, you might be just as satisfied – and Tom, too – with a lesser amount."

"As I said before though, darling, don't take any notice of that girls talk – it means nothing!" Linda told her daughter, in conclusion.

"I *am* listening to every word that *you* say, and taking it all in, Mother," said Alexandra. "When you explain things to me, everything seems so clear. It's when I'm with other girls, that things sometimes get confusing."

"You still need more confidence in yourself, darling," said Linda. "You've come a long way, but I think this is a step back for you, and it'll take a little time for you to make up the ground. But you *will* do Alexandra. Trust me on this. You've got a lot of assets to take advantage of. Don't under-sell yourself. You're one of the most intelligent girls in your year group at school – if not *the* most intelligent! – and you're also very likeable. Add to that, the fact that you're a very attractive girl, who's managed to propose a relationship – and you've got yourself a good young man, too – then I think most people would agree that you've got a lot going for you.

"Once we get you back to Charterhouse, *if* you can pick up where you left off as a candidate for college champion, then it's going to be more important for you than ever, to make this concert a success. I've always said that it will do wonders for your confidence, darling and it'll certainly help restore your reputation to where it was."

"I *will* try my hardest Mother. I promise you that."

Linda touched her daughter's arm. "I know you will, sweetheart," she said, smiling.

"To return to Gillian's taunting of your sexual capabilities though," she continued. "From what you told me last weekend, you certainly have many fantasies in that regard. Well, your fantasies *can* and *will* become reality! But all in good time. Gillian's smutty brain is suggesting that you should 'practice' and I'm pleased to say that help may be on its way. You remember I said that there was something on the market? Well it could be with you soon. But again, I'm not saying anything more about that at the moment. But it will *definitely* be a better way of going about it, than going with escort boys, which Gillian obviously has.

"Let's get your punishment term over with, first though. You still shouldn't have gone shoplifting Alexandra. Whatever the reason behind it, there can be no excuse for stealing. Yes, you didn't want to be thumped, so it was understandable to appear to agree to collaborate with Gillian over it, but then you really should have done something about it, before you actually had to go through with it."

"But what could I have done Mother?" asked Alexandra. "I didn't think any of the staff would do anything about it, and if Gillian found out that I'd told tales on her again, she'd have thumped me for sure!"

"Well, this was a serious matter darling – even more so than the tuck shop affair, which I now know about. It might have been difficult for them to do absolutely nothing, this time. And there was the escort business for you to expose. You did do that in the end, but not before you'd got yourself into trouble in the process! At the very least, you could have tried to slip out to a public phone box at the college, and rung me. I'm sure I'd have had some advice for you."

"I must admit, I didn't think of that, Mother," replied Alexandra.

"You need to get a little stronger Alexandra," said her mother. "If people start to pressurise you, and you feel that what they're proposing is wrong, then go with your instincts and stand your ground. You know that I'll always help you through, but I won't, and I *can't* be physically with you, all the time."

"I do think that I've improved in that respect, Mother," said Alexandra. "I certainly told Gillian, categorically, that I wasn't getting involved with her escort boys, and before we left to go to Rimmingtons, I told her that this was the only time I was doing this. She'd said nothing about any future endeavours, so we'd be even after that."

"Well that was good at least," agreed Linda. "And as I've said, I can see that you were obviously put under heavy pressure, which intimidated you so much, that you felt you had no choice but to commit the offence. And what's more, I think, once they hear the whole evidence, a lot of other people will, too."

"Which brings me on to what we're going to do about all of this," continued Linda. She opened her notepad and began ticking off the details, as she explained them to her daughter.

"Your hearing is obviously on Day 1 of next week, and I'll be with you, so I've taken the day off. Tom may too, so I believe. I was busy making phone calls in here last night. I rang Sergeant Perkins, who informed me who was representing you. It's a lady called Jessica Beale, a solicitor with over ten years of experience, I'm told. I contacted her, and she told me who's going to be the judge. It's Lavinia Mountford, someone who I knew at Charterhouse, in fact. I've asked to be called as a witness, which will enable me to speak on your behalf."

"Oh!" said Alexandra, surprised. "That's good then Mother. Thank you." She wasn't very well informed about what the procedure was, in this type of court. She'd never dreamt that she'd one day be before one. "Will ... Will I have to give evidence too, Mother?" she asked nervously.

"No, darling, so don't start worrying about that," said Linda, gently. "Jessica Beale will be your representative and present your case for you. You'll just need to stand up to confirm your identity at the start, and then stand again at the end, when you're given your sentence.

"Now, I also called the palace, and spoke to Queen Alexandra. She told me that the report on you had already made the news, and afterwards I made a brief statement, through the intercom. The queen was as shocked as the rest of us have been, but she feels that this is outside of your normal character, and that you seem to have been coerced into it, somewhat. She obviously can't be seen to be directly getting involved in your case, but she has very kindly said, that she will supply a reference to the court, commending your usual good character. There'll be no specific mention of this affair."

"I'm extremely grateful for that, Mother!" exclaimed Alexandra.

"Yes, well I think that you should thank her personally, next week Alexandra. Especially if – as I hope – you get a reasonably lenient punishment. Your case will be that, although you realise what you did was wrong, that there is no excuse for it, that you're truly sorry, and that you're prepared to offer a sum of money to Rimmingtons, equivalent to the value of the perfume, as compensation, you were, nevertheless, bullied into it by others, namely your co-accused, which you felt too intimidated by, to resist. That, I'm hopeful will satisfy the juvenile court and convince them to look upon you as favourably as possible. Then, once your suspension from Charterhouse is up, you'll be able to go back and pick up the pieces, from the week after next."

"Yes, Mother. Of course," said Alexandra obediently. "Do you mean that I'll need to come to the palace?"

"Very possibly," replied Linda.

"I've also written a letter, and copied it to every member of the board of governors at Charterhouse, which I'm going to send off in the post, first thing next week. I'm calling for an emergency meeting, which will discuss

Mrs Spencer's future as headmistress. I think that now is the time to get her removed from her post. Although, with the new information that you've now given me, regarding the tuck shop activities, I shall now need to amend it."

Alexandra's eyes widened with amazement.

"You're really going to get her removed, Mother?"

"I'm going to *try*, Alexandra! Charterhouse is likely to be a focus of attention in the media, for a spell now, mainly through the antics of Spencer junior, rather than you, I hope. I imagine that quite a lot of people are going to say Mrs Spencer's incompetent, for not knowing that escort boys were being brought into the college, by her own daughter, and probably also, that Gillian should be expelled. It's even on the cards that she might be sent to a young offenders' institution, given the extent of her misdemeanours, in which case, she'll be gone anyhow. If she should be lucky and escape that, then I think that for as long as Mrs Spencer remains in place, then Gillian's got a chance of remaining, too, but if the pressure becomes too great on her, from the media and public alike, then she may be forced to kick her out. If Elizabeth was to be sacked, then I can't see Gillian being able to stay there either.

"Whatever happens, Gillian can't be considered for college champion now. So you'll probably be the only candidate, as I doubt there'll be time for them to select another now, before the end of term. I don't think there's ever been a champion with a criminal record though, even if yours will be a relatively minor offence, which should get blown over, in time. We'll just have to keep our fingers crossed on that, and hope that the panel who decide it, won't allow this indiscretion to exclude you, but at least up to a point, that would be your own fault, Alexandra. It's only a relatively recently established annual award, but again, I don't think that Charterhouse has ever been in a position, where it cannot send a college champion to a University, one year. That would be a further blow to its reputation! Philippa also wishes you good luck for the hearing, and she's going to send a letter to the judge, telling her that she has found you a very pleasant girl to work with, and that she hopes that with your talent, you'll still be able to perform the concert in her honour.

"So, all in all, Alexandra, I think you'll be alright, but the fact still remains that you've done this, and you've no excuse, and now you must serve your punishment. I know that you're sorry – I believe you completely, and I've already accepted your apology – and I *do* appreciate that there were mitigating circumstances. You're not a bad girl at all, in fact quite the reverse, normally. You've made a mistake, but we all do from time to time."

"When I went to Charterhouse yesterday morning, I never had any thought in my mind that I would try and shoplift from Rimmingtons,

Mother!" said Alexandra. "I would never have done it, if it hadn't have been for Gillian – although I know that's no excuse."

"I know, darling, and that will be stressed at the hearing," said Linda. "Unfortunately," she added, "there will inevitably be a quite a few people from the media there as well, which you won't be used to. Just do as I say, and leave any talking that needs to be done, to me. I'll get you through it."

Linda looked at her checklist. "I think that's all I needed to say to you, Alexandra. Is it all clear to you? Any questions, just ask away."

"No, I don't think there's anything else, Mother," replied her daughter. "Except to say, that I'll be really nervous at the hearing."

"Well yes, I expect you will be," said Linda. "But as I said, you've not got that much to do directly, during the proceedings, so as long as you're looking at your best, are courteous, and accept everything that the judge tells you, then you'll be halfway there.

"So, let's leave it there for now. You'll be serving your punishment for two weeks and we'll try and stay clear of this subject, as much as possible, until then. Once you're due to complete it, we'll speak again, and then hopefully after that, we can draw a line under it."

"Very good, Mother," said Alexandra.

Linda got up from her desk and her daughter followed suit. "So now, you'd better think about getting ready for Tom, hadn't you?" she asked, smiling. "I've told him not to say anything to any journalists, just in case any should try to get into contact with him, as your boyfriend, and also, to come through the wood this evening, and come in through our back entrance, for security."

Alexandra smiled back. "That's probably a good idea, Mother," she replied.

"Meanwhile, I'm going to go down to the grocery store, as you obviously can't this week, now." added Linda.

"Oh! I'm sorry about that, too, Mother!" said Alexandra. Then she thought of something else.

"There is just one more thing Mother," she said. "Tonight, will I be in your bed as usual, on this day of the week, or is that postponed during my punishment term?"

"I don't think that necessarily counts as a treat, darling," said Linda. "It's something intimate and personal, that happens between us once a week, and I think it's something that's important to both of us. After the hurt between us yesterday, I need you particularly badly at the moment. I want you, Alexandra, and you're to go to *my* bedroom, when you retire tonight!"

"You know that I need you more, Mother," replied Alexandra, gratefully. "Thank you!"

# CHAPTER 4

Tom arrived punctually at 6 p.m., and came through the back gate, as Linda had instructed. Alexandra let him into The Grange, through the kitchen porch, when she saw him, just after she'd finished laying the dining room table, for her mother. He was wearing a smart dinner suit and tie.

"Good evening, Tom!" said Linda. She wore a long blue gown, and a pair of long black gloves were on a side table, which she had removed, whilst she was cooking. "I hope you're feeling hungry. Tonight, we can celebrate your birthday properly."

"Very, as a matter of fact, Mrs Radcliffe!" replied Tom, amiably. "What's on the menu?"

"Vegetable soup, followed by one of our favourite earth dishes," she told him. "Chilli con carne."

Mmm, I've had that before. It's delicious!"

"Well, I'd better get on with it then," said Linda. "Darling, you go and entertain Tom for a while. I'll fetch you when I'm ready to serve up the soup."

"Yes, Mother, of course! Anything I can do to help!" said Alexandra, at her most obedient. She was determined to display exemplary behaviour and work exceptionally hard at the jobs that her mother gave her to do, over the next fortnight, whilst she was under punishment, to make up for the trouble that she'd caused.

"Let me take your coat," she said, to Tom, as she led him to the cloakroom. Once there, she took off her own, that she had worn out into the cold evening air to meet him. She was pleased to see his reaction.

"So, you like what you see, then?" she asked.

"Oh yes," answered Tom. "You look gorgeous!"

Alexandra glowed with pleasure, and wrapped her arms around him. She kissed his lips softly, and her aroused geratis pressed against his thigh. For several seconds they exchanged kisses and both murmured with pleasure as their sexual excitement grew.

"Did you bring your bow tie?" she asked, as they eventually separated from their embrace.

Yes. It's in my jacket pocket," replied Tom.

"Good! We'll ask Mother to show us how you tie it, later."

Then Alexandra took him up to her room. She started to load her selection of music, into her music machine.

"Alexandra," said Tom. I've obviously heard about what's happened, and your mother filled me in on some of the details, over the phone, but she said that there was more to it. I imagined there must be. You would never normally do something like that!"

"No. Quite," confirmed Alexandra.

"Well there's been more on the news today, so I know roughly the story, but I assume you want to talk about it?"

"Definitely!" she replied. "I'd have liked to have come over to see you during the day, but unfortunately Mother's gated me here for a week now, as part of my punishment for what I did yesterday."

"OK. Well come and sit with me, and you can pour it all out then," said Tom.

Alexandra started up her music machine and went to her boyfriend, as he sat on her bed. She took his hand and Tom gave hers an encouraging squeeze from the inside. Her heart swelled with her love for him. He was the sweetest and kindest boy she could ever meet; she was certain of that. She'd chosen well, and his understanding of her need to talk, confirmed it.

So she gave Tom an account of what had happened, in her own words, telling him about the escort boys being brought into Charterhouse by Gillian Spencer, how their services had been taken advantage of, by both Gillian and Melanie, and their need for extra cash to pay for it, which they'd procured by shoplifting, and then selling the goods on to other girls at the college.

Then she described how Gillian had tried to bully her into seeing one of the escort boys and when she'd refused, threatened to give her a thumping if she didn't participate in the shoplifting activities. She'd felt that she had no choice, but now she knew she'd been stupid. Once they were at Rimmingtons, and Gillian had ordered her to swipe the perfume bottles into her school bag, she'd been immediately caught, and Gillian and Melanie had gone. She'd realised that Gillian had set her up, and then been arrested. Then she told Tom the reason why she thought Gillian had done it, and of how the headmistress, Gillian's mother, had wanted her reputation tarnished, so that she'd have to withdraw as a candidate for the college Champion, and leave her own daughter to gain the award, unopposed.

"Blimey, this is terrible!" exclaimed Tom. "They can't get away with that. So, what happened after your arrest?"

"Well, they obviously took me to the police station. I realised that I was in a lot of trouble, and that it was pointless lying or covering anything up, or I might get into even deeper hot water, so I decided to tell everything, including the fact that the escorts were coming into Charterhouse. I was told that I'd have to report to Buckmore Juvenile Court, at 8.00 a.m. on Day 1 of Week 34. Mrs Spencer came to collect me, but before she had the chance to take me, a sergeant and a constable came over and said that they'd also like to talk to Gillian, and her friend Melanie. It was obviously because of what I'd revealed in my statement to them, at the station.

"So, they took me back to Charterhouse, and Mrs Spencer drove herself. Then all three of us girls were called into a meeting with the headmistress and the officers. Gillian tried to deny it all, and put the blame on me, but the upshot was that she was eventually forced to admit that she was behind both the escort and the shoplifting schemes, and that I hadn't previously had any involvement with either, before yesterday lunchtime. Gillian and Melanie were then told that they had to report to the juvenile court, next week too.

"Then Mrs Spencer told us that we were all to be suspended for a week, and Melanie and I were caned on our bare bottoms – me six times and Melanie eight, due to her previous misdemeanours with the escorts. She claimed that Gillian had already been punished. And both of them took it in turns to beat us, too!"

"I don't believe it!" said Tom. "But surely the court will be sympathetic with the situation you were in, and be lenient with you? Seeing as you were obviously being coerced. I don't necessarily think you were *that* stupid to do what you did."

"Mother certainly thought I was, and that I couldn't excuse it, and she was right, Tom – now that she's corrected me, I can see that now. She was *furious*! She came to collect me from Charterhouse, and she didn't speak at all, from the time that we left, to when we got home. Then she gave me the biggest telling off of my life. You should have heard her shout and bang her desk in the study! I actually started stammering again, I was so nervous, which I think Mother was upset about, but she felt that I deserved the rollicking."

"Did you get the cane from her, too?"

Alexandra gave Tom a look. "What do *you* think?" she asked.

"Of course afterwards, Mother gated me for next week. I've also had my allowance cancelled for a fortnight, and been disqualified from receiving any special treats, during that period."

"I gather you were also sent to your room, and not allowed out until your mother gave you permission, too," said Tom. "When did you eventually come back downstairs?"

"At lunch time," replied Alexandra.

"Actually, Mother does think that there's a good chance of me getting a reasonably light sentence," she continued, "but she didn't tell me that yesterday! She said that I'd put my whole future at risk, and that she was hurt that I'd thrown everything that she'd done for me recently, back in her face. What she said about our relationship, really did it, and I had a terrible night thinking about it all. Damaging that would be a disaster for me. You know that Tom!

"Anyhow, after I'd been sent up to my room in disgrace, Mother apparently made a lot of phone calls, and it transpires that both Queen Alexandra and Philippa Barrington – who's giving me private tuition, before I *hopefully* organise a concert in her honour – are going to send references to the court, telling of my usual good character, and behaviour. She also knows the judge – she was at Charterhouse with her, apparently – and she seems to feel that the solicitor representing me, should know her stuff. Mother's also asked to be a witness for the defence, so that she can speak on my behalf. Luckily, I don't have to actually give evidence myself. It'll just be my solicitor making my case, for me. I just have to confirm my identity, and then at the end, stand before the court and hear my sentence. There's going to be a lot of media attention, which I'm not looking forward to, but Mother says, that if I do as she says, she can get me through it all. She's basically taken control."

"Well she usually does, doesn't she?" said Tom. "She did tell me last night, when she rang, that you had to play your cards right, and that she was going to play them for you!"

"Did she?" asked Alexandra. "Well yes, I suppose she has done really, and as always, I'm eternally grateful to her."

"Gillian should be expelled!" said Tom furiously. "From what you've told me about her before, she's been getting away with things for ages, and what she's done in total, for this case, is far worse than your crime. I'm sure you'll be alright, and it sounds as if you've got as much support as you could wish for, in this situation."

"Tom," said Alexandra, squeezing his hand. They looked into each other's eyes, as the music played in the background. "It's going to be a really nervous day for me on Day 1 of next week, despite the fact that I won't have to do much myself. I'm scared stiff of being up in front of a court, as a defendant. I never, in my wildest dreams, thought that it would ever happen! Then there'll be all the press people around us, which I'm dreading. And you know what part of the punishment is for some of the girls who get sentenced there? They get horsewhipped, in front of the royal Palace!"

"They won't do that to *you*, will they?" asked Tom. "Just for what you did yesterday? Gillian's done far worse, over a far longer period of time."

"I don't know," said Alexandra, her voice faltering slightly.

"You want me to come as well, to support you?" Tom asked, guessing what was going through her mind.

"Could you? Mother said that she thought you would. Your work will let you have the time off? Mother will be there of course, but to have you both there with me, would be a terrific comfort to me."

"Alexandra, of course I'll be there! If I didn't support you now, in your hour of greatest need, then what kind of a boyfriend would you have proposed a relationship to, last weekend?"

"Oh, thank you, darling!" Alexandra felt her love for Tom swell up inside and her geratis responded accordingly. She took Tom down on her bed, beneath her, and began to give him all the affection that she could muster, which luckily for Tom, was plenty. Suddenly her sexual confidence began to partially return, as she placed soft kisses on his lips, which made his eyes close with pleasure, and a low murmur to escape from him, as his breath shortened with excitement. Alexandra's legs wrapped around Tom's, and he felt the power in her thighs, and of her geratis stabbing between his. She squeezed his shoulders in her arms and engulfed his whole body. The intensity of Tom's arousal made his genus start to balloon. He returned Alexandra's kisses, as she continued to love him, and they both felt ecstasy. Alexandra felt a tingling sensation in her thighs, and feet and a huge wave of pleasure shot through her geratis, making her gasp. Just as she'd experienced four nights ago, she knew that they had gone as far as they possibly could, without fully making love, and she rolled off him, allowing them both to get their breath back.

If any of the previous moments had told Alexandra anything, it was that, if she and Tom had been naked, and she'd been inside of him, she would have come and brought him on as well. She was sure of that. Gillian was at least wrong in her opinion that she couldn't make love to Tom. Whether after truly experiencing a full orgasm, she would be able to summon her energy to do it again, was another matter, but she wasn't going to worry about that at the moment and – as her mother had pointed out – it was nobody else's business anyhow.

"Tom," she said, "When Gillian found out that I had a boyfriend, she insulted me, by casting aspersions about my sexual capabilities, in front of our form class! She said that I ought to go to the 'drama lessons' now, to learn how to do it, and that you'd have to be the one on top – that I could never give you an orgasm, let alone two or three at a time, like most normal Geratican women."

"She said that!" Tom exploded. "That's utter rubbish! After the way you just made me feel, I know that you could! I hope you didn't take any notice?"

"Well, to be honest, I did a bit," admitted Alexandra. "Mother told me that I shouldn't have done, too, but some of the others thought it was very amusing, and it was so embarrassing. She was probably trying to goad me, but I think she really did believe it, too. It knocked my confidence, and started making me wonder if she might be right, and that other people would think it, as well. After tonight though, I may be feeling a little different, again. If we'd been trying to go all the way, then I'd have made love to you just now, Tom! I just know it, *my darling*. I'm certain that I can now, and when we're finally both allowed to do it, and you're ready, then I *want* to!"

"And I want you to make love to me, too, Angel!" replied Tom.

Side by side they kissed again, and Alexandra wrapped him in her arms and he snuggled to her. They continued talking for another couple of minutes, before Alexandra gently eased herself over Tom, and began to kiss him again. Suddenly, there was a knock on the door. It immediately opened and Linda walked in.

"Oh! Sorry to interrupt," she said with a slight smirk. "I just wanted to say, that I'm ready to start serving up now, Alexandra – when you're ready that is!"

Alexandra had leapt to her feet as quickly as she could. "That's OK, Mother!" she said, her cheeks flushing slightly. "I'm ready now. We'll come on downstairs."

She took Tom's hand, and they followed her mother out of the room, and down the stairs.

Alexandra sat Tom down in the dining room, and then went to the kitchen to help her mother dish up and serve the soup.

"Mother," she said quickly. "We weren't about to make love just then. You know that, don't you?"

Linda burst out laughing. "Well of course, Alexandra, unless you young people are now able to do it with your clothes on? Don't worry about what I saw. I may be strict about you having intercourse until you're both above the age of consent, but I'm not a prude when it comes to that sort of thing. You can climb all over Tom, on the sofa before me, and I won't mind, though I would have thought you'd have preferred somewhere a little more private, to be that intimate together!"

"Yes, Mother!" Alexandra giggled.

"Seriously though, darling," continued her mother. "I'm sorry I walked in on you, in the middle of that – perhaps I'll have to ask if I can come in, the next time you're up there with Tom."

A couple of minutes later, they were all seated at the dining room table, with Linda at the head, Alexandra in her usual place, to her first right and Tom to her first left.

"Well, Tom," said Linda, as she poured red wine into his glass. "May I first congratulate you – properly at last – on your fifteenth birthday. You've caught Alexandra up again! And secondly may I also say how pleased I am, that you've now become my prospective son-in-law! You were always my first choice, and it was one of my daughter's better decisions, recently."

"Thank you, Mrs Radcliffe," said Tom politely. "I'm also delighted to have been asked by Alexandra!" He reached across the table and touched her hand. "My answer was never in doubt. And I've always been fond of you, Mrs Radcliffe, so it will feel almost as if I've now got two stepmothers!"

Alexandra smiled at him, as she remembered the comment that he'd made on his birthday, when he'd said that he felt as if her mother had spoken to him, as if he was her own son. She was extremely pleased to hear Tom say such a nice thing to her. She'd always known that he was genuinely fond of her mother, but to actually hear him say it to her, made Alexandra overjoyed. The two people who meant the most to her in all of Geratica, were with her tonight, and they also got on very well with each other. She couldn't ask for mor.!

"Steady on, old boy!" exclaimed Linda. "One child can be quite enough to deal with, at times."

"Mrs Radcliffe," said Tom, "I don't want to talk about this subject much tonight, as we're supposed to be celebrating, but as Alexandra's boyfriend, I feel I must say that, from what she's told me, Gillian Spencer has behaved atrociously towards her, and I hope that the juvenile court takes that into account next week, and treats her leniently."

"Yes, I quite agree, Tom," replied Linda. "Although Alexandra still shouldn't have done what she did. We'll just have to hope so, and wait to see what happens."

After their soup, Alexandra did the same for her mother as earlier, with the chilli.

"Mmm, this is most excellent, Mrs Radcliffe!" said Tom, contentedly.

"Thank you, Tom," said Linda. "I'm glad that you like it. Even if do say so myself, I think that I'm a decent cook, and my daughter certainly seems to think so, as is quite evident from the speed at which she clears her plate, at every meal time in this household!"

"I *love* your cooking, Mother," said Alexandra. "You aren't just a *decent* cook, you're the *best* cook in Geratica! Although, last time I said that you were being unusually modest, you smacked my bottom in Parliament House, for being cheeky, so I won't say it again!"

"Really?" asked Tom. "You'll have to tell me more about that later, Alexandra!"

Linda chuckled and reaching across the table, she wrapped her arms around her daughter's shoulders, and kissed her strongly on the lips. As so often happened, Alexandra lost herself for a moment, in her mother's eyes. The communication between them, made her feel warm, protected and most of all, loved.

Tom had seen, many times, the effect that Linda had on Alexandra. He knew that until the day her mother died, Alexandra would need her more than anyone else – including himself, sometimes. But he didn't mind. He was under no illusions that Linda was the most important person in Alexandra's life, and he'd known it when he'd accepted her proposal for a relationship, seven days ago.

After they had finished their main course, Alexandra asked Linda, "Mother, Tom was astonished on his birthday night, when you came into my bedroom with the coffee, and I told you what we'd been talking about, without saying anything."

Linda laughed. "I'll bet he was! Philippa Barrington was, too, last weekend, wasn't she? Well that's the Radcliffe's secret code, Tom."

"Is it possible for Tom to learn it, Mother?" asked her daughter. "I'm not really sure myself, of how I started to do it with you."

"Well, possibly," said Linda. "But it's not information that I want circulated very far. It comes in very handy sometimes, when we need to be particularly discreet. Also, you need to be *exceptionally* close. You and I are extremely intimate, even by Geratican standards, and we have a very strong relationship, where we each know what the other needs. Without that, it wouldn't be possible to understand what we're feeling, and saying to each other, through both our eyes and fingers. You also have particularly acute senses, which is also a help.

"In the main, it's only of use for communication such as in making a decision or knowing how the other person is feeling, although there can be other times when it's effective. I can read you quite well, and I obviously picked up the subject you were talking about, the other evening."

"Do many other people in Geratica communicate like that, Mother?" asked Alexandra. "I mean, who taught you? Grandmother?" Both of Alexandra's grandparents had died when she was very young.

"No, darling. Nobody taught me. It's just something I've developed between the two of us. Any other Geraticans who have a similarly intimate relationship to us, *might* be capable of doing the same, and maybe some do – most likely between females, if I had to guess. But I don't know. It's certainly not an officially known language, and I've never heard of it being used publicly before. We could equally be the only two Geraticans to do it!"

"We could try an experiment, I suppose," she continued. "If you'll both excuse me for a moment, I'll just go and get something."

"OK, Mother," said Alexandra, as Linda left the room.

"Crikey," remarked Tom. "I always knew that you and your mother were clever, but I didn't realise you'd invented a whole new language!"

"Well, actually Tom, neither did I!" said Alexandra.

Linda returned with a notepad and pen, and sat down again at the table.

"Right," she said. "Alexandra. Think of something very basic that you're feeling at the moment, which you'd like to pass on to Tom, and write it down on this pad." She passed the pen and pad to her daughter.

"Yes, Mother," obeyed Alexandra.

She thought for a few seconds and then wrote, 'It's wonderful to have you here tonight!'

"OK," said Linda, when she'd finished. "Next, rip the page off the notepad and give it to me, and then, as if you were communicating with me, take Tom's hand, look into his eyes, and try sending that message to him."

"Yes, Mother," said Alexandra again.

Linda looked at what her daughter had written and smiled. Alexandra was an extremely nice girl, with a warm, gentle nature. Using her analogy once again, of a box of chocolates, her daughter was the one with the softest centre, and if the box should be full of her, Linda could ravenously eat her up all at once, and still want more, such was the strength of her love and passion. A little later tonight, she was going to do just that, upstairs in her bed. What had happened yesterday was completely out of character, and she intended to hammer that point home vociferously, to the court next week.

Meanwhile Alexandra did as her mother had instructed. She took Tom's hand and was about to slip hers inside of his, as she would do with her mother, when she suddenly had another thought. Alexandra looked into her mother's eyes for a moment and Linda confirmed that she was right. Now, she changed her hold, so that her hand squeezed Tom's inside of hers and looked into his eyes. She gently stroked his fingers and focused her thoughts on him.

Tom looked back at her and for a few seconds felt nothing. Then for a fleeting moment, he experienced a pleasurable feeling of Alexandra's love for him, causing his senses to tingle. Then, that was it.

"Well?" asked Linda. "Did you understand what your girlfriend was trying to tell you?"

"I'm not sure specifically," answered Tom, "but I felt something. I *definitely* felt something!" he continued in amazement. It was a kind of sensation, almost as if Alexandra was loving me!"

"I get that kind of feeling from you often, Mother!" said Alexandra excitedly. "Perhaps I *can* do this with him."

"Hmm, *perhaps*, said Linda ponderously. "As I said, it's possible, as the two of you are very close and becoming more intimate by the day – as I've seen tonight! If you keep practising, then you may get some positive results. But I honestly don't know, if it can truly be as it is between us. Just for reference Tom, this was Alexandra's message."

She handed him what her daughter had written. Tom immediately broke into a broad smile, as he read it.

"Excuse me, Mrs Radcliffe," he said. "Could I ask Alexandra to come around to this side of the table, please?"

"Of course, Tom!" she answered.

Alexandra smiled also, and went to join her boyfriend. As she reached him, Tom looked up at her lovingly, put his arms around her waist and raising himself slightly from his chair, kissed Alexandra's lips.

"It's wonderful to be here with you, too!" he said.

Alexandra wrapped her own arms around his shoulders and leaning over him, softly kissed his lips, three times in return.

"Once you've finished, Alexandra, we'll try the second half of the experiment!" said Linda, her eyes twinkling at her daughter's.

"Oh, OK. At once, Mother," replied Alexandra obediently and went back to her chair.

"Right then," said Linda. "Give the pad and pen to Tom, Alexandra, and this time, he should try sending you a simple thought. Again Tom, write it down and give it to me."

"OK, Mrs Radcliffe!" said Tom cheerfully. He was extremely curious to find out if he could do this.

On the notepad Tom wrote, 'You are the most beautiful girl in all of Geratica!' He ripped off the page, as Alexandra had done and gave it to Linda.

Linda now read Tom's words, and couldn't stop herself releasing a small chuckle. But she also felt a warm glow of pride, that the daughter she had created, with her beloved Robert, was now producing such a reaction in her future son-in-law.

Tom now took Alexandra's hand, and she helped him by placing it outside of his.

"Yes that's right," said Linda. When Alexandra and I communicate, I am usually the dominant one, as a mother should be, therefore my hand is on the outside, and hers is inside. But if the two of you are to have a traditional Geratican relationship, then Alexandra's hand should be in the dominant position."

Tom squeezed Alexandra's hand from the inside and looked into her eyes. He was in a state of deep sexual arousal, though, and he found it difficult to concentrate on them, without looking away to admire her long blonde hair and gorgeous black gown that showed off her perfect figure.

They broke off the connection.

"OK, Alexandra. Results please," said her mother. "What did you detect?"

"Well not much, to be truthful, Mother," admitted Alexandra. "In fact, nothing at all! You're right, Mother, we will need to practice this. Tom needs to concentrate, and focus his thoughts more. I couldn't tell you with any certainty whatsoever, what he was trying to communicate, but since his eyes spent more time devouring all of me, than purely my eyes, then I'd hazard a guess that it was something to do with his physical attraction towards me. He did after all tell me last weekend, that I was his idea of the perfect girl!"

"Well yes, you're right in so many words," replied Linda and gave her daughter Tom's message. "Tom, I think you're about to become the luckiest boy in all of Geratica!" she continued, chuckling again.

"Mother, excuse me, but may I get up from the table and go around to Tom again?" asked Alexandra.

Linda laughed. "I told you so Tom – get ready for it! Certainly, Alexandra. Go ahead."

As quickly as she could, Alexandra was back with Tom. She wrapped him in her arms, as he sat on the chair before her, squeezed him tight, and began to kiss him softly again. "I fancy you more than any other boy, too!" she whispered breathlessly, between the third and fourth one.

Linda cleared her throat. "Yes, well, I'll let you two love birds continue your liaison, whilst I go out and sort out the dessert! Don't worry, you carry on, Alexandra. I can manage this on my own."

***

Whilst they ate their dessert course, Linda announced her conclusion to the experiment.

"I think it does seem that, as I suggested earlier, you two are close enough – and may become intimate enough – to have a chance of perfecting this kind of communication between yourselves, but, as Alexandra says, you'll need to practice it. I'm sure she'll teach you well, Tom, and of course I'm always at hand, too. If it can be done by anyone else besides Alexandra and me, then I'm certain that it will be you."

"But one other thing. This is a very private form of communication and I want it to stay that way. Let's keep it between the three of us, OK? *Discretion* please. Understood? Both of you?"

"Yes, Mother," said Alexandra.

"Of course, Mrs Radcliffe," said Tom.

Once they had finished their meal, Linda rose and started collecting the dishes. "Tom, would you like some tea or coffee?" she asked.

"Yes please Mrs Radcliffe. A black coffee would be lovely," he replied.

"Oh. I'm impressed!" exclaimed Linda. "Alexandra has obviously started to train you, already. We Radcliffes always take our coffee black, but we seem to be somewhat in the minority. It may be a refined taste, but it's the correct way, so there's an end to it. I have spoken!"

Alexandra chuckled at her mother's humour. She appeared to be in another good mood tonight, which bode well for her later. Both mother and daughter were beginning to feel their familiar longings for each other, which always stirred between them around this time of the week, knowing that they were slowly edging towards bedtime together.

"Darling, take Tom through to the parlour then, and make yourselves comfortable," said Linda. "I'll join you with the coffees, in a few minutes."

"Yes, Mother. Of course. Is there anything else that you want me to do, to help?" Alexandra was again at her most willing and obedient.

"No, that's alright, sweetheart," replied Linda, touching her daughter's arm lightly. and planting a soft kiss on her forehead, affectionately. You run along and enjoy each other's company."

"Thank you, Mother," said Alexandra, and taking Tom's hand again, she led him out of the dining room.

As they sat down on the sofa in the parlour, Alexandra slipped her arms around Tom again, and kissed him.

"Your mother and *discretion*," remarked Tom. "That's her favourite word!"

"She means well Tom," replied Alexandra. "She guards our privacy very fiercely, and I'm thankful to her, for that."

"What time do you and your mother normally go to bed on a weekend night? I don't want to keep you up too late."

"Oh. Don't worry. Not for a while yet, Tom. We'll be having the coffee with you, and probably a little something to drink with it, and perhaps even one of our parlour games, that you've often played with us before. Tonight's the night when Mother and I sleep together anyhow, so I'll be going up to her bedroom, not long before she retires. It'll be up to her really. This is always my favourite night of the week. I get two of my favourite things. Mother's cooking – assuming we're at home – and her taking me over in bed."

"Her ... what did you say?" asked Tom.

"Taking me over in bed. It's what I've always called it, when Mother's on top of me, and loving me so dominantly, that I feel as if I've surrendered all control to her. Believe me, it's an incredible feeling, at the moment when I finally lose it! I become breathless, the room spins around, and sometimes I actually feel as if I'm floating. Mother loves doing it to me, too."

"Your mother actually lies on top of you?" Once again Tom was taken aback. "I knew that you shared a bed together once a week, but I didn't realise you were *that* intimate! But there's no actual intercourse, is there?"

"Tom Ryder, really!" exclaimed Alexandra. "I know that most of you boys don't go to school, but I would have thought you would at least know about the facts of Geratican life, by your age. Of course not! You know as well as I do, that it's not possible for same-sex intercourse in our culture. But I'm sure you also know that it's quite common for mothers and daughters to be intimate, usually because, as in *my* mother's case, there is no husband or partner in the household. I suppose I'm a sort of substitute for Father, in that respect. Geratican women are very passionate, and have needs that they must satisfy!"

"Will Fiona be coming to collect you tonight, darling?" asked Alexandra.

"No, I'll walk back – it's only down the drive," said Tom. "I've never been quite sure, why your mother doesn't allow you out after dusk, in the hamlet. The security gate's always locked at the bottom of the drive anyhow!"

"I think it's mainly that she wants to make sure that I don't go into the wood, after that time. After whatever happened with Father, she doesn't want me falling into the river in the dark. Maybe also, she's worried that your stepmother might not see me after dusk, and knock me over with her car! You know she drives quite fast. Mother's often saying that there's no need for her to zoom past The Grange, quite as fast as she does, and that she'll probably get done for speeding soon, as well!"

Tom grinned.

"Your mother didn't worry about asking *me* to come through the wood tonight, though," he pondered.

"Well, I suppose these are unusual circumstances tonight," replied Alexandra. It was a more private way for you to come, and privacy is what we really need this weekend. Anyhow, she probably knows that Fiona doesn't apply the same rule to you."

Linda came into the parlour, and put down the tray with the coffee, on the table in front of Alexandra and Tom. She poured them all a cup, and took her own over to her armchair opposite, where there was another table.

"Now, who's for a drink?" she asked. Alexandra and I will have a port or two – what would you like, Tom?"

"A port would be fine for me, too, Mrs Radcliffe!" said Tom.

"Three ports coming up then!" said Linda. She took three glasses from the sideboard, and filled them with port, from The Grange's extensive alcoholic beverage rack.

"You're certainly easy, Tom," she continued, as she gave him his glass. "You can come again!"

She sat down, and they sipped their drinks.

"So, does Alexandra's gown, and the rest of her appearance, meet with your approval, Tom?" asked Linda.

"Definitely!" he replied.

Linda tapped one of her gloves with her finger. "She's actually asked for a gown with matching long gloves, like this. I'm intending to arrange a fitting for her, though it won't be for another couple of weeks at least, now, as she's currently barred from receiving any special treats."

"Mother! Is that true?" cried Alexandra excitedly.

"I wouldn't have said it, if it wasn't, dear."

"Oh thank you, Mother!" Alexandra got up and went to her, and gave her a grateful kiss.

Linda smiled at her daughter. "That's fine, darling. But you just be a good girl now, or I may have to change my mind. Do I make myself clear?"

"Yes. Definitely, Mother. Crystal clear!"

"Actually Mother," she continued as she re-took her place on the sofa, "we wanted to ask you about something else. You know that I gave Tom a bow tie for his birthday? Could you show him how to tie it, please?"

"You mean he doesn't know?" exclaimed Linda. "Goodness me! Whatever is the modern world coming to?"

Alexandra and Tom smirked at one another.

"I would have taught him myself Mother – but unfortunately I don't know either!"

"Well? Have you brought it with you, boy? asked Linda.

"Yes." He pulled it out of his jacket pocket.

"Right. Take that tie that you're wearing off and come over here. I'll soon have you an expert in this particular art!"

She demonstrated it to him twice, then had him do it himself three times, under her strict scrutiny, before she was finally satisfied.

"I'm surprised your stepmother couldn't have shown you that, Tom," said Linda.

"I've not asked her, actually," confessed Tom.

"We just naturally assumed that you would know, Mother," said Alexandra. "You're usually an expert on the finer things in life – especially the old-fashioned ones. I've learnt a lot from you."

"I hope you're not suggesting that I'm an old fuddy-duddy, my girl!" replied Linda. "But thank you. I'll take that as a compliment."

"Now," she continued. "Do you two want to have a quick game of something? Is there anything in the games cupboard that you could suggest darling?"

Alexandra got up and opened the cupboard. "Is there anything that you fancy, Tom? You know most of what we have."

He thought for a second. "I always enjoy playing Word Mistress, with you two. (This was a Geratican game, similar to the Earth game 'Scrabble'). "It's always entertaining to see you both trying to make the longest and highest scoring words!"

And so, Linda pulled up her armchair, nearer to Alexandra and Tom, and her daughter placed the game on the table. They played one game, and as it happened, Linda made the longest word, which was also the highest scoring, but Alexandra won it overall, much to her mother's only half-joking frustration.

"I've always said that you should get bonus points for making the highest scoring word of the game," she remarked. "I'd have won, if that had been the case."

"Oh, right. And I suppose the bonus points would roughly equal the number you needed to beat me by one, Mother?" retorted Alexandra. "It's funny that you never mention that, if *you* win, but *I* make the highest scoring word!"

"Rubbish! You've just not been paying attention, sweetheart."

"Well of course, that explains it then," said Alexandra, smiling ruefully. "How stupid of me, not to realise!"

"Hmm, quite," said her mother.

Tom chuckled to himself. Linda often gently teased her daughter, and

Alexandra played along, but at the same time he knew that Linda was quite competitive. He'd heard accounts from Alexandra, about the games they played together when they were alone, and the epic struggles the two of them often had. He'd also heard of her reputation as a formidable card player, during after-dinner parties.

A short time later, Alexandra started to feel a little sleepy. She leant against Tom's shoulder, and her eyes closed for a moment.

"I think that, maybe it's time I went," said Tom.

"Alexandra's trying to tell me, that she wants to go to bed," said Linda. "Or else the wine and port has gone to her head!"

Alexandra shook herself. "No. It's just that I didn't sleep very well last night," she said.

Linda got up and sat down beside her daughter, on the sofa, to the other side of Tom. "Well, not long now, darling. After Tom goes, we'll just need to wash up and clear away, and then we'll turn in." She wrapped her arm around Alexandra and pulled her close. Her daughter clung to her waist and snuggled against her chest, looking up at her. Linda saw the need for love in Alexandra's eyes, and her passion grew. She *really* wanted her daughter tonight! For now, she gave her a big affectionate kiss.

Tom could clearly see that it was *definitely* time for him to go.

"Well, thank you so much, Mrs Radcliffe. It's been a wonderful evening, with some excellent entertainment, and the dinner was superb! I'd better be off now, or my stepmother will be wondering where I've got to."

"You're most welcome, Tom!" said Linda. "We must start to get together more regularly from now on."

"I'll fetch your coat for you, darling," said Alexandra, and went out to the cloakroom.

Linda offered her hand. "Goodbye then Tom. Will you definitely be coming to the hearing, next week? I've got the day off, and I expect Alexandra's told you, that I'll be called as a witness, in her defence."

"Yes she has," said Tom. "And rest assured Mrs Radcliffe, I'll be there. I'll be taking the day off too, although I'll have to confirm it with my boss, first thing. So I'll be there a bit after you. It's my duty to support my girlfriend."

"Good! Thank you Tom." Linda embraced him and gave him a kiss on the cheek. This was exactly the response to this kind of situation, that she expected from a Geratican boy.

"See you there then," she said. "Alexandra will show you out. Goodbye." Alexandra was back with his coat and had put her own on, too.

"Is it OK for me to go up the drive, when returning to The Lodge, Mrs Radcliffe?"

"Oh. Yes, I should think so," said Linda. "No one's rung at the gate all day, so I'd assume that there's nobody there now. Hopefully, they've all been to call on the Spencers!" She went to the phone extension in the parlour and pressed the button to switch the screen on. She had a quick scan around.

"Yes. I think the coast is clear, Tom," she confirmed.

"OK then. Goodbye, Mrs Radcliffe, and thanks again," said Tom. "I'll see you next week at the hearing."

"Goodbye, Tom! We'll look forward to seeing you there."

In the porch, Alexandra and Tom kissed and cuddled for a few moments.

"I'd better be going, Alexandra, my Angel," said Tom. "You need to get to bed anyhow, and I don't want to keep you from being under your mother! I hope you really enjoy it, but also, remember that I dream of being under you every night, too!"

Alexandra smiled. "Thank you, Tom. I always *do* enjoy it. That's my natural and favourite position when I'm with Mother, I can't deny it. But I *also* dream every night of being *on top* of you, Tom, *my darling*! When I'm with *you*, something seems to happen inside of me, and I want to love you like a natural Geratican woman!

After exchanging a last few kisses, they finally said goodbye.

Alexandra went and re-joined her mother in the parlour.

"Right then darling," said Linda. "The quicker we get the washing up done, the quicker we can go to bed."

"Yes, Mother," replied Alexandra.

Linda took her hand, and they went into the kitchen. With Linda washing up, and Alexandra drying and both wasting little time, they soon had everything cleared away.

Alexandra's mother drew her close, and kissed her firmly on the mouth. As they embraced, they both felt each other's excitement.

"Right. See you in bed in a moment then, darling," said Linda. "I'll just get everything shut up and secure for the night and then I'll be with you. And I hope I won't come up to find you already asleep. I'm afraid I shall be waking you up, if that's the case!"

Alexandra gripped Linda's waist tighter. "No, Mother, I won't! I promise. I need your dominance tonight. I want you to take control, and make every part of me yours!"

"Of course I will, sweetheart," promised Linda again. "I know that's what you need – and never more so than at the moment, I believe."

She held and kissed her daughter one more time and Alexandra felt tingles all over. "Now get up those stairs darling!" Linda ordered, playfully. "I'm won't be long, assuredly. I want you tonight, and I'm going to have you!"

"At once, Mother!" replied Alexandra, her voice hoarse with excitement and hurried out of the kitchen, down the passage and up the stairs. She went into her room, briefly, to collect her night attire and then went over to her mother's bedroom. There, she quickly undressed, and did her night time ablutions, then put on her nightgown, and got into what was her side of the bed, when she slept with her mother. Her heart was beating fast, and her legs and feet tingled, as she longed more and more for her mother's hugs and kisses.

***

Arriving back at The Lodge, Tom went to the parlour. His father was sitting there, listening to the radio.

"Hello, Tom," said Colin. "Did you have a good time?"

"Fantastic, thanks, Father," Tom replied. "Where's Mother?"

"In her study."

"Oh," said Tom. "Well, I won't disturb her then."

But just then, Fiona called out to him. "Tom! It's alright. You can come in."

He went to the study.

"Hello, Tom. Was it a good night?" asked his stepmother.

"Yes wonderful. Good food, and great entertainment!"

"Hmm, well Linda usually puts on a good show. How was Alexandra? I bet she's worried stiff about appearing in court next week."

"Yes she is, although Mrs Radcliffe's hopeful that they'll be fairly lenient on her, and be harder on Gillian Spencer. I think she's more or less taken control of the situation. She made a lot of phone calls last night, apparently."

"Well, yes," remarked Fiona. "As I've said many times, Alexandra *is* dominated by her mother. I *am* pleased for you, having her as your girlfriend, Tom. I think you'll be very happy together, and probably marry. But *do* just bear in mind that Alexandra is already in a marriage – to Linda Radclffe!"

"Her mother is certainly the most important person in her life," agreed Tom. "She's always going to have a strong influence on her, but I don't mind, because I know that when we're together alone, which will hopefully mean a home of our own, eventually, she's definitely her own person, and quite capable of leading the relationship. Deep inside, she's a traditional Geratican girl."

"And you're a traditional easy-going Geratican boy, Tom," replied his stepmother. "Which is just as well, because you'll need to be, with your mother-in-law in the background!"

"Assuming that I'm allowed the day off, I'm going to the hearing on Day 1 of next week, Mother," said Tom.

"Yes, well naturally you will. Your father will take you there, before he goes to work, once you've rung your boss." That time of the morning was a little early for Fiona's liking.

"OK then," replied Tom.

"So it's to be the Radcliffes versus the Spencers!" remarked Fiona. "A final showdown perhaps? Personally, my money's on the Radcliffes. Linda usually gets her way in the end! I'm only sorry that I won't be able to see it. For once, I'll be in charge of court administration, whilst she sorts her daughter's problem out. She'll probably be thinking about what's going on at the palace, half of the time!"

"I imagine she'll be pretty focused on Alexandra's case, Mother," said Tom. "When it really comes down to it, she means even more to her than *Queen* Alexandra's court. In fact, she might not even think about the latter, at all!"

# CHAPTER 5

Linda came into her bedroom. Alexandra was lying on her back, her long blonde hair pushed forward over her shoulders, so that it fell over her chest. She looked longingly at her mother, with the hint of submissive need that always inflamed Linda's passion.

After undressing, she went through to her bathroom, then came back in to put her nightgown on, and got into bed. She held Alexandra, and gently stroked her hair, giving her daughter familiar tingles.

"Are you alright, *my darling*," said Linda softly, sensing that there was something troubling her.

Alexandra gripped her mother's hand. "Mother," she began, "Do you think that I'm going to be sentenced to a horsewhipping, as part of my sentence? That's what happens to some of the girls who appear in a juvenile court, isn't it?"

Linda looked at her. "Well, I suppose nothing can be ruled out, sweetheart, and unfortunately you're not in much of a position to complain, should it come to that, but I would have thought not, in your case. Gillian and Melanie maybe – perhaps even probably - but I'm sure we can convince the court to be less severe with you. Try not to worry about it, darling!"

"I've already been given ten strokes of the cane from Mrs Spencer at the college, on my bare bottom, Mother, before she told us all that we were going to be suspended. Melanie got twelve. She did it extremely hard, too!"

"Harder than me last night?" asked Linda.

"The last two that she gave me were, Mother. Although I did manage to withstand them."

"Yes, well some mistresses and even headmistresses, are tougher than others." replied Linda. "I don't think that I've ever been soft with you, when you've been deserving of a beating, but I've never considered it necessary to go that far, with you. I don't think you've ever needed to feel it on your bare skin. But in the end, whilst you're at Charterhouse College, she's in charge and if she wants to do that, then there's not a lot I can do about it."

"What about Gillian?" she asked.

"Oh, she joined in, Mother! Mrs Spencer shared out administering the beatings with her."

Linda stopped stroking her daughter's hair and sprang to her knees on the bed.

"What?" she shouted. "That's *totally unacceptable conduct*! Gillian is a pupil there, not a mistress. She should have *received* the most, of all three of you."

Alexandra sat up. "Gillian only beat me, Mother, not Melanie. She gave me four and I actually had six from the headmistress. According to Mrs Spencer, she'd already given Gillian her punishment, although I'm not sure if she was being completely truthful. I've heard several stories of girls being told the same thing, when they were being caned for a misdemeanour that Gillian had also been involved in. Once she realised that her daughter had been bringing in escort boys, she asked the sergeant if she could speak to her in private, and we were all taken out of her study. Outside, I heard her shout 'You stupid girl!' and a sound which I assumed was her striking Gillian once, but it was no more than that. She certainly shouted a lot, too. We could hear her outside the study, and, as the sergeant remarked, probably half of the college could, too!"

Linda was still livid about the way Elizabeth had conducted the punishment. "How *dare* they behave like that!" she cried and banged the headboard with her fist. "Elizabeth Spencer was just furious that her plans had been ruined, and she was taking advantage of a legitimate reason to punish you, to vent her frustration. She was probably trying to get back at me, also. And to allow a pupil – let alone her own daughter – to assist her! That's *disgraceful*! Do you know if this has happened previously?"

"I couldn't say, Mother. Truthfully, I've not heard about the like of it before, therefore perhaps not. They did seem to have a pre-arranged routine for administering the punishment, though."

"Well that's more information for me to add to my letter – and to mention at your hearing too. I'm not letting them get away with this, Alexandra! I'm going to get Spencer Senior removed from her post, and fight for Spencer Junior, to be given a tough, just sentence, *and* for your involvement in this affair to be clearly understood."

Having vented her own frustration, Linda's temper began to cool, but her passion did not. In fact, it possibly inflamed it even more.

"As I said, darling," she told Alexandra more quietly. "You mustn't worry about it. Your strong, dominant Mother, is going to take control, and we'll get through this together, I promise."

"In fact I'm going to demonstrate how strong and dominant I can be, right now darling!" she continued. "If ever it's a dominant loving that you need – and I think you do – then you know that I'm the one to give it to you!"

Linda began to slowly massage her daughter's feet and thighs. Then her fingers opened the front of Alexandra's nightgown, exposing her body. She eased her back on to the sheets and kissed her stomach, followed by her chest, shoulders and neck.

"*I love you, darling!*" she whispered into her daughter's ear. "*I want to eat you all up!*"

The seductive sound of her voice and the thought of having done to her, what her mother desired, slipped softly through Alexandra's mind, and heightened all of her senses

"*I love you Mother!*" she replied softly, a trace of her desperate need betraying her emotions to Linda. "*Do what you want! I'm yours!*"

Her mother smiled and her eyes betrayed to Alexandra, her pleasure and excitement at the invitation.

"*In that case, my darling, I **will** eat you all up! Right now!*" Linda laced her last two words with even more seduction.

She smothered her daughter beneath her body, squeezed her legs inside her own and wrapped her arms tight around Alexandra's shoulders. Somehow, what they'd both been through yesterday night, seemed to make them need each other particularly badly tonight, and the thought of what she needed to do for her daughter next week, combined with her indignance at the news that she'd just learnt, now concentrated Linda's mind, and inspired her to produce her best loving.

The taste of Linda's kisses pouring over her lips, and the aroma of her perfumed body pressing deep into hers, made Alexandra begin to murmur with pleasure in no time at all. She held on to her mother and looked forward to being taken away. Her heartbeat raced, and Linda felt it beneath her chest.

She stopped for a brief moment, to let her daughter get some breath back. She stroked Alexandra's hair again, and as her fingers brushed the tips, Alexandra felt a shiver down her spine, and her legs tingled. She squeezed her mother's legs from the inside.

Linda smiled again, and said lightly into her ear, "*Do you think that your defences can resist me?*"

"*No, definitely not Mother! And I won't want them, too! Please Mother, no other daughter needs her mother like I do. Dominate me and take control!*"

"*Very well then!*" said Linda. "*Here comes the final and most dominant attack of my loving. This **will** defeat you! I won't stop until I've taken you over completely. Now, look into my eyes!*"

Alexandra's heart raced with excitement again. Her legs were squeezed inside her mother's and she was engulfed in her arms. Kisses rained down on her and she felt her mother's tongue inside her mouth, licking hers, which gave her yet more tingles. Looking into her mother's eyes, only intensified her murmurs of pleasure, as Linda told her, again and again, how much she loved her, and would take care of her always, without having to say anything. She felt her mother thrust deep into her, as if she was completely inside of her body, and heard the sound of *her* pleasure becoming more and more audible.

As she continued to gaze into Linda's eyes, she felt her mother's hot passion, and knew it was about to explode, and sweep her away. She clung on tightly to her mother's waist. Linda thrust down deeper than ever before into her body, and they both sighed in ecstasy. Then the explosion came, and tore through Alexandra's defences. Suddenly all of her senses were conquered by her mother. Everything she heard, tasted, felt and smelt, was her mother and she became breathless. She saw stars, and experienced the familiar sensation of her head spinning. She was floating along, being carried by her mother – and her mother was everything. As long as she was there, nothing else mattered. She could face anything, under her protection. It was as if her mother was nourishing her with her strength, and the force of her personality. She knew what was best. She would tell her what to do. And she was grateful for it.

Linda murmured at the ecstasy of loving her daughter. This, she always thought, was the greatest feeling that any mother could wish for, with the exception of the orgasm she experienced when making love to a man.

Alexandra's heart felt like it might soon burst. She groaned softly, and her legs began to twitch inside her mother's. Linda stopped. Alexandra couldn't safely be taken any further – and without resting, she had almost burnt herself out for the moment, anyhow. She rolled off and laid beside her daughter, with her arm gently wrapped around her shoulders, and stroking her hair with her fingers, whilst they both got their breath back.

Eventually, when she was recovered, Alexandra re-fastened her nightgown, rolled to face her mother, and snuggled up to her chest. She looked lovingly up into Linda's eyes.

"Thank you, Mother! That was incredible!" she said.

"My pleasure, as ever, darling," said Linda. "As it happens, it was incredible for me too!"

She pulled Alexandra up to her face. Her daughter kissed her lips three times to show her appreciation, before Linda returned them with gusto and interest.

Then Alexandra's eyes began to close.

"I think someone's starting to feel a bit sleepy again!" said her mother.

"Mmm ..." was all Alexandra could muster.

"Well goodnight then, darling," said Linda, affectionately." Mother loves you very, very much and my arms will be around you, all night long. I promise! Sweet dreams!" Then she kissed her again.

"Goodnight, Mother. Sweet dreams to you too!" replied Alexandra. She was almost gone.

Linda couldn't resist giving her daughter one more kiss, and then Alexandra was fast asleep. Linda reached across and switched off the light, and then settled down herself. Tonight Alexandra's sleep was less troubled, in the warmth and security of her mother's arms.

***

Alexandra awoke the following morning, still in Linda's arms. She looked up at her mother as they lay side by side, and saw that she was awake, also.

"Good morning darling!" said Linda.

"Good morning, Mother!" Alexandra replied.

Both mother and daughter instinctively shifted slightly, as they prepared to exchange their first kiss of the day. As their lips touched, Linda took the initiative and tightening her embrace, she looked down into Alexandra's eyes and gave her not just one, but a whole series of kisses, which her daughter returned, when she got a chance. As usual Linda's passion dominated. In fact, she had always assured her daughter, that if just half of the kisses she gave to her were returned, then she would be quite content.

Linda rocked her daughter gently in her arms, and her fingers slipped through her hair and brushed the tips. For as long as she could remember, her mother had done this to her, and she had always loved the feeling that it gave her. Now as she also felt her mother's seemingly endless kisses, Alexandra oozed with pleasure. This was always her favourite morning of the week, when she woke up with her mother.

Finally, Linda stopped for a moment and held her daughter close to her.

"Did you have a better night, then sweetheart?" she asked.

"Yes. Thank you, Mother. I didn't wake up at all," replied Alexandra.

"Good. Well you went to sleep almost as soon as I took you over, last night – again! You did at least manage to say 'goodnight,' this weekend! But you were obviously tired."

"Yes. As I said when Tom was here yesterday evening, I didn't sleep very well the previous night. I was worrying about things."

"Well, try not to worry too much today. Get some rest before tomorrow! Later, we'll go through that letter together, that I want to send to the other governors, about Mrs Spencer. You can tell me if there's anything that you can think of, that I might have missed."

"Oh yes, of course Mother. That's a good idea," said Alexandra.

"And under the circumstances, darling, just for one occasion only during the year, you can come and sleep with me tonight, too, if it'll make it easier for you, being with me," Linda continued kindly.

Alexandra reached for her mother's hand and stared into her eyes. "Oh! Thank you, Mother!" she said with delight. "That might help me sleep better tonight, I must admit."

"Well, that's a deal then," said Linda. "Now, are you feeling refreshed, after a good night's sleep? If so, then before I get us some breakfast, I should like to have you again!"

"I feel fine, Mother. But probably even better, if you should take me over again!" replied Alexandra. She undid her nightgown again and laid back.

"Right," said Linda and after unfastening her own nightgown, she moved on top of her daughter. A few minutes later, Alexandra saw the room spin around, and she surrendered control, as all of her senses were dominated, whilst she lay underneath her mother.

***

Later on, Alexandra was stretched out in Linda's bed. She could smell the breakfast, that her mother was cooking downstairs in the kitchen. Today was the one day of the week, when the Radcliffes treated themselves to breakfast in bed. Linda let her daughter stay in bed, whilst she prepared it and brought it up to the bedroom.

As she lay there, Alexandra thought ahead to the future, and imagined herself one day, in her own home, in her own mistress bedroom, with – she hoped – Tom on the other side of the bed. She was bound to be the mistress of her own home eventually, and providing that meant living with Tom, then she was looking forward to it.

Having said that though, unlike some of the girls that she knew at Charterhouse, who couldn't wait to leave their parents, she wouldn't really mind if somebody told her that she had to return and live forever with her mother, after finishing University (though she of course knew – that would never happen). She loved her more than anyone else in the world, and probably always would do. Tom was the man that she wanted to be with for the rest of her life, but even he would be a very close second. Only just, but she had to admit that he would. Even though she was definite in her mind, that she wanted to be in charge of her own relationship with him, and their home together, as was traditional, she also knew that if her mother gave her some strong advice, she would almost certainly take it, and that if Linda really put her foot down, then there would be no question of her not doing so. That was the way it had always been between them, and their relationship was so strong and solid, and so important to both of them, that nothing could ever change it. Also, the last thing that Alexandra wanted to do, was to offend her mother, by ignoring her counsel.

She heard her mother coming up the stairs, and she entered the room, carrying a tray with their cooked breakfast on it.

Alexandra's mouth watered. "Mmm, that looks even better than it smells, Mother!" she exclaimed. "I can't wait to taste it – I'm sure that the trend will continue, since you cooked it!"

Linda felt a wave of pleasure, as she heard her daughter's second compliment of the weekend, regarding her cooking. She felt very lucky to have a daughter who clearly appreciated it. She had always enjoyed cooking, and wasn't afraid to say that she considered herself quite expert. In fact, as a girl, she had won a couple of first prizes in competitions, and after doing well in cookery classes at school, it had been one option for her to consider, as a career. She sometimes reflected, that she could have ended up as the head chef, at the palace (a position that Fiona had once held, during what Linda privately regarded as her somewhat meteoric rise through the ranks, since she'd started there). But ultimately, her interests were always in the main affairs of state, and her ambition, intellect, and schooling had all helped to take her right to the top, where she was able to administer those affairs.

"Well, if you wouldn't mind pulling the table across, then I can put the tray down, and you can find out, darling!" she said.

"Oh! Sorry, Mother. At once!" Alexandra sprang up in the bed, and

Linda smiled to herself, at her daughter's obedience.

One of the luxuries of her bed was that a table could be set up, in order to eat and drink whilst you were there. There were two parts – one on either side of the bed, which when pulled out, could be joined together, to form it. This, Alexandra now did and her mother set the tray down before them, and climbed back inside the bed.

"Right. Tuck in then," said Linda,

"With pleasure, Mother," replied Alexandra, happily.

As usual there was a period of quiet, whilst they hungrily ate their first meal of the day. Then Linda went back downstairs, and made toast and coffee for them, which they enjoyed back in the bed, on her return.

"Thank you, Mother. That was scrummy!" said Alexandra, leaning across, and kissing her.

"Good," said Linda, and kissed her back.

"Now, here comes the tickle monster!" said Linda and pushed Alexandra backwards on the bed. This was another thing that she had often done to her daughter, since she was a very young girl. Alexandra had always been extremely ticklish, and for a moment or two, Alexandra writhed and giggled, as her mother's long fingers swept all over her body, and tickled her most sensitive parts, which in Alexandra's case, were many. Soon her giggles became squeals and she thrashed violently up against her mother, before she finally relented. Linda had often remarked that if she hadn't been pinning her down, then she would have nearly hit the ceiling. Despite the fact that Alexandra was now fifteen, she and her mother sometimes still lapsed into some of their earlier games together, such was the intimate connection that they had.

Linda had unfastened her daughter's nightgown again, in order to tickle her bare torso. Now instead, she began to kiss Alexandra all over her body. Then she smothered her, wrapped her arms and legs around her, and took her daughter over for the second time that morning, and the third time that weekend.

*** 

Once they were finally up, dressed, and downstairs, they got washed up and cleared away. After Linda had gone down to the letterbox and picked up her newspaper, she took Alexandra into the study, to go through her letter to the Charterhouse board of governors.

"Right!" she said, picking up a document from her desk. "This is the current mistress-copy of the letter. Have a read of it and tell me what you think. I already know that I need to make one addition, concerning that disgracefully inappropriate behaviour from her, at the end of last week. To encourage her daughter to cane other girls – it really defies belief! Do you know if she's done this before?"

"Well, I wouldn't like to say for certain," replied Alexandra. "The Spencers did seem to have a pre-established method together when they beat us on Day 5 of this week – though I think there was mainly personal animosity at the heart of it. I'm sorry that Melanie got caught up in it."

Linda seethed with rage and her daughter thought that she might bang the desk again, but then she regained her composure. Once again, Alexandra knew that, although her mother was very strict, with a sharp tongue, and could be harsh in her punishment of misdemeanours, she was also very fair and didn't like to see injustice. And injustice perpetrated by authority, angered her most of all, because she believed that such people should set an example.

Linda handed her the letter. Alexandra took a moment to read it, and meanwhile, Linda poured coffee for them both.

"Thank you, Mother," said Alexandra, as Linda stretched over, and placed a cup and saucer on to her desk.

"I see you've already put in the bit about Gillian embezzling money from the tuck shop, Mother," she said, as she finished reading the letter. "I'm sure that Mrs Spencer eventually found out about that too, but made sure that no action was taken against her daughter."

"Oh yes, so am I," replied Linda. "And at your hearing in the juvenile court tomorrow, I shall be spilling the beans in a most public fashion, when I appear as a witness in your defence."

"Well, I can't think of anything much else, Mother," said Alexandra. "I think you've covered everything that *I* know of, at least."

"Excellent!" said Linda. "Right. Let's get this put down on paper, in rough and then type it up. Then they'll have to be copied and circulated. I want them to go out in the first post collection, tomorrow morning. I've already shredded the original ones that I wrote."

Alexandra handed her mother back the letter. Linda took a red pen from her desk and pulled up her sleeves.

Alexandra sipped her coffee, whilst her mother wrote furiously, her pen gliding effortlessly over the page. She was deep in concentration and not for the first time, Alexandra got a glimpse of the speed and efficiency, at which her mother worked. As she'd told her form class last week, her mother was used to drafting documents for another Alexandra – the queen. As well as having a high qualification in finance, Linda had two first class degrees – one was in Geratican law, but the other was in Geratican Language – and Alexandra believed that there were few better than her, at doing this particular task. Her mother had personally tutored her in both Geratican Language, and mathematics, from a very early age, which was something she had found extremely helpful when she'd started school, and it had continued to be an advantage, up to the present day. It was yet another thing that she would always be grateful to her, for doing.

"OK I think that will do," announced Linda, putting down her pen. "Right, Alexandra. You can make yourself useful now – and by the way, I shall be giving you some jobs to do this coming week, whilst you're suspended from Charterhouse, and gated at The Grange! Bring your chair around here, and sit at my word-processor." She switched it on.

"Yes, Mother, of course. I'll do whatever you say," replied Alexandra extremely obediently. She was still determined to please her mother, and be a model daughter for her, over the next fortnight – and forevermore. Now she pushed up her own sleeves, and wheeled her chair around, as instructed.

"Yes you certainly will – particularly whilst you're under punishment – or there'll be trouble!" said Linda firmly. She moved her chair to the side, so that her daughter could take her place at the desk.

In fact, Linda also had other motives. She was fully aware that her daughter's fragile confidence would have been damaged over the past few days, at just the point when it had seemed as if the opposite was happening. She was going to have to do an urgent repair job, before Alexandra returned to Charterhouse and the most effective way do that with her, was to praise her for things done well, so that her belief in her abilities was raised. Linda also knew that she was going to have to try and help her daughter become a slightly stronger person, particularly amongst other females. She wouldn't change their own relationship, at all, because it worked for them, but on the other hand, as she'd already told Alexandra, she wouldn't always be there to guide her, and her daughter needed to be more sure of herself and her own opinions, which might well be correct most of the time, because of her mother's teaching. She mustn't be so easily pressurised into thinking that another, incorrect view, was the only option.

"Now!" she continued. "This is the document on the word-processor." She brought it up on the screen. "Type up what I've written on the hard copy, in the relevant place. You're not a bad typist, so it shouldn't take too long.

And I'll finish my coffee."

"Yes, Mother. At once," said Alexandra.

Linda drank her coffee and watched as her daughter looked at the hard copy of the letter and then brought the curser on the word-processor, to the correct place. She placed the letter on the stand and moved it towards her. Then she started to type. Her mother felt quietly pleased at the way she'd approached the task.

After a couple of minutes, Alexandra had finished. Linda read what she'd typed. There were no mistakes, and nothing had been left out. She was very satisfied.

"Right. Good work, Alexandra," she said. "Now, save that and print off seven copies – one for each member of the board, and one for me to keep."

"Yes, Mother," said Alexandra, and did exactly as she was asked.

"Now. Take those copies out of the printer, whilst I get the address file up."

"Of course, Mother."

"OK. These are the six members that I need to send the copies to. Print out an address label for each one."

"Very good, Mother."

"Right. Nearly finished. Get six envelopes, and put one copy of the letter inside them, and then put an address label on each one. Then seal them, and attach a first class stamp to each. That's all fairly straight forward, isn't it?

"I think so, Mother. Yes."

A couple of minutes later, she was finished. Linda smiled at her.

"There, that was excellent, darling. I'm pleased. I could employ you as my secretary at court! Thank you." She kissed her daughter.

Alexandra was visibly pleased to hear her mother's praise. She wanted and needed it, particularly badly at the moment.

"Now, in view of the fact that tomorrow morning, there could well be some reporters outside the hamlet gates – to see you off, so to speak – I think that it might be best to put these in the post box now. It'll be awkward to stop off at it, on the way out tomorrow. Normally, I'd ask you to do it, but since you're gated, I'll go out and do it now, and then it'll be done."

"Alright Mother," said Alexandra. Then she gripped Linda's hand.

"Mother," she said again. "I know that what I did was stupid and wrong, and it can't be excused, but I'm really grateful for what you're doing for me. I probably don't deserve to be helped."

"Oh no, sweetheart!" cried Linda. "*Do* stop thinking like that. Yes, I was very angry with you on Day 5 of this week, but even then there was never going to be any question that I'd do my best to help you! Queen Alexandra said that nothing inspired me more than fighting for you and she was right. You need someone to play your cards right for you, this weekend, and to do your talking for you, tomorrow. And you know that I'm the best person to do both of those things!"

"Yes, Mother. You definitely are!" remarked her daughter. "I know how lucky I am to have you as my mother, in so many ways. You're my rock that I cling to. You've given me such a fantastic upbringing, in a wonderful place. I love you, Mother!"

"I love you, too, darling, stronger than any other mother loves her daughter!" replied Linda.

They embraced and kissed.

"I don't normally sleep with you on this night of the week, Mother. Will you be taking me over?"

Linda took Alexandra's hand. "Do you want me to, darling?" she asked softly. "It's up to you tonight." Her fingers gently stroked her daughter's.

"If you need help to make up your mind, then I'll tell you that I'd like to, sweetheart," she continued and squeezed her daughter's hand from the outside. As she looked into her eyes, the squeeze grew tighter. Alexandra felt her mother's dominance, and the need for her strength overcame her.

"I'd like you to as well, Mother!" she said.

"Well in that case then, sweetheart, leave your nightgown unfastened tonight, and I'll take care of the rest!" replied Linda.

Alexandra smiled excitedly. "Yes, Mother!"

"Anyhow, I'll just pop out and put these in the box then, darling," said Linda. "I'll only be a moment. Be a good girl whilst I'm gone."

"Yes, of course, Mother. I want to be the best daughter that any Mother has, all for you. "I'll never be naughty again, Mother. I promise that you've caned me for the very last time."

"Well, I certainly hope so, Alexandra!" exclaimed Linda. "But that's down to you of course. Don't worry though. You're already the best daughter that any mother has. I'm very proud of that fact!"

She kissed her daughter again, passionately. Alexandra became lost in her mother's eyes for a moment.

"Can I do anything else to help, whilst you're out, Mother?" she asked.

Linda could tell that her daughter was desperate to please her at the moment.

"Good girl!" she said, smiling. "Alright then, sweetheart, if you wash up these cups and saucers and the coffee pot, put it all away and start preparing our lunchtime snack, then I'm sure that I'll be back by that time, and I promise that you'll have earned yourself another kiss!"

"Oh. Right away then, Mother! said Alexandra, delightedly and immediately gathered everything up, and put it on the tray.

Linda smiled again at her daughter's eagerness.

"Right. I'm gone. See you in a second, darling," She went with the letters to put her coat on, before going out, and Alexandra picked up the tray, and took it to the kitchen.

*\*\**

When Linda returned, and Alexandra had done exactly as she had been asked, her mother kept her promise.

However, whilst she had been posting the letters, Judith had seen her, and come out of the store to speak to her. She'd said that there was a story about her, inside one of the newspapers, written by a feature writer, and wondered whether she might like to read it. Linda had brought a copy from her, and now she flicked through the pages to find the article. She took it to the study, and sat at her desk to read it.

From the kitchen, Alexandra guessed from her mother's furious outbursts, that it did not meet with her approval. She braced herself for the tirade that was bound to be coming. She didn't have to wait long. Linda stormed back into the kitchen, and threw the newspaper across the room, to the waste.

"Blasted rag!" she fumed. "'Weekend People' has always been in the gutter of the press, playing on people's desire for gossip. Half-truths and downright lies, all the way through!"

"What does it say, Mother?" asked Alexandra nervously. She hoped that nothing embarrassing had been printed about *her*, due to her own bad behaviour.

"It claims, darling, that your misdemeanour two days ago, was directly linked to the fact that I am a single mother! What cheek! It highlights the problems that we're all supposed to face, and suggests that this is the reason why you, and some other young people, have 'gone off the rails'.

"This stupid woman, who I can't bring myself to name, has always been one of those confounded 'Male Rights' protesters, and she thinks that there are a growing number of men who can't stand being in a traditional Geratican relationship and want a more dominant role. She claims they are consequently leaving their wives or girlfriends, to look after their children alone – who are then proving unable to control them!"

"It's total poppycock of course. In your case it certainly isn't true, and completely misses the point regarding the cause. But people love to gossip, and when they read this sort of rubbish, they'll believe it. If it's in the paper, then it *must* be true!

"Darn her! There's no hard evidence that there's any direct link between single motherhood and problem children. It may be a factor in a few cases, obviously, but it's usually just one of those excuses used by these 'progressive' thinkers, to excuse the children's bad behaviour. In reality it's just bad parenting, and it shouldn't be beyond any Geratican woman to discipline her children appropriately, regardless of whether her partner is there, or not. We women are the traditional administers of justice in this world, after all. I don't think I've done too badly, bringing you up."

"No, Mother, you certainly haven't," confirmed Alexandra. "I'm really sorry, Mother. I've caused you an embarrassment."

"Don't worry about that," said Linda. "This is just rubbish, and if this rag's circulation want to believe it, then that's up to them. I know the reality, and I sincerely hope that most *sensible* people in Geratica, will realise that too."

"What I *am* going to have to think again about now though, is my plan to get James to leave Elizabeth. If he does it now, firstly, some in the papers, who aren't so familiar with Elizabeth Spencer, will say that this is another case of a man leaving his wife, because he wants a more 'progressive' relationship, despite the fact that exactly the opposite would be true in this case! That would give Mrs Spencer, some short-term negative publicity, which would suit me fine, but I don't want to put James through that, when the reason given by those idiots, is so false."

"Secondly and perhaps more importantly, *I'd* probably be accused of being a single mother, who has broken up another marriage to suit herself, and produced another single parent family, in the process!"

Linda swore, before raging, "Am I never to be able to get the man I love? I *won't* be denied!" and she banged the kitchen table.

The fact that her mother had used such a word, which was an extremely rare occurrence, made it all the clearer to Alexandra, that she was boiling mad. She liked to get her way, and few things irritated her more, than when she didn't get it, or was foiled in a plan. She hated losing.

"I'm sorry, Mother," she said again. "Will you really have to change all of your plans now?"

"Well, we'll have to see what happens in the next few days," said Linda. "I'll only do that extremely reluctantly."

"I'm sorry, I shouldn't have used that word, when talking to you, darling," she continued, feeling a little calmer. "It was very *remiss* of me, especially as you're officially under punishment at the moment, and I should be setting you the right example. Swearing is not part of that example. In fact, as long as you're a *very* good girl during this term of punishment, then I'm prepared to knock a day off, to make up for it."

Alexandra couldn't believe it. "Are you serious, Mother?" she asked.

"Yes, darling, I am," said Linda. In fact, she desperately wanted this whole distasteful affair to be over as soon as possible, so that she and Alexandra could get fully back to normal. She hated anything spoiling her relationship with her daughter. She had some treats planned, that she wanted to share with her, but that wasn't possible at the moment.

"Thank you, Mother!" said Alexandra, still shocked. Her mother had never before shortened a period of punishment, after it's commencement. "I *am* going to be such a good girl – I promise!"

"Good, well we'll see about that, too, then," said Linda. "Now let's change the subject. It's time we had our lunch!"

***

Later that evening, not long before bedtime, Alexandra was on the parlour sofa, curled up in her mother's arms, with her legs up on the cushions. The radio was on in the background, and they had just listened to the latest news, which hadn't reported anything new on 'The Charterhouse Scandal', as it was now beginning to be called. Now as some soft music began to be played, she closed her eyes, and tried to relax as much as possible, before her big day tomorrow. Her mother's arms smothered her as they held her tight, and then she felt fingers running through her hair, and over her shoulders, massaging them. She murmured with pleasure, and Linda held her even tighter. Alexandra opened her eyes slightly, and looking up, glimpsed her mother looking over her. Linda smiled lovingly at her daughter, and leaning her head down, she kissed her lips. Alexandra returned it, and then received some more as she lost herself in her mother's eyes, which looked deep into her. Then Linda took control, as she locked them both together, and pushed herself forward, so that her daughter lay on her back, and she on top. For a few moments she kissed Alexandra's lips, over, and over again. Her daughter murmured again, several times, and gradually Linda did too.

The phone rang, startling them both.

"I wonder who that might be?" asked Linda, as she climbed to her feet. "Whoever it is, I shan't let them stay long. We've got to go to bed soon, particularly if I'm going to take you over, before we settle down!"

She crossed to the phone and answered it. "Oh, hello, Tom!" she said.

Alexandra sat up on the sofa, her eyes suddenly lit with joy.

"Your boyfriend for you, darling!" said Linda, with a twinkle in her eyes. "Take it in here and I'll take our coffee things to the kitchen, and get washed up and cleared away. I won't be able to hear, unless you shout, so don't worry! You can have until I've finished, but no longer, because we *must* go to bed then. Is that clear?"

"Yes, Mother. Crystal clear." replied her daughter, obediently.

"Good girl," said Linda. She put the receiver down, and went to the table, to take the tray out. Alexandra crossed the room to take the call, and waited for a brief moment for her mother to leave the room.

"Hello, *darling*!" she said softly. "Did you hear what Mother said?"

"Hello, Angel!" Tom answered. "Yes I did. Sorry, I know you go to bed a little earlier at The Grange, than we do at The Lodge."

"It's alright, but we'd better be quick," replied Alexandra. My bedtime's at 9.30 and tonight Mother says I can sleep with her again, if it'll help me have a better night. I am a bit worried. So she's coming to bed a bit earlier than her usual time, and she's promised to take me over again, before we settle down to sleep."

"Well, I know I'll see you at the court tomorrow, but I was just calling to see how you're feeling."

"Terrified!" said Alexandra. "Tom. You know that tomorrow I'm going to need Mother, more than ever before, don't you?"

"Of course I do," said Tom.

"But I need you, too, darling! Mother will be on one side of me, holding my hand. I really want you to be doing the same on my other."

"I promise that I will. You've no need to ask, Angel. My father's bringing me to the court tomorrow, once I've got my day off confirmed – which I think they'll be expecting – and before he goes to his own work. Try and get a good night's sleep."

"I wish you were here with me now, Tom," said Alexandra. "I don't want you to go, without me showing you how much I love you. Would you like me to send you some kisses down the phone again, until Mother comes back? It won't be long. There are only some cups and saucers, and the coffee pot to wash up."

"Ooh, yes please *Angel*!" said Tom, feeling aroused, as soon as he thought of his girlfriend's caresses.

Alexandra's geratis became hardened and extended. "OK then! Close your eyes again. *Now! If I was with you in your dreams tonight, what would you be hoping I'd be doing?*" she asked softly.

At The Lodge, Tom looked around to check that his stepmother wouldn't overhear. "*Definitely kissing me all over my body!*" he whispered back.

Alexandra became even more sexually excited. "*Oh! What a coincidence! That's just what I dream of doing to you, every night! Well, here they come then!*"

For the next couple of minutes, they exchanged kisses, making affectionate noises to one another, as they did so. Alexandra traced her finger along the tip of her geratis, inside her skirt, and got a shock of pleasure, which made her exhale deeply down the phone.

Then her mother reappeared and pointed to her watch. Alexandra nodded, and to Linda's pleasure, she instantly began to bring the call to an end.

"Anyhow, Tom, I'd better let you go. Mother's back, therefore our time's up. It's my bedtime. See you at the court tomorrow. Bye then, *darling!* Love you!"

"OK I will do," replied Tom. Try and sleep as best that you can. Bye *Angel!* Love you, too!"

They hung up.

***

And so, that night, after Linda had taken her over for a fourth time that weekend, something Alexandra knew for a fact, had never happened before, she snuggled up to her mother's body, and slept as best she could. The hearing was now, obviously, very close, and it was on her mind constantly. Being with her mother certainly helped, but even so, she woke up three times – on one occasion, with such a start, that she woke Linda, too. Her mother held her tight in her arms, and rocked her gently to and from, beside her. She talked softly and lovingly into her daughter's ear, soothing her with the gentle sound of her voice, and eventually, Alexandra slept once more, helped by the strength of her mother's love and protection.

# CHAPTER 6

At 7.15 a.m. on Day 1 of Week 34, Linda and Alexandra were getting ready to leave for Buckmore Juvenile Court.

Alexandra was wearing her school uniform, as would Gillian and Melanie. It was a standard requirement, for young people appearing before the court. Alexandra's was freshly washed and pressed and her mother had already told her that she looked extremely smart and well presented.

Linda wore a royal blue skirt suit with a white blouse, and a blue bow at her neck, which matched her suit.

After they had put their coats on, Linda took her daughter in her arms. "OK then, darling. Here we go! Now don't worry, I'm going to be with you every step of the way. Just do as I tell you, and you'll be fine, I promise. Is there anyone you trust more than me?"

"No, Mother," declared Alexandra, as she looked up at her mother and clutched at her waist. "I'd go anywhere in Geratica with you, if I was in your arms!"

"Well then. Trust me when I tell you, that you'll be OK," asserted Linda. "The worst bit for you, might be when we get there. You're not used to public attention, but there's sure to be some today. That's guaranteed, unfortunately. I'll talk to you more about that, then. We'll avoid the main entrance, and go through to the car park at the back of the building, in the basement. I went there as an observer a couple of times when I was at Charterhouse, actually, so I know the general layout, unless they've radically changed it since then – admittedly that was thirty years ago now! You'll be pleased to know, too, that the outcome was satisfactory on both occasions!"

"Right," she concluded. "Now we must leave, my love. We must make sure that you're not late for this,"

They went outside and Linda shut the door. "Now, once I've got the car out of the garage, just for this morning only, it might be best if you sit in the back. The reason will become clear in a moment. Understood?"

"Oh! Yes, Mother," said Alexandra, surprised.

So, Linda went to the garage and her daughter walked down to their front gate and opened it. Then she waited for the car to come down. It was another cold day, and her nervousness made it feel even more so. Her coat was buttoned up to the neck, just like her mother's, and she wrapped her scarf tighter around her.

The car drew up and after closing their front gate, she got into the back, as her mother had told her. Linda's car was wide enough to seat three adults in the back, and there were seatbelts for each, on the left side, centre and right side. Although this was a journey that she didn't want to make, at least she would be in the warm now. Her mother had put the heater on, and she soon began to feel the effect in her toes, legs and fingers.

"Right then. First I need to do this," said Linda, and she pressed a button on the dashboard. Immediately, all the windows, apart from the front windscreen, began to tint.

Alexandra looked around in shock. "I never knew your car had that facility, Mother!" she exclaimed.

"Well, it's one of those little extra gizmos that you get as standard on this range. There's no real need to bother with it normally, but today it will certainly be useful to you. You can still see out to an extent, but you'll be protected from the gaze of people outside, who won't be able to see *you* at all. Obviously, I need a fully clear view at the front, so that's why I've put you in the back this morning. OK?"

"Yes, Mother. Thank you. That's a good idea," remarked her daughter.

"Right. Away we go then!" said Linda and she drove down to the end of Elmsbrook's drive. She opened the window and as quickly as she could, swiped the keypad to open the gate, and then shut the window once more. She drove out of the hamlet, and sped away. Alexandra could see the reporters that her mother had warned her about, immediately as they went by. She was sure that she detected some flashes, as photographers took their shots of their car leaving for the hearing. Soon they left them behind, and were headed for Buckmore.

Alexandra put two fingers up to her mouth, but then stopped herself. A short time later, the same thing happened again. Her mother looked back at her, through the rear view mirror.

"Darling, just for now, I'm not going to stop you sucking your fingers, or whatever you need to, if that's going to help," she said kindly. "But please do try and not do it, once we've arrived. I can see pictures of that appearing on certain newspaper front pages, which might not be very pleasant for you!"

"OK, Mother, and thank you," said Alexandra gratefully.

In no time at all, her thumb went into her mouth and she sucked on it, trying to comfort herself, as she contemplated what lay in store for her today.

***

At 7.45 a.m., Linda arrived at the back of Buckmore Juvenile Court and after paying the toll to go through the barrier, drove into the car park. There were a small number of other cars there, but no one else at the moment.

Linda parked the car, and they got out. She made sure that she had her handbag with her. It contained her notes for what she intended to say, when she was called as a witness in her daughter's defence.

She squeezed Alexandra to her. "Right. Once we get out of the car parking area and into the building itself, we might meet a few journalists who have anticipated our entrance route. Now, my arm will be around you the whole time, so I'll be with you all the way. Hold on to me, and I'll walk you through, as quickly as I can. Just keep looking ahead, and don't say anything when the reporters start asking questions. I'll do the talking, if anything needs to be said, no matter what it is. Try to ignore the flashes from the photographers, too. Once we're at reception, we'll hopefully be soon taken elsewhere, and that'll be over for the time being."

"As we walk, think of this." Linda kissed her daughter's mouth and held her tighter. "And I promise to give you *this,* when we reach safety. She did the same again.

"Try and be brave, darling. We're a partnership, and we'll get through this together. And I'll be the dominant one. You've already done well, by giving the police the information they needed to catch Gillian and Melanie, and force them to confess. Now, leave the rest to me!"

"Thank you, Mother. I'm really worried about the punishment that the court might decide for me, but I will try, and I know that I can be, if you keep me strong enough. Please, Mother, empower me with your dominance!"

Linda felt her daughter's legs shake slightly, as she held her. She kissed and squeezed her again.

"Let's take one thing at a time, my baby," she said gently. "Now, we must get inside. You can't be late, reporting to reception. Are you ready?"

Alexandra felt a cold shiver of dread pass through her. "As I'll ever be, Mother!" she said fearfully.

"Right!" said Linda, and opened the door. She took Alexandra up the steps that led to another door at the back entrance of the building. Alexandra gripped her mother's waist tighter, and with a last protective look at her daughter, Linda opened it, and swept them through.

Immediately, there were flashes of light, and a group of women appeared around them, photographers snapping pictures, and journalists hoping for a quote. The questions came thick and fast.

*"Why did you do it, Miss Radcliffe?"*

*"Does this prove that single mothers have difficulty bringing up their children alone, Mrs Radcliffe?"*

*"Should men be more equal in their relationships with women, to stop them feeling the need to leave their partners?"*

*"What sort of punishment are you expecting your daughter to get, Mrs Radcliffe?"*

"I made a statement at the end of last week. I said then that there would be no further comment to the media, and that still applies today," said Linda, as she pushed through the reporters, and sped Alexandra down the corridor. Alexandra kept looking straight ahead as her mother had told her, and tried to completely ignore them. She held on to Linda's waist as she was swept along. A camera flashed in her face, particularly close to her, making her flinch, and almost squeal in alarm, but was comforted by the feeling of her mother's arm tightening around her shoulders, pulling her closer to her body.

Linda could feel her daughter trembling. At last she stopped at another door, and they went through it, into another corridor. This time it was mercifully empty, but some of the reporters followed them through.

She spoke as quietly as possible into her daughter's ear. "It's alright, my baby, we're almost there. The reception is at the end of this corridor.

Linda took them through another door, and they finally arrived next to the reception desk.

"Good morning. This is my daughter, Alexandra Radcliffe," announced Linda. "She is due to appear before a hearing today. The solicitor representing her is Jessica Beale."

"Good morning. Thank you, Mrs Radcliffe," said the receptionist. "If you'd just like to sign the attendance register, and the time of your arrival at the desk, Miss Radcliffe." She indicated to the register on the counter.

Alexandra did as she was asked. Her hand was shaking slightly, but she drew strength from her mother's body, as she was held tightly against it.

"Thank you," said the receptionist. "If you'd both like to follow me?" She showed them into a side room. "Please wait here until your solicitor arrives. Your hearing will take place, along with two other girls', at 9.00 a.m."

She left the room.

"9.00 a.m. Well that's good anyway!" remarked Linda. "Your case will be the first of the day, which gets it over with, early. Perhaps, as this one is likely to be a little more high profile than normal, they're keen to get it over and done with, and they've pushed everything else back. If we're lucky, we'll be home before lunchtime! We won't hang around here for long, once this is finished."

"Now, before anything else," she continued, "let me give you what I promised." She held and kissed her daughter lovingly, inside her arms.

Alexandra was still trembling, slightly. To appear before a juvenile court, was something that she had always thought happened to other girls, who were much worse behaved than she was. Despite what her mother had told her, she couldn't help but think ahead to the end of the hearing, when they would all learn their punishment. Most of all, Alexandra dreaded being sentenced to a horse-whipping. She didn't even like watching it done to others, let alone suffer it herself. Quite apart from the thrashing that she'd experience, the thought of having people watching her ordeal, was too embarrassing for her to bear.

"Are you alright, darling?" asked Linda.

Alexandra tried to speak, but her fear and nerves overcame her, and to her horror, she began to stammer again.

Her mother drew her towards her and kissed her again. "Take it steady, my baby!" she said soothingly into her daughter's ear. "You're with the one who'll protect you the most, and you've nothing to fear. Take a deep breath, and think of what you want to say. You're a bright girl, and nothing you say is going to be stupid. Let it come gradually."

Linda squeezed her daughter's hand as she spoke, and stroked her fingers. Their eyes met and Linda began to read Alexandra's feelings.

"Darling, you must try to stop thinking about the end of the hearing, or you'll work yourself up too much!" she urged her daughter. "Would another kiss help? I've got plenty, and they're all for you this morning!"

Alexandra nodded and looked up, as her mother engulfed her, and gave her one of the most affectionate kisses that she had ever experienced.

Slowly she began to feel calmer, as she felt the love in her mother's eyes and her kiss, and Linda's words registered in her mind.

"Yes, Mother. I'll try not to, but it's difficult," she replied to her mother. "And that camera just now, too! All those reporters and photographers! Your kisses are helping though."

"Well, I'd better give you another for luck then!" said Linda, and repeated what she had just done.

***

Tom arrived, a short time afterwards. He immediately went to his girlfriend. They embraced and for a few seconds, kissed.

Then Linda gave a mock cough and said, "Good morning, Tom! You got here alright then?"

"Good morning Mrs Radcliffe!" replied Tom. "Sorry, I should have greeted you first. Yes. My father brought me, before he went to work."

At almost the same time, Jessica Beale arrived. She was quite short, slim, with long golden hair. She wore a grey suit with a matching bow, at the neck of a white blouse. After they had made their introductions, she opened her briefcase, and took out her notes. Then they began to discuss the case.

Jessica went through the details of Alexandra's crime, and the connection to the other shoplifting offences, and the escort boys visits to Charterhouse, which concerned the other two girls, but that she hadn't been involved in.

"Now, is there anything else that I haven't covered, that you think I need to know, Alexandra?" she asked.

Alexandra's hand was held deep inside her mother's. Linda gently stroked her fingers, coaxing her, and helping to ease her nerves. Her thoughts began to become rational, with their usual logic and perception.

"No, I don't think so," she replied. "For my part, I realise that I've made a serious error of judgement, and deserve whatever punishment that the court wishes to serve upon me, but I want to point out that there was a lot of pressure put on me to commit this offence, by Gillian Spencer, although I know that's no excuse. I felt that I had no option, but to do as she said, but I now realise that I should have reported Gillian's conduct, instead. I've never done anything like this before, and it's at odds with my normal character. I'm truly sorry for what I've done, and will pay Rimmingtons the total amount that the goods were worth."

Jessica made quick notes of everything that Alexandra said, and after she'd finished, Linda looked into her daughter's eyes, and squeezed her hand again. She gave Alexandra's fingertips a light stroke with one of her own, telling her daughter that she had done well. Alexandra began to feel some strength and confidence, beginning to build, inside of her.

Linda then explained to Jessica, what she wanted to say as the witness for her daughter. Jessica confirmed that this could be useful evidence, and that she would ensure Linda was allowed to speak, at the relevant time.

"Would the three of you like a drink?" she asked. "There's a machine over there. I'm going to get a coffee for myself."

Linda glanced at Alexandra and Tom. "Thank you. That would be nice Mrs Beale," she replied. "Three coffees, black with no sugar, please."

Meanwhile, Melanie arrived at the court with her parents and they were taken to another room. She looked distinctly uncomfortable.

Last to arrive was Gillian, with her mother and father making a rare appearance together, and they were taken into the same room. Gillian and Melanie would be jointly represented, by another solicitor.

*** 

At 8.45 a.m., they were all called to the courtroom, and the two separate parties sat at their respective tables. Linda gave a discreet nod of acknowledgement to James, but ignored Elizabeth completely. Alexandra too, avoided all eye contact with Gillian.

Their solicitors made their final preparations, and talked with the clerk of the court, a tall, grey haired woman, who Alexandra guessed must be approaching retirement. The solicitor for the prosecution was also there, with two witnesses. Alexandra also noticed that there were a couple of journalists present too. One of them was from the national radio news.

At 9.00 a.m. precisely, the judge, Lavinia Mountford QC, entered the courtroom, together with two magistrates, both women slightly younger than herself.

"Court will rise!" called the clerk of the court.

Everybody stood up and the four officials took their places.

"Court is now in session," announced the judge.

Lavinia Mountford went through the formalities, and gave a brief assessment of the case that she had been asked to consider. She also noted that all three girls had already pleaded guilty to at least some of their offences. There were three others who had previously seen the escorts, but no longer and had never been involved with the shoplifting. There was to be a separate hearing for them tomorrow. Out of sight, Linda squeezed her daughter's hand inside of hers, and her fingers gently and quickly massaged Alexandra's, to comfort and relax her as much as possible. "Everything's fine, darling," she breathed softly into her daughter's ear, and gave it the softest of kisses. On the other side of her, Tom discreetly held her other hand.

Alexandra was the first to be called, as it had been her offence that had prompted the case.

"Defendant, will rise!" said the clerk of the court.

Linda gave her daughter's hand a final squeeze and then she and Tom let go of Alexandra's hands, and she stood up.

"Do you swear that the evidence heard in your name, before this court, will be the truth, girl?!" demanded the clerk.

"I do!" declared Alexandra.

"Please confirm your name, address and date of birth!" said the clerk.

To Alexandra's immense relief, she managed to supply the relevant information as clearly as she could, without stammering.

The clerk nodded in acknowledgement to the judge, confirming that these were the details held by the court.

"Thank you Miss Radcliffe. Please stand down," said Lavinia Mountford.

"Defendant will stand down!" repeated the clerk.

Alexandra sat back down in her seat and Linda and Tom re-took her hands. "Well done, darling. That was excellent," her mother murmured into her ear, and Alexandra felt another slight surge of strength, flowing through her.

Lavinia asked the solicitor for the prosecution to outline the precise details of Alexandra's crime, and then their two witnesses were called – the sergeant who had arrested her, and the Rimmingtons store detective. The sergeant confirmed that the police station had received a tip off from a Miss Gillian Spencer, at Charterhouse, that there might be an attempted burglary at Rimmingtons at lunchtime, on the day in question, and the store detective described how the police had alerted them of the possible crime, and that she had seen Alexandra Radcliffe put three bottles of perfume into her school bag. Her security had then apprehended her, and the police had arrested her. The sergeant also confirmed that she had not resisted arrest, and that according to the custody sergeant at the police station, she had complied fully, and made a complete confession. In her statement she had given a detailed account of her reasons, and of other allegations of offences, concerning the other two defendants in the case. This had led the police to visit Charterhouse, and speak to all three girls together, where Gillian Spencer and Melanie Patterson had eventually admitted the offences, and confirmed that Alexandra hadn't been a part of them. The clerk approached the bench, and showed the magistrate the statement which Alexandra had signed at the police station. Lavinia Mountford read it, and then passed it to her assistants. After they had finished, Lavinia gave a nod of acknowledgement, and returned it to the clerk.

Then it was the turn of Jessica Beale for the defence. She went through the events of the case, in detail, from Alexandra's point of view, including the previous shoplifting incidents, and the escort visits, which Gillian had organised and taken part in seeing, as well as negotiating a cut of their takings. She explained that Alexandra hadn't been involved in any of these previous activities. Jessica then called her witness for the defence, Alexandra's mother.

"Witness will rise!" commanded the clerk of the court.

Linda picked up her notes. She didn't need to read directly from them as she spoke, but they were there for her as a general crib-sheet, to ensure that she remembered everything that she wished to say.

She stood up and the clerk said, "Do you swear to tell the truth before this court, Madam?"

"I do!" Linda assured everybody present.

She took a deep breath.

"I should like to begin, Your Honour, by saying how sorry my daughter is, for the trouble she has caused. She knows that she has done wrong – and believe me I have made this very clear to her, and punished her severely for her transgression. Alexandra hasn't ever been in trouble at Charterhouse before, let alone the authorities however, and I would humbly ask this court to take into account her usual exemplary behaviour, and popularity with her peers and mistresses alike. This is completely out of character, and although my daughter realises that this is no excuse, she feels that considerable pressure was put on her to commit the offence – pressure which she unfortunately succumbed to. I believe that she is being completely honest about this. She did point out to me, that when she went to the college on the day in question, she had absolutely no thought that she would do such a thing. It was only when she was confronted by Miss Spencer and Miss Patterson, along with, I believe, a pair of Miss Spencer's 'heavies' that she was made to feel as if she had no choice.

"Alexandra told me, that she was indeed threatened with a 'thumping' by Miss Spencer, if she didn't either partake in the two other girls' shoplifting activities that lunchtime – which meant going outside of the college grounds without authorisation - or later that afternoon visit one of the escort boys that the aforementioned was secretly bringing in to Charterhouse, in the guise of 'actors'! She had never shoplifted before – unlike Miss Spencer and Miss Patterson – and she had no intention of going with an escort boy – which again I believe the other two girls regularly did. They needed the stolen goods to sell on to the other girls at Charterhouse, so that they had enough money to continue to see these – ugh-hum – actors! So to avoid being physically hurt, my daughter took the option of agreeing to shoplift, for one occasion only, which as I have said, she now realises was a bad error of judgement, and bitterly regrets. As a gesture of this regret, she is going to make a payment to Rimmingtons, for the exact value of the three bottles of perfume, that she attempted to steal.

"Of course, Alexandra didn't realise that Miss Spencer was going to contact the police and tip them off, in order to set her up. The other girls scarpered just before they arrived and arrested her. I believe the reason for that involves her mother, Mrs Elizabeth Spencer, the headmistress of Charterhouse and owes much to the internal politics of that institution, as well as perhaps some personal vendetta towards Alexandra and myself. However, that being said, my daughter now knows that she still should have alerted someone at the college, or even myself, to Miss Spencer and Miss Patterson's activities, rather than simply doing what they told her to do.

"It has also come to my attention, that on one previous occasion, Alexandra did do just that. Miss Spencer apparently runs the Charterhouse College tuck shop, and it appears that whilst she was ill for a few days, a while ago, the other girls who normally assisted her, had to take over themselves and my daughter was drafted in to keep the accounts. It was then that she realised that Miss Spencer was fiddling the books, and embezzling a considerable amount of the takings into her own pocket! She rightly informed her house mistress, and the staff became aware of Miss Spencer's ruse. However – presumably due to the intervention of her mother – no action was taken against her, although I believe she *was* told that she'd been rumbled. She was I'm told, 'furious,' and gave my daughter a thumping for 'grassing' on her, which completely knocked the wind out of her. She also barred Alexandra from the tuck shop, and forced her to hand over the money that I personally allowed her every week, to buy items from the tuck shop, directly to her instead! This may have been a factor in her decision to appease Miss Spencer, at the end of last week. One would find it understandable in some ways, though once again, I'm sure that she now knows that this does not excuse it. My daughter told me she was hoping, that if she went along with Miss Spencer in this, she would 'get her off her back for a while'. I would urge the court, to look upon this as naive at worst.

"I didn't know about the tuck shop affair, until a couple of days ago. Alexandra was worried that I would complain to the college and make things worse for her. I am outraged that no action was taken against Miss Spencer, and even more so, at the fact that she was simply allowed to go back to running the operation again! It seems to me that she is allowed to do more or less what she wants at Charterhouse, under her mother's protection. She also acts as that woman's eyes and ears, even sometimes engineering situations to get other girls into trouble or cause mistresses problems, on the headmistress's behalf, to the advantage of both of them – Mrs Spencer politically and Miss Spencer personally. Most incredibly I'm told that when Miss Patterson and my daughter were punished by the headmistress for their offences, on Day 5 of last week, Miss Spencer was allowed to assist in the caning of Alexandra, before all three girls were suspended for a week. I think that this is totally inappropriate behaviour, from both of them. My daughter isn't suggesting that it has happened before, but does note that they apparently seemed to have had a pre-arranged routine for administering the caning. Miss Spencer does not appear to have assisted with the punishment of Miss Patterson, though. Mrs Spencer claimed that she'd already 'punished,' her daughter, but Alexandra is not so sure!"

By now, Elizabeth and Gillian Spencer were shifting uncomfortably in their seats.

Linda continued, "If I could just also say, that I *am* aware of the problems of single parenthood – being a single mother myself. However, there is absolutely no solid evidence, that many of the juvenile delinquents who appear before this court, would have behaved any differently, if they were under the supervision of either one, or two parents. As to the suggestion that the men in these relationships would be more likely to stay with their partners, if they had a more dominant role, that is pure speculation, which in my view is completely false, though I've no doubt that Mrs Spencer disagrees! In any case, my husband died and we'd still be together now, if he hadn't – you can be sure of that! But anyhow, that's not relevant to my daughter's case."

"Quite!" Lavinia Mountford intervened. "Please keep to the point, Mrs Radcliffe. I don't wish my court to be turned into a political arena!"

Elizabeth smirked.

"I'm sorry, Your Honour," said Linda. "It's just that there was an article in one of the weekend 'newspapers' about that particular subject, mentioning my name in connection to it, and I was not best pleased. Then, when we got here this morning, there were questions asked about it, by some reporters.

"I've not really got anything else to say anyhow, other than that I believe the court has received references to Alexandra's good character, from a couple of notable sources. I hope that those, together with my own comments, will be taken into account, when the court considers my daughter's punishment."

"Yes. Well of course, we'll study all the evidence, before deciding each individual girl's sentence," said the judge. "That is the purpose of this hearing today. Thank you Mrs Radcliffe. Please stand down."

"Thank you, Your Honour," said Linda.

"Defendant will stand down!" barked the clerk and Linda re-took her seat.

"I can confirm that the court has indeed received two references, Your Honour," added the clerk of the court. "One is from Mrs Philippa Barrington and the other, Her Majesty, the queen!" She reached across from her desk behind the magistrate and handed them over.

Elizabeth's smirk disappeared, and was replaced by an angry glare.

Lavinia Mountford and the magistrates took a few moments to read the references before them Linda looked at Alexandra and they smiled at one another.

Linda put her lips to her daughter's ear. "Alright, my darling?" she asked, planting another soft kiss. Alexandra squeezed her mother's hand from the inside, as she said softly into her ear, "Yes, Mother. Thank you for that," and kissed her back.

Once they had finished their studying, Lavinia passed the documents back and asked Jessica, "Do you have any other witnesses, Mrs Beale?"

"No, Your Honour," she replied.

"Then please conclude your case, Mrs Beale."

"Certainly, Your Honour," said Jessica. She summed up Alexandra's case and made her closing remarks.

"Thank you, Mrs Beale," said the judge, when she had finished. That concludes Miss Radcliffe's case. We will now consider Miss Spencer and Miss Patterson."

"Defendants will rise!" called the clerk.

Gillian and Melanie stood up and went through their identification formalities and both girls swore to tell the truth before the court.

Then their solicitor, Nicola Masters, put forward their case, telling the court what the two girls had told her, about the events of last week. Then she called her own witness. Unsurprisingly to Linda, it was Elizabeth Spencer. She'd been expecting it.

The same formalities were observed again and then Elizabeth began, "Your Honour, my daughter may have admitted to arranging these visits from escort boys, under the cover name of 'actors', and that she negotiated a percentage of their takings, with the massage parlour that employed them. She also organised the shoplifting sprees, which both Miss Patterson and herself carried out. They also admit to selling the stolen items to other Charterhouse College students, to gain extra money to pay for their services. I had no knowledge of any of this, and though it might at least show that my daughter has a natural flair for enterprise, she too apologises unreservedly, offers no excuses and will except any punishment that she is given by this court – as indeed does and will Miss Patterson. I am assured that both of the girls took the necessary precautions, when they saw the escorts – as did the other three who were involved previously. But clearly, their behaviour was unacceptable. I have caned and suspended all of them from the college for a week."

"However, both girls do strongly deny that they in any way coerced Miss Radcliffe into committing the offence at Rimmingtons, on Day 5 of last week. I should like to remind the court, that it was my daughter's prompt actions that prevented the bottles of perfume being stolen, and Miss Radcliffe is simply trying to wriggle out of her predicament, by falsely accusing them of 'setting her up'. She will try anything to keep her 'Goody Two Shoes' reputation intact! I've always said that sometimes it's the quietest members of a school who end up getting into some of the worst mischief, and I think my point may have been illustrated here!"

A murmur went around the courtroom after this remark. At their table, Linda felt her daughter begin to shake. "Mother!" Alexandra whispered into her ear. "She's telling lies! Gillian definitely *did* threaten me and I would never falsely accuse anyone."

Linda murmured back, "Don't panic, darling. This is the last desperate throw of the dice from Mrs Spencer. She knows her daughter's in deep trouble. Believe me, I'm incensed by the bare-faced cheek of the pair of them, and after Mrs Spencer promised to tell the truth, too! I'd like to punish Gillian myself, but let's just wait until we hear what the judge and magistrates ultimately decide, at the end of the hearing."

"Quiet please!" ordered Lavinia Mountford. "Are you accusing Miss Radcliffe of lying, Mrs Spencer?"

"Yes, Your Honour. Unfortunately, I am," said Elizabeth gravely, and Alexandra shook with indignation and fear. If the court decided that she'd lied, then that would increase the severity of her sentence, and might scupper her chances of becoming college champion, for good. The dreaded horsewhip came into her mind again, too.

But, at the same time, her mother's soothing voice came softly into her ear. "Don't worry sweetheart! No one will believe that of you. Trust me, darling!"

"Of course, she does have the most powerful of friends, Your Honour," continued Elizabeth, referring to Queen Alexandra. "As for Philippa Barrington, well she's only known Miss Radcliffe for the briefest of times, so I hardly think that *her* opinion, carries much weight in this court!"

"That is for us to decide, Mrs Spencer!" snapped Lavinia. "Do *you* have anything further to add?"

"Just two more things, Your Honour.

"Firstly, on the matter of Miss Radcliffe's punishment at Charterhouse College last week. It is certainly not a usual occurrence for a pupil to assist the headmistress, or even a mistress, in administering a punishment at the college. But yes, it did happen after the shoplifting affair last week. I am sorry if some are calling my judgement into question – I can categorically state that I have never involved any girl in such a practice before – and I do mean *any* girl But all I will humbly say to this court, is that Miss Radcliffe had committed an offence and my daughter had played a significant part in enabling the police to apprehend her. She believed that Miss Radcliffe should be punished, and I felt there would be justification in allowing her to be part of any action taken."

"She'd set her up in the first place!" shouted Linda, from the Radcliffes' table. "I can't believe I'm hearing such nonsense! And in any case, that's hardly an excuse for a headmistress to allow a pupil to assist her in punishing another pupil – and her own daughter, too! No, this was more about settling old scores."

"If I might continue, Your Honour?" asked Elizabeth, with a wave of her hand. "I can further assure this court that no girl was ever punished by me as Headmistress at Charterhouse College, who either didn't deserve to be, or was excessively so treated. That was the case on Day 5 of last week, and it always will be.

"My second point is this. I think it's obvious to most people, that Mrs Radcliffe feels some animosity towards myself, and in particular my views on Male Rights, and my desire to discover a way to reform our people's characteristics, so that we females are not always the dominant sex on Geratica, and males not so often, subservient. These are always her real consistent issues, and as we all heard during that long winded statement from her, earlier, she likes nothing better than the sound of her own voice and never misses an opportunity to bring these matters up, even when they have no bearing on the subject at hand! It's time she realised that she doesn't rule Geratica, and certainly not Charterhouse, where my ways of running the college are no business of hers. We don't all have to do whatever she says!"

Deep inside her mind, Elizabeth knew that Linda Radcliffe was almost certainly going to emerge from this affair, in the stronger position, which was almost too humiliating for her to bear. She was also now, feeling terribly vulnerable in her position at Charterhouse. Once the hearing was over and she was back at the college, she intended to take steps to save her own neck, and try to restore some of her battered reputation.

For now, though, to finish her statement to the court, in her final remark, Elizabeth's hatred of Linda made her unable to resist hitting where she knew it would hurt most.

"Unlike her subservient mouse of a daughter!" she concluded.

Now Linda lost her temper, just as Elizabeth had known that she would.

She leapt to her feet again. "Your Honour, that's outrageous!" she shouted. "I only wish to set the record straight and help to start to restore my daughter's reputation. How dare Mrs Spencer suggest that any other issue is more important to me than that, and insult my daughter in the process?! Long winded? Rubbish! I ..."

"Mrs Radcliffe, please sit down this instant!" the judge rebuked her. "You've already given your testimony. In your position, allowing your emotions to get the better of you? I'm surprised at you!"

"I'm sorry, Your Honour," said Linda and sat back down.

Elizabeth and Gillian both sniggered.

"Silence in court!" shouted Lavinia Mountford. "Mrs Radcliffe and Mrs Spencer, this hearing is to discuss the behaviour of these three girls, and determine their punishment. It is not a stage, where you can trade insults at one another, to settle personal scores! If this continues, then I shall increase the punishment for each of your respective daughters!"

There was a silence and Lavinia briefly paused to allow the implication of what she'd just threatened, to sink in.

Then she continued, "Now, Mrs Spencer. Have you finished?"

"Yes, Your Honour," said Elizabeth.

"Then please stand down," said the judge.

"Thank you, Your Honour," replied Elizabeth.

"Defendant will stand down!" commanded the clerk of the court, and Elizabeth became seated again.

Then, after confirming that she had no more witnesses, Nicola Masters closed her case.

"Thank you, Miss Masters," said Lavinia Mountford. "We will now retire to consider the overall case, and return when we have reached a decision, regarding the sentences. Court is now adjourned until then."

"Court will rise!" shouted the clerk and everybody stood up. The three women strode out of the courtroom, and into the judge's chambers.

Everyone remaining, made their way out, and back to their respective waiting rooms.

"I think that went quite well!" said Jessica. "Apart from that bit towards the end, when the judge gave that warning. I'm sure I don't need to tell you, Mrs Radcliffe, that it's best to keep on the right side of them!"

"Yes, I'm sorry about that, Mrs Beale," replied Linda. "But that woman always manages to irk me, and I'm sure she does it deliberately, to get at me personally. She made a nasty snide remark about Alexandra, which was completely unnecessary, and once again totally inappropriate for someone in her position. And as for me making a long-winded speech – what poppycock! That was clear and concise. I made all the points I wanted, and unlike Mrs Spencer, I did not resort to purely personal attacks!"

"Please, Mrs Radcliffe! Call me Jessica! Well I'm sure you didn't do your daughter any harm," said Jessica. "I think most mothers would have felt the same, if they'd heard their children being spoken about in that way. No, I honestly think that we've come across as the 'less' guilty party in all of this. Alexandra simply made a mistake, by getting involved with the other two girls, on what she hoped would be a one-off basis, after being threatened. It's the other two who should be a lot more worried."

"You don't think the court will say that I've lied then, Jessica?" asked Alexandra. "Mrs Spencer was lying, when she asserted that everybody she's ever punished deserved it. Gillian's got quite a lot of people into trouble with her, unfairly – including me!"

"No, Alexandra," answered Jessica, reassuringly. "I don't think it's very likely that the court will say that, giving what will have been submitted to them, regarding your character. If they do, then I would suggest that you definitely have grounds for an appeal."

"So, now it's just a question of waiting," she continued. "I shouldn't think that it'll be too long. In the meantime, would you each like another drink?"

Linda glanced briefly at her daughter and Tom and then answered, "Yes please, Jessica. The same again for us all would be nice."

Jessica went to get them from the machine. Linda held Alexandra and kissed her again. "Well, we've done our best, and no woman can do better than that," she remarked. "How are you feeling?"

"Nervous, Mother," replied Alexandra. "I just want to get this over with!"

"Well, as Jessica said, that probably won't be too long now," said Linda.

Tom took her hand and kissed her. "You'll be fine Angel!" he declared. Alexandra kissed him back.

***

At 10.00 a.m. they were all called back into the courtroom. The judge came out of her chambers with the magistrates, and took their places.

"Court will rise!" said the clerk of the court, once again.

Everybody stood up.

"Court is now in session," announced Lavinia.

Then she began her verdict. "In the matter of Miss Radcliffe's attempted theft of three bottles of perfume from Rimmingtons, at 1 p.m. on 5/33/5010, the court notes that the defendant immediately pleaded guilty, and has offered financial compensation. We also note her assertion that she was pressurised into committing the offence. After considering the evidence and reading the references supplied in her defence, we are inclined to believe that this was indeed the case. She has never been in any kind of trouble before, and appears to have been a model student. It seems unlikely that someone in her position, both at Charterhouse and domestically, would suddenly wish to turn to crime, out of the blue, without there being a very dark and pressing reason for it. Her mother has given evidence of a previous occasion when she was 'thumped' for exposing a previous misdemeanour from Miss Spencer, at Charterhouse. This appears to be in keeping with the case before us today, and gives further weight to Miss Radcliffe's claims. We do not believe the denials made by Miss Spencer and Miss Patterson, that coercion was used.

"The other part of this case, relates to the additional allegations from

Miss Radcliffe. Firstly, that escort boys were being smuggled into Charterhouse, posing as 'actors,' by Miss Spencer, for a percentage of their takings, without the actual truth of their identities being known to any of the staff, and secondly that this theft and previous ones at other stores which the police were investigating, were being carried out by Miss Spencer and Miss Patterson, before selling the goods on to other girls at the college, in order for them to obtain sufficient money to pay for the escorts' services.

"The court notes that after initially trying to deny this allegation, Miss Spencer did eventually admit to it, and also that Miss Radcliffe had no involvement in this, or any of the previous shoplifting offences, nor indeed, did she partake in the activities relating to the escorts.

"In conclusion we can say categorically that Miss Spencer organised visits to Charterhouse of escort boys, in the guise of actors. Miss Spencer and Miss Patterson both took advantage of their services and we believe, tried to encourage other girls to join them, including Miss Radcliffe, who vehemently refused. In order to pay these escorts though, the two girls needed extra money and so Miss Spencer organised some shoplifting sprees, which she carried out, together with Miss Patterson, during lunchtimes, and some weekends. They then sold on the stolen items to their fellow pupils at Charterhouse.

"For some reason, which may or may not have been linked to the race for college champion, taking place at Charterhouse this term, and which Mrs Spencer wants her daughter to win – it is not this court's role to determine that – we do believe that Miss Spencer wanted to discredit Miss Radcliffe's reputation, and started to put pressure on her to join with the other two girls, in meeting the escorts. When she realised that this wasn't going to work, she then threatened to physically harm Miss Radcliffe, if she did not go shoplifting with Miss Patterson and herself, at lunchtime on 5/33/5010. We believe that there is little doubt, that under the severe pressure of the bullying she was receiving, Miss Radcliffe felt forced to go along with them, if only to stop them harassing her.

"Miss Spencer then tipped off the police and press. However, we do not believe that she would have done this, had she not been deliberately trying to set Miss Radcliffe up, and that her decision to do it, was unlikely to have had much to do with civic duty. According to Miss Radcliffe's statement, they'd scarped just before the police arrived. Also, although the punishment which Mrs Spencer administered to the girls before their suspension from Charterhouse last week, is ultimately not a concern of this court, we nevertheless find her justification for allowing a girl - who was also her daughter - to assist her as Headmistress, in punishing Miss Radcliffe, to be rather weak, and are inclined to agree with Mrs Radcliffe."

Lavinia paused for a second, to take a sip of water.

"So, we now come to the sentences. Would the defendants please rise?"

"Defendants please rise!" repeated the clerk of the court.

All three girls stood up. Alexandra took a final look at her mother, as she did so. Linda's eyes twinkled reassuringly at her daughter's. She now knew that her assumptions had been correct.

Alexandra still trembled slightly though. In her mind, she pleaded that she wasn't to be horsewhipped.

"Alexandra Radcliffe!" said Lavinia. "You have unquestionably been caught attempting to shoplift from Rimmingtons. This is a serious offence, which you have admitted to and there is indeed, no excuse for it, as I believe you fully realise.

"However, the court acknowledges that you have apologised, and offered to make a payment to Rimmingtons, equivalent to the value of the goods that you attempted to steal. We also, further acknowledge your previously exemplary character, and believe that would not have tried to commit this theft, had considerable pressure not been put on you – and there is evidence that it was.

"Accordingly, the court fines you 100g and your offer of compensation to Rimmingtons will be accepted by it, on their behalf. In addition, you will witness two horse whippings, the details of which will follow in due course."

A small whimper and some heavily whispered comments came from Gillian and Melanie's defence table. They could now guess part of what was coming to them.

Lavinia glanced at Alexandra's table. "May I ask how the payments are to be made?"

Linda reached for her briefcase. "I will write two cheques, Your Honour," she said. "One for 100g, made payable to this court and another for 19g 75d, made payable to Rimmingtons. The total amount will be deducted in instalments, from Alexandra's weekly allowance."

"Thank you, Mrs Radcliffe," said the judge. "The court is now finished with you, Miss Radcliffe, and doesn't expect to see you standing before it again!" she continued. "Please stand down."

"Thank you, Your Honour. I promise that it won't!" answered Alexandra politely.

"Defendant will stand down!" called the clerk and Alexandra did as she was asked, gratefully. Her mother and Tom both smiled at her, and Linda cradled her in her arms and kissed her. "All over now, darling!" she whispered inside her daughter's ear.

"Melanie Patterson!" said Lavinia. "You have admitted assisting Miss Spencer in these shoplifting offences. This is a very serious matter, which is compounded by the fact that you have had sex, below the legal age of consent! I believe that you were strongly influenced by Miss Spencer, but even so, this is no excuse. The court sentences you to a fine of 200g, plus a horsewhipping of 10 lashings, outside of the royal Palace, witnessed by Miss Radcliffe, and Miss Spencer. You will also witness another, which we will come to next. That will be all. Please stand down!"

"Defendant will stand down!" shouted the clerk and Melanie re-took her seat, visibly shaken and distressed.

"Gillian Spencer!" said the judge. "You are without doubt, an extremely naughty girl and a bully. You played truant from school, and visited a massage parlour, to have sex. Then you invited escort boys from the parlour into Charterhouse, and pretended that they were actors. You had underage sex with them, encouraged other girls to do the same, and took a percentage of the parlour's takings from the 'enterprise'.

"You mistress-minded the shoplifting offences, which you committed whilst you should have been on the college premises, and sold the stolen goods on to other girls, in order to pay for the escorts' services. You led Miss Patterson astray, in assisting you, and again you attempted to encourage others to do the same.

"You were clearly the ringleader of these activities, and you tried to coerce Miss Radcliffe into going with an escort boy. When she refused, you threatened her with a physical assault, if she also didn't take part in your next shoplifting operation. When she submitted, you tipped off the police, and press, and she was arrested – we believe you wished to discredit Miss Radcliffe in some way, and were setting her up.

"The court accordingly sentences you to a fine of 300g. After witnessing Miss Patterson's horsewhipping of 10 lashings, you will then receive a horsewhipping of 20 lashings, yourself, outside of the Royal Palace, witnessed by Miss Radcliffe, and Miss Patterson. In addition, you will spend a year in Avermore Young Offenders' Institution!"

"Defence!" she barked, looking at their table. "Please make arrangements for these two girls' fines to be made payable to this court as soon as possible."

She looked back at Gillian. "That will be all. Take Miss Spencer to the

Young Offenders' Institution, immediately. The other two girls are now free to go. That concludes the hearing. Court is dismissed!"

"Court dismissed!" boomed the clerk of the court, although she was nearly drowned out, and there was pandemonium, as Elizabeth Spencer shouted furiously at the judge.

"A slap on the wrist for the Radcliffe girl and then the others take all the rap! A travesty of justice! My daughter shall appeal!"

The courtroom door opened, and two officials entered. They led Gillian away. Amid the hubbub, Linda thanked Jessica Beale for her help, and Alexandra followed suit. She offered Tom a lift back home, which he accepted. Then she wrapped her arm around her daughter's shoulders, and walked her quickly out of the courtroom, with Tom on Alexandra's other side.

At the reception, she placed two cheques on the counter. "These are the payments owed by my daughter, Alexandra Radcliffe," she told the woman at the desk.

"Thank you," replied the receptionist. "If you wouldn't mind confirming your departure time in the register, before you leave, Miss Radcliffe?"

"At once," said Alexandra, and scribbled a time quickly on the page. She desperately wanted to get out of this place, and go back to the safety of home. Now she supposed, there would be another media scrum, on the way back to their car.

"Thank you and goodbye," said Linda, and with that she sped Alexandra and Tom back down the corridor, in the direction of the car park. "I'll do the talking!" she announced firmly to them, as again, a group of reporters from the media surrounded them.

"What is your reaction to your daughter's sentence, Mrs Radcliffe?" asked one.

"I believe that this is an example of Geratican justice being administered at its best," said Linda.

"What do you think of Gillian Spencer's sentence, Mrs Radcliffe?" asked another.

"I am not going to comment on that. That is a matter for Mrs Spencer and Gillian, herself. That is all we wish to say, regarding this affair."

Linda opened the door leading to the final corridor, on the way to the car park. She quickly swept her daughter along to the door leading down to it, and the three of them went through, and down the steps. Opening the door at the bottom, they finally reached their destination.

"You two sit in the back," said Linda, as she unlocked the car. "Let's go home!"

"Yes Mother," said Alexandra. "Before that though, thank you so much, Mother! I couldn't have got through this morning without you, and what you said in the courtroom must have played a significant role, when they decided my sentence, as well as Jessica Beale's defence of me." She looked up and kissed Linda, who returned it.

"Don't forget Queen Alexandra and Philippa Barrington, darling," said Linda. "I must organise a meeting with Her Majesty, for you, as soon as possible, so that you can thank her personally."

"Oh yes. Of course, Mother," replied Alexandra. "And last but not least, you too, Tom, for being there with me. I needed you today and you were fantastic!" She kissed him, too, and they became affectionate.

"Come on you two," said Linda. "You can continue with all that in the car! I want to get us away from here, as quickly as possible, before we meet any more media women."

"Yes, Mother. So do I!" Alexandra ushered Tom into the car. Once they were all inside, Linda drove out of the building and through the barrier, after she had paid another toll fee. Through the tinted windows, Alexandra once again saw the reporters outside the court, and cameras flashed as they swept past. Then Linda turned into a main road and they sped away, back to Greenacres and Elmsbrook.

***

Alexandra sank gratefully into the comfort of the back seat of her mother's car, and puffed out her cheeks.

"Thank the Divine Being for that!" she exclaimed.

"I told you that you'd be OK, darling," said Linda.

"Do you think that there *will* be an appeal, Mother?" asked her daughter.

"I don't know," said Linda. "It's possible, but I very much doubt it. I don't see that Gillian's got any chance at all. Mrs Spencer has a big mouth, but it's whether she's prepared to put her money where that is. The assertion may have been just pure temper. Mrs Spencer's certainly got one of those – even worse than mine, sometimes, I think, which is really saying something!"

Tom exchanged glances with Alexandra. "Would there have to be another hearing, Mrs Radcliffe?" he asked.

"Well, only if she was to be successful in her appeal," replied Linda. "I don't think it'll go that far. Let's not think about that now, anyhow. The important thing is, that Alexandra has received her sentence, and the court has acknowledged the circumstances in which she was bullied into committing the offence. I imagine that the horse whippings will take place very soon, and once Alexandra's witnessed them, and her period of suspension ends, she can then return to Charterhouse next week, and hopefully start to get back to normal. We now know, also, that Gillian Spencer won't be there anymore. She'll be expelled immediately, and taken to Avermore Young Offenders' Institution!"

In the back of the car, Tom took Alexandra's hand, and they smiled at each other.

"You made it through, then?" whispered Tom.

"Yes!" Alexandra whispered back.

They kissed and cuddled for most of the journey back home.

# CHAPTER 7

Back in Elmsbrook, Linda reached The Grange.

"Are you going to come in with us, for a while Tom?" she asked. "I've no doubt that Alexandra will be pleased, and you can stay and have a bit of lunch with us, if you like."

"Thank you, Mrs Radcliffe. That would be nice," replied Tom.

Inside the house, Alexandra went to her bedroom to change out of her school uniform, and Linda sat talking with Tom in the breakfast room, whilst she waited for the kettle to boil in the kitchen, before making coffee. Once she had served it, and Alexandra had re-joined them, she looked at the time. As far as Linda could remember, Queen Alexandra should be free around now.

"If you two will just excuse me for a few moments," she announced, "I'm just going to ring the palace, and confirm what's happened. We'll have some lunch, when I've finished."

"OK, Mother," replied Alexandra.

\*\*\*

Linda went into the study, and after getting through to the palace, immediately enquired whether Queen Alexandra was free. She was soon connected to her.

"Linda!" the queen greeted her.

"Your Majesty!" replied Linda.

"I was just about to listen to the news," continued Queen Alexandra. "How are things?"

"As good as they could be, Ma'am, dare I say it. Our hearing was the first of the day at 9.00 a.m., and it was all over after about an hour and ten minutes. The court accepted that Alexandra was coerced into the attempted theft, and she was fined 100g. She's also made a payment to Rimmingtons, equivalent to the value of the perfume that she tried to steal, as compensation – which was at her instigation. I wrote a cheque for each, and gave them to the court, but I'll deduct the total amount from her weekly allowances. As far as she's concerned, that's it, although she has been ordered to witness two horse whippings."

"Oh, that's wonderful, Linda," remarked the queen. "I'm really pleased and Alexandra must be very relieved that it's all over."

"I think you could say that again, Ma'am," confirmed Linda.

"And the other two girls? I assume that the horse whippings that you referred to concern them?"

"Indeed, Ma'am. You'll soon be making their acquaintances. They've both been fined, and sentenced to a horsewhipping – Gillian Spencer more severely in both cases. And she's also being sent to Avermore Young Offenders' Institute, for a year, with immediate effect. She'll now be expelled from Charterhouse. Mrs Spencer says that her daughter will appeal, though whether she actually will, I don't know – and in any case, I very much doubt that she'd stand much chance of success. I sincerely hope that *my* daughter is now free of her, for good!"

"Yes. Well, as I inferred at the end of last week, that was always on the cards," said the queen. "Well done, Linda! I always knew that you'd get the result you wanted."

"Thank you, Ma'am, but I believe that your contribution to the court, was also most helpful, so I thank you for that! Furthermore, I feel that Alexandra should come to the palace, and express her gratitude to you, personally, as well. Perhaps if I bring her in with me tomorrow, would Your Majesty have any time free to meet with her?"

"Well let me see now," said the queen. "Just bear with me for a moment, would you, Linda?"

"Of course, Ma'am," she replied.

The line went quiet, as the queen consulted with her personal aide.

A moment later she came back. "I have some free time at 9.00 a.m. tomorrow, Linda."

"9.00 a.m. tomorrow, it is then, Ma'am. Thank you."

"Do you wish to be present also?"

"No, Ma'am. I think it would be good for Alexandra to meet with you alone, and say her peace. It might also do her confidence some good, if she can meet with you alone and feel that it's gone well – which I'm sure it will. She does need that at the moment. Ultimately, she needs to become a slightly stronger person. She's improved a lot, but this could set her back a bit."

"Yes, you might be right, Linda," agreed Queen Alexandra. "I might have some words of advice for her, too."

"Very good, Ma'am. Then I shall instruct my daughter to pay strict attention to it!" asserted Linda.

"The other matter that we now need to organise, Ma'am, is the double horsewhipping," she continued. "The court ordered that Alexandra and Gillian witness Melanie's and Alexandra and Melanie witness Gillian's. As I'll be bringing my daughter to the palace tomorrow anyhow, shall we arrange for them both to take place then, also, Ma'am?"

"Hmm, that sounds logical," said the queen. "Very well, I agree Linda. I know that I'm also free at noon tomorrow, so the court will administer the thrashings then. Although of course, if Elizabeth Spencer does carry out her threat to appeal, then we may have to postpone it, at least until after that."

It was customary for the queen and her most senior courtier to carry out this punishment themselves.

"Just one other thing regarding this, Ma'am," said Linda. "My daughter was not sentenced to be horsewhipped, as the other two girls were, but to witness them both. I trust the fact that I am the mother of a co-defendant in their case, will not prevent me from being able to carry out my normal duty?"

"Well, I don't know, Linda," said Queen Alexandra, thoughtfully. "I had been considering asking Fiona to take your place. Your position could be compromised."

Fiona, in her position, normally only deputised for Linda in this particular procedure if the latter was ever unavailable. Other than that, she wasn't involved.

"I do feel *very* strongly about this, Ma'am," pressed Linda. "Obviously, if my own daughter was sentenced to be horsewhipped, then I would step aside immediately, but she hasn't. Her crime was far more limited than that of the other two girls, and although they were linked, they were really two separate cases. It was only because Gillian Spencer tried to discredit Alexandra, that my daughter became involved in their squalid activities! Gillian and Melanie deserve to be punished severely, Ma'am and Gillian in particular. The only way that I will be able to satisfy myself, that the level of severity is high enough, will be to participate in the horse whippings with you, as usual, Ma'am."

"I agree that the level of severity *must* be appropriate to the crime, Linda," asserted the queen. *That* is what concerns me. I hope that you wouldn't attempt to extract any kind of revenge on Gillian, or completely lose your temper."

"Oh no. Of course not, Ma'am. You have my complete assurance on that." Linda had every intention of thrashing Gillian hard, but not excessively so. She was by now, quite skilled with the horsewhip, both through these occurrences with juvenile delinquents and due to occasionally riding to hounds, as a guest of Queen Alexandra, during her hunting expeditions. She was extremely accurate in her placement and knew the particular spots to hit, that would cause Gillian the maximum level of discomfort.

The queen sighed. "Alright then Linda. I'll allow it. But if anyone does accuse you of being unfairly brutal to the wretched Spencer girl, then on your head be it! However, if you will be assisting me, then I don't think it would be appropriate for you to also lead your own daughter out, to witness the horse whippings – especially Spencer's - given the precise personal feelings between all involved, including you. I command that Fiona should at least do that."

"I understand, Ma'am," Linda assured her.

After they had said goodbye until tomorrow, Linda went to the kitchen, and began to prepare their snack for lunch.

Alexandra and Tom were in the parlour. Once the lunch was ready, Linda called them to the dining room, and they sat down to eat. As they did so, she explained to her daughter, the events planned at the palace for tomorrow, which involved her.

Alexandra still felt uncomfortable. "I'd rather *not* watch, to be honest Mother!" she exclaimed. "I hate horse whippings. I think they're barbaric."

"Well I'm sorry, darling, but you've been ordered to witness both of them by the juvenile court, and therefore, witness them you must – and will!"

"Anyhow, Alexandra," she continued, "You're far too soft over this subject. Gillian and Melanie – particularly Gillian – have behaved disgracefully – far worse than you. They need to be taught a lesson, and I intend to do my share in teaching them it!"

"Very well, Mother," replied Alexandra. "I'll just have to grit my teeth, and bear it, I suppose."

"Indeed you will, Alexandra!" Linda told her firmly.

***

Later, Alexandra phoned Philippa, and told her the news. She was pleased to hear it, and hoped that Alexandra would be able to resume her plans for the concert, once she was back at Charterhouse. Alexandra thanked her for the help she'd given her, at the hearing.

*\*\*

That night, James came for dinner, as arranged.

Linda was wearing a long flowing shoulder-less purple gown, with a knee length split at the front, and Alexandra, a blue gown, with straps at the shoulders and pleats at the hem – two at the front and two at the back.

"Well now, I said that I'd get us together again soon," remarked Linda, as they sat down to eat and she poured the wine. "And now, a little later than I'd originally planned, so I have. Welcome to the Radcliffe abode James!"

"Thank you, Linda!" replied James. "Go easy on that wine, won't you? I've got to drive back tonight, remember?"

"Yes, yes, you needn't worry about that, man," said Linda. "We've got to be up early tomorrow morning, anyhow, though Alexandra's day won't be quite the same as usual. Not that today was either, of course."

"Hmm," said James. "This has obviously been a difficult day for all of us, but there's no excusing Gillian's behaviour at all, and I thought the judgement was reasonably fair to all of the girls. I've already told Alexandra, that I was pleased with the way it went for her, Linda."

"Yes," replied Linda. "Well of course I can't excuse *my* daughter's behaviour either, but she was nevertheless pressurised into doing it, against her normal character. Thank you for your generosity, James."

"Children!" she continued. "They don't half cause us some headaches sometimes, don't they James?"

"Yes, but I think that your child is a lot sweeter than mine, Linda," remarked James.

"A lot, I would say, James!" interjected Alexandra.

James chuckled. "I agree with you actually, Alexandra!"

"Do bear in mind the fact that Alexandra is on her *very* best behaviour, during her period of punishment, James," said Linda. "But yes. I think that whenever you're with us, you'll find that she's an extremely easy child to manage. Despite recent events, I'm still, on the whole, very proud of her."

"Thank you, Mother!" Her daughter beamed with pleasure.

"So, has there been anything exciting happening at the palace, in the last few days?" asked Alexandra, a short time later.

"Alexandra!" said Linda. "How many times have I spoken to you about the need for discretion? Do you really think that we, as loyal servants of Her Majesty, are going to reveal details like that? Really! I'm surprised at you!"

However, Alexandra saw the twinkle in her mother's eyes, and she knew that she was only being given a mock rebuke.

"I'm sorry, Mother, I forgot myself. Please forgive me!" she replied. "But I do know for a fact, that Queen Alexandra went to Castra University last week, to give an address. It was on the radio. Was it a good trip? Did you keep the queen amused during the journey?"

Linda and James smiled at each other. "She's determined to get some details, isn't she Linda?" said James. "If you mean, was there any banter between us in the front, well then I think it's fair to say, that we were up to our usual standard."

"Banter? I don't know what you're talking about, James," said Linda. "I don't remember any exchange of 'banter,' between us! I do recall though, that I had to redirect you on a few occasions, during the route. Queen Alexandra obviously would never have made it to the university on time, if I hadn't been there!"

"When we arrived back, the queen thanked me for a very professional drive, actually, Linda," said James, amiably.

"Well naturally, she didn't want to seem ungrateful to you, James, but she knew that it was my meticulous planning and navigational skills, that were the real reason for its successful execution." retorted Linda.

James looked at Alexandra and rolled his eyes. "Yes of course, Linda!" he replied.

***

Later, they finished the evening talking in the parlour. Once again, Alexandra felt that she liked James. She liked most men really – more than some of the girls and women that she'd met. If her mother was going to fall in love, and bring someone into the household, then she couldn't really ask for anyone nicer. If nothing else, The Grange would be a jolly place, given the humour that seemed to naturally flow between the two of them.

She was feeling extremely relieved that today's hearing was over, and that her mother had been correct in her prediction, that she wouldn't get a severe sentence. She was still a bit nervous about tomorrow though. She'd met Queen Alexandra on a few occasions now, and had always liked and respected her. But this would be the very first time that she'd be speaking alone with her, and she would also have to convey appropriately, her gratitude for the character reference that the queen had submitted to the juvenile court.

Then there were the horsewhipping sessions that she was being forced to watch. She was trying hard not to think about it. The only good thing was that she wasn't to suffer one herself. She half hoped that Gillian's mother *would* appeal, and they would have to be postponed, but on the other hand, she wanted all this to be finished, as soon as possible. And in the unlikely event of the appeal being successful, she might not be in quite such a strong position, anyhow.

Once it was all over, she was looking forward to having the rest of the week to herself. As well as doing whatever jobs her mother gave her, whilst she was at work, she was planning to take advantage of this unscheduled period of absence from Charterhouse, by thinking some more about the concert that she still hoped to give at the end of term, as well as swatting up on some schoolwork. She was going to have some catching up to do, on her return, and so she would teach herself, as far as possible, by reading ahead in her text books, and making her own notes, so that she was familiar with the stage that her classes had reached.

***

At the end of the evening, as James was leaving, Linda said to him, "I know that we *officially* said that we needed to discuss confidential arrangements, for the dinner here at the end of the week. I don't think that there's a lot that we can't talk about at the palace though, in fact. That was mainly just an excuse for me to get you over here."

"But there is one thing, James," continued Linda, quietly to him. "Obviously, your wife is on the official guest list. After this though, there's absolutely no possibility of her being invited! I won't be able to keep my manners, and Alexandra is bound to feel uncomfortable, at her presence at a social event."

"I'm not too sure, Linda," James replied, ponderously. "She's her own woman and despite having, what you describe as 'progressive views' on Male Rights, her temperament is actually quite traditional for a Geratican woman! You'd imagine that she'd want to stay away, out of the social spotlight, for a while, after what's happened. She'll probably make some excuse not to attend. On the other hand though, she *is* one of the finest authorities on Geratica's core, so in that capacity, she'll want to come."

"I don't care if she's the daughter of the Divine Being herself, James!" snapped Linda. "She *can't* come and that's final!"

"Meanwhile, we'll have to see if she can survive as headmistress of Charterhouse," she continued. "And the heat is about to turn up considerably for her, in that regard!"

\*\*\*

In fact, the current headmistress of Charterhouse, had that evening visited her daughter, before her first night at Avermore Young Offenders' Institution.

The juveniles were allowed one private visit a week, in their rooms, by their parent or parents.

In her arms, Elizabeth had a box, containing a few possessions, which Gillian could keep there, during her year at the Institution, plus one other item. She dropped the box on to a table, then went to close the door.

"Right, Gillian," she said. "Those are your things, from Charterhouse. You are now officially expelled from that college, and I doubt very much that you'll ever go to Castra University."

Then she gripped her daughter firmly, pulled down her skirt.

"Mother, what in the world are you doing?" exclaimed Gillian, in alarm.

"No, I'm not your mother any more, you pesky girl," said Elizabeth coldly.

"What?" said her daughter, uncomprehendingly.

"But I've not finished with you quite yet! First, I'm going to do something that I should have done a long time ago!"

From the box, Elizabeth pulled out the extra item. It was her cane from Charterhouse. She sat down on Gillian's bed and pulled her daughter over her knees. Then she began to beat her daughter, talking as she did so.

"I've had enough of you. You've overstepped the mark for the last time. I can't defend you anymore, and why should I? You had it all, but now you're an utter failure, and you're no use to me, as one of those! You might have been useful before, but never again after this! I can't believe that I could have bred such a nasty, despicable girl like you, and now I'm disowning you! Find your own way in life – you've got yourself into this position, it's all your own fault, now get yourself out of it. I gave you a fantastic opportunity, but you took advantage of me, and went way too far. You're now an embarrassment to me, and my position is in serious jeopardy!"

Gillian cried out from the blows, and her mind raced as she heard her mother's words. She'd never experienced such a shock in all her life, and couldn't take it in. It seemed totally surreal, and she was utterly confused. She didn't know what to say or do.

Finally, Elizabeth stopped, and pushing Gillian away, she stood up and tucked her cane under her arm. Then she turned to leave.

"I don't wish to have any more contact with you. Goodbye, Gillian and good riddance to you!" was her last comment to her daughter, as she strode towards the door.

"Mother!" screamed Gillian, but Elizabeth ignored her and without another word, or pausing to look back, she opened the door and left.

A warden was on duty in the corridor outside.

"If Gillian Spencer comes out of her room, please do *not* let her follow me," she said to her, as she paced quickly by. "I don't wish to see her!"

Elizabeth went down the stairs, and out of the building, to her car. Putting her cane in the passenger seat, she climbed in and drove away, back to Charterhouse, where she hoped to start rebuilding her reputation.

Once back, Elizabeth immediately contacted the Royal Palace and stated that she *wouldn't* be appealing against her daughter's sentence, after all. It was then confirmed to all three girls that the horsewhipping session would take place at noon the following day.

"As I suspected," remarked Linda to Alexandra. "Mrs Spencer wasn't prepared to put her money where her mouth was."

# CHAPTER 8

Linda and Alexandra left for Avermore at 7.15 a.m. the next morning. Linda had told her daughter to wear her skirt suit and bow, to make herself look smart and business-like for her meeting with Queen Alexandra. It was black with the skirt having a simple short split at the back. Beneath her jacket she wore a white blouse and matching black bow. Linda was wearing the same outfit that she had to Castra University, the previous week.

On their arrival at the palace, Linda took Alexandra into her office and made them both a cup of coffee.

She looked at the clock on the wall. "Right!" she said. "Well you've got just over an hour before you'll need to go for your meeting with Her Majesty. Enjoy your coffee and relax for a bit. Once Veronica comes in, which should be around 8.00, I'll see if there's anything that you can do for her, beforehand."

"Oh. Very good, Mother," replied Alexandra. She felt a shiver of nerves. This would be her very first experience of 'the world of work'. On previous visits, she had just been observing, as a special visitor.

"I hope that I won't mess anything up, Mother," she said anxiously.

"Don't worry, darling, you won't be given anything remotely difficult," her mother reassured her. "You managed perfectly well with me yesterday, didn't you? There's a limit to what we possibly *can* give you anyhow, since you've no experience and don't know any of our procedures. But it'll give you just a smidgeon of work experience, which can only be a good thing, and I hope, it will also help rebuild your confidence.

"I want you to return to Charterhouse next week, feeling that you're still a very intelligent and capable girl and that people will still think highly of you. Some will know that you've made a mistake, but we all do from time to time. The important thing is to learn from it and move on, and most people will let you do that, particularly if they know that you're sorry for what you did. You'll have to work extra hard, and keep your nose clean for a while, but I don't think that'll be a problem for you. You enjoy your studies and don't forget – Gillian will no longer be there to bother you!"

"Yes, Mother. I do think that people will now have a better understanding of what actually happened last week. I don't feel quite as nervous about going back now, as I would have done if the hearing had gone differently for me."

"Good girl! That's what I want to hear," said Linda.

"The first thing *I* need to do, is find out what happened in my absence yesterday," she continued. It looks like Fiona's left me a briefing note, which she must have got Veronica to put into my in-tray, before she left, but I'd expected a bit more information, to be honest! Fiona's approach to things tends to be a bit more laid back than mine, but all the same, there were some urgent matters that needed to be addressed yesterday. I know that she didn't stay long in parliament last night, either, because we both heard her motor past The Grange and up to The Lodge, at her usual high speed, quite a bit earlier than I normally return home."

Sure enough, Veronica arrived at 8.00 on the dot. Linda took Alexandra out to the office that she shared with Carol, Fiona's secretary and asked her if there was anything fairly straightforward that her daughter could do for a while, before her meeting with Queen Alexandra.

Veronica gave Alexandra a couple of filing jobs, after showing her where to put them, and had her sit beside her to do some other tasks, as she directed. She briefly used Veronica's word processor.

"You're certainly very efficient and studious, Alexandra!" said Veronica. "And from what I've seen of your work, very accurate, too. Thank you very much for your help. Well done. Your mother will be pleased to hear what I tell her, when she asks for a report, as I've no doubt will be the case!"

"Thank you, Veronica," replied Alexandra, feeling both happy and relieved that she seemed to have impressed. She hoped that her meeting with the queen would be just as successful.

"Now before you go off to perform the duty that's the main reason for your visit today, come with me into the main office for a moment. It's alright, you're not going to be doing any work in there, but we'd like to say a few words to you, that's all! Carol is going to come, too."

"Oh!" exclaimed Alexandra. This was a complete surprise. She hadn't been expecting anything like that.

"OK, Veronica," she said, and once they were ready, she followed the secretaries, smoothing herself down and checking her hair, as she did so.

As soon as the staff in the office saw Alexandra, rather shyly enter with Veronica and Carol, there was some bustle, as people seemed to get themselves prepared for something. Veronica took Alexandra to one of the desks, where a woman with medium length fair hair and glasses, sat. This, Alexandra believed, was the woman in charge of this room. She'd seen most of the small group of people in here, before, but never really spoken much to them – mainly because she'd not had much cause to do so. She was always a bit nervous around people who she didn't know, especially other women.

After a moment, the office became quiet, and everyone gathered around the woman's desk.

"Good morning, Alexandra!" she said with a smile. "My name is Lucy Worthington, and I'm the chief administration officer."

"Good morning, Lucy!" replied Alexandra politely.

"We'd all just like to say, that we obviously know why you're here today, and your predicament at the end of last week. We do understand the position that you were in. We don't know you very well, personally, but we *do* know you as Mrs Radcliffe's daughter, who has visited us on occasions, and been very popular. Our opinion of you hasn't changed, because of this unfortunate incident."

Alexandra felt her heart lift slightly. "Thank you, Lucy – and to all of you. That's very kind!" she said, with genuine feeling. "It's been a difficult few days and I'm looking forward to getting back to normal, soon."

"Well, we're sure that you'll settle back into Charterhouse fairly quickly, next week," said Lucy. "And we all wish you the best of luck in becoming college champion, at the end of 5010."

"Thank you all again," replied Alexandra. "Of course, I don't know for certain, whether I'll still be allowed to be a candidate!"

"I'm sure that, like us, they'll be understanding of your position last week though, Alexandra," commented Lucy. "Try not to worry, and think positively!"

"Thank you. I'll try. I'm really grateful to you all, for your kind sentiments," remarked Alexandra.

"Don't mention it, Alexandra. Best of luck for your meeting with Her Majesty, too," replied Lucy.

There were murmurs of agreement from the assembled group.

"Thank you all again!" exclaimed Alexandra, and everybody laughed gently.

"Right, well it's almost time for that now," said Veronica. "We'd better get you back to Mrs Radcliffe, so that she can escort you down to the queen's study."

"Yes, of course, Veronica. Goodbye and thank you all," said Alexandra.

"Goodbye and the very best of luck for the rest of 5010!" said Lucy. "I expect we'll see you again, at some point."

The other women indicated their assent, and Alexandra nodded in acknowledgement to them all. Then Veronica and Carol ushered her out, and Veronica took her back to her mother's office.

Linda had a security system on her office door. When it was shut, it automatically locked. If someone wanted to gain entry, they pressed a button on the console, and a buzzer sounded inside her office. If she wasn't there, or was busy, and didn't want to be disturbed, a red light automatically lit up on the console, and the door wouldn't open. The only way it could be unlocked from the outside, was by Linda's key, although Veronica also had a copy of it. If she was free, then she could press a button in her office, which would release the mechanism remotely, and a green light came on. The door could then be pushed open. Alternatively, the door could be manually opened from the inside. On this occasion the green light came on, and Veronica opened the door. However, Linda was on the phone. She acknowledged them, and indicated to Veronica that she could go, then after checking the clock, swiftly brought the call to an end.

"Hello, darling. How did it go?" she asked, as she put down the phone.

"Very well, Mother," Alexandra told her. "And the women of 'Your Little Empire' had some kind words for me, too!"

"I'm sure I'll be told all about it," said her mother. "Now, let's get you down to Her Majesty's study. You mustn't be late for this! And I have some information, which I'll tell you about as we go."

They left Linda's office.

"I shouldn't think you'll be all that long with the queen, so I may be in a meeting with my staff, when you're ready to return," she continued. "That's at 9.00 a.m. too. It's what I normally hold on Day 1 of the week, but as I wasn't here yesterday, I want to catch up. I've arranged for someone from Her Majesty's reception staff, to bring you back, and let you into the court administration department, once you've finished. To get back into my room, this is Veronica's copy of my key." She placed it in Alexandra's hand. "Make sure you don't lose it! Simply unlock the door, push it open and go inside. Hopefully, my meeting won't go on very much longer than yours. I'm due for a meeting with the queen myself, at 10.00 a.m."

"Very good, Mother," said Alexandra.

Linda let them out into the main corridor, leading to Queen Alexandra's study.

"Darling, the newspapers have been delivered, and it's been widely reported that Mrs Spencer visited Gillian at Avermore Young Offenders' Institution, last night, to give some possessions to her. She apparently beat her several times and then disowned her! After she left, she contacted one of the papers and told them what she'd done, and it was in time for this morning's front pages."

"What?" gasped her daughter. "*Disowned* her?"

"Well that's what the papers are saying, anyhow."

"Does James know?"

"Yes. I spoke to him a short while ago. She certainly didn't discuss it with him beforehand, and he was as shocked as anyone! We'll talk more about that, later."

"Now, Alexandra," she continued, as they walked. "Don't forget what I've told you. Address the queen as 'Your Majesty', and curtsey when you greet her and then Ma'am after that. And finish with 'Your Majesty', and curtsey, before you leave!"

"Yes, Mother. I will," replied her daughter, obediently.

"Good girl," said her mother. "How do you feel?"

"A bit nervous, I must admit!"

"Well that's quite natural. But you'll be fine. You've met her on other occasions with me, so you know what she's like. Just relax and be yourself and she'll direct the conversation. Although, of course, make sure that you thank Her Majesty for her help."

"I certainly won't forget that, Mother!" promised her daughter.

As they proceeded, Alexandra was struck by the number of palace staff who acknowledged her, as they passed.

# CHAPTER 9

They reached the lobby reception area, and Linda announced her daughter's arrival.

"Now, good luck," she said. "I must be getting back. See you later my darling." She engulfed Alexandra in a strong embrace, and squeezed it tighter, as she kissed her lips deeply. Alexandra took a last look up into her mother's eyes, and felt a sense of warmth, love and protection, which she resolved to take with her, into the meeting.

"Goodbye, Mother," said Alexandra, and kissed her back.

Linda kissed her once more for luck, and then they parted. Alexandra sat down in the lobby, and watched her mother walk back up the corridor, towards her little empire, sleeves rolled to her elbows.

A short time later, Rebecca Hargreaves, Queen Alexandra's personal aide, came out to the lobby.

"Good morning, Miss Radcliffe! Her Majesty will see you now," she said to Alexandra.

"Thank you!" replied Alexandra. She got up, smoothed herself down again, and made sure that her hair was immaculate, then followed Rebecca into the queen's study.

Inside, Queen Alexandra was waiting to greet her. She wore a black skirt suit and bow and a white blouse with black cuffs.

"Ma'am, this is Miss Radcliffe," said Rebecca.

"Your Majesty!" said Alexandra, curtseying perfectly, and shaking the queen's outstretched hand.

"Good morning, Alexandra! Welcome!" smiled the queen. "Please take a seat" She motioned to the chair opposite her own, at her desk.

"Thank you, Ma'am," replied Alexandra, smoothing the back of her skirt to avoid it being creased, as her mother had always taught her that a lady should do, as she sat down.

"You take a black coffee, like your mother, don't you?" enquired the queen.

"Yes Ma'am," said Alexandra.

Queen Alexandra looked at Rebecca, and she nodded in acknowledgement to both of them. "Very good, Ma'am," she said. "Two black coffees then," and went away to organise their refreshments.

The queen took her seat. "Well Alexandra, thank you for coming to see me today," she began. "I was most distressed to hear about what happened at the end of last week. It certainly seemed *totally* out of character for you, to say the least, as I hope my reference that I supplied to your court hearing, with regards to you, clearly demonstrated."

"Yes, Ma'am, it did, and I would like to express my gratitude to you," replied Alexandra." I think it was of invaluable help to me. Thank you very much. I'm only sorry that I caused you so much trouble, and other people, too. I was wrong to do what I did, and I'm sorry. I offer no excuse, because there isn't one."

"Alexandra," said the queen," You and your mother are almost like family to me. I've known you all your life, and your mother is my most trusted advisor, colleague and even, I might say, friend. I'm well aware that you're one of the most pleasant, impeccably mannered, and intelligent girls, in my queendom, and you're generally a huge credit to your mother, in your exemplary behaviour. I'm quoting half of the reference to you now!

"It was always obvious to me, that there must have been something going on, which none of us were initially aware of, and there was never any question of me not – at least indirectly – lending you some support. I, of course, couldn't comment officially on the actual case, only your character, as I know you. I understand that Philippa Barrington also supplied something similar?"

"Yes, Ma'am, and I thanked her also, yesterday."

"Well that confirms what I've always known, that you're a very respectful girl."

"Thank you, Ma'am."

Rebecca then re-appeared with the coffee. As she poured it into their cups, and placed a biscuit in each of their saucers, Alexandra relaxed slightly. Her greeting had been perfect, she felt and she had now thanked Queen Alexandra for her help, which was the main purpose of their meeting. That was the most formal part over with.

Once Rebecca had left once more, the queen began again, "Now, Alexandra, let's have a bit of a chat. I really feel that it needs to be stressed to you, because I don't think you always realise it yourself, just what a popular and well liked girl you are, amongst all who know you - and your reputation amongst those who don't, is highly favourable, also! I doubt if there were many people listening, who could believe what they were hearing on the news, on Day 5 of last week.

"Miss Gillian Spencer might be a clever girl in her academic studies – especially it seems in science, like her mother – but she certainly isn't in her judgement of people, if this is anything to go by. She was naive in the extreme to think that what she was ultimately attempting to do to you wouldn't be highly likely to backfire on her. If she'd just confined herself to finding a way of discrediting you, within Charterhouse and not tried to involve the authorities, then who knows, she might even have succeeded in fulfilling her mother's ambition, but she went too far, and now, even Mrs Spencer's position might be untenable. She clearly has a lot to learn about other people, as well as the standards of behaviour which are expected, and those that will not be accepted from her, as an individual. I can only hope that the final piece of her punishment, taking place here, at noon today, will go some way to teaching her those standards – and that goes for Miss Melanie Patterson, too. Of course, you'll be there to witness both sets of punishments."

Alexandra shifted slightly in her chair. She wasn't really sure if being flogged in public, outside the royal palace, would really make Gillian change her ways. She'd probably just become even more bitter than she would be already, at having lost the chance of the great prize, that both she and her mother had desired – and *possibly* handed it to her greatest rival, of all people, on a plate. In any case, she hated the whole concept.

"Yes, Ma'am, although I must confess that I'd rather not have to," she replied. "I find horsewhipping of people, horrible to even think about, let alone watch. I'm sorry, Ma'am, but I have to tell you that I think it's barbaric – even if I don't care for Miss Gillian Spencer, one jot, and hope that I'll never meet her again! Incidentally, the papers are apparently saying, that Mrs Spencer has disowned her! My mother told me, when she brought me down here."

"Really?" exclaimed Queen Alexandra. "How extraordinary! I shall have to read that, after we've finished.

"Well, you *have* been ordered by the juvenile court to witness the horse whippings, I'm afraid, Alexandra," continued the queen. She pointed a finger at Alexandra. "There's no getting out of it, and you won't find any support from me, there!"

"Oh no, Ma'am, I'm not suggesting that at all!" said Alexandra quickly. "I said that I'd accept whatever punishment the court decided, and I have done. I *will* be there."

"Good. And I don't doubt that you will fulfil your responsibilities, Alexandra. That's your nature. I also realise that as a very sensitive girl, you probably do feel more uncomfortable about this, than some others. But I *must* and I *will* have discipline in my queendom! Those of us in an official capacity in Geratica, at which of course I am the head, believe that this is the only way to adequately punish those juveniles who commit serious misdemeanours, and to deter them and others watching, from doing such things in the future."

"But, Ma'am, with the greatest respect, when I mistakenly decided to attempt the shoplifting offence last week, I never thought once about a possible horsewhipping, and I've always dreaded the thought of receiving it! All I was thinking was that this would definitely be a one off, and the only reason I was doing it, was in the hope that I might get Gillian Spencer off my back, if I could just get through it. I don't think that very many other people who appear before those courts, think about it either. Many people who commit crimes – no matter what they are – assume that they're not going to get caught themselves, even if a lot of people before them have been, so the 'punishment' becomes irrelevant to them, as a so-called deterrent. I know that there was research carried out, which concluded this, when the abolition of the death penalty was being discussed, and that Your Majesty and my mother, were the principal architects of that endeavour, which was ultimately successful."

"Yes, well this obviously isn't *quite* such a serious and 'final' punishment as that!" remarked the queen.

"No, Ma'am, but surely the principle is the same?" answered Alexandra. "And there's no evidence either, that many juvenile delinquents are necessarily deterred from committing further offences, after a horsewhipping, anyhow. A lot become bitter towards the 'system' and start to try and get revenge on it, which only makes things worse, both for them, *and* the rest of us. It's often really administered, and witnessed by people whose primary desire is to vent and release their anger, although of course, they *claim* that they're doing it purely to provide a 'deterrent'.

"I'm sorry. I meant no disrespect, Ma'am!" she added quickly. "I was thinking of *ordinary* people."

The queen studied Alexandra for a moment. "Goodness me!" she exclaimed. "You certainly feel passionately about this subject, don't you?" How does your mother feel about your position? Have you discussed it with her?"

"Not all that much, Ma'am, but she does know that I'm not comfortable about it. She says that I'm far too soft on this sort of thing! Maybe I am, but softness is part of my make-up, and I can't change it. My boyfriend actually says that it's one of the things he likes about me, anyhow, so naturally that means I don't *want* to change it, either."

"Ah yes, Tom Ryder, Fiona Clark's stepson. I believe I'm going to meet him soon. How are the two of you getting along?"

"Fine, Ma'am," said Alexandra. "We've been together for just over a week now, and he turned fifteen last week, too. We invited him to dinner at The Grange, on Day 1 of the weekend."

"Good," replied the queen. "But to return to the subject of horsewhipping, I imagine your mother puts a lot of pressure on you, to come around to her way of thinking. Am I right?"

"Hmm. Yes, a bit," admitted Alexandra. "And obviously she's one of the people administering them, along with Your Majesty, which makes it a bit awkward. But I think that people do exaggerate slightly, when they're speculating on how our relationship works. My mother is certainly a very dominant and strict woman, and unquestionably the boss in our household. She makes the decisions and does indeed tell me what I should do, quite often, which I need quite badly sometimes, and I wouldn't have it any other way. She's my rock. We do find that method is the one that works best for us. But she's not a complete tyrant! I am allowed my own opinions, and to make my own observations, although Mother will always have the final say. As it happens, I do lean towards her conservative views on many subjects, but this is one of the few things that we radically differ on. We do actually get on extremely well, as a partnership, and love each other to death. We enjoy each other's company, and doing things together – unlike some of the girls I've met at Charterhouse!"

Queen Alexandra chuckled. "I know. You don't have to tell *me* that, Alexandra. You and your mother are exceptionally close. I also know that this whole unpleasant business hurt you both, and came between you, although I believe you're just about back to normal now?

"Yes, Ma'am. You're right. Mother was obviously furious with me, and I was very upset, because I felt that I'd let her down. I was in a terrible state at one point, because I thought I might have damaged our relationship irretrievably, but luckily the following day, Mother forgave me, as far as possible, and I'd already apologised for what I'd done, so we were able to make up – much to my relief!"

"Yes, well I always thought that would happen, too," replied the queen. "Your mother and I had discussed ways that we could make you a little stronger, when you're around other people, so that you can stand your ground more effectively, and not have it swept away by others. But you seem to have been able to argue your point effectively with someone, this morning – and a particularly prominent person, too! Perhaps when you do get passionate about something, it becomes easier for you."

"Well, Ma'am, I've met you before, and we're on a one-to-one basis, so I can be a bit more confident, just as I can with Tom, in our relationship, where I do intend to take the traditional woman's role. But it's true, that I don't find it easy amongst other females, sometimes."

"Yes, we know that," said the queen. "With varying degrees, Geratican females tend to be naturally assertive and confident, as well as passionate, but you do seem to be more towards the lower end of that scale. But that doesn't mean that you can't still have a traditional relationship with Tom. And as far as other women are concerned, with more *confidence* – something which you've already alluded to – it will get easier for you. I'm fairly naturally assertive myself, but anyhow, in my position, it simply would not do for the queen of Geratica to not be able to command authority. It's installed into nobles of my rank, from birth."

"Let me give you some advice on the subject, Alexandra. "You're a clever girl and you must have opinions. Coming from you, they must carry some weight. If you're very certain of something, then keep it in your mind, look the other person in the eye, and tell them firmly what you believe. If anyone else is there, then ignore them and just concentrate on the person that you want to give your opinion to. Of course, maintaining your opinion, during the course of an argument, is the hard part, but you've managed it today and it can only come with experience. Debating societies can be helpful, so I'm told, if you're interested in that type of thing."

"That's just it though, Ma'am," said Alexandra. "I don't like getting into arguments. I *hate* confrontation! With my mother it's always been fine. It works perfectly for us. She likes to take control of everything, and I'm happy to let her. Neither of us really want that to change. I know that, because my mother's told me how she feels about it.

"It's what worries me about the concert, that I *hope* I'll still be giving at Charterhouse, Ma'am. "I'm no good at being the boss of something. That's my mother's area."

"Well the main thing you've got to do there, is try and be assertive," said Queen Alexandra. "You don't have to be overbearing, but be clear and firm in your communication. And sometimes, rather than simply *asking* someone to do something, if necessary you may need to *tell* them to do it. Just out of interest, when your mother gives you an instruction, does she *ask*, or *tell* you to do it?"

Alexandra considered, though the answer wasn't long in coming.

"I suppose she does *tell* me, most of the time, Ma'am. And I'm expected to comply, which I do."

"That's what I expected," said the queen. "Your mother is one of the most assertive women that I've ever met, and the perfect person to help you to try and do that, with any people that come under your control."

"Yes Ma'am. She's already given me some help and advice, in getting things started. And she has also told me, herself, that I need to become stronger, so I think she'll be trying to give me advice on that subject, too."

"Yes. So do I," said the queen. "Well, I've given you *my* advice and we'll both try our best to help you, be assured of that, but ultimately, when it comes to it, the change will have to come from you – if you truly want it, that is."

"Thank you, Ma'am. I *will* take what you've told me on board," promised Alexandra.

"Are you looking forward to your mother's dinner party at the end of the week?" asked the queen.

"Yes, Ma'am, I am, although I always feel a little nervous beforehand. But I'm used to them now. We'll certainly enjoy having you as our honoured guest, once again, Ma'am. Elizabeth Spencer was due to come, but I believe she's no longer invited!"

"No, quite. I don't think that would be very appropriate under the current circumstances," remarked Queen Alexandra. "But that situation should enable you to keep building your confidence when with other women – and you'll certainly be in some very distinguished company, looking at the guest list! I shall look forward to coming, as always!"

"And I hope you'll enjoy meeting Tom, Ma'am, as you mentioned earlier. He's an officially invited guest, chiefly for that purpose."

The queen nodded and then began to conclude the meeting.

"Well, thank you for coming, Alexandra, that was very thoughtful of you. We shall meet again briefly, of course, at midday, but other than that, I shall see you next at the dinner party. I wish you the very best of luck, when you return to Charterhouse, next week, and in your quest to become college champion. I'm sure you'll still be in the running and probably now, the main candidate!"

"Thank you, Ma'am. I hope so!" replied Alexandra.

The queen pressed a button on her desk, then stood up and offered her hand again.

Alexandra got up, shook her hand and said, "Thank you very much for seeing me, Ma'am and for your help yesterday. It was most appreciated. My mother and I will look forward to welcoming you to The Grange on the evening of 5/34/10!"

The queen nodded. "Goodbye, Alexandra!" she said.

"Goodbye, Your Majesty!" replied Alexandra, and curtseyed perfectly once again.

Then, Rebecca appeared, and ushered her out of the study. She went back to the lobby reception, and as Linda had promised, someone escorted her back down the corridor, and let her into the court Administration Department once more. She thanked the woman, and then let herself into her mother's office, with Veronica's copy of her key. It was empty and Alexandra assumed that she was still in the meeting with her staff. She dropped the key onto her mother's desk, and flopped down on the chair opposite, feeling relieved that her most important duty of the day was done.

It was then that she noticed the *Geratica Times* newspaper – her mother's usual personal choice. The front page headline, referred to the story about Elizabeth Spencer, that her mother had told her about. She picked it up, and began to read the story.

***

Linda returned, just a few minutes later. Alexandra thought she looked a little cross. Her face brightened slightly, when she saw her daughter, however.

"Ah, you're back, darling!" she said, warmly. "And I see you've given me Veronica's key copy. Good girl. Well? How was it?"

"Fine, I think, Mother," replied Alexandra. "I thanked Her Majesty for the support that she gave me at the hearing, and she talked about the need for me to become a stronger person, as you did before. The subject of today's horse whippings, also came up and – well, the queen didn't seem to mind, but, er, I, um ..."

"You're floundering again, Alexandra!" said Linda. "What happened? Come on, spit it out!"

"Well, I hope I didn't blot my copybook too much, Mother, but we had an exchange of views!"

Linda's eyes widened slightly. "*You* had an exchange of views with Her Majesty?"

"Y-yes, Mother!" said Alexandra. "I told her that I wasn't comfortable about witnessing it, and found it barbaric, although I did say that I accepted that I had to, as part of my punishment."

"Oh!" exclaimed her mother, with a slight chuckle. "Well, I shouldn't think that there'll be any need to throw you into the Tower, for that! You're certainly developing a habit of causing surprises though, Alexandra. I don't think that either Queen Alexandra or myself, would have expected you to do *that* this morning. You were talking to the reigning monarch of Geratica, after all!"

"She seemed to think it was possible, that if I do feel passionate about something, it makes it easier for me to argue my point effectively Mother," replied Alexandra. "But, do you think that she might actually have been annoyed?" she asked tentatively.

"No, darling!" laughed Linda. "And that's a classic example of precisely why you need more confidence in your abilities! It does indeed just go to show, that you *can* sometimes hold your own in a discussion, and that's all a lot of people can reasonably hope for. I imagine that she was quite impressed with you, to be honest – and so am I. Well done!"

Her daughter felt another sense of relief.

"But as I did point out to Her Majesty, though," she said, "I do know her a bit, and we were talking one-to-one. I always feel more confident then."

"Well, I think you were probably both right, Alexandra," remarked Linda. "But however it came about, I'm very pleased with you this morning, darling. It sounds like you did well with the queen, and I've heard from Veronica, that you were a first class assistant to her, too, earlier!"

She kissed her daughter, and saw Alexandra's eyes light up with pride at her praise.

"How was your meeting, Mother?" asked Alexandra.

"I've had better returns to work, after a day off," replied Linda, simply.

Now, you've done your main duties for today, and all that remains is for you to witness the horse whippings at noon. You'll just have to deal with that, as best you can. Try and concentrate your mind on something completely different, if it's really going to bother you that much! In the meantime, sweetheart, I'll make us both another cup of coffee, and you can sit and relax, for a bit, whilst I get on with some work." She switched her machine on.

"Thank you, Mother," said Alexandra. "Will there be anything else that you'll want me to do?"

"No, that's fine, darling, you deserve a break. You've been through a lot, these past few days, and the worst is nearly over. Once you've finished your coffee, I'll take you over to see James, and you can stay with him until the horse whippings begin. I'll come and get you in good time, beforehand, and then Fiona will escort you to the designated area, just before noon. Once it's all over, I'll drive you back home, and there you'll stay, for the rest of the week. In theory, I could let you stay here all day, but that *might* mean allowing you to come and see me in Parliament House, which would constitute a treat. You aren't allowed any of those, until at least 5/35/10, as I'm sure I don't need to remind you!"

"No, Mother. Whatever you say, it shall be," answered Alexandra obediently.

"Yes, Alexandra, it will!" asserted Linda, looking deep into her daughter's eyes. Although she said no more, Alexandra could read her mother's strict warning not to disobey her, or she would be even more severely punished. She acknowledged her, again without speaking.

"Good," said Linda. "Right! Coffee time!" She poured some into their cups, and just as Rebecca had done in Alexandra's meeting with the queen, she dropped a biscuit into each of their saucers. Handing it to her daughter, who thanked her in her usual deferential way, she kissed her again, and then went back to her desk with her own.

"I've read that story about Mrs Spencer, by the way Mother," said Alexandra. "I still can't believe it! To disown your own daughter! I'm not sure which of those two that I despise most. *You* wouldn't do that to *me* would you?"

"For goodness sake, darling. Of course not!" her mother reassured her. "Mrs Spencer has obviously decided that she needs to try and save herself, and that the best way to do that, is to wash her hands of Gillian, and make sure that everybody knows it. A most bold step! I don't know if it will be enough, though."

Alexandra shuddered at the thought of a mother disowning her daughter. She remembered how desperate and alone she'd felt, when her mother had spoken so harshly to her, when she'd told her off, and sent her to her bedroom, after caning her. She never wanted to feel like that again, but now Gillian might feel like that for the rest of her life! She stood up, and reached across to her mother's hand.

Linda took her daughter's hand, and squeezed it inside hers, running her fingers softly over Alexandra's. She looked into her daughter's eyes, and

Alexandra felt her mother's reassurance, love, and protection. She *knew* that *her* mother would never abandon her.

***

At the same moment, the chair of Charterhouse board of governors, Sonia Eastman, was reading Linda's letter. After finishing, she mopped her brow, and thought for a moment. She'd assumed that she was fully briefed on the situation at Charterhouse, both through her contacts there, and following the news stories. But Mrs Radcliffe had raised more issues, with this letter. She certainly wasn't going to suppress it, to protect Mrs Spencer, and the newspapers were being less than complimentary about her, anyhow. This situation couldn't go on any longer.

She contacted the bursar at Charterhouse, and asked her to arrange an urgent meeting of the board of governors, as Linda had requested.

# CHAPTER 10

About fifteen minutes later, Linda delivered her daughter to James.

"Right!" she announced. I can't stop to chat, because I'm rather busy, but I'll be back to fetch you, before noon, Alexandra. See you then!"

"OK, Mother," replied Alexandra.

"See you later," said James.

"How did your meeting with Her Majesty go, then Alexandra?" he asked.

"Very well, I think. Mother seemed to be quite pleased with my report of it to her, and of my performance generally this morning - and that's always a good gauge to judge these things by!"

"Yes! She's a shrewd woman, your mother. You were very lucky to have her in your corner. I think we all thought it. Well, it's all over now, for you. You can relax a little bit more. You must be glad about that!"

"It's not *quite* over yet, James! I've still got to witness these confounded horse whippings, which I think are awful and of course I'm still suspended from Charterhouse, until the end of the week, as well as gated at The Grange, for the same period. Publicly, yes, it'll then be over for me, but even then, privately, I'll still be under punishment until the end of next week, with no weekly allowance or 'treats,'!"

"You don't like to witness what's happening at noon then?" asked James.

"No! Definitely not!" confirmed Alexandra. "It's a subject which my mother and I differ on, unusually.

"I'll let you into a little secret, Alexandra! I don't like them either and I never go to watch them, even though I'm working right here. I certainly don't wish to see these today, with my own daughter involved! I do occasionally hear some squeals though, even in Her Majesty's garage, on the other side of the building!"

"Oh! And does my mother know about this scandalous, 'progressive' view of yours?" asked Alexandra.

"We don't discuss it!" answered James, with a grin.

Alexandra smirked back at him. "So I have an ally, then?"

"Well, I'm certainly on your side, but then again, your mother's not a woman to be trifled with."

"Oh no. *Definitely* not!" replied Alexandra, "And that was very diplomatically put, James!"

"Why, thank you, Alexandra!" exclaimed James.

"Anyhow," he continued, "Whilst you wait for this tiresome episode to begin, would you like to have a sit in the passenger seat of Her Majesty's car, as your mother normally does?"

"Ooh!" said Alexandra, excitedly. "Yes, I would, please!"

"Right you are then, Miss Radcliffe," said James, and leading her to the door, he opened it and motioned for her to get in.

"Thank you, James!" she said, as she did so.

James shut the door, went around the car, and got in on the driver's side.

"So how does it feel, sitting there then?" he asked.

"I always like to see where my mother does her work, so it's great, thank you James," she replied. "I've sat at her desk, in her office a couple of times before, which was a thrill. I'm very proud of what she administers, and the service she does for Her Majesty and Geratica. She'll be taking me straight home, after the events here today are concluded, but I'm hoping that I may get to see her, actually working in parliament, one day. Mother's promised that if an opportunity comes up, when I can conveniently go, then she'll try and arrange it for me."

"Well then, I'm sure that it *will* happen, one day soon," said James.

"You're sitting in the passenger seat, Alexandra," he continued, trying to push the same subject into a new area of interest, "Do you ever think about learning to drive yourself?"

"To be honest, although I have, it's not really a big ambition for me. I know that some of the girls at Charterhouse are, and I've no doubt that Gillian Spencer plans to, but it's not something I feel confident enough about – at least not at the moment. I know that most Geratican women do drive, privately, and men who drive, usually do so in an occupational capacity, as you do, but I'm not always like 'most Geratican women'! I think that Tom probably will think about it, soon, so if he does and passes his test, then I suppose that might mean that, in the end I won't bother. I'm quite happy for him to do it, instead of me, if it means there's less chance of us causing an accident!

"You have to think hard about these things. I don't think that *everybody* is really capable of driving, and if you really think it's not for you, then that should be the end of it. Nervous drivers are sometimes the worst. They cause their fair share of accidents. It doesn't bother me if other Geratican women think I'm strange, because I don't want to drive, and would prefer my boyfriend, and maybe even husband, to do it instead!"

There was a pause, as James took in Alexandra's words. She was clearly, as he already well knew, a very deep thinker and had her mother's gift of logic, if not her supreme confidence - although no other person that he knew, could match Linda in that respect. He had a specific reason for asking that question, which he couldn't reveal to Alexandra, at this moment. He was under strict instructions to leave that to someone else.

Alexandra moved the conversation on to another area, still related to driving. "So, what exactly does your job involve, apart from the obvious?" she asked.

James smiled. "Well, apart from the chauffeuring, when the queen needs to go out on an official engagement, or something else, there is the planning ahead to consider the best and safest route, etc., which your mother and I so often joke about – I'm sure you noticed that last night. But there are always a few odd jobs to be done with the car, like cleaning and servicing it. Your mother casts her meticulous gaze over that, too, before we leave on an excursion! And if necessary, I can be called upon to help out with the odd manual job around the palace, if I'm free."

"It sounds like quite a nice job. Perhaps when your time here comes to an end, Tom could take over from you."

James laughed heartily. "You cheeky young woman! I'm not going anywhere soon, you know, and your boyfriend hasn't even started to learn to drive yet! I suppose you'll be taking over from your mother, at the same time?"

"Well, yes. That might be a good idea. Keeping it 'in the family' as they say," joked Alexandra. "No! To be serious for a moment, I don't think for one moment, that I'd be the right person to step into Mother's shoes. She's got a high profile job, as was evidenced by the amount of publicity that my misdemeanour caused, as her daughter. That's why she always drums into me – and now Tom and I – about the importance of *discretion*! We joke that it's her favourite word, but I fully realise what she means, particularly after what I've just experienced."

"You wouldn't fancy doing the very top job, then?" asked James. "You know. Being Her Majesty?"

Alexandra looked about quickly. "James!" she exclaimed, with a hint of jest in her eyes, "Of course I don't! It could be considered treason, if I said I did, whilst our current gracious queen is still on the throne. I'm not in line for the succession!"

James laughed at her. "Don't worry. I'm sure no one's listening to us here! I'm not asking if you ever want to take over as queen, just whether you think you *could* do it."

"Not in a thousand years James!" asserted Alexandra. "I'm definitely a backroom girl."

"Why not at least have a sit on the back seat and see how you feel?" suggested James. "Her Majesty sits in the middle, next to her lady-in-waiting, with a bodyguard on either side of her."

Alexandra giggled. "Would that be OK?" she asked.

"Of course!" said James. "I'll come round and let you out and open the back door for you."

He opened the door and got out. As he'd promised, he let Alexandra out and opened the back door on the same side, for her.

"Step inside, Ma'am!" he invited her.

"Thank you, James!" said Alexandra and did so. She shifted over to the centre of the seat.

James shut the door and returned to the driver's seat.

"Where would you like to go then, Ma'am?" he asked.

Alexandra chuckled. "The Grange, please James!"

"Hmm, well sorry, but unfortunately I can't *actually* take you anywhere! I'll be going out to fill the car up with petrol, a bit later, but if anyone found out that I'd had you in the back when I did so, I'd be in big trouble, as you're not a member of staff, and there are security issues. I might even get sacked by Her Majesty! You can't go back to The Grange yet, anyhow, as you've got to witness the 'unmentionables' before you go!"

"I'll tell you what you can do though," he said. "Would you like to give the inside of the car a good clean?"

"Yes, James, I'll do whatever I'm asked – or I'll be in big trouble with Mother, if she finds out!"

And so, James fetched the vacuum cleaner, and Alexandra took off her jacket and rolled up her sleeves. She vacuumed the whole car and put a duster around it. Then she helped James to wash the outside. A little while later, the car was spotless.

"Thank you Alexandra. A very good job!" said James, appreciatively.

"Don't mention it!" replied Alexandra, as she tidied herself up and put her jacket back on.

James let her into the car again, and she sat once more in the centre of the back seat.

"Well? How *does* it feel, sitting there, then Alexandra?" he asked.

"I can't believe that I'm actually sitting where the queen of Geratica does, when she goes on an official engagement!" exclaimed Alexandra.

James sat in the driver's seat and they continued talking for some time. It suddenly struck Alexandra that – apart from a brief mention of the imminent horsewhipping - they hadn't spoken at all about his daughter, and what it appeared his wife had done. But it was obviously a difficult subject for them, at the moment. She decided not to raise it. His mind must be in a bit of a turmoil at the moment. Yet, outwardly at least, he didn't seem to be any different to normal, and he was still carrying on with his duties.

They were interrupted by a knocking on the back door window. James had seen the person coming, but Alexandra jumped slightly and looked around. It was her mother.

James got out and opened the door for Alexandra.

"Uh-hum!" Linda exclaimed. "What's going on here?"

"James let me experience what it's like to sit in Queen Alexandra's place, Mother!"

"Did he indeed? I didn't know he was going to let you do that! I shall speak to him later," she said, with a twinkle in her eyes.

Then she laid her hand firmly on her daughter's shoulder and looked hard into *her* eyes. "Right! I imagine that you've had some fun with James and I don't mind that at all, but you must now settle down and get into a serious mood. Is that understood? It's time!"

Alexandra cleared her throat. "Yes, Mother. Very much so!" She smoothed herself down, and checked her hair, yet again.

"Good," said Linda. "Then follow me."

They said goodbye to James, and Linda escorted her daughter out.

# CHAPTER 11

Linda led Alexandra back into the palace.

"Right!" she asserted to her daughter. "Gillian and Melanie are here, and being prepared. Her Majesty is waiting, in position, outside, in the front courtyard. You'll all come out of the front entrance. As you're a witness for both horse whippings, you'll be first, escorted by Fiona because you're my daughter, and then I'll bring the other two girls out together, afterwards. She'll take you to the place of punishment, where the queen will be. Once you've greeted her in the correct, formal fashion, Fiona will take you to your seat and sit you down. Is that clear?"

"Crystal clear, Mother," said Alexandra.

"Good," said Linda. She put her hand on her daughter's shoulder again and gripped it firmly.

"Right. Walk on!"

Alexandra obeyed, with her mother a step behind.

"Now, don't forget," said Linda, as they walked down towards the entrance. This is designed to teach you a lesson. A sombre expression will be most appropriate. There'll be some microphones situated around the area, to project the ceremony around the palace and to the onlookers, so when you greet Her Majesty, *a lot* of people will hear you. Just be aware also, that there'll be a media presence again, too."

"Yes Mother," said her daughter, preparing herself.

As they reached the front lobby, Linda gave Alexandra's hand a quick, final and discreet squeeze, with her remaining free one. "Now look straight ahead, as you go out and Fiona will lead you!" she instructed her.

"Yes, Mother. You and Her Majesty are in charge," said Alexandra, obediently.

"Good girl," said her mother.

Fiona was waiting by the door, with, Alexandra thought, the faintest hint of a smirk on her face.

"Away you go then," said Linda and with a final glance at her daughter, turned away and went back the way she'd come.

Fiona then escorted Alexandra through the front entrance of the palace, her hand pushed against her shoulder. The atmosphere seemed eerily quiet.

As Alexandra looked ahead, she could see in the distance, people watching outside the palace gates, peering through the railings.

A stage had been prepared in the courtyard. At the far end there were three chairs. At the other end, nearest the palace and facing the gates, there were three others and sitting in the central one with the highest back, was Queen Alexandra, with a horsewhip on her lap.

Fiona escorted her over, her black dress flowing in the wind and Alexandra curtseyed. "Your Majesty!" she said formally and her voice was amplified around the palace grounds, something she'd never experienced before. The queen nodded in acknowledgement.

"Your Majesty!" said Fiona. "This is Miss Alexandra Radcliffe. Buckmore Juvenile Court have sentenced her to witness two horse whippings!"

"Very well, Fiona. Have her be seated!" said Queen Alexandra.

"Ma'am!" Fiona replied, nodding.

Guided by Fiona's firm hand on her shoulder once more, Alexandra was walked across to the other end of the stage and pushed into her seat, in the centre of the row. She was directly opposite the queen. Then Fiona crossed the stage again and sat in the chair to Queen Alexandra's left.

Next, Gillian and Melanie emerged from the front entrance of the palace, flanked by Linda, carrying another horsewhip. There were one or two jeers from the assembled onlookers. They were both naked and shivering in the cold wind and – especially in Melanie's case, Alexandra thought – fear. She also looked humiliated that everybody could see her fully exposed body.

Already Alexandra could feel her revulsion at this type of practice, rising inside of her, but she forced herself to look stoically ahead, and not show any emotion.

As they reached the stage, the two girls greeted the queen, as Alexandra had done, although both struggled slightly with her curtsies, never having met Her Majesty before. They were then forcibly pushed to their seats by Linda – Gillian to Alexandra's left and Melanie on the other. Finally, Linda went across the stage and sat in the one remaining chair, to the right of Queen Alexandra.

Linda had made it very clear to Gillian and Melanie, during their pre-briefing, that there was no point in them trying to run from the stage, as the palace guards who surrounded it, would immediately catch them and in any case, even if they should get out of the palace grounds – which would be nigh on impossible – they had no clothes ...

For a few seconds, they all sat in their seats, a whip resting in the lap of both the queen and Linda. The queen looked across at Alexandra, Linda at Gillian and Fiona at Melanie. Then the palace clock struck noon. As the bell chimed the hour, Linda rose and crossed the stage, to Melanie. She brought her back and stood her before Queen Alexandra, as the sound of the chimes stopped.

"Your Majesty!" said Linda. "This is Miss Melanie Patterson. She has been sentenced by Buckmore Juvenile Court, to ten lashings of the horsewhip!"

"Very well, Linda. Have her lie on the stage, and we will administer the punishment!"

"Ma'am!" replied Linda, as Melanie seemed to wince at the queen's words. Linda turned her around and forced her down onto her stomach, on the floor of the stage, so that Queen Alexandra and herself, were behind Melanie and the people watching, were in front. Then she went back to her chair, and sat down.

The queen stood up and walked over to her, her heels clicking on the stage. Melanie heard them gradually getting louder, the nearer she came, and her chills of dread became colder than ever. Finally, the footsteps stopped.

Queen Alexandra raised her arm, and dealt the first blow to Melanie's naked body, around her shoulders. Melanie flinched, and almost cried out. Then Queen Alexandra made the same motion and whipped her again, further down her back. Melanie flinched again. The queen repeated her action another three times, until she had worked her way all down the rear of Melanie's body, who by which time was gnawing at the stage, with her fingers.

Then Alexandra watched, as the queen walked away, back to her chair, and her mother arrived back at the centre of the stage. She pulled Melanie around, onto her back, and knelt beside her. Alexandra concentrated her mind on the thought of the next time that she'd meet Tom, and kissing him ... anything to try and take her mind away from what was happening.

Linda repeated what the queen had done, only this time it was on Melanie's front. Alexandra could tell from the way her body writhed under the whip, that this was particularly uncomfortable for Melanie and she gritted her teeth, and once again clawed at the stage. To try and distract herself, she glanced at Gillian, next to her. She didn't appear to be showing any emotion, and was looking straight ahead, as Alexandra herself had done.

Then at last, Melanie's ordeal was over, having had her ten lashings – five from the queen, and five from Linda.

Linda looked over to Queen Alexandra. "The punishment is complete, Ma'am!" she told her.

"Very good, Linda. Have her return to her seat!"

"Ma'am!" replied Linda. She pulled Melanie to her feet, and then escorted her back to her seat. Melanie sat down gratefully. Despite her abhorrence of this type of punishment, Alexandra was impressed by the way that Melanie had eventually borne it. Although she had clearly been in agony, she hadn't broken like many others before her. She wondered if Gillian would be the same. It wouldn't be long before she found out.

Her mother now crossed in front of her – though they avoided eye contact – and went to Gillian's seat. She led her to the queen.

"Your Majesty!" said Linda. "This is Miss Gillian Spencer. She has been sentenced by Buckmore Juvenile Court, to twenty lashings of the horsewhip!"

"Very well, Linda," said the queen. "Have her lie on the stage, and we will administer the punishment!"

"Ma'am!" replied Linda and as before, she forced Gillian to the floor of the stage. She allowed her to land roughly on her stomach, making Gillian grimace. Then Linda re-took her chair.

Queen Alexandra stepped forward again, and this time, Gillian heard the click of her heels on the floor, as she approached.

The queen stood over Gillian as she brought down the horsewhip for the first time, in the same place as she had begun with Melanie. However, with ten lashings to administer herself, she made slower progress down Gillian's body, than on the previous occasion. Gillian rocked on her fingers and toes, as she took the blows to her bare skin. She looked directly up to Alexandra – who was again trying to concentrate on something else, as the session continued – and scowled menacingly at her. This was how *she* intended to distract herself from the pain she was receiving. By focusing on the girl who she hated most and who – as she saw it – had wrecked her ambitions and brought her to this state. All that she wanted now, was revenge. After her mother had taken the course of action that had now been reported in the media, she didn't care about anything else, any more.

Alexandra noticed Gillian staring at her, and shifted slightly in her seat. She hoped that, despite the fact that Gillian was James's daughter, she wouldn't be seeing her again for quite some time. She well recognised the hatred on her face – and it scared her.

As she moved slightly, she glanced over Gillian and to her mother. She desperately tried to catch her eye. Linda was watching Gillian's ordeal intensely, but at last her eyes glanced away, and she noticed Alexandra. For a moment they stared into each other's eyes, and then Linda began to understand her daughter's message. She acknowledged Alexandra with a barely distinguishable raising of her eyebrows, as she felt a cold fury well up inside of her and she gripped her horsewhip tight.

Queen Alexandra finished her share of the horsewhipping, and returned to her seat as Linda came to take her place. After the initial shock of the first three lashings, Gillian had barely noticed the rest, so deep had her concentration been on Alexandra.

Now Linda knelt down and roughly pulled Gillian around, onto her back. She locked her eyes onto Gillian's and focused a murderous black gaze on her. Then she slowly began administering her share of the lashings.

As she continued, Linda maintained her gaze. Gillian tried to ignore it, but Alexandra's mother was too strong. After three lashings, Gillian shut her eyes, and tried to re-focus her thoughts.

Linda's mouth moved to Gillian's ear, as she kept slowly thrashing her.

*"So you still think that you can bully Alexandra, even now, do you Gillian?!"* she said in a low menacing voice. *"And you think that she'll be useless in bed? How **dare** you insult my daughter like that! I'm warning you. Stay away from her forever, or I'll give you a private horsewhipping! Your mother's disowned you, and I won't be surprised if your father does, too! You're alone, Gillian and you've lost everything! Face it! You've done wrong, and now you will pay for it!"*

Linda had now reached Gillian's legs. Despite her efforts, Gillian simply couldn't fight Linda off. Her voice penetrated her mind, and the shock of hearing it, had made her open her eyes again. Now she was caught once more, in Linda's gaze, and the words ran through her head. Her concentration was shattered, and this time she certainly *was* feeling the lashings.

Linda thrashed between her inner thighs and she screamed.

*"I warn you one more time!"* said Linda. *"Don't come near Alexandra, or you'll have **me** to face once again! Do you understand?!"*

She whipped Gillian's calves and she gave a groan.

*"Do you understand?!"* she repeated.

She whipped Gillian's ankles.

"**Answer me!**" she hissed, furiously into her ear.

Gillian looked straight up at Linda and raising her head slightly, spat in her face.

Linda had one more lashing left to give, and at this, she dealt a huge blow to her toes. Gillian yelped and her feet twitched as the spasm of pain went through them.

*"I'm not going to let you return to your seat, until I've received an answer, Gillian Spencer!"* said Linda.

Gillian smirked as she recovered and said finally, *"You're out of lashings now, Mrs Radcliffe. You can't hurt me anymore!"*

*"Don't bank on it!"* Linda retorted.

*"What? Mrs Radcliffe, breaking the rules? What is the queendom of Geratica coming to?"* replied Gillian, sarcastically.

Linda glared at her cheek and it took all of her powers of resistance, not to strike her again. But there obviously could be no excuse for such a loss of control, particularly in these public circumstances.

Gillian broke the stalemate between them. She had taunted Linda Radcliffe for long enough – and very much enjoyed it. *"Yes Mrs Radcliffe. I understand!"* she finally answered Linda's question.

After giving Gillian a final look, Linda stood up, and looked across to the queen.

"The punishment is complete, Ma'am!" she told her.

"Very good, Linda," said Queen Alexandra. "Have her return to her seat."

"Ma'am!" replied Linda. She pulled Gillian to her feet, pushed her back across the stage, and deposited her in the seat. Then she returned to her own chair.

There was a pause, as everyone sat in their places in silence, for a moment, before the queen brought the proceedings to an end.

"Girls! I hope that these punishments will be a lesson to you all, and that I am never called upon to see any of you again, under these circumstances." she declared. "That will be all. You are now dismissed!"

All three girls stood up and curtseyed. "Your Majesty!" they chorused, and Queen Alexandra acknowledged them with a nod.

Linda got up and paid her own respects to the queen, before crossing over to the three girls, and escorting them off the stage.

***

As they stepped back on to the palace courtyard, Linda immediately separated her daughter from the other two girls.

"Alexandra, stay here and wait for Fiona. She'll take you back to the office. Wait for me there." She slipped her office key into her daughter's hand.

"Yes Mother," replied Alexandra, obediently.

"You two come with me!" she ordered Gillian and Melanie, and she took them back into the palace, through the front entrance.

Fiona came up to Alexandra, with the queen. "We'll go in the usual way!" Fiona told her, and she and the queen led her around the side of the palace, to the rear entrance.

"Well, Alexandra. I hope that wasn't *too* traumatic for you," said the queen, once they were out of public view.

"No, Ma'am," replied Alexandra. She felt that she could hardly say anything else, just at the moment. "I *am* glad that it's over though. I've served my sentence and I'm sorry for what I did. Now I hope to move on, Ma'am."

"And move on, I'm quite sure you will, now, Alexandra," said the queen. "Back to Charterhouse College to work hard, become college champion, pass your exams, and gain a place at Castra. That's the path you're destined for, and none of these last few days will ultimately change that eventual outcome. You mark my words!"

They re-entered the palace.

"Thank you, Ma'am, for your confidence in me, and your support over this difficult period. It is most appreciated."

Queen Alexandra smiled and nodded in acknowledgement. "Well goodbye then, Alexandra. I shall look forward to coming to your mother's dinner party on 5/34/15!"

"And we shall look forward to inviting you, Ma'am. Goodbye Your Majesty!" replied Alexandra, curtseying.

The queen turned and went up the corridor to her rooms. Fiona let Alexandra back into the court administration department, in the opposite direction.

Alexandra was already pulling out her mother's office key. She didn't want to get tied up talking to Fiona, now. After the morning's activities, she just wanted some peace and quiet, for a moment.

"Thank you, Mrs Clark," she said, as she quickly put the key in the lock. "Do you know how long my mother will be?"

"Not long, probably," answered Fiona. "She's just got to take them to see the palace matron for a medical check-up after the whippings, as part of the official procedure, and then to get dressed in the public convenience! That's where they stripped and left their clothes in lockers. Then, once she's seen them off the premises, she'll be back."

"OK, thank you, Mrs Clark. Goodbye." said Alexandra and turned the key, as she did so. The green light shone on the console, and she pushed the door and darted inside. She saw the door click shut behind her, and puffed out her cheeks in relief, again. Putting her mother's key on her desk, she sat back down on the chair opposite. At last, her unexpected public duties were complete.

Later, there was a knock on the door and she heard her mother's voice. "Alexandra! Can you open the door, please? You've got my key!"

Alexandra quickly leapt from the chair and went to the door. Her mother smiled at her when she opened it, and came inside. As the door clicked shut, she enveloped her daughter in her biggest hug of the day so far, and smothered her lips with an equally big kiss. Alexandra murmured contentedly, and as her mother's eyes fixed on her, she sensed a soothing feeling through her mind and body.

Linda stroked her daughter's hair. "Alright, my darling?" she asked softly. "It's all over now, then."

"Yes, Mother, and I'm very glad about that," affirmed Alexandra.

Linda cradled her daughter's head to her shoulder, and brushed her fingers through the tips of her hair, giving Alexandra one of her favourite tingles.

"Well come with me and we'll have lunch in the palace restaurant, then," she said. "Then afterwards, I'll drive you back home!"

\*\*\*

In the restaurant, Alexandra asked her mother if anything had happened between Gillian and her, after the horse whipping.

"She'd already spat at you, before the end, and then you seemed to be talking to her for a few seconds, Mother," she said, enquiringly.

"Well, darling," said Linda, "I realised from what your eyes were telling me, that she was up to her old tricks. Even in that situation, she still seemed to feel that she could bully you, and I was furious. As well as giving her a harsh horsewhipping, I also warned her of a dire consequence, if she came near you again, as I did it, which I think unsettled her."

"She screamed!" exclaimed Alexandra.

"A lot of girls do, under the horsewhip, sweetheart," replied her mother. "Even the hardest ones! Believe me. I've seen it many times."

"Melanie didn't, Mother. That surprised *me*!" said Alexandra. "Of the two, I thought her the more likely. When Mrs Spencer caned us both, neither of us wanted to be a girl who everybody knew – from Gillian – had broken down in the headmistress's study, but she did, and I surprised m*yself* when I didn't – especially in view of the fact that I'd never had it on my bare bottom before."

"Sometimes people *do* surprise you," remarked Linda. "Melanie has fallen into bad company, but I suspect that she won't be in trouble again. She's been too easily led, but unlike Gillian, I don't think she bears grudges, which will help her to get over this, eventually. Now that Gillian Spencer's out of the way, this may well be her chance to turn herself around, and start to fulfil her potential."

"She isn't the brightest of girls though, Mother,"

"Everyone is capable of contributing something, Alexandra," said her mother. "If they put their mind to it and work hard, then there's no reason why they can't achieve it."

"Anyhow," she continued, "As far as Gillian's concerned, you're correct, there *was* a conversation between us – before she spat at me! I pressed her tell me that she understood, that if she came anywhere near you, she'd have *me* to deal with again. It took a long time, but after the horsewhipping was finished, and she'd imparted some cheek in my direction, she did finally answer in the affirmative! The questions are of course, whether she's going to take any notice, and whether she still has the nerve to defy me. Time will tell!"

"Thank you very much for defending me like that, Mother. You know I need it sometimes, and I don't care what anyone else thinks about it. But I think she'll be after revenge on me!" said Alexandra with trepidation. "Especially if she hears that I *have* been successful in becoming college champion. She'll be in that institution for a year, but when she comes out, I hope she doesn't seek me out, to try something else!"

"Yes, well let's not worry about that, right at this moment, darling. Hopefully you'll be at Castra, this time next year, and there's no way that Gillian will be going anywhere near there, now."

"Has any other girl spat at you before, whilst you've been performing that duty, Mother?"

"Oh yes. Once or twice. Remember that many of the children that go before the juvenile courts, and are found guilty of an offence deserving of a horsewhipping, are quite rough types, from the corresponding background. That's not to say that there haven't been some from Charterhouse, and other such public schools, of course. But most of those tend to be the younger members. It's unusual, I have to admit, for Charterhouse girls of your age, to be sent to the palace to be punished in that way. Normally by that time, they're mostly maturing into respectable Geratican ladies – such as yourself, sweetheart!"

"Thank you, Mother!" said Alexandra, her heart glowing with pride at Linda's observation of her.

Later, Linda dropped Alexandra off at The Grange.

"Have a rest this afternoon, darling. I'm certain that you need it," she told her daughter. "I'll ring later as usual, to make sure you're OK and tell you when to prepare supper for. Then tomorrow, you can start doing some things for me, whist I'm out, and also try to put your unscheduled time off from Charterhouse to good use, in your studying."

"I will, Mother" Alexandra promised.

They embraced and kissed goodbye, and then Linda drove back to work. Alexandra went to the end of Elmsbrook's drive, and pushed their bin up to The Grange, that she'd put out for her mother that morning, as usual. Then she went inside, got changed and relaxed.

One thing that she did eventually decide to do, however, was to jot down a few notes, regarding her feelings towards horsewhippings, and the case against them, as she saw it. Afterwards, she put the paper discreetly away, in a drawer, in her bedroom. She didn't know exactly when, or how, but maybe it would come in useful, one day.

\*\*\*

Tom called Alexandra that evening.

"How, was it?" he asked.

"Awful!" Alexandra told him. "You should have seen those poor girls, coming out of the palace, shivering. I wasn't surprised. It was freezing and they were naked! They'll probably both go down with a chill. It was a bizarre formal ceremony. They've obviously been following the same rituals for centuries! Of course, they were thrashed, which I tried hard to ignore, but it's not exactly easy to do, when you're right there!"

"I suppose that's why they put you there," said Tom. "You *were* sentenced to witness it, after all."

"Never again though, I swear!" said Alexandra firmly. "I wouldn't wish that upon anyone – and I mean anyone! Melanie coped with it better than I expected, but Gillian's was obviously of longer length. Whilst the queen gave her the first half of her lashings due, she was staring threateningly at me, for ages. I think she still wants revenge on me. Mother was furious! During her half, Gillian did start to scream and yelp, towards the end. Mother informed me afterwards, that she gave her a good talking to, whilst she thrashed her, and threatened her with dire consequences, if she dares to come near me again – and that seemed to unsettle her. Before the end, she spat at Mother!"

"Spat at her? Blimey! I bet your mother was even more livid with her then!"

"Yes! She gave her a huge thrash on the toes, to finish! For a few seconds after it finished, Mother was still talking to her, but Gillian was just the same. I don't think anything's changed at all, and I think she'll be even more bitter and vengeful, than before – which rather proves my point about horse whippings."

"Still, at least whilst she's at the Institution, then she's out of the way," said Tom.

"Hmm, for now," replied Alexandra.

"And she's publicly been disowned by her mother?"

"Yes! To try and save her own neck, probably. Mother says she's not sure that it'll be enough though."

"She's not home yet, I assume, since you answered the phone?" asked Tom.

"No, but she'll be here any minute, and I've got to get the supper on the table, so we'd better say goodbye now," said Alexandra.

They agreed that she would ring Tom tomorrow evening, and after declaring their love for each other, they hung up.

***

Lavinia Mountford QC heard the case for the other three girls that day. The juvenile court found that although they had clearly broken the law by seeing the escort boys underage when Gillan Spencer first organised their visits to Charterhouse College, the fact that they'd stopped doing so and had never been involved in the shoplifting meant that they were all fined 200g, but not sentenced to a horsewhipping.

Afterwards, one of the girls' mothers did reveal that she had already given her daughter the whip in private though.

# PART 6

# CHAPTER 1

Alexandra slept soundly that night and was finally awoken by her mother unlocking the door, and coming in. She drew back the curtains, as Alexandra slowly came to.

Linda came over to the bed and leant over to look at her daughter. "Good morning, darling," she said gently.

Alexandra's eyes were still a little heavy, but she focused on her mother and smiled. "Good morning Mother," she replied.

Linda kissed her daughter, and it was returned.

"I trust you slept well?" she asked.

"Hmm, like a log!" confirmed Alexandra.

"You look as if you could fall asleep again!" said her mother. "Well I'll give you two choices. You can either get up now, and have some breakfast with me, before I go, and you start your day here, or you can lie in for a bit longer. But if you do, you'll have to get your own breakfast, and you *must* be up by the time I leave. I'm not giving you the chance to lie in bed all morning, under these circumstances, and somewhere between the two choices, isn't an option. So which will it be?"

Alexandra roused herself. "It will be the first option Mother," she told her. "Because that means that I get to be with you for as long as possible, before you go!"

Now it was Linda's turn to smile – and it was a broad one.

"Oh, sweetheart! That's a *nice thing to say*!" she exclaimed in delight and sitting by the side of her daughter, she bent over her, and gave her lips an affectionate slobbering kiss.

"Mmm, thank you, Mother, that was lovely. Your kisses are the best!" said Alexandra appreciatively.

Linda got off the bed. "Yes I know they are, darling, and if you're a perfectly behaved and hard working girl during your period of punishment, then for your first treat, afterwards, there may be more, exactly like that, as you lie beneath me on the sofa!"

She saw her daughter's eyes light up in excitement.

"Right then! If that's your choice, then get moving, because breakfast won't be long."

"Of course, Mother," said Alexandra and drew back her bedclothes, as Linda disappeared out of the room, and downstairs.

Washed and dressed, she was soon in the breakfast room, laying the table. Her mother brought the breakfast in, of cereal and toast, and they ate.

"Right, Alexandra!" said her mother assertively. "As you know, we have a dinner to prepare for, on Day 5, and a most important guest in attendance. Therefore, as we are 'on show,' I want The Grange to be spotless by then. Because of unfortunate events, which we won't speak of, you are to be here for the rest of the week. So, Alexandra, being an intelligent girl, can you anticipate what order I'm about to give you?"

"Yes Mother. I think so. You want me to clean and tidy The Grange, whilst you're at work?"

"Correct! Pay particular attention to the parlour, dining room and kitchen. In the case of the latter, the last thing that I want is for a guest to be ill, and then blame our cooking facilities. It has been known to happen before, when Her Majesty has been a guest, if another has wanted to embarrass the hostess somewhat. See to it, that we don't suffer the same fate."

"Certainly, Mother!" Alexandra failed to suppress a giggle, as she answered.

"It's no laughing matter, Alexandra!" said Linda. "A stain like that on a woman's reputation as a hostess, can seriously damage her household's chances of holding any more social events, due to people not accepting invitations from her and even – if she's really unlucky – exclude her from the guest lists of others, as well."

"Sorry, Mother," said Alexandra. "I of course realise, that it's a bad thing to happen."

Linda laid her hand on her daughter's and smirked. Her eyes betrayed some of the mirth that she herself felt.

"It's alright, darling. I do acknowledge that this has a funny side to it. If the dinner party is a success, I might even tell you the name of the unfortunate woman concerned."

Alexandra looked at her. "Was it Elizabeth Spencer, Mother?" she asked.

"I'm not saying."

"Mother! Is the woman one of our guests this week?"

"I'm not going to give anything else away, until after the dinner party, sweetheart," Linda munched on her last piece of toast.

Alexandra tried to read her, but her mother was as good as her word. She was always more successful at keeping her thoughts secret, anyhow. Much to her occasional frustration, whilst her mother seemed to read her like a book, she was not quite able to return the compliment – at least not yet. She was becoming quite expert herself, but Linda was still the mistress of the art and Alexandra, still the pupil. It wasn't *just* for Tom's benefit, that she wanted to practice with him.

"Anyhow, all joking apart, this is obviously a big night for us, so make sure you do make a thorough job of everything," said Linda. "We've got some of the leading thinkers on the hottest topics of our time, on the guest list, so it should be a 'lively' evening."

"But not now, Elizabeth Spencer, Mother?" asked Alexandra.

"Oh no! *Definitely* not that woman." Linda assured her.

"And it will also be an opportunity for you to show yourself in your true colours, and hopefully gain a bit more confidence in yourself, when you realise what the people who really matter, think of you," she added.

"I hope so, Mother," said Alexandra.

"I'm *sure* it will be so, darling," remarked Linda.

"I'm glad that Tom will be there this time, Mother. That will definitely make me feel better."

"Yes, I'm sure that it will help, sweetheart," said Linda. "I haven't invited any other family members of the guests, as we'll be discussing some formal matters. But in his case, it will give Queen Alexandra the opportunity of finally getting to meet him."

Then she looked at the clock. "I must get myself ready to leave," she said, gulping down the last of her coffee. "We've been sitting talking, for a bit longer than usual, which I hope pleased you." She patted her daughter's arm. "It did for me! And you can make me even more pleased, if you wash up and clear away for me, this morning."

"Of course, Mother," replied Alexandra, obediently. "I'm here all day, after all."

"Yes, quite!" said Linda. "Right, I'll see you in a moment."

She left to go upstairs. Alexandra started the washing up, as her mother had told her.

A few minutes later, Linda was back with her coat, gloves and scarf on and her briefcase in her hand. She held her daughter tight.

"Now, be a good girl and do all that I've told you. And that includes your studying, and thinking about your concert. Let's be positive and say that you will still be the leading candidate for college champion, after you've returned to Charterhouse, next week. Maybe think about the running order. We'll talk it all through later."

"Yes, Mother. I'm always going to be a *very* good girl for you, from now on! I promise," Alexandra assured her. "And you won't forget the extra promise that you made to me earlier, will you?"

Linda smiled. "I'll be counting down the days, darling."

They kissed, with Alexandra deep within her mother's strong embrace and then, after they'd said goodbye, Linda went out to the garage to get her car. Alexandra went down the drive to their front gate, and opened it, ready for her mother to drive through, and go on her way to work. They waved goodbye to each other as she passed, and then as Linda went down the hamlet drive and out of the main security gate, she went back into The Grange.

\*\*\*

It felt strange to Alexandra, being at home on a school day, with her mother at work. She had very few periods of absence, and it was normally only during the term holidays, that she was at The Grange during the week. Being alone didn't bother her at all, though. She never found it difficult to amuse or stimulate her brain, either in her hobbies, or her studying – and sometimes the two combined. She would have plenty to do for the rest of the week, anyhow. She pulled up her sleeves and began by finishing the washing up.

Over the course of the day, she did most of the task her mother had set her, and also found time to read ahead in some of her textbooks, anticipating what they would be learning at Charterhouse this week, and making her own notes, as she'd planned to. She was always very efficient, and no one had ever accused her of being a 'shirker' when there was work to be done. She now had extra motivation, anyhow. Her mother's promise of more kisses, like the one she'd had earlier, once she'd served her punishment, kept running through her head.

Whilst she ate her lunch, she was following her mother's suggestion, and thinking about the pieces that she wanted to play in her concert, and how she wanted it structured, when the phone rang. It gave her a start, and her heart began to beat a little faster, as a fit of nervousness slipped through her body. She didn't recognise the number on the screen, so she wouldn't know who she'd be speaking to beforehand, and she *hated* that. Her mother wasn't there to help her, if she there was a problem, also. She considered ignoring it, but quickly discounted that notion. If it was important, and her mother found out that they'd missed it whist she was at home, there'd be trouble – and that was the last thing that *she* wanted, at the moment!

By now there had been several rings and if she didn't answer it soon, then she *would* miss it! She summoned up her courage, and picked up the receiver.

"Hello?" she asked nervously.

"Hello, Alexandra, it's Mrs Wood."

"Oh!" Alexandra was taken aback. "Oh, I'm really sorry if you were kept waiting before I answered, Mrs Wood! I'm here on my own and to be absolutely honest, I didn't recognise the number, so I was a little worried about who it might be. I don't like the phone very much!" She felt she could tell Mrs Wood that. She liked her.

"No problem at all, Alexandra," replied Annabel Wood. "I was just calling about a couple of things. Firstly, how are you? We obviously all know what happened last week and heard about the result of your hearing. You must be quite relieved that it's over now."

"Indeed I am, Mrs Wood. I feel a lot better now, than I did a few days ago, thank you! I can't begin to tell you how sorry I am though. I was foolish and there was no excuse for what I did. I deserved my punishment, but I've served it now – publicly at least."

"Well, just put it down to experience, and learn and move on from it," said Annabel. "When you say 'publicly' I assume that means that 'privately' you're still serving a punishment at home?"

"Yes Mrs Wood. For more than a week yet, in fact."

"It was reported in the news, that your mother told the court she'd severely punished you. Again, you'll learn from it! I can tell you that there is generally an understanding of the situation you were in last week, here at Charterhouse – amongst staff and pupils alike, in fact. As you probably know, Gillian Radcliffe has been expelled, which I think it's fair to say, many people are very relieved about."

"I do, Mrs Wood. And she's been 'disowned' by her mother. That was a turn up for the books. I bet no one expected that."

"No, indeed," replied Annabel.

"There is still one issue that troubles me though, Mrs Wood," said Alexandra. "Will I still be a candidate for college champion, when I return to Charterhouse next week?"

"Well, that's the second thing that I was going to talk to you about, Alexandra. As far as most of *us* are concerned, nothing has changed, and as far as I'm aware, the board who decide these things – which is independent of Charterhouse – haven't told us any differently. But to completely clarify the situation, we need to contact them, and really it's only Mrs Spencer who has the authority to do that. Again, as you're probably aware, her own position is now in serious jeopardy, and I can tell you honestly, that she was never very happy that I put you forward as a candidate, against her own daughter – but there was nothing she could do about it."

"I had suspected that, Mrs Wood," Alexandra told her.

"There's obviously just been this juvenile court case and therefore, even though she now claims to have disowned Gillian - despite having defended her as a witness in court, earlier that day - it's going to make things rather awkward in trying to get her to obtain the clarification that we seek. So, in the meantime, although I admit, it's not a very satisfactory position, unless you hear any different, just assume that you're still a candidate."

"OK, Mrs Wood," said Alexandra. She would talk to her mother about this, tonight.

"To that end, Alexandra," continued Annabel, "Let's talk about the concert. I'm pleased to tell you that all four of the people who you invited interest from, in assisting your staging of the event, have answered in the affirmative. I think that they're all quite certain of what role they think they can do.

"Obviously time is of the essence now, so what I believe the girls are thinking is, that maybe they could come and visit you one evening, perhaps even this one, if it isn't too inconvenient. The advantage of tonight, would be that, I believe you have a practice session with Philippa Barrington, anyhow, so you could all meet together. I'll drive them over, sometime after the main curriculum of the day is completed, and wait in the car, whilst they come in and visit you. Then I'll get them back in time for their dinner at Charterhouse."

"So, firstly Alexandra, how would you feel about a meeting, and secondly, would you be free tonight?"

Alexandra thought quickly. She was surprised by this offer, but she could see its merits, due to the time issue, and especially as Philippa was going to be here this evening too. She'd initially planned to talk to her mother tonight, but she would need some advice, so she'd have to move that forward and ring her at work, as soon as Mrs Wood hung up.

"I think it's a good idea, Mrs Wood," she replied. "I'll definitely be here, because I'm gated until the end of the week, and Philippa will be here, as you suggested. I don't think that there'll be a problem, but could I ring my mother to check?"

"Yes of course, Alexandra. I'll be in my chambers until the first afternoon period. It's 1 p.m. now, so you've got another forty-five minutes. When you ring you'll go through to the Charterhouse switchboard, so just ask for me, and they'll put you through. I'll give you the number."

Alexandra winced as she picked up her pen and opened her notebook. She hated doing that, too!

Annabel gave her the number, and she thanked her, and promised to ring her straight back, after she'd spoken to her mother, before 1.45 p.m. They said goodbye and Alexandra cut the line.

She reached for her mother's number, at the palace. This was one phone call that she did feel more comfortable in making. It would only be Veronica, or possibly Carol who she'd speak to, and then they'd put her straight through to her mother. She hoped that she wouldn't be in a meeting.

Alexandra dialled the number and waited.

Veronica answered, and Alexandra announced herself.

"Oh hello, Alexandra," said Veronica. "Nice to hear from you again, but I didn't expect it to be so soon! Is everything alright?"

"Yes fine, thank you Veronica," replied Alexandra. "It's nothing to worry about, but is my mother there please? If she's not too busy, then could I possibly speak to her? If she is, then don't bother her, but could you ask her to ring me when she's free? There is something that's come up that I'd like to speak to her about, although it's not vitally urgent, but if she could ring me in the next half an hour, that would be ideal, or else ..."

"Alexandra, relax!" chuckled Veronica. "If you'll just let me get a word in – she's only in the rest room, having her lunch. She's due back at 1.30. But I'm sure she'll speak to you if I go and fetch her."

"Oh! Good. Thank you very much, Veronica," said Alexandra. She realised that she must have been waffling, and felt slightly embarrassed.

"OK I'll go and get her. Just hold the line," replied Veronica and went off to the rest room.

Linda was in conversation with some of her staff, when Veronica put her head around the door. She looked around as the door opened, and seeing that it was her secretary, realised that she must be required in some way. She looked at her enquiringly.

"Sorry to disturb you when you're at lunch Mrs Radcliffe, but your daughter's on the phone," said Veronica. "I think she really wants to speak to you."

"Oh right," said Linda. "In that case, I'm sorry but I'd better leave you, ladies, and see what she wants."

As a couple of the women offered some pleasantries, Linda picked up her sandwiches, and went out with her secretary.

"Is she alright?" she asked, as they walked down the steps.

"I think so," said Veronica, "but she was babbling little bit on the phone, alternating between stating that there was nothing to worry about, but could she speak to you, to not wanting to bother you if you were busy, because it was nothing urgent, but then asking if you could ring her within the next half an hour!"

"Oh for Geratica's sake, don't tell me the wretched girl's got herself into another pickle! Honestly, I leave her alone for a day ..."

Linda opened her office door. "... Thank you Veronica," she said, acknowledging her with her hand.

Veronica went back to her desk, smiling to herself. She was sure Alexandra wasn't in any kind of trouble, this time.

Linda sat down at her desk. The phone rang, as her secretary put the call through. "Thank you," she said.

"Hello, darling, are you OK?" she asked her daughter. "Veronica said you were 'babbling' a bit on the phone. When you flounder like that, it often means that you think you may have done something wrong, or made a mistake. What's happened, Alexandra?"

"It's alright Mother, nothing bad's happened. I swear to you! I'm sorry I babbled. It was just my nerves on the phone. And I don't normally like to bother you with something that might seem trivial, when I know that you're always very busy."

"Alexandra for you to pick up a phone to speak to me at work, and then to tell my secretary that you'd like me to ring back within half an hour, I'm sure that this isn't entirely trivial. I'm at lunch and not due back for a bit, so

I'm here for you to talk to now. Relax, take a deep breath, and say what you need to tell, or ask me."

Alexandra took her deep breath, and then began. "Well you know Mrs Wood, Mother?"

"Yes darling. I've met her, as *you* well know! Unless there are two of them?"

"No Mother, only one! And she's just rung. She wanted to talk to me about the concert."

"Oh," said Linda. She reached over and pressed the button to show the red light on the console outside, indicating that she was busy, and wasn't going to open the door.

"Well we're not going to be disturbed now, sweetheart, so take your time and tell me about it. I'll be finishing my sandwiches." She stretched out her arm to the photograph of her daughter on her desk, and gently ran her fingers over her face, and long blonde hair. The memory of what she'd promised her daughter that morning, registered in her mind, and she felt a wave of passion beginning to stir.

"Alright, Mother," said Alexandra and outlined almost word for word, what Annabel had told her on the phone, a few minutes before.

"Mother," she added, when she'd finished recounting the information, "I thought I should phone you to ask your advice about the meeting they're proposing. I think it's a good idea, particularly as Philippa will be there too. But I wanted to check with you first. I also need to be sure of what I ought to say, and to ask them to do. You know all about that."

"Right!" asserted Linda. As she'd listened to her daughter's typically detailed and concise account, her mind had been working furiously. Now her own talent as a tactician came to the fold, as she decided on a plan of action.

"I'm sorry, about earlier, darling," she continued, "but I was worried, when I heard that you'd been 'babbling' on the phone. I thought something had gone wrong. You did the right thing in phoning me. I'm in complete agreement with you about the value of this meeting, and I most certainly want to help. So this is what we'll do ..."

\*\*\*

Meanwhile, sat at her desk, in the headmistress's office at Charterhouse,

Elizabeth Spencer spilt her coffee. The reason for it, was not caused directly her own carelessness, or even by someone else's, but by a phone call. It was from Paula Scott, am ally of hers, on the board of governors, and it 'tipped her the wink,' that Linda Radcliffe had called for an emergency meeting of the board members, to recommend that she be removed from her post, and that the chair had called one.

Elizabeth wasn't *entirely* surprised, but it was still a huge shock, which had caused her to lose control of her hand for a split second. She had hoped in vain, that her actions against her daughter, the day before last, might be enough to save her – at least for now – but this was a serious development, and typical of the actions of the mistress tactician, Linda Radcliffe.

"Do you know when it's going to be held?" she asked.

"Well it's an emergency meeting, so it won't be long," replied Paula. Sonia Eastman's secretary has got to sort out everyone's availability first, but perhaps it'll be by the end of the week."

Elizabeth swore, before thanking Paula for the tip-off, and hanging up. Then she called her own secretary in, to help her clean up the mess on her desk.

# CHAPTER 2

Linda arrived back home, earlier than she'd planned. She had also managed to postpone the time of the weekly supermarket delivery, by half an hour. Once Queen Alexandra's question time in parliament was over, she had left as soon as she could, and then quickly sorted her desk, back at the palace. Luckily she had nothing more that she needed to do urgently that day, and no more meetings either. She had got in her car at 4.00, in order to arrive at The Grange, at around 4.30. Alexandra's recruits were due at 5.00 p.m. – the same time that Philippa would arrive.

Alexandra went gratefully to her mother's arms, and they kissed.

"Are you OK, my darling?" asked Linda soothingly.

"I feel better, knowing that you'll be in the room with me," answered her daughter.

"We'll act as a partnership, as always," said Linda.

They spent the next half an hour, preparing themselves, and Linda cast an eye over what Alexandra had done, during her day at The Grange. She was impressed.

She was also pleased to see evidence of her daughter's studying, and her completed – provisional – running order for the concert.

"Hmm. Well done, darling. You certainly *have* been a good girl today," she remarked. "I haven't forgotten what I promised you this morning. You've made the chances of it happening, highly likely, and if you keep this up over the next week, then it'll be a certainty! Let's get this meeting and practice session over, and then we'll have dinner. After we've got cleared away, I'll give you a kiss and cuddle tonight, anyhow!"

Alexandra felt a slither of excitement run through her veins, heightening her senses, and this also helped to ease some of the trepidation that she was feeling. Her mother could often push the right buttons, to inspire her to achieve her goals, and she was starting to believe that this would happen tonight.

The phone rang, punctually at 5.00 p.m. In the parlour with her mother, Alexandra picked up the receiver and looked at the monitor, as it came to life. It was the party from Charterhouse, who were the first to arrive.

"Hello," she said, pressing the button that opened the gate. "Come on up the hamlet drive, to our house. The Grange is the first house you'll see. You can't miss it – there are only two in Elmsbrook! There's a nameplate on the house wall, too."

"Thanks," said Benita Davis, one of the girls present. It was she who hadn't realised that the queen didn't write her own speeches, and had received a scornful remark from Gillian, for her ignorance. Despite this evident naivety in her knowledge of the workings of court affairs, Alexandra knew that she was otherwise, a very intelligent person, and had always liked her the most, in her form class at Charterhouse. They actually had in common that both of their fathers had died when they were very young – though in Benita's case, she'd been just a baby and therefore had no memory of him at all. He'd had a heart attack.

"Right!" said Linda, as Alexandra replaced the receiver. "Part one of the operation begins. Now, as I suggested, first of all, we'll bring them in here, and then you offer them some refreshment. I presume they'll accept, and then you go and attend to their requests. I'll keep them talking in here, and it'll give me a brief chance to get a first impression of each of them. Philippa shouldn't be long, and we'll have to quickly fill her in on the change to the normal routine. Once they're all ready, take them into the study and I'll come too, and then we'll get started. Understood?"

"Yes, Mother," replied her daughter.

"Good luck and remember, I'll be there to guide you, and tell you yes, or no, whenever you need clarification." Linda patted her daughter's arm.

"Thank you, Mother," said Alexandra, just as the doorbell rang.

"Right, here we go then!" said Linda, as her daughter went to open it. At the same time the phone rang again.

"That'll be Philippa!" she called down the passage to her daughter. "I'll let her through the gate."

She quickly picked up the receiver. "Good evening, Philippa," she said. "I'm home a bit earlier today. Alexandra will still have her practice session, but we have something else happening as well, which we'd like you to be involved in. Some girls ..."

Linda explained the situation to Philippa, as she opened the gate for her.

Meanwhile, Alexandra opened the front porch door.

"Good evening!" she said, smiling invitingly. Her mother had taught her the correct Geratican etiquette for receiving visitors. "Please come on in," She motioned with her hand.

"Thank you!" the girls chorused as they entered.

"I'll take your coats from you," said Alexandra. "My mother and I are in the parlour at present. She'll be here in a second, and we'll take you through. Philippa Barrington arrived at the gate, just after you."

"Thank you," said the girls again. By the time Alexandra had all of the coats in her hands, Linda had appeared.

"Good evening girls!" she said warmly and held out her hand.

All four politely replied in kind and shook hands with Linda.

"I see that Alexandra's taken your coats. Whilst she puts them in the cloakroom, would you all like to come into the parlour with me?"

"Yes please Mrs Radcliffe," was the response.

"Good. Follow me then, if you please," Linda led the way, down the passage.

Alexandra put the coats away in the cloakroom, as her mother had said and then the doorbell rang again.

"I'll get that, Mother!" she called and went to the front door.

"Good evening Alexandra," said Philippa, as she came in. "I hear you've got other guests this evening?"

"Good evening Philippa," replied Alexandra. "Yes. Rather short notice, I'm afraid. Has my mother told you why the girls are here?"

"She has. A good idea, I think."

"Great! Well I'll just take your coat, and then I'll take you to meet them all. They're in the parlour, talking with my mother, at the moment."

"Thank you, Alexandra," said Philippa.

Once she'd put Philippa's coat away, Alexandra ushered her into the parlour.

The girls were introduced to 'Mrs Barrington'. "But please call me Philippa!" she told them.

As planned, Alexandra offered refreshments, and after taking the order, went off the kitchen to prepare them.

Linda was settling into her task. The girls were Benita Davis, who seemed to be the most talkative one of the group, Imelda Thomas, Rachel Cuthburn and Emma Thatcher.

Emma was the odd one out, being not a member of Alexandra's form. She was the girl who Alexandra was most friendly with in her music classes.

She seemed pleasant enough, the quietest one of the group, and clearly one who enjoyed her food as much as the Radcliffes, except that she obviously wasn't so blessed with their natural ability not to put on weight. Indeed, it turned out that her main hobby was cooking, which stimulated Linda's interest. She had sold her own homemade cakes, and was also a keen musician, playing the piano, guitar and clarinet. She was a member of the Charterhouse Symphony Orchestra.

Imelda and Rachel seemed to be close friends. They tended to let Benita talk, but when Linda did press them to speak, they appeared well spoken and articulate. She soon discovered that they were both Geratican Language scholars, who were also in the same class as her daughter, in that subject. This greatly interested her, given her own academic qualifications. They also, both seemed to anticipate what the other was going to say, and had a habit of looking at each other before doing so, as if seeking approval. They might almost be as close as she and Alexandra were. She felt a fondness for them.

Benita was in several of Alexandra's classes, most significantly her mathematics class, which it transpired, was her favourite subject. This impressed Linda. With the exception of her daughter, she rarely met women and girls who liked it. In fact, quite a lot hated it. She seemed to be the most confident and outgoing of the four, and also to have quite a caring nature. Linda could understand why Alexandra might like her.

By this time, Alexandra had been back from the kitchen for a while, and had been listening to the conversation. Before they'd arrived, she had briefly told her mother what she knew of all the girls, but all the same, she was amazed at how quickly and easily her mother obtained facts, and was probably already assessing their characters and capabilities. They had only been there for a little over ten minutes.

Linda also studied their manners and general ability to eat and drink in a lady-like manner, which she very much expected from girls who went to Charterhouse. If they were going to work on a classical music production, for her daughter, then she wanted them to have a certain class, and to appreciate the importance of the occasion. She knew that some might accuse her of being a snob, and old fashioned. She strongly rejected the first allegation, but she did plead guilty to the second. She was very much a believer in the old, traditional order of Geratica.

She looked at the clock.

"Right!" she said. "Well, I mustn't keep you chin-wagging any longer, because I know you've got a meeting to hold." She signalled discreetly to Alexandra with her eyes, to prompt her and confirm that she felt all girls were of sufficient quality. They were now about to embark upon stage two of their plan.

Alexandra cleared her throat and pushed up her sleeves. "Yes Mother. I've arranged for us all to be seated around my desk in the study, if that's OK with you?"

"Oh. Yes of course, darling," replied Linda. "I suppose that should be OK. I shall be in there as well, at my own desk, as I've got something rather urgent to do for work tomorrow, which can't wait, but you carry on and I'll be minding my own business."

"Very good then, Mother," said Alexandra.

She looked at the others. "Well, if you'd like to follow me to the study then? The sooner we get our roles and strategies sorted out, the sooner you can all go back to Charterhouse. I know you mustn't be late for your supper, or you might miss it! Bring your drinks with you, if you need to."

"OK, boss. Lead on!" said Benita.

Alexandra raised her eyebrows slightly, and led them out, with Philippa in tow. She'd listened quietly to Linda's conversation, without interjecting very much, as she felt it was really for the girls' benefit, but as they trooped down the passageways to the study, she couldn't help but smile to herself. She didn't think that any of the girls suspected, but *she* was sure that there was something of a set-up going on.

Beginning to get to know these two Radcliffe women as she had, over the last couple of weeks, and the way that their relationship worked, she thought it highly unlikely that Alexandra would have arranged to hold the meeting in the study, without her mother apparently knowing, and having urgent work to do there herself. She had almost laughed out loud in the parlour, when Linda had said that they could carry on, and she'd be minding her own business! *That* was the most unlikely story that she'd heard of, in a long time!

They sat down in the study. Alexandra had indeed found chairs for all five of her guests to sit on, around her desk. Linda followed almost immediately, and sat down at hers.

Alexandra positioned herself, so that she could both address her meeting, *and* clearly see her mother, without having to make any discernible movement, in either direction. The chairs were situated in such a way, that, as the assembled group focused on her, they would not be paying much attention to Linda. This was the essential ingredient in their plan. They could then communicate discreetly to each other, as the meeting progressed, and her mother could make sure that she got things right, without having appeared to have done anything directly, to help her, which she was officially not allowed to do. Linda's communication to her daughter would be of the most subtle kind, and virtually undetectable to anyone but them, but they weren't going to take any chances.

Linda pretended to get on with some work, and Alexandra began the meeting. She had a pen and notepad on her desk, the latter of which contained the main items that she needed to discuss. This was in accordance with her mother's advice.

"Right, well as you all know, I've been asked by Mrs Wood, to organise a concert at Charterhouse, around the end of term, in honour of Mrs Philippa Barrington, one of Geratica's finest composers – if not *the* finest! And due to your timely visit to me today, she happens to be present with us now!"

Philippa smiled and nodded in acknowledgement and at her desk, her mother indicated her approval at her opening. She couldn't have worded it better herself!

Alexandra's confidence grew somewhat. "Well on the last day that I was at Charterhouse, I sent you all letters, asking you if you were interested in helping me to stage it, and detailing the roles you might play, and I gather from Mrs Wood, that you've all answered in the affirmative. Thank you very much for that.

"So firstly we need to establish a board, and decide who should do what. I know I talked of the possibility of three jobs, but there are four of you. I don't really want to not accept any of you, so perhaps we can distribute the work between the four of you." Alexandra had agreed this with Linda, beforehand.

"Let's begin with marketing. We're starting out with nothing, and we'll obviously need to generate money to stage the production, so someone should take responsibility for establishing a fund raising activity. Then they'll need to be able to promote the concert itself. We haven't got many weeks in which to organise it, therefore getting money quickly, has to be our first priority. Are there any volunteers?"

Benita spoke up. "We've already had a think about this Alexandra," she said. "Imelda and Rachel are a rock solid partnership and they've decided to do this, if you're in agreement?"

It had been this pair who'd sniggered when Gillian had cast aspersions on her sexual capability, but Alexandra didn't bear a grudge.

Benita went on. "None of us can honestly say that we've any actual experience of promoting something yet, but they're good organisers and very articulate, so they'd be able to communicate our message about the production. I also know that they've come up with an idea for generating some cash."

Imelda looked at Rachel and then said, "We were thinking of some kind of sponsored walk, which the whole college could participate in, Alexandra. Events like that can generate a reasonable amount, if enough people participate in them. And there are a few girls at Charterhouse, who have connections with some quite wealthy people!"

Rachel looked in a similar fashion at Imelda. "We can produce some posters to promote it and put them up wherever we can at Charterhouse. And we've actually already produced a sample, if you'd like to see it!"

"Oh. Yes, please," said Alexandra. She thought that this might be a good idea. She cast an eye at her mother, who was tapping at her word processor. Linda eyed back at her.

Rachel took a folder out of her school bag and from it, a piece of paper, which she handed to Alexandra.

As she now knew that her mother agreed with her, and thought that it was the best idea that they were likely to come up with, she decided that this was probably what she'd go with. So, she could now give the poster sample, appropriate scrutiny. If her mother had told her that they should think of something else, then there wouldn't have been much point in studying it very much.

Alexandra shifted slightly in her chair and raised the poster, as she looked at it, turning it about in such a way that Linda could get good view of it, too. It seemed quite eye-catching. She knew that Rachel had some skill in an artistic direction, too. She tried to think of other posters that she'd seen and to compare this with them. It seemed OK to her. Again, she secretly sought her mother's opinion, whilst still appearing to give full attention to the sample.

Linda indicated her approval but then gave another piece of advice, which it took Alexandra a few seconds to discern.

"I think this is a good idea and it's an eye-catching poster. I'd like to go with organising a walk, if you're all agreed? As I said, we haven't much time to get things started."

"Yes. We've all discussed this, Alexandra," confirmed Benita. "I don't think you'll find any objections."

"OK that's decided then," said Alexandra. "Have you also discussed *where* we'll hold the event?" This had been the question that her mother had been telling her to ask.

"Well, we haven't reached any definite conclusions, I must admit," Benita spoke for the group. "But somewhere in the Buckmore area would seem obvious, and it's not the biggest place in the world."

"Don't forget that the youngest girls might not be able to walk quite so far as the oldest ones," said Emma, making her first contribution to the meeting. "That's if we're going to involve the whole college, of course."

"Well. I think we really *will* need to do that," remarked Alexandra. "We're going to need as many participants as possible, to gain the amount of money required, and we'll have to discuss that subject too, in due course. But you're right Emma. We can't make it too much of a hike, or some people might not feel able to take part. So we'd better agree on a maximum distance. Does anybody have a suggestion on that? Would three miles, be reasonable?"

Alexandra addressed the question to the group, but at the same time her eye was seeking her mother's advice again. Linda thought briefly and then gave her daughter an affirmative message, as their eyes came together.

"I think that's a fair distance" said Benita. "It obviously can't be *too* far, but equally it's got to be of a reasonable length, in order to excite people's interest, and make them want to rise to the challenge! So if no one else objects, let's call it a 3 mile walk. We can establish the exact route, at a later time."

She looked at Alexandra, touched her arm and said quickly, "Sorry, you're the boss. You make the decision!"

"Apology *not* necessary, thank you, Benita!" exclaimed Alexandra, with some feeling which Linda immediately picked up on and made her smile inside. "But I would like to get this finalised, so if it's OK with the other three of you, then that's what we'll agree on."

Emma, Imelda and Rachel all said that they were happy.

Linda felt her daughter was doing well, despite the fact that she was helping her a little. But one of the qualities that Linda had been looking for most in the group, was an ability to lead. As she'd advised Alexandra before, she needed to be able to spend as much time as possible, working towards the concert itself, so it was essential that she had people who she could delegate responsibilities to. Benita was certainly someone like that and in fact, she felt that Alexandra could probably trust her to take charge of the whole operation – a sort of 'right hand woman' – which could prove extremely beneficial, not to say fortuitous, at the present moment, given the time limits. Alexandra needed someone like that on the board anyway, as leading a group of women – as these girls soon would be – was generally outside of her 'comfort zone' and not something that came naturally to her, or even something that she wanted to do.

"Well now that we've established that, let's talk about your roles," said Alexandra. "You said that you'd agreed on the marketing job, and it'll be

Imelda and Rachel, so that's settled. What about the book keeper? I'd probably go for that role myself, but I'll be busy organising the concert – in between schoolwork! – so I wouldn't have time to do any of these roles full time. That's why I have to delegate them."

"I think you know that's going to be me, Alexandra," said Benita, smiling. "You and I are the numbers girls here, and it's also going to be my specialised subject for a degree and career, I hope. Unlike yourself, whose specialised subject seems to be every one that's known in Geratica! I sometimes wonder if there's a subject that you're *not* an expert on!"

All the girls laughed at that and Alexandra coloured slightly. "Well, I don't know about that!" she exclaimed. "I wouldn't say I'm an 'expert' on anything, particularly, but I suppose my general knowledge is reasonable."

"Reasonable? You're the brainiest girl in Charterhouse, Alexandra!" cried Emma.

At her desk, Linda was still trying to seem in a world of her own, though it was difficult at times, so great was her interest and her desire to help her daughter. But she was managing it. She was finding this little exchange quite illuminating though. And yet again, once this was finished, she was going to have to pull Alexandra up, for underselling herself!

"Well anyhow. We're not talking about *me* here!" retorted Alexandra. "We're talking about what skills *you girls* can bring to the operation."

Linda had to put her hand to her mouth, to stop herself from laughing out loud. *That's better Alexandra!* she thought. She'd remember that remark for a while. It was good to know that her daughter had inherited the Radcliffe talent for the sharp incisive comment.

"Thank you for volunteering then, Benita," continued Alexandra. "I know that you won't let me down."

"No, of course not, Alexandra," replied Benita.

"So that just leaves you Emma," said Alexandra. "And there would appear to be only one vacancy left! Retail and distribution. I hope you don't mind that, and feel that you've drawn the short straw?"

"No! Not at all!" laughed Emma. "I don't really mind what I do. I've sold my own cakes from a market stall before, and that's about the scale of my retail experience, but I'll give it a go. And I'm probably the one of our foursome, who's the most musical, so that's got to mean I can help with this project somehow!"

"That's great, thank you, Emma," said Alexandra, smiling at her 'musical' friend. I probably will need your help at the performance itself, and as for retail and distribution – well at least we'll have some catering sorted out for the girls, during the interval."

"I've got nothing else written down to discuss for now, but I would just like to circulate to you all, a copy of my *provisional* running order for the concert – including you Philippa! I'd be honoured if you told me what you think." She passed them around the group.

Philippa cast her gaze across the single sheet of paper. "Well, you've certainly included all of my most significant pieces," she confirmed, a couple of moments later. "Having got to know you over the last couple of weeks, I've some idea of your tastes, and this list is more or less what I'd have expected. We don't need to confirm anything definite today, but provisionally, I agree that this would be a very good selection, for the discerning listener! Well done, Alexandra!"

Alexandra smiled broadly, feeling a warm flush of pleasure at this compliment from her musical heroine. "Thank you, Philippa!" she said.

"What's your opinion of it, Emma?" she asked.

Emma almost said, "Well, you'd hardly expect me to tell you any different, after that, would you Alexandra?" but instead she said simply, "I agree with Philippa."

"In fact there are a couple of pieces on the list, which I've always wanted to play, but never had the chance to," she added. "That alone will give me all the motivation I need, to make sure that this concert gets staged."

"Has anybody considered giving the concert a specific title?" asked Philippa.

There was a short pause. "How about 'A Tribute to Philippa Barrington'?" suggested Alexandra. "I can't think of anything more appropriate, and succinct, than that."

"Hmm, well I can't argue with that!" remarked Philippa, grinning broadly. "Would that be OK with the rest of you?" She looked around at the group of girls.

"Yes, certainly!" they all assented.

"Great!" enthused Alexandra. "Now, does anybody have anything else that they want to say this evening?"

There was another even shorter silence, before Benita said, "Only to assure you Alexandra, that we'll all work to get this show on for you, and we won't let you down. Don't worry about that. We genuinely miss you at Charterhouse, and you won't be back there until next week, but we can get cracking on things, right away, and don't forget that we can work on it during our extracurricular time, before dinner every day. We'll get the girls bums on the seats, even if I have to personally cane them, in the headmistress's study!"

They all laughed again. *The girl has a sense of humour, too!* thought Linda. She thought that they were collectively a good bunch and her daughter had chosen wisely, but she was particularly impressed with Benita. She would certainly be the boss, and Alexandra could leave much of the behind-the-scenes organisation to her. That was fairly obvious. Providing of course, that she could match her words with deeds. She'd seen a few women fall down in that respect, over the years, but something told her that this wouldn't be one of those occasions. Benita appeared to feel a natural bond with her daughter, which Linda naturally, of course found endearing.

Benita did indeed like Alexandra, and thought she was one of the nicest girls she'd ever met. She was probably the one who knew her the best at Charterhouse, never having been put off by her extremely shy nature. Benita herself was indeed much more outgoing and confident, but she greatly respected Alexandra's intelligence and intellect. On more than one occasion she'd been sitting at her desk in the Prep room in her house at Charterhouse in the evening, and wished that Alexandra was a boarder, so that she could help her in some of her weaker subjects. By the same token, once breakfast was over, every weekday morning, she was often the first to head off to their form class to catch Alexandra before the official day began, and pick her brains, over something.

She had always loathed Gillian Spencer, and been particularly disgusted at the way she'd treated Alexandra, which was partly because of her timid nature, but mainly due to the fact that she'd been the one person who could stop her coming top of the class in a range of subjects, and quite often did. Despite Gillian's obvious academic gifts, her major weaknesses, which had now considerably contributed to her downfall, were, firstly, her inability to control her temper and jealousy, when she was beaten – in a nutshell, she'd been the worst loser in Charterhouse, resulting in her becoming bitter, resentful and vengeful – and secondly, her bullying ways and tendency to take advantage of things, to satisfy her greed. Benita didn't think that she was an evil-minded person, as such, but she'd certainly taken advantage of pupils and staff alike, during her time at the college, and that was partly because she'd been allowed to do things that other girls couldn't, by her mother, the headmistress, for political purposes. With the probable exception of Alexandra, Benita suspected that no one was more glad to see the back of Gillian Spencer, than herself. She was certain that their own classes and Charterhouse as a whole would be a better and nicer place without her.

Alexandra put down her pen and looked around. "Well thank you, everybody. I'm really grateful to all of you for supporting me, and making the effort to come and see me today. I think we can leave it there then, and I'll see you all next week."

She cleared her throat again. "Mother!" she called over to the desk opposite hers. "We've now finished our meeting, and the girls will be heading off back to Charterhouse now."

"Hmm?" asked Linda innocently. "Oh right! Goodness me, I've been so engrossed in what I'm doing, that I'd almost forgotten you were there! I trust you've had a productive discussion?"

"Yes, Mother," I think we're clear on what we're doing now," answered her daughter.

Philippa was still a bit bemused, and deeply sceptical of Linda's claim to be in ignorance of the discussion that had taken place, right in front of her. Alexandra's mother would have normally had plenty to say, during the course of it, and the conversation between mother and daughter, both beforehand and afterwards, seemed rather unnatural to her, knowing them as she did. She remembered her astonishment at the theatre, when they appeared to have come to an agreement just by looking at each other and without Alexandra having said a word. There had been something going on this evening, but she couldn't put her finger on it, and she thought it best not to mention it, after the girls had left.

Everybody stood up. "So I suppose it's back to Charterhouse in time for supper now, then?" asked Linda. "If I remember – and this is going back a bit now – in my time the grub wasn't too bad. I'll let you into a little secret, for you to bear in mind as you proceed through your lives though. If you know where to look, you'll find better!"

"None better than here, though," said her daughter.

"For Geratica's sake, Alexandra, don't tell them that! They'll be running away from Charterhouse to have dinner with us every night, and then I'll be in terrible trouble!"

She slipped her arm around her daughter.

"Although Alexandra does know which side her bread is buttered," she added.

"I'm not just saying it; I really mean it," asserted Alexandra to the other girls.

"Well it's nice to have met you all!" said Linda, shaking all of their hands. "I expect I will again. Goodbye. Alexandra will get your coats, and show you out."

"Goodbye, Mrs Radcliffe!" they all replied, and she disappeared down the passage, with Philippa.

Alexandra fetched the coats from the cloakroom.

"It's a nice place here," remarked Benita. "You're very lucky. And you get to come back, every night."

"Yes, I think I am rather," agreed Alexandra. "And my boyfriend lives in The Lodge, the only other house in Elmsbrook."

"Is that where he lives?" asked Imelda.

"You jammy so-and-so!" she exclaimed, as Alexandra nodded. "To find the boy you love, right on your own doorstep! I bet you and him, are together all day long, every day!"

"No, not really," Alexandra told her. "There certainly aren't many days when we don't talk together, but we do have our own lives to lead. Obviously, during the week, I'm at Charterhouse all day and he's at work as a part time as trainee gardener and general labourer on Lady Sackville's estate, so that only leaves the evenings, when I have prep to do, and I'm not allowed out after dusk. I hope you liked my mother, she's a very hospitable woman, with quite a caring heart, but she's also very strict."

"She seemed really nice in the parlour," said Benita. "She was obviously busy in the study though. It was good of her to let us have the meeting in the study whist she worked. I hope we didn't disturb her too much. Thank her for us, will you?"

The others murmured similar sentiments and Alexandra suppressed a smirk. They all seemed to have been taken in by her mother's little ruse!

"Yes of course," she assured them.

"Find a picture of -Tom, isn't it? We'd all love to see what he looks like," urged Benita.

"Is he good-looking?" asked Rachel.

"Of course!" said Alexandra.

"I bet he is as well!" said Imelda. "And you're a double jammy so-and-so!"

"I'll see what I can find," promised Alexandra.

"Right, well we'd better be getting back to Mrs Wood, girls," said Benita, taking charge once again. "You're right, Alexandra. We can't be late back for our supper. They won't hold it for us, for long. We'll welcome you back to Charterhouse, next week. See you then!"

Alexandra opened the porch door and bid her farewells to the group of girls.

"Once you get to the gate at the end Elmsbrook's drive, I'll let you out," she said. "See you next week!"

***

With the girls having left, Alexandra could now concentrate on her piano practice with Philippa. Linda had promised to pay her time and a half, if she agreed to still give Alexandra her full hour's tuition, after the meeting. Altogether, the girls had been there for just over half an hour. So this was what she did, although not before contacting her family to tell them that she'd be a little later home than previously planned.

To Linda's relief, the supermarket delivery arrived at the time she had re-arranged it for, so that it hadn't interrupted her presence in her daughter's meeting.

Later that evening, after they'd finished dinner and cleared away, Alexandra phoned Tom. She told him about the visit from the girls at Charterhouse, and how her mother had secretly helped her when she'd needed it.

"You've got to teach me more about that type of communication you two use!" he exclaimed. "I can see how useful it can be sometimes."

Then he suddenly had a thought. "Hey, that's not the reason why your mother's so good at cards is it? You don't secretly feed her information about her opponents' hands? My stepmother would be livid if she found out that she'd lost, due to Radcliffe cheating!"

"No of course not!" answered Alexandra indignantly. "How dare you insinuate that, Tom! You take it back immediately, or our relationship might be terminated very quickly. And I certainly won't be teaching you anymore! The Radcliffes *always* play fair!"

"I'm sorry, Alexandra, my Angel," said Tom. "I'm sure you and your mother would never dream of doing such a thing. The Spencer women, when they were together, though ..."

"Oh they'd have been capable of anything, when Gillian was at Charterhouse!" said his girlfriend. "That's why it's so important to keep the technique to ourselves, and not let it fall into enemy hands!"

"Aye, Aye, Captain!" said Tom, teasingly.

*\*\**

Before she went to bed, Alexandra curled up on the sofa, beside her mother, relieved that her unexpected meeting seemed to have gone well.

"I wonder if I might have just one quieter day tomorrow, Mother," she said.

"I can't imagine that you'll have anything out of the ordinary happen tomorrow, darling, but you never know," said Linda. "As I said at dinner though, I thought you did brilliantly this evening, despite still managing to sell yourself short yet again, when your intelligence was commented upon! Tom is quite right. You *are* capable of chairing a meeting. You've just done it!"

"I don't want to make a habit of it though, Mother."

"Well, as I've told you before, I'm afraid that as you go through life, there are inevitably going to be times when you'll have to do things that feel uncomfortable to you, sweetheart. You'll be by no means the only one!"

"If I *have* to do it, then I will, Mother, but I'll never *want* to!" asserted Alexandra.

"I know, sweetheart. That's fair enough," said Linda. "And *you* know that whenever it's you and me, then I'll be leading for you." She kissed her daughter.

"I was grateful for you being there, anyhow, Mother," said Alexandra, kissing her mother back, as she looked up at her. "You gave me confirmation when I needed it, and prompted me when necessary."

"Always, darling!" said Linda. "And that was the general object of the exercise, after all. You aren't officially supposed to get any direct help from me, in that situation. It should be all your own work."

"You prompted me, without the other girls knowing that you were doing it, Mother! So the exercise was a success. Benita even thanked you for letting us use the study, whilst you were working in it!"

"Yes. She was a star! I was most impressed with her. I think she's going to go far. You'll be alright, with her on your board, Alexandra!"

"Do you think that Philippa suspected anything Mother?"

"Possibly, on occasions, but she won't have known *what* exactly, or the specific reason behind it," said Linda. "I wouldn't worry about that."

"Right!" she said. "Time for you to be getting ready for bed. You've had another good day, today. Well done!" She hugged and kissed her daughter.

"Thank you Mother," said Alexandra.

She went up to her bedroom, feeling happy. She quickly got herself ready for bed, and lay there reading her book, whilst she waited for her mother to come and kiss her goodnight, and secure her in her room for the night.

# CHAPTER 3

Alexandra finished her housework tasks the following morning, and did a bit more swatting up. To her relief there were no phone calls at all during the day, and having had a particularly good night's sleep, and a quieter period to herself, she could finally reflect on things properly.

She was certainly feeling more confident about returning to Charterhouse now. If yesterday was any accurate barometer of how the other girls were feeling about her misfortune, then she felt she didn't have *too much* to worry about, and her selected group to form a board to assist her in putting on the concert, seemed only too pleased to help. Benita was proving to be a good friend, she thought. Obviously, when she went into each of her separate subject classes, she would meet some other people, but there wasn't really anybody else who she was particularly close to.

She was still slightly worried about what it would be like with Mrs Spencer still the headmistress though, even though Gillian was no longer there. Also, she couldn't yet be absolutely certain that she would still be eligible as a candidate for college champion, although she did feel that she detected the wind blowing in her favour. If she wasn't, then she supposed the concert could still go ahead if she really wished it, but it would only predominantly be something of importance to her personally, and not of such great significance to her prestige at Charterhouse.

The public side of her punishment was now, thankfully, behind her, and all that remained, was the remainder of the private one that she'd been given by her mother.

All in all, she felt that, after the most difficult week of her life so far, she was finally through the worst of it. She knew that her mother had played a huge role in helping her, and she couldn't have got through it, without her. Once things were *officially* back to normal between them, in a week's time, then she resolved to give her a present of some kind, to show her gratitude.

***

When Linda arrived home that night, she had some news for her daughter.

"The chair of the Charterhouse board of governors has agreed to my request for an emergency meeting!" she declared. "It's to be held there tomorrow at 2.00 p.m., in the boardroom."

Alexandra looked at her for a moment. "So, do you think the board are going to get rid of her mother?" she asked.

"I don't know, but there's obviously a possibility, given the motion that I've proposed," said Linda. "After all the publicity that there's been over the 'Charterhouse Scandal' it was almost inevitable that the chair would have to call this, after one of the members requested it, though, so don't draw any immediate conclusions. It depends how much support she still has on the board. We'll find out tomorrow, and I imagine, if she is to go, Mrs Spencer will be told immediately! So, I should be able to tell you tomorrow evening, whether she's still your headmistress or not!"

"Our dinner party is tomorrow night, too, Mother," remarked Alexandra.

"Yes! It's unfortunate timing in that regard, but that can't be helped. The meeting has to be arranged for the earliest possible time which is convenient to everybody. But I certainly don't want to be too late getting back here tomorrow evening, so that we can make the finishing touches to our preparations in good time, before the party begins. So as soon as we're finished at Charterhouse, I shall come straight home, and not go back to the palace. Tomorrow is going to be another big day!"

# CHAPTER 4

Linda arrived at Charterhouse, just over twenty minutes before the meeting, and after announcing herself to the reception, waited in the college lobby. She heard the college bell ring, signalling the end of lunchtime for the girls, and glimpsed some of them filing back to their form classes for afternoon registration. Her heart was fluttering slightly with excitement. If things went well here this afternoon, then she would achieve something that would bring her immense pleasure, and satisfaction – although she'd have to make sure that wasn't too evident during her motion against Elizabeth Spencer, or she could be accused of purely bearing a personal grudge against her.

Five minutes later, she was shown up to the boardroom, via the lift. She was one of the first to arrive, but the others wouldn't be long in coming. The chair, Sonia Eastman was there, and the two women shook hands.

"It's a pleasure to see you again, Mrs Radcliffe!" said Sonia. "How's life at the palace?"

"The pleasure is mutual, Mrs Eastman!" replied Linda. "All is well, though as ever, extremely busy! I have a dinner party to host tonight too, so I shall be on my way home after we've finished here this afternoon."

"You know that Sonia is acceptable to me! said the chair of the governors. "Yes, I'd heard. The queen herself is attending, so I understand?"

"Yes, that's right," confirmed Linda. "We've entertained her before, but it's obviously always the ultimate honour to have Her Majesty as a guest!"

"Well good luck!" said Sonia. "I'll try and keep things moving along for you, so that you're not too delayed."

She put her mouth to Linda's ear. "To tell you the truth, Mrs Radcliffe, I, too, feel that this arrangement needs to change. Gillian Spencer has caused a major embarrassment to this college, and her mother's apparent ignorance of the goings on, has made things even worse. If what you also allege is true – and I've no reason to doubt your word – then I think her position is untenable and she must go!"

"Thank you, Sonia," said Linda quietly. "Have you any idea of how many are with us on the issue? If you are to vote for her dismissal, then we only need two more members to do the same, and she'll be gone."

"I suspect that Paula Scott is with Elizabeth, as I've heard that she 'tipped the wink' to her, that this meeting was being arranged!"

"Hmm, another of her 'Male Rights Supporters' allies!" remarked Linda, ruefully. "What of the rest of the board?"

"I wouldn't like to say, Mrs Radcliffe," admitted Sonia. "All I will predict, is that it'll be a close run thing!"

"Right. Thank you, Sonia, I'll bear that in mind," said Linda.

***

The meeting started promptly at 2.00 p.m. As there was only the one item on the agenda, it wasn't long before Linda was called upon to deliver her motion. As at the juvenile court, she had some notes, which sat before her on the table, but she spoke directly to the group.

"Madam Chair. Fellow Board Members. Good afternoon!" she began. "Firstly, let me say that it gives me no great pleasure in proposing such a motion, as an old Charterhouse girl. I never thought that such a scenario would ever arise! However, the evidence that has been brought to my attention, chiefly by my daughter, Alexandra, has made me feel that I have no option but to act.

"You will all be only too aware, of the unfortunate mess that my daughter found herself in, a week ago. I don't want to revisit that particular occurrence, accept to say that it has been firmly dealt with by myself, and you will have heard the sentence from the juvenile court. But what I am bringing to your attention, now, came to *my* notice as a direct result of Alexandra confiding in me about her misdemeanour, beforehand.

"And so I'll come to the evidence, which I outlined in my letter to each of you, and indeed I touched on briefly at my daughter's hearing.

"Mrs Spencer runs a fairly strict regime at Charterhouse, and I have no objections to that. I run a similar one both at the royal palace, and in my own household, However, I have heard stories that her daughter Gillian, who until this week of course, boarded here, was more or less allowed to do as she pleased, and if she committed offences – which she did on an almost daily basis - and was excused the usual punishments that any other girl would suffer, for doing the same. This was almost entirely due to Mrs Spencer's influence, and I am sure you will all agree with me, was grossly unfair.

"I believe that she wished her daughter to be her spy in the college, telling tales on other girls to get them into trouble with her, causing problems for mistresses and manipulating situations in order for her to implement her plans for Charterhouse, as she saw fit. In return, she ensured that Gillian was considered 'untouchable' by the mistresses, a privilege which she took full advantage of, and some might say, abused. Despite her disgraceful behaviour, Mrs Spencer still managed to ensure that she was made Head Girl!

"This is what was really going on in relation to my daughter's attempted shoplifting offence, last week. Mrs Spencer's ultimate ambition was for Gillian to go to University as college champion, but Alexandra had the audacity to stand in the way, as a credible alternative candidate, and so she wanted her discredited somehow, so that she could no longer be considered. I think that her personal dislike of me, due to our differences on a certain subject, and the fact that my daughter is only a day pupil here, may have had some bearing on this desire, too, though this should have been irrelevant. Her mistake was to leave it to Gillian's discretion, as to how this was achieved. Gillian overreached herself, when she set Alexandra up, by involving the police, which ultimately led to the Charterhouse escort boys' visits, and the connected shoplifting operation, being exposed by my daughter when they interviewed her. It appears that none of the mistresses, or the headmistress herself, had any knowledge whatsoever of the entire business, which I think shows Mrs Spencer to be incompetent.

"A couple of specific issues, particularly incense me. I mentioned them at Alexandra's hearing. Gillian Spencer was a bully, and it was this method that she used to coerce Alexandra into attempting the shoplifting offence last week, threatening her with a 'thumping' if she didn't comply. I was outraged to discover that the reason that she didn't immediately report what she'd been told to do, was because she *had* reported to her housemistress, a previous misdemeanour from Gillian, that she'd uncovered herself, but that no subsequent action was taken against, by the Charterhouse staff!

"I'm referring to her embezzlement of the profits from the Charterhouse tuck shop, into her own pocket, of course! I simply cannot believe that all this college did, was inform Gillian Spencer that her scam had been discovered, and *then* simply allowed to go back, and resume her position! This, Alexandra assumes, and I imagine that she is correct, was due to the intervention of Elizabeth Spencer. She suspects that her housemistress was asked by the headmistress to alter the figures, in order to cover up the offence. Gillian found out that my daughter had 'grassed' on her, and 'thumped' her on the way out of Charterhouse, one afternoon. She then had the cheek to bar Alexandra from the tuck shop, and forced her to hand over the money that I allowed for her to spend there, directly to her instead, every day! Was it any wonder then, that my daughter felt disinclined to tell the staff at Charterhouse, this time?

"The other thing that came out during my talks with Alexandra, which *really* infuriated me, was that when she was caning my daughter and the other girl involved in the most recent affair, in her study, Mrs Spencer allowed her daughter to be present, and to actually join in with administering the beating to Alexandra! She claimed to have already punished Gillian – which apparently was a story told to many girls who were beaten after misdemeanours chiefly orchestrated by her daughter – however Alexandra is doubtful of this. I too am somewhat sceptical, given rumours which one heard on the grapevine about the frustrations felt by certain mistresses, over the attitude they were expected to take towards Miss Spencer.

"I believe that this is totally unacceptable and inappropriate conduct, and I hope the rest of the board shares my sentiments! For *any* mistress, let alone a headmistress, to allow one pupil to cane another is an abuse of authority, when she *should* be setting an example to the girls in Charterhouse. I will not allege that this has happened before, though my daughter did note that they appeared to have a pre-arranged routine for administering the punishment. Admittedly, Mrs Spencer has recently reminded me personally, that, although I have considerable and broad authority in my own job, *she* is in charge of the girls, when they are here and not me, and that she will deal with them as she sees fit. Well that is all well and good, but what sort of example of authority is this to be setting? That if you are the favourite, or a relative – or both – of authority, you will be excused from all the usual rules and regulations, and never be punished for misdemeanours, and at the same time, when others are seen to have transgressed, be part of that authority, and its implementation of punishment!

"Of course, after defending Gillian so vigorously at the juvenile court on Day 1 of this week, she then claimed to have disowned her, later that evening. I believe that this was, at least partly, a cynical attempt by her, to try and restore her reputation here, and remain in post.

"And so, Madam Chair, and my fellow board members, in conclusion, I ask you to consider, after what I have related to you, whether it is morally right, proper, or fair, to allow someone whose conduct is so inappropriate, is so inconsistent in her judgements, and so incompetent in her knowledge of the recent illicit activities going on in her own college, to remain as headmistress of Charterhouse. I for one, do not, and I accordingly propose this motion of no confidence in Mrs Elizabeth Spencer, and call for her removal from the position, with immediate effect!"

Linda took a long swig of her coffee, as she finished.

Sonia cleared her throat. "Thank you, Mrs Radcliffe," she said. "As usual you've delivered a very clear, and detailed case."

"And so now, what are the thoughts of the rest of you?" she asked the five other board members.

"How do we know that Mrs Radcliffe's claims against Elizabeth Spencer are true?" asked the first member, Paula Scott. "We know that there is personal animosity between the two of them. Mrs Radcliffe may be just trying to take advantage of the outcome of the hearing the other day, to finally get rid of her old sparring partner. Anyhow, as Mrs Spencer has rightly said, Charterhouse *is* her college and she can run it as she sees fit."

"But she still has to be accountable to the governors, though," said a second member.

"Miss Scott, if you pay closer attention to my letter, you will see that it was dated before my daughter's hearing. I did not know what its sentences would be, when I sent it – and all the board members were contacted at the same time.

"As to whether these claims against Mrs Spencer are true, they came from my daughter's lips. If you are suggesting that they are in some way false, then you are insinuating that my daughter is lying!"

"No one is 'insinuating' anything Mrs Radcliffe" said a third member, at which Linda snorted contemptuously. "But we only have your daughter's word against hers."

The member looked over to Sonia. "Perhaps, Chair, we should ask Mrs Spencer to come up here, and then she can answer for herself."

Before Sonia could answer, Linda cut back in. "Before I was interrupted, I was about to say that at my daughter's hearing, the court did say that they were inclined to believe her, and she was given excellent character references. She is categorically not a liar."

"Blast your daughter's hearing!" said Paula. "That's all in the past now. We're talking about her allegations about Mrs Spencer, today."

"But the two things are in some ways connected," retorted Linda. "I realise of course, that you share some of Mrs Spencer's more radical views, so maybe it isn't surprising that you defend her so robustly!"

"Alright, calm down, both of you!" said Sonia. "I'm not going to call Mrs Spencer up here, before we've reached a decision on her future. She will almost certainly vigorously deny everything that Mrs Radcliffe alleges, and we simply cannot allow this affair to drag on any longer. There has been enough publicity in the media over the last week, and both Mrs Radcliffe and Mrs Spencer have been heavily featured. We've already heard what they both said at the hearing, and I agree with Mrs Radcliffe. Some of those matters are linked to the subject that we are discussing in our meeting today. I also am 'inclined to believe' Alexandra Radcliffe. I've never met her, but she strikes me as an honest girl, who unfortunately got tangled up in a web of murky goings on, without wishing, or truly meaning to. She's a most popular girl too, as far as I can tell."

"Hear! Hear!" said the second member. "And I too, think that we must take decisive action this afternoon. All of this publicity is damaging Charterhouse's reputation. In case anyone has forgotten, we make most of our money from the fees that Geraticans pay, to send their girls here. There may well be some who had decided to entrust their daughters' education to this college, who are *now* seriously reconsidering their choice."

Linda sipped some more of her coffee. Of the members who had spoken so far, including the chair and herself, she calculated that she seemed to have at least three" yes" votes, out of the possible seven. Paula Scott was, unsurprisingly, a pretty safe bet for Mrs Spencer, and another seemed to be leaning more towards her, too. If they should all vote in that way, that would be 3 to 2 in her favour. If one of the two members who were yet to comment, was to support her, then she might win. But she kept a grip on herself. She wasn't quite there yet, and she had to keep calm and clear headed. Most of all, she wanted to get her way, because she knew she was right. She was used to that being the normal course of events. She could celebrate later, providing she got the result she wanted, but the remaining two members could yet both vote against her.

"Are there any more comments?" asked Sonia.

"I don't like this business of removing someone from their post, without being able to speak to them personally, beforehand," said the fourth member. "Unless we get her up here to defend herself, and we find that she is indeed guilty of what the Radcliffes allege, then I'm prepared to give her the benefit of the doubt."

Linda had her mind focused on the target. That made it 3 votes each, by her calculation. If she was right, then it would all come down to the remaining member of the board.

"I think I should declare a conflict of loyalties here," said the fifth member.

Everybody looked at her in surprise.

"Oh?" enquired Sonia. "How's that?"

"I am inclined to agree with Mrs Radcliffe. I think Mrs Spencer has acted most unwisely. However, she has offered me a position here, starting in the New Year. So although I don't wish to vote for Mrs Spencer, I think that I should, out of gratitude to her, abstain."

"Oh. Well, if that's how you feel, then so be it," said Sonia.

Normally Linda would have been disappointed to have lost someone's vote, simply through the loyalty that they felt to Mrs Spencer. But now, it was tempered by the fact that, if her she was correct in assessing the members' voting intentions, then that abstention would make it still 3 each. In the event of a tie, the chair had the casting vote. Linda was confident of her support. Therefore, she would win.

Linda sensed that was tantalising close to her goal, and her heart beat faster. She'd always had a natural winner's instinct. She could almost taste victory on her lips, which she now subconsciously licked. She loved to win. After making love to a man, it was her greatest thrill.

"Well, we've now heard from everyone," remarked Sonia. "If there are no more comments, then I propose that we put this motion to a vote."

She waited for a few seconds and when no one else spoke she said, "Can we have a show of hands? All those for?"

Linda, Sonia and the second board member, all raised their hands.

"Three votes for," announced Sonia, making a note for the official record.

"All those against?"

Paula and the third and fourth members raised their hands. The fifth hadn't voted for either, as she had earlier indicated.

"Three votes against," Sonia declared, making another note. "Three for, and three against, with one abstention. So the vote is tied. In that event, the chair has the casting vote. I support Mrs Radcliffe. The motion is carried." She added a couple more notes in confirmation. Linda had won.

Sonia asked her secretary, who had been taking minutes of the meeting, to contact Mrs Spencer, and tell her to come up to the boardroom immediately.

As they waited for Elizabeth Spencer, Linda forced herself to stay in control. She didn't want to show her glee before the now ex-headmistress, even though inside she was feeling triumphant. She looked forward to getting home, and telling Alexandra what was going to happen next.

A few moments later, Elizabeth arrived. "Good afternoon, Mrs Spencer," said Sonia. "Please take a seat." She motioned with her hand.

"Thank you Chair," said Elizabeth.

"I'll come straight to the point, Mrs Spencer," asserted Sonia. "Over the past week there has obviously been a huge amount of publicity surrounding Charterhouse, much of it very damaging to the college's reputation. This cannot continue. We on the board feel that your daughter has been the main cause of it, but that you did, yourself, encourage her to discredit Alexandra Radcliffe, which was grossly inappropriate behaviour. We note that with the expulsion of your daughter, due to her being sent to a Young Offenders' Institution, you have publicly disowned her, but the fact remains that there are serious questions related to some of the methods that you employed, as headmistress, whilst she was here, and your general lack of competence, in relation to the recent scandal.

"Therefore, it is with regret, that I have to inform you, that by a small majority, the board has decided that you can no longer remain in your position as headmistress of Charterhouse. We are extremely sorry, and wish to thank you for your service at Charterhouse, but we really do feel that the time has come for change. So please take whatever personal belongings that you have here, and leave the building. Again, we are sorry, but we must say, 'Goodbye Mrs Spencer!'"

Elizabeth seethed with rage inside, but she kept outwardly calm. "If I am to be dismissed, just like that, might I at least know what the questions are, related to the methods that I have used?" she asked.

"Briefly," Sonia told her, "They relate to your apparent favouritism towards your daughter, and your deliberate overlooking of her misdemeanours, as well as your use of her, to fulfil your own ambitions politically, and your action in allowing Gillian to assist you, in punishing other girls in your charge."

"But that is all we wish to say on the matter," she continued. "Thank you Mrs Spencer, and goodbye once again."

Elizabeth was defiant. "Hmm, well I can't pretend that I'm surprised. One member of your board has been waiting for this moment for weeks! I shall appeal, of course."

"Well you've already said that once this week, in relation to the juvenile court case, and then retracted it!" exclaimed Sonia.

"I mean it this time," said Elizabeth firmly. She rose from the seat. "You've not heard the last of me, I promise you that!" she vowed, as she flounced out of the room.

Sonia mopped her brow. "Phew! Well now that's over, we'd better turn to the matter of a replacement. Obviously it'll be an Acting position, until we formally appoint Mrs Spencer's successor. Does anybody have a particular mistress in mind, or shall we simply allow someone to step up voluntarily?" she asked.

"I think it would be best to allow it to be filled voluntarily," said Linda.

"That way, at least the staff will feel that they've had some say in the matter. And who knows, if the mistress concerned is adjudged successful in her stint at the helm, she may well have a good chance of eventually being given the role permanently, if she's strong enough at the interview stage."

On this issue, the board were in complete agreement.

"Does anybody have any other business?" asked Sonia.

"Just one thing, if you please, Chair," said Linda. "We obviously don't know who will take over from Mrs Spencer, but my daughter is most anxious to know if she will still be eligible as a candidate for college champion, after her recent misfortune. Can I ask that the matter be looked into urgently? Alexandra has brought together a group of girls to assist her in her project, which as you probably know is going to be a concert in tribute to Philippa Barrington. They came to our house and met with her the evening before last, and I believe they made some initial plans. I'd hate to see them waste their time, if my daughter can't be a candidate anyhow!"

"OK, Mrs Radcliffe," said Sonia. "I'll see that message is passed on to whoever takes over as acting headmistress, and treated as urgent. I presume the position will be filled as soon as possible."

"If there's no more business, then that concludes the meeting, women!" she continued. "The next meeting will be the one that was scheduled at our last regular meeting."

The meeting broke up, and Linda started to gather up her things. "Well thank you very much, Sonia," she said a few minutes later, as the room began to empty. "I'm very pleased that went so well! It's a weight off my mind. I genuinely think that the board has done the right thing. Let's hope Mrs Spencer's replacement will restore some proper order to Charterhouse – and that they're appointed soon. And now I must dash home to prepare for our dinner party! Goodbye Sonia."

However, at that moment there was a crashing sound outside. Startled, Linda and Sonia rushed to the window.

"That sounded suspiciously like a car!" said Sonia.

Linda scanned the car park below. There didn't seem to be anybody there, who might be having a "discussion" with another driver, after having been involved in a collision.

Then to her horror, she suddenly realised where the sound had come from.

"Darn and blast it!" she exploded angrily and pointed. "That's my car! Someone's crashed into it, and then just simply driven off! How dare they?"

"Oh goodness me!" said Sonia.

She followed Linda, as she marched out of the room.

# CHAPTER 5

Outside, Linda surveyed the damage. The driver had gone into the rear of her car. The left bumper was dented, and her rear lights on the same side, would need replacing.

She double checked the surrounding cars to make sure that the offender wasn't here, but there was no apparent damage elsewhere, so the driver must have been leaving the car park when it happened.

"I'll have to make a phone call to my insurers!" she groaned. "I'd better do it urgently. The process often takes a while, so I believe, so I might not have time later. Then it's the weekend, and I'll have to wait until 1/35/10. Bang goes my plan to go straight home, as soon as our meeting was over! It's just as well that I wasn't planning to return to the palace, this afternoon."

"I wonder if anybody saw it?" asked Sonia. "They might be able to describe what happened, and maybe even the vehicle involved."

"Hmm," muttered Linda. She was still fuming. "I'd better be careful not to make a specific allegation, without concrete proof, and it *might* be pure coincidence, but who do we know, that would have been leaving Charterhouse at around that time? And she'd have been in a foul temper, with, no doubt, revenge on her mind!"

"Elizabeth Spencer? You think she deliberately crashed her car into yours, as she was driving out?"

"I'm saying that it *might be quite likely* to have been Elizabeth Spencer, Sonia," Linda corrected her. In her own mind, she thought that she could probably find out for definite herself, by asking James whether his wife's car had been damaged in any way, if, as she felt was likely, no one was able to give any firm information, regarding the incident. They would presumably be at home together tonight.

She did notice some girls looking out of a classroom window, not far away, surveying the scene and no doubt, Linda thought, having a good chortle at her misfortune. "Blasted girls!" she thought. "Why doesn't their mistress order them back to their desks?"

Back inside Charterhouse, Linda explained to the reception, what had happened. They had heard the bang, just like her, but they hadn't been in a position where they could see the cause. They generously allowed Linda to use one of their phones, rather than the public one in the lobby, to sort out her affairs.

She'd decided not to bother to inform the police. Whoever this was, they were long gone now, and the authorities had more important matters to attend to. But she did make a claim on her car insurance. As she'd anticipated, by the time she'd got through, and it had all been done, quite some time had passed. There was definitely a need to simplify some of the bureaucracy in Geratica, she thought. Not at the palace of course! She prided herself on ensuring that administrative affairs there were *very* efficient.

Whilst she was on the phone, some general enquiries were made of the class that had been watching her earlier, to see if they could give any more details about the collision, since they'd have been the ones with the best possible view of it.

As Linda came off the phone, there was a dark-haired girl standing behind her waiting. Linda turned around to see her. It was Benita.

"Oh hello again, Benita!" exclaimed Linda in surprise. "I said that I expected to see you again soon, but I didn't think it would be quite this quickly!"

"Good afternoon Mrs Radcliffe," said Benita, politely. "Your car's been hit in the car park."

"Yes thank you girl, I was aware of that!" said Linda, as she began to prepare to leave.

"Mrs Spencer rammed into you, as she was leaving the car park," Benita continued. "Then she took off at high speed."

Linda widened her eyes. "Are you saying, that you think she did it deliberately?" she asked.

"I'm saying that I know she did so!" replied Benita confidently. "When she did it, I was the only one in the room, facing the window, as I happened to be up at the front, talking to the rest of the class at the time. In the corner of my right eye, I saw her drive into the back of your car, then reverse back, and drive like lightening away! I know her car. I've seen her in it, on many occasions. Of course, I didn't know that it was *your* car that she rammed, until we were all asked if we'd seen the incident, just now."

"Are you *absolutely* certain of this, girl? Could you *swear* on it?"

"Yes Mrs Radcliffe," said Benita.

Linda was studying her face, and could find no trace of doubt.

"Well, in that case, Benita, thank you for coming forward. That might be very useful!" she said, gratefully.

"If you don't mind my asking, Mrs Radcliffe, there's a rumour going around that Mrs Spencer's been given her marching orders. Is that true? I know that you're on the board of governors. Is that why you're here this afternoon?"

"I can't comment on that at the moment, girl," replied Linda, looking her in the eye.

"Right. Well I'll draw my own conclusions from that," remarked Benita.

Linda guessed that she'd *concluded*, the reason why she couldn't comment on that, might be because it was true.

"You seem a bright young lady and very confident too," she said. "I meant to ask the evening before last. What does your mother do for a living?"

"She's a lawyer," Benita told her.

"Oh really?" laughed Linda. "How very apt, after what's just happened!"

"If you're ever interested in hiring her, this is her business card," Benita drew it out of her blazer pocket, and handed it to Linda, who was taken aback.

"Do you carry a set of these around with you, touting for your mother's business?" she asked, as she read the details.

Benita smiled. "Well I wouldn't say I 'tout' for business, but I do keep a stock of them, yes! You never know when one of the other girls' parents might need someone like her, so I like to be prepared. My mother's chambers are a private business – and in business, you have to be capable of moving fast to secure a deal. I intend to set up my own accountancy firm, once my education is complete."

"Something tells me that you probably will," remarked Linda.

"There's no 'probably' about it," asserted Benita. "I *will*!"

Linda thought that this was quite the most confident girl, she had ever met. In fact she reminded her of herself when she'd been in her final year at Charterhouse (and Head Girl too).

"Actually," she said, "I'm sure I've heard of your mother, although we've never met. *Claire* Davis! I didn't realise you were her daughter. I know that she's primarily a criminal lawyer."

"Well, I'll certainly keep her card in mind, Benita," she said, dropping it into her handbag. "It's been a pleasure to speak to you again, Miss Davis, but now I must go. I want to see how quickly my local garage can fix my car, and then I have a rather important dinner party to host! I'll see you again. Goodbye!"

She shook her hand, and Benita bid her goodbye, also.

Then, after thanking the reception staff for their kindness, she hurried out to her car. She wanted to get back to Greenacres, and get her car into the garage. She was hoping that they would be able to mend the damage, urgently. Quite apart from the normal inconvenience to her life, that not having a car would bring, on Alexandra's first day back at Charterhouse, 1/35/10, she'd been intending to drive her right to the door. It would be for one day only, just in case there were any press women, interested in covering her daughter's return.

She turned on her car's motor, and drove away.

***

Linda managed to reach the garage, by just after 4.00 p.m. She was relieved that she'd just managed to beat the rush hour, and wasn't too late.

The mechanic looked at the back of Linda's car, her hands on her hips. "That was quite a bang!" she exclaimed.

"Yes, and what's more I believe it might have been deliberate," said Linda. "But never mind about that now. My main concern at the moment is, can the damage be fixed urgently – and I mean urgently! – and if so, then how quickly?"

"We can certainly do it urgently for you Mrs Radcliffe," said the mechanic. In fact, few organisations in Greenacres, *wouldn't* do something urgently for *Mrs Radcliffe*.

"As for how long it will take, I'd say that if you come down here at about 3.30 p.m. tomorrow, then the job should be done," she concluded. "We shut at 4.00 p.m. tomorrow, it being Day 1 of the weekend."

"*Should* be done? I want to know that it *will* be!" demanded Linda.

"Oh yes, of course. It definitely shall be, Mrs Radcliffe." The mechanic crossed her fingers behind her back.

"Good," said Linda. "Then I shall be here at 3.30 p.m. tomorrow, to pick up my car, fully restored to its former glory!"

***

At The Grange, Alexandra was in the parlour. Unlike her mother, she'd had a fairly relaxing afternoon, having already completed her week's tasks set by her mother. She had done her various ablutions, ready for the night ahead, and then settled down to listen to the radio, whilst at the same time reading her book.

It was obviously a rare occurrence for her to be listening to the radio during the week, in term time, and she'd made a few discoveries. Alexandra resolved that once she made it to University (assuming that she did), and there were periods when she didn't have a lecture, then if ever she didn't have a lot of work to do, she would listen to some of them.

Alexandra looked up, and out of the front window of the parlour for a moment, and was surprised to see her mother walking down the drive from their front gate. She put down her book, and hurried to the front door.

"Mother," she said, as Linda reached the house. "Where's the car?"

"At the garage, down the road, being mended!" her mother told her.

"What?" Alexandra exclaimed. "Why? What happened?"

"I've had both a good thing and a bad thing happen to me today, darling," said Linda, as she came inside and Alexandra shut the door. "The good thing was, that the board of governors voted to remove Mrs Spencer from her position, as headmistress of Charterhouse. She's gone!"

"Mother. You won!" cried Alexandra. "That's brilliant news! So both the Spencers are now gone. I assume that the 'bad thing' relates to your car?"

"You are quite correct, Alexandra. Unfortunately, after the meeting, and just as I was about to leave the boardroom, *somebody* smashed into the back of my car! And I have reason to believe that it was done deliberately, by none other than Elizabeth Spencer, herself!"

Alexandra gaped. "She rammed your car, Mother? I don't know what I'm going to hear next, about her!"

"Yes, well of course I heard the crash from the boardroom and then looked out of the window, and eventually saw what had happened, but of course the driver had already left by then. I went out to look at the damage with the Chair of the governors, and I soon suspected that it was probably Mrs Spencer, in a fury at being removed, and wanting revenge on me, though of course I had no real proof."

"Then I went back to the reception and I rang the insurance company to make a claim. It took a long time, with all the bureaucratic red tape, and once I'd finished they'd asked one of the forms that been in a classroom that overlooked the car park, if they had happened to see anything. And would you believe it? Who should spring up, and say that she'd seen it all, but your friend, the ubiquitous Benita Davis!"

"Benita!" exclaimed Alexandra. "Was she certain it was her, Mother?"

"That's precisely what I asked her, sweetheart. And she really did seem to be in no doubt. It appears that she was in front of the rest of the class, addressing them at the time, and was therefore the only one looking out of the window! She says that she knows Mrs Spencer's car, and it came into vision 'in the corner of her right eye' and she saw it drive into the back of mine, then reverse and speed away. Mind you, of course, they all had a good gawp after it had happened!

"I don't know what subject she was in. It must have been her last period of the day."

"Mathematics, Mother. I expect she'd been called up to the front, to demonstrate her knowledge of a particular application."

"Well anyhow, it appeared that the rumour was already spreading, of Mrs Spencer's removal, when we spoke. She asked me to confirm it, and I obviously said that I couldn't comment, but I think she might have guessed the truth. And it turns out that her mother is *Claire* Davis! I've never met her, but I know of her, as a criminal lawyer, and the girl promptly gave me one of her business cards, in case I should ever need her services! Young Miss Davis is going to go far, you mark my words, Alexandra. She's got the right kind of head for business, and I believe her when she says that she *will* set up her own accountancy firm. I've never met a girl so confident and self-assured!"

"So then I brought the car to our local garage and asked if they could fix it urgently, and they've promised me that it will be ready by 3.30 p.m. tomorrow. I really want to be able to drop you to the door, when you return to Charterhouse next week, darling, just in case there should be any media covering it, for a story."

Oh! Very good, Mother," said Alexandra, pleased. "Will you be informing the police about what's happened?"

"Well I wasn't going to bother, initially. I didn't know for certain that it was Elizabeth Spencer – and *whoever* it was had gone – but given what Benita has said, I may do. I can find out from James, whether *her* car has been damaged, and which will more or less prove that it was her. I'm assuming they'll be together at home tonight."

"Well now, *I'm* home. So let's get ready for *our* night!"

# CHAPTER 6

The dinner party was due to start at 7.00 p.m. By 6.15, they were making the finishing touches to their preparations. Linda wore the same royal blue gown, and black gloves that she'd worn for Tom's birthday dinner. Alexandra wore a long flowing navy blue one.

"Right!" said Linda. "It won't be long now, before our guests begin to arrive. As you know, Queen Alexandra should be arriving earlier than the rest of the guests outside of Elmsbrook, at around 6.45." (On Geratica, the queen did not necessarily always arrive last for a dinner party).

"Now, Alexandra!" she continued, assertively, "You know what to do, don't you? As the guests arrive, you greet them and take their coats, then show them into the parlour, where I'll be waiting. Just say their names to me, by way of an official introduction, and then I'll take charge of their hospitality. Once everyone's here, then we'll make sure that everyone is happy, and then I'll get on with the dinner. The main course is going to be fish. You'll stay here and mingle with the guests, and keep their drinks topped up. A little later, we'll serve the first course – the canapés – in here. Once the soup course is ready, which shouldn't be too long afterwards, then I'll come and fetch you, and you'll help me to serve it in the dining room. Then you'll do the same for the rest of the courses. We'll share out the wine pouring duties – I'll serve Queen Alexandra and the guests seated to her left, and you, the ones on our side of the table, and Lady Sackville at the foot."

"Once dinner is finished, then you can start to play some pieces on the piano, and I'll serve the after dinner drinks and mints. I very much expect that there'll be a card game or two later, as well."

"Is that all fairly straight forward? You understand?" she asked her daughter.

Alexandra cleared her throat, which was a bit dry, due to the slight bit of tension that she always felt, before this sort of occasion.

"Yes Mother, I shouldn't have too many problems. I've helped you with a few of these parties now. And Tom will be here with me this time, so I'm looking forward to that. Although he's never met Queen Alexandra before, so he's bound to be a bit nervous!"

Linda noticed a slight tremor in Alexandra's hand, and a hint of anxiety in her eyes. She wrapped her arms around her daughter, and drew her in tight to her chest.

"Are you alright, my darling?" she asked soothingly. "You're feeling nervous too, aren't you?"

"A little, but I'm sure that doesn't surprise you, Mother," replied Alexandra. "You know me! "

"I can't believe that you can keep feeling so relaxed and normal, with the queen coming to dinner, Mother," she added. "You must have nerves of steel!"

"Well, I wouldn't say I felt 'normal' darling! This obviously isn't a 'normal' evening. It's a very significant one for us. But I'm an old hand at this type of thing, and I've never been short of confidence, so any nerves that I feel, don't adversely affect me too much. We all do feel them, sweetheart! You're not alone there."

She tightened her hold. "But you're going to be OK darling. You're doing this with me, and we're a proven successful partnership. I'll be leading as usual, and I'll look after you. Also, you *know* that you can speak very well, and often very knowledgeably, if people talk to you. I've heard you do it and so has Tom, and we're both here with you. Do you want me to hold your hand, under the table, like I've done in the past?"

"Um, oh yes please, Mother," said Alexandra, gratefully, trying unsuccessfully to convey the impression of needing to think, before accepting her offer. It was a gesture which symbolised their relationship. No matter how much her personal confidence grew – and deep down, Alexandra realised that it was – and whatever successes and achievements that she attained in her life, she knew that it would always be her mother's strength, wisdom, and guidance, that would carry her through.

Linda kissed her daughter, and swallowed her up in an embrace, which engulfed her entire body, making her tingle, and inducing the thought of going to bed together, for a brief moment in both of them. Tomorrow night they would do so again. Alexandra gave a low murmur of pleasure.

By now the news had broken, that the headmistress of Charterhouse had been relieved of her duties, and that Annabel Wood would be filling the position of acting headmistress, until a new appointment was made.

A short while later the doorbell rang.

"Right! Here we go then!" announced Linda. "I think we can guess who our first guests are, since they didn't need us to let them through the gate."

She squeezed her daughter's hand encouragingly, and then let her go, to begin her duties for the night.

***

"Good evening, Mrs Clark! Good evening, Tom!" said Alexandra, smiling, as she opened the front porch door of The Grange. "Do come in."

"Good evening, Alexandra!" they both replied, as they stepped inside.

Alexandra closed the door. "Let me take your coats," she said. They slipped them off, and she hung them in the cloakroom.

Tom was wearing his dinner suit, and to Alexandra's pleasure he had his bow tie on, immaculately tied. They kissed briefly.

Fiona was wearing a long flowing red gown with a thigh length split at the front and back, and matching elbow length gloves.

"If you'd like to follow me into the parlour, my mother is there."

She led the way that Fiona and Tom well knew, but given the rank and status of many of the people on the guest list, Linda had given her daughter instructions to observe strict formalities for everybody tonight.

"Mrs Clark and Master Tom Ryder, Mother!" Alexandra announced, as she motioned them into the parlour. She caught Tom's eye as they entered, and both smirked slightly. It felt really strange for her to be calling her boyfriend that.

"Good evening both of you!" said Linda, warmly." Welcome. What would you like to drink?"

"A whisky please, Linda," said Fiona.

"A dry sherry please, Mrs Radcliffe," said Tom.

"Alexandra?"

"The same as Tom, please, Mother,"

"And I'll join you," said Linda. She poured three sherries and a whisky, and handed them to everybody.

"It's nice to be back at The Grange again," said Fiona. She and Linda didn't visit each other's houses very often, despite their close proximity and being the only two in the hamlet. It was largely only on special occasions.

"How were things at work, this afternoon?" asked Linda.

"Fine. Nothing special to report," replied Fiona. "Quite a quiet finish to the week really. I gather that things were rather different at Charterhouse though. You were successful in your motion then, Linda?"

"Indeed I was. It was close though. Three votes each, with one abstention. Luckily the Chair favoured my position, and her casting vote won the day."

"Congratulations on your success." said Fiona. "I'll bet Mrs Spencer's hopping mad!"

"Well it can't have come as *that* much of a surprise to her, given the scandal that's broken out there, over the last week. But she ..."

She was interrupted by the phone ringing. "Oh, if you'll excuse me, that will be our next guest, waiting at the gate."

She went to the phone and the monitor came on, revealing James' face. "Good evening, James!" she said. "Drive on up to The Grange, and Alexandra will greet Her Majesty at the door."

"Right you are Linda! Coming up!"


"I assume you heard that, Alexandra," said Linda. "Our most special guest of the night, has arrived. You'd better run along, and let her in!"

Alexandra gulped slightly, and then stood up, smoothing herself down. She cleared her throat, as she walked out of the parlour, her mother briefly touching her hand, as she passed. Walking down the passage, she checked that her hair looked immaculate.

As this was the queen and her bodyguards arriving, this time, she opened the door, and stood waiting.

James carefully parked the car on their courtyard, at the end of their drive. Before it had even stopped moving, her bodyguards had exited the car, and the door was opened for Queen Alexandra to get out. Then, flanked by her security, lady-in-waiting, and James, she walked to the entrance of The Grange.

Alexandra did a perfect curtsey, as the queen reached her. "Your Majesty!" she said, smiling broadly. She shook the queen's hand. "Welcome to The Grange!"

"Thank you, Alexandra!" said the queen.

"Please come in, Ma'am!" invited Alexandra, motioning with her hand.

As The queen stood in the hallway, her lady-in-waiting slipped the coat that she was wearing, off her shoulders. This would be kept in her possession, throughout the evening. The queen was dressed in a long white gown, with two knee length splits at the front and the same at the back. On her arms she wore a pair of long white gloves, and at her neck, a silver broach.

Meanwhile, Alexandra handed James her swipe card to open the hamlet gate. He nodded, and giving his leave to Queen Alexandra, he went back outside, and hurried down to the end of Elmswood's drive. Linda had arranged that once he'd driven the queen to The Grange, he would then stay by the gate, and swipe it open, as each guest arrived, so that she wouldn't have to keep letting them in herself at the house, and the parlour wouldn't be continually interrupted by the telephone ringing.

"If you'd like to follow me to the parlour, Ma'am, my mother is there. Two guests have already arrived, Mrs Fiona Clark and her stepson, Master Tom Ryder – my boyfriend!"

"Ah, Tom!" said Queen Alexandra. "Good. I've been looking forward to this. Lead on, Miss Radcliffe!"

"Certainly, Ma'am!" Alexandra took the queen and her bodyguards down the passage, to the parlour.

"Her Royal Highness, Queen Alexandra! Mother!" she called at the door. Linda, Fiona and Tom stopped talking and all rose to their feet.

"Your Majesty!" they said together. Linda and Fiona curtseyed, and Tom bowed. As it was his first meeting with the queen, he had been instructed on the correct etiquette, by his stepmother.

Queen Alexandra's bodyguards quickly surveyed the room, and then satisfied, they withdrew.

"Will you have a drink, Ma'am?" asked Linda. "I think you'll find that The Grange is well stocked with just about every alcoholic beverage that exists on Geratica."

"Linda Radcliffe, what sort of a stupid question is that?" demanded the queen. "I intend to indulge the Radcliffes' legendary reputation as dinner party hosts to the maximum. A gin and tonic to start with, please."

"Well, Ma'am, I'm not sure whether to apologise for my foolishness, or thank you for the compliment to my household!" replied Linda.

"Never mind about that, just get me the blasted drink, Linda!" ordered the queen, looking across at Alexandra and winking at her.

"Ma'am!" said Linda compliantly, and immediately applied the mixture to a glass.

Alexandra was just downing the last of her glass of sherry and she very nearly spat the contents straight out of her mouth, so great was her impulse to laugh. She'd never heard anyone *dare* speak to her mother like that before, even though she knew that it was all good-natured high spirits. Still this *was* the reigning monarch of Geratica, so Alexandra supposed that she could say what she liked.

Fiona was also, clearly highly amused, but she could see that Tom was slightly shocked, this being his very first experience of some of the banter that occurred at court. Most Geraticans only got to see the more official, public side of 'the business' as she'd heard her mother describe it before. She'd been lucky enough to peep behind the scenes on a few occasions, and she was quite used to the fun and games that went on in private. She smiled at him and lifted her eyebrows.

In fact, Tom was the next person that the queen turned to.

"Tom," She extended her hand. "I'm delighted to meet you, at long last. Your stepmother seems to keep you so well hidden! I've met your girlfriend on a few occasions now – and a credit to her mother she really is – but all I know of you are the stories I hear from your stepmother, and sometimes indeed, even Miss Radcliffe."

"I'm delighted to meet you, too, Ma'am," replied Tom. "It's a great honour for me, as a loyal Geratican subject of yours."

"I've told Tom, that crawling will get him everywhere, Ma'am!" said Fiona.

"Would the rest of you like a top-up?" asked Linda, "Or in your case, Alexandra, a refill? You seem to be quaffing that down pretty well!"

Everyone answered in the affirmative, and Linda first attended to Fiona and Tom. Then she came to her daughter, but before she could pour her some more sherry, the doorbell rang again.

"Oh dear! Bad luck, darling. Back to work you go," said Linda, withdrawing the bottle.

"Linda, that's not fair!" said the queen. "She's working twice as hard as you. The least she deserves is another drink."

"That's the trouble with being the butler of this household, Ma'am," said Alexandra, as she got up. "I keep missing out, when I have to perform my duties!"

"Don't you be so cheeky, my girl!" said Linda, as she went out of the parlour. "You managed to finish that first one, before than anyone else!"

Alexandra smiled to herself as she walked down the passage. She and her mother shared a similar sense of humour.

At the door this time, was Lady Caroline Sackville. Alexandra went through the same routine as she had earlier with Fiona and Tom, and announced her to her mother in the parlour. Linda greeted her warmly, but Alexandra noticed Fiona's face darken slightly as she came in. She seemed to get over whatever had triggered her annoyance fairly quickly though, and she was soon talking civilly to her.

Alexandra also found her glass refilled when she returned to her chair. Now that there were a group of guests together, the conversation was beginning to bubble up. She looked across to her mother, standing close to Lady Sackville and saw her smile back at her.

"Thank you, Mother," she communicated secretly to her and Linda acknowledged her.

Gradually all the guests arrived, and were greeted and announced in the same way, by Alexandra.

Altogether there were eight guests, Queen Alexandra, Fiona, Tom, Lady Sackville, Teresa Brockenhurst (the local member of parliament), Dr Clarissa Atkins, Edwina Stockton QC (a lawyer, specialising in parliamentary affairs), and Jemima Huddleston (invited by Linda a few days ago, as a late replacement for Elizabeth Spencer, who had been struck off the guest list, due to recent events). With the exception of Tom, no other family members of the guests were present.

With everyone having arrived, and been taken into the parlour, where they enjoyed their pre-dinner drinks, and indulged in good conversation, Linda went to the kitchen to start the cooking, and Alexandra remained to mingle, as planned. She was getting better at this sort of thing, but all the same, it wasn't something that came naturally to her, unlike her mother who she thought was brilliant at the art. It was difficult to find interesting things to talk to people about, after a while. She had begun to realise though, that she could use a certain amount of dry humour to entertain people and having Tom there this evening proved useful, as together, they could bounce things off each other. Once again, she felt sure that she'd made a wise choice in choosing him for a partner.

\*\*\*

James was in the breakfast room, together with the queen's bodyguards and her lady-in-waiting. They had their own food with them and were already beginning to tuck in. As Linda worked in the kitchen, he slipped in to see her, when he got an opportunity.

"Linda," he said. "I know that Elizabeth was relieved of her duties at Charterhouse, this afternoon. I went home briefly, before I brought Her Majesty over here. I expected her to be there, but she wasn't. I don't know where she was, but her car *was* in the drive, so she must have been there, before me. It was damaged at the front though. It looked like she'd hit someone."

Linda stared hard at him. "Goodness me, thank you, James. I was intending to ask you about that when I got a chance, although I didn't know if you'd have gone home before your duties for Her Majesty tonight. That proves I'm right! The car that she *did* hit, is in a garage just down the road from here, being repaired!" She explained to him what had happened that afternoon, in the Charterhouse car park.

"You're joking!" he exclaimed. "She must have been out of her mind. Have you reported it to the police?"

"Not yet. I initially wasn't going to bother as I couldn't be certain of it, but now, after what Miss Davis told me that she saw, and you this, I have the evidence I need. I shall contact them, as soon as I can!"

\*\*\*

Whilst the dinner party's main course was in preparation, Linda served the canapés. Alexandra was relieved. At least now that people had something to eat, they had an additional item to add to their entertainment.

As Linda had promised, she was ready to serve the soup course shortly afterwards, and she fetched her daughter to help her. She told her what James had said, as they did it.

"When are you going to tell the police, Mother?" asked Alexandra.

"Well providing that I'm still sober, then maybe later, after our guests have departed!" said Linda. "I can't really deal with it at the moment."

Then she went back to the parlour.

"Ladies – and 'gentleman,'!" she called. "Dinner is served. If you'll follow me to the dining room?"

"Ah good," said the queen. "I'm famished!"

They all filed out of the parlour, bringing their unfinished drinks with them, and followed Linda along a passage and down the hall.

***

Everybody took their places at the dinner table.

Queen Alexandra was at the head, with Linda to her first right. Alexandra was sat next to her mother, with Tom to her right, and then to *his* right was Fiona.

To the queen's first left was Edwina Stockton QC, with Dr Clarissa Atkins next to her, followed by Jemima Huddleston to her left, and Teresa Brockenhurst MP, to *her* left. Finally, Lady Caroline Sackville was at the foot.

"What is the soup, Linda?" asked the queen.

"Potato, Ma'am," she informed her.

"And the wine is a 5001 Utipidean white," Linda announced, as she opened two bottles. She and Alexandra began their respective pouring duties, with one bottle each.

Each place had a piece of butter on a side plate. As they all began their soup, Alexandra went around the table with a basket, offering them bread, which everyone accepted. Linda fetched two more wine bottles from the kitchen, for refills. She had several more ready in the kitchen.

"Well, I hope you all enjoy your meal," said Linda, as she and Alexandra were both at last ready to eat.

"Thank you Linda," said the queen. "I'm pleased to see Jemima here, from Castra University. I had a very pleasant lunch there, at the beginning of last week."

"I'm pleased that you enjoyed it, Ma'am," replied Jemima. "We were honoured to receive you as our special guest!" Queen Alexandra nodded to her.

"And it's a pleasure for me to be at Mrs Radcliffe's household too," Jemima continued. "I was quite happy to oblige her, when Mrs Spencer suddenly became – unavailable!"

"She's busy visiting those 'drama students' that her daughter brought into Charterhouse!" said Fiona, mischievously.

There were guffaws of laughter from the assembled party.

"Mrs Spencer is in fact no longer at Charterhouse, as you're well aware, Fiona," said Linda. "There was an emergency meeting of the board of governors this afternoon, and it voted to relieve her of her duties, in the light of the college's recent scandal."

"What were the numbers, for and against, just out of interest, Mrs Radcliffe?" asked Edwina Stockton.

"Three each way, with one abstention," Linda told her. "The chair's casting vote, decided her fate."

"You were always a lucky sod, Mrs Radcliffe!" said Teresa Brockenhurst. "We all know that it was your motion, to propose kicking her out."

"I obviously have to admit that it was a close call. The numbers speak for themselves. But I assure you all that it wasn't just 'luck'. The case against her was strong, and I believe that in the end, there was no other outcome that she could reasonably have expected."

"I understand that you weren't so fortunate with your car afterwards, Linda," remarked Queen Alexandra.

"No indeed, I was not," confirmed Linda. "A few minutes after our meeting was finished, but before I'd left the boardroom, somebody crashed their car into the back of mine, in the Charterhouse car park! And I'm now 99% certain that I know who it was – due to having spoken to two witnesses."

"Two?" asked Fiona. "I thought you said that only one girl at Charterhouse, could actually say categorically that they saw Mrs Spencer do it, before speeding away?"

"More evidence has since come to light," said Linda. "As most of you will know, her husband James Spencer, is Her Majesty's chauffeur, and I liaise with him quite regularly. He's obviously here tonight, and he's informed me that he's been home, and noticed that his wife's car has damage to its front. He believes she must have hit something. Unfortunately, she wasn't there, and at this moment, we are unaware of exactly where she is. I'm not going to say any more about it, as it's now likely that I'll be referring the matter on to the authorities."

She stood up and changed the subject. "More wine for anyone?" she asked.

She went round her designated side of the table and topped up the glasses. Alexandra did the same on hers.

Then Linda looked around the table. "Well if you've all finished, I hope you enjoyed the soup, and that you'll be just as approving of the main course. If you'll excuse us for one moment, Alexandra, and I will clear these dishes away, and then it will be time for the main event!"

"Thank you, Linda. I for one, found it delicious," said the queen.

The other guests voiced their concurrence.

"Good. I'm glad," said Linda, and she and Alexandra began their preparations to serve the main course.

# CHAPTER 7

In the kitchen, Linda and Alexandra dished up the fish and then between them, carried the plates into the dining room, and Alexandra brought in some vegetable dishes and placed them on the table. One by one, the guests were served and most were generous with their praise for how it looked, and expressed their impatience to begin tasting it. Once everybody had their main course, Linda told them that they were, of course, welcome to start, and she and Alexandra refilled the wine glasses once more. Linda retrieved two more bottles from the kitchen and then she herself, sat down to eat.

For a while, the conversation of the group was convivial, as they all enjoyed their meal. People chatted lightly to the person next to them. Gradually though, as they neared the end of the course, thoughts began to turn towards current affairs and matters of state, and the talk broadened to more of a group discussion.

The health of the economy was always a popular topic. Teresa and Linda were largely on the same side politically, and the MP was very supportive of Linda's handling of it. She was however becoming concerned, that a growing number of others – a minority, but enough to cause disruption – were beginning to speak about the need for a change of direction. They were tapping into a mood that was becoming popular in certain sections of Geratican life, that there was a prevalent "have and have not" element, running through society.

"Blast it, that's an old, old, story that's been peddled about for generations!" declared Linda contemptuously, as she finished the last of her fish. "No matter what you do, you can't avoid some people being better off than others. That's just a simple fact of life, in any civilised culture."

She took a sip of wine.

"I've said regularly, that I believe that our economy has never been in such good shape, and I strongly argue that since I took over the reins, twelve years ago, there are very few people who haven't become better off!"

"Oh, I certainly agree, Mrs Radcliffe," said Teresa. "But although I personally feel quite safe in this seat in Greenacres, I know that there are others of similar mind to ours, who do not feel so comfortable, and feel that we might need to make some concessions, even though it will be a while before we have another parliamentary election."

"Two and a half years, to be precise," snapped Linda. "You're only halfway through your current term."

"Two and a half years isn't that long, Mrs Radcliffe!" argued Teresa.

"I think that the argument is mainly, that certain groups in society have seen their wealth grow in greater multitude and at a faster rate than others," said Edwina. "Therefore while all have benefited, some have more so than others, and even on occasions, at the expense of those others."

As her mother had promised, she was holding Alexandra's hand, underneath the table. Alexandra sneaked a discreet look at her. She knew that this sort of talk was guaranteed to make her blood boil, and she could already sense her fury growing.

"Richer or poorer. Faster or slower. It all amounts to the same argument!" said Linda angrily. "And my *answer* is just the same! Well, tell me then. What would these people have me do, if I was to take Geratica, in the name of the queen, down this 'change of direction'?"

"Well, I'm not necessarily suggesting that this is a view I favour, but some do desire substantially more public spending, and then that the wealthier members of society, pay higher taxes to help fund it. There are even those who wish for parliament to become independent of the monarch, so that it can make its own laws, and set up state departments to govern and control Geratica."

At this Linda exploded. "What? This is revolutionary talk! At one time these people would have been executed for treason, for spouting such filth! Our whole system of government is based around the ruling monarch, and it's always a female."

"At the risk of sounding patronising, let me remind everyone – I am Her Majesty's senior court administrator, and I advise her, then she decides the laws, and I see that they are administered as efficiently, and effectively as possible, through parliament. MPs get their chance to scrutinise the bills before they're passed, and can get them amended if necessary. If enough MPs refuse to ratify a bill, it can even on occasions be scrapped. They can ask Her Majesty questions in the House on a weekly basis. But they cannot pass their own laws. That is not their role, nor what the people elect them to do. They are in parliament to oversee the bills directed by the court, and primarily to pass them into law effectively. That is all!"

"If I may have a say in how I reign over *my own queendom?*" said Queen Alexandra indignantly. "If parliament and I were to be independent of each other, what do these people whom you speak of, propose that *I* do? Am I not to have a role, in this brave new world that they crave? I have to remain on the throne you know, to ensure the continuity of Geratica!"

"Please, Ma'am, as I said at the start, these are not my views," said

Edwina. "These MPs and those in public life who support them, need to speak for themselves. I can tell you for certain, that proposals such as this would mean major constitutional and legal change, which might cause some severe turbulence to our way of life! As to your role, Ma'am, I'm not sure if any of them have a clear idea, other than to ensure that we always have a queen, and that there is a successor."

"Anyhow, leaving that issue aside, I strongly disagree with the change of direction in economic policy being suggested!" remarked Linda. "I'm certainly not going to pay lip service to it, by making concessions. I believe in private enterprise, and wealth creation for the individual. Any Geratican should have the chance to become better off, through working hard. They should be rewarded for their aspiration, and not be made to feel guilty about having done well for themselves! We endeavour to keep taxation as low as possible for *everybody* and will even cut taxes if we can – thought obviously these must be affordable. The court does ensure that measures exist to provide help for those who need it.

"We consider very carefully, public service needs, and allocate as much of the queendom's budget to it as we can afford. A certain amount of taxation is obviously required, but it simply isn't financially viable to spend and spend money on everything, and then clobber high taxation on 'the rich' when you need even more! It is primarily hard work and thrift, from private enterprise and the individual, that creates the wealth and employment for the economy, not high taxation, which will only discourage and weaken it. I don't think that it's fair, either. We will gradually have to borrow more and more from our banking system, to make up the shortfall and end up bankrupting the queendom! In the end everybody suffers – and actually the poorest most of all. We must keep a tight hold on the purse strings, and not spend money that we don't have. The Bank of Geratica serves the Royal Court, and is fully supportive of its economic policies. And by the way, the court will not reduce funds from the budget towards the Geratican Scientific Research Centre, in order to increase public expenditure either. Those who claim that, since nobody appears to be able to travel between Geratica and Geraticai now, it's a waste of money monitoring the parallel world, need to remember that we can't say for absolute certainty that there are no more mongrels in existence there. We think so, but we must still be alert to any possible threat from Geraticai. And the Research Centre does a lot of fine scientific work besides that."

"I believe that Her Majesty and I are at one on the approach we take, regarding the economy, and I will not allow these 'progressive,' and revolutionary hotheads, who are motivated primarily by envy, to blow us off course, and wreck everything that we've achieved over the past decade!" Linda concluded.

She took another sip from her glass and seeing that more wine was required, got up and started around the table again. Alexandra followed suit on the other side.

"Indeed we are at one, Linda," said the queen. "I am at heart a traditionalist on this subject, and although not an economist, believe that the way we have organised our finances over the years, has served all of Geratica well. I have every confidence in my senior court administrator, to keep my queendom prosperous."

"Thank you, Ma'am," said Linda, as she returned to her chair.

Alexandra squeezed her mother's hand tight from the inside and gripped at her fingers. Linda's eyes shifted ever so slightly to look at her, surprised, sensing that she was seeking to say something that was on her mind, and needed her mother's coaxing to give her the confidence to do it. She stroked her daughter's fingers gently, and engulfed her hand inside of her own.

Somehow Alexandra began to feel some inspiration from somewhere, and for the first time, she believed that she could contribute *something* to this kind of gathering of minds. It was a similar feeling to when she had been in the wood at Elmsbrook with Tom, and suddenly had the confidence to propose a relationship between them.

Then she spoke. "I think it should also be pointed out, that seventy years ago, much the same things were being said!" Everybody looked around at her in surprise, with the exception of Linda, who had correctly anticipated this significant moment.

Her daughter continued, "In those days the nobility held all the power, and there began to be great resentment of them, by the 'common people' thinking that they were out of touch, and having great wealth, whilst the rest of Geratican society was poor. At that time, they might have had a point – sorry Lady Sackville, I mean no personal offence!"

"None taken, Miss Radcliffe!" said Lady Caroline, smiling.

"In those days, there really was a huge gap between the 'rich' and 'poor', but surely it has considerably narrowed now? After the '4941 Budget Crisis', when Lady Monica Dixon-Taylor failed to get her budget passed by parliament, and had to resign, we came nearer than ever, before or since, to having some kind of 'revolution' and it was decided that from then onwards people of my mother's rank in society, should always fill her position, to preserve a link between the nobility and the ordinary people. Feelings were running so high that Queen Matilda the second, almost had to abdicate, in favour of her daughter. But in the end, a way out of the crisis was found, as I mentioned just now, and although I too am not an economist, and therefore not quite as adept as my mother at explaining the exact workings of our financial methods, I think that since then, the lives of most Geraticans have improved dramatically.

"I think that, on balance, our approach since the crisis of 4941, has been the right one. One of my hobbies is researching the affairs of the planet Earth. After scanning their information on this subject, I know that this idea from these 'revolutionary hotheads' was widely tried there. They called it 'socialism'. I must inform you that in several places, it was considered a failure – in one or two cases, even a disaster – and in some parts, officially abandoned – correctly so, in my opinion. I think that we should draw a lesson from that, back home in Geratica. However, just as after 4941, I'm sure that we'll find ways to adapt our policies to suit a changing climate, by peaceful and reasonable means, without abandoning our basic traditional principles. That's what we've always managed to do, throughout our own history. It's the Geratican way!

"Speaking personally, although I *am* of course, naturally biased, I think that my mother has done Geratica a great service, during the tenure of her current position, and we should all be grateful to her. In general, we have greatly prospered from the policies which she's instigated for the queendom."

This time, it was Alexandra who took a grateful sip of wine from her glass, relieved that she seemed to have managed to make her points relatively clearly and covered everything that she'd set out to do. She actually felt quite proud of herself.

Her own pride in her performance, was considerably dwarfed by her mother's however. She, more than anyone else, knew the struggle that her daughter had with her confidence, but she felt she'd spoken brilliantly, considering that this was the first time that she'd really done so, in this sort of company. She was delighted to hear Alexandra's solid support for the basic principles of financial management that she herself believed passionately in, and particularly thrilled by the ringing personal endorsement that she'd been given by her. Tomorrow night she would reward her handsomely, by showing her appreciation upstairs, in the mistress bedroom.

There was a brief silence from the guests, as they digested what Alexandra had said. Some were still recovering from the shock. Teresa was the first to find her voice.

"Alexandra," she asked, "When you eventually finish your education, what are your career plans?"

"To be honest, I'm not entirely decided," replied Alexandra. "My mother is repeatedly admonishing me for 'underselling' myself, so I'll be bold and say, that there seem to be a number of subjects that I could study for a degree, if I get ... sorry 'when' I get to university! Which of them that I choose, I suppose will influence my decision. Plus, if it's not too vulgar a thing to say, the amount of money I'll earn!"

A ripple of laughter broke out around the table. "The girl takes after her mother, there," remarked the queen.

"I do get annoyed with some people who condemn others, for having the audacity to accept another job because it's offering more money," said Linda. "Everybody needs it, after all."

"There's nothing wrong with being motivated by money," said Fiona. "I certainly always have been, above all else. I've no time at all for those – socialists, as Alexandra calls them – either. I'd have them put up against the palace wall and shot!"

"Well, even I wouldn't go that far!" said Linda.

"But then I'm a hanging and horsewhipping supporter!" declared Fiona. "Of course, just before my time, the Court abolished the death penalty."

"I am of course, at one with my Senior Court Administrator over that too, Fiona," asserted Queen Alexandra. "It would not have happened if I wasn't."

"I believe you're hoping to come to Castra, Alexandra?" remarked Jemima Huddleston, changing the subject. "As you probably know, I met your mother last week."

"That's correct, Mrs Huddleston," Alexandra confirmed. "I know that it'll be hard work to get there, but I think I'm capable."

"What I was actually going to suggest, Alexandra," said Teresa, "was that perhaps you might like to consider a career in politics. That little speech you made just then, was one of the finest 'debuts' that I've heard in years! You take after your mother in your articulacy, too."

"No, I don't think that's very likely, Mrs Huddleston!" exclaimed Alexandra. "I'm grateful to you for the compliment, but I actually really *hate* public speaking – and even in a private gathering such as this, or some kind of meeting, I still don't feel particularly comfortable stating my opinions. People tell me that – when I do it – I do it well, and I will if I have to, but it's not something that either comes naturally to me, or I enjoy. I *don't* take after my mother there! She definitely *is* a natural!"

"Well my daughter certainly hasn't done badly tonight!" remarked Linda. "I think she may be becoming the kind of girl, who becomes more emboldened after she's had a certain amount to drink! But to be serious, it *is* probably likely that her future will be more in the background, and I'm perfectly happy about that. That *is* her natural territory, and there she'll do considerable and just as valuable service to Geratica, in her own quiet way. Anyhow, knowing that she's receiving a hefty pay cheque each week, will more than make up for any disappointment that I might feel about her absence from the public arena! I imagine my potential son-in-law will be quite happy with that, too!"

Tom laughed. "Alexandra has all her buttons on," he declared. "I've always thought that she's capable of far more than she realises."

"Tom has the ability to make me see that sometimes, and help me to achieve things," confirmed Alexandra. "That's part of why I proposed a relationship with him."

"Talking of proposing a relationship, I think that it's high time, I made an announcement," said the queen. "A short time ago, I too embarked upon one – with Lord George Sackville! I thought that since we had this dinner party tonight, and Lady Caroline would be in attendance, then today would be an apt day to propose it to him, so that it could be announced tonight. And needless to say he accepted. He would have gone straight to the Tower, if he hadn't!"

First there was a very brief shocked silence at the surprise revelation, followed a big laugh at the queen's humour, and then a succession of congratulatory expressions and good wishes. Linda noticed that Fiona's was muted, bordering in fact on the non-existent.

"Well this calls for a celebration, Ma'am!" she exclaimed. "Alexandra, come and help me fetch some more wine from the kitchen. And whilst we're there, we'll dish up the dessert course."

"Of course, Mother," replied her daughter, obediently.

Between them, they cleared away the main course dishes, and made their way through to the kitchen.

***

"Mother! Did you know about the queen's relationship proposal?" asked Alexandra, as they worked together in the kitchen. "Was that why you invited Lady Caroline?"

"No, darling, I didn't know! I invited Lady Caroline here tonight, for political purposes, more than anything. The question of marriage, and the eventual succession has been a subject of growing importance for a while now, and I've been playing 'matchmaker' and gently trying to bring the queen and Lord George together. Then, at the beginning of last week – the same day that Queen Alexandra went to Castra University, in fact – she indicated to me that he was indeed her most likely suitor, and told me to tell Lady Caroline that Lord George should know that he was in favour. I must confess that I wasn't expecting this stage to be reached quite so quickly, but I'm delighted nonetheless!"

"But that's not all of it," she continued. "That was a wonderful contribution that you made to that discussion. You made the most sensible and wise comments of everybody! Well done! I'm so proud of you!" She kissed her daughter, who beamed with pleasure.

"Yet again, you've surprised us all," she continued. "I realised that something was about to happen, just before you started speaking. Was it just inspiration again, that gave you the confidence to do it?"

"Yes, Mother. I found it from somewhere. I'm not quite sure exactly what came over me!"

"Well let's hope that whatever it was does so again, sweetheart!" exclaimed Linda.

"I could tell that you were becoming boiling mad, when the 'change of direction' in economic policy started to be discussed, Mother," said Alexandra. "Then you really lost your temper, when you found out that some people wanted to, effectively, change our constitution! I suppose I felt that someone needed to say what I did. Maybe it was the same as when I had my meeting with Queen Alexandra. If I do feel strongly enough about something, then it can sometimes help to inspire me with confidence."

"Hmm, maybe," said her mother. "And you're right. I was furious! This kind of revolutionary thinking is seeping into everything, and I'm not standing for it! The economy is booming and the standard of living for everybody, generally, has never been higher. That's beyond question, and as long as it's the case, then our economic policy is working, and there's no need to change it. That's the prime objective of any sensible economic plan, and everything else is secondary. That's obviously a simplified version of what I said, but fundamentally it's true."

"And as for making parliament and the monarch independent of one another, well, I spelt out the court's position, and I will always believe that it's the way things should be done, to make things work efficiently. I do acknowledge that times and attitudes change, and sometimes you have to adapt to meet them, but as you suggest, to do what these people propose, would force us to change the constitution that we've had, for as long as our records go back to, and as an arch-traditionalist, I am *totally* against that!"

"Yes, Mother," said Alexandra, simply.

# CHAPTER 8

Back in the dining room, as they all prepared to eat their dessert, Linda and her daughter went around the table with another bottle of wine each.

Tom was amazed. "Do you usually drink this much at these parties?" he asked Alexandra.

"Oh. Have you had enough?" she asked him with concern and touched his arm. "I won't pour you any more if you have. You don't want to be getting tipsy, especially on the night of your first meeting with the queen! And don't forget, that we'll be offering after dinner drinks in the parlour, a little later too."

"Well, just a small bit, please, then, Angel," he answered.

"Say when then," said Alexandra, as she started to pour the dessert wine.

"When!" said Tom, when his glass was half full.

As Alexandra had expected, when they'd served the desserts, the conversation was presently dominated by Queen Alexandra's news. She stressed that she had made no decision yet, on when she might consider a possible engagement to be married.

"When will you want the news to be officially announced, Ma'am?" asked Linda. "Obviously you can rest assured that no one present here this evening, will speak a word of it to anyone, before then!" She glanced briefly around the table with a warning look to them all.

"Whenever you're ready, Linda," said the queen. "The sooner it's made official, the less chance that there'll be of any accidental leaks to the media!"

"My thoughts exactly, Ma'am" Linda concurred.

"Ma'am, this is of course your decision, and I won't mention it again after tonight, but are you really sure about this? Have you really considered all your possible suitors? You have several – and many other admirers also!"

Queen Alexandra, Linda and Lady Caroline exchanged brief glances.

"Fiona, this is not the place, nor now the time to -" began Linda.

The queen interrupted her. "I am indeed, most certain of this Fiona! As some of you may be aware, I have known Lord George for many years and he was always very much 'in the running for the job', as it were! I love him very much, and I do genuinely believe that he will make a fine consort to me."

"Very good, Ma'am," replied Fiona. "I'm just anxious to ensure that Linda hasn't put undue pressure on you to make a hasty decision. I personally wouldn't be so bold as to suggest a match to you, rather I would leave it entirely up to your discretion."

The queen lost patience. "How *dare* you, Fiona!" she said furiously, banging her spoon against the dish – and this time Alexandra knew it was no jocular admonishment. "I have just told you, that I am certain, and that I believe he will be a fine consort! I cannot be clearer than that. It was *entirely* my decision. I will not tolerate any suggestion that I might have in any way been pressurised into it, by Linda or anyone else! You will withdraw it, or leave this house immediately! Your stepson is welcome to stay, if he wishes, but you will not. This may be Linda's dinner party, but you are embarrassing both her, and my potential mother-in-law, as well as considerably annoying me, the ruling monarch of Geratica. I have made my decision, and yet you continue to question it!"

"I am most sincerely sorry, Ma'am!" said Fiona. "I went too far, and I of course withdraw that allegation. I shall say no more on the subject, and never raise that suggestion again. I meant no disrespect to you, Lady Caroline, or Linda."

"None taken," said Linda.

"Or from me," agreed Lady Caroline – with just the faintest trace of reluctance, Alexandra thought.

"Apology accepted," asserted the queen. "Perhaps we can put it down to you, not being able to hold your drink!"

A couple of stifled laughs followed, and Fiona went nearly as bright red as her gown. She was famous for being prolific in her consumption of alcohol – even more than the average Geratican female – and still rarely suffering any adverse effects. It was a little embarrassing for a woman in her position to be accused of the possibility of being drunk.

"I can *assure* you that I am perfectly sober, Ma'am!" she told Queen Alexandra.

The queen gave her a quizzical look, and then nodded in acknowledgement. She actually hadn't thought that at all, but just wanted to make Fiona sweat a little.

Alexandra glanced at Tom, anxiously. His stepmother had just been given a stern rebuke, and despite their sometimes uneasy feelings about Fiona, she thought that it must have been acutely embarrassing for him to witness. She felt sorry that it had happened, during his first experience of being in the queen's presence.

There was a pause, as everyone waited for someone else to relieve the tension created by the exchange.

Linda eventually obliged. "Dr Atkins, I thought I'd invite you here, just so as we could all have a brief chat about the scientific thinking on the problem with the planet's core. Some of us have already discussed this in great detail with you at the palace, and please be assured, I'm not going to ask you to give another talk!"

"Well I'm quite relieved to hear that, Mrs Radcliffe," she said. "I'm not sure if I could, after such a sumptuous feast!"

"Does anybody have any questions though?" Linda asked the other guests. "I invited Mrs Huddleston along at the last minute, to replace Mrs Spencer as a representative of the educational establishment and – I believe you have a scientific background, like hers?

"That's correct, Mrs Radcliffe," said Jemima.

"I'm sure that most of us here are now aware of the problem," said Teresa. "Although in common with quite a lot of ordinary Geraticans, we probably don't feel quite as obsessive about it, as Elizabeth Spencer! It probably might be worth at least going down there, to have a look and see if anything can be done, but have there been any more developments in achieving the possibility?"

"The technology is still a 'work in progress' and these things can't suddenly happen overnight," said Clarissa. "I wouldn't like to comment on exactly when, but I'm sure that it won't be *too* long, before we are able to say that this can be done safely, and we're ready. There's certainly little doubt that it's *possible* to do it.

"What would happen to the two parallel worlds, should we attempt an operation to fix the problem, we really cannot tell, and we won't know for certain, or even if *that* is possible, until we are actually there."

"Of course it was concluded long ago that, apart from in the mongrels' case, it was not possible to travel between the two parallel worlds," added Jemima. "The numbers of mongrels have decreased rapidly in Geratica in more recent times and they are now, as far as we can tell, extinct. We still don't know what caused their existence and perhaps we never will. Therefore, there's no evidence present, to suspect that we are in any immediate danger from Geraticai and this is probably the reason why for many, this isn't a subject of high priority to them. It tends to be confined more to the scientific fraternity, which as Mrs Radcliffe pointed out earlier, is the specialist area of both Mrs Spencer and myself. Elizabeth's interest is heightened still further, by her feeling that the basic characteristics of the core should be adapted, in order to change the personality traits of Geratican males and females, and further her ambitions for 'Male Rights'. But this is obviously controversial, and does raise some fundamentally ethical questions. I for one would rather not travel down that particular road."

"It potentially raises even more serious questions, than in the case of separating parliament from the monarchy." agreed Edwina.

"Have you any idea of what the cost of the operation might be, Clarissa?" asked Teresa. "Is it affordable?"

"Oh. Well that's not really my area," replied Dr Atkins. "Mrs Radcliffe would be the one to answer that."

"I don't have the precise figures at hand, so I shan't give any quotation, but suffice to say the money will be available," asserted Linda. "I should point out that although my own late husband was the last mongrel that we know of to be living in Geratica – making my daughter a half-mongrel of course – that doesn't necessarily mean that there are none amongst us. It could still be *possible* for spies to infiltrate our society, from Geraticai, though presumably their numbers on that world have diminished in the same way, so there are unlikely to be very many. Therefore, we should still be vigilant and that is why I believe that this isn't *quite* such a low priority issue, as some others suggest.

"In at least one respect, I do find myself in agreement with Mrs Spencer – I think it is important for us to visit the core – and this is indeed the position of Her Majesty's Court. Therefore, the funding for an operation of this kind, would always be set aside, in any yearly budget, regardless of economic circumstance. But it would only happen, providing that it is considered safe to do so, and any alterations that we might make once we were down there, would be in relation to the schism only, and not to change any fundamental personality traits. I recently wrote a letter to Mrs Spencer, on behalf of Her Majesty, setting out this whole position, as far as she and her court were concerned. In it, I said that Her Majesty hoped that this would settle the matter. Time only, will tell whether it ultimately has, or hasn't!.

"I have obviously had many clashes with Mrs Spencer over the issue of 'Male Rights' and I don't want to get into that specific subject, except to say that I would never favour discrimination against them, but I believe in the traditional idea of a Geratican society, where the female is dominant. Again, Her Majesty and her court alluded to this issue, in her recent trip to Castra University, when she said that male schools were a laudable idea, but that we have no plans to extend compulsory education to both sexes at the moment – which you will remember, Mrs Huddleston."

"Of course, Mrs Radcliffe," confirmed Jemima.

Then she looked across the table. "Changing the subject slightly, I gather that you're planning to perform a concert at Charterhouse, in honour of Philippa Barrington, Alexandra? How is that progressing?"

Alexandra coughed lightly before replying, "I am indeed, Mrs Huddleston. It's going well, thank you. I've appointed a board to assist me with the organisation, and we're planning to hold a sponsored walk in Buckmore, for the girls at Charterhouse, to raise money to fund the concert. The board will do most of that side of things for me, so that I can concentrate mainly on the performance itself. If all goes according to plan, it will hopefully be staged shortly before the end of this term, before the Festival of Divinity holiday."

"In time, for you to be judged for the position of college champion?"

"Well, yes. I am hoping to win that honour, I will admit Mrs Huddleston, but as you may be aware, I am something of a fan of Philippa Barrington's music, and just the honour of performing it at Charterhouse, with her in attendance, will be a thrill to me!"

"And you're receiving private tuition from the woman herself, so I understand?"

"Yes, Mrs Huddleston I am. Once a week. She's really nice."

"Good. Well I wish you all the best in your endeavours," said Jemima. "Perhaps this time next year, you'll be the Charterhouse Champion at Castra! And by the way. If you meet me there, then you won't have to call me 'Mrs Huddleston' every time you address me. Nowadays, we aren't averse to a bit of informality at Castra, every now and then!"

"Sorry – er – Jemima," said Alexandra. "It's just the way I've been brought up to address people, by my mother."

"Well you are certainly a credit to her, Alexandra!" remarked Jemima.

Alexandra smiled. "Well! Thank you, Jemima," she replied.

"Yes well I don't care if people consider me old fashioned," said Linda. "Because in many ways, I am! I like to see the correct formalities observed, and children should have respect for their elders – especially their mother, as the head of the household, and I have indeed always been very lucky that my daughter is one of the best, in that regard!"

"And what I like to see is a drink in my hand and a cigar by my side, Linda!" said the queen.

Linda looked around the table. "In that case, would everybody care to withdraw back to the parlour, for some more entertainment?" she asked.

"Certainly Linda. Please lead the way," replied Queen Alexandra, and they all gradually trooped out of the dining room.

***

Linda took an order for tea and coffees, once everyone was seated back in the parlour. She left Alexandra in charge of seeing to their alcoholic drinks, and went off to the kitchen, checking on James in the breakfast room with the rest of the queen's staff, at the same time. She told them of Queen Alexandra's news. Linda had decided to instruct the palace to release the statement, announcing the queen's relationship with Lord George Sackville, immediately, as there was probably still time to get into the following morning's papers. The sooner the news was official, the better, she felt.

She put the kettle on and whilst she waited for it to boil, readied the cups and saucers with one hand and dialled the palace with the other, the receiver under her arm. There were always duty staff there at any time of day, to deal with any important situation or emergency that might come up, outside of normal working hours.

After she got through, there was a slight hint of panic, and Linda suspected that with the queen away for the evening, and not expected back until late, the staff might have been taking the opportunity to have an easy night. They probably weren't expecting to hear from their most senior boss, besides Her Majesty herself, at all.

She informed them of the news, to some excitement on the other end of the line, and dictated a statement off the top of her head, to be released immediately.

That done and with the tea and coffees made, she put some after dinner mints on the tray with them and carried it into the parlour.

"Ma'am," she said quietly into the queen's ear, when she found the right moment, "I have informed the palace of your good news, and asked them to release a statement to the media, immediately."

"Goodness me!" exclaimed Queen Alexandra. "That was quick, Linda!"

"I thought that if we did it now, we should just make tomorrow morning's front pages, Ma'am," she replied.

"Yes, good thinking, Linda," said the queen. "Very wise, as always! Thank you! And now I wish to relax and celebrate!"

# CHAPTER 9

Alexandra went to the piano, and began her next formal duty of the evening, to play some popular pieces of music, to help keep the guests entertained. The conversation turned to their respective plans for the Festival of Divinity, which was now just five weeks away from officially beginning.

Soon afterwards, puffing on a cigar, the queen asked Linda, if she was in the mood for a card game.

"At the risk of appearing impertinent, Ma'am, I think it may now be you who is asking a stupid question!" replied Linda.

The queen's eyebrows rose. "Oh I see! It's like that then, is it? Right, get them out, and we'll begin!"

At the piano, Alexandra was forced to stop for a moment, to put her hand to her mouth. Only her mother, as the queen's closest advisor, could possibly get away with making a comment like that. Beside her, Tom was also in fits.

"Mother will never turn down the challenge of a card game!" remarked Alexandra, quietly.

"Shall we play 'Call!' Ma'am?" asked Linda,

"Excellent!" remarked the queen. "Will anybody else join us?"

Fiona had recovered her usual relaxed manner, after the rather public slap on the wrist that she'd received earlier, and there was less than universal surprise, when she accepted the challenge. Like Linda, she was a keen card player, although less like her, she often frequented bars and casinos during her spare time, and played for money. Although she had lost some, she had won considerably more, swelling her already healthy financial position.

They were also joined by Teresa, and Jemima volunteered to be the dealer.

Teresa was slowly edging towards the limit of her alcohol consumption tolerance. As their game progressed, and the other guests watched, Fiona noticed and she looked across to the piano.

"Alexandra!" she said. "You're neglecting your duties! Teresa's glass is empty!"

Alexandra was still providing some musical accompaniment. After Fiona's request, she looked across to her mother for advice. It wasn't terribly good form to deliberately try to get someone drunk, in order to gain an advantage over them, she felt.

Linda looked back, and acknowledged her concern.

"Do you wish another drink, Mrs Brockenhurst?" she asked.

"Of course. Another stupid question!" replied Teresa, with a very small trace of a slur in her voice.

Well, she'd given her the chance to turn it down. Linda looked across at her daughter, and indicated for her to refill her glass.

It did not take long for Teresa, now slightly the worse for drink, though not embarrassingly so, to be blown out of the game.

The other three competed keenly, before the queen was the next to go out. She lost with the good grace expected from someone in her position, though Alexandra thought it likely that she was hiding some of her true feelings. All the women who she had ever watched her mother play cards with, were highly competitive, and did not take defeat easily.

And so, just Linda and Fiona remained at the card table. Neither women were regular smokers, but they often indulged, during these kinds of activities. Like Queen Alexandra, Linda favoured a cigar, whilst Fiona smoked a pipe.

As they puffed away, regarding each other cautiously, Fiona made a suggestion.

"As it's just the two of us left, shall we spice things up a little, by putting some cash on the table?" she asked, enticingly.

Linda considered. Although, she enjoyed participating in the game, she wasn't by nature a gambler, and didn't play for money all that often. But she did have the occasional flutter, with relatively small amounts. She was sure that, after her earlier embarrassment and obvious displeasure, Fiona would be particularly keen to beat her tonight.

"How much were you thinking of?" she asked, in return.

Fiona reached for her handbag, by her chair, and pulled out some notes. "I'll put down one hundred geros!" she declared.

After a few more seconds of thought, Linda made her decision.

"OK I'll match that!" she replied. "I don't keep cash like that in the house, but I'll write a cheque, made payable to you, from today. If I win, then it will be destroyed immediately."

"Done!" Fiona agreed, and dropped her money on to the table.

Linda glanced at her daughter. "Alexandra, go and retrieve my chequebook!"

"Of course, Mother. Right away," Alexandra left the parlour for the study. She was surprised. As far as she knew, this was the largest sum of money that her mother had ever contributed, to a cash pot such as this. And she had already had one great victory today, at Charterhouse. Presumably she was feeling lucky! Alexandra hurried along the passages. There would be great interest in the final stage of this game, and it wouldn't do to keep the audience waiting, let alone her mother and Fiona.

She opened the study door. Alexandra knew where Linda kept her chequebook. Going to the safe, on the wall, she entered the combination to unlock it. She reached inside and carried out her mother's order, then locked up the safe, and returned immediately to the parlour, closing the study door once more, behind her.

"Thank you, darling," said Linda, as her daughter handed her the chequebook. From a drawer, Linda took out a pen and wrote the cheque, as she had promised. She put the pen back in the drawer and placed the cheque on the table, with Fiona's cash.

Now Jemima dealt the cards again, and the final game began. Alexandra could see the determination in each of their faces. The combination of their mutual strong desire to be the best, the incident earlier, the vast quantity of alcohol that they'd drunk, and now the money on offer, seemed to be concentrating their minds. Although she hadn't yet summoned up enough confidence to play with the other women, herself, she did enjoy watching. As a spectacle, it could be quite exciting and she always found the ultra-competitiveness of some of the women, fascinating. She began to play another piece on the piano, as they started.

The game consisted of fifty-one cards. Eleven of these were 'primary' cards, numbered 1 to 10, and finishing with the highest valued 'Queen'. In addition, there were forty other 'secondary' cards. Someone dealt each player seven cards, and the rest of the pack was placed in the middle of the table. The object of the game was to make a straight consisting of six consecutive numbers, from 1 up to and including the queen, from the seven that you were dealt. One card was immediately discarded, and placed at the bottom of the pack, and then another was taken from the top, alternately by each player. The "secondary" cards were of no value, and were just there as "decoys" to help you when you needed to discard a card. Each player normally had a rack to shield their cards behind, to avoid being detected by their opponents, and to prevent them from being able to watch which card you discarded after picking one up.

Once you had made a straight, you 'called' (literally saying "Call!"), and then each player showed their hand. Alternatively, if you thought that you knew an opponent's cards, and could use their hand to enable you to complete a straight, with some or all of your own hand, then you could 'call' to stop the game, and each player showed their hand in the same way. Using every card from 1 to the queen, was called a 'full house.' Normally the cards were placed face down on the table, before the player 'calling' and the dealer turned them over and checked them, before declaring the winner. If the player 'calling' was not correct, then they forfeited the game, and their opponent was automatically declared the winner. In the event of there not being a straight made, for example if there were only two runs of five, then the person who realised the outcome and 'called' first, to end the game, was declared the winner. If the pack in the centre of the table ran out, before any player had called, then the player with the longest row, was declared the winner. Should this still not prove decisive, then the player with the most rows could be considered the winner.

As with many card games, there was an element of chance in it, but the appeal to many Geratican women, was the additional skill of tying to work out what cards were in your opponents' hands, and knowing when to 'call'."

At first there was the usual jousting, as each of them drew cards, hoping to construct a winning hand, and to begin to try and guess their opponent's hand. It finally reached a stage where, in fact Linda needed just one more card, for a winning straight. She held the 6,7,8,9, and 10, which meant that her winning card could be either the 5, or the queen.

Eventually, Fiona felt confident that she knew what Linda was holding, and what she was waiting for. She thought it was the 1,7,8,9, and 10. Fiona held the 2,3,4,5, and the queen. Therefore, she calculated that as she held the queen, then it would all come down to the 6, which she thought must be in the pack, and surely would come up soon. If she could just draw that, then she would have a run of five cards, and need one more for a straight. She was convinced that Linda had the 1, which would give it to her. Then, if she then called on Linda to show her hand, she would win with a full house.

But of course, Fiona was wrong. The 6 remained elusive to her, and she was unfortunate that Linda did in fact draw the 1 from the pack, giving her the 1,6,7,8,9, and 10. Had the card gone to Fiona, she would have had a run of 1,2,3,4, and 5, plus the queen, which added to Linda's 6,7,8,9, and 10, would have given her another full house, if she had then called to Linda. However, she had no way of knowing any of that.

On her side of the table, Linda observed Fiona closely. She rarely gave anything away in her emotions or expressions, when she was competing, which was what made her so much more difficult to read than the average player. However, once again, Linda knew that she was possibly more pumped up than usual tonight, and she thought she could detect tiny signs that she was seeking something in particular, a card perhaps. She suspected that Fiona thought she would soon be victorious, if she drew something from the pack.

She looked at her cards and thought about what it might be. She had her own run of 6,7,8,9, and 10 of course, so the queen in Fiona's hand would obviously stop her from gaining a straight, in that direction. For Fiona to be near to a straight herself, it was highly likely that she held 2,3,4, and 5. Perhaps she also already had the queen. Linda had just picked up the 1, from the pack. Perhaps that had been the one she was after. That would have given her a run of 1,2,3,4, and 5 and meant that they'd have both had a run of five cards each. If she had called then, she would have been the winner.

On the other hand, though, perhaps Fiona had thought that she had the 1, already. In which case, if she was going for a straight and she had 2,3.4, and 5, then it would be the 6 that she mistakenly thought was in the pack that she was waiting for! It was a long shot, and there was always a mixture of logic, and pure guesswork to this – which was why Linda didn't very often play for money – but it was possible that a full house was on, from their two sets of cards.

She held her breath, as Fiona drew another card, and then discarded one, passing the turn to her once more.

"Call!" she declared, and laid her cards on the table before her, face down.

Fiona looked up in surprise.

"What?" she exclaimed. "You realise that if you're wrong, I take the money?"

"Well I'll just have to take that chance, won't I?" said Linda. "Lay your cards down please."

Fiona did so, again placing them face down, next to Linda's.

Jemima turned over each set of cards, and put them together.

"Linda holds card numbers 1,6,7,8,9,10, and a secondary card!" she announced. "And Fiona holds card numbers 2,3,4,5, the queen, and two secondary cards. Linda has called correctly, and has a full house of primary cards on the table. I declare her the winner!"

Linda swept the money on the table towards her, and ripped up the cheque, which Fiona would now never cash.

"Alexandra," she said, holding out the ripped pieces. "Throw this rubbish on the fire!"

"Yes, Mother," replied Alexandra and did as she was told to, once again.

Fiona was clearly crestfallen. It had turned out to be not a good night for her.

"Hmm, well congratulations then, Linda," she said insincerely.

Then she rose from the chair.

"Tom!" she barked. "It's time for us to leave. Thank you for having us, Linda. Goodnight everybody!"

Tom looked around at everyone, caught off guard by this sudden end to their visit. But Fiona was already turning to Queen Alexandra, so he and Alexandra had a brief kiss, before he quickly got up.

"Thank you, Mrs Radcliffe. Goodnight everybody!" he echoed his stepmother.

"Goodnight, Your Majesty," said Fiona, curtseying. "Have a safe journey home."

"Goodnight, Your Majesty," Tom said, bowing.

"Goodnight, Fiona, and goodnight, Tom," replied the queen.

Also slightly bemused, Alexandra stood up. "I'll see you out," she said, as Fiona ushered her stepson out of the parlour.

"Well, I've seen it all now!" said Linda, after their exit. "Still I've made myself one hundred geros, tonight, so I'm not going to complain about that!"

Alexandra retrieved Fiona and Tom's coats from the cloakroom. Fiona was still in great haste to be gone, so she just had time to give Tom a quick kiss at the front door, before they all bid their farewells, and she returned to the rest of the guests.

Although Fiona's departure at that precise moment, had shocked everyone, about half an hour later, some of the other guests began to indicate that they would soon need to leave, also.

James would obviously be driving Queen Alexandra, and her officials back to the palace, and Lady Caroline's chauffeur would come to fetch her, but for the other guests, who had all taken taxis, to travel to The Grange, this method of transport would to be used again, to take them home to their various destinations. As was often the case after gatherings such as this, none of the women were in any fit state to drive. They had all instructed their drivers to return later in the evening, at roughly the time that they thought the dinner party might finish. Propped up by a considerable amount of strong black coffee, which Alexandra had kindly made for her, Teresa had recovered somewhat. This had also given Alexandra an opportunity to see James, before the end of the evening.

Linda picked up the phone and pressed the button to check the security monitor, and could see some people outside the gate. She spoke into the receiver, making a couple of them jump as her voice suddenly sounded through the intercom, and established that all the taxi drivers and Lady Sackville's chauffeur had arrived back. Then she opened the gate to allow them to drive through, and up to The Grange.

James was once more dispatched by Linda to the gate, this time with her pass, to open it, when all the cars departed with their passengers. The queen would be the last to leave.

In the hall, Alexandra gave each guest their coat, which she'd retrieved from the cloakroom. Lady Caroline, Jemima, Teresa, Clarissa and Edwina, all thanked Linda and her daughter for a marvellous evening. Lady Caroline added that she hoped Fiona would be recovered from her alcoholic misfortune by the morning – a comment which very nearly made Alexandra need to turn her face away and laugh. She was sure that Lady Caroline didn't really think for one moment, that Fiona's earlier comments regarding her son, were at all alcohol related.

Once they had all left, she followed her mother back into the parlour, where their most honoured guest still sat, now surrounded by her staff.

"Well, I must congratulate you both on another excellent night's entertainment," said Queen Alexandra. "Sumptuous food and drink, good conversation, wonderful music and a lively card game to watch with a cigar in my hand! I couldn't ask for better! A rather poor show, that Fiona rushed off so soon though, even if I did nearly dismiss her earlier! I'm sorry I did that in your house Linda, but I really did think she was out of line!"

"Oh that's OK, Ma'am, I understood." Linda reassured her. "I suspect that her sudden decision to leave, was chiefly influenced by the loss of the game. I believe that she made a rare error in reading her opponent's cards. That, on top of the earlier incident to which you refer, I think was too much for her to bear!"

"Yes, well I think we may have to discuss the matter further, next week, Linda," replied the queen. "But whatever the reason, it didn't stop this evening from being a great success, in my opinion." replied the queen. "Well done! Now I must take my leave also."

After they'd made their way to the lobby, Queen Alexandra's lady-in-waiting slipped her coat back around her shoulders, and Linda opened the front door.

"Goodnight and thank you both again," said the queen. "I shall see you again next week Linda. I hope your car is repaired by then."

"Thank *you*, Ma'am," replied Linda. "It was a pleasure to receive you at The Grange, as always. Goodnight, Your Majesty!" she said and curtseyed.

"Thank you, Ma'am, I offer you the same sentiments. Goodnight, Your Majesty!" added Alexandra, curtseying as well.

After acknowledging them both with a nod, the queen went out into the courtyard, with her officials and she was shown into the back of her car. James briefly waved to Linda as he got in, and she and her daughter watched until the car left their drive, and then Linda went quickly back inside to the hall and picked up the phone receiver. She pressed the button to open the gate at the bottom of the hamlet, and they went away. Meanwhile Alexandra went down and closed The Grange's front gate, and then hurried back inside, and out of the cold night air.

***

Linda was still on the phone when Alexandra returned. As she listened, it didn't take her long to deduce that she was reporting the incident with her car at Charterhouse, to the police. Not for the first time, she marvelled at her mother's stamina. After the very big and successful day that she'd had, and the amount that she'd had to drink tonight, she was still able to do that, perfectly effectively, as if she was doing it after having just got up, after a good night's sleep.

Whilst she waited for her mother to finish, she cleared everything away from the parlour, dining room, and breakfast room. They had a mountain of washing up to be done. Luckily for occasions such as these, Linda had invested in a dishwasher. They rarely used it for just themselves, as it wasn't really necessary for the small amount that they generated, by comparison, but its services would certainly be much appreciated tonight.

She began loading it with the all the debris created by the evening's excesses. In fact, there would probably be three or four loads. She had almost finished the first load, when her mother appeared, her phone call completed.

"Oh. Good girl," she said. "That's obviously our final job of the day!" She came over, slipped her arm around her daughter's shoulders and kissed her.

"I take it that was the police, whom you were talking to, Mother?" asked

Alexandra. "What did they say?"

"They'll go around to Mrs Spencer's house tomorrow, and if she's there, they'll question her. I'll have to wait and see what she has to say. If she's *not* – and we still don't know where she is, by that time – then they'll have to start searching for her."

"Anyhow, I've done everything I can, for now. Let's just get this lot done and dusted, and then we can get to bed. It's been a long day – but ultimately quite a successful one, I think!"

"Were you pleased with the way the dinner party went, Mother? asked Alexandra, as she finished loading the dishwasher, switched it on, and moved across to start drying up the dinner dishes, as they came through, washed.

"I was, darling," replied Linda, as she began the second load for the machine. "And I don't just mean my financial earnings! I think everybody genuinely had a good and entertaining time, and we had no problems with the meal, which is obviously the biggest concern for a hostess! So those were the most important things, but we also had some stimulating conversation about a lot of the current main topics of debate, and some lively discussions, which I also aimed to do, and I was delighted to get such a good contribution from you, Alexandra. It won't have gone unnoticed by some quite influential people – not least the Principal at Castra! Once again, well done, sweetheart!"

"Fiona gave us her own brand of 'entertainment' in the dining room, didn't she, Mother?" remarked Alexandra. "What was all that about?"

"I really don't have a clue, darling," said Linda. "It wasn't a total surprise to me though, as she's raised similar concerns before. Ever since Her Majesty indicated that she wanted to settle the issue of her marriage fairly urgently, and that Lord George Sackville was the one she most favoured, she's been very funny about the subject – saying that she's still young, has plenty of time and many suitors, blah, blah, blah! It's true she is still comparatively young, but she'll be thirty next year, and have been on the throne for twelve years. Time is ticking on, and she of course can't leave the other, most important issue, her successor, for too long, either. The younger she is when the child is born, if indeed it is a girl, the longer she'll have to learn her responsibilities, and be moulded into the role, and of course, we women don't have an infinite number of child bearing years, anyhow.

"And you never know what might happen in the future. We all hope that the queen has a long life – and we've no reason to suspect that she won't – but if she was to die without producing an heir ... It's almost as if Fiona doesn't want her to marry at all, but she knows as well as anybody else, the importance of ensuring that we have a queen on the throne. Our tradition prophesises that the survival of Geratica depends upon it!

"It's not *entirely* without precedent, for the monarch to die childless, as I know I don't need to tell a scholar like you, Alexandra! However, on the one occasion before, in our history, that we know of that happening – which was centuries ago – the queen had a sister who could reign, until she died, and then her daughter became Queen. But Her Majesty, like you, is an only child, so she doesn't have that luxury. I suppose our only option *might* be to establish a new Royal House, from somewhere in the Nobility – someone might be able to prove that they're a very distant relative – but we'd be stepping into uncharted territory then!

"And as for leaving like that, well it really wasn't setting a terribly good example to Tom. Rushing away from a dinner party, with the queen in attendance, without a word of explanation, certainly isn't standard etiquette! She's lost one hundred geros as well, though I'm sure that's not going to hurt her bank balance, too much!"

"Mrs Wood is going to be the acting headmistress at Charterhouse too, Mother," said Alexandra.

"Yes and I should have thought that greatly helps you, love," said Linda. "She'll be wanting to make the necessary enquiries about your eligibility as a candidate for college champion, as soon as possible. I imagine that you'll know fairly soon, after you're back at Charterhouse. My hunch is that you will be, and then you'll have to begin your preparations for the concert, in earnest.

"And whilst we're on the subject of your return to Charterhouse, with your suspension lifted from tonight, so your gating at The Grange finishes, too. You'll still not receive any weekly allowance or treats, for this coming week, although I haven't forgotten that I promised to review the length of your punishment, last weekend. At the moment I intend it to finish after Day 4 of next week."

Yes, that's fine, Mother. Whatever you say, goes," said Alexandra.

"Indeed it does when you're in this household, Alexandra," said her mother.

Linda finished loading the fourth cycle into the machine, and with no more to go through, helped her daughter to finish drying up. Then they packed everything away.

"Phew, that's a relief!" exclaimed Linda. "Our night is finally finished."

"Yes, Mother. I did enjoy it, but *I'm* also relieved that it's over. I wouldn't want to do that every week. It'll be nice to have The Grange back to ourselves, and for peace and tranquillity to reign once more."

Linda laughed. "Well I rather like it that way, too, darling, but we *are* both tired, so it's only natural that we'd look forward to that, this weekend!"

"Right, off to bed with you, sweetheart," she continued. "It's considerably past your usual time! I'll be up to kiss you goodnight, and lock up very shortly, so don't take long. I'm extremely keen to hit the hay myself, once I've finished down here for the night."

"At once, Mother," replied Alexandra obediently and went out of the kitchen.

Later after her mother had been into her room, and she was tucked up in her bed, with the light out, and the door locked as usual, she reflected that, although it had been quite a tough week for her, she was certainly in a better position now, than she'd seemed to be a week ago. And now at last, it was the weekend. She curled up, and was asleep in no time.

A moment later Linda came to bed, and it wasn't long before she was, too.

# CHAPTER 10

The next morning both Linda and Alexandra were woken by the sound of the phone ringing. Alexandra rolled over to look at the clock, and to her amazement saw that it was 10.30am. Across the landing she could hear expressions of similar surprise coming from her mother, and realised that they'd slept longer than they'd anticipated. Luckily they didn't have very much planned for today, until later.

The phone stopped ringing, and Alexandra could just hear her mother's voice, telling her that she'd answered it.

A moment later, Linda came out of her bedroom, and across the landing. She unlocked Alexandra's door and opened it. She was in her dressing gown.

"Alexandra it's 10.30!" she said. "There's a police officer at the gate, who's come to talk to us about my car. I've let her through, and she's on her way up. If you want to hear about it at first hand, then get your dressing gown on, and come down!"

She quickly went downstairs, and into the parlour and drew back the front curtains, then went to the door and unlocked it, just as the bell rang.

"Constable Drew!" said Linda. "Please come in!"

"Thank you Mrs Radcliffe!" said Constable Jennifer Drew, stepping through the door.

"If you'd like to come through to the parlour?" Linda offered.

"I'm sorry about my state of dress at this hour of the day," she continued, as she led the constable down the passage. "My daughter and I hosted rather a lavish dinner party last night, and we're only just rising. We are *normally* up a little earlier than this!"

"Oh don't worry about that, Mrs Radcliffe," said Constable Drew. "It is the weekend, after all!"

"Please take a seat," Linda indicated to the parlour sofa. "Can I get you a drink?"

"Oh, no thank you, Mrs Radcliffe! That *is* most kind of you, but I think I'll get straight on with this. It shouldn't take long."

"Ah. Here's my daughter now," said Linda, as Alexandra came in. "Darling, this is Constable Drew. Constable Drew, this is my daughter Alexandra."

They greeted each other, as Alexandra sat in the armchair next to her mother's. She was naturally concerned, and supportive of her mother, but at the same time was pleased that something was happening, that she had no direct involvement with, for a change.

"Well, Mrs Radcliffe," began Constable Drew, "At 9.00 a.m. this morning, I called on Mrs Elizabeth Spencer. Her car was parked outside the front of the house, and I can confirm that its condition matched the description that you reported to us last night, and her husband, James, who I believe is a colleague of yours at the palace, confirmed that he told you about it yesterday."

"Mrs Spencer *was* there and confirmed that she did indeed hit your car, as she was leaving the car park at Charterhouse yesterday afternoon. She apologised profusely, and said that she will of course pay for the damage, if you so wish. However, she does insist that it was an accident."

"An accident? Does she think that I'm stupid?" exploded Linda. "She and I have never been on the best of terms, *particularly recently*, and I convened a meeting of the board of governors, to call for her dismissal, from Charterhouse. The motion was accepted, and she was duly relieved of her duties, with immediate effect. It seems an almighty coincidence that she happened to have an 'accident' crashing into *my* car, on the way out! I don't believe that *her* car was parked anywhere near mine! And if it really was an accident, then why didn't she wait to inform me herself, rather than rush off and only say so upon being questioned by the police?"

The constable raised her eyebrows and continued. "I then put to Mrs Spencer, your claim that one of the girls at Charterhouse, witnessed her 'deliberately' crashing her car into yours. She seemed shocked at being told this, and *did* appear to lose her composure for a moment, before declaring that the girl in question, was a habitual liar and that she shouldn't be believed."

Linda and Alexandra looked at each other in astonishment.

"Constable Drew, really!" exclaimed Linda. "Yesterday was actually the second time in three days that I met Miss Benita Davis, 'the girl in question'. As you probably know, my daughter has been absent from Charterhouse, this past week, and three days ago, Miss Davis and three other girls, came to visit her, here at The Grange, to discuss a matter concerning them all. I have to tell you that I was most impressed by her, and judging by that evening's appearances, I certainly would *not* have described her as a 'habitual liar'! I also know that she is the girl who Alexandra is closest to at Charterhouse."

"Yes indeed Constable Drew!" confirmed Alexandra. "She is no liar. I'm telling you!"

"Well as so often in these cases, it's one person's word against another," said the constable. "There really isn't all that much that we can do, unless you wish to press charges, Mrs Radcliffe?"

Linda considered. She was sorely tempted. But she had already won a victory over her. She was confident that she could win this one too, if she declared the war, but on the other hand, it might interfere with her plans for James, which after the successful events of the previous week, she now felt that she could go ahead with, as originally planned. These would inevitably upset Elizabeth enough already, and this would only make the situation worse between them.

"Well I do believe that I'm right, and nothing will ever change my view," she asserted. "However, I think that my daughter and I have had rather enough of prosecutions and court cases, for the moment! No, I won't press charges against her. I accept her apology. My car is being repaired as we speak, and I hope to retrieve it from the garage, later this afternoon. I'll be claiming off my insurance for the damage, so she needn't worry about that either."

"In that case, Mrs Radcliffe, I think that will be all," remarked Constable Drew. "So, thank you, and I'll be on my way."

After she'd left, Alexandra expressed surprise to her mother that she hadn't pressed charges, against Elizabeth Spencer, of all people.

"I think we'll let this one pass, after what's happened this week, darling," she replied. "And I have certain personal plans, involving her husband, which are now imminent, so I don't want this going on in the middle of them."

"I can't believe how late we slept this morning, Mother!" Alexandra exclaimed.

"No. But we did have rather a lot to drink last night, sweetheart!" answered Linda.

"Mother," said Alexandra, "You know you told me, that if our dinner party was a success, you might tell me which hostess had her cooking blamed for a guest's subsequent illness, when Her Majesty had been in attendance?"

Linda smiled. "Hmm," she confirmed. "Elizabeth Spencer! It was a couple of years ago."

"So, I was right, Mother!" cried Alexandra triumphantly. "And who was the person who made the accusation?"

"Can you not guess, darling?" asked Linda. "It was Fiona!"

***

Apart from a later, and somewhat quicker breakfast than normal, the rest of the morning was, on the whole, routine, with the weekly washing to be put through the machine, and hung out to dry, and Alexandra's weekly trip to buy her mother's groceries, from Judith's store, which she could now make as usual, her gating at The Grange now lifted.

In the afternoon, Alexandra happily called on Tom. Unusually he met her at the door, rather than Fiona. She had apparently been in her study for most of the day, and Tom informed Alexandra that her humour had not markedly improved, since last night.

To Alexandra's disappointment though, Fiona did make the effort to come out, once she'd realised who their visitor was.

"That was a good evening yesterday, Alexandra!" she remarked.

"Thank you. I'm glad you enjoyed it, Mrs Clark," replied Alexandra politely. "We were all surprised when you and Tom left so suddenly, though," she added truthfully.

"Oh, well it was getting late, and near to bedtime, so I thought I'd better take Tom home," replied Fiona.

Alexandra nodded, although she considered this highly unlikely. It had only been around 10.00 p.m., which was certainly not especially late for The Lodge. Fiona and Colin, Tom's father, weren't normally the earliest couple to go to bed in Geratica, although the rumour was that they still enjoyed a particularly healthy sex life. Fiona's gambling hobby often meant that she was out for most of the evening, anyhow.

Today Alexandra and Tom were going to the park, just down the road from Elmsbrook.

"I really didn't want to leave as early as we did yesterday, you know Angel." said Tom, as they went down the drive.

"I know you didn't, *my darling*, and that went double for me, but your stepmother had just lost the card game, and one hundred geros with it, so she was obviously furious, although she hid it reasonably well. After getting her bottom caned by Queen Alexandra earlier, it was altogether, not one of her greatest nights! Mother's not entirely sure what her objection to Her Majesty becoming formally involved in a relationship at the moment, is all about.

You know how important marriage, and the succession are, to the monarchy of Geratica."

"Well done you, last night though," Alexandra continued. "I thought you acquitted yourself well, meeting the queen for the first time. I'm only sorry that your stepmother embarrassed you. Both of those incidents that I mentioned, weren't terribly good etiquette, particularly for someone in her position at court – nor trying to take advantage of Teresa Brockenhurst by getting her inebriated, in order to beat her at 'Call!' either!"

"You were pretty impressive yourself," replied Tom. "Once you get your confidence up, you're a fine speaker, just like your mother!"

"At the risk of incurring her wrath, for 'underselling' myself, no one can match my mother at that," said Alexandra. "But I'm getting more confident, that I *will* grant you."

They walked around the park for a bit, their arms wrapped around each other. There were quite a few people there, it being the weekend, and there were the regular group of brass musicians at the bandstand, helping to keep them entertained. Younger children played on the swings and roundabouts and raced down the slides, causing them great excitement.

Finding a bench in a relatively quiet area of the park, they sat down. It was the first time for a fortnight that Alexandra had been able to actually "go out" with her boyfriend alone – since they'd become an official couple, in fact – and she was feeling a desperate longing. She wanted to show him just how much she loved him, and appreciated the support he'd given her, during her recent trouble.

She slipped her arms around his shoulders, and leaning across him, kissed Tom's lips. He kissed her back lovingly, and her erect geratis throbbed. She continued, savouring the feeling of loving him, as she squeezed him tight in her arms. Tom's pleasure was obvious, as his eyes closed, delighting her and inflaming her desire, all the more. She pressed him against the back of the bench and indulged herself for a few seconds, and Tom murmured in ecstasy, and returned her kisses.

They stopped when their breath ran out, and in each other's arms, they watched the scene at the park for a few more minutes. Tom's genus had been inflated ever since his girlfriend had called on him at The Lodge, and he knew that it would be for the rest of their time together today. He had always loved being with the beautiful Alexandra Radcliffe and now that they were an 'item,' there was the added excitement of what she might do to him, when he was. He dreamed of her kisses every night, and often whilst he was at work, he became sexually aroused thinking of her making love to him.

Linda was planning to walk down to the garage at 3.15 to pick up her car.

She'd suggested to Alexandra that if they wanted, they could go with her, and then she'd bring them back. They left the park, and got to The Grange at 3.00.

They left for the garage as planned, and arrived there at 3.30. Linda went immediately to the office to enquire about her car. She was pleased to hear from the garage manageress, that it was indeed mended, and they were taken out to see it. The mechanic who Linda had met yesterday, was with it.

"As I promised, the job is done, Mrs Radcliffe," she asserted. "I trust it is to your satisfaction?"

"Well, you'll find that out in a moment, girl," Linda said to her. "I must inspect it, before I can tell that!"

"Yes certainly! Be my guest, Mrs Radcliffe!"

Linda looked closely at the back of the car, examined the new bumper and lights that had been fitted, and ran her hands over the bodywork.

She looked back at the mechanic. "Thank you very much. A very good job!

The mechanic smiled. "My pleasure, Mrs Radcliffe!" she said.

They then went back into the office and Linda paid for the job. "I shall be claiming the money back off my insurance," she informed the manageress.

"Of course, Mrs Radcliffe," she replied.

Then they all got into the car, and Linda drove it back to Elmsbrook.

*** 

Tom stayed at The Grange for a little while, before going back home, in time for dinner. Alexandra did her ironing duties, before they had theirs.

Then afterwards, when they were cleared away, they had a relaxing evening, before going to bed together.

Linda remembered her daughter's support for her, during the economic discussion at the dinner party yesterday, and the pride that she'd felt in her being confident enough to speak during it. For this reason alone, she felt passion for her, but there was another reason why she wanted to make this an extremely special night for Alexandra. She wasn't going to mention it yet, though. This week had been quite a week for her daughter. Next week, if her plans went as she wanted them to, would be a momentous one in her own life.

Alexandra lay on her back, as her mother came into the bedroom. Linda immediately came over to her side of the bed, cupped her face in her hands, and kissed her. Then she gently let her fingers brush across her daughter's open nightgown, and briefly touched her exposed chest. Alexandra shivered slightly, as her already heightened senses, tingled in her excitement.

Linda smiled at her. "I'll just go and get myself ready, darling, and then I'll be with you!" she said softly.

"OK, Mother!" replied Alexandra, as Linda went into her bathroom. She pushed her hair forward over her shoulders, to her chest.

When Linda returned, she went to her side of the bed and climbed in. Moving close to her daughter, she kissed her chest and stroked her hair. Alexandra breathed heavily and felt more tingles as she felt her mother's fingers brush through the tips. Her eyes closed in ecstasy, just as Tom's had earlier when she had held and kissed him on the park bench. But Linda had only just begun.

She pulled her daughter close by her side, and squeezed her as tight as she could. Alexandra murmured contentedly, as she snuggled to her mother's chest.

*"I love you, darling! I want you, and I'm going to have you. You're going to let me take control aren't you?"* The soft seductive whispers came into Alexandra ear and wrapped themselves around her brain, inducing a fresh wave of tingles, in all of the most sensitive parts of her young female Geratican body.

*"I love you, Mother. Yes! Take control, and do whatever you want! I'm your baby, and I need you to take me over. Please!"* Alexandra whispered back into her mother's ear, the submissive words that she genuinely meant, and which Linda loved to hear. Her mother could resist no longer.

Linda rolled over on top of her daughter, and locked her arms and legs[Larch4] around her. Her fingers traced all over her body, and stroked her hair. She kissed her lips passionately, and as she saw Alexandra's mouth open slightly, she slipped her tongue inside, and licked her daughter's. Alexandra's legs tingled, and then her tongue itself, making her murmur with pleasure. Her mother's body thrust down into hers, as she lay on top. Her passion already seemed to be reaching a peak, and Alexandra felt that it seemed to be even greater than normal. Her breath was hot, and murmurs of ecstasy were escaping from her, as she loved her on, and on.

As usual there was a brief interlude, as Linda allowed her daughter a breather. But it *was* only briefly.

*"Look into my eyes, my wonderful, sweet baby. My darling!"* she whispered again. Alexandra did so, as her mother squeezed her body, in the tightest grip she'd ever known. Linda's arms and legs lifted her off the sheets and upwards, and then her body thrust down into hers. As kisses smothered her mouth, and her tongue was licked again, she was pinned down beneath Linda's body and held on to it, as she began to feel all of her senses submit to the dominance of her mother's loving. Her mother's eyes sent her a message to do just that.

Linda's breath became heavy and laboured. She wanted to love her daughter forevermore, but she thought that if she didn't stop soon, her heart would burst.

Beneath her, all of Alexandra's senses were now completely dominated and taken over by her mother. There was nothing else but her, and she felt herself get swept up by the strongest tidal wave of her mother's love, that she'd ever known. Everything spun around, as she began to lose her breath. Her eyes closed as she lost all control, and she shuddered and moaned softly in ecstasy.

Linda rolled off her, knowing that she'd given her daughter the feeling that she looked forward to most, every week, and that she looked forward to giving her just as much, if not more so. She would do it again when they awoke tomorrow morning, before she cooked their breakfast in bed.

Beside her, Alexandra was now just about recovered. Linda reached for her and kissed her, as her daughter snuggled up to her once again.

"Thank you, Mother. That was wonderful!" said Alexandra. "I love you!"

"It was a pleasure, as always, darling!" replied Linda. "I love you, too!"

They kissed once more, and said goodnight. Soon they were both asleep in each other's arms.

# PART 7

# CHAPTER 1

Linda drove Alexandra to the door, on her first day back at Charterhouse, as she'd promised.

She had a quick look about. "Well, I think the coast is clear for you darling. Obviously the media have forgotten about you now!"

"Good, Mother!" replied Alexandra firmly.

"Well, I'll be on my way to work then," said Linda. "I'll be later than normal getting there today, because I've brought you here first, but that doesn't matter too much today, and I think it was worth taking the precaution, to ensure you got in the building without any bother,"

"Yes, thank you very much, Mother," replied Alexandra and they kissed.

"Hope you have a good day and maybe we'll both have some news to share, when I get home tonight!"

Alexandra gave her mother a slightly quizzical look, but then opened the car door and got out. She didn't want to keep her waiting.

"Bye, Mother. See you tonight," she said, before she closed the door.

"Yes. Bye, darling,"

Alexandra shut the car door and waved to her mother, as she drove away.

She made her way to her form room. To her surprise, Benita, Imelda and Rachel were already there – plus Emma.

"Welcome back, Alexandra!" said Benita, standing up and gripping her arm. "We thought we'd all make sure we left the dining hall promptly, after we'd finished breakfast today."

"What? Just so that you could be here to welcome me back?" asked Alexandra. "I never expected that."

"It's time you realised how highly we think of you, Alexandra!" exclaimed Benita. "Hopefully with Spencer now gone, you might find it easier."

"Junior *and* Senior now, so I understand," remarked Alexandra, as she took her seat at her desk.

"Yes. And by the way, is your mother pressing charges against Mrs Spencer, for what she did to her car?"

"Oh. I heard you witnessed it. No she's not, as a matter of fact. A police constable visited us at the weekend and said that Mrs Spencer's admitted that she hit my mother's car and apologises, but insists that it was a genuine accident! My mother thinks that's nonsense, but we both want to move on from what's happened just recently, so she's going to let it pass."

Benita couldn't hide her disappointment. "Oh *darn* it!" she exclaimed. "I was hoping to be able to go into a court and be a witness. I've always wanted to do that. I swear that Mrs Spencer did deliberately ram your mother's car."

Alexandra decided not to tell her, that Elizabeth Spencer had told the police, she was a habitual liar. It really was a disgraceful slur, without any foundation. Elizabeth had said it, purely in an attempt to save her neck, once again. Benita would be outraged, and maybe want to take it further, and it was obvious that her mother had decided to drop the matter, so that was that.

"Anyhow," Benita continued, "Now that Mrs Wood's in temporary charge, she's decided it would be best to move Melanie from our form class to the other and do a swap. So from today, as Melanie's back as well, we've got Emma with us. She's not moving anybody to replace Gillian though, therefore there'll just be five in or class, instead of six."

"I wondered why you were here, Emma!" exclaimed Alexandra. "I thought you'd just decided to join the rest of the 'board' to welcome me back, as it's my first day."

"No, I'm afraid you've got me here for good!" said Emma. So, now our form group and board, are one and the same."

"I'll bet that's no coincidence either, now that Mrs Wood's doing Mrs Spencer's job, and she wants us all to work together for Alexandra's concert." remarked Benita.

"If Benita will let the rest of us get a word in," said Rachel, "We've actually made a start on the organisations, that we spoke of at your house last week."

Imelda looked at Rachel and then said, "I don't know if you noticed, but we've put some posters up around the college, regarding the sponsored walk. We're also distributing sponsorship forms to anyone interested in taking part, from the tuck shop."

"I must admit, that when I came in, I was mainly concentrating on getting back into the swing of things, after being away last week, but I may have seen something. Doubtless I'll see them all, over the course of the day. Well that's good then. Well done. Let's hope we get a lot of interest, and some hefty donations. What about the exact route? Any decision on that?"

"As a matter of fact we've thought that the most logical thing would be to make it to Buckmore town square and back again," said Benita. "It's quite an easy walk and as with most areas of this town, very visually appealing. It must be roughly three miles there and back. If it is slightly shorter, then we could always finish it by a circuit of the Charterhouse exercise ground, and even maybe the grounds of the building itself."

"Great! Well you seem to have got things started very well, without me," remarked Alexandra. "That's what I want really, so that I can get on with planning the concert. I'll have to liaise with Emma later, too."

"And now we have a request of you, Alexandra," asserted Benita. "Have you looked out a of photo of Tom, that we can have a peek at?"

"Oh. Yes!" Alexandra opened her school bag and from a protective casing, took out a picture of him. She handed it to Benita.

In a flash, Imelda, Rachel and Emma were at Benita's side and they all gazed at the photograph.

Alexandra looked closely at their reactions and saw all four girls with their tongues almost hanging out of their mouths, drooling over her boyfriend.

"Phwoar, he's gorgeous!" said Imelda. "I knew he would be, you lucky jammer!" She pulled at her skirt slightly, to try and stop her aroused geratis being visible. Imelda was fast maturing, sexually, into a very natural young woman, with traditional desires, and highly erotic fantasies, which made her geratis extend from her vagina, long and thick, whilst she lay in the bed of her chambers at night. She *loved* good-looking men, and although she would never admit it to anyone at all, ever, she had been tempted on a couple of occasions by Gillian's offering of an escort boy, to "break her duck" with. But the consequences of being found out had dissuaded her, and now of course, she was very grateful that she'd resisted. She couldn't wait to turn her fantasies into realities, when she finally *did* lose her virginity, however.

The rest of the girls expressed similar feelings about Tom, as Imelda.

Alexandra smiled. "He is a handsome boy, yes. I fancy him like no other. I am indeed fortunate. But just remember all of you. He's mine! Find your own boyfriends. And now I'll have my photo back, please!"

***

At the palace, when Linda had a convenient moment, she went to seek out James.

She found him in his main working environment, Her Majesty's private garage, where he was running a cloth over her car's right headlamp.

"Good morning, James. How was your weekend?" asked Linda.

"Well, OK I suppose. It was the first weekend that Elizabeth and I had been together, for some time."

Linda closed the doors behind her. "Yes, well that's the subject that I've come to talk about."

She took off the coat that she'd worn to come over to the garage and placed it over a chair. The autumn was gradually getting colder by the week, but the garage was relatively warm, as James kept several electric heaters in there.

Linda was dressed in a grey suit and bow. She also took off the jacket and stood in her cream blouse sleeves, which were rolled to the elbow.

"You'll know that we had a visit from Constable Drew, after she'd questioned Elizabeth, at the weekend, and that I'm not going to take any further action. Although I don't believe for a second, her claim to have damaged my car accidentally, I want to move on from this, and put the whole of the recent chapter at Charterhouse, behind us. I don't want it to interfere with our other matter, regarding your wife!"

"Oh. Right," said James, a little nervously.

"Yes. Right, James!" replied Linda. If you remember, it was two weeks ago today that I gave you an ultimatum, and said that I'd give you a fortnight to tell your wife of our desires, or else I would initiate my own plan, to achieve them. So now, James Spencer, it's the moment of truth. Have you told your wife?"

"No Linda, I haven't," admitted James. "I'm sorry!"

"That's alright. I didn't expect you to tell me that you had, if I'm honest. I know you well, James! And *you* know *me* well, too. I told you a fortnight ago, that having said you wanted to leave Elizabeth and be with me, I wouldn't allow you to turn back – and I meant it."

"*Right!*" she continued, very assertively. James felt the word prickle his skin slightly. "So now, I'll take over. The first thing I want you to do, is go home tonight, and tell Elizabeth that you need to come over to my house on the evening of 3/35/10, to talk about another confidential matter involving one of Her Majesty's engagements, which we need strict privacy for. Then when you come over, I shall have sent Alexandra to The Lodge with Fiona, Colin and Tom, and I'll cook us dinner. And I'll be forward with you now James, I shall be proposing a relationship! That's all for now. Once I've done that, and you've accepted, then we'll take things from there."

"Now, is that clear to you, James?" asked Linda, in conclusion.

"Yes. Very." James assured her. "I only hope that she agrees to let me go over to you again. She may be starting to get a little suspicious of it happening for a second time!"

"Hmm, that's possible, yes," said Linda. "But try your hardest to get her to, James. If necessary I may have to contact her myself and *insist* upon it, but I hope that it won't come to that, nor that we'll need to concoct a story to gain an excuse to see each other, for much longer, either."

James felt a shiver go through him and he wasn't sure if it was due to the excitement of at long last being with Linda, and knowing that she would take control and make things happen, or the trepidation he still felt about telling Elizabeth, that he needed to go to her house for another confidential matter. He also felt a slight knot in his stomach. This was a hugely significant event in his life – and Linda's too of course. In the opposite way, it was also going to be a significant event in Elizabeth's, too, and she'd been through a lot already over the past week and a half. But this had to be done. He couldn't bare the unhappiness that he felt in his marriage any longer, and he'd made a commitment to Linda, before the crisis at Charterhouse had emerged. If he broke that now, he knew that Linda might never forgive him, and he'd lose his chance to be with her, forever.

"OK Linda. I promise I'll speak to her tonight, about needing to see you again in midweek."

"Good! I shall be most disappointed in you – not to say highly annoyed - if you break that promise. I hope I make myself clear?"

"Yes, yes, Linda. Blimey, I can see now, why Alexandra always does as she's told!" exclaimed James.

Linda smirked slightly. "As will you!" she asserted.

"Well I've got a meeting coming up, so I'll leave you to it, James. See you at lunchtime?"

"Right you are, boss!" said James.

***

At Charterhouse, it transpired that Melanie had returned, but suffering from the after-effects of a heavy cold. Alexandra was in no doubt about where she'd caught it from.

The girls had been officially told at the end of last week, that Mrs Spencer was no longer the headmistress, and that Mrs Wood, head of Music, would be 'acting up' in the position, until it was re-filled. It also meant that she would be combining the two roles, and to this end, she would receive assistance in her usual role, to give her more time to deal with her new extra duties. Though she would still be teaching, when another music mistress, Miss Steele, had a free period and it coincided with one in which Mrs Wood was due to teach, then she would take over, and also assist with some of the head of Music's duties.

Before Alexandra's Music theory lesson began, which Miss Steele was due to take, the girls waited for her to arrive. There was little surprise that she had been chosen to assist Mrs Wood, as they knew that she was a rather ambitious young mistress, and considered something of a rising star, amongst the staff.

She was often seen walking around Charterhouse with a couple of other young mistresses, and Gillian Spencer had nicknamed them 'The Charterhouse Steele Band' which had caused some mirth, and, Alexandra thought, might be one of the few things that Gillian would be more affectionately remembered for.

Amongst the pupils, she had a rather formidable reputation, for being rather a strict and hard taskmistress, with a sharp tongue, and an even sharper turn of her wrist, when administering the cane, something which she was not shy of doing. She liked to get good results for her own records, to distinguish herself amongst her peers, and was often intolerant of failure. As a result, there was understandably some trepidation amongst the form. Alexandra wasn't especially troubled by strict mistresses, as she was used to her mother being similar at home, although there was of course, a lot of love and good fun, too.

There was a rumour that Miss Steele had wanted to take on the role of head of Music alone, and for Mrs Wood to be solely the acting headmistress, but that this had been considered infeasible, as that would inevitably leave some music forms without a mistress in charge of them. Despite her brilliance, it was still considered beyond any mistress at Charterhouse College, to take two classes at once.

There was another rumour, that she was unhappy not to have got her way.

Miss Steele arrived and addressed her adopted class.

"Good morning, girls!" she said sharply.

"Good morning, Miss Steele!" said the class.

"Or should we say 'afternoon' Miss!" said one of the girls, Natasha Parker.

"What?" snapped Miss Steele. "Are you being cheeky about my slight tardiness, girl? I was held up on the way here, as a matter of fact. Not that it's any of your business."

"Oh no, Miss Steele. Nothing of the sort," Natasha assured her. "I was simply observing that it's now after midday, so technically we should be saying afternoon."

"Oh I see. You were making a frivolous remark. Well, I should warn you all from the outset, that I don't encourage a lot of levity in my lessons. You're here to work, not mess around!"

Then she took out her cane and Natasha nearly froze. Everyone held their breath. Alexandra couldn't believe that a girl would be beaten, simply for making a witty and very true statement.

However, Miss Steele simply lightly patted her palm with it, a few times, as she walked to the left front desk, as she looked at them, where Alexandra sat. She began to speak to the six girls in the class, walking around the circle of desks, in a clockwise direction and tapping her cane on each of the desks, as she did so.

"Now, I've done some reading up on this class, regarding your general standard of behaviour, which I must admit, sounds reasonable, and your academic results and achievements, which I must say are patchy, indeed!"

The last part of this statement caused a bit of a flutter of indignation, amongst the girls in the class.

"*Be quiet*! screeched Miss Steele, and smacked her cane down hard on whichever desk she happened to be standing next to. She paid no attention to whose it was. It was in fact Emma Thatcher's, sat in the front on the opposite side of Alexandra, and the cane almost caught her finger.

The mistress went to her desk, and picked up a notebook.

"Alexandra Radcliffe, please stand up."

Alexandra jumped. "Yes, Miss Steele," she said obediently, doing as she was told.

"Now class, this girl is the type who will always be welcome in my class, a hard-working, studious, well-mannered, well behaved girl, who always gets good marks."

Alexandra could imagine the thought going through the other girls' heads at that moment. That she was the so-called well behaved girl, who had tried to steal three bottles of perfume from Rimmingtons, the week before last! She hoped that nobody would have the nerve to say that, at the moment. Luckily no one did.

"Please sit down, Alexandra."

"Thank you, Miss Steele," said Alexandra and did so gratefully.

"Harriett Kennedy, please stand up."

"Yes, Miss Steele," Harriett copied Alexandra's most formal style of address.

"Now, this is the type of girl who will *not* be welcome in my class, if her performance does not improve. Consistently low marks and lacking in application. Please hold out your hand, Harriet."

Harriett looked at Miss Steele in horror. "Miss Steele! Please! I do try my best!" she cried.

"Just hold out your hand, girl!" ordered the mistress.

Reluctantly, Harriett complied, assuming the worst.

Miss Steele pressed her cane into Harriett's open hand and ran in it slowly over her palm and down her fingers and then back again.

As she did so, she said quietly, but firmly, "If I do not see an improvement in your performance, when I mark your next work, then you will receive six on the hand. Do you understand, girl?"

"Yes, Miss Steele!" said Harriett, for the moment just relieved that she was not to receive the punishment immediately.

"Good. Please sit down, Harriett," commanded her mistress.

"Thank you, Miss Steele," Harriet did so, even more gratefully than Alexandra had.

Alexandra was appalled. This was the sort of humiliating treatment that she hated to see. Harriett was in no way a bad girl, and she knew that the whole of the music form would agree with her. She'd never been any trouble before. She worked perfectly hard, as far as Alexandra was concerned. She just found the theory side of music difficult to grasp. Unlike the rest of the class, she didn't play a musical instrument, which possibly put her at a disadvantage, as she didn't read music as often as them.

"So, there you have the two opposite ends of the class," said Miss Steele. "I hope that I have made it clear, *which* end I expect you to gravitate to?"

She looked around. "Do you not answer your mistress, when she asks you a question?"

"Yes, Miss Steele!" the girls chorused, quickly.

"Good," The mistress returned to her desk and sat down, laying her cane in full view, in front of her. Then she began the lesson.

She began the class, working through the textbook, demonstrating things on the blackboard, and asking questions to individual members of the class, based on what they were learning. Alexandra hated this sort of approach. Although she often knew the answer (and did today when, due to her position in the room, she was asked a question first), she always felt under pressure.

Alexandra quickly guessed that it was Miss Steele's intention to work her way around the class, in order. She could imagine that Harriett must be in a terrible panic. She was two desks behind her, therefore she would be next in line, after Amanda Hayfield in between them, had answered the question, already asked to her by the mistress. She looked across at Emma and could tell that she was thinking the same.

Sure enough, when Miss Steele did reach her, an agonising pause followed the question, as Harriett desperately tried to work out the answer, and she felt even worse after what had been threatened, if she didn't improve.

"In the name of Divinity, can you not even answer such a simple question as that?" Miss Steele chided her.

There was another silence and Alexandra quickly exchanged a glance with Emma. She began to quickly scribble something on a piece of paper, and Emma nodded slightly to acknowledge her understanding.

"Miss Steele!" Emma suddenly burst out.

The music mistress looked at her. "What is it girl?" she demanded.

"Please, Miss, could you look at this in the text book? I think there's something odd, been written. I'm not sure if it's correct."

"What? Oh *goodness* me!" exclaimed the mistress, impatiently. "Oh, alright then, let me see."

She got up and walked over to Emma's desk. As she reached it, Emma turned slightly and held the text book in such a position that Miss Steele had to turn her back on the class for a moment. Emma pointed to a section in the book. During the distraction, Alexandra quickly passed the piece of paper to Amanda, who in turn handed it to Harriett.

"Oh! I'm terribly sorry, Miss! I made a mistake," said Emma. "The textbook's right after all."

"Yes, that's quite obvious! The textbook rarely isn't. You stupid girl! Wasting my time!" She stomped back to her desk.

"Now where was I? Harriett! Are you any nearer to answering my question? Preferably by lunchtime?"

Harriett cleared her throat and said, "Yes Miss," before reading the answer that Alexandra had given her.

Miss Steele was momentarily shocked, before regaining her composure.

"Ah. Well yes, that's correct," she confirmed. "It took a while, but you got there in the end! Perhaps there's more hope for you, than I'd previously thought. Well done."

Then she moved on to the next girl.

It was an old trick, that had been practised by generations of girls before, at Charterhouse, but perhaps, Alexandra thought – being still a relatively inexperienced mistress, despite her rapid promotion – Miss Steele wasn't yet familiar with it. She wasn't sure if she cared too much for this particular mistress, either.

When the bell finally rang for the end of the lesson and lunchtime, Miss Steele came over to Alexandra and told her that Mrs Wood wished to see her in the headmistress' study, after she'd had her lunch. Alexandra thanked her and left.

Outside the classroom, she could see that Harriett was shaken.

"Well that lesson's clearly going to be a barrel of laughs, every week!" she exclaimed to Emma.

"I'm not sure if she's got any sense of humour at all," agreed Emma.

Luckily it appeared that their Music history and Music practical lessons, would be taken by Mrs Wood, as normal.

\*\*\*

Later, she went to see Mrs Wood, as she'd been asked.

"Good afternoon, Alexandra," said Annabel, at the door of what was now, at least temporarily, her office. "Please take a seat."

"Thank you, Mrs Wood," replied Alexandra.

"It's good to see you back. How was your first morning?" asked Annabel, as she sat down at her desk.

"Not too bad. The girls seem to have been quite friendly to me, and my form class had even left breakfast early, so that they could be in the classroom to welcome me, when I arrived! My mother brought me over here this morning, too, just in case there was any bother from the media, which was nice."

Mrs Wood looked at her with concern.

"Was there any?" she asked.

"No, it was fine," Alexandra reassured her.

"Good," said Annabel. "I certainly wasn't aware of any of those people being here this morning, and I sincerely hope that they won't be back again for a while."

"Well, Alexandra," she continued, "As you know, following Mrs Spencer's sad departure, Charterhouse needed her position covered temporarily, and I have stepped up to the plate, as they say! One of the first things that I did, when I officially started, was to enquire about your continued eligibility as a candidate for college champion, after your recent trouble. It's high time that we got the issue resolved. And I have good news for you Alexandra! It's been officially confirmed that you still are. Gillian Spencer is now obviously gone, and out of the picture, so you're the only candidate that there is now, but of course I can't necessarily predict that you'll automatically win the award. You'll still have to put the work in to get it, and the decision is made by a panel, independent of Charterhouse. Some on the panel may still be influenced by the fact that you were suspended – we've no way of knowing that – so I suggest that you work doubly hard! But I naturally, very much hope that you do, given that I nominated you in the first place – and I wish you the very best of luck. So it's business as usual for you."

"Oh thank you, Mrs Wood," exclaimed Alexandra. "That certainly *is* a weight off my mind."

"I obviously brought some of your friends from here, over to meet with you at your home, last week. I trust that was fruitful?"

"Definitely. I appointed a board, as you suggested and they seem to be getting on very well. I hope that I'll largely be able to leave them to it, so that I can just mainly focus on the performance. They're organising a sponsored walk, to raise money to fund the concert."

"Yes, so we've all seen from the posters, that have sprung up in the last few days. A good idea I think. Good luck! You seem to have made a good start anyhow. How have you found the experience so far?"

"Well, I was a little bit nervous before that meeting last week, but I managed to chair it fairly well in the end, I think. Overall I'm quite pleased with the way it's gone, though it's early days, of course."

"Good," said Annabel. "OK. Well is there anything else that you'd like to discuss, before we finish?"

"Um, well maybe one thing, Mrs Wood." The events of the last period were still resonating in her mind, and she felt confident enough with the acting headmistress, to express her feelings.

"Now that you've become the acting headmistress, I know that you're combining it with your normal head of Music role and that Miss Steele is assisting you with that, so that you have more time to devote to your new extra duties."

Mrs Wood raised her eyebrows. "Yes. What of it?"

"Well, with respect, Mrs Wood, it's Miss Steele! She obviously took us for Music theory, just before lunch and…well, I had some concerns about her conduct."

"What?" Annabel's mind raced. This was the last thing that she wanted to hear! "Alexandra that's a very serious allegation for a girl to make against a mistress! I hope you have very strong evidence to support it."

"Well, I'll tell you what happened, Mrs Wood."

She recounted the details. When she got to the part about Harriett not knowing the answer to Miss Steele's question, she decided to risk making a confession.

"I hope you don't mind me telling you this, Mrs Wood, but we tried the old trick of distracting the mistress, so that we could smuggle the girl struggling with the question, the answer!"

"Oh. That old stunt!" groaned Annabel. "You naughty girls! Yes, I remember falling for that one on a couple of occasions, when I was starting out."

"So did Miss Steele," remarked Alexandra and she saw Mrs Wood's lips twitch, as tried desperately not to laugh.

The acting headmistress coughed, and then recovered. "Right, well I don't wish to know any more about that, Alexandra," she exclaimed.

"As to the lesson itself though, mistresses are by and large allowed the individual freedom to conduct their lessons in the way that they wish. Some are admittedly a little eccentric, and some are stricter and more rigid in their discipline than others, but in the end, as long as they don't overstep the mark, what they do in the classroom is their own, private affair.

"In my opinion you are a pretty good bunch of girls in that class, and there's very little need to impose a lot of discipline. You all work hard, including Harriett, but I know that she struggles with her theory. Personally, I don't believe that she needs to be bullied or humiliated, to make her improve, and indeed, it might even have the opposite effect to what Miss Steele desires, but again, that's at her discretion. She's perfectly entitled to adopt that method, if she thinks it's 'appropriate.'. After all, her results *do* show that many of her pupils flourish under her approach to teaching."

"But Mrs Wood," protested Alexandra. "If Harriett, as we both suspect, not only *doesn't* improve under Miss Steele's approach, but actually *gets worse*, then she'll be punished more and more. That can't be right! She's trying her best, and it's not her fault that she finds it difficult. She shouldn't be made to feel stupid, because she isn't."

"Yes, I agree with you, Alexandra and I do actually think that I perhaps should have a quiet word with Miss Steele. She may indeed be going a little too far, on this occasion. Thank you for bringing this to my attention, Alexandra. You are a good girl, with a very kind heart, and I'm sure that no one here at Charterhouse, now that the previous regime is gone, will begrudge you becoming college champion, if it happens."

"Thank you, Mrs Wood," replied Alexandra. "Well, I'll give her some help, to try and improve, if it'll mean that she won't continually be in trouble with Miss Steele," She felt that Mrs Wood understood that they'd had Harriett's best interests at heart, when they'd done so earlier. "But I promise it will be above board, from now on."

Annabel glanced at her. "Well that's a typically noble gesture from you, Alexandra, but don't forget you're going to be very busy up until the end of term, organising the concert, as well as your regular studies. Leave this to me, and I'll sort it out, as best I can – and you focus on that."

"Yes Mrs Wood. Thank you." said Alexandra.

"Well it won't be long before afternoon registration now Alexandra, so that will be all," declared Mrs Wood. "Well done on how things are going with the concert preparations. Good luck, and I hope to see you become college champion. I'll try and sort out your concerns, on the other matter."

She stood up, and Alexandra followed. "Thank you again Mrs Wood. Goodbye," she said.

"Goodbye Alexandra, and I'll see you for your music history lesson on 4/35/10,"

Alexandra left the study, just as the bell rang for the end of lunchtime, and she made her way to her form class, for afternoon registration.

***

Annabel Wood met Sandra Steele, later, after the main curriculum of the day was completed. They discussed some routine affairs, before Annabel decided to raise the subject that had been troubling Alexandra earlier.

"Sandra," she began, "You took a final year class for me, before lunch – a theory lesson."

"Oh yes, that's the one with Alexandra Radcliffe in," replied Sandra. "I can see that she's a very bright girl. It's a pity that she made an ass of herself the other week, but other than that, I'm sure she'd make a fine candidate for college champion."

"Yes, well that's all settled, Sandra," Annabel informed her. "She is. And I hope that both she, and Charterhouse, can now put that unfortunate business behind us."

"Of course, Annabel," replied Sandra.

"What was your opinion of Harriett Kennedy?" asked Annabel.

"Oh her! Well she's the weak one of that class, there's no doubt. Her marks have been terrible, and she clearly hasn't applied herself properly. I asked her a fairly simple question during the lesson, and I was incredulous that she couldn't give me an answer, although after an interminable amount of thought, she did manage to work it out, which perhaps rather proves my point. If she put more proper thought into this area, she'd probably start improving. I intend to see that she does!"

"Yes, well the first thing to say about that, is that I fear you may have fallen victim to an old Charterhouse girls' trick."

"What?"

"I believe that whilst Harriett was wrestling for an answer, there was something that diverted your attention away?"

Sandra thought back. "Oh yes. One of the other girls, Emma Thatcher I believe, thought that she'd found an error in the textbook. I had thought she was one of the cleverer girls in the class, but when we examined the particular passage in more detail, the idiot girl realised that it was *she* who'd made the error!"

Annabel smiled inwardly to herself. So that was how the rascals had done it!

"And by the time you'd turned your attention back to the class, Harriett suddenly knew the answer to your question?"

"Well, yes, I believe so. Annabel, if you don't my asking, what are you getting at?"

"What I'm 'getting at' Sandra, is that whilst Emma held your attention, the other girls in the class somehow supplied the answer to Harriett."

Sandra's eyes widened as she suddenly understood, and Annabel saw a hot flame of fury burning in them.

"The pesky little scoundrels!" she spat angrily. "I'll give the lot of them six on their bottoms, next week!"

"Well, no, I *don't* think that's a good idea, Sandra," exclaimed Annabel, holding up her hands in a pacifying manner.

"It's my class, I'll do what I like!" retorted Sandra furiously.

"Yes of course, I agree with you, but do please remember that until the end of last week, I was teaching them in this, and I know all the girls well. They had Harriett's best interests at heart, believe me. I would advise you not to be too hard on them."

"They may have been thinking of Harriett's best interests, but they gave *me* a false impression," snapped Sandra. "*I* thought that she at last understood, when in fact she'd been fed the answer."

"Well, yes, of course, that's true again. But I believe that they were concerned that you would punish her, if she didn't manage to answer it. I understand that you started the lesson by giving them all a stern lecture on the standards you expected from them, tapping your cane on their desks, and then singling out Alexandra and Harriett, as the best and worst examples, respectively. You've threatened Harriett with six on the hand, if her marks don't improve and effectively told them all that you expect them to 'gravitate' to Alexandra's position."

"Who *told* you all of this?" demanded Sandra, indignantly. "It must obviously have been Alexandra, when you asked to see her at lunchtime."

"Yes. She had some concerns about what had happened, and I have a very high respect for her, in spite of her recent problem. If she has concerns, *I* listen to them, as I believe would most of the mistresses who know her well, at Charterhouse. She feels that Harriett is hard working, and tries her best, but just finds music theory difficult – and I happen to agree with her. She even implied that she would give Harriett some help with her work, if it meant that you wouldn't be continually punishing her! Again, although it is ultimately your choice, I would strongly advise you that the way to give Harriett a chance to improve, is not to threaten her with punishment if she fails – in my opinion that will only make her 'weaker'– but to encourage her."

"If I might defend myself here, Annabel!" said Sandra hotly. "Firstly, you can say what you like about my methods, but I have a proven track record of getting very good results from the girls in my classes, so I think that speaks for itself, when assessing me as a mistress.

"Secondly, it was my intention right from the start of that lesson, to establish my authority, and make it very clear what I expected from them, and yes, to make an example of one or two people, to highlight the points. I do not care one jot, what anyone else thinks, that is the way that *I* do things! I am sure that, over time, the girls will come to respect and appreciate me.

"Thirdly, it is *not* my intention to 'continually punish' Harriett, for not improving, but I do believe that there is nothing like the cold threat of my cane, on any girl's hand or bottom, to concentrate her mind most effectively!"

Annabel sighed. "Well on your first point, I cannot ague with you, though how many of the girls, *in Harriett's position*, who have actually benefited from your methods, might be debatable.

"On your second point, establishing your authority and expectations, is obviously important, but I personally don't feel that you need to do it in quite such a cold and unfeeling way, and I certainly don't want you to be humiliating a girl in front of the rest, as I think was happening today and which especially upset Alexandra. Remember Sandra, that there are limits to what is considered acceptable in maintaining classroom discipline. I repeat, Sandra, they are a good group of girls. They don't necessarily need the hard approach.

"As for your last point, I am very glad to hear that you won't be continually punishing Harriett, for failing to improve. I will not tolerate that! And I'm afraid I totally disagree with you, about what will most effectively concentrate a girl's mind."

"Could you not perhaps get to know the girls a little, before you judge them?" Annabel continued. "Try and have a joke and exchange pleasantries with them. You never know, they might respect, and appreciate you *more*, with that approach."

"I do not believe in being friendly with the girls," said Sandra flatly. "You will never achieve true discipline in that way. I'm sorry, but in my classes, it's my approach or nothing! Now if you'll excuse me, I must ..."

"No, please wait a moment, Sandra," Annabel told her. This young lady was clearly stubbornly opposed to any other method of achieving discipline than her own. She had been hoping to get her to agree to compromise a little, but that didn't seem to be the girl's style, or maybe it wasn't even in her vocabulary.

"Now listen!" she said assertively. "We've just had the biggest scandal in Charterhouse's history, and part of what inflamed the situation even more, was the revelation of Elizabeth's methods for maintaining school discipline, which *were* considered unacceptable. What you did when you singled out Harriett today, *bordered* on humiliation, which as the acting headmistress, I cannot accept. We simply can't run the risk of attracting more of the kind of bad publicity, that something like that would bring, if it became public. Remember that people pay hefty fees to send their daughters here, and they expect the highest of standards. If they think that we no longer hold true to those standards here, then they will look elsewhere – and we are, after all, a private business.

"These are my girls, who you are in temporary charge of. I'm not asking you to completely abandon your approach when you're in the classroom, but I would like you to moderate it. Now, are you going to do it voluntarily, or do I have to order you?"

Sandra stared at her, looking shocked and thought quickly. She had worked hard to get this position and she wasn't going to throw it away. She was furious at being treated in this way by Mrs Wood, but having to be ordered by her, to do what she wanted, might not look too good, she decided. So, although she completely disagreed with the request, she'd have to swallow her pride, and at least *appear* to do it, of her own free will.

"Mrs Wood," she announced, addressing her formally. "I give you my word that I will moderate my approach, as you wish."

Annabel smiled, feeling relieved, although she still had a few doubts as to whether Miss Steele could entirely keep her promise.

"Good," she replied. "Thank you."

Sandra nodded. "And now if you'll excuse me, I must go," she asserted and got up and left immediately, without waiting for Annabel's response.

Annabel puffed out her cheeks. She hoped that Sandra would at least take some of what she'd said on board. She'd done what she could for the girls.

She'd meant what she'd said about Alexandra. Not only was she extremely gifted academically, in both the sciences and the arts, she also had a particularly good character, which had been clearly demonstrated today.

Gillian Spencer's expulsion, meant that the position of Head Girl at Charterhouse, was now vacant. As far as Annabel was concerned, Alexandra was the girl to fill it. It might not be entirely appropriate for her to take it, so soon after having been suspended, but Annabel wanted to take advantage of being in this position, to push to make it happen. She couldn't say for certain, how long she'd be in the role. It could possibly only be a short time, so she couldn't afford to wait for too long.

She made a note of it, as a priority.

*\*\**

At The Grange over supper that night, Linda and Alexandra compared notes.

Alexandra felt that her first day back had been good. The sponsored walk preparations were underway, and she now knew that she was not only *eligible* as a candidate for college champion, but the *only* one. Her mother was delighted.

When Alexandra told her about the new mistress that they had for music theory, and her concerns, Linda's views were a mixture of Mrs Wood's and Miss Steele's. She was an arch-traditionalist in relation to classroom discipline, and did rather admire much of what she heard of, in the character and general approach to teaching from this 'Miss Steele' but she did agree that she might have gone a bit too far with Harriett, and she didn't believe that punishing a girl, simply because she wasn't getting on very well, was likely to achieve many positive results, either. She told her daughter not to worry too much, and to concentrate as much as she could now, on the concert.

Then Linda told Alexandra about her invitation to James.

"Now, assuming that he manages to convince Mrs Spencer, that he needs to come over here on Palace business, then I want this to be a *private* affair, Alexandra," she declared.

"Therefore, I'm going to ask Fiona, if I can drop you over at The Lodge, and let you stay there until James goes. I'll come back and collect you, then. Have a main meal for your lunch at Charterhouse, that day. I've no doubt that you'll be only too pleased to spend an evening with Tom!"

"Yes Mother, of course," Alexandra assured her. "I don't suppose, there's any point in me asking what this 'private affair' is about?"

"No, there is *not*, Alexandra," asserted Linda. "That is what *private* means! I promise that you will know, straight afterwards, though."

"Oh! OK, Mother. I'll wait with interest," said Alexandra.

# CHAPTER 2

Linda went to see James, the following morning.

"Good morning James," she said. "I'm hoping that you have some news for me."

"Good morning, Linda," he replied. "Well, yes I do. I'll be free to come and join you for dinner tomorrow night. But it wasn't easy. Last time that I did this of course, Elizabeth was still at Charterhouse, so she wasn't living there very much, but now she's at home ... She wasn't at all happy with me spending extra time with you, after we've both been at the palace all day. I decided not to tell her that you'd offered me dinner, just that you wanted me to go to The Grange. I think she suspects something, Linda, and she may have done for some time!"

"Well then that's all the more reason to act decisively now," asserted Linda. "We're reaching the time when this matter will be brought to a head, James."

She rubbed her hands together. "Right! Thank you for that, James. That's excellent news! Now, I want us to be alone this time, given what I have to propose to you, so I'm going to ask Fiona if she'll let her come to The Lodge for the evening, until we've finished. I must go and find her now. See you later, James."

"See you later, Linda," answered James, before she hurried off.

***

Arriving back at her desk, she called Carol, and told her to ask Fiona to come to see her, when she had a moment.

A few minutes later, the buzzer sounded in her office, telling her that someone was at the door. She pressed the button on her desk, to activate the green light, which told her visitor to push the door and enter. As she expected, it was Fiona. Linda asked her to take a seat.

"Just a couple of things, Fiona," she said. "The first is entirely personal. I wonder if The Lodge might be able to take Alexandra off my hands, for a couple of hours tomorrow evening? I want The Grange to be free. I know that she'll be glad of the chance to be with Tom, anyhow."

Fiona studied her, surprised. "Well yes, that should be fine. I'm going out, but Colin will be there all evening. May I ask why?"

"It's a private affair," Linda told her.

"Oh right!" replied Fiona, suppressing a smirk. She was fairly certain that this "private affair" would involve James Spencer. She knew that, apart from the dinner party, he'd visited The Grange once before, on the very day that his daughter had been sent to the Young Offenders' Institution, to discuss some "confidential matters" regarding one of Queen Alexandra's forthcoming engagements. She'd been highly sceptical about that, suspecting that it was just an excuse for them to be together, but she'd said nothing – nor would she this time, either. Things must be serious though, she thought, for Linda to want the house to herself for the evening. Perhaps she was planning to take him to bed! Poor old Elizabeth Spencer! She'd disowned her daughter, lost her job, and now it looked like her husband might be going to have an affair, with the woman who had finally forced her downfall. Things could hardly get much worse for her.

"What time, were you thinking of, Linda?" she asked.

"Around 7.00 p.m., probably. She'll have her main meal at lunchtime, whilst she's at Charterhouse. I'll bring her over, and come back for her once we've finished."

"OK. Agreed," confirmed Fiona.

"Thank you, Fiona," said Linda. She was pleased. Now she could initiate her final plan. But before then, she had a formal matter to attend to, the course of action that she was about to take, having been arranged with Queen Alexandra, yesterday.

With her hand concealed beneath the desk, she took out a remote control device from her skirt pocket. Without looking down, she felt for the button and pressed it, starting up an audio sound recording system, secretly installed around her office, some weeks ago, and which only she and the queen knew about. There was a series of microphones and speakers, discreetly placed around the room. Linda was now able to record any conversations with courtiers that she felt necessary, for security purposes. This was the very first time that she'd used it in an official capacity.

Then she slipped the remote back in her pocket.

Linda continued, "Fiona, the other thing that I must talk to you about, concerns the dinner party at the end of last week. I won't comment on your views regarding Her Majesty's relationship with Lord George Sackville. They are your affair and you apologised for offending the queen, when she rebuked you. But there was also the manner in which you departed. I must formally remind you that you are one of Her Majesty's courtiers and as such, should be especially careful to observe court etiquette at all times! I appreciate that you didn't strictly breach any royal protocol, but to leave my house so abruptly, with no proper reason given, with Her Majesty in attendance, really was most inappropriate and rude, and the queen feels that, given what had already occurred that night, it could have been interpreted as a snub, which she finds most embarrassing!

"Accordingly, I am making a note on your file, and documenting this as an official verbal warning. The conversation has also been audio recorded! That will be all."

Once more, under the cover of her desk, she brought out the remote, pressed the button again to finish the recording and put the device back in her pocket.

Fiona was dumbfounded. "A verbal warning? What in the world do you mean?" she exclaimed. "I wasn't at work; it was a private party!"

"Fiona, when Her Majesty is in attendance, it makes no difference to those of us who work in her court, whether the occasion is a formal or a private affair," remarked Linda. "Both protocol and etiquette must be maintained at all times! I'm a little concerned that I have to tell that, to someone in your position at court."

Fiona's anger, which she often very successfully kept hidden, now began to simmer.

"So, there's a recording of this conversation then, is there?" she demanded, looking about the room. "I see no evidence of that kind, in here!"

For a third time, Linda brought out the remote, this time just edging it far enough out of her skirt to enable it to be operable. She wanted it kept secret, so that no one would attempt to steal the evidence, once they realised that – whatever it was – had been recorded. She pressed another button and immediately her verbal warning to Fiona, was played back.

Fiona nearly jumped out of her chair, when she heard Linda's words repeated. They seemed to be coming from all over the office and she couldn't pinpoint the precise position of whatever device Linda was using.

"You crafty sod!" she shouted, furiously. "I've a good mind to go back on my promise, to let Alexandra come to The Lodge tomorrow night, now!"

Linda shifted slightly in her chair. She'd been slightly worried that Fiona might take that attitude, and she did really need the favour that she'd requested. She *could* keep Alexandra at The Grange, and simply tell her to stay out of the way, whilst she made her proposal to James, but she was hoping to build up the mood romantically with the dinner, and really wanted them to be alone together.

In a conciliatory tone, she said, "Fiona, I'm sorry. Please don't take this personally. I'm just doing my job. This action was carried out by the express order of Her Majesty."

"Hmm," mumbled Fiona. "Very well then. I shall be more mindful of court etiquette at *all times* in the future. You have my word. And Alexandra can come to The Grange tomorrow night."

"Thank you, Fiona," said Linda.

"Now, if you'll excuse me, I'm late for lunch," asserted Fiona.

***

And so that night, Linda confirmed to Alexandra that James was coming to The Grange tomorrow, for dinner, and that Fiona had agreed that she could go to The Lodge with Tom. This would allow her to have The Grange to herself in which to conduct her "private affair," though she still wasn't telling her daughter what that was.

# CHAPTER 3

The next morning – Day 3 of that week, Fiona was in her office when Carol came through on the phone, telling her that she had someone on the line, wishing to speak to her. When Fiona asked who it was, she was surprised by the answer. She had met the woman on one or two occasions, but didn't know her very well.

She decided that she might as well see what she wanted, and told Carol to put her through. Fifteen minutes later she was very glad that she'd made that decision. She was now very much looking forward to allowing Linda Radcliffe the chance to conduct her "private business" for entirely unexpected – and welcome – reasons.

\*\*\*

In the evening, Linda was prepared. She was wearing the same outfit that she had worn when James had driven Alexandra and herself to Avermore, something which was not lost on her daughter, when she went into the parlour, and told her that she was ready to walk her down to The Lodge. Philippa had earlier been there, to give Alexandra another practice session.

Fiona answered the door when they arrived at 6.45, somewhat to Linda's surprise.

"Still here?" she enquired.

"Yes, but I'm just getting ready to go out," explained Fiona. "I'll be leaving in about half an hour."

"Hello, Alexandra," she continued. "Tom is in the parlour, with his father."

"Thank you, Mrs Clark," said Alexandra. She turned to her mother, and they kissed.

"Goodbye Mother. Good luck with whatever it is you're doing tonight!" she said.

"Thank you, darling. See you later," replied Linda and Alexandra hurried to the parlour, grateful that she didn't have to suffer one of Fiona's usual grillings about her everyday affairs, and that the woman would soon be gone for the evening.

"Well I'll be getting back to The Grange, then Fiona," said Linda. "I'll be back later, to fetch Alexandra. Goodbye!"

She turned and hurried away.

"Goodbye, Linda!" Fiona called, as she left.

"Nice to see you again at The Lodge, Alexandra!" said Colin.

"Nice to see you too, Mr Clark!" replied Alexandra, beaming at him. She was much more fond of Tom's father, than she was his stepmother.

"Shall we have a drink then?" asked Tom. "I know that you'll have a black coffee, Alexandra,"

"And I'll have a cup of tea," said Colin.

"Two black coffees and a tea then," confirmed Tom.

Whilst he went to make them, Alexandra talked with Colin. After he'd returned, they settled down for the evening.

***

Once she was back at The Grange, Linda made a final check that all was ready, and that she was looking at her best. This was her biggest night, on a personal level, for many years, and she was excited. She'd waited a long time for this! But she kept a check on her emotions. She wanted tonight to be a success, and that was up to her now, so she had to keep as calm as possible.

James arrived at the gate, punctually, at 7.00 p.m. and Linda let him through the security gate. A couple of minutes later, she opened the door to welcome him in. She saw his eyes transfixed by the vision before him, which indeed, he couldn't fail to remember having seen before.

"Linda, you look fantastic!" he exclaimed.

"Well thank you, James!" replied Linda, smiling. "I thought I'd just spruce myself up a touch – it wasn't much!" She flicked a finger through her blonde hair.

"I'll take your coat, and put it in the cloakroom," she said.

"Thanks," replied James. "I'd have worn my dinner suit tonight, but I couldn't get too dressed up, or Elizabeth would *certainly* have been suspicious! I do feel a little under-dressed, but I don't mind being in inferior to a woman looking as you are!"

Linda felt her sexual arousal deepening, and she was sure James's was, too.

"You are doing well, so far, James Spencer!" she remarked. "And you look fine. Come through to the parlour."

"Thank you again, Linda. The other thing, is that I'd better not drink much tonight. Not only am I driving back home, but we're officially supposed to be working, so it wouldn't seem appropriate to return to Elizabeth with the smell and effects of alcohol, too clearly in evidence."

"Yes, don't worry, James," replied Linda, reassuringly as she motioned for him to take a seat on the sofa. "Everything is in hand. This has been meticulously planned, by myself, as you'll doubtless have expected. I'm not planning anything too elaborate for dinner, but just something to help create a pleasant atmosphere, as we build up to what you know I've really invited you for."

"I'm sure a small pre-dinner drink or two will be fine though," she continued. "Will you have one?"

"Oh. Alright then, yes please," said James. "A dry sherry would be nice."

"Ha! You're stealing my daughter's tipple!" laughed Linda. "She tipped a bit of that back at the dinner party, at the end of last week! And I'll have my usual g and t."

She poured their drinks and handed James his.

"Right!" she announced. "I'd better go and get things started. Would you like a bit of music, whilst you wait?"

"Thanks, yes that would be nice, Linda," said James. "Whatever you've got, that will be fine."

"Well we've got a fair bit," replied Linda. She loaded the player and it started. Then, with a wave of her hand to James, she went out and headed for the kitchen.

\*\*\*

Meanwhile, at 7.15, Fiona left The Lodge and got into her car. She drove down the hamlet drive to the gate. Swiping her card through the console, it opened and she went out.

However, she stopped and parked just outside the entrance. Looking around, Fiona saw the woman who she'd spoken to on the phone earlier, walking towards her car. She got out.

The woman reached Fiona, and handed her an envelope. Fiona briefly checked the contents. Satisfied, she nodded, and went to the gate. She swiped the outside console, and as it opened again, the woman walked through, thanking her, as she passed. The gate automatically closed once more, and Fiona put the envelope in her coat pocket, got back in her car, and drove off to her destination.

\*\*\*

Linda could hear the strains of the music playing in the parlour, and she hummed softly along to it, sipping her gin and tonic, whilst she worked on the dinner. It was a relatively simple affair, for a woman of her culinary skills, a particular traditional Geratican dish, that she knew James liked.

About halfway through the cooking time, with everything progressing well, Linda went back to the parlour to James, and poured them both a top up. She sat down in her armchair briefly, to talk with him, before she needed to go and begin dishing up.

\*\*\*

Outside The Grange, Elizabeth Spencer looked through the gates to the house. It had been her, who had phoned Fiona's extension at the palace this morning. From their brief previous meetings, (including the infamous dinner party, when Fiona had blamed her cooking, for an illness that she'd suffered, subsequently – an allegation which they'd had words about), and hearing of her reputation, Elizabeth had gathered that one of Fiona's biggest weaknesses, was money. She had guessed therefore that she might be susceptible to a bribe, and sure enough Fiona had accepted it – for the right price, eventually agreed by them both (though Fiona had driven a hard bargain and pushed her further than she'd wanted to).

When her husband had told her that he was coming here tonight, she hadn't believed the reason, he gave her. She had wondered for some time about his relationship with the accursed Linda Radcliffe, and even suspected an affair, though she'd had no real evidence. But now, she was starting to become more certain that *something* was happening between them – and not just their so-called heavy workload. Therefore, she had decided to discreetly follow on to Greenacres herself, in her now repaired car, a few minutes after James left, to take a closer look. She knew The Grange. She'd been there before, on one of Linda's previous dinner parties.

Her arrangement with Fiona had been, that if she swiped the gate, and allowed her to enter Elmsbrook in secret, then she would pay her an amount in cash – and this was what had just occurred.

The curtains were all drawn at the front of the house. She looked at a window to the left, where she knew Linda's study was. There was no light on, and no sign of life. If they *were* working, then it certainly wasn't in there! But on the other side she could see through the curtains of the front parlour window, a light burning brightly.

She knew that there was a wood running right around the back of Elmsbrook, starting at this end and coming out outside The Lodge, at the other end of the hamlet. Fiona had told her that there was a rear access to The Grange, if she walked a short distance through the wood, but that at about halfway along the path, there was a perfect vantage point, for looking directly into the back of the house. She began to make her way there.

Elizabeth soon reached the spot that Fiona indicated, a small gap in between two tall bushes. She stopped and peered through. A light could also be seen from the back window of the parlour, on the far side of her. The window nearest her was the dining room and there was a large full length window with a door within, which could open on to a patio. Steps then led down to the spacious garden. The light was on in this room too, but unlike in the rest of the house, the curtains were still pulled back, and the room was illuminated in its full glory to Elizabeth, as she stood in almost total darkness.

*How careless of you, Linda!* thought Elizabeth, wickedly. *Thank you!*

As she watched, she saw Linda enter and start laying dishes on the table. So! They were having dinner together were they? And when she saw the glamorous black gown that Linda was wearing, she could tell that this meeting wasn't purely a business one. She felt the first tickles of a flame of anger, rising inside of her, but she was determined to keep watching. The next half an hour or so, could tell her everything that she needed to know, about her husband and Linda Radcliffe.

# CHAPTER 4

"Dinner is served, James," Linda told him.

"Oh! Right you are, then," he said, as he got up, and followed Linda into the dining room.

They took their places at the table, and began their meal.

From outside in the wood, the spectator of whom they were completely ignorant, looked on. So this was them – together.

There were in fact two wine glasses on the table and a bottle. Linda opened the bottle, and poured a drop into James' glass, for him to taste.

"Mmm. Very nice," he said. "But don't forget what ..."

"It's non-alcoholic wine," Linda explained. "We don't tend to have *too* much call for it, here at The Grange, but today it might prove an appropriate and ideal substitute for the real thing!"

"You're a crafty woman!" exclaimed James. "You think of everything. Anyone looking, would think that this *was* the real thing – as did I before you told me. Thank you!"

He was of course, unaware of the irony in what he'd just said.

"I suppose I can take that as a compliment," mused Linda. "But it's actually the second time this week, that I've been called 'crafty' and on the first occasion the accuser certainly did *not* mean it to express that sentiment! I did tell you of the occasion that I'm referring to, yesterday, in fact."

James looked at her and thought for a moment, as he ate. Then he took a sip of wine.

"Oh, you mean Fiona," he said, finally.

"I do," Linda confirmed.

"Well you told me confidentially that you'd given her a verbal warning, but how did *that* word come up out of it, for goodness sake?"

"I suppose now that Fiona's seen it demonstrated, it will get out, so I might as well tell you, I suppose."

And so Linda proceeded to tell James about her new audio recording machine.

James' eyebrows rose. "Well! Perhaps she had a point!" he exclaimed.

"Yes, well up until yesterday, only Her Majesty and I knew about its installation in my office, and what I *don't* want to reveal, to *anyone* – even including *you,* I'm afraid, James – is exactly how I record, play back and store the sound. I don't want anyone rummaging around, hoping to find out, because they want to destroy any evidence of information, that I've recorded them giving me."

"Oh go on. Don't be rotten!" said James playfully.

"No, I will *not*!" insisted Linda. "Don't you go thinking that I'm going to start giving you any special treatment, either." She pointed her fork at him.

James chuckled. "It's alright, Linda. I understand. I won't ask any more."

"How has your car been?" he asked, changing the subject.

"It's fine. No problems. Has Elizabeth had hers fixed now, after 'accidentally' crashing in to mine?"

"She has, yes. And talking of driving, have you decided whether you want to try and encourage Alexandra to start learning?"

"Well, not entirely, but I don't think I'll push it too hard, after what she told you last week," replied Linda, as she refilled James' glass. "I can't fault her reasoning, that a nervous driver can be a dangerous one, and she probably *will* be a nervous one, especially to begin with. I think that, as with most things, she would gradually get more confident, but if she's set her heart on not wanting to do it, and would really prefer Tom to, then there's no point in making her. Most women do drive, and it's usually us who take the *main* responsibility for it, in relationships and families, but men can obviously drive too – you being an a case in point - and I don't suppose it would *really* matter if Tom did it, and Alexandra didn't."

They finished their main course, and Linda gathered up their plates and took them to the kitchen. James helped with the other dishes.

Then she served up their dessert, and they began to eat again, together with another top up of wine.

From her vantage point outside, Elizabeth still watched. It was cold and she pulled her coat tighter around her shoulders, but she was determined to see every moment of this liaison.

As they reached the end of the course, there was a brief pause in the pair's conversation. Linda decided that the moment had arrived.

"Right, James!" she said. "It's time to get down to business. You know the matter that I'm going to propose, and that it's traditional for me to talk, and you to listen, for a while."

She cleared her throat. "We've been colleagues at the palace, for a number of years now, and I think you'll agree that we've developed a strong rapport together, and our relationship has gradually become closer. We've already established the fact, that our feelings are such that we would both like to be together on a permanent basis. I certainly feel that there is no one else who's company I enjoy and crave for more, we have a great sense of humour together, which seems to entertain others – including my daughter! – and we both, broadly speaking, like to do similar things, especially if it means that we are with each other. I also find you extremely desirable sexually, and believe that you find me attractive, too!"

"I have been a widow for ten years, and although I will obviously always have Robert in my heart, I do desire another relationship, and to move on. Alexandra will almost certainly be moving out of The Grange to go to University next year, so I will be here on my own. But she and I have had a discussion on this subject, and I know that in the meantime, whilst she is still here, she would be quite happy to see me become settled with another man, and maybe even have him move in. So, James Spencer, that is basically what I am proposing. I love you most deeply and I wish to establish a permanent romantic union between ourselves, and for it to be based at The Grange!

"Now, you know the type of woman that I am, James. I am very traditional in temperament, and in the form of relationship that I want. I am dominant and I want to lead, and be in total control of every part of it. If necessary I will force the issue, but if a man will naturally let me take over, and have my way, then it makes things all the easier, and it's the ideal state of affairs for me! I admit that if I *don't* get my way – or if someone does something, or something happens that I don't like – then I can have a temper, and I am, it goes without saying, very assertive. But I'm also very loving and affectionate, and when it really comes down to it, I want a man who will need me to take control and to lead, guide and take care of him, and trust in my judgement completely.

"*I* know the type of man that you are, too, James. You seek a traditional Geratican relationship, and although we may joke about things, when it really comes down to it for you, it's a woman with my personality that you feel most comfortable with, and are most attracted to. I also know that you don't get that from your wife, and that she even likes you to take a more dominant role than you prefer. If you come and live here, you *know* that this will *not* happen, and that I *will* give you the type of relationship that we both want. That relationship will never alter and once a marriage contract is agreed and signed, it isn't the done thing to change the terms.

"So James Spencer, leaving to one side for a moment, the fact that you're married, and haven't yet broached the subject of leaving your wife, do you broadly agree with what I propose? If so, then I shall shortly come on to my solution to your problem."

James took a deep breath. "Yes, I do agree with what you propose, Linda," he said. "I don't like the way my marriage has gone, mainly due to the role that my wife now wants me to play in it, and I'd much prefer the type of relationship that I know you'd provide. She's changing the original terms of our marriage contract. You also have a strength of personality, that attracts me like no other woman, and I can't deny that I've always found you the most beautiful woman at the palace! I enjoy your company, too, and the humour that always exists between us. I'd happily do anything with you, or for you, because I love you!"

"Good!" said Linda smiling. "Well, now we must deal with the terms. Firstly, I want you to promise me that you'll always be totally loyal, faithful and respectful to me, and that you'll never question, or try to change, the nature of our relationship. I'm almost as sure as I can be of all these things being the case, but I still need to hear you promise them – and if you break that promise ..." She deliberately broke off and left the comment hanging in mid-air, for maximum effect.

"You have my promise, Linda!" said James reassuringly. "You know that, underneath the humour, I have enormous respect for you, and I'll never leave or be unfaithful to you. If you take control of the relationship in the way you propose, then why would I ever want to? It's what I want."

"Excellent!" asserted Linda. "Well the other term, which is the most obvious, relates to you still being in your relationship with Elizabeth, and that, in order for us to proceed with this one, you will have to tell her that you want to leave! If, after that happens, she should eventually grant you a divorce, I am giving you an assurance that a proposal of marriage will follow. If you are correct in your thinking, then that may never happen, but in any case, we must deal with the first part of the issue, before anything else can happen.

"So, to that end, this is what I want you to do. You must go home tonight, and tell Elizabeth that *I* want to see you both at The Grange, tomorrow night. Just that, and no more. Then, assuming that all goes according to plan, and you both come, then I shall invite you both into the parlour. I shall sit in my armchair, and you and Elizabeth will be on the sofa. You will then tell your wife, the situation between us, that you're not happy being with her, and that you'd rather be living here with me. Once that is finally said, then you will cross over to the armchair next to mine, where Alexandra normally sits, when we aren't on the sofa. That's all you'll have to do, and then I'll take over from there. But the actual statement, telling Elizabeth that you want to leave her, *must* come from you, James."

"Is that clear, and do you think that you can do it?" she asked.

"Assuming that I can get Elizabeth to agree to come over here with me tomorrow, then yes, I believe that with you present in the room, I will feel able to tell her what we desire," confirmed James.

"Thank you," said Linda. "In actual fact, you have another valid reason for wanting to leave her now, of course. After the scandal that's developed on her watch at Charterhouse, and especially the way it's emerged that she's treated some of the girls there – including my daughter, Alexandra – you'd surely be fully justified in wishing to distance yourself from her."

"Hmm, you may be right, Linda, yes," replied James.

"Of course I am!" asserted Linda dominantly. "Well, I think that's about all we need to say then, unless you want to add anything?"

"No. I'm sure we've covered everything most thoroughly, Linda," replied James. "No one would have expected anything different from you – least of all me!"

"Well let's leave it there for now, and hope that our plans come to fruition, tomorrow," said Linda. She reached out, and lightly ran her gloved fingers over James' hand. "Now, shall we have a little something to celebrate? I'm going to have my usual black coffee, and port."

"That'll be fine for me, too, thanks, Linda," James told her.

Linda did the honours, slipping a mint into both of their saucers, and then they sat on the couch in the dining room, so that they could look out into the night, through the full length window, as they sipped their after dinner drinks and talked.

She had slipped her arm around James's shoulders, an action that had thrilled him, and heightened his sexual arousal. His genus ballooned, and he naturally shifted himself even closer to Linda's body. Her own sexual hunger was like nothing she had experienced for a very long time, and she desperately wanted to, at least partly, satisfy it.

As she held him close, her geratis throbbed inside her gown. It had extended several inches outside of her vagina, and was aggressively seeking James' genus, in direct relation to Linda's longing for him.

She whispered into his ear, "I love you, James. I've wanted you for so long!" and began to kiss him, softly.

"I love you too, Linda," James answered. "You don't know for how long I've wanted you!"

He kissed her back in response, but then Linda's became stronger and more dominant, gradually overpowering him. His breathing became more laboured in his excitement, and he looked submissively and invitingly, into her eyes.

Nothing turned Linda on more, than to sense those sentiments from a man. She always took the initiative in carnal matters anyhow, but even more than the average Geratican woman, she found it particularly stimulating when a man openly encouraged her, and let her do what she wanted.

She leant over, and pushed James down beneath her on the couch. As she lay atop of him, she wrapped her arms around him, and squeezed his legs inside of hers. After so long, the feeling of an actual man's body beneath her, and her hugely erect geratis throbbing against his thigh, as it ached to go inside James, and grind his genus, was exquisite. She kissed him passionately, slipping her tongue into his mouth, and finding his own easily, and as she licked it, James became even more aroused. His mind couldn't help but think of bed, and he thought it inevitable that Linda would be thinking of the same thing. He'd not had the slightest thought that events might turn out that way, when he'd come here this evening, but from the extent of Linda's desire, he began to wonder if it was her intention.

He studied her face, which Linda noticed.

"What are you thinking?" she asked.

"Well," he said, cautiously. He didn't want to offend Linda, with an inappropriate suggestion. "After what you've just done, I was wondering if you wanted to go upstairs?"

"As a matter of fact James, I do," admitted Linda. "But it won't be happening tonight. We have to go about this in the correct manner. You must have left Elizabeth first. I won't be accused of being the cause of you being unfaithful to your wife. Once you have, and you're living here, though, *then my darling, I'm **going** to make love to you!*" Linda said the last words, very softly, and licked her lips seductively at James, whilst slipping two fingers through her hair. She felt his body stiffen with excitement, and he murmured slightly, as he briefly lost his breath, and his genus ballooned further.

Outside, Elizabeth had finally seen enough. She hurried back out of the wood, and opened the front gate of The Grange. Then she marched up the long drive, to the front door.

Linda was still on top of James, when the doorbell rang. She froze.

"Who in the world can that be?" she exclaimed, hopping off the couch. "It must be someone from The Lodge, because no one's buzzed the intercom to be let into Elmsbrook – unless someone from The Lodge did it, or Fiona's just returned, and it's her. But she's not expected back for a while yet."

"Well, I suppose I'd better go and find out," Linda continued. She laid a hand on James's arm. "Stay in here!" she told him quietly, but firmly. She smoothed her gown and went out.

Before Linda reached the front porch door, the bell rang again. "Alright, I'm coming!" she said.

As she opened it, she could just see an elbow, to the side of the door. Suddenly, Elizabeth Spencer barged her way in.

"Elizabeth! How ..." Linda began, horrified, before Elizabeth cut her off.

"You *bitch*!" she screamed and struck Linda across the mouth, drawing blood, and momentarily knocking her off balance.

As she recovered, Linda wiped her lip. "Elizabeth, calm down!" she exclaimed. "What are you talking about? Who let you into Elmsbrook?"

"Oh-Ho! I'd bet you'd like to know!" laughed Elizabeth sarcastically. "Your neighbour very kindly obliged – for a consideration – before she left tonight!"

"Fiona?" spat Linda, incredulously, her eyes wide. "The little–"

"She also gave me some rather useful information, about where to best position myself, to watch your little performance in the dining room. Oh yes, I saw it all – from the wood outside! And *what* I saw, confirmed what I've long suspected. That *you* are having an affair with *my* husband!"

Linda gaped at her for a second, and then quickly ushered Elizabeth into hall, shutting the porch and house doors behind her.

"Where is he then?" demanded Elizabeth, looking about. "James! Come on out!" she shouted at the top of her voice. "There's no point in hiding! This might be a big house, but I'll find your cubbyhole! And then I'll give you a tongue lashing that you'll never forget!"

"You will do no such thing, whilst he is a guest in my house, Elizabeth!" retorted Linda. "Now please. I'll willingly tell you where James is. If, as you claim, you've been snooping on us, then he's still in the place where you saw him. If you'll come with me, I'll take you there, and we'll discuss this civilly. It isn't quite as you think."

"Not quite as I think?" exploded Elizabeth. "Do you think that I'm an idiot? I've just seen you, climbing all over my husband!"

"For the very first time!" Linda told her. "Now please, come and sit down, and we'll explain the exact situation."

"Pah!" spat Elizabeth. "Take me to your little theatre stage, then."

She followed Linda down the hall to the dining room.

James had heard the commotion at the door, and jumped when he'd realised who Linda's visitor was. A feeling of dread gripped him, as he heard Elizabeth coming.

As Linda and Elizabeth entered the room, James desperately tried to avoid eye contact with his wife.

Elizabeth scowled as she saw him. "You cheating–" she began.

"*Elizabeth!*" thundered Linda. "I will not have you say another word in this house, until we've had a chance to explain the situation! Now please, take a seat." She motioned to the couch, next to James.

Linda drew up her dining room chair, and placed the one that James had been sat on, adjacent to it. She sat down. Elizabeth looked at her expectantly.

"Right," began Linda, "Elizabeth, your husband has done nothing wrong, and he most certainly has *not* been unfaithful to you. We can both swear truthfully, that what you've just witnessed has not happened before, though *not* that it won't happen again in the future. And this is due to the reason for our meeting this evening. I'm sorry if James misled you slightly, but he was under my instructions. My original plan was for James to ask you to come here tomorrow night with him, as I had something that I wished to discuss with you, but as you have so unexpectedly arrived *tonight*, instead, then I shall move it forward, accordingly."

"I still don't understand, Linda," said Elizabeth, impatiently. "What 'reason' did you have for this 'meeting' tonight?"

"If you listen, Elizabeth, James has something he wishes to tell you," announced Linda. She looked across, and prompted him with a movement of her eyes.

James's heart beat fast. He'd expected to be doing this tomorrow, which would have given him time to prepare. But at least this unexpected development would get it over with. He understood now, the significance of the extra chair, that Linda had set out. He cleared his throat.

"Elizabeth," he said, "For some time now, I believe that neither of us have been terribly happy in our marriage, and I've felt very uncomfortable with the role that you like me to play in it. I prefer to be in a traditional

Geratican relationship. Under the original terms of the marriage contract, ours was more like that. I have known Linda at work, for a number of years now, and we've grown fond of each other, to the point where I have feelings for her. She likes a traditional Geratican relationship too, has been a widow for ten years. and is seeking someone new. As she can offer me the kind of relationship that I crave – and added to that, the recent events at Charterhouse, where I feel that you've let our daughter behave disgracefully, and that Linda's daughter and others have sometimes been treated rather unfairly – then I'm truly sorry Elizabeth, but I wish to leave you, and move in to The Grange, with Linda."

As Linda had told him, he then got up from the couch, and sat on the chair, beside Linda. She reached across, and took his hand in hers. Linda was pleased. He had, in the end, managed to put his feelings across, very well. His role in their plan, was now over. She would finish the job.

Elizabeth sat open mouthed. She folded her arms. "Well I can see you're still in the middle of your performance, in this theatre!" she declared caustically.

"I assure you, this is no performance, Elizabeth," replied Linda.

Elizabeth rounded on James. "So that's it, is it? You think you can just walk across the room, to hide behind Linda's skirt, and that will be the end of it, do you?"

"Elizabeth!" he protested.

"This decision has been jointly agreed by both of us, Elizabeth," Linda informed her. "This evening, I proposed a relationship with James, in the traditional Geratican manner, and he accepted in the same way. That was my true reason for inviting him here tonight. Of course the main issue to resolve, was the fact that he was still living with you. That was why I intended for you to be invited over tomorrow, so that James could tell you then, as he has been finding it difficult to face telling you, without me being there to support him, for some time now."

"Has *she* put you up to this?" demanded Elizabeth to James. Then she attempted a more conciliatory approach. "It's not too late to turn back you know. If you stay with me, I promise to make some compromises, and then I'm sure that we'll be able to come to an amicable arrangement."

"No Elizabeth, Linda *didn't* 'put me up to this," he declared. "I've come to decide this for myself, and wanted it for a long time. And I won't turn back now. It's too late for you to promise a 'compromise' to me. I don't believe that you will, when it really comes down to it. I'm certain that you've known my feelings for a long time, yet you've never shown the slightest inclination to compromise before. I'm sorry Elizabeth, but I've made my final decision. I want to be with Linda."

Elizabeth glared, and at the same time, there was a hint of a tear in her eye. "So be it, then!" she snarled. "You're a weak lily-livered man, James, and regrettably there are still a lot like you in this world." Her voice became bitter in tone, and laced with sarcasm. *"No doubt from what I've seen, she's going to give you what you want in bed!"*

"Take him if you must, Linda," she continued, "but you mark my words, I will *never*, I repeat *never*, grant James a divorce! You'll *never* marry him. You may have succeeded in getting rid of me at Charterhouse College, and I may now be estranged from my daughter, but you aren't going to take my husband for your own, as well!"

She got up. "I'll see myself out. Please let me out of this blasted hamlet, when I reach the gate, so that I can return to my car. Let me know when you want to collect your things, James – so that *I* can arrange to be out."

"I'll come back tonight, Elizabeth," James told her. "I've brought nothing with me, even for an overnight stay. I'll collect my things, and officially move out, tomorrow night, after work."

"Well, I will have gone to bed," Elizabeth replied. "I don't wish to see you. I shall lock the bedroom door, and you can sleep in the spare room. Tomorrow morning, I want you gone to work by the time I get up. In the evening, I shall be out until late, so you can take whatever you need, before I return. Goodnight!"

With that, she flounced out, finding her way back down the passages to the front porch. Linda and James heard the doors bang shut, as she left.

They were silent for a moment or two.

"Well, at least it's done now," remarked Linda. "You did well, James. I was proud of you. You are *not* a lily-livered man!"

"I think she was a bit more upset, than she was letting on." replied James.

"I'm sure that she was," said Linda. "And much as I loathe the woman, I *am* genuinely sorry for that. But it can't be helped. Sometimes these things have to happen, to enable us all to move on."

"From what she said just then, do you think Elizabeth's not appealing against her dismissal from Charterhouse College, after all?" wondered James. "The last I knew, she was still minded to."

"Perhaps," replied Linda. "I don't think she stands much chance of success if she does appeal. But either way, I'm sure that we'll find out eventually."

Linda checked the monitor, and saw Elizabeth. She pressed the button to open the gate, and watched her go through, and leave Elmsbrook. She secretly hoped that she would never return.

# CHAPTER 5

Fiona left the card table at the club, with her total winnings for the night. She went to the desk, and confirmed that she wished them to be transferred to her personal bank account. The woman retrieved a box, and Fiona took out a remote device, from her handbag. She entered a password, known only to her, and the box opened. The official placed Fiona's cash inside. Fiona re-entered her password, and the box closed again. It was now security sealed and could not be opened by anyone else, but her. The box would be sent to her bank, and when they were ready to make the transaction, she would be contacted, and asked to open it in the same way. Once it was completed, she would close it with her password again, and the box would be returned to the club, ready for her next visit.

When Elizabeth Spencer had contacted her earlier in the day, Fiona had indeed, been unable to resist the offer of such easy money. Had it not been for the humiliation that she'd felt, after receiving the verbal warning from Linda, she might not have quite so readily obliged Elizabeth with her request, since she was not personally close to her, and didn't share all of her most 'radical' views, either. But after that, added to having lost one hundred geros to Linda last week, and the stinging rebuke that she'd also received from the queen, she'd felt in a mood for vengeance.

Elizabeth had been so desperate to gain entry to Elmsbrook, that Fiona had easily managed to raise the price for her assistance, substantially. She had added some extra information, relating to a particular spot in the wood, where the back of the house could be most clearly viewed, into the mix, which had secured the deal in her favour.

She had then taken the money that Elizabeth had given her, together with that which she'd already been planning to use, and increased its value still further, at the card table.

Fiona hadn't quite handed all the money to the desk, however. She'd kept a small proportion back. One of the reasons why she favoured this club, was that it catered for the kind of Geratican woman, who, flushed with success and a certain amount of cash to spend, wished to celebrate with a glass of the house red, and a man of her choice, in one of the private rooms, behind the bar. Privately, she'd been much amused by the fuss over Gillian Spencer, and the escort boys at Charterhouse. Perhaps a public school *was* a highly unusual place for such an activity, but Fiona knew of numerous places in Geratica, which a woman could frequent, if she was looking for that kind of thing. And this was one of them.

Particularly in matters of money or sex, Fiona was a greedy woman. As well as a particularly healthy sex life with her husband (to whom she was happily married), she also sought more on the side (and as much of it as possible). Colin knew nothing of this part of her life.

Walking away from the desk, her erect and extended geratis throbbing against her thigh, Fiona slipped quietly into an empty, dimly lit area. She opened a door, and disappeared into the discreet corridor that was concealed behind it.

A girl in a smart business suit, sat behind another desk. She smiled knowingly at Fiona, as she came in. All women who found their way into this corridor, were looking for the same thing.

"Good evening, Mrs Clark," she said.

"Good evening," replied Fiona, and laid her money on the desk. "Room 6, please!"

The girl checked the cash.

"Very good, Mrs Clark," she replied. "You just want the standard position then? You know that it's extra, for an alternative one?"

"No, that won't be necessary," Fiona declared. "Nathan won't be moving off his back at all, for the next half an hour!"

The girl chuckled, naughtily. "That's fine," she said. "Virtually every woman chooses the same – as would I – but I still have to ask. If you'd like to follow me, then?"

She led the way down the corridor to Room 6, at the far end, her tight black skirt straining against her thighs as she walked.

She opened the door. Inside was Nathan, a tall blonde-haired and handsome man – the type that Fiona found irresistible. He was her personal favourite out of the selection at this club, and she'd been choosing him for some time, now.

"Nathan, this woman wishes a half hour session with you – standard mode," she announced.

She glanced at Fiona. "Enjoy your session!" she said.

"Thank you," replied Fiona, as the girl withdrew, closing the door behind her.

Nathan looked at her. "Hello darling!" he said huskily.

"Hello Nathan!" Fiona replied, a hungry, wolfish smirk on her face.

Nathan stepped to the bed and lay down stretched out on his back. He stared into Fiona's eyes seductively. There was really no need for the girl outside, to tell him what 'mode' this woman wanted. By now, he knew what Fiona's favourite position was. The same as virtually every other woman that he'd ever met!

Fiona licked her lips in anticipation, her green eyes gleaming with desire. Her heart beat fast, and her geratis extended out of her vagina, as far as it could possibly go, as she undressed. Nathan's arousal grew stronger, as he saw it – not quite the longest, but in the top three or four of all the many women that he'd been with. His genus couldn't wait for it to do its work, inside of his vagina.

At last Fiona climbed on top of Nathan. She took a sip from the glass of wine beside her that was automatically provided, and went down over his body. His fragrance was intoxicating. Her geratis instantly shot inside him, and found his genus.

She had her way with him twice, during the half hour session, before finishing her wine, getting back dressed, leaving the room, and exiting the club. Getting into her car, she began her drive home.

***

Back at The Grange, Linda checked the time.

"Well. I suppose I'd better think about going to fetch Alexandra from The Lodge," she said.

"Do you want me to help you clear away, Linda?" asked James. "It's the least I can do, and after all, I'll be living here, from tomorrow night!"

Linda thought about it. "Yes, I suppose you could. It can be your first test, to show me your drying up skills! I've always been quite lucky with my daughter. She's dropped very little of my crockery, over the years. If you make the grade, I might just give her the night off, once in a while!"

"Oh, thank you, Linda. I know exactly what's going to happen now!" groaned James.

Linda laughed. "Well let's get started then, and we'll see if you can withstand the pressure of my beady eye watching you!"

And so they went to the kitchen and Linda washed up, and James dried.

"I'm going to have some strong words with Fiona later," announced Linda. "How *dare* she allow Elizabeth bribe her, to let her into Elmsbrook, and spy on The Grange?"

"Hmm." said James. "It's going to be strange, with three people who work at the palace, all living in the one small hamlet."

"Well, the Festival of Divinity is getting close, once again, and traditionally on Divinity Day, the people at The Lodge, come and join us at The Grange," Linda told him. "Fiona and I do have our ups and downs though, and it's been particularly rocky just recently, so it remains to be seen, how well we can put aside our differences, for the holiday."

"You don't have to tell *me* that you two have your differences," remarked James.

Linda glanced at him as she washed a plate. "No, I don't suppose I do. But I do try to hide them as much as possible, where Alexandra is concerned. She and Tom have always been best friends, and now boyfriend and girlfriend of course, so I don't want to make things awkward for them."

Luckily James *did* withstand the pressure, and *didn't* drop any of Linda's crockery, even when it came to packing it away in the cupboards.

"Hmm ... You did *quite* well," commented Linda, as she took off her rubber gloves and apron. "Seven out of ten, I'd say!"

"Seven?" exclaimed James. "I've always known that you're a hard task mistress, Linda, but surely that was worth at least a nine? There can't have been much, I could have done better!"

Linda was finishing putting her long black evening gloves back on. She smiled.

"In fact, nothing at all, my love," she said gently, taking him in her arms. "Darling, you've made me the happiest woman in Geratica tonight!"

Then she whispered into his ear, "*And **tomorrow** night, I'm going to show you just **how** much! No more having to go on top, for you, my baby! In The Grange mistress bedroom, the lady of the house is dominant in bed. It's **my** role to be on top, and **yours** to be underneath. And I'm an excellent lover, James. Your submissiveness will be rewarded – with interest!*"

James shook with excitement in his partner's arms. "Blimey, Linda, you really know how to turn me on!" he gasped, as he tried to catch his breath. "I'm going to be thinking about that at the palace, all day tomorrow, now!"

Linda squeezed and kissed him, and he felt her erect geratis through her gown. "So shall I!" she asserted.

"Now, I must go and fetch Alexandra, James. It's getting towards her bedtime, and she'll be wondering where I've got to. You'd better be off, too, for your final night in Elizabeth's house."

At the front door, they hugged and kissed again. It was so long since she'd done that, Linda felt almost like a teenager again. Her geratis throbbed against James's thigh as she squeezed him as tight as she could, and kissed his lips passionately.

After they'd finally said goodbye, James got into his car and drove out of The Grange towards the hamlet gate. Linda let him out, when she saw him on the monitor. Then she put on her coat and scarf and went out, to walk along the drive to The Lodge.

\*\*\*

When she arrived, she was greeted by Colin.

"Fiona's not back yet then?" she enquired.

"No. It might not be too much longer, but she doesn't usually get back here until the late evening, after one of these excursions," he answered.

"If you don't mind, as long as it doesn't get too late, I'll wait until she does, before I take Alexandra back," said Linda. "I need to have a word with her about something."

"Of course, Linda. That's fine," Colin assured her. "Did you have a successful evening?"

"Oh yes. I certainly did!" exclaimed Linda.

In the parlour, Linda was reunited with her daughter.

"If you don't mind, Colin, I'd like to just have a word with Alexandra outside, for a moment," she said.

"No problem. Go ahead." he replied.

Out in the hallway, Linda closed the door behind them.

"Mother! How was your evening with James?" asked her daughter.

"The actual purpose of the evening was achieved perfectly, Alexandra," remarked Linda. "I have some news to give you. Tomorrow night, James will be moving into The Grange with us!"

Alexandra's eyes opened wide. "Oh!" she exclaimed. "Right, very good, Mother."

"I proposed a relationship with him this evening, and he accepted. I was intending for him to get Elizabeth to come over with him tomorrow, so that he could finally tell her that he wanted to leave her, but then you'll never guess, but who should turn up at the door, without me having let her in through the hamlet gate, but the woman herself!"

"Elizabeth came here?" asked Alexandra. "But if you didn't let her in, then who did? We didn't, here at The Lodge."

"Fiona! It appears that Elizabeth bribed her with a certain amount of cash, to let her through the gate, when she went out tonight, so that she could come and spy on The Grange! She also told her of a place in the wood, near the house, where she could get a good clear view of the back. I still had the dining room curtains open, and she seems to have witnessed the entire meal, as well as some affection that I gave James on the couch, after he'd accepted my proposal. She came to the front door in a fury, called me a bitch, socked me one, and generally shouted her mouth off!

"Anyhow, the upshot is, that James has now told her officially, that he's leaving her. He's gone back to their house tonight – he's been ordered to sleep in the spare room! – and then tomorrow evening, after he's finished at the palace, he's going to go and pick up his things, and bring them over to The Grange. Elizabeth has vowed to be out at the time."

Alexandra gaped at her. "I can't believe it!" she gasped. "Fiona accepted a bribe? How much was it?"

"I've no real idea, darling," said her mother. "But I think that it was probably a decent amount, to have tempted her. I haven't told Tom's father about it yet, but I *have* said that I'd like to hang on here, until Fiona gets back, providing it doesn't get too late. I'm outraged that she did this and I want to give her a piece of my mind! I'm sorry it's getting so late sweetheart. I'll get you home to bed soon, I promise."

"That's OK, Mother," Alexandra assured her. She was enjoying taking advantage of every moment that she got to spend with Tom.

All the same, as they waited in the parlour, Alexandra was beginning to feel tired. Normally she was tucked up in bed with the light out by this time, especially on a school night. She yawned and rested her head on Tom's shoulder.

Linda was just about to say that they should be leaving now, and she'd see Fiona tomorrow, when a car raced up outside.

"Ah, that must be Fiona now," said Colin.

Fiona liked to drive fast. On occasion, Linda had spoken to her about the speed which with she went around the hamlet, feeling that it was sometimes dangerous.

Colin got up, and peeped through the curtain. "Yes," he confirmed. "She's just putting her car in the garage."

Moments later, they heard the front door open and close, and Fiona's footsteps in the hall.

She entered the parlour. "Oh, goodness, quite a reception party!" she exclaimed, as she saw them.

Linda launched straight in.

"How *dare* you, Fiona! And don't try to pretend that you don't know what I'm talking about. You let Elizabeth Spencer into the hamlet, to spy on The Grange, after she offered you cash, as an inducement!"

"Oh! You caught her then, did you?" asked Fiona, raising her eyebrows.

"No, I did not catch her. She eventually came to the door herself. I'm told that with your help, she was able to gain a perfect view into my dining room, from the wood. The curtains were open, and she didn't like what she saw. You had no right to do that Fiona!"

Fiona sat down. "Well I'm sorry, Linda. I admit that I did let her in, but you rather angered me with that 'verbal warning' yesterday, so I thought I'd ... show you that I won't be pushed around."

"What's that got to do with anything?" shouted Linda, indignantly. "Was that *really* why you agreed to this? For revenge on me? I can't believe that you could be so petty!"

"I apologise again, Linda," replied Fiona. "But if you hadn't done what you did yesterday, then I might not have done it. It was a one off. It won't happen again."

"Pah!" said Linda. "I told you yesterday, that I had no choice but to do that. *This* is a serious breach of trust, between The Grange and The Lodge. How do I know, that this is a 'one off' and that you won't let anybody else in, who happens to be passing the hamlet gate, to view The Grange without my consent – for a high enough price? The whole point of having the security gate there, is to stop anybody but hamlet residents from entering, unless one of us allows them through, after speaking to them through the intercom, and viewing them on a scanner. That's the only way people *should* be allowed in!"

"You have my word, Linda," Fiona assured her.

Linda looked coldly at her for a moment. "Hmm, well see that you don't go back on it!" she warned her.

"Anyhow, the main news, which I informed Alexandra of, when I arrived, is that James Spencer has told Elizabeth that he wants to leave her. I have proposed a relationship with him, this evening, which he accepted. He will be moving into The Grange, tomorrow night."

There was a moment of shocked silence, from Fiona, Colin and Tom. Linda grabbed the opportunity to make an exit. She was tired also.

"Well, now I must be getting Alexandra back to The Grange. It's high time that both of us got to bed. Tomorrow, at the palace, Fiona, I should advise you to stay out of my way, until I've calmed down a little!"

By the time she finally got to bed at The Lodge, Fiona's sexual appetite had returned. Despite her earlier extra-marital liaison, of which Colin was totally unsuspecting, she still made love to her husband five times, before sleep finally overcame them both.

# CHAPTER 6

Alexandra sat down to breakfast with Linda, the next morning.

"So this is the last breakfast for just the two of us, then Mother," she remarked.

"Indeed it is darling, yes," said Linda. "Obviously you only found out officially about James joining us, last night, and although I've hinted that it could happen soon, it must still have been a shock to you. How are you feeling this morning, after having a night to sleep on it?"

"It does feel strange, Mother, I must admit," confessed her daughter. "As I've said before, for almost as long as I can remember, it's just been you and me. But I do like James, a lot, and I want you to be happy, so I'm as pleased with it, as I *can* be!"

"Yes. That's understandable my poppet," said Linda. "And I promise that I'll do all that I can to make you feel as comfortable as possible. Don't forget that it's going to be strange for James too, though."

"I know Mother, and I promise *you* that I'll make him feel as welcome as possible. What concerns me most though, is our relationship. I'm sure that we'll still be close, but this is bound to have at least some effect on it. You now have a man to take charge of and look after, which I know you'll love doing. You're not going to have *quite* so much time for me!" Alexandra's voice shook slightly.

"Oh, darling!" cried Linda. She got up and leant over her daughter. Wrapping her arms around her shoulders, she gave her a huge, long kiss on the lips, making a sound of affectionate pleasure, as she did so. Alexandra's legs tingled. and she murmured back to her mother.

"Now, *that's* not going to stop. I can guarantee it!" said Linda. "As a matter of fact, I'm going to make a point of making sure that we continue to do some things together, on our own. We'll take this gradually. But you're growing up now, and you've got Tom also. You won't be here with me forever, whereas James and I will hopefully be together at The Grange, for the rest of our lives. Whatever happens though, I'm not going to neglect my wonderful daughter, my proudest achievement in all of Geratica. For goodness sake, *don't* get yourself into a state over *that!*" She kissed Alexandra again.

"Thank you, Mother. And I know that I'll come to *love* James, in time. But *you* know that I'll always be closest to you! I love you more than anyone else in the world. I know that it's probably wrong of me to admit it, Mother, but I think I might always love you ever so slightly more than Tom!"

"No, it's not necessarily wrong for a Geratican female to admit that, sweetheart," Linda reassured her. "There's often a particularly strong bond between mothers and daughters, in our race. Some of us go to bed together, after all!"

"Actually that was something that I wanted to mention, darling," she continued. "Now that James will be here, it obviously means that we won't be spending the night together, once a week, anymore."

"Yes, Mother. I did think of that last night, just before I went to sleep," said Alexandra, glumly.

"Having said that though, our feelings for each other will remain, and for as long as you're living here at The Grange, then I don't think it would be fair on either of us, not to act on them, as we desire. I'd like to continue doing to you what I have been, in the last couple of years."

Alexandra's eyes lit up, and she broke into a broad smile.

"It goes without saying, that I'd like you to, as well Mother!" she exclaimed, excitedly. "Thank you! I thought that would all finish now, too."

"Well, I've thought about it, and decided that, even though I shall have James to make love to from now onwards, I shall still want to express how I feel about *you*, too. And as you know, darling, that's usually quite passionate! I'll have to think some more, about how to create the circumstance, to regularly do it."

"I'll leave it for you to decide, Mother," said Alexandra, happily. "You're the one who has the running of this house, anyhow. I hope James realises that!"

"Of *course* he does, Alexandra!" said Linda. "Do you think that I would invite a man who didn't, to become my partner here?"

"No, Mother," her daughter assured her.

"Also, sweetheart, I think it highly likely that I will make love to James in my bed, at least a couple of times, tonight. You *are* obviously getting older now, and will understand these things, but all the same, if you're still awake, you may hear certain sounds that you haven't done previously at The Grange. Basically, it'll be the first time that you'll have heard me in the throes of passion with a man. You'll be alright, won't you?"

Alexandra giggled. "You mean I might hear you have an orgasm, Mother?"

"In a nutshell, yes, darling," said Linda. "And James, too, of course. Since you were small, there's never been another in my bed, at The Grange, other than you, therefore you've never really experienced hearing your mother making love to a man before. Most girls and boys, obviously hear such a thing, much earlier, so they're used to it by the time they get to your age, and you're a very sensitive girl."

"I think I'll be able to bear it, Mother!" said Alexandra, still smiling.

"That's alright then. Good!" replied her mother.

Linda looked at the clock. "Goodness me, look at the time!" she exclaimed. "We must get a move on, or you'll be late for your train."

\*\*\*

At the palace, Linda spoke with James, and then, when she had a convenient moment, gathered her little empire staff together, and made a brief announcement, that he was leaving his wife today, and of their official, personal relationship.

There were expressions of good wishes, all around. It didn't come as a complete surprise to some of the women, who had been gossiping behind the scenes for a while, at their obvious closeness. A couple of the boldest, had even speculated that Linda might be having an affair with Her Majesty's chauffeur, though they'd also made very sure, that their allegations didn't reach the ears of anyone remotely near, or close to her.

Fiona was conspicuous by her absence from the party, but Linda explained that as her neighbour, she was already aware of the situation. It hadn't taken Veronica and Carol long to deduce that their superiors were having one of their occasional "tiffs" and that they should "keep their heads down" until the two women resumed more normal communications.

Queen Alexandra, too, was delighted for them both. Secretly, she had long suspected that this day would eventually come. She was also certain, that Elizabeth Spencer would be beside herself with anguish, and rage.

\*\*\*

Alexandra arrived back home from Charterhouse at her usual time. Her mother had told her that she wouldn't be too late home, as she wanted to be there to get James settled in, when he arrived. Then they would be having their first dinner together, as a threesome.

She'd just made herself a cup of coffee, and begun her prep, when the doorbell rang. For a terrible moment, Alexandra feared that Elizabeth Spencer might have got into Elmsbrook again. No one had buzzed the intercom at the gate, and it was unusual to get a visit by somebody from The Lodge, at this time of day.

She got up from her desk and peeped out of the window. To her relief, and considerable joy, she saw that it was Tom, and she hurried to greet him.

They embraced, and kissed in the porch.

"I thought I'd pop into see you tonight, after work," said Tom.

Alexandra smiled softly, and looked tenderly into his eyes, which always seemed to do something to him, inside. "Thank you *darling*!" she said, and the sound of her voice on the last word, sent tingles through his neck and chest. He hadn't stopped thinking about her, since she'd left The Lodge last night.

"I've just made myself a cup of coffee, actually," said Alexandra. "Come into the kitchen, and I'll make you one, too."

She took his hand, and led him down the hall. "How was your day?" she asked.

"Not too bad, but a lot better for seeing you, now," he replied.

Alexandra looked at him as they went into the kitchen, and smiled again. "And me, you," she admitted.

"That was a bit of a shock last night!" said Tom, as Alexandra poured the kettle.

"What? James? Not so much for me really, Tom," said Alexandra. "I've known since we went to Avermore, that he and Mother want to get together, but the problem was always that James couldn't face telling his wife – my ex-headmistress Elizabeth Spencer! I didn't necessarily know that it was going to happen this quickly, but there had to be some reason why Mother wanted them to be alone at The Grange tonight. Their need to discuss 'confidential work matters' was always just a front – including when he came to dinner with us last week!"

"Hmm!" said Tom, with a smirk on his face. "Scandalous goings on at The Grange, then! It's a good job the media didn't get wind of that story, when you got mixed up with that Charterhouse business."

"Quite! And I can tell you now that Mother was very cross with me about that too. She made it very clear to me, that I'd better hope her plans to get them together, didn't get messed up, because of what I'd done! Luckily, things worked out OK in the end. In any case, she was always very careful to keep their growing feelings for each other, discreet."

"That word again – discretion!" remarked Tom.

"Yes," replied Alexandra. "I'll bet that your stepmother had a few suspicions though."

"Well, if she did, she never spoke of them to me," Tom told her.

"Mother doesn't tell me a great deal about how she feels about Fiona, either. They probably both feel they don't want to make it difficult for us. But we both saw last night, how furious she was, that Fiona let Elizabeth Spencer bribe her into allowing her access to Elmsbrook, and I think they've had one or two ups and downs, since they've been working together at the palace."

"And they let it slip, that your mother gave my stepmother a verbal warning!" exclaimed Tom.

"Well exactly. That proves my point. They don't like to tell us too much about what's going on between them, for our sake, and therefore I don't like to ask Mother too much about it either."

"Fiona doesn't tell me *anything* about the palace goings on." said Tom. "I envy you sometimes. I've never even been there!"

"Well maybe that'll change, now that you're my boyfriend," replied Alexandra, as she poured Tom his coffee.

"Are you feeling alright about James coming to live here?" he asked.

"Yes. He's a very nice man, with a great sense of humour, and I'm happy for my Mother to have found love again. It's going to be strange at first, and I've always liked it being just Mother and I here, and I'll always be closest to her, but I expect I'll get used to it. Mother promises me that they'll both try to make it as easy as possible for me – and James will need time to settle, too, of course. Next year, I should be going to University anyhow, so they'll have The Grange to themselves."

"Oh, by the way," she continued, "I wish you'd been here at breakfast this morning. Mother is sometimes quite frank with me, and today she's told me that it's highly likely, she will make love to James tonight! She wanted to check that I wouldn't be too alarmed at the sounds they made, as I'll never have heard her do that before!"

They both chuckled.

"Oh I *do* know all about that," remarked Tom. "If your mother's anything like my stepmother, then once she gets' going, there'll be no stopping her. I've been lying in bed sometimes, and counted her and my father, having five or six orgasms in a night! And there'll be plenty of noise, too. I remember once, thinking that you must have heard Fiona at The Grange, when she came!"

He smiled naughtily. "Are you going to deliberately stay awake, so that you can hear them?"

Alexandra smirked. "Something tells me that they won't be far behind me, going to bed tonight! So I'll probably still be awake. I've heard some stories from Charterhouse, of girls peeping through the keyhole of their parents' bedroom door, to 'watch the action', but that *definitely* won't be happening here. For one thing, Mother would kill me, if she caught me, and for another, I'll be locked in my room for the night, as usual, so I can't do it anyhow!"

They went into the study and Alexandra continued with her prep, as they talked.

Soon after, from the window, Alexandra could see her mother's car coming through the front gates. She quickly got up from her desk.

"Tom!" she said urgently. "Mother's coming. Let's nip into the parlour. If she sees me doing my prep, *and* talking to you, at the same time, then she might be annoyed with me – saying that I'm not concentrating properly."

She handed Tom his coffee, and ushered him out of the room, before he could reply.

"Sorry," he said eventually, as they neared the end of the passage to the parlour. "I didn't mean to drop in and get you into trouble!" Not for the first time, he was getting a glimpse of the strict rod of iron, that Alexandra's mother ruled with, at The Grange.

"Oh no, don't be silly!" replied Alexandra, as they went to the sofa, sat themselves down, and placed their cups on the coffee table, just as Linda came through the front door. She was surprised to find Tom there, at this time.

"It's alright, Mrs Radcliffe," he said. "I'd better be off to have my dinner, or my stepmother won't be pleased. And I think I'm keeping Alexandra from her prep, too."

"No, it's OK!" Alexandra exclaimed. "I haven't got too much to do tonight, anyhow."

"All the same, I really *do* think I ought to be making tracks," said Tom.

He was still feeling a little guilty.

"I hope that it all goes well tonight, Mrs Radcliffe," he added, politely.

"Thank you Tom," replied Linda. "I'm sure we'll all be fine, once James has settled in. It's bound to feel a little strange at first, but we'll get past that. We aren't going to have any serious problems with this new arrangement." She looked at her daughter. "*Are we Alexandra?*"

Alexandra could tell be the slightly hard tone of her mother's voice and the way that her eyes sent a similarly slight message of warning to her, that she was not being given an option of choice, in her answer to this question. Only one would be acceptable. She was being told, in the unlikely event that she didn't already realise it, that her mother wasn't going to tolerate any dissent from her.

"No of course not, Mother," she answered obediently. "I like James very much. I think it'll be quite good fun, with him living here, as a matter of fact!"

"Good," said Linda, softening her expression, and kissing her daughter.

Tom knew that his stepmother considered his girlfriend to be "under the thumb" of her mother. He felt that it was difficult to disagree sometimes, but he did think that Alexandra was genuine in her sentiments, regarding James Spencer.

He said his goodbyes, and Alexandra saw him out, with several long soft kisses, and licks of her tongue on his. She finished by planting a kiss on either side of his sensitive neck. He became breathless, and shuddered with ecstasy, and he knew as he walked back to The Lodge, that his current state of sexual arousal would last all night long, and throughout his day at work tomorrow, too.

As a result of her recent exposure in the media, many of the men who he worked with on Lady Sackville's estate, had now seen Alexandra for the first time. There had been one or two lustful comments, and several of them had remarked on how lucky he was, to have had such a beautiful girl propose a relationship with him. He had not hesitated to agree with them. Only he, however, knew quite *how* lucky he was, due to her fantastic skills as a lover.

Alexandra finished her prep. James would be here soon, with all of his things. Alexandra realised that this was a very big night indeed, for her mother personally. She seldom saw her in any way nervous, but as Linda busied herself with the final preparations, Alexandra thought that she could detect a hint of it now, which was fully understandable.

***

James arrived soon afterwards. Linda went out to his car, and greeted him with a big welcome kiss – the first time Alexandra had seen her do that, in fact. She could immediately see the affection, and attraction that they felt for each other.

With both Linda and Alexandra helping him, it didn't take long for James to get his things unloaded from the car, and put in place at The Grange. Then they went to the parlour.

"Do you want to sit in the armchair, alongside Mother's, James?" asked Alexandra. She thought that perhaps James' status in the household would entitle him to sit there, from now onwards, and that she should take the sofa.

"Oh, I don't want to deprive you of your normal place, if that's where you usually sit, Alexandra," he exclaimed.

"Perhaps you could both sit on the sofa, just for a short while," suggested Linda, which Alexandra suspected meant that she was telling them to.

"Oh. OK. Very good Mother," she replied, and ushered James to the sofa, with a smile. She assumed that her mother was planning to address them both, and the confirmation wasn't long in coming.

"Now, I'll just make us all a cup of coffee, and then I'd like to say a couple of brief things. It shouldn't take long, and then we'll have our dinner." She left for the kitchen.

Alexandra smiled at James again. He was by no means the first, to find its soft warmth extremely attractive, and endearing.

"You're here then?" she said. "Was your wife out tonight, when you went back to collect your stuff, as she promised she'd be?"

James lifted his eyebrows slightly. "Your mother told you about that, did she? Yes, she was. I haven't seen her since she left here, yesterday."

"I've said it before, but you're certainly *very* polite to your mother, Alexandra," he said, changing the subject.

"And as *I've* said before, to various people, it's the way I was brought up to address her," replied Alexandra. "You know Mother is an arch-traditionalist in most things, and she expects me to be deferential – in much the same manner that Her Majesty expects it of her, and all the rest of her subjects. And I'm sure you also know that even more than most traditional women, she rules the roost in her household!"

James chuckled. "As if I couldn't! I only have to think back to when she told us both off at the palace, the other week, for getting over-excited before our audience with the queen. And she certainly left me in no doubt, when she eventually came on *very* strong at me, and told me that she wanted us to get serious, and tell my wife I wanted to leave her."

Alexandra giggled. "She 'came on' at you, did she? It seems really strange for me, to think of people of your generation, doing that sort of thing."

"What do you mean?" asked James indignantly. "We're not decrepit old fogies you know! As a matter of fact, your mother can be quite seductive when she wants to be. She pinned me down on the bonnet of Her Majesty's private car."

Alexandra gaped at him. "Really?"

James smirked. "I made that last bit up!"

"Oh you swine, you had me going there!" exclaimed Alexandra, slapping his arm playfully.

"I did, didn't I?" he grinned. Then he added, "I think there's a chance that she might do so in bed tonight, though!"

Now they both laughed. Alexandra considered telling James that her mother had indeed asserted similar intentions, this morning at breakfast, but at that moment, Linda returned.

"I see you're both already starting to giggle together," she remarked, as she carried the tray in, and set it down on the coffee table. She took her own to her armchair, and sat down.

"I was just telling Alexandra about how we finally got together, after you came on strong at me, at the palace," James told her.

"What? I don't know what you're talking about," said Linda indignantly. "Honestly James, there are times when you do talk utter rubbish. I do hope that you're not going to be a bad influence on Alexandra, now that you're finally here with us at The Grange. She does occasionally come out with some errant nonsense, too, but I soon put her right, as I shan't hesitate to do in your case, also!"

"Mother will allow us to express our own opinions, if they're different from hers, and even have a discussion with her about them, but then we realise that she's right, and do what she thinks is best!" said Alexandra.

"Quite correct, Alexandra," said Linda. "You've learnt well. You would do well to listen to *her* advice on this subject, James. Perhaps she'll be a good influence on *you*, here!"

"Yes Linda," replied James, winking at Alexandra.

Then Linda tapped her table with her coffee spoon.

"Right!" she said. "Let's just put the joking to one side for a moment. Welcome to The Grange, James! You know how long I've wanted this to happen. and I know that Alexandra is happy, too. We both think that you'll fit in very well here, and we'll do our very best to help you settle. You'll pick up the house rules soon enough. It's true that I run a strict regime here, but I hope that there's a lot of love, warmth and good fun, too. I run and control the household, and take charge of all the aspects related to it. You know the traditional male role that I expect from you, and I know that you want to perform it, so we should have no problems there.

"Alexandra, as far as you're concerned, I know that it might be a bit strange, and even a bit hard for you, to adapt to this new situation, but I know you're going to try your best, and you certainly like James. For our part, James and I will make every effort to be understanding to you, darling. I don't anticipate that we'll have any serious problems there, either.

"The only other thing I want to mention, Alexandra, is that your recent punishment was originally scheduled to finish tomorrow night, but I did promise to end it a day earlier, if your behaviour was good enough to warrant it. I can confirm that it's been exemplary, so from bedtime tonight, it will be lifted. That will obviously mean that, with James having arrived tonight, we can start tomorrow morning afresh, and as I mean us to go on, a traditional – and I hope, happy – family.

"I hope that you've learnt your lesson, Alexandra. Certain unusual circumstances, considerably contributed to you doing what you did, but you still transgressed from the correct path that I've always taught you to follow, which necessitated the punishment."

"I know Mother and I'm sorry," Alexandra assured her. "Stealing is morally wrong, and I shouldn't have attempted it. I've got to make sure that I don't allow other people to push me into doing something that I know is wrong, no matter how much they pressure me to."

"Good girl!" said her mother. "With that understanding between us, we will say no more about the unpleasant matter again, after bedtime tonight, though we won't forget it. Is that clear?"

"Crystal clear, Mother," Alexandra assured her again.

"Good," said Linda in a gentler tone, and gave her daughter a warm smile.

"Well that's all I wanted to say," she concluded. "Any questions?"

"I've got just one, Mother," said Alexandra. "Are we going to have two cars now? Who's going to be the driver, now that James is here?"

"Firstly, I must point out, that was two questions, Alexandra," remarked Linda. "It's not you to make such a basic arithmetical mistake! You'd better brush up on it, before you take your final Mathematics exam at Charterhouse, next year."

"To answer them directly, I imagine that James and I will travel to and from work together, from now on. There shouldn't be too many occasions when he'll need to stay very much later than me, and he'll hang on until I'm finished, on the days that I work late. I shall be doing most of the driving for the household, though James will obviously be able to, should there be a need for it. Therefore, I think that it's quite likely that I'll be selling his car at some point in the near future, though I'm not sure when yet. Let's get James settled into the swing of things here, first."

"OK Thank you, Mother," replied Alexandra.

"Well if that's all, then, I'll get the dinner on," announced Linda.

An hour later, they sat down to eat in the dining room, with Linda and Alexandra in their usual places, and James sat opposite Alexandra, to the other side of his partner. As this was their first meal together as an official item, Linda had laid on a bottle of wine. Just the one, as they would all have to be up for the last working day of the week, tomorrow morning.

After their main course, as Alexandra helped Linda with taking the dishes to the kitchen, and to serve the dessert, she noticed a significant bulge in her mother's skirt. She managed to hide her amusement. Her mother's thoughts were clearly turning towards bedtime, with James!

By the time they'd finished their meal and talked quite a bit during the course of it, the time on the clock told Linda that it was getting late. She was keen to get her daughter to bed, so that she and James could do the same, as soon as possible. She was becoming more sexually excited by the minute.

She cleared her throat, to get her daughter's attention.

"Well, Alexandra, it's almost your bedtime now, and it's a week night. James and I will get cleared away, whilst you get yourself ready, and then I'll be in to say 'good night,' as usual, just before 9.30."

"Yes, Mother," She got up and went around the table. "Goodnight

James," said Alexandra politely, and kissed him.

"Good night, Alexandra, Sleep well," replied James, kissing her back. They smiled happily at one another. Already they each felt a bond with one another, through their mutual love for Linda.

"And you too, James," said Alexandra, even though she knew that sleep wasn't quite the first thing on both his mind and her mother's.

As Linda had said, whilst she readied herself for bed, her mother washed up, with James drying. Then she came up and said goodnight to Alexandra, with a big kiss, and then locked her door for the night. Then she returned to James, who was now back in the parlour.

# CHAPTER 7

Linda crossed to the sofa where James sat. Slipping down close beside him, she immediately began to kiss his mouth. She held him tight, and moved on to his neck, letting her hands glide over his back. James' genus inflated more than it had done for many weeks, with the anticipation of what was in store tonight. He had always had to make the first move with Elizabeth, but he had never been in any doubt that Linda would take the initiative. His dreams were about to come true. Finally, he was together with the right woman for him.

His eyes couldn't fail to see Linda's erect geratis, which was now a long thick bulge, pulsating inside her skirt. He lightly stroked it with his finger, knowing full well what a pleasurable feeling that was for a Geratican woman to experience. He had often used that method to stimulate his wife's interest. It had usually driven her wild, and the next thing he'd known, she would have pulled him down on top of her, and begged him to make love to her. As a traditional man, this wasn't something that he felt naturally comfortable doing, and he'd never found the feeling of coming in that position, as pleasurable as the standard one, despite Elizabeth's eagerness, and passion beneath him. When they'd first married their sex had been traditional, but gradually his wife had become more and more obsessed with 'Male Rights' and her taste had shifted. Now she considered it best for the man if he was on top, and she was never satisfied until she'd come beneath him. He was in fact, not really sure if she genuinely cared for his feelings anymore, so long as her geratis got the pleasure that she desired.

Linda's geratis became even more aroused as James touched it, but her experienced body didn't flinch. Instead she pushed forward, and launched herself on top of him. James felt a blast of hot breath over his face, as Linda exhaled deeply from the pleasure she felt, as her geratis pressed down over his thigh. For a moment she ravished him, moving dominantly all over his body, and kissing his lips deeply. She murmured with pleasure as she thrust powerfully against him. He murmured back. Her pants had a slight dampness in them, as her geratis had emitted a small amount of sticky fluid – "pre-come" as some called it. She could wait no longer.

She whispered into James's ear.

*"That's the way a traditional woman loves a traditional man. And that's the way it will be here, every night – starting **tonight**!* "

James's heart beat fast with excitement.

Then Linda whispered again, seductively.

"*Again, I want to make love to you tonight. And **this** time I **will**! I'm **going** to make love to you **tonight**, James!*"

The sexy seductiveness of Linda's voice, and the message it conveyed to his ear, almost made James lose control. He gasped with pleasure as his genus ballooned, bigger than he could ever remember feeling before.

Linda rose from the sofa.

"Go upstairs and get ready for bed, whilst I shut up shop for the night, down here!" she told James. "Then I'll be up. All I ask is that when I come in, you are presented to me in submissive fashion in the bed. I want to be able to see your naked body, ready and waiting for me to do as I please with – which I guarantee will please you, too!"

"Oh! Of course, Linda! Willingly!" groaned James, unable to wait any longer, either. He leapt off the sofa, and was gone in no time.

\*\*\*

Linda locked up the house and did her nightly checks, then shut everything up, and went up to – what was now "their" bedroom.

Her excitement built as she mounted the stairs. It was so long since she'd made love to a man – the night before Robert had died, in fact – and she had to admit that she'd been longing for it for some time. These longings had got steadily stronger, since she and James had started to get close. She'd been sorely tempted to start an affair with him, but she had given her feelings a severe check. Now he was finally available to her, and tonight she was going to satisfy her desire, and show him just how much she loved and wanted him.

From the bedroom, James could hear the click of Linda's heels as she approached. He hadn't thought that he could get any more excited, but that was undoubtedly what was happening to him now.

As she entered the room, Linda was pleased to see that James had done as she'd asked. He was lying spread-eagled on the sheets, with the bedspread pulled back, so that she got a full view of his body. She liked to come in to that, every night, but tonight was extra special, because it was the very first time that she'd seen James naked. She liked what she saw, and licked her lips hungrily. Her geratis responded in tandem with her thoughts. It twitched madly in her pants, extending further than ever from her vagina, as it sought out James's genus, and he could see the trace of its movement through Linda's skirt. His genus reacted to Linda's geratis, desperately wanting it to come into James's vagina, and thrust over it.

Linda smiled seductively at James. "I'll just go into the bathroom and get ready, then darling!" she said softly. "Then I'll be back to take control!"

"OK!" said James breathlessly.

Linda quickly did her ablutions, applied some red lipstick and then put on a sexy black nightgown. with long black silk gloves. Then she went back into the main bedroom.

James's reaction to the way he looked, was much as she'd anticipated. She knew exactly what turned him on, and by good fortune, they were genuinely some of her favourite outfits. They had very similar tastes.

James writhed in the bed, with even greater excitement. "Oh Linda! Wow, you look gorgeous!" he exclaimed. "I'm yours, Linda! I need you! Make love to me. You're the one who knows how to do it best!"

Linda was thrilled. Those were exactly the kind of words that she loved to hear, and they were now the catalyst that inflamed her desire to its maximum.

She smiled sexily, as she walked to the bed. "Well!" she declared, "I can't say no to that!" She got in beside James, and seductively licked her red lips at him. He moaned softly. Linda knew that she had him in a state of total excitement. Now that the moment that they'd both been waiting for, all evening had finally arrived, she was going to make the most of it.

Linda leant over James, and whispered into his ear, "**Darling, I love you so much!** *I'm going to cover you in kisses, and touch you all over your body! I'll squeeze you very tight, and when I come down over you, I'll be so deep, that you'll disappear beneath me!*" He nearly lost his breath.

She kissed his mouth, then slipped her tongue inside, and found his. As she licked it, James felt his genus aroused even more. Her fingers ran softly down his chest.

Then she worked her way down his body, kissing his neck, shoulders and chest. He shuddered as all of his most sensitive parts became aflame.

Linda's throbbing geratis brushed against the sheet and she experienced another emission, causing a small stain. She had to have James, right now!

She lifted her leg over, so that she straddled him, and her geratis raced inside the left-hand hole of his vagina. It slithered down the left-hand wall, draped itself over James's genus, and then ran back along the other side of his vagina and out through his right-hand hole. Then it re-entered Linda. The feeling of contact inside each of them, made them both gasp with pleasure. Linda licked her lips with a sexy smile and James's excitement finally reached its zenith.

Linda dived flat on top of James and ravished him again, just as she'd done earlier on the sofa. She gripped his legs in a vice–like grip inside of hers, and squeezed him between her thighs. She wrapped her arms around him in a cradling embrace. Her body moved over his, and she thrust herself down deep into him. She ran her fingers through his hair. Her kisses smothered his lips, and his breath shortened.

As she loved James on, and on, Linda's geratis thrust hard over his genus, in direct proportion to her passion. It was expanding in width, inside his vagina, with every thrust. He groaned and his head began to rock from side to side.

Knowing that she had him on the brink, Linda whispered into his ear again, "*I've got you so close now,* **darling**! *I'm going to make you come!*" She ran a finger down his neck, and across his chest, feeling his heartbeat, and quickening it even further. Then she crushed his whole body inside of hers, and pressed herself down deep into it, pinning James to the sheets, whilst at the same time, kissing his mouth hungrily. Her tongue forced its way back over his, and her geratis thrust over his genus harder than ever. The genus finally burst its load, and a huge orgasm ripped through James's entire body, making him convulse beneath Linda, and he screamed loudly with ecstasy, as he came, longer and harder than he had done for years.

Linda felt James's sticky come, seeping into the pores of her geratis, and flowing through it to her own vagina, and she murmured at the deeply pleasurable feeling. Her geratis grew in thickness, until it finally fully engulfed his vagina, and pressed against its walls, as she became aroused to the full. With James still moaning, she squeezed, kissed and thrust again, all in tandem, her own heart now pounding against his chest, and her breath hot and panting. She was coming, and she knew it. Linda's geratis finally lost control, and she orgasmed with a huge force, as it deposited a vast amount of juice around the walls of James's vagina. She squealed even louder than James and her eyes watered. He murmured appreciatively, as Linda's juice transmitted a sweet taste to his veins. In all his years with Elizabeth, she had never produced anything quite so delicious – and in such a quantity.

***

In her own bedroom, Alexandra had been surprised that James and her mother hadn't come up immediately after her "lights out" time. Even so, she *had* managed to stay awake to hear them make love. She knew that she was being nosy – and maybe even a little naughty! – but she simply couldn't resist it. In any case, her mother, even if she ever guessed that she might have done so, could never know for certain.

It *was* the first time that she'd ever listened to a couple copulating, let alone one involving her mother. The sheer intensity of their cries, whilst in the throes of passion, was indeed a shock to her – particularly when she heard her mother scream, and realised that she must have just come, after making love to James. His own, had been mighty loud, too! Tom had certainly not been exaggerating, when he'd commented on the subject earlier.

Ten minutes later, Alexandra was actually almost drifting off to sleep, when to her amazement she heard more sounds of orgasmic pleasure, coming from their bedroom, albeit a touch quieter. She couldn't believe that they'd recovered so quickly, and that her mother was clearly hungry for more. Alexandra, of all people, knew that her mother was a dominant lover, and she was in no doubt that she'd been on top again, the woman's traditional position. Inevitably, her thoughts again moved forward, to when she might be in that same position, with Tom. Would she be able to manage that too? But then she remembered her mother's advice to her, regarding her thinking, and she put the thought from her mind. It wasn't important, and certainly not anyone else's business, and she would never know until they were legally able to do it, anyhow.

She *did* wonder how long the newly established partners would go on for, though. She sat up in bed and looked at her bedside clock. She really should go to sleep, but she was still curious. The girls at Charterhouse had often seemed to talk knowledgeably of their parents' bedroom antics. Now she could judge for herself, whether the some of the stories they told, were true.

A few minutes later she heard the sound that was now unmistakable to her – of James coming again, with a squeal. Her mother followed, almost immediately afterwards, with a slightly bigger one. It certainly seemed to be true that the woman's orgasm was the strongest and most dominant, bringing on the man's, before reaching its own climax, though as hr mother had explained to her, after the first, the subsequent ones gradually lessened in power.

Shortly after that they each came for a fourth time. Just as Alexandra was beginning to wonder whether her mother would make love to James all night, she heard the sound of snoring coming from across the landing. It didn't sound like her mother – and she should know that also – so she assumed that James had finally run out of energy.

She lay back down in her bed, and was asleep almost immediately.

***

James was indeed asleep, too, content in Linda's arms. At last he was snuggled up to the woman he truly loved, and wanted to be with.

Linda was delighted with the way the night had gone. James was finally here – she hoped for good – and already seemed to be having a good time with Alexandra. They'd all had their first official meal as a family, and now she felt that both of them had been more than satisfied, during their first night in bed together. Making love to him four times, was a pretty good beginning, she thought.

It wasn't long before she, too, was asleep.

# CHAPTER 8

Next morning, Linda came into her daughter's bedroom as usual, to start her day.

"Good morning, darling!" she said cheerfully, as she pulled back the curtains.

Alexandra groaned slightly at the sudden awakening. After finally going to sleep last night, this was her first moment of consciousness, and now – even more than on most school day mornings – she really wished that she could sleep on for a bit longer. She squinted at the bedroom light, and buried her face inside her pillow.

Then she felt her mother's arms wrap around her body, and turn her over onto her back. Before she knew it, Linda was leaning over her, and lifting her slightly off the sheet, to give her a kiss. It was a big and strong one, the kind that always got her moving in the morning, as well as the thought of the breakfast that her mother was about to make – two things that she would never tire of.

"I said, good morning darling," Linda repeated, smiling softly.

"Sorry, Mother. Good morning," Alexandra began to gather her wits. She returned Linda's kiss, looking up at her, and they gazed into each other's eyes for a couple of seconds. In that brief time, they both expressed their love for each other, without having to say any words.

"Right, up you get now!" ordered Linda. "Breakfast in twenty minutes!"

"Yes, Mother," answered Alexandra, as she watched her go.

Normally Alexandra was then up immediately, but today proved slightly different. When she next looked at the clock, to her horror she realised that ten minutes had already gone by. She must have dozed off! She sprang out of bed, and slipped out of her nightgown, almost in one movement, then raced to her bathroom, and had a very quick wash. Hoping that she hadn't misjudged the considerably reduced time she now had, she rushed back into the main part of her bedroom and put her school uniform on, checking the time, as she did so. She should *just* be OK. She was usually down just in time to prepare the table in the breakfast room, before they ate, but she wouldn't be able to that today. She ran her comb through her hair, and brushed it by her dressing table.

Her mother's voice suddenly called shrilly from downstairs, making her jump and almost drop the brush.

"Alexandra you have thirty seconds to come to breakfast, or you'll get three strokes on your right hand, before we leave this morning!"

Alexandra finished and darted towards her bedroom door.

"I'm sorry, Mother! That won't be necessary! I'm coming down at once!" she called back from the landing. She scampered down the stairs as quick as she could. Her mother was returning to the breakfast room, and Alexandra got there, just as she was making a final check of her watch.

"That's not like you, to nearly be late for your breakfast, Alexandra!" she exclaimed. "James laid the table for me, but I told him that you were normally here to do that. What happened?"

"I'm sorry I was nearly late, Mother, but I dozed off just after you left," said her daughter. "If it's not inappropriate for me to say it, I was kept awake a little later than usual, by the two of you, last night, after you came to bed!"

"What?" asked Linda, looking up in surprise, as she sat down to eat, "You mean you weren't asleep by then?"

"Er, no Mother," answered Alexandra. "I don't think that you weren't *too* long after me."

James laughed cheekily. "I know why she was ..."

"Be quiet James!" Linda interrupted him.

"Alexandra, I hope you didn't force yourself to stay awake *deliberately,* so that you might hear what you *claim* to have kept you from sleeping last night. If you did, then you've only got yourself to blame, for not being able to get up on time this morning – as well as having been a naughty girl!"

"Oh no, Mother," Alexandra lied to Linda. "I would never *dream* of doing such a thing."

James snorted, as he tried desperately not to laugh again, and this time Linda couldn't resist having a smirk, too.

"Hmm, well I'll give you the benefit of the doubt!" she said. "And in actual fact, whether you did, or you didn't, I'm not going to worry too much, either way." Her eyes twinkled at her daughter's, and Alexandra couldn't help but smile back at her, with the faintest trace of guilt. Linda knew her daughter like no one else did, and was now fairly convinced that she *had* deliberately kept herself awake. Alexandra was never very successful at keeping things from her, once she was under suspicion. She usually either yielded to the dominance of her mother's probing, or was outwitted by her tactics. Still, it wasn't a terrible crime, despite the fact that her daughter had just lied about it. She'd done similar herself, when she was young.

She reached across and laid her hand on Alexandra's arm, just as she was beginning her first piece of toast.

"Just to be serious for a moment though, darling. Please don't make a habit of forcing yourself to stay awake after lights out – for whatever the occasion might be. There's a reason why I turn them out then, and tell you to go to sleep. *You need your rest!* It's not *quite* so vital at the weekend, but particularly on week nights, you *must* be fresh for school the following morning!"

"No, I won't, Mother," Alexandra assured her. "Er, well, I mean, not that I did that last night, in any case!"

Linda and James both hooted with laughter.

"Anyhow, I'm sorry if we *did* disturb you last night, sweetheart," said Linda. "But it was James' first night living here, and I know that he agrees with me, that it was *most* satisfactory."

"*You* were a *huge* amount more than satisfactory, Linda" confirmed James. "More like an 'A' plus, I'd say!"

"My pleasure, darling!" said Linda, as they both smiled at each other. She leant across and kissed him, her geratis slithering out of her vagina, as she felt a stirring of sexual arousal again.

Alexandra had heard her mother use those words, many times, to her. She hoped very much, that her mother would keep her promise that they could still have an intimate time alone together, even though James would be in her bed every night, from now on. Actually, she was sure that she would. Such things were very important between them.

For the rest of breakfast, Alexandra noted that her mother and James were in extremely good humour. She wasn't surprised after last night. Something told her that tonight would be much the same, too – and *this* time it would be the weekend!

***

At 7.15 a.m., they all set off together as a threesome, for the first time. James left his own car in the garage, and Linda drove them. From now onwards, James would be in the passenger seat and Alexandra in the back. Just before they dropped Alexandra off at the station, in time for her train, Linda made an offer to her.

"Darling, would you like to be picked up from Charterhouse tonight?

James and I both shouldn't be too late finishing, at the palace."

"Oh! Yes, please!" said Alexandra, both surprised and delighted.

Just hang on in the lobby, until we get there, then," said Linda. "Perhaps we'll start to do it at the end of every week, from now on. It'll be a nice thing to look forward to. There's no real reason why I can't go early on Day 5, normally, and James can probably fit in. Things are usually winding down for the weekend then, anyhow."

"Thank you *very* much, Mother!" replied Alexandra, excitedly. "I definitely *will* look forward to that, every week!"

"Good. Well that's settled then," announced Linda. "We'll see you tonight, at Charterhouse."

After kissing both her mother and James goodbye, Alexandra walked over to the station platform, already counting down the hours, to when she'd be back in the car with them again, on her way home to the very first weekend that James would spend, living at The Grange.

# PART 8

# CHAPTER 1

At Charterhouse, that day, Alexandra's "board" met in their form class. It was now officially decided that they would hold the sponsored walk on the next weekend. The overall response had been very good, and Imelda and Rachel had gathered together a sample of the sponsorship forms, completed so far.

"By my calculations, if all these girls complete the course, and collect the amount of money that's been pledged to them, then projecting that figure over the total number of participants, we should make a decent return from it," announced Benita confidently. Alexandra trusted Benita's confidence. It was what attracted her most to the best female friend that she had. She'd often given her assistance academically – though mainly, only in fairly complicated things – and Benita had always looked out for her.

Emma had also been in touch with the Charterhouse catering staff, and arranged for them to provide sufficient refreshments for all the participants, during the course of the walk. She would arrange their distribution on the day.

Alexandra *was* surprised by what Benita told her next though. The two of them were to be excused by Mrs Wood, the last period of the morning, and given special permission to leave the college grounds. The reason being, that Benita had arranged for them both to visit a local restaurant, for a meeting with the manager. And the purpose of that, was that Benita was hoping to persuade the manager, to provide Alexandra's concert with additional sponsorship from her business.

The two of them had discussed the possibility of doing something like this, two days earlier, after Benita had suggested it. It was her brainchild, and Alexandra had been happy to let her get on with trying to arrange it. Not only was she far more confident in this sort of thing than herself, but Benita had the best understanding of business, of all of them, and was an open admirer of her mother's economic policies.

With everything that had been going on at The Grange this week, she hadn't got around to telling her mother about this yet, but it had happened quickly, and was at very short notice. It appeared that Benita had clinched the meeting, only last night, and lunchtime today was when the woman had said she was available. As Benita said also, they didn't have long to get things organised, anyhow, so they shouldn't delay.

Alexandra's natural inclination would have been to ask her mother's advice first, but since she'd been caught out by the speed that Benita conducted business, and wouldn't really get much of a chance to call the palace from Charterhouse, this morning, she'd just have to tell her about it, after the event, later this afternoon.

*\*\*\**

The restaurant in question was called Rumbold's, and was both owned and managed by Miranda Rumbold. She actually owned a chain of three, but the one in Buckmore was her base, as it was her home town. It catered for a wide variety of Geratican tastes, from the traditional home grown dishes, to imported ones learnt from researching Earth's cuisine.

Benita suggested that Alexandra should make their introductions, and briefly explain about the operation that they were planning, but then she would do the talking, regarding their business proposal. Alexandra more than readily agreed to the second part of her suggestion. She knew that Benita had firm ambitions in that field, after she left formal education, but she was so much more confident than her in general, that she never minded her taking the lead. Benita, for her part, never minded doing that, either. Alexandra would still be in overall charge, when it came to the actual finances though. They'd agreed what they thought that they'd probably still need, after the sponsored walk, and Benita would negotiate the best possible deal for them, but she'd still defer to Alexandra for the final decision. Numbers were a particular speciality of hers, and Benita knew that Alexandra had no confidence issues, there. Also, it was *ultimately* her project, anyhow. But they could potentially be a very good partnership.

All the same, Alexandra still felt very nervous beforehand. This was *totally* new territory to her. She was grateful for the encouraging tight squeeze of her arm, from Benita, as they went in. Benita was the nicest and most thoughtful girl that she knew, and the bond between them was deepening. In some ways she reminded her of her mother.

After they had met, Miranda Rumbold, dressed in a simple white blouse and red skirt, invited the girls up to her private flat, above the restaurant, and offered them refreshment. They sat down in the chairs offered to them, taking their school blazers off, and placing them over the backs.

Miranda had never been approached to do anything like this before, and she was amazed that such a bold request could come from a pair so young, and still in school. The girl on the phone, Benita, had certainly been most forthright in her ambition, and she'd gathered that Alexandra Radcliffe was hosting the concert herself. *That* girl had obviously had a bit of exposure in the media recently, so she knew of her, and had also met her mother on a couple of occasions, as Linda Radcliffe was a frequenter of one of her other restaurants in Avermore, and she'd happened to have been over there at the time. She also knew Fiona Clark, who she knew was the stepmother of her boyfriend. They had clashed swords over cards on occasions, sometimes in a back room at one of her restaurants, or else a casino, where she went to relax and enjoy herself.

A mature woman, blonde, of average height and slightly portly, she'd been in a long term relationship for many years, with a man she loved a lot and did a lot of things with – including having fantastic sex – but still hadn't got around to proposing marriage to him. She had never really wished for children of her own. She'd become a successful and relatively wealthy businesswoman, and her restaurants were her real babies, where her heart truly belonged.

As they'd planned, Alexandra told Miranda about the concert that she was going to stage in honour of Philippa Barrington, just before the end of term, at Charterhouse. Miranda knew of the quality of standards that the college had a reputation for, leaving aside its recent misfortune, and actually had quite a high regard for Philippa Barrington's work, herself. She was quite impressed with the pair, and thought the concert a nice idea, but she was interested in the exact details of what they were proposing.

She wasn't disappointed. Benita launched into her task, with the ease of a veteran. After explaining their basic catering requests for the night, she then gave Miranda a detailed, word perfect, cost analysis, that she and Alexandra had worked out, before handing her their written figure work, as proof. They hoped that their sponsored walk would raise a certain amount of capital, but they felt that they would need more, to really give the audience watching, value for money. Therefore, if Rumbold's agreed to sponsor the concert, providing the rest of the money, Benita would guarantee that any profits made from it, would go straight back to her, though she respectfully asked if, having put the business her way, Miranda wouldn't mind cutting the five of them organising it, a small share.

Miranda turned over the cuffs of her blouse sleeves a notch, as she pored over the figures. They seemed to be perfectly reasonable. These two girls clearly understood accounts, and Benita was obviously the businesswoman of their group. And she *might* be a young woman who she *could* do business with. Her eyebrows rose slightly in wonder, as she raised the possibility of a share in the profits. The girl was a revelation to her! Alexandra was quieter, and similar to how she'd expected her to be, going by the little attention that she paid to the grapevine, which specifically included Fiona Clark. But she'd understood her to be a gifted mathematician, amongst other things, and possibly going to Castra, so she suspected, correctly, that she'd had a major input with regard to their accounts.

Benita wasn't quite finished yet, though. There was one more thing up her sleeve (both of which in reality were pushed to the elbow). She understood that this restaurant had been targeted recently by burglars.

Miranda's face darkened, and Alexandra saw a hint of cold fury in her eyes.

"Yes! They seem to be after money. And so far they seem to have evaded capture. Shame on our police force! If I ever catch them myself, they'll be sorry, I tell you! And if it turns out to be kids and they're sentenced to a horsewhipping, then I hope that Alexandra's mother does it hard!"

Alexandra shifted uncomfortably in her chair. Benita reached out and gave her arm another comforting squeeze. She knew that was a slightly distasteful subject for her, and she wasn't an overwhelming fan, herself. Alexandra felt a warm glow of gratitude to her best school friend. She understood her, in a way that not all girls did. Miranda couldn't fail to see Benita's gesture.

"Well, I'm sure that our police force is doing its best," exclaimed Benita. "Personally I'd rather leave it for them to deal with. You never know exactly *what* you might come up against. And *I* consider myself to be quite a tough girl."

"Oh, I'm tougher than *them*, don't you worry about that," said Miranda, darkly.

Benita exchanged glances with Alexandra.

"In any case if it does prove to be kids, then it would be up to a juvenile court to decide their punishment," remarked Benita. "The reason why I mention the problem, is this. Are you aware that my mother is a criminal lawyer?"

Miranda had never heard of this girl, let alone her mother, before yesterday.

"No, I wasn't," she confessed.

Reaching behind to her blazer pocket, Benita pulled out another business card, and handed it to Miranda.

"Those are her details, if you should need the services of a lawyer to represent you in a court of law," she told her. "Her firm does specialise in this area of it, and I know that, as a business partner of mine, she would be prepared to offer you a very favourable rate, well below the normal fee that they would normally charge."

Miranda's eyes widened. Now the girl was bargaining with her! She reached a decision. Obviously the potential profit that she could make from this would not be huge, but a profit was a profit, and she was highly driven by that. There was also the possible future business that might come from those watching the concert on the night. Her tongue ran over her lips. Making money aroused her like nothing else – even more than making love to her boyfriend, and *that* turned her on, plenty enough.

"Right you two, I'll declare my hand," she announced, taking charge of the proceedings. "I like you two girls, very much, and you're clearly very professional in your business acumen. I think you deserve some reward, and I'm prepared to make an amount of money available to you, which will certainly fund your concert, and the cuisine of this restaurant can certainly be at your disposal. In exchange, I want the name of Rumbold's to be heavily in evidence at Charterhouse, so that I get maximum exposure for my restaurants and I wish to benefit from the profit that I'm confident that you'll make. As I'm in a generous mood, I think it's only fair that I allow you a share, too."

Alexandra and Benita looked at each other, both smiling softly. It looked as if they were going to pull this off!

"Thank you Miss Rumbold," said Alexandra.

"You may call me Miranda,"

"So let's confirm the final details," she continued. "Are you happy for me to supply the exact amount of money that you think you'll need, according to your figures?"

"Well," asserted Benita. "That's obviously a rough, but I believe, accurate assessment. However, perhaps a slightly higher amount would make things a little more comfortable – if that was possible."

Miranda smiled. Somehow she'd expected this from Benita. "How *much* higher?" she asked. She saw that Alexandra had pen, notepad and calculator at hand.

Benita bartered with Miranda. Now Alexandra was truly grateful for Benita being there. Things like that had never been her strong point, in her life up to now. It didn't take them long to agree a possible deal and then Benita looked across at Alexandra, to indicate that it was now down to her to decide.

She quickly started crunching some numbers. Now that Benita had so skilfully negotiated for them both, she felt quite calm and composed. A lot more so, than if she'd been there alone.

Eventually, she looked back at Benita, and nodded.

"OK, Miranda, that's a deal," announced Benita. "All that remains to discuss now, is the amount of the profits you're prepared to give away to us."

"70-30, in my favour," proposed Miranda.

Benita pursed her lips. "Is there any room for negotiation on that?" she asked.

Alexandra could see the determination on both of their faces. They were really getting to the fundamentals now. She'd seen her mother in similar mood, when she'd been negotiating a price for something, to her satisfaction.

Miranda chuckled. "I can see that you and I were cut from the same cloth, Miss Davis!" she asserted. "60-40, then. I think that's quite generous. I want to make it clear, that unless I receive a share of more than 50%, then the deal is off, so consider that very carefully."

"55-45, maybe then?" ventured Benita, cautiously.

Alexandra breathed in deeply. Benita was really pushing it to the limit.

Miranda swore inwardly. She'd hoped that Benita wouldn't have the nerve to push her any further, but the girl didn't miss a trick, if she saw that there was still an opportunity. She considered insisting on 60-40, but then decided against it. She wouldn't put it past Miss Davis to convince Alexandra to pull out of the deal herself, if she didn't get the share she wanted for the girls, and take their business elsewhere. Miranda had set her sights on this deal, and she wasn't going to let it go to someone else, now.

"Done!" she replied. "And if I *do* end up looking for a lawyer, for my current troubles here, then I may well look up your mother's firm."

Alexandra smiled warmly at her. "Thank you, Miranda," she said, getting up and shaking hands with her. "I think that will conclude our business for today."

Miranda shook hands with both girls.

"If you don't mind, I'd like to come back here for another meeting soon, Miranda," said Benita. A girl called Emma Thatcher, will be in charge of the catering, during the concert, so she'll need to let you know what she wants to have."

"Of course," agreed Miranda. "Get in touch to arrange it, whenever you want."

"I'll be focusing mainly on the concert itself now, Miranda," said Alexandra. "I'm sort of 'Executive Producer" of it, and officially I'm the chair of the board organising it, but Benita will be the real boss, in terms of arranging it. She's the one to deal with, for any queries, or problems. She's my right-hand woman."

"Fine," said Miranda. She'd concluded that Benita was the organiser some time ago.

And so, after saying goodbye to Miranda, the girls made their way back to Charterhouse. Benita needed to be back for her cooked dinner, whereas Alexandra would just be having her sandwiches. Her mother was cooking tonight.

As they walked, Alexandra returned a squeeze to Benita's arm. "Thanks Benita, you were fantastic!" she enthused. "I think that we stand a good chance of staging this now!" She couldn't resist giving her a kiss on the cheek, to show her appreciation.

Benita smiled and took her hand. "That's alright. I said that I'd make sure that you got this concert staged, and I won't let you down." She kissed Alexandra's cheek, also.

"I didn't realise that you were calling yourself 'Executive Producer' though!" she exclaimed. "That's a new one on me!"

"Well, that's how it feels, really," replied Alexandra.

"I wouldn't want to get on the wrong side of that woman though," she continued. I think that she wants to dish out her own dose of punishment, to whoever it is that keeps breaking in and stealing from her. Do you think that she *will* contact your mother's firm, for a lawyer, seeing as she'll be getting a discounted fee?"

"Well, actually I don't *know* that for certain," confessed Benita. "Sometimes you just have to take a chance. But I'm sure my mother *would* do what I said, now that we need Miranda's restaurant's sponsorship."

Alexandra looked at her in shock. "Blimey!" she exclaimed. "I wouldn't *dare* promise something like that, without having discussed it fully with my mother first. She'd go mad!"

"Yes, well I suppose that you have more opportunity, going home every night," replied Benita, thoughtfully. "I only really speak to my mother about once a week, on the phone."

"Hmm!" murmured Alexandra. She wasn't convinced *her* mother would consider that any excuse.

# CHAPTER 2

Alexandra told her mother about their meeting, as she went out of Charterhouse to the car with her, later that afternoon. She was delighted about it, and once again thought that Benita was a marvel. She confirmed that she knew Miranda Rumbold, a little, and her restaurant in Avermore, even better.

Once they were back at The Grange, Alexandra presented her mother with a gift of a box of chocolates, which she'd brought from Judith's store, to thank her for her help, during the hearing. She also kissed her, and had it returned with interest.

"They'll be gone, by tomorrow night!" Linda asserted, her mouth already watering in anticipation. "Thank you, darling."

She would prove to be correct in her prediction.

Linda then took her daughter up to her bedroom, and fulfilled two promises that she'd made to her.

Firstly, she smothered Alexandra's body under hers, on the bed. She'd actually said the sofa, but the bed was just as good, and in any case, James was downstairs! She pressed down on her, and kissed her lips deeply. Their tongues connected, and Linda licked her daughter's softly. Alexandra looked into her mother's eyes, and murmured in ecstasy.

Eventually, Linda got up, and told her daughter to wait, whilst she fetched something from her own room. It turned out to be the blow-up man, with a fake genus, that she'd been waiting to give Alexandra, once her punishment was over. She showed her how to pump it up, and fix the head to its body, and gave her a brief explanation of how it worked.

Alexandra's heart began to race, and her geratis extended far, thickening all the while in her excitement. She already knew exactly what photo she'd use, for the machine to stimulate her mind. The one that she'd shown her form class, at the beginning of the week.

"Use it whenever you really need to, and however you want to," said her mother. James and I aren't going to worry about anything that we might 'overhear'! But at the same time, please use your common sense, and try to be as discreet as possible!"

"Yes, Mother," promised Alexandra. "Thank you."

"That's alright. I hope it'll help you to satisfy some of your stronger urges, as well as to convince you once and for all, that you *can* make love to

Tom!"

She left her alone, and it wasn't long before Alexandra had the photo downloaded into the machine. That night, after her mother had said goodnight and locked her in her bedroom, she made her first experiment of the toy.

She attached the eyepiece that allowed the image of Tom to register in her mind. Her geratis raced hungrily into the man's hole, and slithered across it's vagina walls, making her shiver, as she felt the sensation for the first time in her life. It slipped back outside of the man's other hole, and re-entered her. She was already struggling to stay in control. She felt her geratis touch a genus, bringing forth a further new sensation, and electricity shot through her. The image of Tom kept appearing intermittently in her head, and she squeezed the man's body inside her arms and legs, as she thrust her own body deep into it, imagining – of course – that it was Tom. Her geratis filled the vagina and rubbed against its walls, as it grew bigger than ever before, and so hard did it thrust over the genus, that it burst in no time. As Alexandra felt the fake sperm first trickle into the pores of her geratis, she came immediately. The orgasm made her scream long and hard, and her eyes watered so much, that she couldn't see, as the sticky substance ran through her geratis and inside of her. She filled the walls with her own juice and the image of Tom glowed in her mind, as if she'd just given him tremendous pleasure.

She couldn't believe the power of what had just happened to her. And her mother had told her, *that* wasn't as strong as the real thing! How could women take that, and then do it over and over again?

Downstairs, Linda and James looked at each other knowingly, when Alexandra screamed. It was quite a moment for Linda. Her daughter had just had her first sexual experience. She was fast becoming a woman.

Their own passion showed no sign of diminishing. In fact, that night, they reached six times. Alexandra heard none of them tonight, though. After experiencing her first stimulated orgasm, she was wiped out. She fell asleep immediately, and didn't wake up for several hours. When she did, she was still tired. She packed her toy away, and was soon fast asleep again, until her mother woke her again, next morning.

Linda slipped her arms around her daughter in the bed, smiling, and asked her how it had felt. She and James had heard her experience, which didn't surprise Alexandra at all. She told her mother that it had been incredible, though the power had shocked her. Linda assured her, that was normal to feel at first, but she'd soon get used to it. In her own mind, she'd noted that Alexandra had only done it the once, and she was sure that at her age, she personally would have gone on to experiment further, had the toy been invented then, but her daughter was different, and the fact that she hadn't didn't surprise *her* at all, either. In all of the time that she'd been using her own toy, she'd never come like her daughter appeared to have done last night. That would have knocked even the strongest of girls out for the night, on their first experience of an orgasm. Once Alexandra and Tom finally did it for real, then clearly everyone would have to batten down the hatches, as goodness only knew, what she'd be like then.

Linda also promised her daughter, that she'd keep thinking about how to maintain the most intimate side, of their own relationship.

***

Over the first day of that weekend, James got more settled into The Grange. One immediate change was that Linda would no longer be paying for Mike, who had been their gardener for much of the time, since Robert's demise, as James would be taking over the duties from now on. Mike paid a final visit this weekend, and Linda took them both outside to supervise the 'handover'. Alexandra went with them, but her mother had also decided, that as a "thank you," it would be nice for them to cook him a small treat, before he left. Alexandra was tasked with baking some cakes, and after a while, Linda dismissed her from the garden and told her to go to the kitchen, and begin. It was another cold day, and Alexandra was quite pleased enough, to obey her mother, and get back inside.

Later, they all sat down in the parlour, with a cup of coffee, and ate the cakes. Alexandra was praised for her efforts, which pleased her, but she pointed out that her mother had taught her baking skills, just as she had, everything else. She was still a novice, and Linda was the expert. She still regarded her mother as the best cook in Geratica, a compliment she had paid on several occasions, and one that, as usual, earned her a big kiss.

Linda also gave Mike a card and a cheque for 50g, to help him on his way. His eyes widened in astonishment, when he saw the amount.

"Goodness me, Tina *will* be pleased when I give her this!" he exclaimed. Tina – his wife – worked in a local factory. He was a miner, and Linda had got to know him, through Robert, when he'd been alive. He had worked for Linda, on an occasional basis, to earn them some extra money. Her gift would certainly help cushion the disappointment of losing the surplus income.

"Thank you, Mrs Radcliffe! That really is most kind," he remarked, gratefully.

"Oh, don't mention it," said Linda. "Never let it be said that the Radcliffes aren't generous in their gratitude, for a job well done!"

\*\*\*

James was introduced to some of The Grange's parlour activities, that evening, and he also witnessed some of Linda and Alexandra's logic games, which they both enjoyed playing, when their weekends weren't too busy. Linda had always considered herself a mistress of this particular genre, but mother and daughter each had the most ideal of minds, for the strategies involved, and gradually, as she'd got older, Alexandra had begun to at least hold her own, against her, and sometimes even to beat her. After often epic battles of will, Linda still managed to win plenty of times, but her losses were invariably accompanied by some barbed comments about her daughter's luck, which Alexandra knew were mostly meant in jest, but she suspected also, that some were based on true sentiment, on occasions. Though not exactly a bad loser, she hated to do so, and didn't like it when she failed to make her daughter yield to the strength of her mind.

At the end of the evening, Linda and Alexandra took James up a small staircase to the loft and showed him their telescope. They spent a few minutes looking up at the sky through a window in the ceiling. Linda commented on Geratica's two moons and expounded her knowledge of the stars. She and Alexandra believed that although they should be grateful that the Divine Being had constructed a force-field around Geratica to protect it from invasion, they should also be outward looking to beyond their world. And somewhere, in another galaxy, across the universe, was planet Earth…

\*\*\*

On the second day of the weekend, 7/35/10, Linda was taking part in a hunting outing, in the land owned by the Sackville Estate. Linda didn't ride regularly, but she participated in this activity once or twice, during a season. Alexandra usually accompanied her, but she stayed well away from the horses, as she wasn't fond of them. She thought that they could give her a nasty kick, or a bite. Her mother had tried to introduce her to riding when she was younger, but she'd been so frightened, that they'd had to take her off the pony that she was training on. She hadn't sat on a horse of any kind, since, and she had no intention of doing so, at any time in the future. In any case, she couldn't really see the attraction of riding around a wood, often on a bitterly cold day, to try and hunt for quarry. She didn't mind watching from a safe distance though, even if it wasn't very pleasant to see a pack of animals, attack another individual one.

It was early morning, when they arrived, with James and Tom too, this time. Again, this was the first time that Tom had experienced this kind of event, now that Alexandra was able to invite him as her guest. Fiona, who was quite an accomplished horsewoman, and a keen rider to hounds, had come as well. Queen Alexandra was also participating.

Her mother looked very smart in her tunic and jodhpurs, Alexandra thought.

A horn sounded and they watched the party set off. A carriage enabled them to travel some distance behind them, to watch the proceedings. Alexandra actually saw some of the hounds assigned to her mother's charge, attack a couple of rabbits, and a fox, and by the time they finished, at midday, it appeared, that though considered a relative novice, she had actually been one of the most successful members of the party, though she (some thought uncharacteristically) modestly put it down to luck. This was something that seemed to have deserted Fiona, during the trip, much to her frustration. She blamed it on her inexperienced horse not being quick enough, her usual one having gone lame this very morning.

Later they enjoyed a lunch at the palace. Some of the guests were eating rabbit. Alexandra dryly wondered to herself, if the meat was from the same ones that her mother had caught earlier. It wouldn't be, of course.

In the afternoon, the party turned its attention to shooting birds. As this didn't involve having to be with a horse, Alexandra didn't mind helping her mother with this, loading the gun for her, so that it was ready for her to shoot. Linda was a quite a decent shot, and she'd won some trophies, in the past.

After her disappointment in the hunting, Fiona was determined to make up for it, in this discipline, and she set about the task with gusto. She still finished third in the overall tally of birds felled though, behind Linda in second place and the queen herself, as the winner.

After some drinks back at the palace, afterwards, the party broke up, and everybody returned home.

# CHAPTER 3

On 1/36/10, at Charterhouse, Sandra Steele once again took Annabel Wood's Music theory lesson, for the final year pupils.

At the start, she made a reference to the previous week's events, walking up and down the two rows of desks, and tapping her cane on each of them, as she passed.

"So! I am told that I was taken for a fool last week, by you girls," she remarked. "And I have been 'dropped in it', as they say! Very well, I have taken notice of your feelings, and will endeavour to show you in future, that I do genuinely have a sense of humour, and that I am not always *quite* as intolerant of slow progress, as some of you seem to think."

Having crossed back to her own desk, she continued, looking around at each member of the class and beating her cane several times, as she spoke.

"But let me just say this. If *any* girl, no matter who it might be, *dares* to go behind my back, to a higher authority, and criticise *my* teaching methods, again, then I shall come down on her, like a ton of bricks! *I* am the mistress and *you* are the pupils. If you don't like my approach, then you can get out! I will *not* be lectured to by *my* pupils. And you *are* my pupils, when Mrs Wood is unable to teach you, whilst she attends to her new duties."

"I trust that makes the position clear?" she asked the class.

"Yes, Miss Steele!" chorused the girls, and Alexandra squirmed slightly in her chair.

"Good," said the mistress, as she placed her cane at the front of her desk, and sat down.

Then Sandra started the lesson, though its general tone was markedly less severe, than the previous week's. But Miss Steele had made her point, and her pupils had taken note of it.

\*\*\*

That weekend, Linda gave Alexandra gave her daughter another treat, as she fulfilled her promise to take Alexandra back to Avermore, with James – and this time, Tom, as well. Alexandra was delighted that she could give Tom a first experience of something that was more common to her.

As a special surprise, Linda revealed as they left The Grange, on the morning of 6/36/10, that she wasn't going to drive there, but they would instead take the train. Travelling direct wouldn't take long, but their train would take a more circuitous route, thus allowing them some more time to enjoy the ride.

After she'd driven them to the station, they all stood in the foyer, and Linda looked up at the timetable board, flashing above them. Alexandra was always completely dumbfounded when she saw all the information, and could never understand how her mother could determine the correct platform to go to, in order to meet their train. It wasn't quite as simple as *one* train, at *one* platform, as she was used to on a daily basis, during the week. Somehow her mother always did however, and even though Tom was with her in her arms, she instinctively moved them both closer to Linda.

"Mother," she urged, "Don't get separated from us. I'll be lost without you to take us to the right place!"

"Yes, don't worry, darling! I'll look after you all," Linda assured her, and slipped her arm around her shoulder. With Tom pulled to her on one side, she snuggled to her mother's body on the other. She felt Linda's embrace tighten, and then the next thing she knew, she was receiving a kiss. Alexandra looked up happily at her mother. Now she certainly *did* feel looked after.

When they eventually did reach their platform, and their train arrived, they got settled into their first class compartment. Linda sat with James, opposite Alexandra and Tom. Only once they were underway, did Linda make a further revelation. She announced that before they got to Avermore, they would be stopping off in Liverton. The significance of this was largely lost on James and Tom, but Alexandra's eyes suddenly began to shine, as she guessed what might be coming.

"Are we going to visit Camilla Forbes' shop, Mother?" she asked excitedly. "Am I having a fitting for the new gown that I asked you about?"

Linda smiled and her eyebrows twitched up and down, always a clue to her daughter, that she was on the right track. Her eyes twinkled at Alexandra, and as she met them with her own, she knew that it was true, without her mother having to confirm it.

"Ooh, thank you, Mother!" she cried, beaming with pleasure, all over her face. She leant forward to Linda opposite, and kissed her three times.

"*Mmm,*" murmured Linda, appreciatively, speaking softly into her daughter's ear, so that only she could hear. "*Those were nice. Some of your very best, in fact! But you know, that I can always best you in that regard, and I know that you don't mind at all!*"

She locked Alexandra's shoulders inside her arms, and kissed her lips deeply, four times. Alexandra murmured as she felt tingles in her thighs.

"*You always win in that regard, Mother!*" she asserted, before they withdrew from each other. "*I'll always be learning from you!*"

They smiled at one another as they each sat back on their seats. Tom reflected once again, on how close his girlfriend was – and always would be – to her mother.

Camilla Forbes was a private dressmaker, and Alexandra had been taken to her shop on several occasions, over the years. Linda brought all of their gowns from her, and consequently they knew her quite well.

When the guard came around, Linda showed her their tickets, and then arranged some refreshments.

By the time they'd finished their coffee and scones, the next stop was Liverton. At the station, they disembarked, and Linda led the way out. Then they made their way to Camilla Forbes' shop.

Camilla worked by an appointment basis, therefore she was expecting them when they arrived. She was pleased to see them again. Alexandra was taken into the fitting room, with Camilla and her mother, and they discussed what she was looking for, from her catalogue.

"You'll be looking quite the young lady, with this new gown!" said Camilla to Alexandra, with a smile, as she measured her up.

Alexandra looked at her mother. "Well, I hope so," she replied. "I've got one or two responsibilities now, including a particularly important engagement, coming up just before the Festival of Divinity. I want to look my best."

"Ah yes, your concert," said Camilla. "I'd heard about that. Is there any chance of me getting a seat in the audience, seeing as I'm supplying you with a gown for it, or is it just for the girls only?"

"Well, you can, as long as you buy one from the girls in charge of selling them, like everybody else!" retorted Linda.

"Oh well, naturally, of course I will," Camilla assured her. "I wasn't trying to gain preferential treatment! When will they be on sale, and how much will they be?"

"We'll be putting the tickets up for sale, at Charterhouse, by the middle of next week," Alexandra informed her. "We haven't made a final decision on the price, yet."

"Well, I shall look forward to purchasing one, whatever the price," remarked Camilla.

"Thank you Mrs Forbes," said Alexandra, politely. "And I hope that this gown, won't just be worn to this concert, but to many other functions, besides!"

After her fitting was completed, Linda requested that the gown be made ready, as soon as possible. Camilla promised that it would be available for collection or delivery, by a fortnight's time, at the latest. Linda agreed and said that she would collect it, once it was ready.

Once they'd left the shop, they went back to the station, and caught another train to Avermore. It was around lunchtime when they arrived, and Linda took them to eat in Rumbold's. She thought that it was only fair for them to show their support, in return for Miranda's agreement to sponsor Alexandra's concert. It transpired that Miranda was expected, but not until this evening, so Linda asked the manager there, to pass on her personal thanks. She promised that she would.

Then, in the afternoon, Tom was taken on an official sight-seeing tour of Avermore, co-ordinated, naturally, by Linda. He saw every major attraction, and landmark that there was, for the first time, including of course, the royal Palace, though they didn't go inside on this occasion.

By the time they were finished, it was time to return home, and they caught the train back to Greenacres.

# CHAPTER 4

The sponsored walk took place the following day. Linda drove her daughter to Charterhouse, early in the morning, along with James and – much to Alexandra's pleasure – Tom. She was looking forward to getting the opportunity to show him around the college, later.

It seemed strange to her to be at Charterhouse at the weekend, as she met her board before the walk, to go through the final preparations. They were all participating themselves, and each had secured healthy sponsorship. Linda had taken Alexandra's form around the palace, and she personally was pledging a considerable amount. The route had been confirmed, and they would go to Buckmore town centre and back, and then finishing with a circuit of the college grounds. The walk would be followed by lunch for the girls, and any of their relatives visiting.

At 11.00 a.m. the girls were lined up, and ready to start. Emma handed a bottle of water to each of them, for refreshment during the walk, although at this time of year, it obviously wouldn't be too hot.

Mrs Wood rang the bell, and they began. There was a nip in the air, but it was warmer in the sun as they walked, and at least it wasn't raining.

It took about an hour to complete the walk, and by the end, Alexandra was glad to be back. That was far enough, as far as she was concerned, and she'd worked up an appetite, which she wanted to satisfy.

A short time later, everybody was sat in the dining hall. Some of the girls were flanked by their parents, and other family members, who had come along to support them, therefore extra seating had been arranged. Linda was particularly pleased to meet Benita's mother, Claire Davis.

Imelda was on the next table to Alexandra, with her parents. She was especially excited at seeing Tom in the flesh, for the first time. He looked even better than his picture had suggested, she thought. Whenever she could catch his eye, she smiled at him. Although she didn't do it deliberately, on a couple of occasions her tongue ran over her lips as she did it, so desirable did she find him, which gave a slightly sexy element to it.

Tom had no idea who the girl was, but he thought it fairly obvious that she fancied him. For the record, the feeling was mutual. She was blonde like Alexandra, though not quite as stunning, and as a natural Geratican man, he couldn't help but feel sexual arousal at her advances. If it weren't for the fact that he loved Alexandra more than anyone else in the world, and wanted to be with her for the rest of his life, without betrayal, he could probably be successfully seduced by her, he thought.

Meanwhile, Imelda's young, inexperienced, but confident geratis, was going wild inside her pants, as she surveyed Tom's features, and fantasised about him being spread before her in her chambers bed, and casting away her virginity at last, as she made love to him. She discreetly put her hand down on her lap, beneath the table, and stroked the bulge in her skirt with her finger. Immediately she felt an enormously strong bolt of energy rip through her, causing an emission in her pants. Unfortunately for Imelda, she was holding a cup and saucer in her other hand, at the time. She jumped so violently from the shock, that the cup toppled from the saucer, spilling some of its contents onto her mother's lap, beside her, and landing on the dining hall floor, smashing on impact.

Her mother shrieked slightly with shock, and then scolded her, as she cleaned her skirt with a serviette. "Imelda, you *stupid* girl! What in the world is the matter?" she demanded.

"I'm sorry, Mother! It was an accident. I don't know what came over me."

The last part of Imelda's assertion was a lie. Her face was as red as a beetroot, and her embarrassment was made all the more acute, by the fact that she could see Tom was highly amused by her misfortune. He was however, as ignorant as her mother, about its exact cause.

After lunch, Alexandra showed Tom around Charterhouse, as she'd planned. He saw her form room, some of her other classrooms, her science laboratory and music room, as well as the assembly hall, library and her house prep room. She also showed him where the house dormitories were, but as she explained to him, even she hadn't been into one of those, as she didn't board. They finished in the exercise yard, Alexandra's least favourite place in the whole college, though it might gain a slightly more favourable impression on her from now onwards, as here they exchanged kisses in each other's arms. The tip of her geratis tingled, and she murmured in ecstasy.

"Thank you for bringing me here," said Tom. "It's nice to finally see where you go every weekday. It's a lovely place!"

"I've wanted to for a long time, but until now, there's never been a proper reason for you to come," replied Alexandra. "I'm glad that you like it."

Tom asked her about the girl in the dining hall. After he'd described her accident, she realised who he was referring to.

"Oh, that's Imelda," she said.

"I think that she fancies me!" Tom told her.

"I think that *all* of my form class do, Tom," remarked his girlfriend. "Benita asked me to bring a picture in, so that they could see what you looked like, and they all drooled over you. I warned every one of them to keep their hands off you, as you're mine!"

Tom looked shocked. "Oh my goodness!" he exclaimed. "You didn't tell me that I was such an object of desire, before you invited me here. You must look after me! You know I'm yours, and nothing will ever change that."

Alexandra smiled with pride, and took him in her arms. It did seem that Imelda was the one most attracted to Tom, she thought. Perhaps she'd better watch her!

"Well let's get back to Mother and James," she said. "It'll soon be time for us to leave anyhow." She kissed him again and he returned it. She held him close to her, as she led the way back to reunite them with Linda and James.

***

At the beginning of Week 37, after the sponsored walk, Alexandra looked over the accounts and agreed with Benita's assessment of their financial status. Only a couple of the girls, who'd said they'd participate, hadn't in the end, due to illness, and all who'd started had finished. Assuming that everyone obtained their sponsorship money by the end of the week, as they wanted them to, then they would have done well. It would be Imelda and Rachel's job to collect the money, as it was given to them, and Benita's to store and account for it, though she also asserted that she'd personally take action if there were any late payers. Benita had also been told that Charterhouse had received a cheque from Rumbold's restaurant, to cover the sponsorship of the concert.

Imelda and Rachel printed concert tickets, and started selling them, from the next day onwards. Benita had arranged for them to have a small advertising space, in the local paper. This caused her slight friction with Imelda and Rachel, who felt that organising this, should have been part of their role. There was a feeling, particularly from Imelda, that Benita was becoming too dominant.

This was something that Alexandra had always dreaded. If there was going to be a personality clash, then it was always likely to be between these two. She hated confrontation and avoided it as much as possible, preferring to just quietly get on with whatever she had to do and not get involved, at all. It was one of the reasons why she didn't think that management would ever suit her. She didn't like dealing with people very much.

Benita was a very confident person, and could indeed dominate. That was the reason why Alexandra found her so invaluable as a board member. She *could* take over, and run the operation for her, which had taken the pressure off her considerably, and she was extremely grateful for that. It would also allow her to concentrate on the concert performance from now on. But they had all done a fantastic job for her so far, and she was certain that would continue to be the case, until the concert was over.

Alexandra tried her best to be diplomatic.

"You've all been really helpful, and I'm really pleased to have you all on the board, helping me!" she remarked. "I really don't mind who does things, as long as when they need to be done, they are! But I think we're all agreed that Benita is an integral part of our group. We wouldn't be in such a healthy overall position now, if it wasn't for her. She's the one with the best head for business, undoubtedly!"

She looked at Benita and was about to speak again, when her friend touched her arm and more or less said it for her.

"I'm sorry, Imelda. I should have spoken to you two about it first, and maybe let you do it. It's just that there's always the time element to consider. We've only got another fortnight, until this concert will be staged. I just wanted to get the advert in the paper as quickly as possible. I'll admit it, I messed up!"

"No that's OK, Benita," replied Imelda. "You and Alexandra are both right. You *are* the most capable of all of us, in doing this sort of thing. That *was* an important job that needed to be done urgently. Thank you for doing it. I'm sorry I spoke out of turn!"

Benita nodded in acknowledgement and Alexandra hoped that the matter was now resolved. Afterwards Benita was appreciative of her support. She knew that Alexandra hadn't been comfortable with the notion of intervening. She gave her a hug, squeezing her tight.

Together with Emma and Benita, Alexandra had a meeting with the Charterhouse Symphony Orchestra, to discuss the performance, and then rehearsals finally began. Emma had also met Miranda Rumbold, with Benita, and was now making plans for the catering, and what food they would ask to be brought from Rumbold's restaurant to the Charterhouse kitchen, for the audience to eat during the concert.

\*\*\*

Alexandra and Tom also practised their communication without words that they'd first tried at The Grange, during Tom's birthday dinner. It was a slow process, and Alexandra had to work hard, to get Tom to focus his thoughts sufficiently. But when he did, the intense concentration of her mind was able to make a certain amount of impact, and Tom continued to feel something, when their eyes met, and Alexandra's fingers glided softly over his.

# CHAPTER 5

In the very early morning of 5/37/10, both The Grange and The Lodge were woken by a loud bang, which echoed all around Elmsbrook. The vibration could be felt in both households.

Alexandra could hear shouts of exclamation from her mother and James' bedroom, across the landing. She sprang out of bed and went to the window, but before she reached it, there was another sound, of something coming up the hamlet drive, and getting nearer and nearer. As she pulled the curtain back, and looked through the darkness, she saw the headlamp of a motorbike stopping outside The Grange gates. The rider fiddled with the latch and forced it open. Then, to her amazement the rider raced their bike down the private driveway of their home, stopping outside their parlour window. The Grange's security light came on, shrouding the rider in its glow. They were dressed all in black, with the same colour helmet, which had a thick visor, so their features couldn't be seen, but Alexandra guessed from their general physique, that it was likely to be a man.

Then she heard her mother's voice shout from their bedroom.

"*Hey, who* **are** *you? Get out! How dare you trespass on private property?*"

She had obviously done the same as her, on the other side of the house, and had opened the window to remonstrate with the intruder. The rider ignored her, and took something out of his saddlebag. He hurled it at the parlour window, and there was a smash as it came through, and then a thud as it landed on the room floor. Then the rider turned their motorbike around, and sped away, back the way they'd come.

"What in the name of ...!" Alexandra heard her mother begin, as their bedroom door opened and she stomped across the landing. She went down the stairs, and once she was in the parlour there were further shouts. She heard James following on, down the stairs. But of course, until her mother let her out of her own bedroom, she couldn't join them.

As if her mother had read her mind, Alexandra heard her come back up the stairs.

"Mother!" she cried, through the closed door. "What's happened?"

"Just a minute, Alexandra, I'll get the key," replied Linda.

Then Alexandra heard the front door open and close. Looking out of the window again, the security light came on once more, and she saw the figure of James, hurrying down the drive, with his overcoat and scarf over his pyjamas.

A few seconds later, she opened the door. "Darling, you'd better come down. Something rather unpleasant has been 'delivered' to The Grange!"

"Yes Mother," Alexandra pulled her dressing gown tighter around herself, and followed her downstairs.

In the parlour there were bits of broken glass on the floor around the front window area, and a brick lay on the carpet, further inside.

Linda had a piece of paper in her hand, and her expression was grave.

"*This,* was attached to *that,* when it came through the window!" She held up the piece of paper, and pointed to the brick.

"It's a note," she continued. "It says, 'To The Grange and The Lodge. Rich scum women will pay for their privileges. Men will be educated and take their places. Stay away from your workplace and your college of elitism. We will be watching you always! Take great care! Have a happy Festival of Divinity. From The Oppressed Men of Geratica.'

"The security scanner on the gate, also isn't working," Linda added. "James has gone down to check it, but I would think that the bang that woke us all up, was our intruder, blasting their way through it, to force entry into Elmsbrook!"

Alexandra stared at her mother, unable to speak. Linda laid her hands on her shoulders. Her eyes offered comfort to her, but she could also tell her mother was incandescent with rage.

"Now don't you worry. We *won't* be intimidated by this. These barbarians won't stop us from going about our normal daily lives, by threatening us, although just to be on the safe side, I think it's best if we both take today off! You'll be having a long weekend, sweetheart. Forget about Charterhouse for today! I'm going to phone the police immediately, and then there'll be things that I'll need to do!"

The phone immediately rang. Linda went and looked at the display. "It's The Lodge," she said.

"Good morning Fiona," she said, after she'd answered it.

She explained what had just happened. Alexandra heard her mother vent her full fury. She wasn't sure if she'd ever seen her so angry. When she could get a word in, Fiona assured her that this time, the intrusion was nothing to do with her.

"They've gone too far this time!" Linda was raging. "Those damned Male Rights Protestors! They should all be locked up, and then I'll throw away the keys myself!"

She was still fuming down the phone, when James returned and confirmed that the gate had been forced open. It looked as if a small explosive had been used, to blow open the security lock.

Linda suggested that Fiona should stay at home today too, but Fiona pointed out that one of them at least should go to work as normal, to show that they wouldn't be bullied. She declared that Colin and Tom were already doing so... After some consideration, Linda agreed, although she then suggested that rather than go alone, Fiona should let James take her. He needed to go in today, as he had some important work to do on Queen Alexandra's private car. After some more discussion between the three of them, this was agreed also.

Fiona rang off, and Linda immediately contacted the police. She was shocked to discover that there had been several more incidents of this kind, reported this morning, all over Castra. The officer promised that they would come to The Grange, as soon as possible.

"It's worse than we thought!" exclaimed Linda, as she came off the phone. "We're not the only ones to have suffered this, today."

She put the radio on. There was a special bulletin on the day's attacks. It appeared that there had been six in total. Apart from The Grange, three were households owned by women of the nobility – including Lady Caroline Sackville – and the others by Teresa Brockenhurst MP, and Edwina Stockton QC.

"Outrageous!" spat Linda.

"Right!" she said, assertively, "Alexandra, I want you to make the breakfast, this morning. I must ring the palace, the police will be here shortly, and James must go to work with Fiona. Not to mention the repair work that I'm now going to have to get organised. We'd better quickly get dressed, and then we're in for a busy morning!"

"Yes, Mother. Of course," replied her daughter, obediently.

*** 

Queen Alexandra had heard the reports, and was deeply alarmed by the early morning's events.

"I knew that there was an element of strong feeling, amongst a minority of people in my queendom, but I never thought that anything like this would happen," she said, worriedly.

"They're nothing but a band of ruffians Ma'am!" asserted Linda. "We mustn't give any quarter to them,"

"There hasn't been any incident at the palace, I trust, Ma'am?" she asked.

"No. Not that I'm aware of, anyhow," replied the queen.

"Perhaps even those scum don't have the nerve to go that far, Ma'am!" said Linda. "I'm not giving in to this pressure, but if you don't mind, Ma'am, would it be possible for me not to come in today? Fiona wants to, and I've suggested that she travel with James, rather than on her own. I shall have things to do here now. I'm keeping Alexandra off school today, too."

"Of course Linda. That's perfectly alright. I understand," Queen Alexandra assured her. "You must tend to your own affairs."

"I would strongly advise you to stay in the palace today, Ma'am. In this climate, we can't predict for certain, what might happen. I always said that this 'Male Rights' business, would lead to a breakdown in law and order, and now I've been proved right!"

"As always, you are very wise Linda," said the queen. "I *will* stay here. My guards will certainly earn their keep, today!"

"I wouldn't be at all surprised if dear Elizabeth Spencer is involved in this, Ma'am," said Linda. "After all, this has always been her hobby horse, and she herself gained unauthorised access to Elmsbrook, only a couple of weeks ago – with the help of Fiona, of course! She could easily have supplied some information on our security system to whoever it was who broke in this morning."

"Well, let's not make any hasty accusations, without any direct proof, Linda!" exclaimed Queen Alexandra. "Once Fiona gets here, I want her to immediately arrange me a meeting with Geratica's Head of Security, to try and establish what we *do* know about these people – if anything. I assume the police might be able to tell you what they know, when they visit you, presently."

"I hope so, Ma'am," remarked Linda. "In the meantime, I think we need to put out some kind of statement about this. And I recommend a very robust response, making it very clear what we think of these activists and their methods, and stating that we will not be cowed by their threats."

"Hmm," began the queen. "I think I would favour a slightly more conciliatory tone, Linda. Something along the lines of, acknowledging their concerns, stating that we are reviewing the situation and promising to bear them in mind, when considering a possible future solution, but making no specific pledges or proposals."

Linda had to make a huge effort to stay calm. This was far *too* conciliatory for her liking.

"Ma'am, this is a crisis, potentially the biggest of your reign! With respect, you must be strong and resolute in your response to this. I don't think that now is the time, to be hinting at possible concessions! If we don't stamp this out firmly, now, then it may well come back on us again later, with even greater force. We'll be storing problems for ourselves in the future."

"I quite agree with you, about the need to be strong over this, Linda. And I am not promising these people anything, other than that their concerns will be borne in mind. But at the same time, we must be careful not to inflame the situation further. I'm sorry Linda, but I want a calming influence, to cool things down for a while. I realise that your feelings over this are particularly raw at the moment, after what's happened at The Grange this morning, but you're certainly strong enough to survive that! This response, that *I* propose, is my final decision, Linda. I'll have *my* will implemented!"

"As you wish, Ma'am" conceded Linda. Queen Alexandra could be highly assertive when she needed to be, and once she'd made up her mind about a course of action, she demanded compliance. She was, it went without saying, the one person in Geratica, who Linda had no choice but to defer to, and indeed, the only person that she ever did so to.

"As you're not going to be here today, are you happy to let Fiona draft the statement?" asked the queen. "It must be done with the utmost urgency."

"Of course, Ma'am," Linda told her.

"Good. Well that settles that, at least. I'm sure we'll get through this Linda. And I'm equally sure that your contribution will end up playing a crucial role in our survival. It usually does!" Queen Alexandra tried to end on a positive note, with her most trusted and loyal advisor, whose opinion she had always valued above all others.

"You can be doubly certain of that, Ma'am!" declared Linda, confidently.

***

After her phone call with the queen, Linda sat down for a quick breakfast with James and Alexandra.

"Mmm! Well done Alexandra! Despite your acknowledgement of who is the mistress cook of this household, I must ask that you don't put yourself down quite so readily in the future! As I've told you countless times – don't undersell yourself!" After getting some of her anger out of her system, Linda was beginning to regain her humour.

"Thank you, Mother!" said Alexandra, beaming at her.

Shortly afterwards, Fiona arrived, and she and James left for the palace. Then Linda rang Charterhouse, to tell them that her daughter wouldn't be attending today, due to unforeseen circumstances.

***

A little later two police officers arrived. One introduced herself as Sergeant Marshall, and the other was Constable Drew, who had visited them before, when Elizabeth Spencer had crashed her car into Linda's at Charterhouse.

Linda explained exactly what had happened, and Sergeant Marshall confirmed that this incident, followed much the same pattern – though not necessarily involving the blasting of a security gate – as others that had taken place, in various locations in Castra, that same morning.

"These people are obviously Male Rights Supporters," remarked Linda. "But do we have any idea of the individual identities of the culprits? They need to be prosecuted."

"Quite!" agreed Sergeant Marshall. "At the moment, no we don't, on the uniform side, though I suspect our plain clothes detective colleagues, probably have some leads."

"I can't say that I'm surprised to have been targeted, though," said Linda. "Not only am I what *some* sections of society like to call *rich,* but I have also been one of the most outspoken critics of this issue. I imagine, I was at the top of their list!"

"Possibly, but I think that any prominent woman in Geratica could have been targeted today," said the sergeant. "The statement that you've given us, will go on to the central file, relating to this case, and we'll take things from there."

"And because any woman could be targeted, we're asking all to be especially vigilant over the next few days, in case there are any more attacks in the pipeline," said Constable Drew.

"We certainly will be, here at Elmsbrook!" vowed Linda. "But if someone is determined enough to blast through a security gate with an explosive, in order to get in, then it just goes to show that you can only do so much! I've already been in touch with the company who installed it, and they're sending a couple of people to fix it, later this morning."

"Well that's good news, at least," said Sergeant Marshall. "Don't worry, Mrs Radcliffe. The perpetrators of this crime will soon be caught!"

"Hmm. I hope so!" exclaimed Linda, ruefully.

\*\*\*

At lunchtime, as two women worked at the bottom of the hamlet drive, to get Elmsbrook's security gate in operation again, and a man from a window fitting company replaced the broken one in the parlour of The Grange, Linda and Alexandra listened to the news. As they expected, it was dominated by the events of early that morning.

The statement that Queen Alexandra had wanted drafted, was now published and it was read on the bulletin. It was largely as the queen had asserted, during her phone call with Linda earlier, but one sentence had slipped in, declaring that:

*'Her Majesty very much hopes that a diplomatic solution, suiting both sides, can be reached, rather than one obtained through confrontation with each other.'*

In addition, it was noted that Fiona Clark had drafted the statement, rather than Linda Radcliffe, the latter of whom was thought to favour the more confrontational approach. This was leading to speculation amongst some commentators, that Linda Radcliffe had been deliberately "snubbed" by Queen Alexandra.

Linda lost her temper for the second time that day, at such an erroneous report, slapping the dining room table with her fist and startling Alexandra. However, she forced herself – helped by years of disciplining her mind to keep thinking rationally, when dealing with court affairs – to regain her composure, whilst she listened to the rest of the broadcast.

It also appeared that, according to an interview with Henrietta Kelly,

Geratica's Head of Security, the authorities were in fact closing in on those they suspected of carrying out the attacks. Their names and addresses were known – and two of the six were women – which made Linda's blood begin to boil again. She even went so far as to name the suspected ring-leader, Ralph Smith.

Linda turned off the radio at the end of the bulletin and exploded.

"So, I have been snubbed by Queen Alexandra have I? What poppycock! Honestly, some people will try and make a story out of nothing!" Although she didn't say it to her daughter, she also suspected that Fiona had put the contentious sentence in deliberately, hoping to cause her some embarrassment at court. It was probably more retaliation for the warning she'd been given.

On her own in the study, she rang through to the palace once again and was put through to the queen. After the initial formalities, she came to the point.

"Ma'am, I've heard the latest news reports, and there's some twaddle of a story, that you've somehow 'snubbed me', with the statement that was issued earlier!"

"Yes, I'm sorry about that, Linda," replied Queen Alexandra. "I don't know where they got that idea from!"

"Well, obviously it was that sentence that the media are quoting, Ma'am. I'd like to know where exactly it came from!"

"It was penned by Fiona," admitted Queen Alexandra. "I didn't think anything much of it, when I cleared it for release, but maybe with hindsight, I should have got it amended slightly. I'm sorry. What they're saying in the news, on that particular subject, is clearly slightly wide of the mark."

"Yes, Ma'am, I'd guessed it probably came chiefly from Fiona. And I suspect that she put it in deliberately, to try and cause me some embarrassment!"

The queen thought so too. Fiona had seen a way to manipulate the circumstances to Linda's disadvantage. She was treading a very thin line, at the moment, after having already being disciplined for her poor etiquette, and this might very well be revenge against Linda, for that. But Fiona hadn't technically done anything wrong here. The sentence had been passed by herself, and in any case, it was indeed true, that Linda had argued for a tougher stance to be taken.

"Is there anything you want to do about it?" she asked.

"Well, since you ask, Ma'am, I'd like to draft my own statement, putting the record straight, as I see it, and release it to the media as soon as possible."

Queen Alexandra considered.

"Well I don't see why not," she replied. She wanted to help Linda feel better, after the day she'd had. "But I'd like to clear it myself, after you've written it, before it goes out."

"It is already on my desk here, awaiting your approval, Ma'am," revealed Linda.

"Oh!" exclaimed the queen. "Well I suppose I might have known. You're as keen and determined as ever, Linda!"

"Never doubt it, Ma'am!" asserted Linda. "If I may, I'll read it to you."

"*With reference to the reports amongst certain elements of the media, that I have been somehow 'snubbed' by Her Majesty, I wish to totally refute this suggestion, and put the record straight.*

"*Whilst it is true that I am hostile to the apparent aims of the Male Rights Supporters, in relation to Geratican society as a whole, I would not wish to take any action which might provoke even more breakdown in law and order. I wholeheartedly support the statement, issued earlier, by the palace.*

"*The only reason why I did not draft the aforementioned, myself, was because I am not at my desk today. My household has been damaged and both my daughter and I have been threatened, so I am sure that most people will understand that I feel my place should be at home, at the moment. Do not fear, though. I shall be back at the palace, with renewed vigour, on Day One of next week!"*

Queen Alexandra smiled to herself. Linda had done it again. She was sure that most people, would find Linda's position entirely reasonable.

"That sounds fine, Linda," she confirmed to her. "Have the palace put it out, straight away!"

"Thank you, Ma'am!" replied Linda.

Later that afternoon, Linda and Alexandra heard the exact, same statement, read out word for word, on the radio.

\*\*\*

By this time, the gate and window were fixed and the repairers had left. Alexandra sat with her mother, on the sofa in the parlour.

"Mother," said Alexandra, grabbing her hand.

Linda instinctively let her daughter's hand slip inside of hers, and then squeezed it.

"What, darling?" she said encouragingly, realising that there was something on Alexandra's mind.

"Do you think that there'll be any more attacks? Will I be safe on the train, going to and from Charterhouse?"

"Well I'm hopeful that these half dozen will be caught fairly quickly," replied Linda. "And it sounds as if one of them is the ring-leader. Let's hope that they're the only ones militant enough to go to the extremes that we've witnessed today! Try not to worry, my baby. I know this has probably frightened you, but you know that whenever we're together, I'll protect you!"

Alexandra squeezed her Linda's hand from the inside. "I know you will, Mother. Thank you!" she said.

They kissed and then Alexandra continued, "And you know, Mother, that you also said, you could still take me over sometimes!"

Linda looked at her daughter for a moment and then at the clock. All of a sudden her desire to look after Alexandra, ignited her passion.

She smiled. "Well, I suppose there's no time like the present," she declared. "We'll be alone for a little bit longer yet!"

Alexandra's eyes shone bright in her delight. Her mother stood up and lifted her off the sofa.

"Come upstairs to my bedroom, darling!" said Linda, and led her daughter out of the parlour.

***

Twenty minutes later, Alexandra lay gasping on James's side of the bed, after her mother had just given her the loving of her life. She'd never felt so dominated, and it hadn't taken long at all, for her defences to be defeated, and to have all control taken away.

Suddenly the phone rang. Linda eased herself up and reaching across, picked up the extension.

It turned out to be Fiona. She'd just found out, that all of the people involved in the morning's attacks had now been caught – except one, Ralph Smith. He had gone on the run and was now at Lady Sackville's estate – and holding Lady Caroline, her steward, Lord George, and Tom, as hostages.

# CHAPTER 6

Linda and Alexandra jumped into the car and raced over to Lady Sackville's estate. At the palace, James and Fiona, together with Queen Alexandra and her bodyguards, did likewise.

Alexandra was shaking, in her fear for Tom's safety. According to Fiona, Smith reportedly had access to a bomb.

They'd left in such a hurry, that Linda hadn't had much of a chance to give her daughter any precise explanation of the situation.

"Mother, what does this man want?" asked Alexandra.

"He's doing a bit more than 'wanting', darling. He's 'demanding' that what this gang have done, be seen as a 'political action' and thus they be granted immunity from prosecution and allowed to make a broadcast of their views on the radio! If we refuse, he will ... harm everyone in the house!"

Fiona had actually told her that Smith had apparently already shot dead every one of Lady Caroline's staff inside the Manor and reportedly stated that he would kill all of the family, Tom and himself, if his demands weren't met, but she didn't want to alarm her daughter even further.

As it was, Alexandra shuddered and struggled to stop herself from stammering. "W-Will they be given what they demand, Mother?"

"Certainly not!" declared Linda, indignantly. "Whether this be seen as a 'political' act or not, they've still committed crimes, and you don't reward *that* with immunity from prosecution and provide it with a worldwide public platform. And *particularly* not when their ringleader holds people hostage, to try and *force* us to agree to his demands. What a cheek!"

"How did Tom get caught up in it all though, Mother? Obviously, he works there, but only outside. How would he?" Alexandra broke off, struggling to put her confused thoughts into words.

"I don't know really know any exact details of what happened yet, darling. Maybe we'll find out some more when we get there, and meet the detective squad. In actual fact, although I don't handle Geratican security directly, I am kept abreast of some of the issues, and I have vaguely heard this man's name mentioned before, but I know nothing more about him."

Alexandra couldn't stop thinking about what might be happening to Tom.

***

When they arrived at the estate, they were met by a Detective Sergeant, who was working with a group of other detectives under her command. She immediately ushered them to a safe area.

She introduced herself as Detective Sergeant Jill Baynton.

"How are things going?" asked Linda. "You're aware I'm sure, that my daughter's boyfriend is one of the hostages in the house?"

"We certainly are Mrs Radcliffe," replied the detective. "Miss Radcliffe, if you like, you can go with one of my officers, who is trained to deal with the traumatic feelings that you're probably experiencing."

Alexandra squeezed hard inside her mother's hand. Linda squeezed back in acknowledgement.

"I think that she'd prefer to stay with me, therefore she will, if it's alright with you, Detective Sergeant Baynton. Thank you."

Jill Baynton, like countless others before her, decided not to argue with Linda Radcliffe.

"As you wish, Mrs Radcliffe. That's not a problem," she replied.

"How exactly did this happen?" asked Linda.

"Well, all we know, is that the assailant somehow gained access to the Sackville estate, and then managed to get inside. There are no signs of a break in, so as Tom Ryder is one of the hostages, then it's possible that he was commandeered to assist him, against his will, no doubt. I believe he is a trainee gardener here?"

"That's correct, Detective Sergeant Baynton," confirmed Alexandra. "And he would *never* have helped this man voluntarily, I can assure you of that!"

"Do we know for certain, that he's set up a bomb?" asked Linda.

"Unfortunately, yes we know that he has," replied Jill. "Security scanners picked up the signal of its source and it was traced to the manor house."

"There are actually armed police surrounding the manor," she continued. Linda and Alexandra looked around and could just make out some women dotted around, with guns aimed in the direction of the estate home.

"Commander Henrietta Kelly, who I'm sure you're acquainted with Mrs

Radcliffe, is here and in overall charge of the operation."

"Of course," replied Linda. "In fact, I can see her coming now."

Henrietta joined them. "Good afternoon, Mrs Radcliffe, Miss Radcliffe," she said. "I saw you arrive earlier. I presume that Sergeant Baynton has appraised you of the facts? We have in fact had some dialogue with Smith. He appears to have a device with which he can communicate with our own radios. But it's an ongoing situation."

"I sincerely hope you've no intention of agreeing to his demands?" demanded Linda. "The court will not tolerate that!"

"Oh no, absolutely not! But it might be useful to offer the hint of a possible broadcast, if he co-operates, just to keep him happy, and maybe even tempt him to surrender."

"Very well."

There was tension in the air. This sort of thing, whilst not unheard of, was still a relatively rare occurrence in Geratica. Alexandra shivered, and pushed herself against her mother's body. Linda squeezed her inside of her arm, and softly kissed her forehead.

"Don't worry, my darling," she said reassuringly to her daughter. "These people know what they're doing. They'll get everyone out safely. It's just one man, against all of them! How can he possibly hope to win?"

Alexandra didn't reply. She found it impossible. Although she appreciated her mother's words of comfort, she couldn't help but worry. She buried her face deeper into Linda's chest, and held on to her waist. Once again, she would need her mother's strength to endure this.

***

Ralph Smith, the man who had attacked The Grange, first thing this morning, had spent some hours endeavouring to evade capture by the police. Eventually after lunchtime he had come to the Sackville Estate, which had earlier been attacked by one of his fellow protestors - throwing another message attached to a brick, over one of the walls. The police had since left.

He had managed to disable the estate's security system, climb a wall, and drop into the grounds, undetected. By chance, he'd come across Tom, and forced him at gunpoint to take him into the Manor House. On the way he had ascertained that the mistress of the estate, Lady Caroline and her son,

Lord George, were in the parlour. After Tom knocked on the door, opened it and entered the room, he'd burst in and forced them out into the lobby at gunpoint. Then he had ordered Tom to round up every member of staff working in the manor. Once they were all assembled in the lobby, he'd told all except Tom and the steward of the estate, Collette Braithwaite, to go outside, or he would shoot Lady Caroline. They had soon complied and were now being attended to by the police.

Next, he had wired a mobile device to the front door. It was a brand new, cunning piece of technology, designed and built by a young scientific mistress, who'd shown him how to work it, and sold it to him, for a tidy sum. He also had a lover who was now the boss of their organisation, and he'd used some of her money, to help him pay for the service, without her knowledge, or consent.

The device was connected to a bomb, back at his own home, which had also been built for him by the same girl. If he set it in motion, it would start the timer on the bomb ticking. It was set for ninety minutes. However, if the bomb went off, then instead of exploding at his home, its energy would be reflected back to the location of its detonation. In this case, that would be Lady Caroline Sackville's manor, and it would be blown to smithereens, along with anybody within. He would be killed, too. But that didn't matter. He would be honoured to be a martyr for their organisation's cause. Finally, he'd ordered the steward, at gunpoint, to lock every point in the manor which could be accessed from outside. If anybody attempted to enter by breaking a window or forcing a door, then the device would pick up the sound and detonate the bomb instantly.

Satisfied that all was prepared, he had then switched on his radio – the same type as the police used to communicate with each other, and calmly informed the first woman that he'd pick up over the airwaves, of what he'd just done at Lady Caroline Sackville's estate. It hadn't taken long for the security force and police to gather outside.

***

Queen Alexandra's private car drew up, and James and Fiona got out. The queen was following her bodyguard's advice, to stay inside, with them.

Fiona immediately enquired about Tom, and both she and James were brought up to date with the current situation.

"When are you going to go in and shoot Smith?" demanded Fiona.

Henrietta's jaw dropped slightly. "Well let's not get too ahead of ourselves!" she exclaimed. "We'll do what we can to end this peacefully, by trying to talk him into giving himself up, but if that fails, then we may have to think of alternative solutions."

"Oh rubbish!" said Fiona impatiently. "The stupid little man's only got himself to blame. My stepson's in there! Let's get rid of the bomber, and all go home!"

"Fiona! For goodness sake, let these people do their jobs!" cried Linda. "Show a bit of trust in our world's security force."

"The trouble is," said Henrietta, "that we would have to find a way of entering the building, without detonating the bomb, and to be able to get to the front door to disable the mobile detonator and stop the timer."

Just then though, there was a crackling on Henrietta's radio ...

*\*\**

When Ralph had first entered the house and realised who he had as hostages, he hadn't been able to believe his luck. To have chanced upon both Lady Caroline *and* Lord George Sackville at home, was certainly fortunate, he thought. And Lord George was Queen Alexandra's intended! As a bonus there was Tom Ryder, who he'd recognised from his picture in the paper, during his girlfriend's recent embarrassment. He knew that his stepmother worked at the queen's court, as did his girlfriend's mother, who everybody in Geratica was aware of. He'd been confident that with those three people in his capture, along with the steward, it wouldn't be long before the authorities agreed to his demands. To lose them, would surely be a devastation to several prominent people, and a massive blow to Geratica's morale.

But now as the minutes ticked by, he was becoming more anxious. There was less than half an hour to go, and he'd heard nothing of any consequence from the woman running the show outside. He wanted to bring this to an end, and he had never been a patient man. Also, as the deadline approached, after which he would know np more, he was slightly less certain than he had been an hour ago, that he *did* want to be a martyr after all.

He had heard another car arrive outside, and his desire to find out what was going on grew irresistible. He picked up his radio and spoke.

"Kelly, what's happening out there!" he demanded. "I've been waiting over an hour and still nothing's happened. You know that you've only got another 25 minutes, and this whole place goes boom! I won't be stopping the timer on the bomb now!" He crossed his fingers behind his back.

"Now, just hold your horses, Smith," replied Henrietta. "We can sort this out. We're looking into the possibility of your group making a broadcast this evening, though I can't promise anything definite at the moment."

"Well it's about time that you *could!*" snapped Ralph. "And what about our immunity from prosecution?"

"Yes, we've taken note of your desire on that subject too and it will all go into the mix for discussion."

"Pah! Discussion! That's all you clever clog, privileged women ever do. Well my people want action! And starting from today, it's going to begin!"

Suddenly, Lady Sackville's voice could be heard in the background.

"You'll never get away with this, you scoundrel of a man! If I had my way, you'd be horsewhipped at the Royal Palace!"

"Shut your trap, you hoity-toity, posh nob!" replied Ralph, rudely. "Or I'll shut it for you. Permanently!"

Then he went back off the air again.

"Charming fellow," remarked Linda.

"We must do something soon," argued Fiona. "In that respect only, I agree with Smith. The time for discussion is drawing short. Action needs to be taken from our side, and to our own advantage."

"That's all very well, but we still don't know how to get into the house, without getting everybody in the manor killed in the process," said Jill.

"I think I might know a way," said Alexandra, suddenly.

Everybody turned to her in surprise.

"*You* know a way, darling?" said Linda, taking her hand and encouraging her daughter with her fingers.

"Yes Mother," replied Alexandra. "You know that on a couple of occasions, we've been here as guests at one of Lady Caroline's dinner parties? Well the last time, Tom was here as well, and as he worked here by then, he showed me around. And one of the most fascinating features of the house that we discovered, was a secret passageway. It opens in the lobby, but you'd never know it was there, unless you had some prior knowledge of the building. And it comes out around the side of the house, through another secret door! Unless those have now been locked up, I'm sure that you could get in that way. Smith won't know about it."

Linda squeezed her hand. "Sweetheart, you're absolutely sure about this?" She looked searchingly into her daughter's eyes, the way she had done many times previously to test her daughter's honesty, or certainty.

Alexandra looked back firmly into her mother's eyes and they met. "Yes Mother, I am. I remember it distinctly," she declared, as she felt her mother's probe.

Linda looked back at Henrietta and Jill. "My daughter knows a way in," she confirmed. "Nobody knows her better than me, and if she says she knows something and I believe her, then she does. End of story. The one thing that she cannot do is lie to me. I *always* know!"

"Well in that case, Miss Radcliffe, take me to this entrance that you speak of!" ordered Henrietta. "We'll see if it's open. Jill, you stay with your women here, and keep in radio contact."

"Yes Madam," said Detective Sergeant Baynton.

"I shall come, too," said Linda.

Henrietta didn't really expect anything else from her, and she wasn't going to object.

"By all means, Mrs Radcliffe," she confirmed.

"I'm coming as well," said Fiona.

\*\*\*

As they went off around the estate to the side of the manor, Ralph Smith came back on the radio.

"Where's Kelly?" he asked, when he heard Jill Baynton's voice.

"*Commander* Kelly is involved in some negotiations on your behalf, at the moment," the Detective Sergeant lied. "You can speak to me for a while, instead."

This caused another furious outburst, and gradually, as the minutes ticked by, his appearances over the airwaves became more frequent, and his demands more desperate.

"You know, I'm not so sure that this chap really does wish to be dead in a few minutes' time," remarked Jill, dryly to her fellow officers.

Just then though, another car pulled up. And out of it stepped –

Elizabeth Spencer ...

***

Elizabeth had already had quite a stressful afternoon. She'd noticed that a withdrawal had been made from her bank account, that she knew hadn't been transacted by her, and had gone to the branch to investigate. It had taken a while, but eventually she'd discovered that Ralph had somehow managed to make a copy of her bank card, and withdraw the money himself. Outraged, she had gone to his house, to remonstrate with him.

He hadn't been there, but she'd let herself in with her copy of his door key. She'd put the radio on to listen to the news, specifically to find out what was being said about the band of protestors. Then she'd seen the box, containing the bomb and noticed, with horror, the timer ticking down! By the side of it, there was a detailed plan of its construction and its mobile detonator, which she'd realised with almost equal horror, bore the unmistakeable hallmark of Gillian's handy work. Then she'd seen a receipt beside the plan, which her ex-daughter had obviously written out, especially for him. That confirmed what he'd done with the money withdrawn from her account. Finally, she'd heard the report on the news about what Ralph had done and was threatening to do next, if his demands weren't met. She'd sworn loudly, rushed out back to her car, and driven to Lady Caroline Sackville's estate, as fast as she dared. She'd hoped she wouldn't be too late to prevent a major catastrophe ...

***

"Elizabeth!" exclaimed James. "What are you doing here?"

"Never mind about that!" she replied quickly. "I've only just heard about this on the radio. What's the latest position? It's vital that I know! I'm acquainted with Ralph Smith."

Jill Baynton was well aware of Elizabeth Spencer, and her support for the Male Rights Supporters. Over the last couple of weeks, since she'd been removed from Charterhouse, and her husband had left her, Jill's team had become aware of her increasingly frequent visits to the organisation's members, especially to one in particular, and started maintaining a discreet surveillance on her movements. She suspected that Elizabeth was hoping to help Smith. Jill had no intention of telling her anything.

However, she was saved from having to do so, anyhow, as at that very moment, Ralph Smith's voice came back on her radio.

As soon as she heard his voice, Elizabeth was on to it.

"Give me that radio!" she demanded. "I must speak to him."

She moved towards it, but Jill held it out of her reach. Then she made a full-blown lunge for it, and grappled with the Detective Sergeant.

Finally, in desperation, she shouted so that Smith would hear her, "Ralph, you damn fool, turn that device off, this instant. I order you, as your superior!"

James looked at her in astonishment. Very slowly Jill released her grip on her radio. Perhaps Mrs Spencer didn't want to help him destroy Lady Sackville's home, after all. Elizabeth clutched hold of it.

"Elizabeth, is that you?" asked Ralph.

"Yes of course it is!" snapped Elizabeth. "What in the name of Geratica do you think you're playing at? I've never authorised murdering people! And how dare you spend my money to pay for that bomb! My ex-daughter should never have even made it, let alone sold it to you!"

"But I won't have to kill anyone, if my demands are met," protested Ralph.

"They're never going to agree to that, you silly idiot!" cried Elizabeth. "They might string you along for a while, but believe me, they've no intention of giving you what you want. You might very well end up dead. Besides which, we want Male Rights, but two of your three key hostages are men. Think on that. And please Ralph, think also of what *I've* already lost – my job, my daughter, my husband – you're all I've got left! It's been you that I've been living for, this past half-year – and for what you've done to me in bed! I do love you, you know. I can't bear the thought of losing you too!"

James stared at her, open-mouthed. He couldn't believe what he was hearing.

"I'm not going to give up now, Elizabeth!" shouted Ralph, through the radio. "They surely won't let Lady Caroline and Lord George Sackville, as well as Tom Ryder, die. I won't believe it. I'll never surrender and that's my final decision – I swear!"

"Ralph please!" begged Elizabeth ...

***

Meanwhile, Alexandra had successfully found the outside entrance, to the secret passageway. It wasn't locked.

"Well done girl!" enthused Henrietta.

She spoke into her radio.

"Baynton? We've found the secret passageway entrance. Do you think there's there any chance that Smith might surrender?"

"I'm not sure if he really wants to die, Madam," replied Jill. "But he seems to believe that with Lady Caroline and Lord George Sackville, as well as Tom Ryder, all held hostage to him, he holds all of the cards. He thinks that we won't be prepared to let them die and therefore we'll eventually have to give into his demands. He actually said that he'll never surrender and swears that's his final decision."

"Alright, Baynton," said Commander Kelly. "We're running out of time. If he's said that, then I'm going in. Stand by."

"Right, now I *can* get this over with," she continued, after cutting her radio. "The end of this passageway opens directly into the lobby, you say, Miss Radcliffe?"

"Yes, Commander Kelly," replied Alexandra. She looked at her mother, and squeezed at her hand over hers. She would be frightened, but she thought she should ask Henrietta anyhow, and she also desperately wanted to get to Tom.

"Do you want me to show you?" she asked.

Henrietta looked at her and thought quickly. "Well, I'll go first. I intend to try and convince Smith to surrender. But if he refuses, then I must warn you that I'll shoot to kill. I could wound him, but then it would still be likely he'd interfere with me, whilst I tried to disable the bomb. Whatever happens, don't go out into the lobby when I enter, until I give you the all clear. Understood?"

"Perfectly, Commander Kelly. Don't worry. I've no intention of doing so!"

"And that goes for you too, Mrs Radcliffe!" Henrietta had no doubt that if Miss Radcliffe went, then Mrs Radcliffe would be sure to, as well.

Then to everybody's astonishment, Fiona pulled out a gun from her briefcase.

"Let me make another suggestion, Commander Kelly," she began. "I'll go in there with you. I may not have worked in Geratican Security, but I'm quite sure I can take care of Smith. As I'm doing that, you can disable the bomb. Then there'll be no need for either of the Radcliffes to be put in danger."

"Fiona, have you gone mad?" exclaimed Linda. "The actual job of disabling an armed assailant, is one for the security service only. As your superior, I order you not to get involved. And do you always carry a gun around with you?"

Henrietta stared at Fiona. "That's very noble of you, Madam, and I appreciate that your stepson is one of the hostages. However, I really am sorry. I could never allow an untrained civilian to undertake such a task. Leave it to me, please."

"I'm-" began Fiona, but then stopped. She flushed with annoyance. "I *want* to do it!" she continued, finally.

"But I refuse to allow it," replied Henrietta. "I suggest that you go back and join the others at the front of the manor."

"We're wasting time!" declared Linda, impatiently.

"Oh, very well!" snapped Fiona. She turned and stomped off.

"Now lead on, Commander Kelly," said Linda.

Henrietta nodded and they started up the passageway. It wasn't long, and soon they came to the door that Alexandra had spoken of earlier. They could clearly hear Ralph Smith on the other side, in the lobby, talking on his radio. Alexandra's heart beat furiously, and Linda's was by no means regular, either.

Henrietta crouched down with her gun, her back to the wall, and prepared herself. Very gently she eased the secret door open, revealing just a small crack in the doorway to the lobby. She peeped around, and spied Ralph Smith, stood close to the detonator, still in full flow, with his back to her. Lady Caroline and Prince George were sat on chairs on the left of the lobby, with Tom and Collette on ones to the right. In one movement, she turned, and sprang from the doorway, with her gun raised and aimed right at Ralph. He spun around in shock.

"Switch off the detonator timer, Smith!" she said. "Or stand aside and let me do it."

"Never!" he cried.

"Don't be an idiot," said Commander Kelly. "Do as I ask, or I'll have to use force. I'd rather not, but I'll fire if I have to. There's not much time left."

"I told the other woman, I'll never surrender, and I meant it!" asserted Ralph.

Henrietta glanced at the timer on the detonator. She could see there just 10 minutes to go. If the bomb was to be disabled in time, the job had to begin now.

"Smith, I tell you, this is your last chance!" she declared.

He didn't move.

Then Henrietta fired her gun three times. Ralph Smith slumped to the floor.

For a moment everybody stared at Henrietta.

"Lady Sackville!" she said. "I am Commander Kelly of Geratican Security. I must now ask all of you to remain still, whilst I disable the bomb."

Quickly, Henrietta raced to the front door. The timer on the mobile detonator was now showing just 9 minutes to go. But that hopefully should be enough for her to disable it. She was quite an expert with technology, though great care still needed to be taken. Not all devices were the same and this one was certainly unique. She'd never come across this kind of bomb before.

Linda and Alexandra waited nervously in the passageway, Alexandra tight within her mother's arms. Much to Linda's surprise though, through the radio that Ralph Smith had dropped as he fell, she heard a woman's voice, calling him – which sounded very much like Elizabeth Spencer's.

***

Elizabeth heard the shots coming from inside the house.

"What was that?" she asked, with dread in her voice.

There was a silence.

Then Elizabeth began shouting Ralph's name. Everyone lost count of the number of times that she did it, but her angst grew ever more evident, each time.

At last Henrietta's voice came through on the radio.

"Mission accomplished. Bomb disabled – assailant dead."

Elizabeth let out a wail, as her worst fears were realised.

Commander Kelly had completed her job with only three minutes to spare.

Inside the manor, Henrietta let Linda and Alexandra enter the lobby from the secret passageway and they met the others. Alexandra ran to Tom, and they had an emotional reunion.

Outside, Fiona informed Queen Alexandra of the mission's successful outcome, and she hurried inside to conduct her own reunion with Lord George.

It was finally over – but at the price of a life.

\*\*\*

In the aftermath, Elizabeth was questioned by Detective Sergeant Baynton, and another of her colleagues. She was still distraught at the death of Ralph Smith. Since her removal from Charterhouse, she'd finally given up on any hopes of returning and was not appealing against the decision. Elizabeth had been looking for a job which would gain her re-entry into the Scientific field, but admitted that in the meantime, she'd taken over the running of the Male Rights Protestors, and had planned the morning's attacks. Linda had been correct in her original suspicion. Elizabeth claimed that she had left it to the individual protestors to decide what message they wanted to attach to the bricks, that they'd lobbed through the windows, or over walls. Her justification for it, was that they were now in a desperate situation, especially since the letter she'd received from Her Majesty's court, effectively ruling out any change of policy in the near future. She strongly denied any prior knowledge, or any involvement in the planning, of Ralph Smith's siege at Lady Caroline's estate, and wholeheartedly condemned it and also her "ex-daughter" for constructing and selling the bomb to him, though she did admit that they had been lovers, for half a year. After being dismissed from Charterhouse and accidentally crashing her car into Linda's on the way out, his house was where she'd gone to, after leaving her damaged vehicle at her own.

She was arrested, and taken away to the police station, charged with conspiracy to damage private property, and threaten the occupiers. Gillian Spencer would now be charged with conspiracy to murder.

Linda and Alexandra were also shocked by Elizabeth's revelations.

"To think that whilst I was carefully planning to have you leave her in a dignified manner, she was, all the time, having it off with a Male Rights Protestor!" exclaimed Linda to James. "And after calling *me* a 'bitch' because she thought that *I* was having an affair with her husband. We all knew that she was passionate about the cause, but even I didn't realise that she was quite as *intimately* involved as that!"

"I honestly didn't suspect a thing," confessed James. "Although admittedly, we didn't see as much of each other, in more recent times."

"Now we also know, that after she was removed from Charterhouse, she decided to convert her strong support for the Male Rights Protestors, into direct control of their organisation," added Linda. "I can't believe that she decided to resort to the sort of tactics that we witnessed this morning. Still, I'm not sure, if Mr Smith has done their cause any favours, by his actions this afternoon, and I'm not sure what the scientific community is going to make of Mrs Spencer, after this, either!"

"And *Gillian* Spencer would appear to have taken to the making and selling of homemade bombs, Mother," remarked Alexandra.

"What a waste of a fine scientific brain," said Linda.

She had been surprised by Fiona's desire to be the one who disabled Ralph Smith and spoke to her about it.

"If you wish to become more involved in resolving matters such as these, then I'm sure that the court could arrange for you to spend some time with Geratican Security. Of course, it would have to be fitted around your existing official duties at the palace."

"My motives were obviously heightened by the fact that Tom was one of the hostages," declared Fiona. "But that might indeed be something which would interest me."

"I will discuss this with Queen Alexandra, then," said Linda.

"Thank you. Linda," replied Fiona.

The media had arrived earlier, and now that the affair was ended, they were allowed into the grounds of the estate. Linda and Alexandra, as well as Fiona and Tom, found themselves being interviewed for a live broadcast on the radio.

Linda was then interviewed further, this time linked together with an MP in a radio studio. The woman, Louise Bond, was outraged at the events of first thing that morning, and said that there were many women who were now deeply worried that they might suffer the same fate. She also claimed that a number of MPs wanted a special session of parliament to be called, urgently, possibly even tomorrow, to debate the issue, and for Her Majesty to be invited to attend. Linda agreed that the attacks had been appalling – she spoke from personal experience – and that security would need to be tightened. She didn't know at this stage, whether there were any more protestors, planning similar attacks. About the siege at the Sackville Estate, Linda said it was tragic that Ralph Smith had lost his life, but that Commander Kelly had been left with no choice. The man appeared to have been a fanatic.

Afterwards, Linda discussed with the queen, the possibility of a special session of parliament tomorrow morning, for an Emergency Debate. They agreed that after the grievous events of today, it might be a good idea. Linda contacted the palace and asked them to put out a statement, informing all MPs that a session of parliament would indeed take place tomorrow morning at 10.00 a.m., with Her Majesty in attendance. Queen Alexandra also agreed that Fiona could be allowed to gain some experience with Geratican Security, when time allowed after her official duties.

"Well, darling, at least one good thing has come out of today, for you," said Linda to her daughter. "Parliament is meeting on the first morning of a weekend. You are welcome to come and watch. I've no doubt that I shall be saying much!"

"Oh, thank you, Mother!" said Alexandra, delightedly. She kissed her. "Can Tom come, too?"

"Of course. Though maybe Fiona will come, too, in which case she might be taking him."

"Has there ever been a session of parliament at the weekend, before, Mother?" asked Alexandra.

"Well, it's certainly very rare," Linda told her. "It hasn't happened before, in my time at least."

James and Fiona took Queen Alexandra back to the palace, and then they were able to take James' car back home. Fiona had confirmed that she wanted to see the parliamentary session tomorrow, so she would bring Tom, if he did also. He didn't hesitate to answer in the affirmative. It would mean being with his girlfriend again, and after what he'd been through today, he wanted that particularly badly tomorrow.

Eventually, Linda was able to drive Alexandra and Tom back to Elmsbrook too.

Alexandra was pleased and touched, to get a phone call from Benita, at Charterhouse, that evening. She wanted her to know, that everyone had been deeply shocked by what they'd heard of the events of the day, and wanted to send their best wishes. Benita especially, was thinking of her. They'd all been following the dramatic siege at Lady Sackville's estate, on the radio, with their main curriculum studies having been completed for the week, and had heard Alexandra speaking with her mother, live on the radio, afterwards. Alexandra thanked Benita warmly for her concern, and asked her to pass it on to the other girls at the college. She was genuinely delighted, and both girls felt a strong affection for one another.

The day that had begun so dramatically, did however, also end with another bombshell.

Gillian Spencer had absconded from the Buckmore Young Offenders' Institution, and vanished.

# CHAPTER 7

The day began early once again, at The Grange on 6/37/10, as they all prepared to leave for Avermore, and the special session of parliament.

Despite the seriousness of the subject matter, Alexandra couldn't help but feel excited at the prospect of finally seeing her mother speak in the chamber.

Linda was wearing her best suit. Her black skirt suit was immaculately pressed. Although she would only be watching from the gallery, Alexandra was wearing her suit, too, for the occasion. She knew that this was a big day for her mother. James was dressed in his usual uniform. He would be driving Queen Alexandra, the short distance from the palace to Parliament House.

Upon their arrival at the palace, James went off to attend to his duties, and Linda took Alexandra into her office, where she made them a quick cup of coffee, and began her final preparations for the debate. She'd had another lengthy discussion with the queen last night, on the phone at The Grange, when they had established their official policy statement.

At 9.45, Linda and Alexandra walked through the entrance and into the lobby of Parliament House. Now they would go their separate ways.

"Right, well I hope we put on a good show for you, darling!" Linda said, as she pulled her daughter close. "I'll see you afterwards then."

Alexandra stretched up the short distance to her mother's lips, and kissed her. "Good luck, Mother," she said.

Linda smiled lovingly. "Thank you, darling," she replied, and held and kissed her daughter strongly.

"You remember the way, don't you?" she checked, although she was fairly certain that Alexandra did.

"Yes, Mother," her daughter confirmed.

They said goodbye and then went in opposite directions, Alexandra up the steps to the public gallery, and Linda towards the chamber.

***

Alexandra selected a seat in the gallery, and looked down at the chamber. It was almost full to capacity now, with the debate due to start in a matter of moments. She checked her watch against the clock in the chamber. They agreed. Her mother had given her the watch for her fifteenth birthday, and so far it had kept excellent time.

There were a few other people in the gallery, but no sign of Fiona and Tom yet. She hoped Tom wouldn't miss the start of the debate. His stepmother was usually on the later, rather than earlier side for things, but Alexandra did think that she might want to be in good time for this. It was an Emergency Debate, after all.

She'd chosen a place to sit, where she would get the best view possible of her mother. Looking down again, she could see her taking her place. Linda cast an eye up to the gallery, and saw her daughter. They acknowledged each other discreetly, before Linda busied herself with her notes. Alexandra studied her features to see if she could detect any sign of nerves, but she found none of any great consequence. Her mother wasn't that type, and in any case, she had years of experience. Alexandra knew that *she* would be shaking like a leaf, in the same situation.

Then the speaker of the house, Maureen Chesterton, addressed the chamber.

"Honourable Ladies, all please rise for Her Majesty, the queen!"

Everybody stood, including those in the public gallery, and Queen Alexandra swept in, wearing her parliamentary gown and the monarch's crown on her head. Alexandra could just see one of her bodyguards as they melted discreetly into the background, and then the queen took her place, in front of her mother.

At the very moment that everyone re-took their seats, Fiona and Tom scrambled in, and sat down on either side of Alexandra.

"You missed Her Majesty coming into the chamber!" said Alexandra, quietly to Tom. "Where've you been?"

"Fiona overslept," he replied. "She said that she worked such a long day yesterday, she was exhausted!"

Alexandra struggled to keep a straight face. Her mother often worked those kind of hours, yet she couldn't remember a single time that she'd overslept on a weekday, or when there was an important engagement of some kind, in the morning of any other day.

"Did she go out gambling last night?" she asked.

Tom grinned. "Yes!"

"Serves her right then. She could obviously find the energy for that – and I bet she had a skin full too."

"Order!" the speaker shouted. Queen Alexandra had indicated to her that she was ready to begin. A hush fell on the chamber.

"Emergency Debate called to discuss law and order, specifically the security of private properties!" announced Speaker Chesterton. "Senior Court Administrator, Mrs Linda Radcliffe!"

Alexandra felt her heart flutter as her mother rose to speak. Tom slipped his hand in hers, and smiled. He knew that this was a very special moment for his girlfriend.

Linda began.

*"Honourable Ladies! Yesterday, was indeed a black day for all of Geratica, and especially for those of us who were unfortunate enough to have been personally targeted by the 'Male Rights Protestors'. As Her Majesty's court stated yesterday, we do appreciate this group's concerns, and we will endeavour to incorporate their views into any future solution, but the kind of violent acts that were perpetrated yesterday can never be justified, and we will not be intimidated by them. I can assure this house, that no such act will ever result in the furtherance of 'Male Rights'. Especially not the outrageous kind which occurred at the Sackville Estate. It was tragic that the perpetrator was killed, but under the circumstances, Geratican Security ultimately had no choice but to take the action which they did. The man appeared to be a fanatic. Peaceful protests will be tolerated, so long as they do not inconvenience too many people. Negotiations might be possible in the future, but only by constructive dialogue, and not by violence!*

*"Her Majesty's court, wishes to make it clear to the House, though, that for as long as this group's opinions remain a minority view in the queendom of Geratica, it has no plans to bring in any new legislation, or amend any existing laws, to accommodate it. A minority does not have the right to lecture or bully the majority!"*

Linda saw Louise Bond, who she'd spoken on the national radio to, yesterday, standing up and indicating that she wished to intervene.

"I give way to the Honourable Lady, Madam Speaker," she declared, and sat down.

"I thank the Honourable Lady, Madam Speaker," said Louise, as she rose to intervene, acknowledging Linda.

"You speak of new legislation. Does the court propose to implement any imminently, with regards to the public order and trespassing offences, that occurred yesterday?"

Louise Bond sat down, and Linda rose once more.

"I thank the honourable lady for her intervention." She returned to her statement.

"I can confirm that Her Majesty has given me the necessary power, to implement emergency legislation, with immediate effect.

"The minimal penalty for trespassing on private property, will now rise from 200 geros to 1000 geros, and criminal damage, from 500 geros to 2000 geros, to be paid within 5 working days! We will also be endeavouring to tighten security procedures in all areas of Geratican working life, and to update as many of the existing security systems as possible, in all public places. We hope that this sends out a clear message to anyone who would behave in the manner witnessed yesterday, that we will not tolerate it, and will clamp down severely on those who attempt to defy the supreme, and unquestionable order of Geratican law!

"Her Majesty will now happily answer any questions which you may have."

Linda sat down.

Speaker Chesterton, then began calling members who had submitted questions beforehand, and allowing any other members to respond to what they had just heard. There were quite a wide range of views.

One asked whether any consideration had been made to horsewhipping the offenders from yesterday, and making that part of the penalty for any future transgressions of a similar nature. Apparently certain noblewomen had made comments suggesting that they would do this themselves, if they found anybody trespassing on their estates.

The queen informed her that there were no plans to take this measure, and reminded the members that indeed Queen Beatrix's court had abolished the practice of horsewhipping for adults' misdemeanours in 4990. It was of course still technically within the right of a woman to horsewhip her husband in private – or even her fiancé if he should back out of an official contract for engagement or marriage after signing it. But in more general matters, Queen Alexandra didn't recommend or condone women – or men – taking the law into their own hands. Geratican justice would ensure that the perpetrators were appropriately punished.

A second, asked whether it was known exactly how many members there were in the Male Rights Protestors group, and if they were planning any more attacks.

The queen looked towards Linda, who stood up again.

"According to Geratican security, it is thought that, besides their new leader, Elizabeth Spencer, there are around twenty members," she attested. One is now dead, and five others – all men are in police custody. Of the remaining members, there are a minority of females. It is thought that most are not as radical, therefore the worst of their organisation's threat may be over, for the time being. But you obviously can never be completely sure, so we must all be vigilant. From the point of view of attracting any new members, their cause may not have been served well. by yesterday afternoon's siege at Lady Sackville's estate, and even Mrs Elizabeth Spencer has distanced herself from it. There are surely *very* few Geraticans, who would condone such a callous and barbaric threat."

Someone else pointed out that there would likely be several people who committed these types of offences, who would not be able to afford the fines that were imposed upon them, and certainly not within 5 working days.

Queen Alexandra hotly replied that this was tough luck, and reminded the member that the penalties were designed to be a punishment, and to act as a deterrent to wayward Geraticans.

Gradually the debate wound up, and Speaker Chesterton declared time, and the end of business for the day.

The members began to file out, anxious to return to their constituencies as quickly as possible, for the rest of the weekend.

Alexandra, Fiona, and Tom, met Linda back in the lobby.

"Well, my girl, was it worth the wait?" Linda asked her daughter.

Alexandra beamed. "It certainly was Mother!" she replied, kissing her again. "*I thought you spoke brilliantly. Thank you for bringing me here today!*" she said softly into her mother's ear.

Now Linda beamed back. "*Thank you darling! And it was my pleasure!*" She gave her daughter a deep hug and kiss, which swallowed her up.

"Congratulations Linda!" said Fiona. "Let's hope that keeps the members satisfied for a little while. We don't want too much discord, over the next few weeks, with the Festival of Divinity almost upon us."

"Thank you Fiona! That's most true," replied Linda.

Then Fiona left with Tom, and Alexandra went with her mother, back to the palace. James had brought Queen Alexandra back, and after he'd finished his duties, Linda, Alexandra and himself, returned to The Grange.

On the way, Linda put the radio on, and they listened to the report of the emergency debate in parliament. Overall, the reaction seemed to be, that Her Majesty's court had responded well to the crisis.

# CHAPTER 8

Over the course of Week 38, Alexandra was busy with the Charterhouse Symphony Orchestra, rehearsing for the concert taking place next week. Alexandra was pleased, and relieved that the girls seemed to have a lot of respect for her. She obviously was friends with Emma, but she found all of the girls quite easy to get on with. The running order was decided.

She was however, a little disconcerted, that Gillian Spencer was now back on the loose.

On the night of 3/38/10, she had her final practice session with Philippa Barrington. She told Alexandra that she was confident that her evening was going to be a tremendous success. Alexandra told Philippa that she hoped she wouldn't let her down, after all her help.

At the end of the week, Linda brought home Alexandra's new gown. She immediately tried it on. Her mother agreed with her, that it was perfect.

On 6/38/10, the first day of the weekend, Linda and James were working overtime with court business. Alexandra was used to her mother sometimes having to work on this day – often it was only the morning. Queen Alexandra had an official engagement, visiting a hospital for sick children, in Avermore, during the run up to the Festival of Divinity. James was chauffeuring her, and Linda co-ordinating the visit. Whilst they were out working, Alexandra did some domestic duties, that she'd been given by her mother.

The traditional preparations were being made for the Festival of Divinity, too. The Grange was lavishly decorated, and there was a special atmosphere this year, as James was now there, too. All over Geratica, the trimmings were going up, and the streets were lit up with bright decorative lights.

# CHAPTER 9

At lunchtime on 3/39/10, Alexandra and the Charterhouse Symphony Orchestra had their dress rehearsal. It seemed to go quite well, but Alexandra was beginning to feel extremely nervous, as she'd fully expected. The concert would take place at 8.00 p.m. tonight!

Benita, Imelda, Rachel and Emma, had all worked their hardest, and everything was prepared. The tickets had all been sold, and the tables and chairs were arranged in the assembly hall, where the event would take place. The choice of dishes that they had selected for the girls to eat during the performance, had been put onto menus by Emma, with additional help with their design from Imelda and Rachel. Miranda Rumbold would be bringing the food over to Charterhouse from her restaurant, with some of her staff, this evening, a couple of hours before it began, together with Benita and Emma, and they would prepare it in the college kitchen and serve it to the girls themselves. In addition to her role in the symphony orchestra, Emma would also be in charge of the refreshments of tea and coffee, during the interval. Benita, Imelda and Rachel, would all be on hand, to look after any of the girls' needs, during the concert.

As Miranda had requested, Imelda and Rachel had also ensured that there could be no doubt to anybody present, that it was being sponsored by Rumbold's restaurant.

\*\*\*

Linda and James picked up Alexandra from Charterhouse at 3.30. Arriving home, Alexandra immediately began getting herself ready. She was going to be back again, dressed in her new gown, at 6.00 p.m., in plenty of time before her performance was due to begin. She looked at the book, that Philippa had given her, to give her a final reminder about one or two scores, and cradled it to her chest, in a kind of good luck gesture to herself.

\*\*\*

Meanwhile, Benita and Emma left Charterhouse, for Rumbold's. They met Miranda there at 5.45. She was in a particularly good humour today, as it appeared that her burglar had finally been caught. It wasn't a juvenile, but an employee from a rival restaurant! Miranda told Benita, that if the offer still stood, she *would* be interested in hiring her mother's services. She suspected that the rival owner, might have had a hand in the crime, behind the scenes. Benita promised to inform her mother, as soon as the concert was over.

They loaded up a van with various food products, and set off for the college.

\*\*\*

Alexandra arrived back at Charterhouse with Linda and James, at 6.00 p.m., as planned. Linda accompanied her daughter, as she went into the hall, and got settled down. Gradually the symphony orchestra began assembling, and Linda stayed for as long as possible, to give Alexandra any last minute help and advice, and also for moral support. She knew that her daughter was *very* nervous.

It had been decided that Alexandra wouldn't do a lot of talking, during the concert – this was going to be her greatest fear – but she would make a brief introduction at the beginning, say one or two things during it, and then some closing remarks before the finale.

Benita and Emma arrived with Miranda's staff, shortly afterwards, and Miranda was shown into the Charterhouse kitchen. She immediately put her women to work, once their van was unloaded. Then Emma took her place with the symphony orchestra, and Benita went to Alexandra.

She touched her arm. "Are you alright? How do you feel?" she asked gently.

"Truthfully, I've never felt so nervous in all of my life!" admitted Alexandra.

"Well just think, in about four hours' time, it will all be over. Try and stay calm. You're a good pianist and you know Philippa Barrington's work. None of the other girls could do this as well as you! Remember what we said I'd do. I'll be sat not far from the edge of the stage, where you'll be able to see me, the whole time. Hopefully the knowledge that your mother, Tom, James Spencer and myself, are all behind you, will help get you through it. I'm sure that you're going to be fine!"

She kissed Alexandra on the cheek. Alexandra followed suit.

"Thank you," she replied. "You're a good friend, Benita. I can't thank you enough for co-ordinating everything, to get me to this point. I just hope that I won't let you down, now!"

"No you won't, Alexandra, believe me, I know it! And it was my pleasure to help you, as well."

*** 

At 7.30, Linda gave her daughter one of her strongest hugs, and kissed her deeply, so that Alexandra tingled.

"Well, you must start warming up with the orchestra now," she said. "I'd better go and take my seat. The very best of luck to you. Remember what I said. Just imagine that you're playing to the guests at a dinner party, at The Grange! You're going to be fine!"

"Thank you, Mother," said Alexandra, kissing her back. "I love you!"

"I love you too, darling!" said Linda, before the parted.

Philippa Barrington also came to wish her luck beforehand, too.

"You've done everything that I've asked of you, when we've been practising, over the last few weeks," she said. "And your friends have done a marvellous job, helping you to organise this performance. I'm looking forward to it! I *know* that it's going to be a great success!"

"Thank you Philippa. That's what everybody's telling me!" replied Alexandra. "I hope so too."

"You should *believe* what everybody is telling you, Alexandra," Philippa told her.

Fiona didn't arrive until quite late, as usual, which annoyed Alexandra a little, as it meant that she didn't see much of Tom before the performance. They did manage to have a brief hug and kiss though, and Tom gripped her hand, and wished her luck.

By now the assembly hall was filling up with all of the girls who had tickets, some of whom had relatives with them, too. Then there were Philippa Barrington, Annabel Wood and Sandra Steele. One or two other notable people had decided to come, too, following the advert in the newspaper, including Camilla Forbes. Benita, Imelda and Rachel attended to their duties, as required, getting the audience settled. Their orders for their meal were taken, and the food began to be cooked.

***

At 8.00 p.m., on the dot, the Charterhouse Symphony Orchestra began its overture to Alexandra's concert.

For those who had ordered first, the food wouldn't be long in coming.

As the last notes of the overture died away, and a hushed silence fell upon the hall, the curtain lifted and Alexandra walked out on to the stage. The audience applauded and she sat down at the piano. Then she lowered her mouth to the microphone before her, as near to it as possible. One of her biggest worries was that people might not be able to hear her, so she needed to make full use of it. It had been turned up to a high volume. Linda had also suggested that she keep notes of what she wanted to say, discreetly near to her, to minimise the chances of her "drying up" on stage. She could see her mother in the audience, as well as Benita in her selected place at the edge of the stage. Alexandra took a deep breath, and spoke.

"Thank you everybody. Welcome to 'A Tribute to Philippa Barrington'. I hope that you will enjoy the performance! I will start with one of her most popular pieces."

She took another deep breath, put her hands to the piano keyboard, and began. As the first chords rippled through the hall, the audience applauded appreciatively, and she was away.

***

Benita sat near the stage. From now onwards, Imelda and Rachel should be able to manage together, without her. She saw her main duty now, as being to help Alexandra get through the concert, with moral support.

She did, however, keep some of her attention on the rest of the hall.

At the back, by the entrance, she suddenly caught a glimpse of Melanie Patterson, in the corner of her eye.

Since returning from her suspension from Charterhouse, Melanie had made a determined effort to "turn over a new leaf." Without Gillian's influence, which she now cursed herself for falling under, she had begun to improve in her work, and not been in any kind of trouble, whatsoever. Her mother had remonstrated with her, and advised her in the strongest possible terms, to have nothing more to do with Gillian Spencer. Since their relationship had got her into so much trouble and Gillian was now expelled, this had not been much of a hardship. She'd had no wish to see her again.

Her mother, Rosemary Patterson, had not been especially gifted at school, and had left aged 14, without many noteworthy qualifications, becoming a shop assistant and marrying a train driver. However, she had inherited a substantial amount of money from a distant aunt, and not being an entirely stupid woman, had employed an accountant to assist in the management of her financial affairs. As a result of some shrewd investments, she and her husband had done considerably better for themselves, than they'd previously thought would be possible. They had moved into a smart new house and been able to send Melanie to Charterhouse – an astonishing achievement, for which she was most proud.

She had therefore been most alarmed when she'd discovered what her daughter had been up to at the college, given what a tremendous opportunity she'd been presented with, and implored upon her, with the aid of a beating, the need to change her ways – and fast. Her daughter had already severely damaged her reputation, with a criminal record, and unlike in the case of Alexandra Radcliffe, hers could not be expected to be viewed so leniently.

Melanie had fancied coming to the concert herself, but had in the end decided, that it might be more diplomatic for her to stay away.

But now she stood, trying to gain Benita's attention, and beckoning to her to come over.

Benita cursed inwardly. What in the world did *she* want now? Reluctantly, she decided that she'd better go and find out. She looked back at Alexandra, who was now into her second piece, and indicated as best she could, that she was leaving her seat for a moment. Then she slipped quietly down the side of the hall, to the entrance.

"What do *you* want?" she demanded. "This is for ticket holders only, you know!"

"Yes I do know!" said Melanie. "But I've got something urgent to tell you. I've just seen Gillian Spencer!"

"What?" exclaimed Benita, in alarm, "Where?"

"I saw her slipping out of the front door of the kitchen, just now. You won't believe it, though. She was in disguise! But I still recognised her. She was dressed as a Rumbold's kitchen assistant, but I could tell by her gait that it was her, and she was the same height and build – and her eyes, I'd never mistake them, for anybody! She also had a bag with her, that I recognised. It looked as if she was heading for the side entrance, leading up to the storage area, above the hall."

Benita looked at her quizzically. "Are you absolutely *certain* that it was her? And if you're lying, and this is some sort of trick to divert my attention, so that you can ..."

"It's not a trick, Benita!" Melanie urged her. "I'm telling the truth! I think she may be intending something nasty, to avenge Alexandra! In any case, why would a kitchen assistant from Rumbold's be going there?"

"Well if you're right, and it's her, then *of course* her intentions are hostile!" replied Benita, tersely.

She glanced back at the hall one more time. "Oh alright then! We'd better go up to the storage area and check," she continued. "Come with me."

There were steps leading up to the storage area, from the other side of the hall to where Gillian – if it was her – would have entered from the outside. They bounded up them, as quickly as they could.

***

A few weeks before, Gillian Spencer had received a phone call at Buckmore Young Offenders' Institution, from Ralph Smith. He'd told the receptionist that he was a relative of hers, and she had put it through to the public phone, for Gillian to take. It was then that he'd requested that she make the bomb for him, and she'd agreed, in return for a hefty fee. Gillian had also been the person who'd supplied Smith with a copy of her mother's bankcard.

She'd told the institution governess, afterwards, that he was a distant family member, and that he'd be visiting her at a later date. As a result, he'd eventually been able to come directly to her room, to receive it. She'd shown him how it worked and how to operate it, and he'd paid her, and taken it away with him.

Once she'd heard about what had happened, and realised the likely consequences for her, she'd moved fast.

On occasions, as a way of entertaining the offenders, a group of actors would visit the Institution and perform – genuine ones this time. They also gave opportunities for any of the juveniles who were interested, to participate in their productions. This didn't interest Gillian at all, however, what *did,* was a room just down the corridor from hers, which stored props and costumes, for the actors to use, when they visited. One of her work duties was to clean various rooms of the Institution, and whilst in there one day, not long ago, she'd swiped a number of items, and smuggled them back to her room, thinking that they might be useful, in any escape opportunity.

After Smith's attempt to use her bomb to blow up Lady Sackville's house, she'd made certain changes to her facial features, put on a brunette wig and some different clothes, until, looking in the mirror, she'd been transformed. She'd packed a few things, and then managed to get past the reception staff, unseen, when their attention had been pre-occupied, and walked out. It had been a simple matter to convince the guard at the gate, that she was a visitor, who'd been there since before he had reported for duty, and was now on her way out. Then she had made her escape, with the money that she'd earned from the sale of the bomb, in her handbag.

She'd gone to a bed and breakfast accommodation, and stayed there until now. Reading the paper had told her, that Rumbold's were sponsoring Mouse's concert at Charterhouse. Today, she'd visited Rumbold's restaurant, and asked Miranda Rumbold to hire her as a kitchen assistant. She'd told Miranda that her name was Mary Jones and that she'd just left school, and needed a temporary job, urgently. She'd work hard, just so long as she could earn some money. She produced a passport, as proof of her identity – a forgery that she'd managed to produce, over the last few days. Miranda had agreed, but told her that if she wanted to be taken on permanently, then she'd need to see a reference. 'Mary Jones' had assured her that she'd get that from her school, as soon as possible, although in reality, Gillian intended to have left Rumbold's employment, far behind, after tonight.

Therefore, she'd been one of the staff who had come over in the van tonight, with the food from the restaurant. Security had been tightened after the recent attacks from the Male Rights Protestors, and she'd known that she wouldn't be able to get into Charterhouse without some kind of cover, or deception. It had been slightly tense, when she'd been travelling with Benita and Emma, but luckily her disguise had been good enough, and she hadn't been recognised. Now she was confident, that no one could tell who she really was.

Once they'd arrived and gone into the kitchen, she'd slipped out at the first opportunity, after she'd heard the concert beginning. In her bag, she carried a small item. It was in fact, a small explosive device, which she had also produced over the past few days. She intended to plant it directly over the stage, where Alexandra would be playing.

When she'd made the bomb for Smith, she'd been able to satisfy her conscience, by telling herself that she was simply selling it to him, and that it's use was purely his concern. In fact, she hadn't known of his exact intentions – and didn't think that he did either. But she herself, despite being many things, wasn't really up to being a murderess. The explosion wouldn't, she thought, cause any loss of life. It would, however, cause some damage, and she hoped, force the abandonment of Radcliffe's concert.

Now she reached the storage area, above the stage in the assembly hall.

She could see her most hated enemy, playing below. Taking out the explosive from her bag, she set to work ...

\*\*\*

From the top of the steps, Benita and Melanie approached the storage area from the opposite side to Gillian. It was around the corner of a wall. Benita indicated to Melanie to hide behind it. Then she peeped around the corner. Sure enough someone was there, and they were definitely up to something. She realised with a shock that it was one of the kitchen assistants, who she'd travelled with in the van, earlier. When she looked very closely, she could see that Melanie was right. It *was* Gillian Spencer! She cursed herself for not recognising her before. Clearly, though, Melanie was very observant!

Gillian had almost completed her task. Benita signalled for Melanie to follow her.

"Gillian!" she shouted, as she ran out from their hiding place, with Melanie close behind. Gillian looked around in shock, both at being caught in the act of administering her dirty work, and being addressed by her real name, whilst in her disguise, which she had thought infallible. Then she recovered her wits, and turned back to try and complete her work, but Benita reached her, grabbed at her arm, and caught it. Gillian fought furiously to free it, and then made to strike Benita with her free hand. But Melanie was too quick for her, and grabbed that arm too. For a few more seconds they grappled with her, and Gillian, with a huge effort, temporarily broke free, before Melanie's outstretched foot, sent her sprawling. As she picked herself up, Melanie's fist followed, and struck a hard, perfectly placed blow, to the side of her head. Gillian saw stars, and lost consciousness, slumping to her knees, and just being caught, limp in Benita's arms, before her whole body crashed to the floor.

Benita laid her down, and searched around the storage area, quickly. There were some discarded pieces of rope, in a corner.

"Help me tie her hands and feet!" she ordered to Melanie.

They soon had her bound, still out cold.

"I'll call the police!" said Benita. "Stay with her!"

She raced back around the corner, and down the steps. In the lobby, she picked up the public phone. Getting through to the emergency services switchboard she asked for the police, and reported what they'd just witnessed Gillian attempting to do – in disguise. After being told that they would be there right away – Gillian was a wanted girl – Benita raced back to check on Melanie, with Gillian. Gillian had regained consciousness, and was snarling and trying to free herself, but without success.

"The police are on their way," Benita informed Melanie. She paid a glance at Gillian. "*You're* going back to where you came from!" she said sternly.

"I'll go down to the hall and get Mrs Wood!" Benita hurried away.

Re-entering the hall, she went to where Annabel Wood sat, and spoke quietly in her ear.

"Excuse me Headmistress, but could I have a word with you outside, for a second? It's rather urgent!"

Annabel looked at her, surprised, and not a little annoyed, at this interruption to her enjoyment of the performance. "Oh, very well then," she replied, eventually.

Outside of the entrance to the hall, Benita told her what had happened.

Now Annabel realised why Benita had brought her out. "Good grief!" she exclaimed, and hurried up the steps to the storage area, without another moment's hesitation.

Gillian was still struggling frantically, and hurling obscenities. Mrs Wood marched right up to her, and struck her face.

"Shut up, Spencer!" she shouted. "And you've no idea how long I've wanted to do that!"

Then there were the sounds of sirens, above the noise of the music being played below, telling them that the police had arrived. Annabel rushed down to meet them. A couple of minutes later, Gillian Spencer was arrested and handcuffed to an officer. She was quickly taken away, as was her explosive device, to serve as further evidence against her, in a growing dossier of crimes.

Back in the hall, Benita sat back down. She could see that Alexandra was puzzled, as to her disappearance. She gave her a reassuring look.

***

Before the interval, Alexandra told the audience that she hoped they'd enjoyed the performance so far, and that the orchestra would continue after the intermission, during which they could have some tea or coffee. There was applause from the audience, and the curtain went down.

Benita rushed backstage and told Alexandra what had happened. Annabel soon appeared, as well.

"I always feared that something like this might happen!" said Alexandra. "Especially after we heard that Gillian had absconded from the Young Offenders' Institution. She was bound to want to seek vengeance on me. The last couple of weeks *prove* that horse whippings certainly do *not* always deter juveniles from committing even worse crimes, later on!"

"Well, she's back in police custody, now," said Mrs Wood. "And a good job too!"

"Perhaps, in acknowledgement of Melanie's role in catching Gillian, we should let her come into the hall and see the second half performance, free of charge, Mrs Wood," said Alexandra. "I *am* genuinely grateful to her. It's the least I can do to show it to her!"

"That's very generous of you, Alexandra and not a gesture that surprises me in the least, coming from you! Imelda and Rachel, please find Melanie and tell her that she's welcome in the hall to enjoy the second half performance, if she so wishes."

"Yes, Mrs Wood!" they said, together, and went away.

Benita gave Alexandra a hug. "Don't let all that nonsense from Gillian, put you off!" she urged her. "It's all over now."

Tom did likewise, when he and Linda came to see her, and said, "You were fantastic in the first half, Angel! You'll knock them dead in the second. I know it! I bet no one in this college, knows half of what you do, about Philippa Barrington's music. Have confidence in yourself. You can do so much more than you think!" They kissed. Tom had given her some uplifting words again.

"It's all gone without a hitch so far, darling, despite the best efforts of that blasted Spencer girl!" said Linda. "Just one more effort now and you'll be through." She held and kissed her daughter, once more.

"Keep it up, old girl! You're doing fine!" said James, as he embraced her.

"I couldn't have played better myself!" said Philippa, when she joined her. "All the hard work is paying off."

The audience had all tucked heartily into their meals, during the performance, and they were now served either tea or coffee, depending on their preference, by the Charterhouse catering staff, with Emma supervising, during the intermission period.

Soon after, the orchestra started again, the curtain rose and Alexandra began the second half of her performance.

# CHAPTER 10

As the concert finally drew to a close, Alexandra began to prepare herself for the finale. She was relieved that she and the orchestra seemed to have performed well, with no mistakes. She'd had one or two dicey moments, but she'd kept her cool, and nothing noticeable had been detected by anybody else.

They finished the last piece before the finale, and there was applause from the audience. Then Alexandra addressed the audience again.

"Well, I hope that you all enjoyed this 'Tribute to Philippa Barrington' and been sufficiently satisfied by the catering, offered by the staff of Rumbold's restaurant, which I thank Miranda Rumbold, for making available tonight. I also thank her, for allowing her restaurant to become the official sponsor of tonight's event!"

There was a round of applause from the audience.

"I'd also like to thank the Charterhouse Symphony Orchestra, for accompanying me so well. I couldn't have performed without them backing me!"

More applause ensued.

"I'd also like to give special thanks to my small group of girls who more or less organised the event for me, behind the scenes – Benita Davis, Imelda Thomas, Rachel Cuthburn and Emma Thatcher!"

All four girls rose and acknowledged the applause awarded to them, Benita seemingly to do it naturally, as if it was a common occurrence for her, whilst Imelda, Rachel and Emma, were slightly more shy.

"It only remains for me to thank you all for coming – and to ask the subject of the evening, herself, Philippa Barrington, to join me on stage for our finale!"

This was something that she and Philippa had planned together, but only they and the orchestra had known about it. There were exclamations of delight from some members of the audience, as Philippa made her way to the stage. A curtain was pulled back by Emma, revealing another piano, which she sat down at, as the audience gasped in amazement.

Then the two of them led the orchestra in a medley of some of her most popular pieces. When they finished, Alexandra said simply, "Thank you everybody, and goodnight!"

There was thunderous applause in the hall. Alexandra half beamed with pride, and half blushed with embarrassment. She and Philippa joined hands and curtseyed to the audience. Then they were joined on stage by Annabel Wood, who presented each of them, with a bouquet of flowers. The traditional calls for an encore, followed. Alexandra did a reprise – and this time joined by Philippa – of her signature, "Opus 1" piece. Then, after yet more fabulous applause, the curtain finally came down.

***

The next few minutes were all a blur to Alexandra, as she received congratulations from everyone, and hugs and kisses from her mother, Tom, James, Fiona, Benita and Philippa. Annabel asserted that there surely could be no doubt, now, that she would be named college champion. When Miranda greeted her, Alexandra thanked her profusely again, for her help in sponsoring the concert, and for her staff's hospitality at the college. Miranda had been shocked to learn of Gillian's deception.

"She told me that her name was Mary Jones," she said. "I was asking where in the name of Geratica, she'd got to, from not long after the performance started. If I'd known I was employing the notorious Gillian Spencer, I'd have soon sent her packing, believe me!"

"Don't worry," Linda comforted her. "You wouldn't be the first to be deceived by that little scoundrel!"

As the girls left for their dormitories, and the other guests departed, the hall began to be cleared away. Annabel gave Alexandra a final word of congratulation, and then told her to go home and get some rest. As a special favour, she was being allowed tomorrow off, to recover. There were only two more days left before the Festival of Divinity school holiday, so she wouldn't be missing much.

Before she left though, Melanie came to her and thanked her for the generosity she'd shown in allowing her into the hall, even though she had no official ticket. Alexandra told her that was no problem, and that it was she who should be giving the thanks, as Gillian was now safely out of the way again. Although she didn't say it, Alexandra felt that the two of them were finally on the same wavelength, and could now be friends.

Linda and James escorted her back to the car. Fiona and Tom had left a little while ago. As Linda drove away, Alexandra collapsed into the back seat, with total relief. She'd done it! Now, whether she became college champion or not, was down to the panel, but she couldn't have done any better, and in any case, the honour and prestige of successfully performing a tribute concert to Philippa Barrington, in her very presence, was more than enough. Even if she did nothing else of any great significance in her life, she could now always say, that she'd done that.

An hour later, she was tucked up in bed, and had fallen asleep immediately after her mother had kissed her goodnight, and locked her door – exhausted by her evening's exertions.

# CHAPTER 11

On the last day of term, Alexandra's board met for the final time. Everybody congratulated her on a fine performance. Alexandra looked over Benita's figures and agreed with them. They had made a substantial profit, which they would split with Miranda Rumbold 55-45, in her favour, as agreed. Mrs Wood had confirmed that, as it was all earned by their own efforts, they could keep their share for themselves. This obviously meant, effectively, that each girl would receive 9% of the total profits, each – an early Festival of Divinity present for all of them all. Alexandra thanked all the girls for their help.

At lunchtime, Alexandra and Benita were once again granted special permission to leave the college grounds, and delivered a cheque for Miranda's share, at her restaurant. Miranda's tongue ran across her lips, as she read the amount. She never turned down any money, no matter what the amount – and this had actually exceeded her expectations for the night's work.

"Thank you very much!" she said gratefully. "It was a pleasure doing business with you both."

When they returned to Charterhouse, Miss Ford asked Alexandra to report to Mrs Wood's study, following afternoon registration.

Upon her arrival, Annabel greeted her warmly, and asked her to take a seat. Then she gave her four pieces of information.

Firstly, a short time ago, she'd received confirmation via a telephone call, that the panel of judges, had decided to award the title of Charterhouse college champion to her. She'd get a certificate of confirmation, sent to The Grange, in the next few days. Alexandra was thrilled. After all the hard work, and despite her misfortune of a few weeks ago, she had finally achieved her goal. But Mrs Wood had further good news for her.

Secondly, it had been agreed by herself, and the various Charterhouse Heads of Departments, that if willing, she would, from next term, become Head Girl, filling the position vacated by Gillian Spencer, on her expulsion. Alexandra couldn't believe it.

"Thank you, Mrs Wood!" she exclaimed. "That's a great honour. I will accept!"

She couldn't wait to tell her mother and James, later, as well as Tom. As Mrs Wood remarked, now two generations of Radcliffes would have held the post.

Thirdly, Benita and Melanie were to get special, personal letters of commendation from Charterhouse College, due to their prompt actions, in preventing Gillian Spencer from causing the damage that she'd intended, during the concert. This would be particularly good news for Melanie, in her efforts to redeem her reputation – which still seemed to be progressing well.

Finally, Mrs Wood informed Alexandra, that she had also received further news regarding her own position. It was confirmed that she was now the permanent headmistress at Charterhouse. Miss Steele would become the new head of music and a new mistress, a Miss Whitmore, would take over her position, in the New Year. This would mean that Mrs Wood would no longer be teaching Alexandra's music class in any of their lessons, nor any others, and they would now have Miss Steele in charge of them, three times a week. Those girls who were formerly Miss Steele's pupils, would now be under Miss Whitmore.

It was a bit of a blow to be losing Mrs Wood, and having Miss Steele's rod of discipline, in all of their music lessons, but on the other hand, after the distinctly frosty start, between her, and the class, relations had thawed somewhat since. An understanding had been reached.

In any case, nothing could dampen Alexandra's enthusiasm this afternoon, and she left Mrs Wood's study, elated. All the girls, led by Benita, congratulated her on her double achievement – and promised to stay on their best behaviour, for Alexandra's last three terms at Charterhouse!"

\*\*\*

As was now normal, Alexandra was picked up from Charterhouse at 3.45 p.m., by Linda and James, and driven home. They were equally delighted with her news.

"I always knew you'd do it, darling!" said her mother. "And Head Girl, to boot! So, at least in that regard, you're following in my footsteps! Well done! How do you feel? Has it made you feel more confident?"

"Possibly, Mother," replied Alexandra. "It's a bit early to say at the moment. I still just feel incredibly happy!"

"Yes. Well I suppose that's fair enough sweetheart." said Linda.

"Did you enjoy the experience of doing what you had to do, to become college champion, though, Alexandra?" asked James.

"No! And I never want to step on to another stage in my life. I mean it!"

vowed Alexandra. "My nerves won't stand any more of that. I'm not a performer and I most certainly do *not* want a career as an entertainer, in *any* capacity!"

"James Spencer, you would have to put a dampener on things, by asking a question like that!" Linda chided him. "Of course she didn't really enjoy it, and probably won't want to do it again, but the point is, that having done it, her confidence to face difficult challenges will hopefully now increase. That's one of the reasons for the exercise, you silly man, as well as achieving something significant for the college."

"Sorry. Of course, Linda," said James, suitably chastened.

"Anyhow, tonight I intend us to have a suitable celebration at The Grange," asserted Linda. "We shall drink the barrels dry!"

Alexandra chuckled. When her mother got into this kind of mood, things usually became very merry. She was clearly delighted and proud of her achievement, and as usual Alexandra was thrilled to have pleased her.

She settled back into the back seat of the car. She was truly happy now. She had two weeks off and the Festival of Divinity officially began on Day 1 of next week – a bank holiday. The big day – Divinity Day, would be a week later. Her mother was on holiday all the way through, as well, and with James now at The Grange too, it promised to be a jolly fortnight. The first few flakes of snow were beginning to fall. By Divinity Day, there would be a blanket of white covering everything.

\*\*\*

At The Grange that night, Alexandra phoned Philippa Barrington and told her the news. She was proud to have had her work showcased by Alexandra at Charterhouse, and that the net result had been gaining her the title of Charterhouse college champion, as well as becoming Head Girl. Alexandra thanked her for all her help.

Then she rang Tom.

"I knew you'd do it!" said Tom. "I said so, didn't I? You're a fine pianist. Your skills are going to be much in demand, on Divinity Day, when we're all together at The Grange!"

"Well, at least *that* shouldn't be a problem, after performing for all those people at the concert," remarked Alexandra. "But as I told Mother and James, I'm never going to do what I did at Charterhouse, again. I'm going to return to being a back room girl."

After that Alexandra was indeed treated to a sumptuous feast, cooked by her mother, with six bottles of wine drunk between Linda, James and herself. They followed this up, after dinner, with coffees and ports, and some mint chocolates, and Linda smoked a cigar.

Linda also suggested a game of Word Mistress, whilst they enjoyed their drinks in the parlour. Despite the amount of alcohol that they'd drunk, Alexandra and her mother was still keen to compete with each other and it wasn't long before Alexandra had the board out of the cupboard. James felt that his brain might not be quite at its best at that time, and he wasn't quite in the Radcliffes' league, but he agreed to play - or rather he was told to by his wife. Alexandra and her mother were still remarkably strong of mind, and soon it became a battle between themselves, which on this occasion, Linda won, putting her in an even better mood.

She commiserated with her daughter.

"Well bad luck, darling, you lost again, but you put up a good fight. I'm proud of you."

Alexandra was a little stung by her mother's observation that she'd 'lost again'.

"Well perhaps if I'd got bonus points for the highest scoring word, *I* might have won this time, Mother!" she said, indignantly.

"What?" said Linda, "You can't make up the rules as you go along you know! Goodness me, whatever will you come out with next, dear?"

Alexandra couldn't resist pressing the issue. "If you remember, Mother, the last time we played, was when Tom came here for his birthday dinner. I won then, and you claimed to have always said that the person making the highest scoring word in the game, should get bonus points! Bonus points which would have doubtless been enough for you to pip me at the post."

James snorted with laughter. "Despite your mother's many and varied talents, which make her almost the perfect woman, losing gracefully is one of the few things that she struggles with on occasions!"

"How dare you, James!" said Linda. "I never have a problem with losing! It doesn't happen to be something that's a regular occurrence for me, that's all. I've no memory whatsoever of saying that the last time I played this game. And what do you mean, 'almost' the perfect woman? I can't think of a single traditional woman's role, that I can be bested in!"

"I would contend that *modesty* is another thing that you struggle with, Mother," said Alexandra, looking at her mother with a twinkle of merriment in her eyes.

Linda's eyes widened slightly. "The cheek of it! After I treat you, to what you yourself describe as a wonderful dinner, to celebrate your successful term at Charterhouse, you accuse me of that! I think maybe the two of you had better be getting to bed. The drink is getting to your brains – I've not heard such nonsense, since the last time I heard a Male Rights Protestor speak!"

Alexandra and James both burst out laughing. Alexandra crossed over to Linda and kissed her.

"I love you, Mother, and I wouldn't change anything about you. You're perfect in every way," she said, lovingly.

"I'll second that," said James.

Linda couldn't stop herself from smiling. "Hmm, that's a little better from the two of you," she replied. "Alright, you're both forgiven!"

She looked at the clock. "I do think that maybe it is time we all thought about bedtime though! Drink up, and then up you go Alexandra. "I'll come and kiss you goodnight in a few moments time, so make sure you're in bed by then."

"Yes, Mother," said Alexandra obediently. She drained her glass and got up. "Goodnight James. See you tomorrow!" she said, as she kissed him.

"Goodnight, Alexandra. Sleep well!" replied James, kissing her back.

Alexandra left the parlour. In fact, Linda had a rather pressing reason, for wanting everyone to get to bed, as soon as possible.

After being kissed goodnight, Alexandra went straight to sleep.

A short time later, Linda and James were in bed as well. They went to sleep too – but not before Linda had satisfied her throbbing geratis and made love to James three times – and forcing him to admit that she was '*the* perfect woman'.

# CHAPTER 12

It was 1/40/10 - Tribute Day - and the Festival of Divinity had begun. The atmosphere was happier, friendlier and lighter, there was festive music on the radio, and outside the snow continued to fall. At The Grange, everybody exchanged Divinity cards, and later Alexandra did the same with Tom. Presents were arranged around both sides of the fireplace, in the parlour.

In the evening, Greenacres's official service took place, in the town hall, marking the start of The Festival. Alexandra always felt that Greenacres was the prettiest town in Geratica, at this time of year, when it was fully decorated with every conceivable light, lantern and ornament. In the town square, there was a message wishing everybody a Merry Festival of Divinity.

The traditional story was performed. It was narrated by Linda, as the most prominent member of the town. Alexandra had never wanted to take part in this. She was content to join her mother, James, Tom, Fiona and Colin, in the choir, accompanying it. There were speeches afterwards, including one from her mother, and then some traditional festive songs were sung, again by the choir, and the whole audience joined in.

\*\*\*

Linda always brought a chicken from Lady Sackville's estate, for Divinity Day, and on 2/40/10, as happened every year, a selection had been brought to The Grange. for her to choose from.

Alexandra stood beside her mother in the kitchen, as she looked them over. There were four laid out on the table.

"Well, darling," said Linda. "You're fast becoming a young lady! Which would you choose, for your own household?"

Alexandra examined the birds, looking for all the things that her mother had taught her to spot, both positive and negative. She concentrated furiously, wanting to make the choice that she knew her mother had already made. She was *the* expert, as far as Alexandra was concerned.

Eventually she decided. She pointed to the one, second from the right. "That one?" Although Linda had asked her which one she would choose herself, she still made her answer, a question. She wanted to learn from her mother and choose as she would. Her heart beat slightly faster than normal, as she waited for her mother's verdict on her decision.

Linda smiled. "That's what I would choose, too," she said. "Well done. You're going to be a fine housekeeper, and make Tom a happy man and me a proud mother!" She slipped an arm around her daughter's shoulders and kissed her. Alexandra smiled back broadly, in ecstatic pleasure and returned her mother's kiss.

"We'll take that one, please," Linda said to the girl who had brought the chickens to The Grange. She pointed to their selected bird.

"Very good, Mrs Radcliffe, she said.

Linda paid for the chicken. It was expensive, but she was paying for quality.

***

On the evening of 3/40/10, it was the court Administration Festival of Divinity meal. Although Linda was on holiday for the entire Festival of Divinity, she always made a special trip to Avermore, for it, and recently Alexandra had started accompanying her. This year the office was eating at Rumbold's, so it had an extra significance for Alexandra. For the first time James was coming too, as Linda's guest. He was still working this week, but would be on holiday for the rest of the Festival period. As usual, Avermore was lavishly decorated, with lights, lanterns and messages of good will, adorning every street.

Linda sat at the head of the table in the restaurant and presided over the proceedings. Fiona was at the foot. Alexandra sat on one side of her, and James on the other. Both were happy to stay in the wings, so to speak, whilst Linda took centre stage. Linda held her daughter's hand under the table.

There was a certain amount of interest in James, given that his was the first year that he was officially Linda's partner, but some of Linda's staff also congratulated Alexandra on her achievements that term. Alexandra thanked them, but to the question of whether she was considering a career in musical performance, she gave an emphatic "No, definitely not!" response.

"Alexandra isn't a natural performer," Linda explained. "She had to have her arm lightly twisted, in order to finally agree to give the concert."

"Lightly twisted?! I've never heard that particular version of the saying, before!" remarked Lucy Worthington. "I suppose it was you, who did the twisting, Mrs Radcliffe?"

Linda's eyebrows twitched up and down. "And others as well," she declared.

Lucy smiled. Like many of the women present, she was sure that the rumour that Alexandra's mother made most of her decisions for her, was true, if, as seemed likely, Linda was as dominant at home, as she was at work. If their boss made a decision, they followed it to the letter, and if they were told to do something, they did it, without question or delay.

Miranda made a visit to this one, of her three restaurants, tonight. She greeted Linda and Alexandra, and spoke to Linda at length.

As she would be driving home with James and Alexandra, Linda made sure to watch her alcohol consumption, and they didn't stay all that late.

They were back at The Grange, in time for their usual bedtimes.

*** 

On 4/40/10, Alexandra certificate came through, confirming that she was the Charterhouse college champion for 5010. She proudly showed it to Linda, James and Tom, and kept it in a safe place, in her bedroom.

That day, they also found out, that Elizabeth Spencer had been fined 2000 geros, and received a ten week suspended sentence, for her role in organising the Male Rights' attacks.

Meanwhile, Gillian Spencer had been sentenced to a further five years, in an Avermore adult prison, after her current year long one, finished at Buckmore Young Offenders' Institution, for conspiracy to commit murder, and criminal damage.

***

With James at work that week, and The Grange to themselves, Linda and Alexandra had plenty of opportunity to be at their most intimate together, and this they duly did – on no less than three occasions. Alexandra felt as if she was the luckiest girl in Geratica, each time her mother took her to the mistress bedroom, and took her over.

Tom was also working this week, but he came over on most evenings, and he, too, would be off for all of Week 1 of 5011. They practised their wordless communication again, and Alexandra felt that Tom was improving. His concentration was better, and she could read his thoughts more easily. It was a particularly special and exciting time for them, this year, as it was their first Festival of Divinity together, in an official relationship. Alexandra showed her boyfriend how much she cared about him, on her bed, as they listened to festive music on her music machine.

Linda was also especially passionate with James, during this period, making love to him with gusto and in many multiples, each night. Even though she didn't deliberately set out to do it anymore, Alexandra still heard their squeals of ecstasy, echoing around The Grange, on several occasions.

She herself experimented more in this regard, with her toy. She started to get used to the feeling of coming atop of a man, and she liked it, as most Geratican women did, but once was still generally enough for her. The force of the orgasm, nearly always exhausted her anyhow, and she went straight to sleep, waking up later, still laid over the man. But instead of immediately becoming aroused and doing it again, as many Geratican women would, she simply packed the toy away, and went straight back to sleep.

*****

On the final weekend of the year, Alexandra and Tom enjoyed Elmsbrook wood together, trudging through the snow, which was now becoming quite crisp and deep, and throwing snowballs at each other.

Back at The Grange, the phone rang, and when Linda answered it, the scanner came on, and immediately a choir could be seen and heard singing. Linda opened the gate and they came up to the house, whereupon she gave them some money for their efforts.

*****

On 1/1/11, Divinity Day dawned. Alexandra was awoken by Linda coming into her room. After pulling the curtains back a touch, to allow some light into the room, she crossed over to her daughter's bed and went down over her, on top of the bedspread.

"Good morning darling," she said, giving Alexandra a kiss. "Happy Divinity Day!"

She kissed her daughter's lips again, this time for longer, and slipped her tongue inside Alexandra's slightly open mouth. Her daughter felt it lick over hers, and she murmured with deep pleasure, as her thighs tingled. She kissed her mother back, as she began to fully wake up.

"Good morning, Mother. Happy Divinity Day!" she replied, happily.

When she came downstairs, a short time later, she met James, in the breakfast room.

"Happy Divinity Day, James!" she said with a smile. "You're first at The Grange!"

"Happy Divinity Day, Alexandra, my sweetheart!" he replied. "Indeed it is!" They exchanged kisses. James had grown very fond of Alexandra. There was something about her that people couldn't fail to like, and she was a credit to her mother, he felt.

Alexandra laid the table for her mother, and then they all enjoyed a cooked breakfast, with – much to Alexandra's delight - seconds.

There was festive music on the radio, and Linda put on some of The Grange's own collection too.

Traditionally Linda and Alexandra always had a present in mid-morning, as they enjoyed their first tipple of the day, and the tradition continued, though this year it was of course extended to James, as well.

Another tradition was that after a light lunch, The Grange inhabitants walked down to The Lodge, and officially invited its inhabitants to spend the rest of the day with them. With the traditional acceptance from The Lodge having taken place, they trudged back through the snowy hamlet, to The Grange.

During the afternoon, they opened their presents in the parlour. Linda, naturally, marshalled the operation.

Alexandra got a box of her favourite chocolates from Tom, a bottle of sherry from James, and amongst other things, a new classical compilation recording, for her music machine, from Linda.

She gave Tom, a couple of new books that she thought he might enjoy, Fiona and Colin, a new mug, James, a box of chocolates, and her mother, another box of chocolates, plus a bottle of wine.

Tom gave Fiona, a new make-up kit, his father, a new shirt and Linda and James, a bottle of port.

Fiona and Colin, gave Tom, amongst other things, a watch, Alexandra, some perfume, and Linda and James, a new matching pair of gloves each. Fiona gave Colin, a pair of cuff-links and Colin gave her, some perfume.

Linda gave James, a new tool kit, and she and James, gave Tom, another bow tie, and Fiona and Colin, a new pipe and cigarettes, respectively. She got a bouquet of flowers from James, who had managed to smuggle them into The Grange and keep them hidden, until this afternoon. (When she received this, Alexandra saw the pleasure on her mother's face and her whispering something into James's ear. From the look of excitement on his face, which he'd failed to conceal, Alexandra guessed that he'd just been promised a treat in bed tonight!)

There was entertainment on the radio, and Linda began to prepare the Divinity Day dinner, with Alexandra helping. As the evening approached and their traditional feast grew nearer, everybody dressed for dinner, as was another tradition. Fiona, Colin, and Tom, always brought clothes with them for the occasion, and changed in the spare rooms. Alexandra wore her new gown, Linda, the one that was James' favourite, and Fiona, a new flowing blue velvet one, with matching elbow length gloves.

James, Colin and Tom, were all in their dinner suits, with bow ties. As they ate, their starter, all three of them thought that their respective partner was the most beautiful woman that they'd ever seen. The main course followed – the chicken that Linda and Alexandra had chosen last week, together with all 'the trimmings'. As bottle after bottle was opened, the wine flowed copiously and the mood grew ever more merry. After their dessert, they retired to the parlour for coffee and after dinner drinks, with chocolates, a cigar for Linda, and Fiona a pipe of tobacco.

It was no surprise to anyone, when Fiona suggested a game of cards, to Linda. She very likely wanted revenge for her humiliation, received the last time that she'd visited The Grange.

This time Fiona suggested *two* hundred geros, as a prize. This was more than Linda would normally play for, but she decided that refusing, might make Fiona claim that she was afraid to challenge her again. She agreed, and once again, Alexandra was despatched to fetch her chequebook. Alexandra realised that Fiona hoped to win back the previous one hundred, and then gain another, to put herself back into the winner's position.

When she returned, her mother wrote a cheque for two hundred geros, and announced that, as before, it would be paid into Fiona's bank account if *she* won, but if Linda won, it would be immediately destroyed.

Alexandra dealt this time, and the game began. Remarkably the 6 card, which Fiona had mistakenly thought was in the pack, at the end of the last came, became the key to this one, as incredibly, Linda held a run of 1,2,3,4, and 5 and Fiona 7,8,9,10, and the queen. This time neither woman had made a mistake, and both knew what was needed for them to win – the same card, that was somewhere in the pack. They would both keep discarding the decoy cards until one of them was lucky enough to draw the winning card.

Finally, after an agonising few seconds, Linda said "Call!" and put her cards down on the table, face down.

Fiona eyed her for a moment, desperately hoping that she might have made a mistake, after all.

"Lay your cards down, please Fiona," said Linda, with a hint of triumph in her voice, and a gleam in her eyes.

Fiona did so, showing no emotion.

Alexandra turned the cards over, put them together, and checked them. "Fiona has cards 7, 8, 9, 10, and the queen, plus two secondary cards, and Mother has cards 1, 2, 3, 4, 5, and 6, plus one secondary card. She is the winner."

Linda gave her the cheque. "Destroy that!" she ordered.

"Yes, Mother," said Alexandra. She ripped it up, and threw the pieces on to the fire.

Linda scooped up the cash from the table. "Thank you, Fiona!" she said. "That came down to pure luck, I must admit – you can't get a closer result than that. But it's all in the game."

Fiona nodded. "Hmm, congratulations, Linda. You're right. Whichever one of us had one that game, would have had the run of the cards to thank for it."

She didn't suggest another game, but simply got up and returned to her easy chair, with her drink and pipe.

More parlour games followed, and Alexandra entertained the party on the piano.

Finally, Linda and Alexandra played the first in a series of logic games, which would continue each night, and end on the last day of the Festival of Divinity (seven in all). After one of their usual epic struggles, the first round went to Linda. She felt that she'd had a good night!

In more general terms, everybody agreed that it had been a most agreeable day, when Fiona, Colin and Tom, took their leave. Alexandra and Tom kissed goodnight. They'd be seeing each other every day this week.

Linda and James got washed up and cleared away, whilst Alexandra got ready for bed. Later, after Alexandra had been kissed goodnight by her mother and was safely tucked up and secure in her bedroom, James was given the night of his life in the mistress bedroom, on the other side of the landing. Over a period of two hours, Linda made love to him ten times, with barely a break in between each one. Alexandra had certainly been correct in her guess, that afternoon.

# CHAPTER 13

The following day, 2/1/11, was Queen's Day. After their sumptuous Divinity Day dinner party, and subsequent marathon in the bedroom, the previous night, Linda and James had a leisurely start to the day.

Later on, they would all be going to the palace, for the annual dinner, being held this evening, as was traditional, in Her Majesty's honour.

Before that though, at 2.00 p.m., Queen Alexandra would be making her annual Festival of Divinity address to Geratica, on the radio (a tradition which went back to the year 4951). This had been drafted for her by Linda, on her last day at work, before the Festival began.

At 10.00 a.m., just as Linda, James and Alexandra were starting on their breakfast, the phone rang.

"Blast it! Who can that be now?" exploded Linda. She went to the extension and paused in surprise, when she saw the number.

"Goodness! It's Her Majesty!" she exclaimed, looking at James. "I hope everything's alright."

She cleared her throat and picked up the receiver.

"Your Majesty," she said.

"Happy New Year, Linda," said Queen Alexandra. "I hope you had a good Divinity Day yesterday, and that you're enjoying the Festival?"

"And to you, Ma'am," replied Linda. "And yes, Ma'am, it's been wonderful. I hope that the same can be said for you?"

"Yes, indeed it can," replied the queen. "Linda, I'll come straight to the point. I have some very happy news to report, and it will affect my radio address this afternoon, as I want to announce it to my queendom then. I've ..."

Alexandra and James watched Linda, as they ate their breakfast. They saw her eyes widen slightly, as she heard whatever the queen was telling her. Over the course of the next few moments, Linda congratulated Queen Alexandra, agreed that if she wanted to announce it this afternoon, her address would need to be amended, and assured her that, yes of course she could draft something urgently and get it added to the original speech. She promised to ring back in a few moments and said goodbye.

"Stop the presses!" asserted Linda. "Queen Alexandra has got engaged to Lord George Sackville. She proposed to him yesterday, on Divinity Day, and naturally he accepted!"

Alexandra and James cheered. "That's wonderful news, Mother!" exclaimed Alexandra.

"Indeed it is, darling. But unfortunately, it means that my services have been called upon urgently. The queen wants to announce it personally, in her address this afternoon. Therefore, I'm going to have to draft an additional part, and get it attached to the planned address that I prepared for her before the holiday. My work is never done – even when I'm on leave! I'll be back in a moment. I must get the copy of this afternoon's speech. Luckily, I've got it with me, in the study."

She rushed out.

Alexandra smiled at James. "I'll bet you, Mother's loving this situation, already! She's the best there is, at coming up with the goods quickly, when they're needed, urgently. I've seen her do it, before."

"Yes," replied James. "She's certainly the one to rely on, under pressure. She's the strongest woman I know."

Linda arrived back in the breakfast room, with the document in her hand and a pen. She sat back at the table, and pulled up her sleeves.

"Now I want silence, for a few moments, is that clear?" she asked.

"Yes, Mother," said Linda.

"Of course, dear," replied James.

Concentrating furiously, Linda wrote quickly on the copy of the original speech, whilst at the same time, eating her breakfast, which had been delayed by this sudden development.

A few minutes later she went to her study and closed the door behind her. She was soon back on the phone to the palace, and put through to Her Majesty. Queen Alexandra agreed to the amendment that Linda had made, and told her to see that it was added to the original speech, in time for her address this afternoon.

Linda immediately contacted the palace press office, who had a skeleton staff working over the Bank Holiday, and were shocked to hear from their most senior boss, today. She told them to carry out Her Majesty's wishes, urgently. She also ordered them to keep the news secret, until after the address, this afternoon, and said that she would sack anyone who disobeyed her, over this.

The girl on the other end of the phone trembled slightly.

"Yes, Mrs Radcliffe," she replied. "We'll get on to it straight away. And not a word will come out, until after the transmission, I assure you!"

"Good," said Linda, and they hung up.

At 2.00 p.m., Linda, Alexandra and James, heard the queen's address, live on the radio, with the additional announcement that Linda had drafted at The Grange's breakfast room table, less than four hours previously, slotted in.

\*\*\*

At the palace that evening, the annual dinner was held in Her Majesty's honour. Alexandra was delighted to have Tom with her, for the first time, as her official guest. It was his first ever visit inside. Fiona would also be attending in her own right, of course. They were there in good time before the dinner was due to start, so that she and Linda could show him around. They of course had a quick look at the currently empty office, of her mother's "little empire."

"There'll be a few people in tomorrow morning," said Linda. "Including your stepmother of course! That's her office in there – locked I'm afraid! I shan't be back here again, until next week, though."

The dinner began at 8.00 p.m., attended by many dignitaries and important people, and including of course Lady Caroline and Lord George Sackville, the latter of whom was now making his first official appearance as the queen's fiancé, and appeared to be quite popular.

Alexandra was flanked by her mother and James, with Tom opposite her, with Fiona. She always enjoyed coming to the palace, but these occasions in the State Dining Room, were always a bit overawing for her. She slipped her hand inside her mother's in between courses, and was grateful to feel her comforting and protective fingers, fold around hers. She smiled at Tom across the table. It wasn't very easy to talk to someone opposite you in this room, as there was quite a distance in between, but it was still good to have him there with her, to experience all of this for the first time. She couldn't really understand why Fiona didn't involve him more, particularly now he was older, as her mother did with her. Perhaps it was partly because he was a mere boy.

In fact, it didn't appear that Fiona was in a very good mood. She remarked upon it to her mother, next to her.

"Well, I think we can guess what the reason for that is," said Linda, in her ear. "And I'm not talking about her financial loss, yesterday! I imagine she listened to Her Majesty's address, and wasn't at all pleased to hear of the late announcement, given what she's said previously on the subject. Why, I still don't know."

Later that night, the dinner was finished, but there was a dance afterwards, in the State Ballroom. Fiona cheered up a little then, and began to enthusiastically seek out male partners to dance with, but Linda and Alexandra made their excuses, and prepared to leave with James and Tom, in tow. They bid farewell to Her Majesty and Lord George, and all congratulated them once again, on their news, and wished them both happiness and success in their future relationship.

*\*\*

Late that night, back at The Grange, Linda and Alexandra, had their second round of their logic game. Linda won again.

Alexandra had never won a series like this against her mother, yet, but she'd run her close, in the last couple of years. She could sense that her mother was starting to feel confident, that she would win again. At two up, with five to play, she only needed to win another two, and it would be over – though they would still play out whatever rounds still remained. She was determined to fight back though. She might not be a hugely combative person, in most areas of life, but when it came to this sort of thing, she had to admit, she enjoyed the competition.

*\*\*

The next evening, and for the rest of the Festival of Divinity, Tom was there to witness the contest, with James present too. The game was much closer than the previous one, and Alexandra finally got her name on the board, with a win of her own.

"Hmm, well I'll give you that one, darling," said Linda. "But I'm still ahead 2-1. Tomorrow will be a big game. Another one to me, and I'll be two up with three to play."

"Yes, Mother. I am aware of that," said Alexandra, her eyes twinkling, as they exchanged gentle banter. "Maths is quite a strong subject for me, you know."

"Well we'll see what your results are at the end of your school year, before you go making assertions like that!" retorted her mother. "For now, let's just repeat the facts. If I win tomorrow, you'll need to win all the three remaining games."

"You won't, Mother," said Alexandra, simply.

James and Tom guffawed with laughter.

"You tell her, Alexandra!" urged James.

"Be quiet, James!" snapped Linda.

*\*\**

The following evening, on 4/1/11, Alexandra was proved correct in her prediction. They were now all square, at 2-2.

"I said that you wouldn't win, Mother," she reminded her.

Linda was noticeably less vocal, than on the previous night.

Then on 5/1/11, after another close and epic battle of wills, Alexandra actually won again, to move ahead. Alexandra couldn't quite keep a smirk off her face, at this dramatic reversal in their respective fortunes.

"I shall come back and win tomorrow, to force a decider," her mother vowed.

This time, Linda proved to be right, and by the end of the sixth night of their challenge, it was 3-3. Everything would be decided on the final game.

And so, on 7/1/11, the last night of the Festival of Divinity, with the trimmings coming down, and 5011 about to begin in earnest, tomorrow, they began their final showdown. Alexandra started strongly, but her mother came back, and towards the end it seemed that she was favourite to be the series champion again. But Alexandra again fought back, and then the outcome seemed unclear. After one more final tussle – Alexandra won.

Tom couldn't resist cheering at his girlfriend's success. He'd surprised himself, by becoming quite excited at the end, even though the game was a little beyond him. James was more reserved, out of respect for his partner, although he was also pleased for Alexandra. He did secretly hope though, that Linda's disappointment at having finally been beaten, in this annual battle of the brains at The Grange, wouldn't result in a loss of motivation in the bedroom later.

Linda shook her daughter's hand.

"Well done, Alexandra!" she said, with a smile, which her daughter thought was almost genuine. "You played very well this year, and I can't deny that you fully deserved to win."

Alexandra waited for a moment, to see if her mother's generous words would be followed by some of her usual caustic and barbed wit, that normally accompanied her defeats, but nothing came. For once it appeared that her mother was accepting her daughter's victory over her, with heartfelt good grace.

"Thank you, Mother!" she said, happily, and kissed her, as they embraced.

Linda kissed her back, twice. "Hostilities over for another year, then, darling," she said.

"Until next year, then, Mother," remarked Alexandra.

"Indeed," said Linda. "Well that's the Festival of Divinity over for another year too, then! 1/2/11, tomorrow, and back to work. Let's hope the new year brings us success – I hope that you'll go to Castra, for a start! But I fear with these Male Rights Protestors, seemingly stepping up their cause, and the mutterings that we hear that there are those who want, effectively a change in our constitution, not to mention the fact that there are some who would have us alter the planet's core to achieve their objectives, then we may be heading for turbulent times, ahead!"

End of Volume 1.


Volume 2 of this Chronicle – *'The Two Worlds Of Geratica – The Mistress Of Geratica'* starts eleven years before this first volume ends. Just who is the mystery Fiona? Was Robert Radcliffe's death really an accident?


Ensure that you read that Volume, before starting the second Chronicle!

Printed in Great Britain
by Amazon